‘Howard was the Thomas Wolfe [illegible]
Conan tales seem to almost fall over themselves in their need
to get out’

Stephen King

‘A hero of mythic proportion, fashioned by a storyteller who
helped define what modern fantasy should be’

Raymond E. Feist

‘Pure adventure yarns with a touch of weirdness’

H.P. Lovecraft

‘The bloodiest hero in all fantasy fiction’

Brian Lumley

The ULTIMATE FANTASIES sequence

Conan

Elric

Lankhmar

Lud-in-the-Mist

Lyonesse

The Broken Sword

The Chronicles of Amber

The Dragon Waiting

THE CONAN CHRONICLES

ROBERT E. HOWARD

Edited by Stephen Jones

This edition published in Great Britain in 2008 by
Gollancz
An imprint of the Orion Publishing Group
Orion House, 5 Upper Saint Martin's Lane
London WC2H 9EA

1 3 5 7 9 10 8 6 4 2

A CIP catalogue record for this book is available from the British Library.

ISBN 978 0 57508 2 731

Typeset by Deltatype Ltd, Birkenhead, Merseyside

Printed and bound at Mackays of Chatham plc, Chatham, Kent

The Orion Publishing Group's policy is to use papers that are natural, renewable and recyclable products and made from wood grown in sustainable forests. The logging and manufacturing processes are expected to conform to the environmental regulations of the country of origin.

www.orionbooks.co.uk

In memory of
KARL EDWARD WAGNER
who began this project
more than a quarter of a century ago.

THE HYBORIAN AGE

(Nothing in this article is to be considered as an attempt to advance any theory in opposition to accepted history. It is simply a fictional background for a series of fiction-stories. When I began writing the Conan stories a few years ago, I prepared this 'history' of his age and the peoples of that age, in order to lend him and his sagas a greater aspect of realness. And I found that by adhering to the 'facts' and spirit of that history, in writing the stories, it was easier to visualize (and therefore to present) him as a real flesh-and-blood character rather than a ready-made product. In writing about him and his adventures in the various kingdoms of his Age, I have never violated the 'facts' or spirit of the 'history' here set down, but have followed the lines of that history as closely as the writer of actual historical-fiction follows the lines of actual history. I have used this 'history' as a guide in all the stories in this series that I have written.)

Of that epoch known by the Nemedian chroniclers as the Pre-Cataclysmic Age, little is known except the latter part, and that is veiled in the mists of legendry. Known history begins with the waning of the Pre-Cataclysmic civilization, dominated by the kingdoms of Kamelia, Valusia, Verulia, Grondar, Thule and Commoria. These peoples spoke a similar language, arguing a common origin. There were other kingdoms, equally civilized, but inhabited by different, and apparently older races.

The barbarians of that age were the Picts, who lived on islands far out on the western ocean; the Atlanteans, who dwelt on a small continent between the Pictish Islands and the main, or Thurian Continent; and the Lemurians, who inhabited a chain of large islands in the eastern hemisphere.

There were vast regions of unexplored land. The civilized kingdoms, though enormous in extent, occupied a comparatively small portion of the whole planet. Valusia was the western-most kingdom of the Thurian Continent; Grondar the eastern-most. East of Grondar, whose people were less highly cultured than those of their kindred kingdoms, stretched a wild and barren expanse of deserts. Among the less arid stretches of desert, in the jungles, and among the mountains, lived scattered clans and tribes of primitive savages. Far to the south there was a mysterious civilization, unconnected with the Thurian culture, and apparently pre-human in its nature. On the far-eastern shores of the Continent there lived another race, human, but mysterious and non-Thurian, with which the Lemurians from time to time came in contact. They apparently came from a shadowy and nameless continent lying somewhere east of the Lemurian Islands.

The Thurian civilization was crumbling; their armies were composed largely of barbarian mercenaries. Picts, Atlanteans and Lemurians were their generals, their statesmen, often their kings. Of the bickerings of the kingdoms, and the wars between Valusia and Commoria, as well as the conquests by which the Atlanteans founded a kingdom on the mainland, there were more legends than accurate history.

Then the Cataclysm rocked the world. Atlantis and Lemuria sank, and the Pictish Islands were heaved up to form the mountain peaks of a new continent. Sections of the Thurian Continent vanished under the waves, or sinking, formed great inland lakes and seas. Volcanoes broke forth and terrific earthquakes shook down the shining cities of the empires. Whole nations were blotted out.

The barbarians fared a little better than the civilized races. The inhabitants of the Pictish Islands were destroyed, but a great colony of them, settled among the mountains of Valusia's southern frontier, to serve as a buffer against foreign invasion, was untouched. The Continental kingdom of the Atlanteans likewise escaped the common ruin, and to it came thousands of their tribesmen in ships from the sinking land. Many Lemurians escaped to the eastern coast of the Thurian Continent, which was comparatively untouched. There they were enslaved by the ancient race which already dwelt there, and their history, for thousands of years, is a history of brutal servitude.

In the western part of the Continent, changing conditions created strange forms of plant and animal life. Thick jungles covered the plains, great rivers cut their roads to the sea, wild mountains were heaved up, and lakes covered the ruins of old cities in fertile valleys. To the Continental kingdom of the Atlanteans, from sunken areas, swarmed myriads of beasts and savages – ape-men and apes. Forced to battle continually for their lives, they yet managed to retain vestiges of their former state of highly advanced barbarism. Robbed of metals and ores, they became workers in stone like their distant ancestors, and had attained a real artistic level, when their struggling culture came into contact with the powerful Pictish nation. The Picts had also reverted to flint, but had advanced more rapidly in the matter of population and war-science. They had none of the Atlanteans' artistic nature; they were a ruder, more practical, more prolific race. They left no pictures painted or carved on ivory, as did their enemies, but they left remarkably efficient flint weapons in plenty.

These stone-age kingdoms clashed, and in a series of bloody wars, the outnumbered Atlanteans were hurled back into a state of savagery, and the evolution of the Picts was halted. Five hundred years after the Cataclysm the barbaric kingdoms have vanished. It is now a nation of savages – the Picts – carrying on continual warfare with tribes of savages – the Atlanteans. The Picts had the advantage of numbers and unity, whereas the Atlanteans had fallen into loosely knit clans. That was the west of that day.

In the distant east, cut off from the rest of the world by the heaving up of gigantic mountains and the forming of a chain of vast lakes, the Lemurians are toiling as slaves of their ancient masters. The far south is still veiled in mystery. Untouched by the Cataclysm, its destiny is still pre-human. Of the civilized races of the Thurian Continent, a remnant of one of the non-Valusian nations dwells among the low mountains of the southeast – the Zhemri. Here and there about the world are scattered clans of apish savages, entirely ignorant of the rise and fall of the great civilizations. But in the far north another people are slowly coming into existence.

At the time of the Cataclysm, a band of savages, whose development was not much above that of the Neanderthal, fled to the north to escape destruction. They found the snow-countries inhabited only by a species of ferocious snow-apes – huge shaggy white animals, apparently native to that climate. These they fought and drove beyond the Arctic circle, to perish, as the savages thought. The latter, then, adapted themselves to their hardy new environment and throve.

After the Pictish–Atlantean wars had destroyed the beginnings of what might have been a new culture, another, lesser cataclysm further altered the appearance of the original continent, left a great inland sea where the chain of lakes had been, to further separate west from east, and the attendant earthquakes, floods and volcanoes completed the ruin of the barbarians which their tribal wars had begun.

A thousand years after the lesser cataclysm, the western world is seen to be a wild country of jungles and lakes and torrential rivers. Among the forest-covered hills of the northwest exist wandering bands of ape-men, without human speech, or the knowledge of fire or the use of implements. They are the descendants of the Atlanteans, sunk back into the squalling chaos of jungle-bestiality from which ages ago their ancestors so laboriously crawled. To the southwest dwell scattered clans of degraded, cave-dwelling savages, whose speech is of the most primitive form, yet who still retain the name of Picts, which has come to mean merely a term designating men – themselves, to distinguish them from the true beasts with which they contend for life and food. It is their only link with their former stage. Neither the squalid Picts nor the apish Atlanteans have any contact with other tribes or peoples.

Far to the east, the Lemurians, levelled almost to a bestial plane themselves by the brutishness of their slavery, have risen and destroyed their masters. They are savages stalking among the ruins of a strange civilization. The survivors of that civilization, who have escaped the fury of their slaves, have come westward. They fall upon that mysterious pre-human kingdom of the south and overthrow it, substituting their own culture, modified by contact with the older one. The newer kingdom is called Stygia, and remnants of the older nation seemed to have survived, and even been worshipped, after the race as a whole had been destroyed.

Here and there in the world small groups of savages are showing signs of an upward trend; these are scattered and unclassified. But in the north, the tribes are growing. These people are called Hyborians, or Hybori; their god was Bori – some great chief, whom legend made even more ancient as the king who led them into the north, in the days of the great Cataclysm, which the tribes remember only in distorted folklore.

They have spread over the north, and are pushing southward in leisurely treks. So far they have not come in contact with any other races; their wars have been with one another. Fifteen hundred years in the north country have made them a tall, tawny-haired, grey-eyed race, vigorous and warlike, and already exhibiting a well-defined artistry and poetism of nature. They still live mostly by the hunt, but the southern tribes have been raising cattle for some centuries. There is one exception in their so far complete isolation from other races: a wanderer into the far north returned with the news that the supposedly deserted ice wastes were inhabited by an extensive tribe of ape-like men, descended, he swore, from the beasts driven out of the more habitable land by the ancestors of the Hyborians. He urged that a large war-party be sent beyond the arctic circle to exterminate these beasts, whom he swore were evolving into true men. He was jeered at; a small band of adventurous young warriors followed him into the north, but none returned.

But tribes of the Hyborians were drifting south, and as the population increased this movement became extensive. The following age was an epoch of wandering and conquest. Across the history of the world tribes and drifts of tribes move and shift in an everchanging panorama.

Look at the world five hundred years later. Tribes of tawny-haired Hyborians have moved southward and westward, conquering and destroying many of the small unclassified clans. Absorbing the blood of conquered races, already the descendants of the older drifts have begun to show modified racial traits, and these mixed races are attacked fiercely by new, purer-blooded drifts, and swept before them, as a broom sweeps debris impartially, to become even more mixed and mingled in the tangled debris of races and tag-ends of races.

As yet the conquerors have not come in contact with the older races. To the southeast the descendants of the Zhemri, given impetus by new blood resulting from admixture with some unclassified tribe, are beginning to seek to revive some faint shadow of their ancient culture. To the west the apish Atlanteans are beginning the long climb upward. They have completed the cycle of existence; they have long forgotten their former existence as men; unaware of any other former state, they are starting the climb unhelped and unhindered by human memories. To the south of them the Picts remain savages, apparently defying the laws of Nature by neither progressing nor retrogressing. Far to the south dreams the ancient mysterious kingdom of Stygia. On its eastern borders wander clans of nomadic savages, already known as the Sons of Shem.

Next to the Picts, in the broad valley of Zingg, protected by great mountains, a nameless band of primitives, tentatively classified as akin to the Shemites, has evolved an advanced agricultural system and existence.

Another factor has added to the impetus of Hyborian drift. A tribe of that race has discovered the use of stone in building, and the first Hyborian kingdom has come into being – the rude and barbaric kingdom of Hyperborea, which had its beginning in a crude fortress of boulders heaped to repel tribal attack. The people of this tribe soon abandoned their horse-hide tents for stone houses, crudely but mightily built, and thus protected, they grew strong. There are few more dramatic events in history than the rise of the rude, fierce kingdom of Hyperborea, whose people turned abruptly from their nomadic life to rear dwellings of naked stone, surrounded by cyclopean walls – a race scarcely emerged from the polished stone age, who had by a freak of chance, learned the first rude principles of architecture.

The rise of this kingdom drove forth many other tribes, for, defeated in the war, or refusing to become tributary to their castle-dwelling kinsmen, many clans set forth on long treks that took them halfway around the world. And already the more northern tribes are beginning to be harried by gigantic blond savages, not much more advanced than ape-men.

The tale of the next thousand years is the tale of the rise of the Hyborians, whose warlike tribes dominate the western world. Rude kingdoms are taking shape. The tawny-haired invaders have encountered the Picts, driving them into the barren lands of the west. To the northwest, the descendants of the Atlanteans, climbing unaided from apedom into primitive savagery, have not yet met the conquerors. Far to the east the Lemurians are evolving a strange semi-civilization of their own. To the south the Hyborians have founded the kingdom of Koth, on the borders of those pastoral countries known as the Lands of Shem, and the savages of those lands, partly through contact with the Hyborians, partly through contact with the Stygians who have ravaged them for centuries, are emerging from barbarism. The blond savages of the far north have grown in power and numbers so that the northern Hyborian tribes move southward, driving their kindred clans before them. The ancient kingdom of Hyperborea is overthrown by one of these northern tribes, which, however, retains the old name. Southeast of Hyperborea a kingdom of the Zhemri has come into being, under the name of Zamora. To the southwest, a tribe of Picts have invaded the fertile valley of Zingg, conquered the agricultural people there, and settled among them. This mixed race was in turn conquered later by a roving tribe of Hybori, and from these mingled elements came the kingdom of Zingara.

Five hundred years later the kingdoms of the world are clearly defined. The kingdoms of the Hyborians – Aquilonia, Nemedia, Brythunia, Hyperborea, Koth, Ophir, Argos, Corinthia, and one known as the Border Kingdom – dominate the western world. Zamora lies to the east, and Zingara to the southwest of these kingdoms – people alike in darkness of complexion and exotic habits, but otherwise unrelated. Far to the south sleeps Stygia, untouched by foreign invasion, but the peoples of Shem have exchanged the Stygian yoke for the less galling one of Koth. The dusky masters have been driven south of the great river Styx, Nilus, or Nile, which, flowing north from the shadowy hinterlands, turns almost at right angles and flows almost due west through the pastoral meadowlands of Shem, to empty into the great sea. North of Aquilonia, the western-most Hyborian kingdom, are the Cimmerians, ferocious savages, untamed by the invaders, but advancing rapidly because of contact with them; they are the descendants of the Atlanteans, now progressing more steadily than their old enemies the Picts, who dwell in the wilderness west of Aquilonia.

Another five centuries and the Hybori peoples are the possessors of a civilization so virile that contact with it virtually snatched out of the wallow of savagery such tribes as it touched. The most powerful kingdom is Aquilonia, but others vie with it in strength and mixed race; the nearest to the ancient root-stock are the Gundermen of Gunderland, a northern province of Aquilonia. But this mixing has not weakened the race. They are supreme in the western world, though the barbarians of the wastelands are growing in strength.

In the north, golden-haired, blue-eyed barbarians, descendants of the blond arctic savages, have driven the remaining Hyborian tribes out of the snow countries, except the ancient kingdom of Hyperborea, which resists their onslaught. Their country is called Nordheim, and they are divided into the red-haired Vanir of Vanaheim, and the yellow-haired Æsir of Asgard.

Now the Lemurians enter history again as Hyrkanians. Through the centuries they have pushed steadily westward, and now a tribe skirts the southern end of the great inland sea – Vilayet – and establishes the kingdom of Turan on the southwestern shore. Between the inland sea and the eastern borders of the native kingdoms lie vast expanses of steppes and in the extreme north and extreme south, deserts. The non-Hyrkanian dwellers of these territories are scattered and pastoral, unclassified in the north, Shemitish in the south, aboriginal, with a thin strain of Hyborian blood from wandering conquerors. Toward the latter part of the period other Hyrkanian clans push westward, around the northern extremity of the inland sea, and clash with the eastern outposts of the Hyperboreans.

Glance briefly at the peoples of that age. The dominant of Hyborians are no longer uniformly tawny-haired and grey-eyed. They have mixed with other races. There is a strong Shemitish, even a Stygian strain among the peoples of Koth, and to a lesser extent, of Argos, while in the case of the latter, admixture with the Zingarans has been more extensive than with the Shemites. The eastern Brythunians have intermarried with the dark-skinned Zamorians, and the people of southern Aquilonia have mixed with the brown Zingarans until black hair and brown eyes are the dominant type in Poitain, the southern-most province. The ancient kingdom of Hyperborea is more aloof than the others, yet there is alien blood in plenty in its veins, from the capture of foreign women – Hyrkanians, Æsir and Zamorians. Only in the province of Gunderland, where the people keep no slaves, is the pure Hyborian stock found unblemished. But the barbarians have kept their bloodstream pure; the Cimmerians are tall and powerful, with dark hair and blue or grey eyes. The people of Nordheim are of similar build, but with white skins, blue eyes and golden or red hair. The Picts are of the same type as they always were – short, very dark, with black eyes and hair. The Hyrkanians are dark and generally tall and slender, though a squat slant-eyed type is more and more common among them, resulting from mixture with a curious race of intelligent, though stunted, aborigines, conquered by them among the mountains east of Vilayet, on their westward drift. The Shemites are generally of medium height, though sometimes when mixed with Stygian blood, gigantic, broadly and strongly built, with hook noses, dark eyes and blue-black hair. The Stygians are tall and well made, dusky, straight-featured – at least the ruling classes are of that type. The lower classes are a down-trodden, mongrel horde, a mixture of negroid, Stygian, Shemitish, even Hyborian bloods. South of Stygia are the vast black kingdoms of the Amazons, the Kushites, the Atlaians and the hybrid empire of Zembabwe.

Between Aquilonia and the Pictish wilderness lie the Bossonian marches, peopled by descendants of an aboriginal race, conquered by a tribe of Hyborians, early in the first ages of the Hyborian drift. This mixed people never attained the civilization of the purer Hyborians, and was pushed by them to the very fringe of the civilized world. The Bossonians are of medium height and complexion, their eyes brown or grey, and they are mesocephalic. They live mainly by agriculture, in large walled villages, and are part of the Aquilonian kingdom. Their marches extend from the Border Kingdom in the north to Zingara in the southwest, forming a bulwark for Aquilonia against both the Cimmerians and the Picts. They are stubborn defensive fighters, and centuries of warfare against northern and western barbarians have caused them to evolve a type of defense almost impregnable against direct attack.

Five hundred years later the Hyborian civilization was swept away. Its fall was unique in that it was not brought about by internal decay, but by the growing power of the barbarian nations and the Hyrkanians. The Hyborian peoples were overthrown while their vigorous culture was in its prime.

Yet it was Aquilonia's greed which brought about that overthrow, though indirectly. Wishing to extend their empire, her kings made war on their neighbors. Zingara, Argos and Ophir were annexed outright, with the western cities of Shem, which had, with their more eastern kindred, recently thrown off the yoke of Koth. Koth itself, with Corinthia and the eastern Shemitish tribes, was forced to pay Aquilonia tribute and lend aid in wars. An ancient feud had existed between Aquilonia and Hyperborea, and the latter now marched to meet the armies of her western rival. The plains of the Border Kingdom were the scene of a great and savage battle, in which the northern hosts were utterly defeated, and retreated into their snowy fastnesses, whither the victorious Aquilonians did not pursue them. Nemedia, which had successfully resisted the western kingdom for centuries, now drew

Brythunia and Zamora, and secretly, Koth, into an alliance which bade fair to crush the rising empire. But before their armies could join battle, a new enemy appeared in the east, as the Hyrkanians made their first real thrust at the western world. Reinforced by adventurers from east of Vilayet, the riders of Turan swept over Zamora, devastated eastern Corinthia, and were met on the plains of Brythunia by the Aquilonians who defeated them and hurled them flying eastward. But the back of the alliance was broken, and Nemedia took the defensive in future wars, aided occasionally by Brythunia and Hyperborea, and, secretly, as usual, by Koth. This defeat of the Hyrkanians showed the nations the real power of the western kingdom, whose splendid armies were augmented by mercenaries, many of them recruited among the alien Zingarans, and the barbaric Picts and Shemites. Zamora was reconquered from the Hyrkanians, but the people discovered that they had merely exchanged an eastern master for a western master. Aquilonian soldiers were quartered there, not only to protect the ravaged country, but also to keep the people in subjection. The Hyrkanians were not convinced; three more invasions burst upon the Zamorian borders, and the Lands of Shem, and were hurled back by the Aquilonians, though the Turanian armies grew larger as hordes of steel-clad riders rode out of the east, skirting the southern extremity of the inland sea.

But it was in the west that a power was growing destined to throw down the kings of Aquilonia from their high places. In the north there was incessant bickering along the Cimmerian borders between the black-haired warriors and the Nordheimir; and the Æsir, between wars with the Vanir, assailed Hyperborea and pushed back the frontier, destroying city after city. The Cimmerians also fought the Picts and Bossonians impartially, and several times raided into Aquilonia itself, but their wars were less invasions than mere plundering forays.

But the Picts were growing amazingly in population and power. By a strange twist of fate, it was largely due to the efforts of one man, and he an alien, that they set their feet upon the ways that led to eventual empire. This man was Arus, a Nemedian priest, a natural-born reformer. What turned his mind toward the Picts is not certain, but this much is history – he determined to go into the western wilderness and modify the rude ways of the heathen by the introduction of the gentle worship of Mitra. He was not daunted by the grisly tales of what had happened to traders and explorers before him, and by some whim of fate he came among the people he sought, alone and unarmed, and was not instantly speared.

The Picts had benefited by contact with Hyborian civilization, but they had always fiercely resisted that contact. That is to say, they had learned to work crudely in copper and tin, which were found scantily in their country, and for which latter metal they raided into the mountains of Zingara, or traded hides, whale's teeth, walrus tusks and such few things as savages have to trade. They no longer lived in caves and tree-shelters, but built tents of hides, and crude huts, copied from those of the Bossonians. They still lived mainly by the chase, since their wilds swarmed with game of all sorts, and the rivers and sea with fish, but they had learned how to plant grain, which they did sketchily, preferring to steal it from their neighbors the Bossonians and Zingarans. They dwelt in clans which were generally at feud with each other, and their simple customs were blood-thirsty and utterly inexplicable to a civilized man, such as Arus of Nemedia. They had no direct contact with the Hyborians, since the Bossonians acted as a buffer between them. But Arus maintained that they were capable of progress, and events proved the truth of his assertion – though scarcely in the way he meant.

Arus was fortunate in being thrown in with a chief of more than usual intelligence – Gorm by name. Gorm cannot be explained, any more than Genghis Khan, Othman, Attila, or any of those individuals, who, born in naked lands among untutored barbarians, yet possess the instinct for conquest and empire-building. In a sort of bastard-Bossonian, the priest made the chief understand his purpose, and though extremely puzzled, Gorm gave him permission to remain among his tribe unbutchered – a case unique in the history of the race. Having learned the language Arus set himself to work to eliminate the more unpleasant phases of Pictish life – such as human sacrifice, blood-feud, and the burning alive of captives. He harangued Gorm at length, whom he found to be an interested, if unresponsive listener. Imagination reconstructs the scene – the black-haired chief, in his tiger-skins and necklace of human teeth, squatting on the dirt floor of the wattle hut, listening intently to the eloquence of the priest, who probably sat on a carven, skin-covered block of mahogany provided in his honor – clad in the silken robes of a Nemedian priest, gesturing with his slender white hands as he expounded the eternal rights and justices which were the truths of Mitra. Doubtless he pointed with repugnance at the rows of skulls which adorned the walls of the hut and urged Gorm to forgive his enemies instead of putting their bleached remnants to such use. Arus was the highest product of an innately artistic race, refined by centuries of civilization; Gorm had behind him a heritage of a hundred thousand years of screaming savagery – the pad of the tiger was in his stealthy step, the grip of the gorilla in his black-nailed hands, the fire that burns in a leopard's eyes burned in his.

Arus was a practical man. He appealed to the savage's sense of material gain; he pointed out the power and splendor of the Hyborian kingdoms, as an example of the power of Mitra, whose teachings and works had lifted them up to their high places. And he spoke of cities, and fertile plains, marble walls and iron chariots, jeweled towers, and horsemen in their glittering armor riding to battle. And Gorm, with the unerring instinct of the barbarian, passed over his words regarding gods and their teachings, and fixed on the material powers thus vividly described. There in that mud-floored wattle hut, with the silk-robed priest on the mahogany block, and the dark-skinned chief crouching in his tiger-hides, was laid the foundations of empire.

As has been said, Arus was a practical man. He dwelt among the Picts and found much that an intelligent man could do to aid humanity, even when that humanity was cloaked in tiger-skins and wore necklaces of human teeth. Like all priests of Mitra, he was instructed in many things. He found that there were vast deposits of iron ore in the Pictish hills, and he taught the natives to mine, smelt and work it into implements – agricultural implements, as he fondly believed. He instituted other reforms, but these were the most important things he did: he instilled in Gorm a desire to see the civilized lands of the world; he taught the Picts how to work in iron; and he established contact between them and the civilized world. At the chief's request he conducted him and some of his warriors through the Bossonian marches, where the honest villagers stared in amazement, into the glittering outer world.

Arus no doubt thought that he was making converts right and left, because the Picts listened to him, and refrained from smiting him with their copper axes. But the Pict was little calculated to seriously regard teachings which bade him forgive his enemy and abandon the warpath for the ways of honest drudgery. It has been said that he lacked artistic sense; his whole nature led to war and slaughter. When the priest talked of the glories of the civilized nations, his dark-skinned listeners were intent, not on the ideals of his religion, but on the loot which he unconsciously described in the narration of rich cities and shining lands. When he told how Mitra aided certain kings to overcome their enemies, they paid scant heed to the miracles of Mitra, but they hung on the description of battle-lines, mounted knights, and maneuvers of archers and spearmen. They harkened with keen dark eyes and inscrutable countenances, and they went their ways without comment, and heeded with flattering intentness his instructions as to the working of iron, and kindred arts.

Before his coming they had filched steel weapons and armor from the Bossonians and Zingarans, or had hammered out their own crude arms from copper and bronze. Now a new world opened to them, and the clang of sledges re-echoed throughout the land. And Gorm, by virtue of this new craft, began to assert his dominance over other clans, partly by war, partly by craft and diplomacy, in which latter art he excelled all other barbarians.

Picts now came and went freely into Aquilonia, under safe-conduct, and they returned with more information as to armor-forging and sword-making. More, they entered Aquilonia's mercenary armies, to the unspeakable disgust of the sturdy Bossonians. Aquilonia's kings toyed with the idea of playing the Picts against the Cimmerians, and possibly thus destroying both menaces, but they were too busy with their policies of aggression in the south and east to pay much heed to the vaguely known lands of the west, from which more and more stocky warriors swarmed to take service among the mercenaries.

These warriors, their service completed, went back to their wilderness with good ideas of civilized warfare, and that contempt for civilization which arises from familiarity with it. Drums began to beat in the hills, gathering-fires smoked on the heights, and savage sword-makers hammered their steel on a thousand anvils. By intrigues and forays too numerous and devious to enumerate, Gorm became chief of chiefs, the nearest approach to a king the Picts had had in thousands of years. He had waited long; he was past middle age. But now he moved against the frontiers, not in trade, but in war.

Arus saw his mistake too late; he had not touched the soul of the pagan, in which lurked the hard fierceness of all the ages. His persuasive eloquence had not caused a ripple in the Pictish conscience. Gorm wore a corselet of silvered mail now, instead of the tiger-skin, but underneath he was unchanged – the everlasting barbarian, unmoved by theology or philosophy, his instincts fixed unerringly on rapine and plunder.

The Picts burst on the Bossonian frontiers with fire and sword, not clad in tiger-skins and brandishing copper axes as of yore, but in scale-mail, wielding weapons of keen steel. As for Arus, he was brained by a drunken Pict, while making a last effort to undo the work he had unwittingly done. Gorm was not without gratitude; he caused the skull of the slayer to be set on the top of the priest's cairn. And it is one of the grim ironies of the universe that the stones which covered Arus's body should have been adorned with that last touch of barbarity – above a man to whom violence and blood-vengeance were revolting.

But the newer weapons and mail were not enough to break the

lines. For years the superior armaments and sturdy courage of the Bossonians held the invaders at bay, aided, when necessary, by imperial Aquilonian troops. During this time the Hyrkanians came and went, and Zamora was added to the empire.

Then treachery from an unexpected source broke the Bossonian lines. Before chronicling this treachery, it might be well to glance briefly at the Aquilonian empire. Always a rich kingdom, untold wealth had been rolled in by conquest, and sumptuous splendor had taken the place of simple and hardy living. But degeneracy had not yet sapped the kings and the people; though clad in silks and cloth-of-gold, they were still a vital, virile race. But arrogance was supplanting their former simplicity. They treated less powerful people with growing contempt, levying more and more tributes on the conquered. Argos, Zingara, Ophir, Zamora and the Shemite countries were treated as subjugated provinces, which was especially galling to the proud Zingarans, who often revolted, despite savage retaliations.

Koth was practically tributary, being under Aquilonia's 'protection' against the Hyrkanians. But Nemedia the western empire had never been able to subdue, although the latter's triumphs were of the defensive sort, and were generally attained with the aid of Hyperborean armies. During this period Aquilonia's only defeats were: her failure to annex Nemedia; the rout of an army sent into Cimmeria; and the almost complete destruction of an army by the Æsir. Just as the Hyrkanians found themselves unable to withstand the heavy cavalry charges of the Aquilonians, so the latter, invading the snow-countries, were overwhelmed by the ferocious hand-to-hand fighting of the Nordics. But Aquilonia's conquests were pushed to the Nilus, where a Stygian army was defeated with great slaughter, and the king of Stygia sent tribute – once at least – to divert invasion of his kingdom. Brythunia was reduced in a series of whirlwind wars, and preparations were made to subjugate the ancient rival at last – Nemedia.

With their glittering hosts greatly increased by mercenaries, the Aquilonians moved against their old-time foe, and it seemed as if the thrust were destined to crush the last shadow of Nemedian independence. But contentions arose between the Aquilonians and their Bossonian auxilliaries.

As the inevitable result of imperial expansion, the Aquilonians had become haughty and intolerant. They derided the ruder, unsophisticated Bossonians, and hard feeling grew between them – the Aquilonians despising the Bossonians and the latter resenting the attitude of their masters – who now boldly called themselves such, and treated the Bossonians like conquered subjects, taxing them exorbitantly, and conscripting them for their wars of territorial expansion – wars the profits of which the Bossonians shared little. Scarcely enough men were left in the marches to guard the frontier, and hearing of Pictish outrages in their homelands, whole Bossonian regiments quit the Nemedian campaign and marched to the western frontier, where they defeated the dark-skinned invaders in a great battle.

This desertion, however, was the direct cause of Aquilonia's defeat by the desperate Nemedians, and brought down on the Bossonians the cruel wrath of the imperialists – intolerant and short-sighted as imperialists invariably are. Aquilonian regiments were secretly brought to the borders of the marches, the Bossonian chiefs were invited to attend a great conclave, and, in the guise of an expedition against the Picts, bands of savage Shemitish soldiers were quartered among the unsuspecting villagers. The unarmed chiefs were massacred, the Shemites turned on their stunned hosts with torch and sword, and the armored imperial hosts were hurled ruthlessly on the unsuspecting people. From north to south the marches were ravaged and the Aquilonian armies marched back from the borders, leaving a ruined and devastated land behind them.

And then the Pictish invasion burst in full power along those borders. It was no mere raid, but the concerted rush of a whole nation, led by chiefs who had served in Aquilonian armies, and planned and directed by Gorm – an old man now, but with the fire of his fierce ambition undimmed. This time there were no strong walled villages in their path, manned by sturdy archers, to hold back the rush until the imperial troops could be brought up. The remnants of the Bossonians were swept out of existence, and the blood-mad barbarians swarmed into Aquilonia, looting and burning, before the legions, warring again with the Nemedians, could be marched into the west. Zingara seized this opportunity to throw off the yoke, which example was followed by Corinthia and the Shemites. Whole regiments of mercenaries and vassals mutinied and marched back to their own countries, looting and burning as they went. The Picts surged irresistibly eastward, and host after host was trampled beneath their feet. Without their Bossonian archers the Aquilonians found themselves unable to cope with the terrible arrow-fire of the barbarians. From all parts of the empire legions were recalled to resist the onrush, while from the wilderness horde after horde swarmed forth, in apparently inexhaustible supply. And in the midst of this chaos, the Cimmerians swept down from their hills, completing the ruin. They looted cities, devastated the country, and retired into the hills with their plunder, but the Picts occupied the land they had over-run. And the Aquilonian empire went down in fire and blood.

Then again the Hyrkanians rode from the blue east. The withdrawal of the imperial legions from Zamora was their incitement. Zamora fell easy prey to their thrusts, and the Hyrkanian king established his capital in the largest city of the country. This invasion was from the ancient Hyrkanian kingdom of Turan, on the shores of the inland sea, but another, more savage Hyrkanian thrust came from the north. Hosts of steel-clad riders galloped around the northern extremity of the inland sea, traversed the icy deserts, entered the steppes, driving the aborigines before them, and launched themselves against the western kingdoms. These newcomers were not at first allies with the Turanians, but skirmished with them as with the Hyborians; new drifts of eastern warriors bickered and fought, until all were united under a great chief, who came riding from the very shores of the eastern ocean. With no Aquilonian armies to oppose them, they were invincible. They swept over and subjugated Brythunia, and devastated southern Hyperborea, and Corinthia. They swept into the Cimmerian hills, driving the black-haired barbarians before them, but among the hills, where cavalry was less effectual, the Cimmerians turned on them, and only a disorderly retreat, at the end of a whole day of bloody fighting, saved the Hyrkanian hosts from complete annihilation.

While these events had been transpiring, the kingdoms of Shem had conquered their ancient master, Koth, and had been defeated in an attempted invasion of Stygia. But scarcely had they completed their degradation of Koth, when they were over-run by the Hyrkanians, and found themselves subjugated by sterner masters than the Hyborians had ever been. Meanwhile the Picts had made themselves complete masters of Aquilonia, practically blotting out the inhabitants. They had broken over the borders of Zingara, and thousands of Zingarans, fleeing the slaughter into Argos, threw themselves on the mercy of the westward-sweeping Hyrkanians, who settled them in Zamora as subjects. Behind them as they fled, Argos was enveloped in the flame and slaughter of Pictish conquest, and the slayers swept into Ophir and clashed with the westward-riding Hyrkanians. The latter, after their conquest of Shem, had overthrown a Stygian army at the Nilus and over-run the country as far south as the black kingdom of Amazon, of whose people they brought back thousands as captives, settling them among the Shemites. Possibly they would have completed their conquests in Stygia, adding it to their widening empire, but for the fierce thrusts of the Picts against their western conquests.

Nemedia, unconquerable by Hyborians, reeled between the riders of the east and the swordsmen of the west, when a tribe of Æsir, wandering down from their snowy lands, came into the kingdom, and were engaged as mercenaries; they proved such able warriors that they not only beat off the Hyrkanians, but halted the eastward advance of the Picts.

The world at that time presents some such picture: a vast Pictish empire, wild, rude and barbaric, stretches from the coasts of Vanaheim in the north to the southern-most shores of Zingara. It stretches east to include all Aquilonia except Gunderland, the northern-most province, which, as a separate kingdom in the hills, survived the fall of the empire, and still maintains its independence.

The Pictish empire also includes Argos, Ophir, the western part of Koth, and the western-most lands of Shem. Opposed to this barbaric empire is the empire of the Hyrkanians, of which the northern boundaries are the ravaged lines of Hyperborea, and the southern, the deserts south of the lands of Shem. Zamora, Brythunia, the Border Kingdom, Corinthia, most of Koth, and all the eastern lands of Shem are included in this empire. The borders of Cimmeria are intact; neither Pict nor Hyrkanian has been able to subdue these warlike barbarians. Nemedia, dominated by the Æsir mercenaries, resists all invasions. In the north Nordheim, Cimmeria and Nemedia separate the conquering races, but in the south, Koth has become a battle-ground where Picts and Hyrkanians war incessantly. Sometimes the eastern warriors expel the barbarians from the kingdom entirely; again the plains and cities are in the hands of the western invaders. In the far south, Stygia, shaken by the Hyrkanian invasion, is being encroached upon by the great black kingdoms. And in the far north, the Nordic tribes are restless, warring continually with the Cimmerians, and sweeping the Hyperborean frontiers.

Gorm was slain by Hialmar, a chief of the Nemedian Æsir. He was a very old man, nearly a hundred years old. In the seventy-five years which had elapsed since he first heard the tale of empires from the lips of Arus – a long time in the life of a man, but a brief space in the tale of nations – he had welded an empire from straying savage clans, he had overthrown a civilization. He who had been born in a mud-walled, wattle-roofed hut, in his old age sat on golden thrones, and gnawed joints of beef presented to him on golden dishes by naked slave-girls who were the daughters of kings. Conquest and the acquiring of wealth altered not the Pict; out of the ruins of the crushed civilization no new culture arose phoenix-like. The dark hands which shattered the artistic glories of the conquered never tried to copy them. Though he sat among the glittering ruins of shattered palaces and clad his hard body in the silks of vanquished kings, the Pict remained the eternal barbarian, ferocious, elemental, interested only in the naked primal principles of life, unchanging, unerring in his instincts which were all for war and plunder, and in which arts and the cultured progress of humanity had no place. Not so with the Æsir who settled in Nemedia. These soon adopted many of the ways of their civilized allies, modified powerfully, however, by their own intensely virile and alien culture.

For a short age Pict and Hyrkanian snarled at each other over the ruins of the world they had conquered. Then began the glacier ages, and the great Nordic drift. Before the southward moving ice-fields the northern tribes drifted, driving kindred clans before them. The Æsir blotted out the ancient kingdom of Hyperborea, and across its ruins came to grips with the Hyrkanians. Nemedia had already become a Nordic kingdom, ruled by the descendants of the Æsir mercenaries. Driven before the onrushing tides of Nordic invasion, the Cimmerians were on the march, and neither army nor city stood before them. They surged across and completely destroyed the kingdom of Gunderland, and marched across ancient Aquilonia, hewing their irresistible way through the Pictish hosts. They defeated the Nordic-Nemedians and sacked some of their cities, but did not halt. They continued eastward, overthrowing a Hyrkanian army on the borders of Brythunia.

Behind them hordes of Æsir and Vanir swarmed into the lands, and the Pictish empire reeled beneath their strokes. Nemedia was overthrown, and the half-civilized Nordics fled before their wilder kinsmen, leaving the cities of Nemedia ruined and deserted. These fleeing Nordics, who had adopted the name of the older kingdom, and to whom the term Nemedian henceforth refers, came into the ancient land of Koth, expelled both Picts and Hyrkanians, and aided the people of Shem to throw off the Hyrkanian yoke. All over the western world, the Picts and Hyrkanians were staggering before this younger, fiercer people. A band of Æsir drove the eastern riders from Brythunia and settled there themselves, adopting the name for themselves. The Nordics who had conquered Hyperborea assailed their eastern enemies so savagely that the dark-skinned descendants of the Lemurians retreated into the steppes, pushed irresistibly back toward Vilayet.

Meanwhile the Cimmerians, wandering southeastward,

destroyed the ancient Hyrkanian kingdom of Turan, and settled on the southwestern shores of the inland sea. The power of the eastern conquerors was broken. Before the attacks of the Nordheimr and the Cimmerians, they destroyed all their cities, butchered such captives as were not fit to make the long march, and then, herding thousands of slaves before them, rode back into the mysterious east, skirting the northern edge of the sea, and vanishing from western history, until they rode out of the east again, thousands of years later, as Huns, Mongols, Tatars and Turks. With them in their retreat went thousands of Zamorians and Zingarans, who were settled together far to the east, formed a mixed race, and emerged ages afterward as gypsies.

Meanwhile, also, a tribe of Vanir adventurers had passed along the Pictish coast southward, ravaged ancient Zingara, and come into Stygia, which, oppressed by a cruel aristocratic ruling class, was staggering under the thrusts of the black kingdoms to the south. The red-haired Vanir led the slaves in a general revolt, overthrew the reigning class, and set themselves up as a caste of conquerors. They subjugated the northern-most black kingdoms, and built a vast southern empire, which they called Egypt. From these red-haired conquerors the earlier Pharaohs boasted descent.

The western world was now dominated by Nordic barbarians. The Picts still held Aquilonia and part of Zingara, and the western coast of the continent. But east to Vilayet, and from the Arctic circle to the lands of Shem, the only inhabitants were roving tribes of Nordheimr, excepting the Cimmerians, settled in the old Turanian kingdom. There were no cities anywhere, except in Stygia and the lands of Shem; the invading tides of Picts, Hyrkanians, Cimmerians and Nordics had levelled them in ruins, and the once dominant Hyborians had vanished from the earth, leaving scarcely a trace of their blood in the veins of their conquerors. Only a few names of lands, tribes and cities remained in the languages of the barbarians, to come down through the centuries connected with distorted legend and fable, until the whole history of the Hyborian age was lost sight of in a cloud of myths and fantasies. Thus in the speech of the gypsies lingered the terms Zingara and Zamora; the

Æsir who dominated Nemedia were called Nemedians, and later figured in Irish history, and the Nordics who settled in Brythunia were known as Brythunians, Brythons or Britons.

There was no such thing, at that time, as a consolidated Nordic empire. As always, the tribes had each its own chief or king, and they fought savagely among themselves. What their destiny might have been will not be known, because another terrific convulsion of the earth, carving out the lands as they are known to moderns, hurled all into chaos again. Great strips of the western coast sank; Vanaheim and western Asgard – uninhabited and glacier-haunted wastes for a hundred years – vanished beneath the waves. The ocean flowed around the mountains of western Cimmeria to form the North Sea; these mountains became the islands later known as England, Scotland and Ireland, and the waves rolled over what had been the Pictish wilderness and the Bossonian marches. In the north the Baltic Sea was formed, cutting Asgard into the peninsulas later known as Norway, Sweden and Denmark, and far to the south the Stygian continent was broken away from the rest of the world, on the line of cleavage formed by the river Nilus in its westward trend. Over Argos, western Koth and the western lands of Shem, washed the blue ocean men later called the Mediterranean. But where land sank elsewhere, a vast expanse west of Stygia rose out of the waves, forming the whole western half of the continent of Africa.

The buckling of the land thrust up great mountain ranges in the central part of the northern continent. Whole Nordic tribes were blotted out, and the rest retreated eastward. The territory about the slowly drying inland sea was not affected, and there, on the western shores, the Nordic tribes began a pastoral existence, living in more or less peace with the Cimmerians, and gradually mixing with them. In the west the remnants of the Picts, reduced by the cataclysm once more to the status of stone-age savages, began, with the incredible virility of their race, once more to possess the land, until, at a later age, they were overthrown by the westward drift of the Cimmerians and Nordics. This was so long after the breaking-up of the continent that only meaningless legends told of former empires.

This drift comes within the reach of modern history and need not be repeated. It resulted from a growing population which thronged the steppes west of the inland sea – which still later, much reduced in size, was known as the Caspian – to such an extent that migration became an economic necessity. The tribes moved southward, northward and westward, into those lands now known as India, Asia Minor and central and western Europe.

They came into these countries as Aryans. But there were variations among these primitive Aryans, some of which are still recognized today, others which have long been forgotten. The blond Achaians, Gauls and Britons, for instance, were descendants of pure-blooded Æsir. The Nemedians of Irish legendry were the Nemedian Æsir. The Danes were descendants of pure-blooded Vanir; the Goths – ancestors of the other Scandinavian and Germanic tribes, including the Anglo-Saxons – were descendants of a mixed race whose elements contained Vanir, Æsir and Cimmerian strains. The Gaels, ancestors of the Irish and Highland Scotch, descended from pure-blooded Cimmerian clans. The Cymric tribes of Britain were a mixed Nordic–Cimmerian race which preceded the purely Nordic Britons into the isles, and thus gave rise to a legend of Gaelic priority. The Cimbri who fought Rome were of the same blood, as well as the Gimmerai of the Assyrians and Grecians, and Gomer of the Hebrews. Other clans of the Cimmerians adventured east of the drying inland sea, and a few centuries later mixed with Hyrkanian blood, returned westward as Scythians. The original ancestors of the Gaels gave their name to modern Crimea.

The ancient Sumerians had no connection with the western race. They were a mixed people, of Hyrkanian and Shemitish bloods, who were not taken with the conquerors in their retreat. Many tribes of Shem escaped that captivity, and from pure-blooded Shemites, or Shemites mixed with Hyborian or Nordic blood, were descended the Arabs, Israelites, and other straighter-featured Semites. The Canaanites, or Alpine Semites, traced their descent from Shemitish ancestors mixed with the Kushites settled among them by their Hyrkanian masters; the Elamites were a typical race of this type. The short, thick-limbed Etruscans, base of the Roman race, were descendants of a people of mixed Stygian, Hyrkanian and Pictish strains, and originally lived in the ancient kingdom of Koth. The Hyrkanians, retreating to the eastern shores of the continent, evolved into the tribes later known as Tatars, Huns, Mongols and Turks.

The origins of other races of the modern world may be similarly traced; in almost every case, older far than they realize, their history stretches back into the mists of the forgotten Hyborian age . . .

THE TOWER OF THE ELEPHANT

1

Torches flared murkily on the revels in the Maul, where the thieves of the east held carnival by night. In the Maul they could carouse and roar as they liked, for honest people shunned the quarter, and watchmen, well paid with stained coins, did not interfere with their sport. Along the crooked, unpaved streets with their heaps of refuse and sloppy puddles, drunken roisterers staggered, roaring. Steel glinted in the shadows where wolf preyed on wolf, and from the darkness rose the shrill laughter of women, and the sounds of scufflings and strugglings. Torchlight licked luridly from broken windows and wide-thrown doors, and out of these doors, stale smells of wine and rank sweaty bodies, clamor of drinking-jacks and fists hammered on rough tables, snatches of obscene songs, rushed like a blow in the face.

In one of these dens merriment thundered to the low smoke-stained roof, where rascals gathered in every stage of rags and tatters – furtive cut-purses, leering kidnappers, quick-fingered thieves, swaggering bravoes with their wenches, strident-voiced women clad in tawdry finery. Native rogues were the dominant element – dark-skinned, dark-eyed Zamorians, with daggers at their girdles and guile in their hearts. But there were wolves of half a dozen outland nations there as well. There was a giant Hyperborean renegade, taciturn, dangerous, with a broadsword strapped to his great gaunt frame – for men wore steel openly in the Maul. There was a Shemitish counterfeiter, with his hook nose and curled blue-black beard. There was a bold-eyed Brythunian wench, sitting on the knee of a tawny-haired Gunderman – a wandering mercenary soldier, a deserter from some defeated army. And the fat gross rogue whose bawdy jests were causing all the shouts of mirth was a professional kidnapper come up from distant Koth to teach woman-stealing to Zamorians who were born with more knowledge of the art than he could ever attain.

This man halted in his description of an intended victim's charms, and thrust his muzzle into a huge tankard of frothing ale. Then blowing the foam from his fat lips, he said, 'By Bel, god of all thieves, I'll show them how to steal wenches: I'll have her over the Zamorian border before dawn, and there'll be a caravan waiting to receive her. Three hundred pieces of silver, a count of Ophir promised me for a sleek young Brythunian of the better class. It took me weeks, wandering among the border cities as a beggar, to find one I knew would suit. And is she a pretty baggage!'

He blew a slobbery kiss in the air.

'I know lords in Shem who would trade the secret of the Elephant Tower for her,' he said, returning to his ale.

A touch on his tunic sleeve made him turn his head, scowling at the interruption. He saw a tall, strongly made youth standing beside him. This person was as much out of place in that den as a gray wolf among mangy rats of the gutters. His cheap tunic could not conceal the hard, rangy lines of his powerful frame, the broad heavy shoulders, the massive chest, lean waist and heavy arms. His skin was brown from outland suns, his eyes blue and smoldering; a shock of tousled black hair crowned his broad forehead. From his girdle hung a sword in a worn leather scabbard.

The Kothian involuntarily drew back; for the man was not one of any civilized race he knew.

'You spoke of the Elephant Tower,' said the stranger, speaking Zamorian with an alien accent. 'I've heard much of this tower; what is its secret?'

The fellow's attitude did not seem threatening, and the Kothian's courage was bolstered up by the ale, and the evident approval of his audience. He swelled with self-importance.

'The secret of the Elephant Tower?' he exclaimed. 'Why, any fool knows that Yara the priest dwells there with the great jewel men call the Elephant's Heart, that is the secret of his magic.'

The barbarian digested this for a space.

'I have seen this tower,' he said. 'It is set in a great garden above the level of the city, surrounded by high walls. I have seen no guards. The walls would be easy to climb. Why has not somebody stolen this secret gem?'

The Kothian stared wide-mouthed at the other's simplicity, then burst into a roar of derisive mirth, in which the others joined.

'Harken to this heathen!' he bellowed. 'He would steal the jewel of Yara! – Harken, fellow,' he said, turning portentously to the other, 'I suppose you are some sort of a northern barbarian—'

'I am a Cimmerian,' the outlander answered, in no friendly tone. The reply and the manner of it meant little to the Kothian; of a kingdom that lay far to the south, on the borders of Shem, he knew only vaguely of the northern races.

'Then give ear and learn wisdom, fellow,' said he, pointing his drinking-jack at the discomfited youth. 'Know that in Zamora, and more especially in this city, there are more bold thieves than anywhere else in the world, even Koth. If mortal man could have stolen the gem, be sure it would have been filched long ago. You speak of climbing the walls, but once having climbed, you would quickly wish yourself back again. There are no guards in the gardens at night for a very good reason – that is, no human guards. But in the watch-chamber, in the lower part of the tower, are armed men, and even if you passed those who roam the gardens by night, you must still pass through the soldiers, for the gem is kept somewhere in the tower above.'

'But if a man *could* pass through the gardens,' argued the Cimmerian, 'why could he not come at the gem through the upper part of the tower and thus avoid the soldiers?'

Again the Kothian gaped at him.

'Listen to him!' he shouted jeeringly. 'The barbarian is an eagle who would fly to the jeweled rim of the tower, which is only a hundred and fifty feet above the earth, with rounded sides slicker than polished glass!'

The Cimmerian glared about, embarrassed at the roar of

mocking laughter that greeted this remark. He saw no particular humor in it, and was too new to civilization to understand its discourtesies. Civilized men are more discourteous than savages because they know they can be impolite without having their skulls split, as a general thing. He was bewildered and chagrined, and doubtless would have slunk away, abashed, but the Kothian chose to goad him further.

'Come, come!' he shouted. 'Tell these poor fellows, who have only been thieves since before you were spawned, tell them how you would steal the gem!'

'There is always a way, if the desire be coupled with courage,' answered the Cimmerian shortly, nettled.

The Kothian chose to take this as a personal slur. His face grew purple with anger.

'What!' he roared. 'You dare tell us our business, and intimate that we are cowards? Get along; get out of my sight!' And he pushed the Cimmerian violently.

'Will you mock me and then lay hands on me?' grated the barbarian, his quick rage leaping up; and he returned the push with an open-handed blow that knocked his tormentor back against the rude-hewn table. Ale splashed over the jack's lip, and the Kothian roared in fury, dragging at his sword.

'Heathen dog!' he bellowed. 'I'll have your heart for that!'

Steel flashed and the throng surged wildly back out of the way. In their flight they knocked over the single candle and the den was plunged in darkness, broken by the crash of upset benches, drum of flying feet, shouts, oaths of people tumbling over one another, and a single strident yell of agony that cut the din like a knife. When a candle was relighted, most of the guests had gone out by doors and broken windows, and the rest huddled behind stacks of wine-kegs and under tables. The barbarian was gone; the center of the room was deserted except for the gashed body of the Kothian. The Cimmerian, with the unerring instinct of the barbarian, had killed his man in the darkness and confusion.

2

The lurid lights and drunken revelry fell away behind the Cimmerian. He had discarded his torn tunic, and walked through the night naked except for a loin-cloth and his high-strapped sandals. He moved with the supple ease of a great tiger, his steely muscles rippling under his brown skin.

He had entered the part of the city reserved for the temples. On all sides of him they glittered white in the starlight – snowy marble pillars and golden domes and silver arches, shrines of Zamora's myriad strange gods. He did not trouble his head about them; he knew that Zamora's religion, like all things of a civilized, long-settled people, was intricate and complex, and had lost most of the pristine essence in a maze of formulas and rituals. He had squatted for hours in the courtyard of the philosophers, listening to the arguments of theologians and teachers, and come away in a haze of bewilderment, sure of only one thing, and that, that they were all touched in the head.

His gods were simple and understandable; Crom was their chief, and he lived on a great mountain, whence he sent forth dooms and death. It was useless to call on Crom, because he was a gloomy, savage god, and he hated weaklings. But he gave a man courage at birth, and the will and might to kill his enemies, which, in the Cimmerian's mind, was all any god should be expected to do.

His sandalled feet made no sound on the gleaming pave. No watchmen passed, for even the thieves of the Maul shunned the temples, where strange dooms had been known to fall on violators. Ahead of him he saw, looming against the sky, the Tower of the Elephant. He mused, wondering why it was so named. No one seemed to know. He had never seen an elephant, but he vaguely understood that it was a monstrous animal, with a tail in front as well as behind. This a wandering Shemite had told him, swearing that he had seen such beasts by the thousands in the country of the Hyrkanians; but all men knew what liars were the men of Shem. At any rate, there were no elephants in Zamora.

The shimmering shaft of the tower rose frostily in the stars. In the sunlight it shone so dazzlingly that few could bear its glare, and men said it was built of silver. It was round, a slim perfect cylinder, a hundred and fifty feet in height, and its rim glittered in the starlight with the great jewels which crusted it. The tower stood among the waving exotic trees of a garden raised high above the general level of the city. A high wall enclosed this garden, and outside the wall was a lower level, likewise enclosed by a wall. No lights shone forth; there seemed to be no windows in the tower – at least not above the level of the inner wall. Only the gems high above sparkled frostily in the starlight.

Shrubbery grew thick outside the lower, or outer wall. The Cimmerian crept close and stood beside the barrier, measuring it with his eyes. It was high, but he could leap and catch the coping with his fingers. Then it would be child's play to swing himself up and over, and he did not doubt that he could pass the inner wall in the same manner. But he hesitated at the thought of the strange perils which were said to await within. These people were strange and mysterious to him; they were not of his kind – not even of the same blood as the more westerly Brythunians, Nemedians, Kothians and Aquilonians, whose civilized mysteries had awed him in times past. The people of Zamora were very ancient, and, from what he had seen of them, very evil.

He thought of Yara, the high priest, who worked strange dooms from this jeweled tower, and the Cimmerian's hair prickled as he remembered a tale told by a drunken page of the court – how Yara had laughed in the face of a hostile prince, and held up a glowing, evil gem before him, and how rays shot blindingly from that unholy jewel, to envelop the prince, who screamed and fell down, and shrank to a withered blackened lump that changed to a black spider which scampered wildly about the chamber until Yara set his heel upon it.

Yara came not often from his tower of magic, and always to work evil on some man or some nation. The king of Zamora feared him more than he feared death, and kept himself drunk all the time because that fear was more than he could endure sober.

Yara was very old – centuries old, men said, and added that he would live for ever because of the magic of his gem, which men called the Heart of the Elephant, for no better reason than they named his hold the Elephant's Tower.

The Cimmerian, engrossed in these thoughts, shrank quickly against the wall. Within the garden someone was passing, who walked with a measured stride. The listener heard the clink of steel. So after all a guard did pace those gardens. The Cimmerian waited, expected to hear him pass again, on the next round, but silence rested over the mysterious gardens.

At last curiosity overcame him. Leaping lightly he grasped the wall and swung himself up to the top with one arm. Lying flat on the broad coping, he looked down into the wide space between the walls. No shrubbery grew near him, though he saw some carefully trimmed bushes near the inner wall. The starlight fell on the even sward and somewhere a fountain tinkled.

The Cimmerian cautiously lowered himself down on the inside and drew his sword, staring about him. He was shaken by the nervousness of the wild at standing thus unprotected in the naked starlight, and he moved lightly around the curve of the wall, hugging its shadow, until he was even with the shrubbery he had noticed. Then he ran quickly toward it, crouching low, and almost tripped over a form that lay crumpled near the edges of the bushes.

A quick look to right and left showed him no enemy in sight at least, and he bent close to investigate. His keen eyes, even in the dim starlight, showed him a strongly built man in the silvered armor and crested helmet of the Zamorian royal guard. A shield and a spear lay near him, and it took but an instant's examination to show that he had been strangled. The barbarian glanced about uneasily. He knew that this man must be the guard he had heard pass his hiding-place by the wall. Only a short time had passed, yet in that interval nameless hands had reached out of the dark and choked out the soldier's life.

Straining his eyes in the gloom, he saw a hint of motion through the shrubs near the wall. Thither he glided, gripping his sword. He made no more noise than a panther stealing through the night, yet the man he was stalking heard. The Cimmerian had a dim glimpse of a huge bulk close to the wall, felt relief that it was at least human; then the fellow wheeled quickly with a gasp that sounded like panic, made the first motion of a forward plunge, hands clutching, then recoiled as the Cimmerian's blade caught the starlight. For a tense instant neither spoke, standing ready for anything.

'You are no soldier,' hissed the stranger at last. 'You are a thief like myself.'

'And who are you?' asked the Cimmerian in a suspicious whisper.

'Taurus of Nemedia.'

The Cimmerian lowered his sword.

'I've heard of you. Men call you a prince of thieves.'

A low laugh answered him. Taurus was tall as the Cimmerian, and heavier; he was big-bellied and fat, but his every movement betokened a subtle dynamic magnetism, which was reflected in the keen eyes that glinted vitally, even in the starlight. He was barefooted and carried a coil of what looked like a thin, strong rope, knotted at regular intervals.

'Who are you?' he whispered.

'Conan, a Cimmerian,' answered the other. 'I came seeking a way to steal Yara's jewel, that men call the Elephant's Heart.'

Conan sensed the man's great belly shaking in laughter, but it was not derisive.

'By Bel, god of thieves!' hissed Taurus. 'I had thought only myself had courage to attempt *that* poaching. These Zamorians call themselves thieves – bah! Conan, I like your grit. I never shared an adventure with anyone, but by Bel, we'll attempt this together if you're willing.'

'Then you are after the gem, too?'

'What else? I've had my plans laid for months, but you, I think, have acted on a sudden impulse, my friend.'

'You killed the soldier?'

'Of course. I slid over the wall when he was on the other side of the garden. I hid in the bushes; he heard me, or thought he heard something. When he came blundering over, it was no trick at all to get behind him and suddenly grip his neck and choke out his fool's life. He was like most men, half blind in the dark. A good thief should have eyes like a cat.'

'You made one mistake,' said Conan.

Taurus's eyes flashed angrily.

'I? I, a mistake? Impossible!'

'You should have dragged the body into the bushes.'

'Said the novice to the master of the art. They will not change the guard until past midnight. Should any come searching for him now, and find his body, they would flee at once to Yara, bellowing the news, and give us time to escape. Were they not to find it, they'd go on beating up the bushes and catch us like rats in a trap.'

'You are right,' agreed Conan.

'So. Now attend. We waste time in this cursed discussion. There are no guards in the inner garden – human guards, I mean, though there are sentinels even more deadly. It was their presence which baffled me for so long, but I finally discovered a way to circumvent them.'

'What of the soldiers in the lower part of the tower?'

'Old Yara dwells in the chambers above. By that route we will come – and go, I hope. Never mind asking me how. I have arranged a way. We'll steal down through the top of the tower and strangle old Yara before he can cast any of his accursed spells on us. At least we'll try; it's the chance of being turned into a spider or a toad, against the wealth and power of the world. All good thieves must know how to take risks.'

'I'll go as far as any man,' said Conan, slipping off his sandals.

'Then follow me.' And turning, Taurus leaped up, caught the wall and drew himself up. The man's suppleness was amazing, considering his bulk; he seemed almost to glide up over the edge of the coping. Conan followed him, and lying flat on the broad top, they spoke in wary whispers.

'I see no light,' Conan muttered. The lower part of the tower seemed much like that portion visible from outside the garden – a perfect, gleaming cylinder, with no apparent openings.

'There are cleverly constructed doors and windows,' answered Taurus, 'but they are closed. The soldiers breathe air that comes from above.'

The garden was a vague pool of shadows, where feathery bushes and low spreading trees waved darkly in the starlight. Conan's wary soul felt the aura of waiting menace that brooded over it. He felt the burning glare of unseen eyes, and he caught a subtle scent that made the short hairs on his neck instinctively bristle as a hunting dog bristles at the scent of an ancient enemy.

'Follow me,' whispered Taurus, 'keep behind me, as you value your life.'

Taking what looked like a copper tube from his girdle, the Nemedian dropped lightly to the sward inside the wall. Conan was close behind him, sword ready, but Taurus pushed him back, close to the wall, and showed no indication to advance, himself. His whole attitude was of tense expectancy, and his gaze, like Conan's, was fixed on the shadowy mass of shrubbery a few yards away. This shrubbery was shaken, although the breeze had died down. Then two great eyes blazed from the waving shadows, and behind them other sparks of fire glinted in the darkness.

'Lions!' muttered Conan.

'Aye. By day they are kept in subterranean caverns below the tower. That's why there are no guards in this garden.'

Conan counted the eyes rapidly.

'Five in sight; maybe more back in the bushes. They'll charge in a moment—'

'Be silent!' hissed Taurus, and he moved out from the wall, cautiously as if treading on razors, lifting the slender tube. Low rumblings rose from the shadows and the blazing eyes moved forward. Conan could sense the great slavering jaws, the tufted tails lashing tawny sides. The air grew tense – the Cimmerian gripped his sword, expecting the charge and the irresistible hurtling of giant bodies. Then Taurus brought the mouth of the tube to his lips and blew powerfully. A long jet of yellowish powder shot from the other end of the tube and billowed out instantly in a thick green-yellow cloud that settled over the shrubbery, blotting out the glaring eyes.

Taurus ran back hastily to the wall. Conan glared without understanding. The thick cloud hid the shrubbery, and from it no sound came.

'What is that mist?' the Cimmerian asked uneasily.

'Death!' hissed the Nemedian. 'If a wind springs up and blows it back upon us, we must flee over the wall. But no, the wind is still, and now it is dissipating. Wait until it vanishes entirely. To breathe it is death.'

Presently only yellowish shreds hung ghostily in the air; then they were gone, and Taurus motioned his companion forward. They stole toward the bushes, and Conan gasped. Stretched out in the shadows lay five great tawny shapes, the fire of their grim eyes dimmed for ever. A sweetish cloying scent lingered in the atmosphere.

'They died without a sound!' muttered the Cimmerian. 'Taurus, what was that powder?'

'It was made from the black lotus, whose blossoms wave in the lost jungles of Khitai, where only the yellow-skulled priests of Yun dwell. Those blossoms strike dead any who smell of them.'

Conan knelt beside the great forms, assuring himself that they were indeed beyond power of harm. He shook his head; the magic of the exotic lands was mysterious and terrible to the barbarians of the north.

'Why can you not slay the soldiers in the tower in the same way?' he asked.

'Because that was all the powder I possessed. The obtaining of it was a feat which in itself was enough to make me famous among the thieves of the world. I stole it out of a caravan bound for Stygia, and I lifted it, in its cloth-of-gold bag, out of the coils of the great serpent which guarded it, without awaking him. But come, in Bel's name! Are we to waste the night in discussion?'

They glided through the shrubbery to the gleaming foot of the tower, and there, with a motion enjoining silence, Taurus unwound his knotted cord, on one end of which was a strong steel hook. Conan saw his plan, and asked no questions as the Nemedian gripped the line a short distance below the hook, and began to swing it about his head. Conan laid his ear to the smooth wall and listened, but could hear nothing. Evidently the soldiers within did not suspect the presence of intruders, who had made no more sound than the night wind blowing through the trees. But a strange nervousness was on the barbarian; perhaps it was the lion-smell which was over everything.

Taurus threw the line with a smooth, rippling motion of his mighty arm. The hook curved upward and inward in a peculiar manner, hard to describe, and vanished over the jeweled rim. It apparently caught firmly, for cautious jerking and then hard pulling did not result in any slipping or giving.

'Luck the first cast,' murmured Taurus. 'I—'

It was Conan's savage instinct which made him wheel suddenly; for the death that was upon them made no sound. A fleeting glimpse showed the Cimmerian the giant tawny shape, rearing upright against the stars, towering over him for the death-stroke. No civilized man could have moved half so quickly as the barbarian moved. His sword flashed frostily in the starlight with every ounce of desperate nerve and thew behind it, and man and beast went down together.

Cursing incoherently beneath his breath, Taurus bent above the mass, and saw his companion's limbs move as he strove to drag himself from under the great weight that lay limply upon him. A glance showed the startled Nemedian that the lion was dead, its slanting skull split in half. He laid hold of the carcass, and by his aid, Conan thrust it aside and clambered up, still gripping his dripping sword.

'Are you hurt, man?' gasped Taurus, still bewildered by the stunning swiftness of that touch-and-go episode.

'No, by Crom!' answered the barbarian. 'But that was as close a call as I've had in a life noways tame. Why did not the cursed beast roar as he charged?'

'All things are strange in this garden,' said Taurus. 'The lions strike silently – and so do other deaths. But come – little sound was made in that slaying, but the soldiers might have heard, if they are not asleep or drunk. That beast was in some other part of the garden and escaped the death of the flowers, but surely there are no more. We must climb this cord – little need to ask a Cimmerian if he can.'

'If it will bear my weight,' grunted Conan, cleansing his sword on the grass.

'It will bear thrice my own,' answered Taurus. 'It was woven from the tresses of dead women, which I took from their tombs at midnight, and steeped in the deadly wine of the upas tree, to give it strength. I will go first – then follow me closely.'

The Nemedian gripped the rope and, crooking a knee about it, began the ascent; he went up like a cat, belying the apparent clumsiness of his bulk. The Cimmerian followed. The cord swayed and turned on itself, but the climbers were not hindered; both had made more difficult climbs before. The jeweled rim glittered high above them, jutting out from the perpendicular – a fact which added greatly to the ease of the ascent.

Up and up they went, silently, the lights of the city spreading out further and further to their sight as they climbed, the stars above them more and more dimmed by the glitter of the jewels along the rim. Now Taurus reached up a hand and gripped the rim itself, pulling himself up and over. Conan paused a moment on the very edge, fascinated by the great frosty jewels whose gleams dazzled his eyes – diamonds, rubies, emeralds, sapphires, turquoises, moonstones, set thick as stars in the shimmering silver. At a distance their different gleams had seemed to merge into a pulsing white glare; but now, at close range, they shimmered with a million rainbow tints and lights, hypnotizing him with their scintillations.

'There is a fabulous fortune here, Taurus,' he whispered; but the Nemedian answered impatiently. 'Come on! If we secure the Heart, these and all other things shall be ours.'

Conan climbed over the sparkling rim. The level of the tower's top was some feet below the gemmed ledge. It was flat, composed of some dark blue substance, set with gold that caught the starlight, so that the whole looked like a wide sapphire flecked with shining gold-dust. Across from the point where they had entered there seemed to be a sort of chamber, built upon the roof. It was of the same silvery material as the walls of the tower, adorned with designs worked in smaller gems; its single door was of gold, its surface cut in scales, and crusted with jewels that gleamed like ice.

Conan cast a glance at the pulsing ocean of lights which spread far below them, then glanced at Taurus. The Nemedian was drawing up his cord and coiling it. He showed Conan where the hook had caught – a fraction of an inch of the point had sunk under a great blazing jewel on the inner side of the rim.

'Luck was with us again,' he muttered. 'One would think that our combined weight would have torn that stone out. Follow me; the real risks of the venture begin now. We are in the serpent's lair, and we know not where he lies hidden.'

Like stalking tigers they crept across the darkly gleaming floor and halted outside the sparkling door. With a deft and cautious hand Taurus tried it. It gave without resistance, and the companions looked in, tensed for anything. Over the Nemedian's shoulder Conan had a glimpse of a glittering chamber, the walls, ceiling and floor of which were crusted with great white jewels which lighted it brightly, and which seemed its only illumination. It seemed empty of life.

'Before we cut off our last retreat,' hissed Taurus, 'go you to the rim and look over on all sides; if you see any soldiers moving in the gardens, or anything suspicious, return and tell me. I will await you within this chamber.'

Conan saw scant reason in this, and a faint suspicion of his companion touched his wary soul, but he did as Taurus requested. As he turned away, the Nemedian slipt inside the door and drew it shut behind him. Conan crept about the rim of the tower, returning to his starting-point without having seen any suspicious movement in the vaguely waving sea of leaves below. He turned toward the door – suddenly from within the chamber there sounded a strangled cry.

The Cimmerian leaped forward, electrified – the gleaming door swung open and Taurus stood framed in the cold blaze behind him. He swayed and his lips parted, but only a dry rattle burst from his throat. Catching at the golden door for support, he lurched out upon the roof, then fell headlong, clutching at his throat. The door swung to behind him.

Conan, crouching like a panther at bay, saw nothing in the room behind the stricken Nemedian, in the brief instant the door was partly open – unless it was not a trick of the light which made it seem as if a shadow darted across the gleaming door. Nothing followed Taurus out on the roof, and Conan bent above the man.

The Nemedian stared up with dilated, glazing eyes, that somehow held a terrible bewilderment. His hands clawed at his throat, his lips slobbered and gurgled; then suddenly he stiffened, and the astounded Cimmerian knew that he was dead. And he felt that Taurus had died without knowing what manner of death had stricken him. Conan glared bewilderedly at the cryptic golden door. In that empty room, with its glittering jeweled walls, death had come to the prince of thieves as swiftly and mysteriously as he had dealt doom to the lions in the gardens below.

Gingerly the barbarian ran his hands over the man's half-naked body, seeking a wound. But the only marks of violence were between his shoulders, high up near the base of his bull-neck – three small wounds, which looked as if three nails had been driven deep in the flesh and withdrawn. The edges of these wounds were black, and a faint smell as of putrefaction was evident. Poisoned darts? thought Conan – but in that case the missiles should be still in the wounds.

Cautiously he stole toward the golden door, pushed it open, and looked inside. The chamber lay empty, bathed in the cold, pulsing glow of the myriad jewels. In the very center of the ceiling he idly noted a curious design – a black eight-sided pattern, in the center of which four gems glittered with a red flame unlike the white blaze of the other jewels. Across the room there was another door, like the one in which he stood, except that it was not carved in the scale pattern. Was it from that door that death had come? – and having struck down its victim, had it retreated by the same way?

Closing the door behind him, the Cimmerian advanced into the chamber. His bare feet made no sound on the crystal floor. There were no chairs or tables in the chamber, only three or four silken couches, embroidered with gold and worked in strange serpentine designs, and several silver-bound mahogany chests. Some were sealed with heavy golden locks; others lay open, their carven lids thrown back, revealing heaps of jewels in a careless riot of splendor to the Cimmerian's astounded eyes. Conan swore beneath his breath; already he had looked upon more wealth that night than he had ever dreamed existed in all the world, and he grew dizzy thinking of what must be the value of the jewel he sought.

He was in the center of the room now, going stooped forward, head thrust out warily, sword advanced, when again death struck at him soundlessly. A flying shadow that swept across the gleaming floor was his only warning, and his instinctive sidelong leap all that saved his life. He had a flashing glimpse of a hairy black horror that swung past him with a clashing of frothing fangs, and something splashed on his bare shoulder that burned like drops of liquid hellfire. Springing back, sword high, he saw the horror strike the floor, wheel and scuttle toward him with appalling speed – a gigantic black spider, such as men see only in nightmare dreams.

It was as large as a pig, and its eight thick hairy legs drove its ogreish body over the floor at headlong pace; its four evilly gleaming eyes shone with a horrible intelligence, and its fangs dripped venom that Conan knew, from the burning of his shoulder where only a few drops had splashed as the thing struck and missed, was laden with swift death. This was the killer that had dropped from its perch in the middle of the ceiling on a strand of its web, on the neck of the Nemedian. Fools that they were not to have suspected that the upper chambers would be guarded as well as the lower!

These thoughts flashed briefly through Conan's mind as the monster rushed. He leaped high, and it passed beneath him, wheeled and charged back. This time he evaded its rush with a sidewise leap, and struck back like a cat. His sword severed one of the hairy legs, and again he barely saved himself as the monstrosity swerved at him, fangs clicking fiendishly. But the creature did not press the pursuit; turning, it scuttled across the crystal floor and ran up the wall to the ceiling, where it crouched for an instant, glaring down at him with its fiendish red eyes. Then without warning it launched itself through space, trailing a strand of slimy grayish stuff.

Conan stepped back to avoid the hurtling body – then ducked frantically, just in time to escape being snared by the flying web-rope. He saw the monster's intent and sprang toward the door, but it was quicker, and a sticky strand cast across the door made him a prisoner. He dared not try to cut it with his sword; he knew the stuff would cling to the blade, and before he could shake it loose, the fiend would be sinking its fangs into his back.

Then began a desperate game, the wits and quickness of the man matched against the fiendish craft and speed of the giant spider. It no longer scuttled across the floor in a direct charge, or swung its body through the air at him. It raced about the ceiling and the walls, seeking to snare him in the long loops of sticky gray web-strands, which it flung with a devilish accuracy. These strands were thick as ropes, and Conan knew that once they were coiled about him, his desperate strength would not be enough to tear him free before the monster struck.

All over the chamber went on that devil's game, in utter silence except for the quick breathing of the man, the low scuff of his bare feet on the shining floor, the castanet rattle of the monstrosity's fangs. The gray strands lay in coils on the floor; they were looped along the walls; they overlaid the jewel-chests and silken couches, and hung in dusky festoons from the jeweled ceiling. Conan's steel-trap quickness of eye and muscle had kept him untouched, though the sticky loops had passed him so close they rasped his naked hide. He knew he could not always avoid them; he not only had to watch the strands swinging from the ceiling, but to keep his eye on the floor, lest he trip in the coils that lay there. Sooner or later a gummy loop would writhe about him, python-like, and then, wrapped like a cocoon, he would lie at the monster's mercy.

The spider raced across the chamber floor, the gray rope waving out behind it. Conan leaped high, clearing a couch – with a quick wheel the fiend ran up the wall, and the strand, leaping off the floor like a live thing, whipped about the Cimmerian's ankle. He caught himself on his hands as he fell, jerking frantically at the web which held him like a pliant vise, or the coil of a python. The hairy devil was racing down the wall to complete its capture. Stung to frenzy, Conan caught up a jewel chest and hurled it with all his strength. It was a move the monster was not expecting. Full in the midst of the branching black legs the massive missile struck, smashing against the wall with a muffled sickening crunch. Blood and greenish slime spattered, and the shattered mass fell with the burst gem-chest to the floor. The crushed black body lay among the flaming riot of jewels that spilled over it; the hairy legs moved aimlessly, the dying eyes glittered redly among the twinkling gems.

Conan glared about, but no other horror appeared, and he set himself to working free of the web. The substance clung tenaciously to his ankle and his hands, but at last he was free, and taking up his sword, he picked his way among the gray coils and loops to the inner door. What horrors lay within he did not know. The Cimmerian's blood was up, and since he had come so far, and overcome so much peril, he was determined to go through to the grim finish of the adventure, whatever that might be. And he felt that the jewel he sought was not among the many so carelessly strewn about the gleaming chamber.

Stripping off the loops that fouled the inner door, he found that it, like the other, was not locked. He wondered if the soldiers below were still unaware of his presence. Well, he was high above their heads, and if tales were to be believed, they were used to strange noises in the tower above them – sinister sounds, and screams of agony and horror.

Yara was on his mind, and he was not altogether comfortable as he opened the golden door. But he saw only a flight of silver steps leading down, dimly lighted by what means he could not ascertain. Down these he went silently, gripping his sword. He heard no sound, and came presently to an ivory door, set with blood-stones. He listened, but no sound came from within; only thin wisps of smoke drifted lazily from beneath the door, bearing a curious exotic odor unfamiliar to the Cimmerian. Below him the silver stair wound down to vanish in the dimness, and up that shadowy well no sound floated; he had an eery feeling that he was alone in a tower occupied only by ghosts and phantoms.

3

Cautiously he pressed against the ivory door and it swung silently inward. On the shimmering threshold Conan stared like a wolf in strange surroundings, ready to fight or flee on the instant. He was looking into a large chamber with a domed golden ceiling; the walls were of green jade, the floor of ivory, partly covered by thick rugs. Smoke and exotic scent of incense floated up from a brazier on a golden tripod, and behind it sat an idol on a sort of marble couch. Conan stared aghast; the image had the body of a man, naked, and green in color; but the head was one of nightmare and madness. Too large for the human body, it had no attributes of humanity. Conan stared at the wide flaring ears, the curling proboscis, on either side of which stood white tusks tipped with round golden balls. The eyes were closed, as if in sleep.

This then, was the reason for the name, the Tower of the Elephant, for the head of the thing was much like that of the beasts described by the Shemitish wanderer. This was Yara's god; where then should the gem be, but concealed in the idol, since the stone was called the Elephant's Heart?

As Conan came forward, his eyes fixed on the motionless idol, the eyes of the thing opened suddenly! The Cimmerian froze in his tracks. It was no image – it was a living thing, and he was trapped in its chamber!

That he did not instantly explode in a burst of murderous frenzy is a fact that measures his horror, which paralyzed him where he stood. A civilized man in his position would have sought doubtful refuge in the conclusion that he was insane; it did not occur to the Cimmerian to doubt his senses. He knew he was face to face with a demon of the Elder World, and the realization robbed him of all his faculties except sight.

The trunk of the horror was lifted and quested about, the topaz eyes stared unseeingly, and Conan knew the monster was blind. With the thought came a thawing of his frozen nerves, and he began to back silently toward the door. But the creature heard. The sensitive trunk stretched toward him, and Conan's horror froze him again when the being spoke, in a strange, stammering voice that never changed its key or timbre. The Cimmerian knew that those jaws were never built or intended for human speech.

'Who is here? Have you come to torture me again, Yara? Will you never be done? Oh, Yag-kosha, is there no end to agony?'

Tears rolled from the sightless eyes, and Conan's gaze strayed to the limbs stretched on the marble couch. And he knew the monster would not rise to attack him. He knew the marks of the rack, and the searing brand of the flame, and tough-souled as he was, he stood aghast at the ruined deformities which his reason told him had once been limbs as comely as his own. And suddenly all fear and repulsion went from him, to be replaced by a great pity. What this monster was, Conan could not know, but the evidences of its sufferings were so terrible and pathetic that a strange aching sadness came over the Cimmerian, he knew not why. He only felt that he was looking upon a cosmic tragedy, and he shrank with shame, as if the guilt of a whole race were laid upon him.

'I am not Yara,' he said. 'I am only a thief. I will not harm you.'

'Come near that I may touch you,' the creature faltered, and Conan came near unfearingly, his sword hanging forgotten in his hand. The sensitive trunk came out and groped over his face and shoulders, as a blind man gropes, and its touch was light as a girl's hand.

'You are not of Yara's race of devils,' sighed the creature. 'The clean, lean fierceness of the wastelands marks you. I know your people from of old, whom I knew by another name in the long, long ago when another world lifted its jeweled spires to the stars. There is blood on your fingers.'

'A spider in the chamber above and a lion in the garden,' muttered Conan.

'You have slain a man too, this night,' answered the other. 'And there is death in the tower above. I feel; I know.'

'Aye,' muttered Conan. 'The prince of all thieves lies there dead from the bite of a vermin.'

'So – and so!' The strange inhuman voice rose in a sort of low chant. 'A slaying in the tavern and a slaying on the road – I know; I feel. And the third will make the magic of which not even Yara dreams – oh, magic of deliverance, green gods of Yag!'

Again tears fell as the tortured body was rocked to and fro in the grip of varied emotions. Conan looked on, bewildered.

Then the convulsions ceased; the soft, sightless eyes were turned toward the Cimmerian, the trunk beckoned.

'Oh man, listen,' said the strange being. 'I am foul and monstrous to you, am I not? Nay, do not answer; I know. But you would seem as strange to me, could I see you. There are many worlds besides this earth, and life takes many shapes. I am neither god nor demon, but flesh and blood like yourself, though the substance differ in part, and the form be cast in a different mold.

'I am very old, oh man of the waste countries; long and long ago I came to this planet with others of my world, from the green planet Yag, which circles for ever in the outer fringe of this universe. We swept through space on mighty wings that drove us through the cosmos quicker than light, because we had warred with the kings of Yag and were defeated and outcast. But we could never return, for on earth our wings withered from our shoulders. Here we abode apart from earthly life. We fought the strange and terrible forms of life which then walked the earth, so that we became feared, and were not molested in the dim jungles of the east, where we had our abode.

'We saw men grow from the ape and build the shining cities of Valusia, Kamelia, Commoria and their sisters. We saw them reel before the thrusts of the heathen Atlanteans and Picts and Lemurians. We saw the oceans rise and engulf Atlantis and Lemuria, and the isles of the Picts, and shining cities of civilization.

We saw the survivors of Pictdom and Atlantis build their stone-age empires, and go down to ruin, locked in bloody wars. We saw the Picts sink into abysmal savagery, the Atlanteans into apedom again. We saw new savages drift southward in conquering waves from the Arctic circle to build a new civilization, with new kingdoms called Nemedia, and Koth, and Aquilonia and their sisters. We saw your people rise under a new name from the jungles of the apes that had been Atlanteans. We saw the descendants of the Lemurians who had survived the cataclysm, rise again through savagery and ride westward as Hyrkanians. And we saw this race of devils, survivors of the ancient civilization that was before Atlantis sank, come once more into culture and power – this accursed kingdom of Zamora.

'All this we saw, neither aiding nor hindering the immutable cosmic law, and one by one we died; for we of Yag are not immortal, though our lives are as the lives of planets and constellations. At last I alone was left, dreaming of old times among the ruined temples of jungle-lost Khitai, worshipped as a god by an ancient yellow-skinned race. Then came Yara, versed in dark knowledge handed down through the days of barbarism, since before Atlantis sank.

'First he sat at my feet and learned wisdom. But he was not satisfied with what I taught him, for it was white magic, and he wished evil lore, to enslave kings and glut a fiendish ambition. I would teach him none of the black secrets I had gained, through no wish of mine, through the eons.

'But his wisdom was deeper than I had guessed; with guile gotten among the dusky tombs of dark Stygia, he trapped me into divulging a secret I had not intended to bare; and turning my own power upon me, he enslaved me. Ah, gods of Yag, my cup has been bitter since that hour!

'He brought me up from the lost jungles of Khitai where the gray apes danced to the pipes of the yellow priests, and offerings of fruit and wine heaped my broken altars. No more was I a god to kindly jungle-folk – I was slave to a devil in human form.'

Again tears stole from the unseeing eyes.

'He pent me in this tower which at his command I built for him in a single night. By fire and rack he mastered me, and by strange unearthly tortures you would not understand. In agony I would long ago have taken my own life, if I could. But he kept me alive – mangled, blinded, and broken – to do his foul bidding. And for three hundred years I have done his bidding, from this marble couch, blackening my soul with cosmic sins, and staining my wisdom with crimes, because I had no other choice. Yet not all my ancient secrets has he wrested from me, and my last gift shall be the sorcery of the Blood and the Jewel.

'For I feel the end of time draw near. You are the hand of Fate. I beg of you, take the gem you will find on yonder altar.'

Conan turned to the gold and ivory altar indicated, and took up a great round jewel, clear as crimson crystal; and he knew that this was the Heart of the Elephant.

'Now for the great magic, the mighty magic, such as earth has not seen before, and shall not see again, through a million million of millenniums. By my life-blood I conjure it, by blood born on the green breast of Yag, dreaming far-poised in the great blue vastness of Space.

'Take your sword, man, and cut out my heart; then squeeze it so that the blood will flow over the red stone. Then go you down these stairs and enter the ebony chamber where Yara sits wrapped in lotus-dreams of evil. Speak his name and he will awaken. Then lay this gem before him, and say "Yag-kosha gives you a last gift and a last enchantment". Then get you from the tower quickly; fear not, your way shall be made clear. The life of man is not the life of Yag, nor is human death the death of Yag. Let me be free of this cage of broken blind flesh, and I will once more be Yogah of Yag, morning-crowned and shining, with wings to fly, and feet to dance, and eyes to see, and hands to break.'

Uncertainly Conan approached, and Yag-kosha, or Yogah, as if sensing his uncertainty, indicated where he should strike. Conan set his teeth and drove the sword deep. Blood streamed over the blade and his hand, and the monster started convulsively, then lay back quite still. Sure that life had fled, at least life as he understood it, Conan set to work on his grisly task and quickly brought forth something that he felt must be the strange being's heart, though it differed curiously from any he had ever seen. Holding the pulsing organ over the blazing jewel, he pressed it with both hands, and a rain of blood fell on the stone. To his surprise, it did not run off, but soaked into the gem, as water is absorbed by a sponge.

Holding the jewel gingerly, he went out of the fantastic chamber and came upon the silver steps. He did not look back; he instinctively felt that some transmutation was taking place in the body on the marble couch, and he further felt that it was of a sort not to be witnessed by human eyes.

He closed the ivory door behind him and without hesitation descended the silver steps. It did not occur to him to ignore the instructions given him. He halted at an ebony door, in the center of which was a grinning silver skull, and pushed it open. He looked into a chamber of ebony and jet, and saw, on a black silken couch, a tall, spare form reclining. Yara the priest and sorcerer lay before him, his eyes open and dilated with the fumes of the yellow lotus, far-staring, as if fixed on gulfs and nighted abysses beyond human ken.

'Yara!' said Conan, like a judge pronouncing doom. 'Awaken!'

The eyes cleared instantly and became cold and cruel as a vulture's. The tall silken-clad form lifted erect, and towered gauntly above the Cimmerian.

'Dog!' His hiss was like the voice of a cobra. 'What do you here?'

Conan laid the jewel on the ebony table.

'He who sent this gem bade me say "Yag-kosha gives you a last gift and a last enchantment".'

Yara recoiled, his dark face ashy. The jewel was no longer crystal-clear; its murky depths pulsed and throbbed, and curious smoky waves of changing color passed over its smooth surface. As if drawn hypnotically, Yara bent over the table and gripped the gem in his hands, staring into its shadowed depths, as if it were a magnet to draw the shuddering soul from his body. And as Conan looked, he thought that his eyes must be playing him tricks. For when Yara had risen up from his couch, the priest had seemed gigantically tall; yet now he saw that Yara's head would scarcely come to his shoulder. He blinked, puzzled, and for the first time that night, doubted his own senses. Then with a shock he realized that the priest was shrinking in stature – was growing smaller before his very gaze.

With a detached feeling he watched, as a man might watch a play; immersed in a feeling of overpowering unreality, the Cimmerian was no longer sure of his own identity; he only knew that he was looking upon the external evidence of the unseen play of vast Outer forces, beyond his understanding.

Now Yara was no bigger than a child; now like an infant he sprawled on the table, still grasping the jewel. And now the sorcerer suddenly realized his fate, and he sprang up, releasing the gem. But still he dwindled, and Conan saw a tiny, pygmy figure rushing wildly about the ebony table-top, waving tiny arms and shrieking in a voice that was like the squeak of an insect.

Now he had shrunk until the great jewel towered above him like a hill, and Conan saw him cover his eyes with his hands, as if to shield them from the glare, as he staggered about like a madman. Conan sensed that some unseen magnetic force was pulling Yara to the gem. Thrice he raced wildly about it in a narrowing circle, thrice he strove to turn and run out across the table; then with a scream that echoed faintly in the ears of the watcher, the priest threw up his arms and ran straight toward the blazing globe.

Bending close, Conan saw Yara clamber up the smooth, curving surface, impossibly, like a man climbing a glass mountain. Now the priest stood on the top, still with tossing arms, invoking what grisly names only the gods know. And suddenly he sank into the very heart of the jewel, as a man sinks into a sea, and Conan saw the smoky waves close over his head. Now he saw him in the crimson heart of the jewel, once more crystal-clear, as a man sees a scene far away, tiny with great distance. And into the heart came a green, shining winged figure with the body of a man and the head of an elephant – no longer blind or crippled. Yara threw up his arms and fled as a madman flees, and on his heels came the avenger. Then, like the bursting of a bubble, the great jewel vanished in a rainbow burst of iridescent gleams, and the ebony table-top lay bare and deserted – as bare, Conan somehow knew, as the marble couch in the chamber above, where the body of that strange transcosmic being called Yag-kosha and Yogah had lain.

The Cimmerian turned and fled from the chamber, down the silver stairs. So mazed was he that it did not occur to him to escape from the tower by the way he had entered it. Down that winding, shadowy silver well he ran, and came into a large chamber at the foot of the gleaming stairs. There he halted for an instant; he had come into the room of soldiers. He saw the glitter of their silver corselets, the sheen of their jeweled sword-hilts. They sat slumped at the banquet board, their dusky plumes waving somberly above their drooping helmeted heads; they lay among their dice and fallen goblets on the wine-stained lapis-lazuli floor. And he knew that they were dead. The promise had been made, the word kept; whether sorcery or magic or the falling shadow of great green wings had stilled the revelry, Conan could not know, but his way had been made clear. And a silver door stood open, framed in the whiteness of dawn.

Into the waving green gardens came the Cimmerian, and as the dawn wind blew upon him with the cool fragrance of luxuriant growths, he started like a man waking from a dream. He turned back uncertainly, to stare at the cryptic tower he had just left. Was he bewitched and enchanted? Had he dreamed all that had seemed to have passed? As he looked he saw the gleaming tower sway against the crimson dawn, its jewel-crusted rim sparkling in the growing light, and crash into shining shards.

THE HALL OF THE DEAD

(Synopsis)

A squad of Zamorian soldiers, led by the officer Nestor, a Gunderman mercenary, were marching down a narrow gorge, in pursuit of a thief, Conan the Cimmerian, whose thefts from rich merchants and nobles had infuriated the government of the nearest Zamorian city. Conan had left the city and been followed into the mountains. The walls of the gorge were steep and the gorge floor grown thickly with high rich grass. Striding through this grass at the head of his men, Nestor tripped over something and fell heavily. It was a rawhide rope stretched there by Conan, and it tripped a spring-pole which started a sudden avalanche that overwhelmed all the soldiers except Nestor, who escaped, bruised, and with his armor scratched and dented. Enraged, he followed the trail alone, and emerging into an upland plateau, came into the deserted city of the ancients, where he met Conan. He instantly attacked the Cimmerian, who, after a desperate battle, knocked him senseless with a sword-stroke on his helmet, and went on into the deserted city, thinking him dead. Nestor recovered and followed the Cimmerian. Conan, meanwhile, had entered the city, clambering over the walls, the gates being locked, and had encountered the monstrous being which haunted the city. This he slew by casting great blocks of stone upon it from an elevation, and then descending and hacking it to pieces with his sword. He had made his way to the great palace which was hewn out of a single monstrous hill of stone in the center of the city. He was seeking an entrance, when Nestor came upon him again, sword in hand, having followed him over the wall. Conan disgustedly advised him to aid him in securing the vast fabulous treasure instead of fighting. After some argument the Gunderman agreed, and they made their way into the palace, eventually coming to the great treasure chamber, where warriors of a by-gone age lay about in life-like positions. The companions made up packages of gold and precious stones, and threw dice to decide which should take a set of perfectly matched uncanny gems which adorned an altar, on which lay a jade serpent, apparently a god. Conan won the toss, and gave all the gold and the other jewels to Nestor. He himself swept up the altar-gems and the jade serpent – but when he lifted it off the altar, the ancient warriors came terrifically to life, and a terrible battle ensued, in which the thieves barely managed to escape with their lives. Hewing their way out of the palace, they were followed by the giant warriors who, upon coming into the sunlight, crumpled into dust. A terrific earthquake shook down the deserted city, and the companions were separated. Conan made his way back to the city, and entering a tavern, where his light-of-love was guzzling wine, spilled the jewels out on the ale-splashed table, in the Maul. To his amazement, they had turned to green dust. He then prepared to examine the jade serpent, who was still in the leather sack. The girl lifted the sack and dropped it with a scream, swearing that something moved inside it. At this instant a magistrate entered with a number of soldiers and arrested Conan, who set his back to a wall, and drew his sword. Before the soldiers could close in, the magistrate thrust his hand into the sack. Nestor had regained the city, with the coins which had not crumpled, and drunk, had told of the exploit. They had sought to arrest him, but drunk though he was, he had cut his way through and escaped. Now as the magistrate thrust his fat hand into the sack, he shrieked and jerked it forth, a living serpent fast to his fingers. The turmoil which followed gave Conan and the girl an opportunity to escape.

THE GOD IN THE BOWL

Arus the watchman grasped his crossbow with shaky hands, and he felt beads of clammy perspiration on his skin as he stared at the unlovely corpse sprawling on the polished floor before him. It is not pleasant to come upon Death in a lonely place at midnight.

Arus stood in a vast corridor, lighted by huge candles in niches along the walls. These walls were hung with black velvet tapestries, and between the tapestries hung shields and crossed weapons of fantastic make. Here and there, too, stood figures of curious gods – images carved of stone or rare wood, or cast of bronze, iron or silver – mirrored in the gleaming black mahogany floor.

Arus shuddered; he had never become used to the place, although he had worked there as watchman for some months. It was a fantastic establishment, the great museum and antique house which men called Kallian Publico's Temple, with its rarities from all over the world – and now, in the lonesomeness of midnight, Arus stood in the great silent hall and stared at the sprawling corpse that had been the rich and powerful owner of the Temple.

It entered even the dull brain of the watchman that the man looked strangely different now, than when he rode along the Palian Way in his golden chariot, arrogant and dominant, with his dark eyes glinting with magnetic vitality. Men who had hated and feared Kallian Publico would scarcely have recognized him now as he lay like a disintegrated tun of fat, his rich robe half torn from him, and his purple tunic awry. His face was blackened, his eyes almost starting from his head, and his tongue lolled blackly from his gaping mouth. His fat hands were thrown out as in a gesture of curious futility. On the thick fingers gems glittered.

'Why didn't they take his rings?' muttered the watchman uneasily, then he started and glared, the short hairs prickling at the nape of his neck. Through the dark silken hangings that masked one of the many doorways opening into the hallway, came a figure.

Arus saw a tall powerfully built youth, naked but for a loincloth, and sandals strapped high about his ankles. His skin was burned brown as by the suns of the wastelands, and Arus glanced nervously at the broad shoulders, massive chest and heavy arms. A single look at the moody, broad-browed features told the watchman that the man was no Nemedian. From under a mop of unruly black hair smoldered a pair of dangerous blue eyes. A long sword hung in a leather scabbard at his girdle.

Arus felt his skin crawl, and he fingered his crossbow tensely, of half a mind to drive a bolt through the stranger's body without parley, yet fearful of what might happen if he failed to inflict death at the first shot.

The stranger looked at the body on the floor more in curiosity than surprise.

'Why did you kill him?' asked Arus nervously.

The other shook his tousled head.

'I didn't kill him,' he answered, speaking Nemedian with a barbaric accent. 'Who is he?'

'Kallian Publico,' replied Arus, edging back.

A flicker of interest showed in the moody blue eyes.

'The owner of the house?'

'Aye.' Arus had edged his way to the wall, and now he took hold of a thick velvet rope which swung there, and jerked it violently. From the street outside sounded the strident clang of the bell that hung before all shops and establishments to summon the watch.

The stranger started.

'Why did you do that?' he asked. 'It will fetch the watchman.'

'I am the watchman, knave,' answered Arus, bracing his rocking courage. 'Stand where you are; don't move or I'll loose a bolt through you.'

His finger was on the trigger of his arbalest, the wicked square head of the quarrel leveled full on the other's broad breast. The stranger scowled, and his dark face was lowering. He showed no fear, but seemed to be hesitating in his mind as to whether he should obey the command or chance a sudden break of some kind. Arus licked his lips and his blood turned cold as he plainly saw indecision struggle with a murderous intent in the foreigner's cloudy eyes.

Then he heard a door crash open, and a medley of voices, and he drew a deep breath of amazed thankfulness. The stranger tensed and glared worriedly, like a startled hunting beast, as half a dozen men entered the hall. All but one wore the scarlet tunic of the Numalian police, were girt with stabbing swords and carried bills – long-shafted weapons, half pike, half axe.

'What devil's work is this?' exclaimed the foremost man, whose cold gray eyes and lean keen features, no less than his civilian garments, set him apart from his burly companions.

'By Mitra, Demetrio!' exclaimed Arus thankfully. 'Fortune is assuredly with me tonight. I had no hope that the watch would answer the summons so swiftly – or that you would be with them!'

'I was making the rounds with Dionus,' answered Demetrio. 'We were just passing the Temple when the watch-bell clanged. But who is this? Mitra! The master of the Temple himself!'

'No other,' replied Arus. 'And foully murdered. It is my duty to walk about the building steadily all night, because, as you know, there is an immense amount of wealth stored here. Kallian Publico had rich patrons – scholars, princes and wealthy collectors of rarities. Well, only a few minutes ago I tried the door which opens on the portico, and found it to be only bolted. The door is provided with a bolt, which works both from within or without, and a great lock which can be worked only from without. Only Kallian Publico had a key to that, the key which you see now hanging at his girdle.

'Naturally my suspicions were roused, for Kallian Publico always locks the door with the great lock when he closes the Temple; and I had not seen him return since he left earlier in the evening for his villa in the eastern suburbs of the city. I have a key that works the bolt; I entered and found the body lying as you see. I have not touched it.'

'So,' Demetrio's keen eyes swept the somber stranger. 'And who is this?'

'The murderer, without doubt!' cried Arus. 'He came from that door yonder. He is a northern barbarian of some sort – a Hyperborean or a Bossonian, perhaps.'

'Who are you?' asked Demetrio.

'I am Conan,' answered the barbarian. 'I am a Cimmerian.'

'Did you kill this man?'

The Cimmerian shook his head.

'Answer me!' snapped the questioner.

An angry glint rose in the moody blue eyes.

'I am no dog,' he replied resentfully.

'Oh, an insolent fellow!' sneered Demetrio's companion, a big man wearing the insignia of prefect of police. 'An independent cur! One of these citizens with rights, eh? I'll soon knock it out of him! Here, you! Come clean! Why did you murder—'

'Just a moment, Dionus,' ordered Demetrio curtly. 'Fellow, I am chief of the Inquisitorial Council of the city of Numalia. You had best tell me why you are here, and if you are not the murderer, prove it.'

The Cimmerian hesitated. He was not afraid, but slightly bewildered, as a barbarian always is when confronted by the evidence of civilized networks and systems, the workings of which are so baffling and mysterious to him.

'While he's thinking it over,' rapped Demetrio, turning to Arus, 'tell me – did you see Kallian Publico leave the Temple this evening?'

'No, he's usually gone when I arrive to begin my sentry-go. But the great door was bolted and locked.'

'Could he have entered the building again without your having seen him?'

'Why, it's possible, but hardly probable. The Temple is large, and I walk clear around it in a few minutes. If he had returned from his villa, he would of course have come in his chariot, for it is a long way – and who ever heard of Kallian Publico travelling otherwise? Even if I had been on the other side of the Temple, I'd have heard the wheels of the chariot on the cobblestones, and I've heard no such thing, nor seen any chariots, except those which always pass along the streets just at dusk.'

'And the door was locked earlier in the night?'

'I'll swear to it. I try all doors several times during the night. The door was locked on the outside until perhaps half an hour ago – that was the last time I tried it, until I found it unlocked.'

'You heard no cries or struggles?'

'No. But that's not strange. The walls of the Temple are so thick, they're practically sound-proof – an effect increased by the heavy hangings.'

'Why go to all this trouble of questions and speculations?' complained the burly prefect. 'It's much easier to beat a confession out of a suspect. Here's our man, no doubt about it. Let's take him to the Court of Justice – I'll get a statement if I have to smash his bones to pulp.'

Demetrio looked at the barbarian.

'You understand what he said?' asked the Inquisitor. 'What have you to say?'

'That any man who touches me will quickly be greeting his ancestors in hell,' the Cimmerian ground between his powerful teeth, his eyes glinting quick flames of dangerous anger.

'Why did you come here, if not to kill this man?' pursued Demetrio.

'I came to steal,' sullenly answered the other.

'To steal what?' rapped the Inquisitor.

'Food,' the reply came after an instant's hesitation.

'That's a lie!' snapped Demetrio. 'You knew there was no food here. Don't lie to me. Tell me the truth or—'

The Cimmerian laid his hand on his sword hilt, and the gesture was as fraught with menace as the lifting of a tiger's lip to bare his fangs.

'Save your bullying for the fools who fear you,' he growled, blue fires smoldering in his eyes. 'I'm no city-bred Nemedian to cringe before your hired dogs. I've killed better men than you for less than this.'

Dionus, who had opened his mouth to bellow in wrath, closed it suddenly. The watchmen shifted their bills uncertainly and glanced at Demetrio for orders. They were struck speechless at hearing the all-powerful police thus bearded and expected a command to seize the barbarian. But Demetrio did not give it. He knew, if the others were too stupid to know, the steel-trap muscles and blinding quickness of men raised beyond civilization's frontiers where life was a continual battle for existence, and he had no desire to loose the barbaric frenzy of the Cimmerian if it could be avoided. Besides, there was a doubt in his mind.

'I have not accused you of killing Kallian,' he snapped. 'But you must admit the appearances are against you. How did you enter the Temple?'

'I hid in the shadows of the warehouse which stands behind this building,' Conan answered grudgingly. 'When this dog –' jerking a thumb at Arus – 'passed by and rounded the corner, I ran quickly to the wall and scaled it—'

'A lie!' broke in Arus. 'No man could climb that straight wall!'

'Did you ever see a Cimmerian scale a sheer cliff?' asked Demetrio impatiently. 'I am conducting this investigation. Go on, Conan.'

'The corner is decorated with carvings,' said the Cimmerian. 'It was easy to climb. I gained the roof before this dog came around the building again. I went across the roof until I came upon a trap-door which was fastened with an iron bolt that went through it and was locked on the inside. I was forced to hew the bolt in twain with my sword—'

Arus, remembering the thickness of that bolt, gulped involuntarily and moved further back from the barbarian, who scowled abstractedly at him, and continued.

'I feared the noise might wake somebody, but it was a chance I had to take. I passed through the trap-door and came into an upper chamber. I didn't pause there, but came straightway to the stair—'

'How did you know where the stair was?' snapped the Inquisitor. 'I know that only Kallian's servants and his rich patrons were ever allowed in those upper rooms.'

A dogged stubbornness shadowed Conan's eyes and he remained silent.

'What did you do after you reached the stair?' demanded Demetrio.

'I came straight down it,' muttered the Cimmerian. 'It let into the chamber behind yonder curtained door. As I came down the stairs I heard the noise of a door being opened. When I looked through the hangings I saw this dog standing over the dead man.'

'Why did you come from your hiding place?'

'It was dark when I saw the watchman outside the Temple. When I saw him here I thought he was a thief too. It was not until he jerked the watch-bell rope and lifted his bow that I knew he was the watchman.'

'But even so,' persisted the Inquisitor, 'why did you reveal yourself?'

'I thought perhaps he had come to steal what—' the Cimmerian checked himself suddenly as if he had said too much.

'—What you had come after, yourself!' finished Demetrio. 'You have told me more than you intended! You came here with a definite purpose. You did not, by your own admission, tarry in the upper rooms, where the richest goods are generally stored. You knew the plan of the building – you were sent here by someone who knows the Temple well to steal some special thing!'

'And to kill Kallian Publico!' exclaimed Dionus. 'By Mitra, we've hit it! Grab him, men! We'll have a confession before morning!'

With a heathen curse Conan leaped back, whipping out his sword with a viciousness that made the keen blade hum.

'Back, if you value your dog-lives!' he snarled, his blue eyes blazing. 'Because you dare to torture shopkeepers and strip and beat harlots to make them talk, don't think you can lay your fat paws on a hillman! I'll take some of you to hell with me! Fumble with your bow, watchman – I'll burst your guts with my heel before this night's work is over!'

'Wait!' interposed Demetrio. 'Call your dogs off, Dionus. I'm not convinced that he is the murderer. You fool,' he added in a whisper, 'wait until we can summon more men, or trick him into laying down his sword.' Demetrio did not wish to forgo the advantage of his civilized mind by allowing matters to change to a physical basis, where the wild beast ferocity of the barbarian might even balance the odds against him.

'Very well,' grunted Dionus grudgingly. 'Fall back, men, but keep an eye on him.'

'Give me your sword,' said Demetrio.

'Take it if you can,' snarled Conan. Demetrio shrugged his shoulders.

'Very well. But don't try to escape. Four men with crossbows watch the house on the outside. We always throw a cordon about a house before we enter it.'

The barbarian lowered his blade, though he only slightly relaxed the tense watchfulness of his attitude. Demetrio turned again to the corpse.

'Strangled,' he muttered. 'Why strangle him when a sword-stroke is so much quicker and surer? These Cimmerians are a bloody race, born with a sword in their hand, as it were; I never heard of them killing a man in this manner.'

'Perhaps to divert suspicion,' muttered Dionus.

'Possibly.' He felt the body with experienced hands. 'Dead possibly half an hour,' he muttered. 'If Conan tells the truth about when he entered the Temple he would hardly have had time to commit the murder before Arus entered. But he may be lying – he might have broken in earlier.'

'I climbed the wall after Arus made the last round,' Conan growled.

'So *you* say.' Demetrio brooded for a space over the dead man's throat, which had been literally crushed to a pulp of purplish flesh. The head sagged awry on splintered vertebrae. Demetrio shook his head in doubt.

'Why should a murderer use a pliant cable apparently thicker than a man's arm?' he muttered. 'And what terrible constriction was applied to so crush the man's heavy neck.'

He rose and walked to the nearest door opening into the corridor.

'Here is a bust knocked from a stand near the door,' he said, 'and here the polished floor is scratched and the hangings in the doorway are pulled awry as if a clutching hand had grasped them – perhaps for support. Kallian Publico must have been attacked in that room. Perhaps he broke away from the assailant, or dragged the fellow with him as he fled. Anyway, he ran staggeringly out into the corridor where the murderer must have followed and finished him.'

'And if this heathen isn't the murderer, where is he?' demanded the prefect.

'I haven't exonerated the Cimmerian yet,' snapped the Inquisitor. 'But we'll investigate that room and—'

He halted and wheeled, listening. From the street had sounded a sudden rattle of chariot wheels, which approached rapidly, then ceased abruptly.

'Dionus!' snapped the Inquisitor. 'Send two men to find that chariot. Bring the driver here.'

'From the sound,' said Arus, who was familiar with all the noises of the street, 'I'd say it stopped in front of Promero's house, just on the other side of the silk-merchant's shop.'

'Who is Promero?' asked Demetrio.

'Kallian Publico's chief clerk.'

'Bring him here with the chariot driver,' snapped Demetrio. 'We'll wait until they come before we examine that room.'

Two guardsmen clomped away. Demetrio still studied the body; Dionus, Arus and the remaining policemen watched Conan, who stood, sword in hand, like a bronze figure of brooding menace. Presently sandalled feet re-echoed outside, and the two guardsmen entered with a strongly built, dark-skinned man in the helmet and tunic of a charioteer, with a whip in his hand; and a small, timid-looking individual, typical of that class which, risen from the ranks of artisans, supplies righthand men for wealthy merchants and traders.

This one recoiled with a cry from the sprawling bulk on the floor.

'Oh, I knew evil would come of this!'

'You are Promero, the clerk, I suppose. And you?'

'Enaro, Kallian Publico's charioteer.'

'You do not seem overly moved at the sight of his corpse,' observed Demetrio.

'Why should I be moved?' the dark eyes flashed. 'Someone has only done what I dared not, but longed to do.'

'So!' murmured the Inquisitor. 'Are you a free man?'

Enaro's eyes were bitter as he drew aside his tunic, showing the brand of the debtor-slave on his shoulder.

'Did you know your master was coming here tonight?'

'No. I brought the chariot to the Temple this evening for him as usual. He entered it and I drove toward his villa. But before we came to the Palian Way, he ordered me to turn and drive him back. He seemed much agitated in his mind.'

'And did you drive him back to the Temple?'

'No. He bade me stop at Promero's house. There he dismissed me, ordering me to return there for him shortly after midnight.'

'What time was this?'

'Shortly after dusk. The streets were almost deserted.'

'What did you do then?'

'I returned to the slave quarters where I remained until it was time to return to Promero's house. I drove straight there, and your men seized me as I talked with Promero in his door.'

'You have no idea why Kallian went to Promero's house?'

'He didn't speak of his business to his slaves.'

Demetrio turned to Promero. 'What do you know about this?'

'Nothing.' The clerk's teeth chattered as he spoke.

'Did Kallian Publico come to your house as the charioteer says?'

'Yes.'

'How long did he stay?'

'Only a few minutes. Then he left.'

'Did he come from your house to the Temple?'

'I don't know!' The clerk's voice was shrill with taut nerves.

'Why did he come to your house?'

'To – to talk matters of business with me.'

'You're lying,' snapped Demetrio. *'Why did he come to your house?'*

'I don't know! I don't know anything!' Promero was growing hysterical. 'I had nothing to do with it—'

'Make him talk, Dionus,' snapped Demetrio, and Dionus grunted and nodded to one of his men who, grinning savagely, moved toward the two captives.

'Do you know who I am?' he growled, thrusting his head forward and staring domineeringly at his shrinking prey.

'You're Posthumo,' answered the charioteer sullenly. 'You gouged out a girl's eye in the Court of Justice because she wouldn't give you information incriminating her lover.'

'I always get what I go after!' bellowed the guardsman, the veins in his thick neck swelling, and his face growing purple, as he seized the wretched clerk by the collar of his tunic, twisting it so the man was half strangled.

'Speak up, you rat!' he growled. 'Answer the Inquisitor.'

'Oh Mitra, mercy!' screamed the wretch. 'I swear that—'

Posthumo slapped him terrifically first on one side of the face and then on the other, and continued the interrogation by flinging him to the floor and kicking him with vicious accuracy.

'Mercy!' moaned the victim. 'I'll tell – I'll tell anything—'

'Then get up, you cur!' roared Posthumo, swelling with self-importance. 'Don't lie there whining.'

Dionus cast a quick glance at Conan to see if he were properly impressed.

'You see what happens to those who cross the police,' he said.

The Cimmerian spat with a sneer of cruel contempt for the moaning clerk.

'He's a weakling and a fool,' he growled. 'Let one of you touch me and I'll spill his guts on the floor.'

'Are you ready to talk?' asked Demetrio tiredly. He found these scenes wearingly monotonous.

'All I know,' sobbed the clerk, dragging himself to his feet and whimpering like a beaten dog in his pain, 'is that Kallian came to my house shortly after I arrived – I left the Temple at the same time he did – and sent his chariot away. He threatened me with discharge if I ever spoke of it. I am a poor man, without friends or favor. Without my position with him, I would starve.'

'What's that to me?' snapped Demetrio. 'How long did he remain at your house?'

'Until perhaps half an hour before midnight. Then he left, saying that he was going to the Temple, and would return after he had done what he wished to do there.'

'What was he going to do there?'

Promero hesitated at revealing the secrets of his dreaded employer, then a shuddering glance at Posthumo, who was grinning evilly as he doubled his huge fist, opened his lips quickly.

'There was something in the Temple he wished to examine.'

'But why should he come here alone in so much secrecy?'

'Because it was not his property. It arrived in a caravan from the south, at dawn. The men of the caravan knew nothing of it, except that it had been placed with them by the men of a caravan from Stygia, and was meant for Kalanthes of Hanumar, priest of Ibis. The master of the caravan had been paid by these other men to deliver it directly to Kalanthes, but he's a rascal by nature, and wished to proceed directly to Aquilonia, on the road to which Hanumar does not lie. So he asked if he might leave it in the Temple until Kalanthes could send for it.

'Kallian agreed, and told him he himself would send a runner to inform Kalanthes. But after the men had gone, and I spoke of the runner, Kallian forbade me to send him. He sat brooding over what the men had left.'

'And what was that?'

'A sort of sarcophagus, such as is found in ancient Stygian tombs, but this one was round, like a covered metal bowl. Its composition was something like copper, but much harder, and it was carved with hieroglyphics, like those found on the more ancient menhirs in southern Stygia. The lid was made fast to the body by carven copper-like bands.'

'What was in it?'

'The men of the caravan did not know. They only said that the men who gave it to them told them that it was a priceless relic, found among the tombs far beneath the pyramids and sent to Kalanthes "because of the love the sender bore the priest of Ibis". Kallian Publico believed that it contained the diadem of the giant-kings, of the people who dwelt in that dark land before the ancestors of the Stygians came there. He showed me a design carved on the lid, which he swore was the shape of the diadem which legend tells us the monster-kings wore.

'He determined to open the Bowl and see what it contained. He was like a madman when he thought of the fabled diadem, which myths say was set with the strange jewels known only to that ancient race, a single one of which is worth more than all the jewels of the modern world.

'I warned him against it. But he stayed at my house as I have said, and a short time before midnight, he came along to the Temple, hiding in the shadows until the watchman had passed to the other side of the building, then letting himself in with his belt key. I watched him from the shadows of the silk shop, saw him enter the Temple, and then returned to my own house. If the diadem was in the Bowl, or anything else of great value, he intended hiding it somewhere in the Temple and slipping out again. Then on the morrow he would raise a great hue and cry, saying that thieves had broken into his house and stolen Kalanthes's property. None would know of his prowlings but the charioteer and I, and neither of us would betray him.'

'But the watchman?' objected Demetrio.

'Kallian did not intend being seen by him; he planned to have him crucified as an accomplice of the thieves,' answered Promero. Arus gulped and turned pale as this duplicity of his employer came home to him.

'Where is this sarcophagus?' asked Demetrio. Promero pointed, and the Inquisitor grunted. 'So! The very room in which Kallian must have been attacked.'

Promero turned pale and twisted his thin hands.

'Why should a man in Stygia send Kalanthes a gift? Ancient gods and queer mummies have come up the caravan roads before, but who loves the priest of Ibis so well in Stygia, where they still worship the arch-demon Set who coils among the tombs in the darkness? The god Ibis has fought Set since the first dawn of the earth, and Kalanthes has fought Set's priests all his life. There is something dark and hidden here.'

'Show us this sarcophagus,' commanded Demetrio, and Promero hesitantly led the way. All followed, including Conan, who was apparently heedless of the wary eye the guardsmen kept on him, and seemed merely curious. They passed through the torn hangings and entered the room, which was rather more dimly lighted than the corridor. Doors on each side gave into other chambers, and the walls were lined with fantastic images, gods of strange lands and far peoples. And Promero cried out sharply.

'Look! The Bowl! It's open – and empty!'

In the center of the room stood a strange black cylinder, nearly four feet in height, and perhaps three feet in diameter at its widest circumference, which was halfway between the top and bottom. The heavy carven lid lay on the floor, and beside it a hammer and a chisel. Demetrio looked inside, puzzled an instant over the dim hieroglyphs, and turned to Conan.

'Is this what you came to steal?'

The barbarian shook his head.

'How could I bear it away? It is too big for one man to carry.'

'The bands were cut with this chisel,' mused Demetrio, 'and in haste. There are marks where misstrokes of the hammer dented the metal. We may assume that Kallian opened the Bowl. Someone was hiding nearby – possibly in the hangings in the doorway. When Kallian had the Bowl open, the murderer sprang on him – or he might have killed Kallian and opened the Bowl himself.'

'This is a grisly thing,' shuddered the clerk. 'It's too ancient to be holy. Who ever saw metal like it in a sane world? It seems less destructible than Aquilonian steel, yet see how it is corroded and eaten away in spots. Look at the bits of black mold clinging in the grooves of the hieroglyphics; they smell as earth smells from far below the surface. And look – here on the lid!' The clerk pointed with a shaky finger. 'What would you say it is?'

Demetrio bent closer to the carven design.

'I'd say it represents a crown of some sort,' he grunted.

'No!' exclaimed Promero. 'I warned Kallian, but he would not believe me! It is a scaled serpent coiled with its tail in its mouth. It is the sign of Set, the Old Serpent, the god of the Stygians! This Bowl is too old for a human world – it is a relic of the time when Set walked the earth in the form of a man! The race which sprang from his loins laid the bones of their kings away in such cases as these, perhaps!'

'And you'll say that those moldering bones rose up and strangled Kallian Publico and then walked away, perhaps,' derided Demetrio.

'It was no man who was laid to rest in that bowl,' whispered the clerk, his eyes wide and staring. 'What human could lie in it?'

Demetrio swore disgustedly.

'If Conan is not the murderer,' he snapped, 'the slayer is still somewhere in this building. Dionus and Arus, remain here with me, and you three prisoners stay here too. The rest of you search the building. The murderer could only have escaped – if he got away before Arus found the body – by the way Conan used in entering, and in that case the barbarian would have seen him, if he's telling the truth.'

'I saw no one but this dog,' growled Conan, indicating Arus.

'Of course not, because you're the murderer,' said Dionus. 'We're wasting time, but we'll search the building as a formality. And if we find no one, I promise you shall burn! Remember the law, my black-haired savage – you go to the mines for killing a commoner, you hang for killing a tradesman, and for murdering a rich man, you burn!'

Conan answered with a wicked lift of his lip, baring his teeth, and the men began their search. The listeners in the chamber heard them stamping upstairs and down, moving objects, opening doors and bellowing to one another through the rooms.

'Conan,' said Demetrio, 'you know what it means if they find no one?'

'I didn't kill him,' snarled the Cimmerian. 'If he had sought to hinder me I'd have split his skull. But I did not see him until I saw his corpse.'

'I know that someone sent you here tonight, to steal at least,' said Demetrio. 'By your silence you incriminate yourself in this murder as well. You had best speak. The mere fact of your being here is sufficient to send you to the mines for ten years, anyhow, whether you admit your guilt or not. But if you tell the whole tale, you may save yourself from the stake.'

'Well,' answered the barbarian grudgingly, 'I came here to steal the Zamorian diamond goblet. A man gave me a diagram of the Temple and told me where to look for it. It is kept in that room –' Conan pointed – 'in a niche in the floor under a copper Shemitish god.'

'He speaks truth there,' said Promero. 'I'd thought that not half a dozen men in the world knew the secret of that hiding place.'

'And if you had secured it,' asked Dionus sneeringly, 'would you really have taken it to the man who hired you? Or would you have kept it for yourself?'

Again the smoldering eyes flashed resentment.

'I am no dog,' the barbarian muttered. 'I keep my word.'

'Who sent you here?' Demetrio demanded, but Conan kept a sullen silence.

The guardsmen were straggling back from their search.

'There's no man hiding in this building,' they growled. 'We've ransacked the place. We found the trap-door in the roof through which the barbarian entered, and the bolt he cut in half. A man escaping that way would have been seen by the guards we posted about the building, unless he fled before we came. Then, besides, he would have had to stack tables or chairs or cases upon each other to reach it from below, and that has not been done. Why couldn't he have gone out the front door just before Arus came around the building?'

'Because the door was bolted on the inside, and the only keys which will work that bolt are the one belonging to Arus and the one which still hangs on the girdle of Kallian Publico.'

'I've found the cable the murderer used,' one of them announced.

'A black cable, thicker than a man's arm, and curiously splotched.'

'Then where is it, fool?' exclaimed Dionus.

'In the chamber adjoining this one,' answered the guard. 'It's wrapped about a marble pillar, where no doubt the murderer thought it would be safe from detection. I couldn't reach it. But it must be the right one.'

He led the way into a room filled with marble statuary, and pointed to a tall column, one of several which served a purpose more of ornament to set off the statues, than of utility. And then he halted and stared.

'It's gone!' he cried.

'It never was there!' snorted Dionus.

'By Mitra, it was!' swore the guardsman. 'Coiled about the pillar just above those carven leaves. It's so shadowy up there near the ceiling I couldn't tell much about it – but it was there.'

'You're drunk,' snapped Demetrio, turning away. 'That's too high for a man to reach; and nothing but a snake could climb that smooth pillar.'

'A Cimmerian could,' muttered one of the men.

'Possibly. Say that Conan strangled Kallian, tied the cable about the pillar, crossed the corridor and hid in the room where the stair is. How then, could he have removed it after you saw it? He has been among us ever since Arus found the body. No, I tell you Conan didn't commit the murder. I believe the real murderer killed Kallian to secure whatever was in the Bowl, and is hiding now in some secret nook in the Temple. If we can't find him, we'll have to put the blame on the barbarian to satisfy Justice, but – where is Promero?'

They had returned to the silent body in the corridor. Dionus bellowed threateningly for Promero, and the clerk came suddenly from the room in which stood the empty Bowl. He was shaking and his face was white.

'What now, man?' exclaimed Demetrio irritably.

'I found a symbol on the bottom of the Bowl!' chattered Promero. 'Not an ancient hieroglyphic, but a symbol recently carved! The mark of Thoth-amon, the Stygian sorcerer, Kalanthes's deadly foe!

He found it in some grisly cavern below the haunted pyramids! The gods of old times did not die, as men died – they fell into long sleeps and their worshippers locked them in sarcophagi so that no alien hand might break their slumbers. Thoth-amon sent death to Kalanthes – Kallian's greed caused him to loose the horror – and it is lurking somewhere near us – even now it may be creeping upon us—'

'You gibbering fool!' roared Dionus disgustedly, striking him heavily across the mouth. Dionus was a materialist, with scant patience for eery speculations.

'Well, Demetrio,' he said, turning to the Inquisitor, 'I see nothing else to do other than to arrest this barbarian—'

The Cimmerian cried out suddenly and they wheeled. He was glaring toward the door of a chamber that adjoined the room of statues.

'Look!' he exclaimed. 'I saw something move in that room – I saw it through the hangings. Something that crossed the floor like a long dark shadow!'

'Bah!' snorted Posthumo. 'We searched that room—'

'He saw something!' Promero's voice shrilled and cracked with hysterical excitement. 'This place is accursed! Something came out of the sarcophagus and killed Kallian Publico! It hid from you where no human could hide, and now it is in that room! Mitra defend us from the powers of Darkness! I tell you it was one of Set's children in that grisly Bowl!' He caught Dionus's sleeve with claw-like fingers. 'You must search that room again!'

The prefect shook him off disgustedly, and Posthumo was inspired to a flight of humor.

'You shall search it yourself, clerk!' he said, grasping Promero by neck and girdle, and propelling the screaming wretch forcibly toward the door, outside of which he paused and hurled him into the room so violently the clerk fell and lay half stunned.

'Enough of this,' growled Dionus, eyeing the silent Cimmerian. The prefect lifted his hand, Conan's eyes began to burn bluely, and a tension crackled in the air, when an interruption came. A guardsman entered, dragging a slender, richly dressed figure.

'I saw him slinking about the back of the Temple,' quoth the guard, looking for commendation. Instead he received curses that lifted his hair.

'Release that gentleman, you bungling fool!' swore the prefect. 'Don't you know Aztrias Petanius, the nephew of the city's governor?'

The abashed guard fell away and the foppish young nobleman brushed his embroidered sleeve fastidiously.

'Save your apologies, good Dionus,' he lisped affectedly. 'All in line of duty, I know. I was returning from a late revel and walking to rid my brain of the wine fumes. What have we here? By Mitra, is it murder?'

'Murder it is, my lord,' answered the prefect. 'But we have a man who, though Demetrio seems to have doubts on the matter, will doubtless go to the stake for it.'

'A vicious looking brute,' murmured the young aristocrat. 'How can any doubt his guilt? I have never seen such a villainous countenance before.'

'Yes, you have, you scented dog,' snarled the Cimmerian, 'when you hired me to steal the Zamorian goblet for you. Revels, eh? Bah! You were waiting in the shadows for me to hand you the goblet. I would not have revealed your name if you had given me fair words. Now tell these dogs that you saw me climb the wall after the watchman made the last round, so that they'll know I didn't have time to kill this fat swine before Arus entered and found the body.'

Demetrio looked quickly at Aztrias, who did not change color.

'If what he says is true, my lord,' said the Inquisitor, 'it clears him of the murder, and we can easily hush up the matter of attempted theft. He is due ten years at hard labor for house-breaking, but if you say the word, we'll arrange for him to escape and none but us will ever know anything about it. I understand – you wouldn't be the first young nobleman who had to resort to such things to pay gambling debts and the like. You can rely on our discretion.'

Conan looked at the young nobleman expectantly, but Aztrias shrugged his slender shoulders and covered a yawn with a delicate white hand.

'I know him not,' he answered. 'He is mad to say I hired him. Let him take his just desserts. He has a strong back and the toil in the mines will be well for him.'

Conan's eyes blazed and he started as if stung; the guards tensed, grasping their bills, then relaxed as he dropped his head suddenly, as if in sullen resignation, and not even Demetrio could tell that he was watching them from under his heavy black brows, with eyes that were slits of blue bale-fire.

He struck with no more warning than a striking cobra; his sword flashed in the candlelight. Aztrias shrieked and his head flew from his shoulders in a shower of blood, the features frozen in a white mask of horror. Cat-like, Conan wheeled and thrust murderously for Demetrio's groin. The Inquisitor's instinctive recoil barely deflected the point which sank into his thigh, glanced from the bone and ploughed out through the outer side of the leg. Demetrio went to his knee with a groan, unnerved and nauseated with agony.

Conan had not paused. The bill which Dionus flung up saved the prefect's skull from the whistling blade which turned slightly as it cut through the shaft, and sheared his ear cleanly from his head. The blinding speed of the barbarian paralyzed the senses of the police and made their actions futile gestures. Caught flat-footed and dazed by his quickness and ferocity, half of them would have been down before they had a chance to fight back, except that Posthumo, more by luck than skill, threw his arms about the Cimmerian, pinioning his sword-arm. Conan's left hand leaped to the guard's head, and Posthumo fell away and writhed shrieking on the floor, clutching a gaping red socket where an eye had been.

Conan bounded back from the waving bills and his leap carried him outside the ring of his foes, to where Arus stood fumbling at his crossbow. A savage kick in the belly dropped him, green-faced and gagging, and Conan's sandalled heel crunched square in the watchman's mouth. The wretch screamed through a ruin of splintered teeth, blowing bloody froth from his mangled lips.

Then all were frozen in their tracks by the soul-shaking horror of a scream which rose from the chamber into which Posthumo had hurled Promero, and from the velvet-hung door the clerk came reeling, and stood there, shaking with great silent sobs, tears running down his pasty face and dripping off his loose sagging lips, like an idiot-babe weeping.

All halted to stare at him aghast – Conan with his dripping sword, the police with their lifted bills, Demetrio crouching on the floor and striving to staunch the blood that jetted from the great gash in his thigh, Dionus clutching the bleeding stump of his severed ear, Arus weeping and spitting out fragments of broken teeth – even Posthumo ceased his howls and blinked whimpering through the bloody mist that veiled his half-sight.

Promero came reeling out into the corridor and fell stiffly before them. Screeching in an unbearable high-pitched laughter of madness, he cried shrilly, 'The god has a long neck! Ha! ha! ha! Oh, a long, a cursed long neck!' And then with a frightful convulsion he stiffened and lay grinning vacantly at the shadowy ceiling.

'He's dead!' whispered Dionus, awedly, forgetting his own hurt, and the barbarian who stood with his dripping sword so near him. He bent over the body, then straightened, his eyes flaring. 'He's not wounded – *in Mitra's name what is in that chamber?*'

Then horror swept over them and they ran screaming for the outer door, jammed there in a clawing shrieking mob, and burst through like madmen. Arus followed and the half-blind Posthumo struggled up and blundered blindly after his fellows, squealing like a wounded pig and begging them not to leave him behind. He fell among them and they knocked him down and trampled him, screaming in their fear. But he crawled after them, and after him came Demetrio. The Inquisitor had the courage to face the unknown, but he was unnerved and wounded, and the sword that had struck him down was still near him. Grasping his blood-spurting thigh, he limped after his companions. Police, charioteer and watchman, wounded or whole, they burst screaming into the street, where the men watching the building took panic and joined in the flight, not waiting to ask why. Conan stood in the great corridor alone, save for the corpses on the floor.

The barbarian shifted his grip on his sword and strode into the chamber. It was hung with rich silken tapestries; silken cushions and couches lay strewn about in careless profusion; and over a heavy gilded screen a face looked at the Cimmerian.

Conan stared in wonder at the cold classic beauty of that countenance, whose like he had never seen among the sons of men. Neither weakness nor mercy nor cruelty nor kindness, nor any other human emotion was in those features. They might have been the marble mask of a god, carved by a master hand, except for the unmistakable life in them – life cold and strange, such as the Cimmerian had never known and could not understand. He thought fleetingly of the marble perfection of the body which the screen concealed – it must be perfect, he thought, since the face was so inhumanly beautiful. But he could see only the god-like face, the finely molded head which swayed curiously from side to side. The full lips opened and spoke a single word in a rich vibrant tone that was like the golden chimes that ring in the jungle-lost temples of Khitai. It was an unknown tongue, forgotten before the kingdoms of man arose, but Conan knew that it meant, 'Come!'

And the Cimmerian came, with a desperate leap and a humming slash of his sword. The beautiful head rolled from the top of the screen in a jet of dark blood and fell at his feet, and he gave back, fearing to touch it. Then his skin crawled, for the screen shook and heaved with the convulsions of something behind. Conan had seen and heard men die by the scores, and never had he heard a human being make such sounds in the death-throes. There was a thrashing, floundering noise, as if a great cable were being lashed violently about.

At last the movements ceased and Conan looked gingerly behind the screen. Then the full horror of it all rushed over the Cimmerian, and he fled, nor did he slacken his headlong flight until the spires of Numalia faded into the dawn behind him. The thought of Set was like a nightmare, and the children of Set who once ruled the earth and who now sleep in their nighted caverns far below the black pyramids. Behind that gilded screen there had been no human body – only the shimmering, headless coils of a gigantic serpent.

ROGUES IN THE HOUSE

'One fled, one dead, one sleeping in a golden bed'

OLD RIME

1

At a court festival, Nabonidus, the Red Priest, who was the real ruler of the city, touched Murilo, the young aristocrat, courteously on the arm. Murilo turned to meet the priest's enigmatic gaze, and to wonder at the hidden meaning therein. No words passed between them, but Nabonidus bowed and handed Murilo a small gold cask. The young nobleman, knowing that Nabonidus did nothing without reason, excused himself at the first opportunity and returned hastily to his chamber. There he opened the cask and found within a human ear, which he recognized by a peculiar scar upon it. He broke into a profuse sweat, and was no longer in doubt about the meaning in the Red Priest's glance.

But Murilo, for all his scented black curls and foppish apparel, was no weakling to bend his neck to the knife without a struggle. He did not know whether Nabonidus was merely playing with him, or giving him a chance to go into voluntary exile, but the fact that he was still alive and at liberty proved that he was to be given at least a few hours, probably for meditation. But he needed no meditation for decision; what he needed was a tool. And Fate furnished that tool, working among the dives and brothels of the squalid quarters even while the young nobleman shivered and pondered in the part of the city occupied by the purple-towered marble and ivory palaces of the aristocracy.

There was a priest of Anu whose temple, rising at the fringe of the slum district, was the scene of more than devotions. The priest was fat and full-fed, and he was at once a fence for stolen articles and a spy for the police. He worked a thriving trade both ways, because the district on which he bordered was The Maze, a tangle of muddy winding alleys and sordid dens, frequented by the boldest thieves in the kingdom. Daring above all were a Gunderman deserter from the mercenaries and a barbaric Cimmerian. Because of the priest of Anu, the Gunderman was taken and hanged in the market-square. But the Cimmerian fled, and learning in devious ways of the priest's treachery, he entered the temple of Anu by night, and cut off the priest's head. There followed a great turmoil in the city, but search for the killer proved fruitless until his punk betrayed him to the authorities, and led a captain of the guard and his squad to the hidden chamber where the barbarian lay drunk.

Waking to stupefied but ferocious life when they seized him, he disemboweled the captain, burst through his assailants and would have escaped, but for the liquor that still clouded his senses. Bewildered and half blinded, he missed the open door in his headlong flight, and dashed his head against the stone wall so terrifically that he knocked himself senseless. When he came to, he was in the strongest dungeon in the city, shackled to the wall with chains not even his barbaric thews could break.

To this cell came Murilo, masked and wrapped in a wide black cloak. The Cimmerian surveyed him with interest, thinking him the executioner sent to dispatch him. Murilo set him at rights, and regarded him with no less interest. Even in the dim light of the dungeon, with his limbs loaded with chains, the primitive power of the man was evident. His mighty body and thick-muscled limbs combined the strength of a grizzly with the quickness of a panther. Under his tangled black mane his blue eyes blazed with unquenchable savagery.

'Would you like to live?' asked Murilo. The barbarian grunted, new interest glinting in his eyes.

'If I arrange for your escape will you do a favor for me?' the aristocrat asked.

The Cimmerian did not speak, but the intentness of his gaze answered for him.

'I want you to kill a man for me.'

'Whom?'

Murilo's voice sank to a whisper. 'Nabonidus, the king's priest!'

The Cimmerian showed no sign of surprise or perturbation. He had none of the fear or reverence for authority that civilization instills in men. King or beggar, it was all one to him. Nor did he ask why Murilo had come to him, when the quarters were full of cutthroats outside prisons.

'When am I to escape?' he demanded.

'Within the hour. There is but one guard in this part of the dungeon at night. He can be bribed; he *has* been bribed. See, here are the keys to your chains. I'll remove them, and after I have been gone an hour, the guard, Athicus, will unlock the door to your cell. You will bind him with strips torn from your tunic; so when he is found, the authorities will think you were rescued from the outside, and will not suspect him. Go at once to the house of the Red Priest, and kill him. Then go to the Rats' Den, where a man will meet you and give you a pouch of gold and a horse. With those you can escape from the city and flee the country.'

'Take off these cursed chains now,' demanded the Cimmerian. 'And have the guard bring me food. By Crom, I have lived on moldy bread and water for a whole day and I am nigh to famishing.'

'It shall be done; but remember – you are not to escape until I have had time to reach my house.'

Freed of his chains, the barbarian stood up and stretched his heavy arms, enormous in the gloom of the dungeon. Murilo again felt that if any man in the world could accomplish the task he had set, this Cimmerian could. With a few repeated instructions he left the prison, first directing Athicus to take a platter of beef and ale in to the prisoner. He knew he could trust the guard, not only because of the money he had paid, but also because of certain information he possessed regarding the man.

When he returned to his chamber, Murilo was in full control of his fears. Nabonidus would strike through the king – of that he was certain. And since the royal guardsmen were not knocking at his door, it was as certain that the priest had said nothing to the king, so far. Tomorrow he would speak, beyond a doubt – if he lived to see tomorrow.

Murilo believed the Cimmerian would keep faith with him. Whether the man would be able to carry out his purpose remained to be seen. Men had attempted to assassinate the Red Priest before, and they had died in hideous and nameless ways. But they had been products of the cities of men, lacking the wolfish instincts of the barbarian. The instant that Murilo, turning the gold cask with its severed ear in his hands, had learned through his secret channels that the Cimmerian had been captured, he had seen a solution of his problem.

In his chamber again, he drank a toast to the man, whose name was Conan, and to his success that night. And while he was drinking, one of his spies brought him the news that Athicus had been arrested and thrown into prison. The Cimmerian had not escaped.

Murilo felt his blood turn to ice again. He could see in this twist of fate only the sinister hand of Nabonidus, and an eery obsession began to grow on him that the Red Priest was more than human – a sorcerer who read the minds of his victims and pulled strings on which they danced like puppets. With despair came desperation. Girding a sword beneath his black cloak, he left his house by a hidden way, and hurried through the deserted streets. It was just at midnight when he came to the house of Nabonidus, looming blackly among the walled gardens that separated it from the surrounding estates.

The wall was high but not impossible to negotiate. Nabonidus did not put his trust in mere barriers of stone. It was what was inside the wall that was to be feared. What these things were Murilo did not know precisely. He knew there was at least a huge savage dog that roamed the gardens and had on occasion torn an intruder to pieces as a hound rends a rabbit. What else there might be he did not care to conjecture. Men who had been allowed to enter the house on brief, legitimate business, reported that Nabonidus dwelt among rich furnishings, yet simply, attended by a surprisingly small number of servants. Indeed, they mentioned only one as having been visible – a tall silent man called Joka. Someone else, presumably a slave, had been heard moving about in the recesses of the house, but this person no one had ever seen. The greatest mystery of that mysterious house was Nabonidus himself, whose power of intrigue and grasp on international politics had made him the strongest man in the kingdom. People, chancellor and king moved puppet-like on the strings he worked.

Murilo scaled the wall and dropped down into the gardens, which were expanses of shadow, darkened by clumps of shrubbery and waving foliage. No light shone in the windows of the house which loomed so blackly among the trees. The young nobleman stole stealthily yet swiftly through the shrubs. Momentarily he expected to hear the baying of the great dog, and to see its giant body hurtle through the shadows. He doubted the effectiveness of his sword against such an attack, but he did not hesitate. As well die beneath the fangs of a beast as the ax of the headsman.

He stumbled over something bulky and yielding. Bending close in the dim starlight, he made out a limp shape on the ground. It was the dog that guarded the gardens, and it was dead. Its neck was broken and it bore what seemed to be the marks of great fangs. Murilo felt that no human being had done this. The beast had met a monster more savage than itself. Murilo glared nervously at the cryptic masses of bush and shrub; then with a shrug of his shoulders, he approached the silent house.

The first door he tried proved to be unlocked. He entered warily, sword in hand, and found himself in a long shadowy hallway dimly illumined by a light that gleamed through the hangings at the other end. Complete silence hung over the whole house. Murilo glided along the hall and halted to peer through the hangings. He looked into a lighted room, over the windows of which velvet curtains were drawn so closely as to allow no beam to shine through. The room was empty, in so far as human life was concerned, but it had a grisly occupant, nevertheless. In the midst of a wreckage of furniture and torn hangings that told of a fearful struggle, lay the body of a man. The form lay on its belly, but the head was twisted about so that the chin rested behind a shoulder. The features, contorted into an awful grin, seemed to leer at the horrified nobleman.

For the first time that night, Murilo's resolution wavered. He cast an uncertain glance back the way he had come. Then the memory of the headsman's block and ax steeled him, and he crossed the room, swerving to avoid the grinning horror sprawled in its midst. Though he had never seen the man before, he knew from former descriptions that it was Joka, Nabonidus's saturnine servant.

He peered through a curtained door into a broad circular chamber, banded by a gallery halfway between the polished floor and the lofty ceiling. This chamber was furnished as if for a king. In the midst of it stood an ornate mahogany table, loaded with vessels of wine and rich viands. And Murilo stiffened. In a great chair whose broad back was toward him, he saw a figure whose habiliments were familiar. He glimpsed an arm in a red sleeve resting on the arm of the chair; the head, clad in the familiar scarlet hood of the gown, was bent forward as if in meditation. Just so had Murilo seen Nabonidus sit a hundred times in the royal court.

Cursing the pounding of his own heart, the young nobleman stole across the chamber, sword extended, his whole frame poised for the thrust. His prey did not move, nor seem to hear his cautious advance. Was the Red Priest asleep, or was it a corpse which slumped in that great chair? The length of a single stride separated Murilo from his enemy, when suddenly the man in the chair rose and faced him.

The blood went suddenly from Murilo's features. His sword fell from his fingers and rang on the polished floor. A terrible cry broke from his livid lips; it was followed by the thud of a falling body. Then once more silence reigned over the house of the Red Priest.

2

Shortly after Murilo left the dungeon where Conan the Cimmerian was confined, Athicus brought the prisoner a platter of food which included, among other things, a huge joint of beef and a tankard of ale. Conan fell to voraciously, and Athicus made a final round of the cells, to see that all was in order, and that none should witness the pretended prison-break. It was while he was so occupied that a squad of guardsmen marched into the prison and placed him under arrest. Murilo had been mistaken when he assumed this arrest denoted discovery of Conan's planned escape. It was another matter; Athicus had become careless in his dealings with the underworld, and one of his past sins had caught up with him.

Another jailer took his place, a stolid, dependable creature whom no amount of bribery could have shaken from his duty. He was unimaginative, but he had an exalted idea of the importance of his job.

After Athicus had been marched away to be formally arraigned before a magistrate, this jailer made the rounds of the cells as a matter of routine. As he passed that of Conan, his sense of propriety was shocked and outraged to see the prisoner free of his chains, and in the act of gnawing the last shreds of meat from a huge beef-bone. The jailer was so upset that he made the mistake of entering the cell alone, without calling guards from other parts of the prison. It was his first mistake in the line of duty, and his last. Conan brained him with the beef-bone, took his poniard and his keys, and made a leisurely departure. As Murilo had said, only one guard was on duty there at night. The Cimmerian passed himself outside the walls by means of the keys he had taken, and presently emerged into the outer air, as free as if Murilo's plan had been successful.

In the shadows of the prison walls, Conan paused to decide his next course of action. It occurred to him that since he had escaped through his own actions, he owed nothing to Murilo; yet it had been the young nobleman who had removed his chains and had the food sent to him, without either of which his escape would have been impossible. Conan decided that he was indebted to Murilo, and, since he was a man who discharged his obligations eventually, he determined to carry out his promise to the young aristocrat. But first he had some business of his own to attend to.

He discarded his ragged tunic and moved off through the night naked but for a loin-cloth. As he went he fingered the poniard he had captured – a murderous weapon with a broad double-edged blade nineteen inches long. He slunk along alleys and shadowed plazas until he came to the district which was his destination – The Maze. Along its labyrinthian ways he went with the certainty of familiarity. It was indeed a maze of black alleys and enclosed courts and devious ways; of furtive sounds, and stenches. There was no paving on the streets; mud and filth mingled in an unsavory mess. Sewers were unknown; refuse was dumped into the alleys to form reeking heaps and puddles. Unless a man walked with care he was likely to lose his footing and plunge waist-deep into nauseous pools. Nor was it uncommon to stumble over a corpse lying with its throat cut or its head knocked in, in the mud. Honest folk shunned The Maze with good reason.

Conan reached his destination without being seen, just as one he wished fervently to meet was leaving it. As the Cimmerian slunk into the courtyard below, the girl who had sold him to the police was taking leave of her new lover in a chamber one flight up. This young thug, her door closed behind him, groped his way down a creaking flight of stairs, intent on his own meditations, which, like those of most of the denizens of The Maze, had to do with the unlawful acquirement of property. Part-way down the stairs, he halted suddenly, his hair standing up. A vague bulk crouched in the darkness before him, a pair of eyes blazed like the eyes of a hunting beast. A beast-like snarl was the last thing he heard in life; as the monster lurched against him, a keen blade ripped through his belly. He gave one gasping cry, and slumped down limply on the stairway.

The barbarian loomed above him for an instant, ghoul-like, his eyes burning in the gloom. He knew the sound was heard, but the people in The Maze were careful to attend to their own business. A death-cry on darkened stairs was nothing unusual. Later, some one would venture to investigate, but only after a reasonable lapse of time.

Conan went up the stairs and halted at the door he knew well of old. It was fastened within, but his blade passed between the door and the jamb and lifted the bar. He stepped inside, closing the door after him, and faced the girl who had betrayed him to the police.

The wench was sitting cross-legged in her shift on her unkempt bed. She turned white and stared at him as if at a ghost. She had heard the cry from the stairs, and she saw the red stain on the poniard in his hand. But she was too filled with terror on her own account to waste any time lamenting the evident fate of her lover. She began to beg for her life, almost incoherent with terror. Conan did not reply; he merely stood and glared at her with his burning eyes, testing the edge of his poniard with a calloused thumb.

At last he crossed the chamber, while she cowered back against the wall, sobbing frantic pleas for mercy. Grasping her yellow locks with no gentle hand, he dragged her off the bed. Thrusting his blade back in its sheath, he tucked his squirming captive under his left arm, and strode to the window. Like most houses of that type, a ledge encircled each story, caused by the continuance of the window-ledges. Conan kicked the window open and stepped out on that narrow band. If any had been near or awake, they would have witnessed the bizarre sight of a man moving carefully along the ledge, carrying a kicking, half-naked wench under his arm. They would have been no more puzzled than the girl.

Reaching the spot he sought, Conan halted, gripping the wall with his free hand. Inside the building rose a sudden clamor, showing that the body had at last been discovered. His captive whimpered and twisted, renewing her importunities. Conan glanced down into the muck and slime of the alleys below; he listened briefly to the clamor inside and the pleas of the wench; then he dropped her with great accuracy into a cesspool. He enjoyed her kickings and flounderings and the concentrated venom of her profanity for a few seconds, and even allowed himself a low rumble of laughter. Then he lifted his head, listened to the growing tumult within the building, and decided it was time for him to kill Nabonidus.

3

It was a reverberating clang of metal that roused Murilo. He groaned and struggled dazedly to a sitting posture. About him all was silence and darkness, and for an instant he was sickened with the fear that he was blind. Then he remembered what had gone before, and his flesh crawled. By the sense of touch he found that he was lying on a floor of evenly joined stone slabs. Further groping discovered a wall of the same material. He rose and leaned against it, trying in vain to orient himself. That he was in some sort of a prison seemed certain, but where and how long he was unable to guess. He remembered dimly a clashing noise, and wondered if it had been the iron door of his dungeon closing on him, or if it betokened the entrance of an executioner.

At this thought he shuddered profoundly and began to feel his way along the wall. Momentarily he expected to encounter the limits of his prison, but after a while he came to the conclusion that he was travelling down a corridor. He kept to the wall, fearful of pits or other traps, and was presently aware of something near him in the blackness. He could see nothing, but either his ears had caught a stealthy sound, or some subconscious sense warned him. He stopped short, his hair standing on end; as surely as he lived, he felt the presence of some living creature crouching in the darkness in front of him.

He thought his heart would stop when a voice hissed in a barbaric accent: 'Murilo! Is it you?'

'Conan!' Limp from the reaction, the young nobleman groped in the darkness and his hands encountered a pair of great naked shoulders.

'A good thing I recognized you,' grunted the barbarian. 'I was about to stick you like a fattened pig.'

'Where are we, in Mitra's name?'

'In the pits under the Red Priest's house; but why—'

'What is the time?'

'Not long after midnight.'

Murilo shook his head, trying to assemble his scattered wits.

'What are you doing here?' demanded the Cimmerian.

'I came to kill Nabonidus. I heard they had changed the guard at your prison—'

'They did,' growled Conan. 'I broke the new jailer's head and walked out. I would have been here hours agone, but I had some personal business to attend to. Well, shall we hunt for Nabonidus?'

Murilo shuddered. 'Conan, we are in the house of the archfiend! I came seeking a human enemy; I found a hairy devil out of hell!'

Conan grunted uncertainly; fearless as a wounded tiger as far as human foes were concerned, he had all the superstitious dreads of the primitive.

'I gained access to the house,' whispered Murilo, as if the darkness were full of listening ears. 'In the outer gardens I found Nabonidus's dog mauled to death. Within the house I came upon Joka, the servant. His neck had been broken. Then I saw Nabonidus himself seated in his chair, clad in his accustomed garb. At first I thought he too was dead. I stole up to stab him. He rose and faced me. God!' The memory of that horror struck the young nobleman momentarily speechless as he relived that awful instant.

'Conan,' he whispered, 'it was no *man* that stood before me! In body and posture it was not unlike a man, but from the scarlet hood of the priest grinned a face of madness and nightmare! It was covered with black hair, from which small pig-like eyes glared redly; its nose was flat, with great flaring nostrils; its loose lips writhed back, disclosing huge yellow fangs, like the teeth of a dog. The hands that hung from the scarlet sleeves were misshapen and likewise covered with black hair. All this I saw in one glance, and then I was overcome with horror; my senses left me and I swooned.'

'What then?' muttered the Cimmerian uneasily.

'I recovered consciousness only a short time ago; the monster must have thrown me into these pits. Conan, I have suspected that Nabonidus was not wholly human! He is a demon – a were-thing! By day he moves among humanity in the guise of men, and by night he takes on his true aspect.'

'That's evident,' answered Conan. 'Everyone knows there are men who take the form of wolves at will. But why did he kill his servants?'

'Who can delve the mind of a devil?' replied Murilo. 'Our present interest is in getting out of this place. Human weapons can not harm a were-man. How did you get in here?'

'Through the sewer. I reckoned on the gardens being guarded. The sewers connect with a tunnel that lets into these pits. I thought to find some door leading up into the house unbolted.'

'Then let us escape by the way you came!' exclaimed Murilo. 'To the devil with it! Once out of this snake-den, we'll take our chance with the king's guardsmen, and risk a flight from the city. Lead on!'

'Useless,' grunted the Cimmerian. 'The way to the sewers is barred. As I entered the tunnel an iron grille crashed down from the roof. If I had not moved quicker than a flash of lightning, its spear-heads would have pinned me to the floor like a worm. When I tried to lift it, it wouldn't move. An elephant couldn't shake it. Nor could anything bigger than a rabbit squirm between the bars.'

Murilo cursed, an icy hand playing up and down his spine. He might have known Nabonidus would not leave any entrance into his house unguarded. Had Conan not possessed the steel-spring quickness of a wild thing, that falling portcullis would have skewered him. Doubtless his walking through the tunnel had sprung some hidden catch that released it from the roof. As it was, both were trapped living.

'There's but one thing to do,' said Murilo, sweating profusely. 'That's to search for some other exit; doubtless they're all set with traps, but we have no other choice.'

The barbarian grunted agreement, and the companions began

groping their way at random down the corridor. Even at that moment, something occurred to Murilo.

'How did you recognize me in this blackness?' he demanded.

'I smelled the perfume you put on your hair, when you came to my cell,' answered Conan. 'I smelled it again a while ago, when I was crouching in the dark and preparing to rip you open.'

Murilo put a lock of his black hair to his nostrils; even so the scent was barely apparent to his civilized senses, and he realized how keen must be the organs of the barbarian.

Instinctively his hand went to his scabbard as they groped onward, and he cursed to find it empty. At that moment a faint glow became apparent ahead of them, and presently they came to a sharp bend in the corridor, about which the light filtered grayly. Together they peered around the corner, and Murilo, leaning against his companion, felt his huge frame stiffen. The young nobleman had also seen it – the body of a man, half naked, lying limply in the corridor beyond the bend, vaguely illumined by a radiance which seemed to emanate from a broad silver disk on the farther wall. A strange familiarity about the recumbent figure, which lay face down, stirred Murilo with inexplicable and monstrous conjectures. Motioning the Cimmerian to follow him, he stole forward and bent above the body. Overcoming a certain repugnance, he grasped it and turned it on its back. An incredulous oath escaped him; the Cimmerian grunted explosively.

'Nabonidus! The Red Priest!' ejaculated Murilo, his brain a dizzy vortex of whirling amazement. 'Then who – what—?'

The priest groaned and stirred. With cat-like quickness Conan bent over him, poniard poised above his heart. Murilo caught his wrist.

'Wait! Don't kill him yet—'

'Why not?' demanded the Cimmerian. 'He has cast off his were-guise, and sleeps. Will you awaken him to tear us to pieces?'

'No, wait!' urged Murilo, trying to collect his jumbled wits. 'Look! He is not sleeping – see that great blue welt on his shaven temple? He has been knocked senseless. He may have been lying here for hours.'

'I thought you swore you saw him in beastly shape in the house above,' said Conan.

'I did! Or else – he's coming to! Keep back your blade, Conan; there is a mystery here even darker than I thought. I must have words with this priest, before we kill him.'

Nabonidus lifted a hand vaguely to his bruised temple, mumbled, and opened his eyes. For an instant they were blank and empty of intelligence; then life came back to them with a jerk, and he sat up, staring at the companions. Whatever terrific jolt had temporarily addled his razor-keen brain, it was functioning with its accustomed vigor again. His eyes shot swiftly about him, then came back to rest on Murilo's face.

'You honor my poor house, young sir,' he laughed coolly, glancing at the great figure that loomed behind the young nobleman's shoulder. 'You have brought a bravo, I see. Was your sword not sufficient to sever the life of my humble self?'

'Enough of this,' impatiently returned Murilo. 'How long have you lain here?'

'A peculiar question to put to a man recovering consciousness,' answered the priest. 'I do not know what time it now is. But it lacked an hour or so of midnight when I was set upon.'

'Then who is it that masquerades in your own gown in the house above?' demanded Murilo.

'That will be Thak,' answered Nabonidus, ruefully fingering his bruises. 'Yes, that will be Thak. And in my gown? The dog!'

Conan, who comprehended none of this, stirred restlessly, and growled something in his own tongue. Nabonidus glanced at him whimsically.

'Your bully's knife yearns for my heart, Murilo,' he said. 'I thought you might be wise enough to take my warning and leave the city.'

'How was I to know that was to be granted me?' returned Murilo. 'At any rate, my interests are here.'

'You are in good company with that cutthroat,' murmured Nabonidus. 'I had suspected you for some time. That was why I caused that pallid court secretary to disappear. Before he died he told me many things, among others the name of the young nobleman who bribed him to filch state secrets, which the nobleman in turn sold to rival powers. Are you not ashamed of yourself, Murilo, you white-handed thief?'

'I have no more cause for shame than you, you vulture-hearted plunderer,' answered Murilo promptly. 'You exploit a whole kingdom for your personal greed, and under the guise of disinterested statesmanship, you swindle the king, beggar the rich, oppress the poor, and sacrifice the whole future of the nation for your ruthless ambition. You are no more than a fat hog with his snout in the trough. You are a greater thief than I am. This Cimmerian is the most honest man of the three of us, because he steals and murders openly.'

'Well, then, we are all rogues together,' agreed Nabonidus equably. 'And what now? My life?'

'When I saw the ear of the secretary that had disappeared, I knew I was doomed,' said Murilo abruptly, 'and I believed you would invoke the authority of the king. Was I right?'

'Quite so,' answered the priest. 'A court secretary is easy to do away with, but you are a bit too prominent. I had intended telling the king a jest about you in the morning.'

'A jest that would have cost me my head,' muttered Murilo. 'Then the king is unaware of my foreign enterprises?'

'As yet,' sighed Nabonidus. 'And now, since I see your companion has his knife, I fear that jest will never be told.'

'You should know how to get out of these rat-dens,' said Murilo. 'Suppose I agree to spare your life. Will you help us to escape, and swear to keep silent about my thievery?'

'When did a priest keep an oath?' complained Conan, comprehending the trend of the conversation. 'Let me cut his throat; I want to see what color his blood is. They say in The Maze that his heart is black, so his blood must be black too—'

'Be quiet,' whispered Murilo. 'If he does not show us the way out of these pits, we may rot here. Well, Nabonidus, what do you say?'

'What does a wolf with his leg in the trap say?' laughed the priest. 'I am in your power and if we are to escape, we must aid one another. I swear, if we survive this adventure, to forget all your shifty dealings. I swear by the soul of Mitra!'

'I am satisfied,' muttered Murilo. 'Even the Red Priest would not break that oath. Now to get out of here. My friend here entered by way of the tunnel, but a grille fell behind him and blocked the way. Can you cause it to be lifted?'

'Not from these pits,' answered the priest. 'The control lever is in the chamber above the tunnel. There is only one other way out of these pits, which I will show you. But tell me, how did you come here?'

Murilo told him in a few words, and Nabonidus nodded, rising stiffly. He limped down the corridor, which here widened into a sort of vast chamber, and approached the distant silver disk. As they advanced the light increased, though it never became anything but a dim shadowy radiance. Near the disk they saw a narrow stair leading upward.

'That is the other exit,' said Nabonidus. 'And I strongly doubt if the door at the head is bolted. But I have an idea that he who would go through that door had better cut his own throat first. Look into the disk.'

What had seemed a silver plate was in reality a great mirror set in the wall. A confusing system of copper-like tubes jutted out from the wall about it, bending down toward it at right angles. Glancing into these tubes, Murilo saw a bewildering array of smaller mirrors. He turned his attention to the larger mirror in the wall, and ejaculated in amazement. Peering over his shoulder, Conan grunted.

They seemed to be looking through a broad window into a well-lighted chamber. There were broad mirrors on the walls, with velvet hangings between; there were silken couches, chairs of ebony and ivory, and curtained doorways leading off from the chamber. And before one doorway which was not curtained, sat a bulky black object that contrasted grotesquely with the richness of the chamber.

Murilo felt his blood freeze again as he looked at the horror which seemed to be staring directly into his eyes. Involuntarily he recoiled from the mirror, while Conan thrust his head truculently forward, till his jaws almost touched the surface, growling some threat or defiance in his own barbaric tongue.

'In Mitra's name, Nabonidus,' gasped Murilo, shaken, 'what is it?'

'That is Thak,' answered the priest, caressing his temple. 'Some would call him an ape, but he is almost as different from a real ape as he is different from a real man. His people dwell far to the east, in the mountains that fringe the eastern frontiers of Zamora. There are not many of them, but if they are not exterminated, I believe they will become human beings, in perhaps a hundred thousand years. They are in the formative stage; they are neither apes, as their remote ancestors were, nor men, as their remote descendants may be. They dwell in the high crags of well-nigh inaccessible mountains, knowing nothing of fire or the making of shelter or garments, or the use of weapons. Yet they have a language of a sort, consisting mainly of grunts and clicks.

'I took Thak when he was a cub, and he learned what I taught him much more swiftly and thoroughly than any true animal could have done. He was at once bodyguard and servant. But I forgot that being partly a man, he could not be submerged into a mere shadow of myself, like a true animal. Apparently his semi-brain retained impressions of hate, resentment, and some sort of bestial ambition of its own.

'At any rate, he struck when I least expected it. Last night he appeared to go suddenly mad. His actions had all the appearance of bestial insanity, yet I know that they must have been the result of long and careful planning.

'I heard a sound of fighting in the garden, and going to investigate – for I believed it was yourself, being dragged down by my watch-dog – I saw Thak emerge from the shrubbery dripping with blood. Before I was aware of his intention, he sprang at me with an awful scream and struck me senseless. I remember no more, but can only surmise that, following some whim of his semi-human brain, he stripped me of my gown and cast me still living into the pit – for which reason, only the gods can guess. He must have killed the dog when he came from the garden, and after he struck me down, he evidently killed Joka, as you saw the man lying dead in the house. Joka would have come to my aid, even against Thak, whom he always hated.'

Murilo stared at the mirror at the creature which sat with such monstrous patience before the closed door. He shuddered at the sight of the great black hands, thickly grown with hair that was almost fur-like. The body was thick, broad and stooped. The unnaturally wide shoulders had burst the scarlet gown, and on these shoulders Murilo noted the same thick growth of black hair. The face peering from the scarlet hood was utterly bestial, and yet Murilo realized that Nabonidus spoke truth when he said that Thak was not wholly a beast. There was something in the red murky eyes, something in the creature's clumsy posture, something in the whole appearance of the thing that set it apart from the truly animal. That monstrous body housed a brain and soul that were just budding awfully into something vaguely human. Murilo stood aghast as he recognized a faint and hideous kinship between his kind and that squatting monstrosity, and he was nauseated by a fleeting realization of the abysses of bellowing bestiality up through which humanity had painfully toiled.

'Surely he sees us,' muttered Conan. 'Why does he not charge us? He could break this window with ease.'

Murilo realized that Conan supposed the mirror to be a window through which they were looking.

'He does not see us,' answered the priest. 'We are looking into the chamber above us. That door that Thak is guarding is the one at the head of these stairs. It is simply an arrangement of mirrors. Do you see those mirrors on the walls? They transmit the reflection of the room into these tubes, down which other mirrors carry it to reflect it at last on an enlarged scale in this great mirror.'

Murilo realized that the priest must be centuries ahead of his generation, to perfect such an invention; but Conan put it down to witchcraft, and troubled his head no more about it.

'I constructed these pits for a place of refuge as well as a dungeon,' the priest was saying. 'There are times when I have taken refuge here, and through these mirrors, watched doom fall upon those who sought me with ill intent.'

'But why is Thak watching that door?' demanded Murilo.

'He must have heard the falling of the grating in the tunnel. It is connected with bells in the chambers above. He knows someone is in the pits, and he is waiting for him to come up the stairs. Oh, he has learned well the lessons I taught him. He has seen what happened to men who come through that door, when I tugged at the rope that hangs on yonder wall, and he waits to mimic me.'

'And while he waits, what are we to do?' demanded Murilo.

'There is naught we can do, except watch him. As long as he is in that chamber, we dare not ascend the stairs. He has the strength of a true gorilla, and could easily tear us all to pieces. But he does not need to exert his muscles; if we open that door he has but to tug that rope, and blast us into eternity.'

'How?'

'I bargained to help you escape,' answered the priest; 'not to betray my secrets.'

Murilo started to reply, then stiffened suddenly. A stealthy hand had parted the curtains of one of the doorways. Between them appeared a dark face whose glittering eyes fixed menacingly on the squat form in the scarlet robe.

'Petreus!' hissed Nabonidus. 'Mitra, what a gathering of vultures this night is!'

The face remained framed between the parted curtains. Over the intruder's shoulder other faces peered – dark, thin faces, alight with sinister eagerness.

'What do they here?' muttered Murilo, unconsciously lowering his voice, although he knew they could not hear him.

'Why, what would Petreus and his ardent young nationalists be doing in the house of the Red Priest?' laughed Nabonidus. 'Look how eagerly they glare at the figure they think is their arch-enemy. They have fallen into your error; it should be amusing to watch their expressions when they are disillusioned.'

Murilo did not reply. The whole affair had a distinctly unreal atmosphere. He felt as if he were watching the play of puppets, or as a disembodied ghost himself, impersonally viewing the actions of the living, his presence unseen and unsuspected.

He saw Petreus put his finger warningly to his lips, and nod to his fellow-conspirators. The young nobleman could not tell if Thak were aware of the intruders. The apeman's position had not changed, as he sat with his back toward the door through which the men were gliding.

'They had the same idea you had,' Nabonidus was muttering at his ear. 'Only their reasons were patriotic rather than selfish. Easy to gain access to my house, now that the dog is dead. Oh, what a chance to rid myself of their menace once and for all! If I were sitting where Thak sits – a leap to the wall – a tug on that rope—'

Petreus had placed one foot lightly over the threshold of the chamber; his fellows were at his heels, their daggers glinting dully. Suddenly Thak rose and wheeled toward him. The unexpected horror of his appearance, where they had thought to behold the hated but familiar countenance of Nabonidus, wrought havoc with their nerves, as the same spectacle had wrought upon Murilo. With a shriek Petreus recoiled, carrying his companions backward with him. They stumbled and floundered over each other, and in that instant Thak, covering the distance in one prodigious, grotesque leap, caught and jerked powerfully at a thick velvet rope which hung near the doorway.

Instantly the curtains whipped back on either hand, leaving the door clear, and down across it something flashed with a peculiar silvery blur.

'He remembered!' Nabonidus was exulting. 'The beast is half a man! He had seen the doom performed, and he remembered! Watch, now! Watch! Watch!'

Murilo saw that it was a panel of heavy glass that had fallen across the doorway. Through it he saw the pallid faces of the conspirators. Petreus, throwing out his hands as if to ward off a charge from Thak, encountered the transparent barrier, and from his gestures, said something to his companions. Now that the curtains were drawn back, the men in the pits could see all that took place in the chamber that contained the nationalists. Completely unnerved, these ran across the chamber toward the door by which they had apparently entered, only to halt suddenly, as if stopped by an invisible wall.

'The jerk of the rope sealed that chamber,' laughed Nabonidus. 'It is simple; the glass panels work in grooves in the doorways. Jerking the rope trips the spring that holds them. They slide down and lock in place, and can only be worked from outside. The glass is unbreakable; a man with a mallet could not shatter it. Ah!'

The trapped men were in a hysteria of fright; they ran wildly from one door to another, beating vainly at the crystal walls, shaking their fists wildly at the implacable black shape which squatted outside. Then one threw back his head, glared upward, and began to scream, to judge from the working of his lips, while he pointed toward the ceiling.

'The fall of the panels released the clouds of doom,' said the Red Priest with a wild laugh. 'The dust of the gray lotus, from the Swamps of the Dead, beyond the land of Khitai.'

In the middle of the ceiling hung a cluster of gold buds; these had opened like the petals of a great carven rose, and from them billowed a gray mist that swiftly filled the chamber. Instantly the scene changed from one of hysteria to one of madness and horror. The trapped men began to stagger; they ran in drunken circles. Froth dripped from their lips, which twisted as in awful laughter. Raging, they fell upon one another with daggers and teeth, slashing, tearing, slaying in a holocaust of madness. Murilo turned sick as he watched, and was glad that he could not hear the screams and howls with which that doomed chamber must be ringing. Like pictures thrown on a screen, it was silent.

Outside the chamber of horror Thak was leaping up and down in brutish glee, tossing his long hairy arms on high. At Murilo's shoulder Nabonidus was laughing like a fiend.

'Ah, a good stroke, Petreus! That fairly disemboweled him! Now one for you, my patriotic friend! So! They are all down, and the living tear the flesh of the dead with their slavering teeth.'

Murilo shuddered. Behind him the Cimmerian swore softly in

his uncouth tongue. Only death was to be seen in the chamber of the gray mist; torn, gashed and mangled, the conspirators lay in a red heap, gaping mouths and blood-dabbled faces staring blankly upward through the slowly swirling eddies of gray.

Thak, stooping like a giant gnome, approached the wall where the rope hung, and gave it a peculiar sidewise pull.

'He is opening the farther door,' said Nabonidus. 'By Mitra, he is more human than even I had guessed! See, the mist swirls out of the chamber, and is dissipated. He waits, to be safe. Now he raises the other panel. He is cautious – he knows the doom of the gray lotus, which brings madness and death. By Mitra!'

Murilo jerked about at the electric quality of the exclamation.

'Our one chance!' exclaimed Nabonidus. 'If he leaves the chamber above for a few minutes, we will risk a dash up those stairs.'

Suddenly tense, they watched the monster waddle through the doorway and vanish. With the lifting of the glass panel, the curtains had fallen again, hiding the chamber of death.

'We must chance it!' gasped Nabonidus, and Murilo saw perspiration break out on his face. 'Perhaps he will be disposing of the bodies as he has seen me do. Quick! Follow me up those stairs!'

He ran toward the steps and up them with an agility that amazed Murilo. The young nobleman and the barbarian were close at his heels, and they heard his gusty sigh of relief as he threw open the door at the top of the stairs. They burst into the broad chamber they had seen mirrored below. Thak was nowhere to be seen.

'He's in that chamber with the corpses!' exclaimed Murilo. 'Why not trap him there as he trapped them?'

'No, no!' gasped Nabonidus, an unaccustomed pallor tingeing his features. 'We do not know that he is in there. He might emerge before we could reach the trap-rope, anyway! Follow me into the corridor; I must reach my chamber and obtain weapons which will destroy him. This corridor is the only one opening from this chamber which is not set with a trap of some kind.'

They followed him swiftly through a curtained doorway opposite the door of the death-chamber, and came into a corridor, into which various chambers opened. With fumbling haste Nabonidus began to try the doors on each side. They were locked, as was the door at the other end of the corridor.

'My God!' The Red Priest leaned against the wall, his skin ashen. 'The doors are locked, and Thak took my keys from me. We are trapped, after all.'

Murilo stared appalled to see the man in such a state of nerves, and Nabonidus pulled himself together with an effort.

'That beast has me in a panic,' he said. 'If you had seen him tear men as I have seen – well, Mitra aid us, but we must fight him now with what the gods have given us. Come!'

He led them back to the curtained doorway, and peered into the great chamber in time to see Thak emerge from the opposite doorway. It was apparent that the beast-man had suspected something. His small, close-set ears twitched; he glared angrily about him, and approaching the nearest doorway, tore aside the curtains to look behind them.

Nabonidus drew back, shaking like a leaf. He gripped Conan's shoulder. 'Man, do you dare pit your knife against his fangs?'

The Cimmerian's eyes blazed in answer.

'Quick!' the Red Priest whispered, thrusting him behind the curtains, close against the wall. 'As he will find us soon enough, we will draw him to us. As he rushes past you, sink your blade in his back if you can. You Murilo, show yourself to him, and then flee up the corridor. Mitra knows, we have no chance with him in hand-to-hand combat, but we are doomed anyway when he finds us.'

Murilo felt his blood congeal in his veins, but he steeled himself, and stepped outside the doorway. Instantly Thak, on the other side of the chamber, wheeled, glared, and charged with a thunderous roar. His scarlet hood had fallen back, revealing his black misshapen head; his black hands and red robe were splashed with a brighter red. He was like a crimson and black nightmare as he rushed across the chamber, fangs bared, his bowed legs hurtling his enormous body along at a terrifying gait.

Murilo turned and ran back into the corridor, and quick as he was, the shaggy horror was almost at his heels. Then as the monster rushed past the curtains, from among them catapulted a great form that struck full on the apeman's shoulders, at the same instant driving the poniard into the brutish back. Thak screamed horribly as the impact knocked him off his feet, and the combatants hit the floor together. Instantly there began a whirl and thrash of limbs, the tearing and rending of a fiendish battle.

Murilo saw that the barbarian had locked his legs about the apeman's torso, and was striving to maintain his position on the monster's back, while he butchered it with his poniard. Thak, on the other hand, was striving to dislodge his clinging foe, to drag him around within reach of the giant fangs that gaped for his flesh. In a whirlwind of blows and scarlet tatters they rolled along the corridor, revolving so swiftly that Murilo dared not use the chair he had caught up, lest he strike the Cimmerian. And he saw that in spite of the handicap of Conan's first hold, and the voluminous robe that lashed and wrapped about the apeman's limbs and body, Thak's giant strength was swiftly prevailing. Inexorably he was dragging the Cimmerian around in front of him. The apeman had taken punishment enough to have killed a dozen men. Conan's poniard had sunk again and again into his torso, shoulders and bull-like neck; he was streaming blood from a score of wounds, but unless the blade quickly reached some absolutely vital spot, Thak's inhuman vitality would survive to finish the Cimmerian, and after him, Conan's companions.

Conan was fighting like a wild beast himself, in silence except for his gasps of effort. The black talons of the monster and the awful grasp of those misshapen hands ripped and tore at him, the grinning jaws gaped for his throat. Then Murilo, seeing an opening, sprang and swung the chair with all his power, and with force enough to have brained a human being. The chair glanced from Thak's slanted black skull; but the stunned monster momentarily relaxed his rending grasp, and in that instant Conan, gasping and streaming blood, plunged forward and sank his poniard to the hilt in the apeman's heart.

With a convulsive shudder the beastman started from the floor, then sank limply back. His fierce eyes set and glazed, his thick limbs quivered and became rigid.

Conan staggered dizzily up, shaking the sweat and blood out of his eyes. Blood dripped from his poniard and fingers, and trickled in rivulets down his thighs, arms and breast. Murilo caught at him to support him, but the barbarian shook him off impatiently.

'When I cannot stand alone, it will be time to die,' he mumbled, through mashed lips. 'But I'd like a flagon of wine.'

Nabonidus was staring down at the still figure as if he could not believe his own eyes. Black, hairy, abhorrent, the monster lay, grotesque in the tatters of the scarlet robe; yet more human than bestial, even so, and possessed somehow of a vague and terrible pathos.

Even the Cimmerian sensed this, for he panted: 'I have slain a *man* tonight, not a *beast*. I will count him among the chiefs whose souls I've sent into the dark, and my women will sing of him.'

Nabonidus stooped and picked up a bunch of keys on a golden chain. They had fallen from the apeman's girdle during the battle. Motioning his companions to follow him, he led them to a chamber, unlocked the door, and led the way inside. It was illumined like the others. The Red Priest took a vessel of wine from a table and filled crystal beakers. As his companions drank thirstily, he murmured: 'What a night! It is nearly dawn, now. What of you, my friends?'

'I'll dress Conan's hurts, if you will fetch me bandages and the like,' said Murilo, and Nabonidus nodded, and moved toward the door that led into the corridor. Something about his bowed head caused Murilo to watch him sharply. At the door the Red Priest wheeled suddenly. His face had undergone a transformation. His eyes gleamed with his old fire, his lips laughed soundlessly.

'Rogues together!' his voice rang with its accustomed mockery. 'But not fools together. You are the fool, Murilo!'

'What do you mean?' the young nobleman started forward.

'Back!' Nabonidus's voice cracked like a whip. 'Another step and I will blast you!'

Murilo's blood turned cold as he saw that the Red Priest's hand grasped a thick velvet rope which hung among the curtains just outside the door.

'What treachery is this?' cried Murilo. 'You swore—'

'I swore I would not tell the king a jest concerning you! I did not swear not to take matters into my own hands if I could. Do you think I would pass up such an opportunity? Under ordinary circumstances I would not dare kill you myself, without sanction of the king, but now none will ever know. You will go into the acid-vats along with Thak and the nationalist fools, and none will be the wiser. What a night this has been for me! If I have lost some valuable servants, I have nevertheless rid myself of various dangerous enemies. Stand back! I am over the threshold, and you cannot possibly reach me before I tug this cord and send you to hell. Not the gray lotus, this time, but something just as effective. Nearly every chamber in my house is a trap. And so, Murilo, fool that you are—'

Too quickly for the sight to follow, Conan caught up a stool and hurled it. Nabonidus instinctively threw up his arm with a cry, but not in time. The missile crunched against his head, and the Red Priest swayed and fell face-down in a slowly widening pool of dark crimson.

'His blood was red, after all,' grunted Conan.

Murilo raked back his sweat-plastered hair with a shaky hand as he leaned against the table, weak from the reaction of relief.

'It is dawn,' he said. 'Let us get out of here, before we fall afoul of some other doom. If we can climb the outer wall without being seen, we won't be connected with this night's work. Let the police write their own explanation.'

He glanced at the body of the Red Priest where it lay etched in crimson, and shrugged his shoulders.

'He was the fool, after all; had he not paused to taunt us, he could have trapped us easily.'

'Well,' said the Cimmerian tranquilly, 'he's travelled the road all rogues must walk at last. I'd like to loot the house, but I suppose we'd best go.'

As they emerged from the dimness of the dawn-whitened garden, Murilo said: 'The Red Priest has gone into the dark, so my road is clear in the city, and I have nothing to fear. But what of you?

There is still the matter of that priest in The Maze, and—'

'I'm tired of this city anyway,' grinned the Cimmerian. 'You mentioned a horse waiting at the Rats' Den. I'm curious to see how fast that horse can carry me into another kingdom. There's many a highway I want to travel before I walk the road Nabonidus walked this night.'

THE HAND OF NERGAL

(Fragment)

1

The battlefield stretched silent, crimson pools among the still sprawling figures seeming to reflect the lurid red-streamered sunset sky. Furtive figures slunk from the tall grass; birds of prey dropped down on mangled heaps with a rustle of dusky wings. Like harbingers of Fate a wavering line of herons flapped slowly away toward the reed-grown banks of the river. No rumble of chariot wheel or peal of trumpet disturbed the unseeing stillness. The silence of death followed the thundering of battle.

Yet one figure moved through that wide-strewn field of ruin – pygmy-like against the vast dully crimson sky. The fellow was a Cimmerian, a giant with a black mane and smoldering blue eyes. His girdled loin-cloth and high-strapped sandals were splashed with blood. The great sword he trailed in his right hand was stained to the cross-piece. There was a ghastly wound in his thigh, which caused him to limp as he walked. Carefully yet impatiently he moved among the dead, limping from corpse to corpse, and swearing wrathfully as he did so. Others had been before him; not a bracelet, gemmed dagger, or silver breastplate rewarded his search. He was a wolf who had lingered too long at the blood-letting while jackals stripped the prey.

Glaring out across the littered plains, he saw no body unstripped or moving. The knives of the mercenaries and camp-followers had been at work. Straightening up from his fruitless quest, he glanced uncertainly afar off across the deepening plain, to where the towers of the city gleamed faintly in the sunset. Then he turned quickly as a low tortured cry reached his ears. That meant a wounded man, living, therefore presumably unlooted. He limped quickly toward the sound, and coming to the edge of the plain, parted the first straggling reeds and glared down at the figure which writhed feebly at his feet.

It was a girl that lay there. She was naked, her white limbs cut and bruised. Blood was clotted in her long dark hair. There was unseeing agony in her dark eyes and she moaned in delirium.

The Cimmerian stood looking down at her, and his eyes were momentarily clouded by what would have been an expression of pity in another man. He lifted his sword to put the girl out of her misery, and as the blade hovered above her, she whimpered again like a child in pain. The great sword halted in midair, and the Cimmerian stood for an instant like a bronze statue. Then sheathing the blade with sudden decision, he bent and lifted the girl in his mighty arms. She struggled blindly but weakly. Carrying her carefully, he limped toward the reed-masked riverbank some distance away.

2

In the city of Yaralet, when night came on, the people barred windows and bolted doors, and sat behind their barriers shuddering, with candles burning before their household gods until dawn etched the minarets. No watchmen walked the streets, no painted wenches beckoned from the shadows, no thieves stole nimbly through the winding alleys. Rogues, like honest people, shunned the shadowed ways, gathering in foul-smelling dens, or candle-lighted taverns. From dusk to dawn Yaralet was a city of silence, her streets empty and desolate.

Exactly what they feared, the people did not know. But they had ample evidence that it was no empty dream they bolted their doors against. Men whispered of slinking shadows, glimpsed from barred windows – of hurrying shapes alien to humanity and sanity.

They told of doorways splintering in the night, and the cries and shrieks of humans followed by significant silence; and they told of the rising sun etching broken doors that swung in empty houses, whose occupants were seen no more.

Even stranger, they told of the swift rumble of phantom chariot wheels along the empty streets in the darkness before dawn, when those who heard dared not look forth. One child looked forth, once, but he was instantly stricken mad and died screaming and frothing, without telling what he saw when he peered from his darkened window.

On a certain night, then, while the people of Yaralet shivered in their bolted houses, a strange conclave was taking place in the small velvet-hung taper-lighted chamber of Atalis, whom some called a philosopher and others a rogue. Atalis was a slender man of medium height, with a splendid head and the features of a shrewd merchant. He was clad in a plain robe of rich fabric, and his head was shaven to denote devotion to study and the arts. As he talked he unconsciously gestured with his left hand. His right arm lay across his lap at an unnatural angle. From time to time a spasm of pain contorted his features, at which time his right foot, hidden under the long robe, would twist back excruciatingly upon his ankle.

He was talking to one whom the city of Yaralet knew, and praised, as Prince Than. The prince was a tall lithe man, young and undeniably handsome. The firm outline of his limbs and the steely quality of his grey eyes belied the slightly effeminate suggestion of his curled black locks, and feathered velvet cap.

THE FROST-GIANT'S DAUGHTER

The clangor of the swords had died away, the shouting of the slaughter was hushed; silence lay on the red-stained snow. The bleak pale sun that glittered so blindingly from the ice-fields and the snow-covered plains struck sheens of silver from rent corselet and broken blade, where the dead lay as they had fallen. The nerveless hand yet gripped the broken hilt; helmeted heads, back-drawn in the death throes, tilted red beards and golden beards grimly upward, as if in last invocation to Ymir the frost-giant, god of a warrior-race.

Across the red drifts and mail-clad forms, two figures glared at each other. In that utter desolation only they moved. The frosty sky was over them, the white illimitable plain around them, the dead men at their feet. Slowly through the corpses they came, as ghosts might come to a tryst through the shambles of a dead world. In the brooding silence they stood face to face.

Both were tall men, built like tigers. Their shields were gone, their corselets battered and dented. Blood dried on their mail; their swords were stained red. Their horned helmets showed the marks of fierce strokes. One was beardless and black-maned. The locks and beard of the other were red as the blood on the sunlit snow.

'Man,' said he, 'tell me your name, so that my brothers in Vanaheim may know who was the last of Wulfhere's band to fall before the sword of Heimdul.'

'Not in Vanaheim,' growled the black-haired warrior, 'but in Valhalla will you tell your brothers that you met Conan of Cimmeria.'

Heimdul roared and leaped, and his sword flashed in a deathly arc. Conan staggered and his vision was filled with red sparks as the singing blade crashed on his helmet, shivering into bits of blue fire. But as he reeled he thrust with all the power of his broad shoulders behind the humming blade. The sharp point tore through brass scales and bones and heart, and the red-haired warrior died at Conan's feet.

The Cimmerian stood upright, trailing his sword, a sudden sick weariness assailing him. The glare of the sun on the snow cut his eyes like a knife and the sky seemed shrunken and strangely apart. He turned away from the trampled expanses where yellow-bearded warriors lay locked with red-haired slayers in the embrace of death. A few steps he took, and the glare of the snow-fields was suddenly dimmed. A rushing wave of blindness engulfed him and he sank down into the snow, supporting himself on one mailed arm, seeking to shake the blindness out of his eyes as a lion might shake his mane.

A silvery laugh cut through his dizziness, and his sight cleared slowly. He looked up; there was a strangeness about all the landscape that he could not place or define – an unfamiliar tinge to earth and sky. But he did not think long of this. Before him, swaying like a sapling in the wind, stood a woman. Her body was like ivory to his dazed eyes, and save for a light veil of gossamer, she was naked as the day. Her slender bare feet were whiter than the snow they spurned. She laughed down at the bewildered warrior. Her laughter was sweeter than the rippling of silvery fountains, and poisonous with cruel mockery.

'Who are you?' asked the Cimmerian. 'Whence come you?'

'What matter?' Her voice was more musical than a silver-stringed harp, but it was edged with cruelty.

'Call up your men,' said he, grasping his sword. 'Yet though my strength fail me, they shall not take me alive. I see that you are of the Vanir.'

'Have I said so?'

His gaze went again to her unruly locks, which at first glance he had thought to be red. Now he saw that they were neither red nor yellow, but a glorious compound of both colors. He gazed spellbound. Her hair was like elfin-gold; the sun struck it so dazzingly that he could scarcely bear to look upon it. Her eyes were likewise neither wholly blue nor wholly grey, but of shifting colors and dancing lights and clouds of colors he could not define. Her full red lips smiled, and from her slender feet to the blinding crown of her billowy hair, her ivory body was as perfect as the dream of a god. Conan's pulse hammered in his temples.

'I cannot tell,' said he, 'whether you are of Vanaheim and mine enemy, or of Asgard and my friend. Far have I wandered, but a woman like you I have never seen. Your locks blind me with their brightness. Never have I seen such hair, not even among the fairest daughters of the Æsir. By Ymir—'

'Who are you to swear by Ymir?' she mocked. 'What know you of the gods of ice and snow, you who have come up from the south to adventure among an alien people?'

'By the dark gods of my own race!' he cried in anger. 'Though I am not of the golden-haired Æsir, none has been more forward in sword-play! This day I have seen four score men fall, and I alone have survived the field where Wulfhere's reavers met the wolves of Bragi. Tell me, woman, have you seen the flash of mail out across the snow-plains, or seen armed men moving upon the ice?'

'I have seen the hoar-frost glittering in the sun,' she answered. 'I have heard the wind whispering across the everlasting snows.'

He shook his head with a sigh.

'Niord should have come up with us before the battle was joined. I fear he and his fighting-men have been ambushed. Wulfhere and his warriors lie dead.

'I had thought there was no village within many leagues of this spot, for the war carried us far, but you cannot have come a great distance over these snows, naked as you are. Lead me to your tribe, if you are of Asgard, for I am faint with blows and the weariness of strife.'

'My village is further than you can walk, Conan of Cimmeria,' she laughed. Spreading her arms wide, she swayed before him, her golden head lolling sensuously, her scintillant eyes half shadowed beneath their long silken lashes. 'Am I not beautiful, oh man?'

'Like Dawn running naked on the snows,' he muttered, his eyes burning like those of a wolf.

'Then why do you not rise and follow me? Who is the strong warrior who falls down before me?' she chanted in maddening mockery. 'Lie down and die in the snow with the other fools, Conan of the black hair. You cannot follow where I would lead.'

With an oath the Cimmerian heaved himself up on his feet, his blue eyes blazing, his dark scarred face contorted. Rage shook his soul, but desire for the taunting figure before him hammered at his temples and drove his wild blood fiercely through his veins. Passion fierce as physical agony flooded his whole being, so that earth and sky swam red to his dizzy gaze. In the madness that swept upon him, weariness and faintness were swept away.

He spoke no word as he drove at her, fingers spread to grip her soft flesh. With a shriek of laughter she leaped back and ran, laughing at him over her white shoulder. With a low growl Conan followed. He had forgotten the fight, forgotten the mailed warriors who lay in their blood, forgotten Niord and the reavers who had failed to reach the fight. He had thought only for the slender white shape which seemed to float rather than run before him.

Out across the white blinding plain the chase led. The trampled red field fell out of sight behind him, but still Conan kept on with the silent tenacity of his race. His mailed feet broke through the frozen crust; he sank deep in the drifts and forged through them by sheer strength. But the girl danced across the snow light as a feather floating across a pool; her naked feet barely left their imprint on the hoar-frost that overlaid the crust. In spite of the fire in his veins, the cold bit through the warrior's mail and fur-lined tunic; but the girl in her gossamer veil ran as lightly and as gaily as if she danced through the palm and rose gardens of Poitain.

On and on she led, and Conan followed. Black curses drooled through the Cimmerian's parched lips. The great veins in his temples swelled and throbbed and his teeth gnashed.

'You cannot escape me!' he roared. 'Lead me into a trap and I'll pile the heads of your kinsmen at your feet! Hide from me and I'll tear apart the mountains to find you! I'll follow you to hell!'

Her maddening laughter floated back to him, and foam flew from the barbarian's lips. Further and further into the wastes she led him. The land changed; the wide plains gave way to low hills, marching upward in broken ranges. Far to the north he caught a glimpse of towering mountains, blue with the distance, or white with the eternal snows. Above these mountains shone the flaring rays of the borealis. They spread fan-wise into the sky, frosty blades of cold flaming light, changing in color, growing and brightening.

Above him the skies glowed and crackled with strange lights and gleams. The snow shone weirdly, now frosty blue, now icy crimson, now cold silver. Through a shimmering icy realm of enchantment Conan plunged doggedly onward, in a crystalline maze where the only reality was the white body dancing across the glittering snow beyond his reach – ever beyond his reach.

He did not wonder at the strangeness of it all, not even when two gigantic figures rose up to bar his way. The scales of their mail were white with hoar-frost; their helmets and their axes were covered with ice. Snow sprinkled their locks; in their beards were spikes of icicles; their eyes were cold as the lights that streamed above them.

'Brothers!' cried the girl, dancing between them. 'Look who follows! I have brought you a man to slay! Take his heart that we may lay it smoking on our father's board!'

The giants answered with roars like the grinding of icebergs on a frozen shore and heaved up their shining axes as the maddened Cimmerian hurled himself upon them. A frosty blade flashed before his eyes, blinding him with its brightness, and he gave back a terrible stroke that sheared through his foe's thigh. With a groan the victim fell, and at the instant Conan was dashed into the snow, his left shoulder numb from the blow of the survivor, from which the Cimmerian's mail had barely saved his life. Conan saw the remaining giant looming high above him like a colossus carved of ice, etched against the cold glowing sky. The axe fell, to sink through the snow and deep into the frozen earth as Conan hurled himself aside and leaped to his feet. The giant roared and wrenched his axe free, but even as he did, Conan's sword sang down. The giant's knees bent and he sank slowly into the snow, which turned crimson with the blood that gushed from his half-severed neck.

Conan wheeled, to see the girl standing a short distance away, staring at him in wide-eyed horror, all the mockery gone from her face. He cried out fiercely and the blood-drops flew from his sword as his hand shook in the intensity of his passion.

'Call the rest of your brothers!' he cried. 'I'll give their hearts to the wolves! You cannot escape me—'

With a cry of fright she turned and ran fleetly. She did not laugh now, nor mock him over her white shoulder. She ran as for her life, and though he strained every nerve and thew until his temples were like to burst and the snow swam red to his gaze, she drew away from him, dwindling in the witch-fire of the skies, until she was a figure no bigger than a child, then a dancing white flame on the snow, then a dim blur in the distance. But grinding his teeth until the blood started from his gums, he reeled on, and he saw the blur grow to a dancing white flame, and the flame to a figure big as a child; and then she was running less than a hundred paces ahead of him, and slowly the space narrowed, foot by foot.

She was running with effort now, her golden locks blowing free; he heard the quick panting of her breath, and saw a flash of fear in the look she cast over her white shoulder. The grim endurance of the barbarian had served him well. The speed ebbed from her flashing white legs; she reeled in her gait. In his untamed soul leaped up the fires of hell she had fanned so well. With an inhuman roar he closed in on her, just as she wheeled with a haunting cry and flung out her arms to fend him off.

His sword fell into the snow as he crushed her to him. Her lithe body bent backward as she fought with desperate frenzy in his iron arms. Her golden hair blew about his face, blinding him with its sheen; the feel of her slender body twisting in his mailed arms drove him to blinder madness. His strong fingers sank deep into her smooth flesh; and that flesh was cold as ice. It was as if he embraced not a woman of human flesh and blood, but a woman of flaming ice. She writhed her golden head aside, striving to avoid the fierce kisses that bruised her red lips.

'You are cold as the snows,' he mumbled dazedly. 'I will warm you with the fire in my own blood—'

With a scream and a desperate wrench she slipped from his arms, leaving her single gossamer garment in his grasp. She sprang back and faced him, her golden locks in wild disarray, her white bosom heaving, her beautiful eyes blazing with terror. For an instant he stood frozen, awed by her terrible beauty as she posed naked against the snows.

And in that instant she flung her arms toward the lights that glowed in the skies above her and cried out in a voice that rang in Conan's ears forever after: 'Ymir! Oh, my father, save me!'

Conan was leaping forward, arms spread to seize her, when with a crack like the breaking of an ice mountain, the whole sky leaped into icy fire. The girl's ivory body was suddenly enveloped in a cold blue flame so blinding that the Cimmerian threw up his hands to shield his eyes from the intolerable blaze. For a fleeting instant, sky and snowy hills were bathed in crackling white flames, blue darts of icy light, and frozen crimson fires. Then Conan staggered and cried out. The girl was gone. The glowing snow lay empty and bare; high above his head the witch-lights flashed and played in a frosty sky gone mad, and among the distant blue mountains there sounded a rolling thunder as of a gigantic war-chariot rushing behind steeds whose frantic hoofs struck lightning from the snows and echoes from the skies.

Then suddenly the borealis, the snow-clad hills and the blazing heavens reeled drunkenly to Conan's sight; thousands of fire-balls burst with showers of sparks, and the sky itself became a titanic wheel which rained stars as it spun. Under his feet the snowy hills heaved up like a wave, and the Cimmerian crumpled into the snows to lie motionless.

In a cold dark universe, whose sun was extinguished eons ago, Conan felt the movement of life, alien and unguessed. An earthquake had him in its grip and was shaking him to and fro, at the same time chafing his hands and feet until he yelled in pain and fury and groped for his sword.

'He's coming to, Horsa,' said a voice. 'Haste – we must rub the frost out of his limbs if he's ever to wield sword again.'

'He won't open his left hand,' growled another. 'He's clutching something—'

Conan opened his eyes and stared into the bearded faces that bent over him. He was surrounded by tall golden-haired warriors in mail and furs.

'Conan! You live!'

'By Crom, Niord,' gasped the Cimmerian. 'Am I alive, or are we all dead and in Valhalla?'

'We live,' grunted the Æsir, busy over Conan's half-frozen feet. 'We had to fight our way through an ambush, or we had come up with you before the battle was joined. The corpses were scarce cold when we came upon the field. We did not find you among the dead, so we followed your spoor. In Ymir's name, Conan, why did you wander off into the wastes of the north? We have followed your tracks in the snow for hours. Had a blizzard come up and hidden them, we had never found you, by Ymir!'

'Swear not so often by Ymir,' uneasily muttered a warrior, glancing at the distant mountains. 'This is his land and the god bides among yonder mountains the legends say.'

'I saw a woman,' Conan answered hazily. 'We met Bragi's men in the plains. I know not how long we fought. I alone lived. I was dizzy and faint. The land lay like a dream before me. Only now do all things seem natural and familiar. The woman came and taunted me. She was beautiful as a frozen flame from hell. A strange madness fell upon me when I looked at her, so I forgot all else in the world. I followed her. Did you not find her tracks? Or the giants in icy mail I slew?'

Niord shook his head.

'We found only your tracks in the snow, Conan.'

'Then it may be I am mad,' said Conan dazedly. 'Yet you yourself are no more real to me than was the golden-locked witch who fled naked across the snows before me. Yet from under my very hands she vanished in icy flame.'

'He is delirious,' whispered a warrior.

'Not so!' cried the older man, whose eyes were wild and weird.

'It was Atali, the daughter of Ymir, the frost-giant! To fields of the dead she comes, and shows herself to the dying! Myself when a boy I saw her, when I lay half-slain on the bloody field of Wolraven. I saw her walk among the dead in the snows, her naked body gleaming like ivory and her golden hair unbearably bright in the moonlight. I lay and howled like a dying dog because I could not crawl after her. She lures men from stricken fields into the wastelands to be slain by her brothers the ice-giants, who lay men's red hearts smoking on Ymir's board. The Cimmerian has seen Atali, the frost-giant's daughter.'

'Bah!' grunted Horsa. 'Old Gorm's mind was touched in his youth by a sword cut on the head. Conan was delirious from the fury of battle – look how his helmet is dented. Any of those blows might have addled his brain. It was an hallucination he followed into the wastes. He is from the south; what does he know of Atali?'

'You speak truth, perhaps,' muttered Conan. 'It was all strange and weird – by Crom!'

He broke off, glaring at the object that still dangled from his clenched left fist; the others gaped silently at the veil he held up – a wisp of gossamer that was never spun by human distaff.

QUEEN OF THE BLACK COAST

1

Conan Joins the Pirates

Believe green buds awaken in the spring,
That autumn paints the leaves with somber fire;
Believe I held my heart inviolate
To lavish on one man my hot desire.

THE SONG OF BÊLIT

Hoofs drummed down the street that sloped to the wharfs. The folk that yelled and scattered had only a fleeting glimpse of a mailed figure on a black stallion, a wide scarlet cloak flowing out on the wind. Far up the street came the shout and clatter of pursuit, but the horseman did not look back. He swept out onto the wharfs and jerked the plunging stallion back on its haunches at the very lip of the pier. Seamen gaped up at him, as they stood to the sweep and striped sail of a high-prowed, broad-waisted galley. The master, sturdy and black-bearded, stood in the bows, easing her away from the piles with a boat-hook. He yelled angrily as the horseman sprang from the saddle and with a long leap landed squarely on the mid-deck.

'Who invited you aboard?'

'Get under way!' roared the intruder with a fierce gesture that spattered red drops from his broadsword.

'But we're bound for the coasts of Kush!' expostulated the master.

'Then I'm for Kush! Push off, I tell you!' The other cast a quick glance up the street, along which a squad of horsemen were galloping; far behind them toiled a group of archers, crossbows on their shoulders.

'Can you pay for your passage?' demanded the master.

'I pay my way with steel!' roared the man in armor, brandishing the great sword that glittered bluely in the sun. 'By Crom, man, if you don't get under way, I'll drench this galley in the blood of its crew!'

The shipmaster was a good judge of men. One glance at the dark scarred face of the swordsman, hardened with passion, and he shouted a quick order, thrusting strongly against the piles. The galley wallowed out into clear water, the oars began to clack rhythmically; then a puff of wind filled the shimmering sail, the light ship heeled to the gust, then took her course like a swan, gathering headway as she skimmed along.

On the wharfs the riders were shaking their swords and shouting threats and commands that the ship put about, and yelling for the bowmen to hasten before the craft was out of arbalest range.

'Let them rave,' grinned the swordsman hardily. 'Do you keep her on her course, master steersman.'

The master descended from the small deck between the bows, made his way between the rows of oarsmen, and mounted the mid-deck. The stranger stood there with his back to the mast, eyes narrowed alertly, sword ready. The shipman eyed him steadily, careful not to make any move toward the long knife in his belt. He saw a tall powerfully built figure in a black scale-mail hauberk, burnished greaves and a blue-steel helmet from which jutted bull's horns highly polished. From the mailed shoulders fell the scarlet cloak, blowing in the sea-wind. A broad shagreen belt with a golden buckle held the scabbard of the broadsword he bore. Under the horned helmet a square-cut black mane contrasted with smoldering blue eyes.

'If we must travel together,' said the master, 'we may as well be at peace with each other. My name is Tito, licensed master-shipman of the ports of Argos. I am bound for Kush, to trade beads and silks and sugar and brass-hilted swords to the black kings for ivory, copra, copper ore, slaves and pearls.'

The swordsman glanced back at the rapidly receding docks, where the figures still gesticulated helplessly, evidently having trouble in finding a boat swift enough to overhaul the fast-sailing galley.

'I am Conan, a Cimmerian,' he answered. 'I came into Argos seeking employment, but with no wars forward, there was nothing to which I might turn my hand.'

'Why do the guardsmen pursue you?' asked Tito. 'Not that it's any of my business, but I thought perhaps—'

'I've nothing to conceal,' replied the Cimmerian. 'By Crom, though I've spent considerable time among you civilized peoples, your ways are still beyond my comprehension.

'Well, last night in a tavern, a captain in the king's guard offered violence to the sweetheart of a young soldier, who naturally ran him through. But it seems there is some cursed law against killing guardsmen, and the boy and his girl fled away. It was bruited about that I was seen with them, and so today I was haled into court, and a judge asked me where the lad had gone. I replied that since he was a friend of mine, I could not betray him. Then the court waxed wrath, and the judge talked a great deal about my duty to the state, and society, and other things I did not understand, and bade me tell where my friend had flown. By this time I was becoming wrathful myself, for I had explained my position.

'But I choked my ire and held my peace, and the judge squalled that I had shown contempt for the court, and that I should be hurled into a dungeon to rot until I betrayed my friend. So then, seeing they were all mad, I drew my sword and cleft the judge's skull; then I cut my way out of the court, and seeing the high constable's stallion tied near by, I rode for the wharfs, where I thought to find a ship bound for foreign parts.'

'Well,' said Tito hardily, 'the courts have fleeced me too often in suits with rich merchants for me to owe them any love. I'll have questions to answer if I ever anchor in that port again, but I can prove I acted under compulsion. You may as well put up your sword. We're peaceable sailors, and have nothing against you.

Besides, it's as well to have a fighting-man like yourself on board. Come up to the poop-deck and we'll have a tankard of ale.'

'Good enough,' readily responded the Cimmerian, sheathing his sword.

The *Argus* was a small sturdy ship, typical of those trading-craft which ply between the ports of Zingara and Argos and the southern coasts, hugging the shoreline and seldom venturing far into the open ocean. It was high of stern, with a tall curving prow; broad in the waist, sloping beautifully to stem and stern. It was guided by the long sweep from the poop, and propulsion was furnished mainly by the broad striped silk sail, aided by a jibsail. The oars were for use in tacking out of creeks and bays, and during calms. There were ten to the side, five fore and five aft of the small mid-deck. The most precious part of the cargo was lashed under this deck, and under the fore-deck. The men slept on deck or between the rowers' benches, protected in bad weather by canopies. With twenty men at the oars, three at the sweep, and the shipmaster, the crew was complete.

So the *Argus* pushed steadily southward, with consistently fair weather. The sun beat down from day to day with fiercer heat, and the canopies were run up – striped silken cloths that matched the shimmering sail and the shining goldwork on the prow and along the gunwales.

They sighted the coast of Shem – long rolling meadowlands with the white crowns of the towers of cities in the distance, and horsemen with blue-black beards and hooked noses, who sat their steeds along the shore and eyed the galley with suspicion. She did not put in; there was scant profit in trade with the sons of Shem.

Nor did master Tito pull into the broad bay where the Styx river emptied its gigantic flood into the ocean, and the massive black castles of Khemi loomed over the blue waters. Ships did not put unasked into this port, where dusky sorcerers wove awful spells in the murk of sacrificial smoke mounting eternally from blood-stained altars where naked women screamed, and where Set, the Old Serpent, arch-demon of the Hyborians but god of the Stygians, was said to writhe his shining coils among his worshippers.

Master Tito gave that dreamy glass-floored bay a wide berth, even when a serpent-prowed gondola shot from behind a castellated point of land, and naked dusky women, with great red blossoms in their hair, stood and called to his sailors, and posed and postured brazenly.

Now no more shining towers rose inland. They had passed the southern borders of Stygia and were cruising along the coasts of Kush. The sea and the ways of the sea were never-ending mysteries to Conan, whose homeland was among the high hills of the northern uplands. The wanderer was no less of interest to the sturdy seamen, few of whom had ever seen one of his race.

They were characteristic Argosean sailors, short and stockily built. Conan towered above them, and no two of them could match his strength. They were hardy and robust, but his was the endurance and vitality of a wolf, his thews steeled and his nerves whetted by the hardness of his life in the world's wastelands. He was quick to laugh, quick and terrible in his wrath. He was a valiant trencherman, and strong drink was a passion and a weakness with him. Naïve as a child in many ways, unfamiliar with the sophistry of civilization, he was naturally intelligent, jealous of his rights, and dangerous as a hungry tiger. Young in years, he was hardened in warfare and wandering, and his sojourns in many lands were evident in his apparel. His horned helmet was such as was worn by the golden-haired Æsir of Nordheim; his hauberk and greaves were of the finest workmanship of Koth; the fine ring-mail which sheathed his arms and legs was of Nemedia; the blade at his girdle was a great Aquilonian broadsword; and his gorgeous scarlet cloak could have been spun nowhere but in Ophir.

So they beat southward, and master Tito began to look for the high-walled villages of the black people. But they found only smoking ruins on the shore of a bay, littered with naked black bodies. Tito swore.

'I had good trade here, aforetime. This is the work of pirates.'

'And if we meet them?' Conan loosened his great blade in its scabbard.

'Mine is no warship. We run, not fight. Yet if it came to a pinch, we have beaten off reavers before, and might do it again; unless it were Bêlit's *Tigress*.'

'Who is Bêlit?'

'The wildest she-devil unhanged. Unless I read the signs a-wrong, it was her butchers who destroyed that village on the bay. May I some day see her dangling from the yard-arm! She is called the queen of the black coast. She is a Shemite woman, who leads black raiders. They harry the shipping and have sent many a good tradesman to the bottom.'

From under the poop-deck Tito brought out quilted jerkins, steel caps, bows and arrows.

'Little use to resist if we're run down,' he grunted. 'But it rasps the soul to give up life without a struggle.'

It was just at sunrise when the lookout shouted a warning. Around the long point of an island off the starboard bow glided a long lethal shape, a slender serpentine galley, with a raised deck that ran from stem to stern. Forty oars on each side drove her swiftly through the water, and the low rail swarmed with naked blacks that chanted and clashed spears on oval shields. From the masthead floated a long crimson pennon.

'Bêlit!' yelled Tito, paling. 'Yare! Put her about! Into that creek-mouth! If we can beach her before they run us down, we have a chance to escape with our lives!'

So, veering sharply, the *Argus* ran for the line of surf that boomed along the palm-fringed shore, Tito striding back and forth, exhorting the panting rowers to greater efforts. The master's black beard bristled, his eyes glared.

'Give me a bow,' requested Conan. 'It's not my idea of a manly weapon, but I learned archery among the Hyrkanians, and it will go hard if I can't feather a man or so on yonder deck.'

Standing on the poop, he watched the serpent-like ship skimming lightly over the waters, and landsman though he was, it was evident to him that the *Argus* would never win that race. Already arrows, arching from the pirate's deck, were falling with a hiss into the sea, not twenty paces astern.

'We'd best stand to it,' growled the Cimmerian; 'else we'll all die with shafts in our backs, and not a blow dealt.'

'Bend to it, dogs!' roared Tito with a passionate gesture of his brawny fist. The bearded rowers grunted, heaved at the oars, while their muscles coiled and knotted, and sweat started out on their hides. The timbers of the stout little galley creaked and groaned as the men fairly ripped her through the water. The wind had fallen; the sail hung limp. Nearer crept the inexorable raiders, and they were still a good mile from the surf when one of the steersmen fell gagging across a sweep, a long arrow through his neck. Tito sprang to take his place, and Conan, bracing his feet wide on the heaving poop-deck, lifted his bow. He could see the details of the pirate plainly now. The rowers were protected by a line of raised mantelets along the sides, but the warriors dancing on the narrow deck were in full view. These were painted and plumed, and mostly naked, brandishing spears and spotted shields.

On the raised platform in the bows stood a slim figure whose white skin glistened in dazzling contrast to the glossy ebon hides about it. Bêlit, without a doubt. Conan drew the shaft to his ear – then some whim or qualm stayed his hand and sent the arrow through the body of a tall plumed spearman beside her.

Hand over hand the pirate galley was overhauling the lighter ship. Arrows fell in a rain about the *Argus*, and men cried out. All the steersmen were down, pincushioned, and Tito was handling the massive sweep alone, gasping black curses, his braced legs knots of straining thews. Then with a sob he sank down, a long shaft quivering in his sturdy heart. The *Argus* lost headway and rolled in the swell. The men shouted in confusion, and Conan took command in characteristic fashion.

'Up, lads!' he roared, loosing with a vicious twang of cord. 'Grab your steel and give these dogs a few knocks before they cut our throats! Useless to bend your backs any more: they'll board us ere we can row another fifty paces!'

In desperation the sailors abandoned their oars and snatched up their weapons. It was valiant, but useless. They had time for one flight of arrows before the pirate was upon them. With no one at the sweep, the *Argus* rolled broadside, and the steel-baked prow of the raider crashed into her amidships. Grappling-irons crunched into the side. From the lofty gunwales, the black pirates drove down a volley of shafts that tore through the quilted jackets of the doomed sailormen, then sprang down spear in hand to complete the slaughter. On the deck of the pirate lay half a dozen bodies, an earnest of Conan's archery.

The fight on the *Argus* was short and bloody. The stocky sailors, no match for the tall barbarians, were cut down to a man. Elsewhere the battle had taken a peculiar turn. Conan, on the high-pitched poop, was on a level with the pirate's deck. As the steel prow slashed into the *Argus*, he braced himself and kept his feet under the shock, casting away his bow. A tall corsair, bounding over the rail, was met in midair by the Cimmerian's great sword, which sheared him cleanly through the torso, so that his body fell one way and his legs another. Then, with a burst of fury that left a heap of mangled corpses along the gunwales, Conan was over the rail and on the deck of the *Tigress*.

In an instant he was the center of a hurricane of stabbing spears and lashing clubs. But he moved in a blinding blur of steel. Spears bent on his armor or swished empty air, and his sword sang its death-song. The fighting-madness of his race was upon him, and with a red mist of unreasoning fury wavering before his blazing eyes, he cleft skulls, smashed breasts, severed limbs, ripped out entrails, and littered the deck like a shambles with a ghastly harvest of brains and blood.

Invulnerable in his armor, his back against the mast, he heaped mangled corpses at his feet until his enemies gave back panting in rage and fear. Then as they lifted their spears to cast them, and he tensed himself to leap and die in the midst of them, a shrill cry froze the lifted arms. They stood like statues, the black giants poised for the spear-casts, the mailed swordsman with his dripping blade.

Bêlit sprang before the blacks, beating down their spears. She turned toward Conan, her bosom heaving, her eyes flashing. Fierce fingers of wonder caught at his heart. She was slender, yet formed like a goddess: at once lithe and voluptuous. Her only garment was a broad silken girdle. Her white ivory limbs and the ivory globes of her breasts drove a beat of fierce passion through the Cimmerian's pulse, even in the panting fury of battle. Her rich black hair, black as a Stygian night, fell in rippling burnished clusters down her supple back. Her dark eyes burned on the Cimmerian.

She was untamed as a desert wind, supple and dangerous as a she-panther. She came close to him, heedless of his great blade, dripping with blood of her warriors. Her supple thigh brushed against it, so close she came to the tall warrior. Her red lips parted as she stared up into his somber menacing eyes.

'Who are you?' she demanded. 'By Ishtar, I have never seen your like, though I have ranged the sea from the coasts of Zingara to the fires of the ultimate south. Whence come you?'

'From Argos,' he answered shortly, alert for treachery. Let her slim hand move toward the jeweled dagger in her girdle, and a buffet of his open hand would stretch her senseless on the deck. Yet in his heart he did not fear; he had held too many women, civilized or barbaric, in his iron-thewed arms, not to recognize the light that burned in the eyes of this one.

'You are no soft Hyborian!' she exclaimed. 'You are fierce and hard as a gray wolf. Those eyes were never dimmed by city lights; those thews were never softened by life amid marble walls.'

'I am Conan, a Cimmerian,' he answered.

To the people of the exotic climes, the north was a mazy half-mythical realm, peopled with ferocious blue-eyed giants who occasionally descended from their icy fastnesses with torch and sword. Their raids had never taken them as far south as Shem, and this daughter of Shem made no distinction between Æsir, Vanir or Cimmerian. With the unerring instinct of the elemental feminine, she knew she had found her lover, and his race meant naught, save as it invested him with the glamor of far lands.

'And I am Bêlit,' she cried, as one might say, 'I am queen.'

'Look at me, Conan!' She threw wide her arms. 'I am Bêlit, queen of the black coast. Oh, tiger of the North, you are cold as the snowy mountains which bred you. Take me and crush me with your fierce love! Go with me to the ends of the earth and the ends of the sea! I am a queen by fire and steel and slaughter – be thou my king!'

His eyes swept the blood-stained ranks, seeking expressions of wrath or jealousy. He saw none. The fury was gone from the ebon faces. He realized that to these men Bêlit was more than a woman: a goddess whose will was unquestioned. He glanced at the *Argus*, wallowing in the crimson sea-wash, heeling far over, her decks awash, held up by the grappling-irons. He glanced at the blue-fringed shore, at the far green hazes of the ocean, at the vibrant figure which stood before him; and his barbaric soul stirred within him. To quest these shining blue realms with that white-skinned young tiger-cat – to love, laugh, wander and pillage—

'I'll sail with you,' he grunted, shaking the red drops from his blade.

'Ho, N'Yaga!' her voice twanged like a bowstring. 'Fetch herbs and dress your master's wounds! The rest of you bring aboard the plunder and cast off.'

As Conan sat with his back against the poop-rail, while the old shaman attended to the cuts on his hands and limbs, the cargo of the ill-fated *Argus* was quickly shifted aboard the *Tigress* and stored in small cabins below deck. Bodies of the crew and of fallen pirates were cast overboard to the swarming sharks, while wounded blacks were laid in the waist to be bandaged. Then the grappling-irons were cast off, and as the *Argus* sank silently into the blood-flecked waters, the *Tigress* moved off southward to the rhythmic clack of the oars.

As they moved out over the glassy blue deep, Bêlit came to the poop. Her eyes were burning like those of a she-panther in the dark as she tore off her ornaments, her sandals and her silken girdle and cast them at his feet. Rising on tiptoe, arms stretched upward, a quivering line of naked white, she cried to the desperate horde: 'Wolves of the blue sea, behold ye now the dance – the mating-dance of Bêlit, whose fathers were kings of Askalon!'

And she danced, like the spin of a desert whirlwind, like the leaping of a quenchless flame, like the urge of creation and the urge of death. Her white feet spurned the blood-stained deck and dying men forgot death as they gazed frozen at her. Then, as the white stars glimmered through the blue velvet dusk, making her whirling body a blur of ivory fire, with a wild cry she threw herself at Conan's feet, and the blind flood of the Cimmerian's desire swept all else away as he crushed her panting form against the black plates of his corseleted breast.

2

The Black Lotus

In that dead citadel of crumbling stone
Her eyes were snared by that unholy sheen,
And curious madness took me by the throat,
As of a rival lover thrust between.

THE SONG OF BÊLIT

The *Tigress* ranged the sea, and the black villages shuddered. Tom-toms beat in the night, with a tale that the she-devil of the sea had found a mate, an iron man whose wrath was as that of a wounded lion. And survivors of butchered Stygian ships named Bêlit with curses, and a white warrior with fierce blue eyes; so the Stygian princes remembered this man long and long, and their memory was a bitter tree which bore crimson fruit in the years to come.

But heedless as a vagrant wind, the *Tigress* cruised the southern coasts, until she anchored at the mouth of a broad sullen river, whose banks were jungle-clouded walls of mystery.

'This is the river Zarkheba, which is Death,' said Bêlit. 'Its waters are poisonous. See how dark and murky they run? Only venomous reptiles live in that river. The black people shun it. Once a Stygian galley, fleeing from me, fled up the river and vanished. I anchored in this very spot, and days later, the galley came floating down the dark waters, its decks blood-stained and deserted. Only one man was on board, and he was mad and died gibbering. The cargo was intact, but the crew had vanished into silence and mystery.

'My lover, I believe there is a city somewhere on that river. I have heard tales of giant towers and walls glimpsed afar off by sailors who dared go part-way up the river. We fear nothing: Conan, let us go and sack that city!'

Conan agreed. He generally agreed to her plans. Hers was the mind that directed their raids, his the arm that carried out her ideas. It mattered little to him where they sailed or whom they fought, so long as they sailed and fought. He found the life good.

Battle and raid had thinned their crew; only some eighty spearmen remained, scarcely enough to work the long galley. But Bêlit would not take the time to make the long cruise southward to the island kingdoms where she recruited her buccaneers. She was afire with eagerness for her latest venture; so the *Tigress* swung into the river mouth, the oarsmen pulling strongly as she breasted the broad current.

They rounded the mysterious bend that shut out the sight of the sea, and sunset found them forging steadily against the sluggish flow, avoiding sandbars where strange reptiles coiled. Not even a crocodile did they see, nor any four-legged beast or winged bird coming down to the water's edge to drink. On through the blackness that preceded moonrise they drove, between banks that were solid palisades of darkness, whence came mysterious rustlings and stealthy footfalls, and the gleam of grim eyes. And once an inhuman voice was lifted in awful mockery – the cry of an ape, Bêlit said, adding that the souls of evil men were imprisoned in these man-like animals as punishment for past crimes. But Conan doubted, for once, in a gold-barred cage in an Hyrkanian city, he had seen an abysmal sad-eyed beast which men told him was an ape, and there had been about it naught of the demoniac malevolence which vibrated in the shrieking laughter that echoed from the black jungle.

Then the moon rose, a splash of blood, ebony-barred, and the jungle awoke in horrific bedlam to greet it. Roars and howls and yells set the black warriors to trembling, but all this noise, Conan noted, came from farther back in the jungle, as if the beasts no less than men shunned the black waters of Zarkheba.

Rising above the black denseness of the trees and above the waving fronds, the moon silvered the river, and their wake became a rippling scintillation of phosphorescent bubbles that widened like a shining road of bursting jewels. The oars dipped into the shining water and came up sheathed in frosty silver. The plumes on the warrior's head-piece nodded in the wind, and the gems on sword-hilts and harness sparkled frostily.

The cold light struck icy fire from the jewels in Bêlit's clustered black locks as she stretched her lithe figure on a leopardskin thrown on the deck. Supported on her elbows, her chin resting on her slim hands, she gazed up into the face of Conan, who lounged beside her, his black mane stirring in the faint breeze. Bêlit's eyes were dark jewels burning in the moonlight.

'Mystery and terror are about us, Conan, and we glide into the realm of horror and death,' she said. 'Are you afraid?'

A shrug of his mailed shoulders was his only answer.

'I am not afraid either,' she said meditatively. 'I was never afraid. I have looked into the naked fangs of Death too often. Conan, do you fear the gods?'

'I would not tread on their shadow,' answered the barbarian conservatively. 'Some gods are strong to harm, others, to aid; at least so say their priests. Mitra of the Hyborians must be a strong god, because his people have builded their cities over the world. But even the Hyborians fear Set. And Bel, god of thieves, is a good god. When I was a thief in Zamora I learned of him.'

'What of your own gods? I have never heard you call on them.'

'Their chief is Crom. He dwells on a great mountain. What use to call on him? Little he cares if men live or die. Better to be silent than to call his attention to you; he will send you dooms, not fortune! He is grim and loveless, but at birth he breathes power to strive and slay into a man's soul. What else shall men ask of the gods?'

'But what of the worlds beyond the river of death?' she persisted.

'There is no hope here or hereafter in the cult of my people,' answered Conan. 'In this world men struggle and suffer vainly, finding pleasure only in the bright madness of battle; dying, their souls enter a gray misty realm of clouds and icy winds, to wander cheerlessly throughout eternity.'

Bêlit shuddered. 'Life, bad as it is, is better than such a destiny. What do you believe, Conan?'

He shrugged his shoulders. 'I have known many gods. He who denies them is as blind as he who trusts them too deeply. I seek not beyond death. It may be the blackness averred by the Nemedian skeptics, or Crom's realm of ice and cloud, or the snowy plains and vaulted halls of the Nordheimer's Valhalla. I know not, nor do I care. Let me live deep while I live; let me know the rich juices of red meat and stinging wine on my palate, the hot embrace of white arms, the mad exultation of battle when the blue blades flame and crimson, and I am content. Let teachers and priests and philosophers brood over questions of reality and illusion. I know this: if life is illusion, then I am no less an illusion, and being thus, the illusion is real to me. I live, I burn with life, I love, I slay, and am content.'

'But the gods are real,' she said, pursuing her own line of thought. 'And above all are the gods of the Shemites – Ishtar and Ashtoreth and Derketo and Adonis. Bel, too, is Shemitish, for he was born in ancient Shumir, long, long ago and went forth laughing, with curled beard and impish wise eyes, to steal the gems of the kings of old times.

'There is life beyond death, I know, and I know this, too, Conan of Cimmeria –' she rose lithely to her knees and caught him in a pantherish embrace – 'my love is stronger than any death! I have lain in your arms, panting with the violence of our love; you have held and crushed and conquered me, drawing my soul to your lips with the fierceness of your bruising kisses. My heart is welded to your heart, my soul is part of your soul! Were I still in death and you fighting for life, I would come back from the abyss to aid you – aye, whether my spirit floated with the purple sails on the crystal sea of paradise, or writhed in the molten flames of hell! I am yours, and all the gods and all their eternities shall not sever us!'

*

A scream rang from the lookout in the bows. Thrusting Bêlit aside, Conan bounded up, his sword a long silver glitter in the moonlight, his hair bristling at what he saw. The black warrior dangled above the deck, supported by what seemed a dark pliant tree trunk arching over the rail. Then he realized that it was a gigantic serpent which had writhed its glistening length up the side of the bow and gripped the luckless warrior in its jaws. Its dripping scales shone leprously in the moonlight as it reared its form high above the deck, while the stricken man screamed and writhed like a mouse in the fangs of a python. Conan rushed into the bows, and swinging his great sword, hewed nearly through the giant trunk, which was thicker than a man's body. Blood drenched the rails as the dying monster swayed far out, still gripping its victim, and sank into the river, coil by coil, lashing the water to bloody foam, in which man and reptile vanished together.

Thereafter Conan kept the lookout watch himself, but no other horror came crawling up from the murky depths, and as dawn whitened over the jungle, he sighted the black fangs of towers jutting up among the trees. He called Bêlit, who slept on the deck, wrapped in his scarlet cloak; and she sprang to his side, eyes blazing. Her lips were parted to call orders to her warriors to take up bow and spears; then her lovely eyes widened.

It was but the ghost of a city on which they looked when they cleared a jutting jungle-clad point and swung in toward the in-curving shore. Weeds and rank river grass grew between the stones of broken piers and shattered paves that had once been streets and spacious plazas and broad courts. From all sides except that toward the river, the jungle crept in, masking fallen columns and crumbling mounds with poisonous green. Here and there buckling towers reeled drunkenly against the morning sky, and broken pillars jutted up among the decaying walls. In the center space a marble pyramid was spired by a slim column, and on its pinnacle sat or squatted something that Conan supposed to be an image until his keen eyes detected life in it.

'It is a great bird,' said one of the warriors, standing in the bows.

'It is a monster bat,' insisted another.

'It is an ape,' said Bêlit.

Just then the creature spread broad wings and flapped off into the jungle.

'A winged ape,' said old N'Yaga uneasily. 'Better we had cut our throats than come to this place. It is haunted.'

Bêlit mocked at his superstitions and ordered the galley run inshore and tied to the crumbling wharfs. She was the first to spring ashore, closely followed by Conan, and after them trooped the ebon-skinned pirates, white plumes waving in the morning wind, spears ready, eyes rolling dubiously at the surrounding jungle.

Over all brooded a silence as sinister as that of a sleeping serpent. Bêlit posed picturesquely among the ruins, the vibrant life in her lithe figure contrasting strangely with the desolation and decay about her. The sun flamed up slowly, sullenly, above the jungle, flooding the towers with a dull gold that left shadows lurking beneath the tottering walls. Bêlit pointed to a slim round tower that reeled on its rotting base. A broad expanse of cracked, grass-grown slabs led up to it, flanked by fallen columns, and before it stood a massive altar. Bêlit went swiftly along the ancient floor and stood before it.

'This was the temple of the old ones,' she said. 'Look – you can see the channels for the blood along the sides of the altar, and the rains of ten thousand years have not washed the dark stains from them. The walls have all fallen away, but this stone block defies time and the elements.'

'But who were these old ones?' demanded Conan.

She spread her slim hands helplessly. 'Not even in legendary is this city mentioned. But look at the handholes at either end of the altar! Priests often conceal their treasures beneath their altars. Four of you lay hold and see if you can lift it.'

She stepped back to make room for them, glancing up at the tower which loomed drunkenly above them. Three of the strongest blacks had gripped the handholes cut into the stone – curiously unsuited to human hands – when Bêlit sprang back with a sharp cry. They froze in their places, and Conan, bending to aid them, wheeled with a startled curse.

'A snake in the grass,' she said, backing away. 'Come and slay it; the rest of you bend your backs to the stone.'

Conan came quickly toward her, another taking his place. As he impatiently scanned the grass for the reptile, the giant blacks braced their feet, grunted and heaved with their huge muscles coiling and straining under their ebon skin. The altar did not come off the ground, but it revolved suddenly on its side. And simultaneously there was a grinding rumble above and the tower came crashing down, covering the four black men with broken masonry.

A cry of horror rose from their comrades. Bêlit's slim fingers dug into Conan's arm-muscles. 'There was no serpent,' she whispered. 'It was but a ruse to call you away. I feared; the old ones guarded their treasure well. Let us clear away the stones.'

With herculean labor they did so, and lifted out the mangled bodies of the four men. And under them, stained with their blood, the pirates found a crypt carved in the solid stone. The altar, hinged curiously with stone rods and sockets on one side, had served as its lid. And at first glance the crypt seemed brimming with liquid fire, catching the early light with a million blazing facets. Undreamable wealth lay before the eyes of the gaping pirates; diamonds, rubies, bloodstones, sapphires, turquoises, moonstones, opals, emeralds, amethysts, unknown gems that shone like the eyes of evil women. The crypt was filled to the brim with bright stones that the morning sun struck into lambent flame.

With a cry Bêlit dropped to her knees among the blood-stained rubble on the brink and thrust her white arms shoulder-deep into that pool of splendor. She withdrew them, clutching something that brought another cry to her lips – a long string of crimson stones that were like clots of frozen blood strung on a thick gold wire. In their glow the golden sunlight changed to bloody haze.

Bêlit's eyes were like a woman's in a trance. The Shemite soul finds a bright drunkenness in riches and material splendor, and the sight of this treasure might have shaken the soul of a sated emperor of Shushan.

'Take up the jewels, dogs!' her voice was shrill with her emotions.

'Look!' a muscular black arm stabbed toward the *Tigress*, and Bêlit wheeled, her crimson lips a-snarl, as if she expected to see a rival corsair sweeping in to despoil her of her plunder. But from the gunwales of the ship a dark shape rose, soaring away over the jungle.

'The devil-ape has been investigating the ship,' muttered the blacks uneasily.

'What matter?' cried Bêlit with a curse, raking back a rebellious lock with an impatient hand. 'Make a litter of spears and mantles to bear these jewels – where the devil are you going?'

'To look to the galley,' grunted Conan. 'That bat-thing might have knocked a hole in the bottom, for all we know.'

He ran swiftly down the cracked wharf and sprang aboard. A moment's swift examination below decks, and he swore heartily, casting a clouded glance in the direction the bat-being had vanished. He returned hastily to Bêlit, superintending the plundering of the crypt. She had looped the necklace about her neck, and on her naked white bosom the red clots glimmered darkly. A huge naked black stood crotch-deep in the jewel-brimming crypt, scooping up great handfuls of splendor to pass them to eager hands above. Strings of frozen iridescence hung between his dusky fingers; drops of red fire dripped from his hands, piled high with starlight and rainbow. It was as if a black titan stood straddle-legged in the bright pits of hell, his lifted hands full of stars.

'That flying devil has staved in the water-casks,' said Conan. 'If we hadn't been so dazed by these stones we'd have heard the noise. We were fools not to have left a man on guard. We can't drink this river water. I'll take twenty men and search for fresh water in the jungle.'

She looked at him vaguely, in her eyes the blank blaze of her strange passion, her fingers working at the gems on her breast.

'Very well,' she said absently, hardly heeding him. 'I'll get the loot aboard.'

*

The jungle closed quickly about them, changing the light from gold to gray. From the arching green branches creepers dangled like pythons. The warriors fell into single file, creeping through the primordial twilights like black phantoms following a white ghost.

Underbrush was not so thick as Conan had anticipated. The ground was spongy but not slushy. Away from the river, it sloped gradually upward. Deeper and deeper they plunged into the green waving depths, and still there was no sign of water, either running stream or stagnant pool. Conan halted suddenly, his warriors freezing into basaltic statues. In the tense silence that followed, the Cimmerian shook his head irritably.

'Go ahead,' he grunted to a sub-chief, N'Gora. 'March straight on until you can no longer see me; then stop and wait for me. I believe we're being followed. I heard something.'

The blacks shuffled their feet uneasily, but did as they were told. As they swung onward, Conan stepped quickly behind a great tree, glaring back along the way they had come. From that leafy fastness anything might emerge. Nothing occurred; the faint sounds of the marching spearmen faded in the distance. Conan suddenly realized that the air was impregnated with an alien and exotic scent. Something gently brushed his temple. He turned quickly. From a cluster of green, curiously leafed stalks, great black blossoms nodded at him. One of these had touched him. They seemed to beckon him, to arch their pliant stems toward him. They spread and rustled, though no wind blew.

He recoiled, recognizing the black lotus, whose juice was death, and whose scent brought dream-haunted slumber. But already he felt a subtle lethargy stealing over him. He sought to lift his sword, to hew down the serpentine stalks, but his arm hung lifeless at his side. He opened his mouth to shout to his warriors, but only a faint rattle issued. The next instant, with appalling suddenness, the jungle waved and dimmed out before his eyes; he did not hear the screams that burst out awfully not far away, as his knees collapsed, letting him pitch limply to the earth. Above his prostrate form the great black blossoms nodded in the windless air.

3

The Horror in the Jungle

Was it a dream the nighted lotus brought?
Then curst the dream that bought my sluggish life;
And curst each laggard hour that does not see
Hot blood drip blackly from the crimsoned knife.

THE SONG OF BÊLIT

First there was the blackness of an utter void, with the cold winds of cosmic space blowing through it. Then shapes, vague, monstrous and evanescent, rolled in dim panorama through the expanse of nothingness, as if the darkness were taking material form. The winds blew and a vortex formed, a whirling pyramid of roaring blackness. From it grew Shape and Dimension; then suddenly, like clouds dispersing, the darkness rolled away on either hand and a huge city of dark green stone rose on the bank of a wide river, flowing through an illimitable plain. Through this city moved beings of alien configuration.

Cast in the mold of humanity, they were distinctly not men. They were winged and of heroic proportions; not a branch on the mysterious stalk of evolution that culminated in man, but the ripe blossom on an alien tree, separate and apart from that stalk. Aside from their wings, in physical appearance they resembled man only as man in his highest form resembles the great apes. In spiritual, esthetic and intellectual development they were superior to man as man is superior to the gorilla. But when they reared their colossal city, man's primal ancestors had not yet risen from the slime of the primordial seas.

These beings were mortal, as are all things built of flesh and blood. They lived, loved and died, though the individual span of life was enormous. Then, after uncounted millions of years, the Change began. The vista shimmered and wavered, like a picture thrown on a windblown curtain. Over the city and the land the ages flowed as waves flow over a beach, and each wave brought alterations. Somewhere on the planet the magnetic centers were shifting; the great glaciers and ice-fields were withdrawing toward the new poles.

The littoral of the great river altered. Plains turned into swamps that stank with reptilian life. Where fertile meadows had rolled, forests reared up, growing into dank jungles. The changing ages wrought on the inhabitants of the city as well. They did not migrate to fresher lands. Reasons inexplicable to humanity held them to the ancient city and their doom. And as that once rich and mighty land sank deeper and deeper into the black mire of the sunless jungle, so into the chaos of squalling jungle life sank the people of the city. Terrific convulsions shook the earth; the nights were lurid with spouting volcanoes that fringed the dark horizons with red pillars.

After an earthquake that shook down the outer walls and highest towers of the city, and caused the river to run black for days with some lethal substance spewed up from the subterranean depths, a frightful chemical change became apparent in the waters the folk had drunk for millenniums uncountable.

Many died who drank of it; and in those who lived, the drinking wrought change, subtle, gradual and grisly. In adapting themselves to the changing conditions, they had sunk far below their original level. But the lethal waters altered them even more horribly, from generation to more bestial generation. They who had been winged gods became pinioned demons, with all that remained of their ancestors' vast knowledge distorted and perverted and twisted into ghastly paths. As they had risen higher than mankind might dream, so they sank lower than man's maddest nightmares reach. They died fast, by cannibalism, and horrible feuds fought out in the murk of the midnight jungle. And at last among the lichen-grown ruins of their city only a single shape lurked, a stunted abhorrent perversion of nature.

Then for the first time humans appeared: dark-skinned, hawk-faced men in copper and leather harness, bearing bows – the warriors of pre-historic Stygia. There were only fifty of them, and they were haggard and gaunt with starvation and prolonged effort, stained and scratched with jungle-wandering, with blood-crusted bandages that told of fierce fighting. In their minds was a tale of warfare and defeat, and flight before a stronger tribe which drove them ever southward, until they lost themselves in the green ocean of jungle and river.

Exhausted they lay down among the ruins where red blossoms that bloom but once in a century waved in the full moon, and sleep fell upon them. And as they slept, a hideous shape crept red-eyed from the shadows and performed weird and awful rites about and above each sleeper. The moon hung in the shadowy sky, painting the jungle red and black; above the sleepers glimmered the crimson blossoms, like splashes of blood. Then the moon went down and the eyes of the necromancer were red jewels set in the ebony of night.

When dawn spread its white veil over the river, there were no men to be seen: only a hairy winged horror that squatted in the center of a ring of fifty great spotted hyenas that pointed quivering muzzles to the ghastly sky and howled like souls in hell.

Then scene followed scene so swiftly that each tripped over the heels of its predecessor. There was a confusion of movement, a writhing and melting of lights and shadows, against a background of black jungle, green stone ruins and murky river. Black men came up the river in long boats with skulls grinning on the prows, or stole stooping through the trees, spear in hand. They fled screaming through the dark from red eyes and slavering fangs. Howls of dying men shook the shadows; stealthy feet padded through the gloom, vampire eyes blazed redly. There were grisly feasts beneath the moon, across whose red disk a bat-like shadow incessantly swept.

Then abruptly, etched clearly in contrast to these impressionistic glimpses, around the jungled point in the whitening dawn swept a long galley, thronged with shining ebon figures, and in the bows stood a white-skinned ghost in blue steel.

It was at this point that Conan first realized that he was dreaming. Until that instant he had had no consciousness of individual existence. But as he saw himself treading the boards of the *Tigress*, he recognized both the existence and the dream, although he did not awaken.

Even as he wondered, the scene shifted abruptly to a jungle glade where N'Gora and nineteen black spearmen stood, as if awaiting someone. Even as he realized that it was he for whom they waited, a horror swooped down from the skies and their stolidity was broken by yells of fear. Like men maddened by terror, they threw away their weapons and raced wildly through the jungle, pressed close by the slavering monstrosity that flapped its wings above them.

Chaos and confusion followed this vision, during which Conan feebly struggled to awake. Dimly he seemed to see himself lying under a nodding cluster of black blossoms, while from the bushes a hideous shape crept toward him. With a savage effort he broke the unseen bonds which held him to his dreams, and started upright.

Bewilderment was in the glare he cast about him. Near him swayed the dusky lotus, and he hastened to draw away from it.

In the spongy soil near by there was a track as if an animal had put out a foot, preparatory to emerging from the bushes, then had withdrawn it. It looked like the spoor of an unbelievably large hyena.

He yelled for N'Gora. Primordial silence brooded over the jungle, in which his yells sounded brittle and hollow as mockery. He could not see the sun, but his wilderness-trained instinct told him the day was near its end. A panic rose in him at the thought that he had lain senseless for hours. He hastily followed the tracks of the spearmen, which lay plain in the damp loam before him. They ran in single file, and he soon emerged into a glade – to stop short, the skin crawling between his shoulders as he recognized it as the glade he had seen in his lotus-drugged dream. Shields and spears lay scattered about as if dropped in headlong flight.

And from the tracks which led out of the glade and deeper into the fastnesses, Conan knew that the spearmen had fled, wildly. The footprints overlay one another; they weaved blindly among the trees. And with startling suddenness the hastening Cimmerian came out of the jungle onto a hill-like rock which sloped steeply, to break off abruptly in a sheer precipice forty feet high. And something crouched on the brink.

At first Conan thought it to be a great black gorilla. Then he saw that it was a giant black man that crouched ape-like, long arms dangling, froth dripping from the loose lips. It was not until, with a sobbing cry, the creature lifted huge hands and rushed towards him, that Conan recognized N'Gora. The black man gave no heed to Conan's shout as he charged, eyes rolled up to display the whites, teeth gleaming, face an inhuman mask.

With his skin crawling with the horror that madness always instils in the sane, Conan passed his sword through the black man's body; then, avoiding the hooked hands that clawed at him as N'Gora sank down, he strode to the edge of the cliff.

For an instant he stood looking down into the jagged rocks below, where lay N'Gora's spearmen, in limp, distorted attitudes that told of crushed limbs and splintered bones. Not one moved. A cloud of huge black flies buzzed loudly above the blood-splashed stones; the ants had already begun to gnaw at the corpses. On the trees about sat birds of prey, and a jackal, looking up and seeing the man on the cliff, slunk furtively away.

For a little space Conan stood motionless. Then he wheeled and ran back the way he had come, flinging himself with reckless haste through the tall grass and bushes, hurdling creepers that sprawled snake-like across his path. His sword swung low in his right hand, and an unaccustomed pallor tinged his dark face.

The silence that reigned in the jungle was not broken. The sun had set and great shadows rushed upward from the slime of the black earth. Through the gigantic shades of lurking death and grim desolation Conan was a speeding glimmer of scarlet and blue steel. No sound in all the solitude was heard except his own quick panting as he burst from the shadows into the dim twilight of the river-shore.

He saw the galley shouldering the rotten wharf, the ruins reeling drunkenly in the gray half-light.

And here and there among the stones were spots of raw bright color, as if a careless hand had splashed with a crimson brush.

Again Conan looked on death and destruction. Before him lay his spearmen, nor did they rise to salute him. From the jungle-edge to the riverbank, among the rotting pillars and along the broken piers they lay, torn and mangled and half devoured, chewed travesties of men.

All about the bodies and pieces of bodies were swarms of huge footprints, like those of hyenas.

Conan came silently upon the pier, approaching the galley above whose deck was suspended something that glimmered ivory-white in the faint twilight. Speechless, the Cimmerian looked on the Queen of the Black Coast as she hung from the yard-arm of her own galley. Between the yard and her white throat stretched a line of crimson clots that shone like blood in the gray light.

4

The Attack from the Air

The shadows were black around him,
The dripping jaws gaped wide,
Thicker than rain the red drops fell;
But my love was fiercer than Death's black spell,
Nor all the iron walls of hell
Could keep me from his side.

THE SONG OF BÊLIT

The jungle was a black colossus that locked the ruin-littered glade in ebon arms. The moon had not risen; the stars were flecks of hot amber in a breathless sky that reeked of death. On the pyramid among the fallen towers sat Conan the Cimmerian like an iron statue, chin propped on massive fists. Out in the black shadows stealthy feet padded and red eyes glimmered. The dead lay as they had fallen. But on the deck of the *Tigress*, on a pyre of broken benches, spear-shafts and leopardskins, lay the Queen of the Black Coast in her last sleep, wrapped in Conan's scarlet cloak. Like a true queen she lay, with her plunder heaped high about her: silks, cloth-of-gold, silver braid, casks of gems and golden coins, silver ingots, jeweled daggers and teocallis of gold wedges.

But of the plunder of the accursed city, only the sullen waters of Zarkheba could tell where Conan had thrown it with a heathen curse. Now he sat grimly on the pyramid, waiting for his unseen foes. The black fury in his soul drove out all fear. What shapes would emerge from the blackness he knew not, nor did he care.

He no longer doubted the visions of the black lotus. He understood that while waiting for him in the glade, N'Gora and his comrades had been terror-stricken by the winged monster swooping upon them from the sky, and fleeing in blind panic, had fallen over the cliff, all except their chief, who had somehow escaped their fate, though not madness. Meanwhile, or immediately after, or perhaps before, the destruction of those on the riverbank had been accomplished. Conan did not doubt that the slaughter along the river had been massacre rather than battle. Already unmanned by their superstitious fears, the blacks might well have died without striking a blow in their own defense when attacked by their inhuman foes.

Why he had been spared so long, he did not understand, unless the malign entity which ruled the river meant to keep him alive to torture him with grief and fear. All pointed to a human or superhuman intelligence – the breaking of the water-casks to divide the forces, the driving of the blacks over the cliff, and last and greatest, the grim jest of the crimson necklace knotted like a hangman's noose about Bêlit's white neck.

Having apparently saved the Cimmerian for the choicest victim, and extracted the last ounce of exquisite mental torture, it was likely that the unknown enemy would conclude the drama by sending him after the other victims. No smile bent Conan's grim lips at the thought, but his eyes were lit with iron laughter.

The moon rose, striking fire from the Cimmerian's horned helmet. No call awoke the echoes; yet suddenly the night grew tense and the jungle held its breath. Instinctively Conan loosened the great sword in its sheath. The pyramid on which he rested was four-sided, one – the side toward the jungle – carved in broad steps. In his hand was a Shemite bow, such as Bêlit had taught her pirates to use. A heap of arrows lay at his feet, feathered ends towards him, as he rested on one knee.

Something moved in the blackness under the trees. Etched abruptly in the rising moon, Conan saw a darkly blocked-out head and shoulders, brutish in outline. And now from the shadows dark shapes came silently, swiftly, running low – twenty great spotted hyenas. Their slavering fangs flashed in the moonlight, their eyes blazed as no true beast's eyes ever blazed.

Twenty: then the spears of the pirates had taken toll of the pack, after all. Even as he thought this, Conan drew nock to ear, and at the twang of the string a flame-eyed shadow bounded high and fell writhing. The rest did not falter; on they came, and like a rain of death among them fell the arrows of the Cimmerian, driven with all the force and accuracy of steely thews backed by a hate hot as the slag-heaps of hell.

In his berserk fury he did not miss; the air was filled with feathered destruction. The havoc wrought among the onrushing pack was breathtaking. Less than half of them reached the foot of the pyramid. Others dropped upon the broad steps. Glaring down into the blazing eyes, Conan knew these creatures were not beasts; it was not merely in their unnatural size that he sensed a blasphemous difference. They exuded an aura tangible as the black mist rising from a corpse-littered swamp. By what godless alchemy these beings had been brought into existence, he could not guess; but he knew he faced diabolism blacker than the Well of Skelos.

Springing to his feet, he bent his bow powerfully and drove his last shaft point blank at a great hairy shape that soared up at his throat. The arrow was a flying beam of moonlight that flashed onward with but a blur in its course, but the were-beast plunged convulsively in midair and crashed headlong, shot through and through.

Then the rest were on him, in a nightmare rush of blazing

eyes and dripping fangs. His fiercely driven sword shore the first asunder; then the desperate impact of the others bore him down. He crushed a narrow skull with the pommel of his hilt, feeling the bone splinter and blood and brains gush over his hand; then, dropping the sword, useless at such deadly close quarters, he caught at the throats of the two horrors which were ripping and tearing at him in silent fury. A foul acrid scent almost stifled him, his own sweat blinded him. Only his mail saved him from being ripped to ribbons in an instant. The next, his naked right hand locked on a hairy throat and tore it open. His left hand, missing the throat of the other beast, caught and broke its foreleg. A short yelp, the only cry in that grim battle, and hideously human-like, burst from the maimed beast. At the sick horror of that cry from a bestial throat, Conan involuntarily relaxed his grip.

One, blood gushing from its torn jugular, lunged at him in a last spasm of ferocity, and fastened its fangs on his throat – to fall back dead, even as Conan felt the tearing agony of its grip.

The other, springing forward on three legs, was slashing at his belly as a wolf slashes, actually rending the links of his mail. Flinging aside the dying beast, Conan grappled the crippled horror and, with a muscular effort that brought a groan from his blood-flecked lips, he heaved upright, gripping the struggling, tearing fiend in his arms. An instant he reeled off balance, its fetid breath hot on his nostrils; its jaws snapping at his neck; then he hurled it from him, to crash with bone-splintering force down the marble steps.

As he reeled on wide-braced legs, sobbing for breath, the jungle and the moon swimming bloodily to his sight, the thrash of bat-wings was loud in his ears. Stooping, he groped for his sword, and swaying upright, braced his feet drunkenly and heaved the great blade above his head with both hands, shaking the blood from his eyes as he sought the air above him for his foe.

Instead of attack from the air, the pyramid staggered suddenly and awfully beneath his feet. He heard a rumbling crackle and saw the tall column above him wave like a wand. Stung to galvanized life, he bounded far out; his feet hit a step, halfway down, which rocked beneath him, and his next desperate leap carried him clear. But even as his heels hit the earth, with a shattering crash like a breaking mountain the pyramid crumpled, the column came thundering down in bursting fragments. For a blind cataclysmic instant the sky seemed to rain shards of marble. Then a rubble of shattered stone lay whitely under the moon.

Conan stirred, throwing off the splinters that half covered him. A glancing blow had knocked off his helmet and momentarily stunned him. Across his legs lay a great piece of the column, pinning him down. He was not sure that his legs were unbroken. His black locks were plastered with sweat; blood trickled from the wounds in his throat and hands. He hitched up on one arm, struggling with the debris that prisoned him.

Then something swept down across the stars and struck the sward near him. Twisting about, he saw it – *the winged one!*

With fearful speed it was rushing upon him, and in that instant Conan had only a confused impression of a gigantic man-like shape hurtling along on bowed and stunted legs; of huge hairy arms outstretching misshapen black-nailed paws; of a malformed head, in whose broad face the only features recognizable as such were a pair of blood-red eyes. It was a thing neither man, beast, nor devil, imbued with characteristics subhuman as well as characteristics superhuman.

But Conan had no time for conscious consecutive thought. He threw himself toward his fallen sword, and his clawing fingers missed it by inches. Desperately he grasped the shard which pinned his legs, and the veins swelled in his temples as he strove to thrust it off him. It gave slowly, but he knew that before he could free himself the monster would be upon him, and he knew that those black-taloned hands were death.

The headlong rush of the winged one had not wavered. It towered over the prostrate Cimmerian like a black shadow, arms thrown wide – a glimmer of white flashed between it and its victim.

In one mad instant she was there – a tense white shape, vibrant with love fierce as a she-panther's. The dazed Cimmerian saw between him and the onrushing death, her lithe figure, shimmering like ivory beneath the moon; he saw the blaze of her dark eyes, the thick cluster of her burnished hair; her bosom heaved, her red lips were parted, she cried out sharp and ringing at the ring of steel as she thrust at the winged monster's breast.

'Bêlit!' screamed Conan. She flashed a quick glance at him, and in her dark eyes he saw her love flaming, a naked elemental thing of raw fire and molten lava. Then she was gone, and the Cimmerian saw only the winged fiend which had staggered back in unwonted fear, arms lifted as if to fend off attack. And he knew that Bêlit in truth lay on her pyre on the *Tigress*'s deck. In his ears rang her passionate cry: 'Were I still in death and you fighting for life I would come back from the abyss—'

With a terrible cry he heaved upward hurling the stone aside. The winged one came on again, and Conan sprang to meet it, his veins on fire with madness. The thews started out like cords on his forearms as he swung his great sword, pivoting on his heel with the force of the sweeping arc. Just above the hips it caught the hurtling shape, and the knotted legs fell one way, the torso another as the blade sheared clear through its hairy body.

Conan stood in the moonlit silence, the dripping sword sagging in his hand, staring down at the remnants of his enemy. The red eyes glared up at him with awful life, then glazed and set; the great hands knotted spasmodically and stiffened. And the oldest race in the world was extinct.

Conan lifted his head, mechanically searching for the beast-things that had been its slaves and executioners. None met his gaze. The bodies he saw littering the moon-splashed grass were of men, not beasts: hawk-faced, dark-skinned men, naked, transfixed by arrows or mangled by sword-strokes. And they were crumbling into dust before his eyes.

Why had not the winged master come to the aid of its slaves when he struggled with them? Had it feared to come within reach of fangs that might turn and rend it? Craft and caution had lurked in that misshapen skull, but had not availed in the end.

Turning on his heel, the Cimmerian strode down the rotting wharfs and stepped aboard the galley. A few strokes of his sword cut her adrift, and he went to the sweep-head. The *Tigress* rocked slowly in the sullen water, sliding out sluggishly toward the middle of the river, until the broad current caught her. Conan leaned on the sweep, his somber gaze fixed on the cloak-wrapped shape that lay in state on the pyre the richness of which was equal to the ransom of an empress.

5

The Funeral Pyre

Now we are done with roaming, evermore;
No more the oars, the windy harp's refrain;
Nor crimson pennon frights the dusky shore;
Blue girdle of the world, receive again
Her whom thou gavest me.

THE SONG OF BÊLIT

Again dawn tinged the ocean. A redder glow lit the river-mouth. Conan of Cimmeria leaned on his great sword upon the white beach, watching the *Tigress* swinging out on her last voyage. There was no light in his eyes that contemplated the glassy swells. Out of the rolling blue wastes all glory and wonder had gone. A fierce revulsion shook him as he gazed at the green surges that deepened into purple hazes of mystery.

Bêlit had been of the sea; she had lent it splendor and allure. Without her it rolled a barren, dreary and desolate waste from pole to pole. She belonged to the sea; to its everlasting mystery he returned her. He could do no more. For himself, its glittering blue splendor was more repellent than the leafy fronds which rustled and whispered behind him of vast mysterious wilds beyond them, and into which he must plunge.

No hand was at the sweep of the *Tigress*, no oars drove her through the green water. But a clean tanging wind bellied her silken sail, and as a wild swan cleaves the sky to her nest, she sped seaward, flames mounting higher and higher from her deck to lick at the mast and envelop the figure that lay lapped in scarlet on the shining pyre.

So passed the Queen of the Black Coast, and leaning on his red-stained sword, Conan stood silently until the red glow had faded far out in the blue hazes and dawn splashed its rose and gold over the ocean.

THE VALE OF LOST WOMEN

1

The thunder of the drums and the great elephant-tusk horns was deafening, but in Livia's ears the clamor seemed but a confused muttering dull and far away. As she lay on the *angareb* in the great hut, her state bordered between delirium and semi-unconsciousness. Outward sounds and movements scarcely impinged upon her senses. Her whole mental vision, though dazed and chaotic, was yet centered with hideous certitude on the naked, writhing figure of her brother, blood streaming down his quivering thighs. Against a dim nightmare background of dusky interweaving shapes and shadows, that white form was limned in merciless and awful clarity. The air seemed still to pulsate with an agonized screaming, mingled and interwoven obscenely with a rustle of fiendish laughter.

She was not conscious of sensation as an individual, separate and distinct from the rest of the cosmos. She was drowned in a great gulf of pain – was herself but pain crystalized and manifested in flesh. So she lay without conscious thought or motion, while outside the drums bellowed, the horns clamored, and barbaric voices lifted hideous chants, keeping time to naked feet slapping the hard earth and open palms smiting one another softly.

But through her frozen mentality individual consciousness at last began to seep. A dull wonder that she was still bodily unharmed first made itself manifest. She accepted the miracle without thanksgiving. The matter seemed meaningless. Acting mechanically, she sat up on the *angareb* and stared dully about her. Her extremities made feeble beginnings of motions, as if responding to blindly awakening nerve centers. Her naked feet scruffed nervously at the hard-beaten dirt floor. Her fingers twitched convulsively at the skirt of the scanty undertunic which constituted her only garment. Impersonally she remembered that once, it seemed long, long ago, rude hands had torn her other garments from her body, and she had wept with fright and shame. It seemed strange, now, that so small a wrong should have caused her so much woe. The magnitude of outrage and indignity was only relative, after all, like everything else.

The hut door opened, and a black woman entered – a lithe pantherish creature, whose supple body gleamed like polished ebony, adorned only by a wisp of silk twisted about her strutting loins. The white of her eyeballs reflected the firelight outside, as she rolled them with wicked meaning.

She bore a bamboo dish of food – smoking meat, roasted yams, mealies, unwieldy ingots of native bread – and a vessel of hammered gold, filled with *yarati* beer. These she set down on the *angareb*, but Livia paid no heed; she sat staring dully at the opposite wall, hung with mats woven of bamboo shoots. The young black woman laughed evilly, with a flash of dark eyes and white teeth, and with a hiss of spiteful obscenity and a mocking caress that was more gross than her language, she turned and swaggered out of the hut, expressing more taunting insolence with the motions of her hips than any civilized woman could with spoken insults.

Neither the wench's words nor her actions had stirred the surface of Livia's consciousness. All her sensations were still turned inward. Still the vividness of her mental pictures made the visible world seem like an unreal panorama of ghosts and shadows. Mechanically she ate the food and drank the liquor without tasting either.

It was still mechanically that at last she rose and walked unsteadily across the hut, to peer out through a crack between the bamboos. It was an abrupt change in the timbre of the drums and horns that reacted upon some obscure part of her mind and made her seek the cause, without sensible volition.

*

At first she could make out nothing of what she saw; all was chaotic and shadowy, shapes moving and mingling, writhing and twisting, black formless blocks hewed out starkly against a setting of blood-red that dulled and glowed. Then actions and objects assumed their proper proportions, and she made out men and women moving about the fires. The red light glinted on silver and ivory ornaments; white plumes nodded against the glare; naked black figures strutted and posed, silhouettes carved out of darkness and limned in crimson.

On an ivory stool, flanked by giants in plumed headpieces and leopardskin girdles, sat a fat, squat shape, abysmal, repulsive, a toad-like chunk of blackness, reeking of the dank rotting jungle and the nighted swamps. The creature's pudgy hands rested on the sleek arch of his belly; his nape was a roll of sooty fat that seemed to thrust his bullet-head forward. His eyes gleamed in the firelight, like live coals in a dead black stump. Their appalling vitality belied the inert suggestion of the gross body.

As the girl's gaze rested on that repellant figure her body stiffened and tensed as frantic life surged through her again. From a mindless automaton, she changed suddenly to a sentient mold of live, quivering flesh, stinging and burning. Pain was drowned in hate, so intense it in turn became pain; she felt hard and brittle, as if her body were turning to steel. She felt her hate flow almost tangibly out along the line of her vision; so it seemed to her that the object of her emotion should fall dead from his carven stool because of its force.

But if Bajujh, king of Bakalah, felt any psychic discomfort because of the concentration of his captive, he did not show it. He continued to cram his frog-like mouth to capacity with handfuls of mealies scooped up from a vessel held up to him by a kneeling woman, and to stare down a broad lane which was being formed by the action of his subjects in pressing back on either hand.

Down this lane, walled with sweaty black humanity, Livia vaguely realized some important personage would come, judging from the strident clamor of drum and horn. And as she watched, one came.

A column of fighting-men, marching three abreast, advanced toward the ivory stool, a thick line of waving plumes and glinting spears meandering through the motley crowd. At the head of the ebon spearmen strode a figure at the sight of which Livia started violently; her heart seemed to stop, then began to pound again, suffocatingly. Against that dusky background, this man stood out with vivid distinctness. He was clad like his followers in leopardskin loin-cloth and plumed headpiece, but he was a white man.

It was not in the manner of a supplicant or a subordinate that he strode up to the ivory stool, and sudden silence fell over the throng as he halted before the squatting figure. Livia felt the tenseness, though she only dimly knew what it portended. For a moment Bajujh sat, craning his short neck upward, like a great frog; then, as if pulled against his will by the other's steady glare, he shambled up off his stool, and stood grotesquely bobbing his shaven head.

Instantly the tension was broken. A tremendous shout went up from the massed villagers, and at a gesture from the stranger, his warriors lifted their spears and boomed a salute royale for King Bajujh. Whoever he was, Livia knew the man must indeed be powerful in that wild land, if Bajujh of Bakalah rose to greet him. And power meant military prestige – violence was the only thing respected by those ferocious races.

Thereafter Livia stood with her eyes glued to the crack in the hut wall, watching the white stranger. His warriors mingled with the Bakalas, dancing, feasting, swigging beer. He himself, with a few of his chiefs, sat with Bajujh and the headmen of Bakalah, cross-legged on mats, gorging and guzzling. She saw his hands dipped deep into the cooking-pots with the others, saw his muzzle thrust into the beer vessel out of which Bajujh also drank. But she noticed, nevertheless, that he was accorded the respect due to a king. Since he had no stool, Bajujh renounced his also, and sat on the mats with his guest. When a new pot of beer was brought, the king of Bakalah barely sipped it before he passed it to the white man.

Power! All this ceremonial courtesy pointed to power – strength – prestige! Livia trembled in excitement as a breathless plan began to form in her mind.

So she watched the white man with painful intensity, noting every detail of his appearance. He was tall; neither in height nor in massiveness was he exceeded by many of the giant blacks. He moved with the lithe suppleness of a great panther. When the firelight caught his eyes, they burned like blue fire. High-strapped sandals guarded his feet, and from his broad girdle hung a sword in a leather scabbard. His appearance was alien and unfamiliar. Livia had never seen his like, but she made no effort to classify his position among the races of mankind. It was enough that his skin was white.

The hours passed, and gradually the roar of revelry lessened, as men and women sank into drunken sleep. At last Bajujh rose tottering, and lifted his hands, less a sign to end the feast, than a token of surrender in the contest of gorging and guzzling, and stumbling, was caught by his warriors, who bore him to his hut. The white man rose, apparently none the worse for the incredible amount of beer he had quaffed, and was escorted to the guest hut by such of the Bakalah headmen as were able to reel along. He disappeared into the hut, and Livia noticed that a dozen of his own spearmen took their places about the structure, spears ready. Evidently the stranger was taking no chances on Bajujh's friendship.

Livia cast her glance about the village, which faintly resembled a dusky Night of Judgment, what with the straggling streets strewn with drunken shapes. She knew that men in full possession of their faculties guarded the outer boma, but the only wakeful men she saw inside the village were the spearmen about the white man's hut – and some of these were beginning to nod and lean on their spears.

With her heart beating hammer-like, she glided to the back of her prison hut and out the door, passing the snoring guard Bajujh had set over her. Like an ivory shadow she glided across the space between her hut and that occupied by the stranger. On her hands and knees she crawled up to the back of that hut. A black giant squatted here, his plumed head sunk on his knees. She wriggled past him to the wall of the hut. She had first been imprisoned in that hut, and a narrow aperture in the wall, hidden inside by a hanging mat, represented her weak and pathetic attempt at escape. She found the opening, turned sidewise and wriggled her lithe body through, thrusting the inner mat aside.

Firelight from without faintly illumined the interior of the hut. Even as she thrust back the mat, she heard a muttered curse, felt a vise-like grasp in her hair, and was dragged bodily through the aperture and plumped down on her feet.

Staggering with the suddenness of it, she gathered her scattered wits together, and raked her disordered tresses out of her eyes to stare up into the face of the white man who towered over her, amazement written on his dark scarred face. His sword was naked in his hand, and his eyes blazed like bale-fire, whether with anger, suspicion or surprize she could not judge. He spoke in a language she could not understand – a tongue which was not a negro guttural, yet did not have a civilized sound.

'Oh, please!' she begged. 'Not so loud. *They* will hear ...'

'Who are you?' he demanded, speaking Ophirean with a barbarous accent. 'By Crom, I never thought to find a white girl in this hellish land!'

'My name is Livia,' she answered. 'I am Bajujh's captive. Oh, listen, please listen to me! I cannot stay here long. I must return before they miss me from my hut.

'My brother ...' a sob choked her, then she continued: 'My brother was Theteles, and we were of the house of Chelkus, scientists and noblemen of Ophir. By special permission of the king of Stygia, my brother was allowed to go to Kheshatta, the city of magicians, to study their arts, and I accompanied him. He was only a boy – younger than myself ...' her voice faltered and broke. The stranger said nothing, but stood watching her with burning eyes, his face frowning and unreadable. There was something wild and untamable about him that frightened her and made her nervous and uncertain.

'The black Kushites raided Kheshatta,' she continued hurriedly. 'We were approaching the city in a camel caravan. Our guards fled and the raiders carried us away with them. But they did us no harm, and let us know that they would parley with the Stygians and accept a ransom for our return. But one of the chiefs desired all the ransom for himself, and he and his followers stole us out of the camp one night, and fled far to the southeast with us, to the very borders of Kush. There they were attacked and cut down by a band of Bakalah raiders. Theteles and I were dragged into this den of beasts ...' she sobbed convulsively. '... This morning my brother was mutilated and butchered before me ...' She gagged and went momentarily blind at the memory. 'They fed his body to the jackals. How long I lay in a faint I do not know ...'

Words failing her, she lifted her eyes to the scowling face of the stranger. A mad fury swept over her; she lifted her fists and beat futilely on his mighty breast, which he heeded no more than the buzzing of a fly.

'How can you stand there like a dumb brute?' she screamed in a ghastly whisper. 'Are you but a beast like these others? Ah, Mitra, once I thought there was honor in men. Now I know each has his price. You – what do you know of honor – or of mercy or decency? You are a barbarian like these others – only your skin is white; your soul is black as theirs. You care naught that a man of your own colour has been foully done to death by these black dogs – that a white woman is their slave! Very well.'

She fell back from him, panting, transfigured by her passion.

'I will give you a price,' she raved, tearing away her tunic from her ivory breasts. 'Am I not fair? Am I not more desirable than these soot-coloured wenches? Am I not a worthy reward for blood-letting? Is not a fair-skinned virgin a price worth slaying for?

'Kill that black dog Bajujh! Let me see his cursed head roll in the bloody dust! Kill him! *Kill him!*' She beat her clenched fists together in the agony of her intensity. 'Then take me and do as you wish with me. I will be your slave!'

*

He did not speak for an instant, but stood like a giant brooding figure of slaughter and destruction, fingering his hilt.

'You speak as if you were free to give yourself at your pleasure,' he said, 'as if the gift of your body had power to swing kingdoms. Why should I kill Bajujh to obtain you? Women are cheap as plantains in this land, and their willingness or unwillingness matters as little. You value yourself too highly. If I wanted you, I wouldn't have to fight Bajujh to take you. He would rather give you to me than to fight me.'

Livia gasped. All the fire went out of her, the hut reeled dizzily before her eyes. She staggered and sank in a crumpled heap on an *angareb*. Dazed bitterness crushed her soul as the realization of her utter helplessness was thrust brutally upon her. The human mind clings unconsciously to familiar values and ideas, even among surroundings and conditions alien and unrelated to those environs to which such values and ideas are adapted. In spite of all Livia had experienced, she had still instinctively supposed a woman's consent the pivotal point of such a game as she proposed to play. She was stunned by the realization that nothing hinged upon her at all. She could not move men as pawns in a game; she herself was the helpless pawn.

'I see the absurdity of supposing that any man in this corner of the world would act according to rules and customs existent in another corner of the planet,' she murmured weakly, scarcely conscious of what she was saying, which was indeed only the vocal framing of the thought which overcame her. Stunned by that newest twist of fate, she lay motionless, until the white barbarian's iron fingers closed on her shoulder and lifted her again to her feet.

'You said I was a barbarian,' he said harshly, 'and that is true, Crom be thanked. If you had had men of the outlands guarding you instead of soft gutted civilized weaklings, you would not be the slave of a black pig this night. I am Conan, a Cimmerian, and I live by the sword's edge. But I am not such a dog as to leave a white woman in the clutches of a black man; and though your kind call me a robber, I never forced a woman against her consent.

Customs differ in various countries, but if a man is strong enough, he can enforce a few of his native customs anywhere. And no man ever called me a weakling!

'If you were old and ugly as the devil's pet vulture, I'd take you away from Bajujh, simply because of the colour of your hide. But you are young and beautiful, and I have looked at black sluts until I am sick at the guts. I'll play this game your way, simply because some of your instincts correspond with some of mine. Get back to your hut, Bajujh's too drunk to come to you tonight, and I'll see that he's occupied tomorrow. And tomorrow night it will be Conan's bed you'll warm, not Bajujh's.'

'How will it be accomplished?' She was trembling with mingled emotions. 'Are these all your warriors?'

'They're enough,' he grunted. 'Bamulas, every one of them, and suckled at the teats of war. I came here at Bajujh's request. He wants me to join him in an attack on Jihiji. Tonight we feasted. Tomorrow we hold council. When I get through with him, he'll be holding council in Hell.'

'You will break the truce?'

'Truces in this land are made to be broken,' he answered grimly. 'He would break his truce with Jihiji. And after we'd looted the town together, he'd wipe me out the first time he caught me off guard. What would be blackest treachery in another land, is wisdom here. I have not fought my way alone to the position of war-chief of the Bamulas without learning all the lessons the black country teaches. Now go back to your hut and sleep, knowing that it is not for Bajujh but for Conan that you preserve your beauty!'

2

Through the crack in the bamboo wall, Livia watched, her nerves taut and trembling. All day, since their late waking, bleary and sodden from their debauch of the night before, the black people had prepared the feast for the coming night. All day Conan the Cimmerian had sat in the hut of Bajujh, and what had passed between them, Livia could not know. She had fought to hide her excitement from the only person who entered her hut – the vindictive black girl who brought her food and drink. But that ribald wench had been too groggy from her libations of the previous night to notice the change in her captive's demeanor.

Now night had fallen again, fires lighted the village, and once more the chiefs left the king's hut and squatted down in the open space between the huts to feast and hold a final, ceremonious council. This time there was not so much beer-guzzling. Livia noticed the Bamulas casually converging toward the circle where sat the chief men. She saw Bajujh, and sitting opposite him across the eating pots, Conan, laughing and conversing with the giant Aja, Bajujh's war-chief.

The Cimmerian was gnawing a great beef-bone, and as she watched, she saw him cast a glance across his shoulder. As if it were a signal for which they had been waiting, the Bamulas all turned their gaze toward their chief. Conan rose, still smiling, as if to reach into a near-by cooking pot; then quick as a cat he struck Aja a terrible blow with the heavy bone. The Bakalah war-chief slumped over, his skull crushed in, and instantly a frightful yell rent the skies as the Bamulas went into action like blood-mad panthers.

Cooking pots overturned, scalding the squatting women, bamboo walls buckled to the impact of plunging bodies, screams of agony ripped the night, and over all rose the exultant '*Yee! yee! yee!*' of maddened Bamulas, the flame of spears that crimsoned in the lurid glow.

Bakalah was a madhouse that reddened into a shambles. The action of the invaders paralyzed the luckless villagers by its unexpected suddenness. No thought of attack by their guests had ever entered their woolly pates. Most of the spears were stacked in the huts, many of the warriors already half drunk. The fall of Aja was a signal that plunged the gleaming blades of the Bamulas into a hundred unsuspecting bodies; after that it was massacre.

At her peep-hole Livia stood frozen, white as a statue, her golden locks drawn back and grasped in a knotted cluster with both hands at her temples. Her eyes were dilated, her whole body rigid. The yells of pain and fury smote her tortured nerves like a physical impact, the writhing, slashing forms blurred before her, then sprang out again with horrifying distinctness. She saw spears sink into writhing black bodies, spilling red. She saw clubs swing and descend with brutal force on kinky heads. Brands were kicked out of the fires, scattering sparks; hut-thatches smoldered and blazed up. A fresh stridency of anguish cut through the cries, as living victims were hurled head-first into the blazing structures. The scent of scorched flesh began to sicken the air, already rank with reeking sweat and fresh blood.

Livia's overwrought nerves gave way. She cried out again and again, shrill screams of torment, lost in the roar of flames and slaughter. She beat her temples with her clenched fists. Her reason tottered, changing her cries to more awful peals of hysterical laughter. In vain she sought to keep before her the fact that it was her enemies who were dying thus horribly – that this was as she had madly hoped and plotted – that this ghastly sacrifice was a just repayment for the wrongs done her and hers. Frantic terror held her in its unreasoning grasp.

She was aware of no pity for the victims who were dying, wholesale under the dripping spears. Her only emotion was blind, stark, mad, unreasoning fear. She saw Conan, his white form contrasting with the blacks. She saw his sword flash, and men went down around him. Now a struggling knot swept around a fire, and she glimpsed a fat squat shape writhing in its midst. Conan ploughed through and was hidden from view by the twisting black figures. From the midst a thin squealing rose unbearably. The press split for an instant, and she had one awful glimpse of a reeling desperate squat figure, streaming blood. Then the throng crowded in again, and steel flashed in the mob like a beam of lightning through the dusk.

A beast-like baying rose, terrifying in its primitive exultation. Through the mob Conan's tall form pushed its way. He was striding toward the hut where the girl cowered, and in his hand he bore a ghastly relic – the firelight gleamed redly on King Bajujh's severed head. The black eyes, glassy now instead of vital, rolled up, revealing only the whites; the jaw hung slack as if in a grin of idiocy; red drops showered thickly along the ground.

Livia gave back with a moaning cry. Conan had paid the price and was coming to claim her, bearing the awful token of his payment. He would grasp her with his hot bloody fingers, crush her lips with mouth still panting from the slaughter. With the thought came delirium.

With a scream Livia ran across the hut, threw herself against the door in the back wall. It fell open, and she darted across the open space, a flitting white ghost in a realm of black shadows and red flame.

Some obscure instinct led her to the pen where the horses were kept. A warrior was just taking down the bars that separated the horse-pen from the main boma, and he yelled in amazement as she darted past him. A dusky hand clutched at her, closed on the neck of her tunic. With a frantic jerk she tore away leaving the garment in his hand. The horses snorted and stampeded past her, rolling the black warrior in the dust – lean, wiry steeds of the Kushite breed, already frantic with the fire and the scent of blood.

Blindly she caught at a flying mane, was jerked off her feet, struck the ground again on her toes, sprang high, pulled and scrambled herself upon the horse's straining back. Mad with fear the herd plunged through the fires, their small hoofs knocking sparks in a blinding shower. The startled black people had a wild glimpse of the girl clinging naked to the mane of a beast that raced like the wind that streamed out his rider's loose yellow hair. Then straight for the boma the steed bolted, soared breathtakingly into the air, and was gone into the night.

3

Livia could make no attempt to guide her steed, nor did she feel any need of so doing. The yells and the glow of the fires were fading out behind her; the wind tossed her hair and caressed her naked limbs. She was aware only of a dazed need to hold to the flowing mane and ride, ride, ride over the rim of the world and away from all agony and grief and horror.

And for hours the wiry steed raced, until, topping a starlit crest, he stumbled and hurled his rider headlong.

She struck on soft cushioning sward, and lay for an instant half stunned, dimly hearing her mount trot away. When she staggered up, the first thing that impressed her was the silence. It was an almost tangible thing – soft, darkly velvet – after the incessant blare of barbaric horns and drums which had maddened her for days. She stared up at the great white stars clustered thickly in the dark blue sky. There was no moon, yet the starlight illuminated the land, though illusively, with unexpected clusterings of shadow. She stood on a swarded eminence from which the gently molded slopes ran away, soft as velvet under the starlight. Far away in one direction she discerned a dense dark line of trees which marked the distant forest. Here there was only night and trance-like stillness and a faint breeze blowing through the stars.

The land seemed vast and slumbering. The warm caress of the breeze made her aware of her nakedness, and she wriggled uneasily, spreading her hands over her body. Then she felt the loneliness of the night, and the unbrokenness of the solitude. She was alone; she stood naked on the summit of the land and there was none to see; nothing but night and the whispering wind.

She was suddenly glad of the night and the loneliness. There was none to threaten her, or to seize her with rude violent hands. She looked before her and saw the slope falling away into a broad valley; there fronds waved thickly and the starlight reflected whitely on many small objects scattered throughout the vale. She thought they were great white blossoms and the thought gave rise to vague memory; she thought of a valley of which the blacks had spoken with fear; a valley to which had fled the young women of a strange brown-skinned race which had inhabited the land before the coming of the ancestors of the Bakalahs. There, men said, they had turned into white flowers, had been transformed by the old gods to escape their ravishers. There no black man dared go.

But into that valley Livia dared go. She would go down those grassy slopes which were like velvet under her tender feet; she would dwell there among the nodding white blossoms and no man would ever come to lay hot, rude hands on her. Conan had said that pacts were made to be broken; she would break her pact with him. She would go into the vale of the lost women; she would lose herself in solitude and stillness ... even as these dreamy and disjointed thoughts floated through her consciousness, she was descending the gentle slopes, and the tiers of the valley walls were rising higher on each hand.

But so gentle were their slopes that when she stood on the valley floor she did not have the feeling of being imprisoned by rugged walls. All about her floated seas of shadow, and great white blossoms nodded and whispered to her. She wandered at random, parting the fronds with her small hands, listening to the whisper of the wind through the leaves, finding a childish pleasure in the gurgling of an unseen stream. She moved as in a dream, in the grasp of a strange unreality. One thought reiterated itself continually: there she was safe from the brutality of men. She wept, but the tears were of joy. She lay full-length upon the sward and clutched the soft grass as if she would crush her new-found refuge to her breast and hold it there for ever.

She plucked the petals of the blossoms and fashioned them into a chaplet for her golden hair. Their perfume was in keeping with all other things in the valley, dreamy, subtle, enchanting.

So she came at last to a glade in the midst of the valley, and saw there a great stone, hewn as if by human hands, and adorned with ferns and blossoms and chains of flowers. She stood staring at it, and then there was movement and life about her. Turning, she saw figures stealing from the denser shadows – slender brown women, lithe, naked, with blossoms in their night-black hair. Like creatures of a dream they came about her, and they did not speak. But suddenly terror seized her as she looked into their eyes. Those eyes were luminous, radiant in the starshine, but they were not human eyes. The forms were human but in the souls a strange change had been wrought; a change reflected in their glowing eyes. Fear descended on Livia in a wave. The serpent reared its grisly head in her new-found Paradise.

But she could not flee. The lithe brown women were all about her. One, lovelier than the rest, came silently up to the trembling girl, and enfolded her with supple brown arms. Her breath was scented with the same perfume that stole from the white blossoms that waved in the starshine. Her lips pressed Livia's in a long terrible kiss. The Ophirean felt coldness, running through her veins; her limbs turned brittle; like a white statue of marble she lay in the arms of her captress, incapable of speech or movement.

Quick soft hands lifted her and laid her on the altar-stone amidst a bed of flowers. The brown women joined hands in a ring and moved supplely about the altar, dancing a strange dark measure. Never the sun or the moon looked on such a dance, and the great white stars grew whiter and glowed with a more luminous light as if its dark witchery struck response in things cosmic and elemental.

And a low chant arose, that was less human than the gurgling of the distant stream; a rustle of voices like the whispering of the great white blossoms that waved beneath the stars. Livia lay, conscious but without power of movement. It did not occur to her to doubt her sanity. She sought not to reason or analyze; she *was* and these strange beings dancing about her *were*; a dumb realization of existence and recognition of the actuality of nightmare possessed her as she lay helplessly gazing up at the star-clustered sky, whence, she somehow knew with more than mortal knowledge, some*thing* would come to her, as it had come long ago to make these naked brown women the soulless beings they now were.

First, high above her, she saw a black dot among the stars, which grew and expanded; it neared her; it swelled to a bat; and still it grew, though its shape did not alter further to any great extent. It hovered over her in the stars, dropping plummet-like earthward, its great wings spread over her; she lay in its tenebrous shadow.

And all about her the chant rose higher, to a soft paean of soulless joy, a welcome to the god which came to claim a fresh sacrifice, fresh and rose-pink as a flower in the dew of dawn.

Now it hung directly over her, and her soul shriveled and grew chill and small at the sight. Its wings were bat-like; but its body and the dim face that gazed down upon her were like nothing of sea or earth or air; she knew she looked upon ultimate horror, upon black cosmic foulness born in night-black gulfs beyond the reach of a madman's wildest dreams.

Breaking the unseen bonds that held her dumb, she screamed awfully. Her cry was answered by a deep menacing shout. She heard the pounding of rushing feet; all about her there was a swirl as of swift waters; the white blossoms tossed wildly, and the brown women were gone. Over her hovered the great black shadow, and she saw a tall white figure, with plumes nodding in the stars, rushing toward her.

'*Conan!*' The cry broke involuntarily from her lips. With a fierce inarticulate yell, the barbarian sprang into the air, lashing upward with his sword that flamed in the starlight.

The great black wings rose and fell. Livia, dumb with horror, saw the Cimmerian enveloped in the black shadow that hung over him. The man's breath came pantingly; his feet stamped the beaten earth, crushing the white blossoms into the dirt. The rending impact of his blows echoed through the night. He was hurled back and forth like a rat in the grip of a hound, blood splashed thickly on the sward, mingling with the white petals that lay strewn like a carpet.

And then the girl, watching that devilish battle as in a nightmare, saw the black-winged thing waver and stagger in mid-air; there was a threshing beat of crippled wings and the monster had torn clear and was soaring upward to mingle and vanish among the stars. Its conqueror staggered dizzily, sword poised, legs wide-braced, staring upward stupidly amazed at victory, but ready to take up again the ghastly battle.

An instant later, Conan approached the altar, panting, dripping blood at every step. His massive chest heaved, glistening with perspiration. Blood ran down his arms in streams from his neck and shoulders. As he touched her, the spell on the girl was broken and she scrambled up and slid from the altar, recoiling from his hand. He leaned against the stone, looking down at her, where she cowered at his feet.

'Men saw you ride out of the village,' he said. 'I followed as soon as I could, and picked up your track, though it was no easy task following it by torchlight. I tracked you to the place where your horse threw you, and though the torches were exhausted by then, and I could not find the prints of your bare feet on the sward, I felt sure you had descended into the valley. My men would not follow me, so I came alone on foot. What vale of devils is this? What was that thing?'

'A god,' she whispered. 'The black people spoke of it – a god from far away and long ago!'

'A devil from the Outer Dark,' he grunted. 'Oh, they're nothing uncommon. They lurk as thick as fleas outside the belt of light which surrounds this world. I've heard the wise men of Zamora talk of them. Some find their way to Earth, but when they do they have to take on Earthly form and flesh of some sort. A man like myself, with a sword, is a match for any amount of fangs and talons, infernal or terrestrial. Come; my men await me beyond the ridge of the valley.'

She crouched motionless, unable to find words, while he frowned down at her. Then she spoke: 'I ran away from you. I planned to dupe you. I was not going to keep my promise to you; I was yours by the bargain we made but I would have escaped from you if I could. Punish me as you will.'

He shook the sweat and blood from his locks, and sheathed his sword.

'Get up,' he grunted. 'It was a foul bargain I made. I do not regret that black dog Bajujh, but you are no wench to be bought and sold. The ways of men vary in different lands, but a man need not be a swine, wherever he is. After I thought awhile, I saw that to hold you to your bargain would be the same as if I had forced you. Besides, you are not tough enough for this land. You are a child of cities and books and civilized ways – which isn't your fault, but you'd die quickly following the life I thrive on. A dead woman would be no good to me. I will take you to the Stygian borders. The Stygians will send you home to Ophir.'

She stared up at him as if she had not heard aright. 'Home?' she repeated mechanically. 'Home? Ophir? My people? Cities, towers, peace, my *home*?' Suddenly tears welled into her eyes, and sinking to her knees, she embraced his knees in her arms.

'Crom, girl,' grunted Conan, embarrassed. 'Don't do that; you'd think I was doing you a favor by kicking you out of this country; haven't I explained that you're not the proper woman for the war-chief of the Bamulas?'

THE SNOUT IN THE DARK

(Draft)

1

Amboola awakened slowly, his senses still sluggish from the wine he had guzzled the night before. For a muddled moment he could not remember where he was; the moonlight, streaming through the barred window, shone on unfamiliar surroundings. Then he remembered that he was lying in the upper cell of the prison where the anger of Tananda, sister to the king of Kush, had consigned him. It was no ordinary cell, for even Tananda had not dared to go too far in her punishment of the commander of the black spearmen which were the strength of Kush's army. There were carpets and tapestries and silk-covered couches, and jugs of wine – he remembered that he had been awakened and wondered why.

His gaze wandered to the square of barred moonlight that was the window, and he saw something that partially sobered him, and straightened his blurred gaze. The bars of that window were bent and buckled and twisted back. It must have been the noise of their rending that had awakened him. But what could have bent them? And where was whatever had so bent them? Suddenly he was completely sober, and an icy sensation wandered up his spine. *Something* had entered through that window, something was in the room with him.

With a low cry he started up on his couch and stared about him; and he froze at the sight of the motionless figure that stood at the head of his couch. An icy hand clutched the heart of Amboola which had never known fear. That silent, greyish shape did not move nor speak; it stood there in the shadowy moonlight, misshapen, deformed, its outline outside the bounds of sanity. Staring wildly, Amboola made out a pig-like head, snouted, covered with coarse bristles – but the thing stood upright and its thick hair-covered arms ended in rudimentary hands –

Amboola shrieked and sprang up – and then the motionless thing moved, with the paralyzing speed of a monster in a nightmare. The black man had one frenzied vision of champing, foaming jaws, of great chisel-like tusks flashing in the moonlight ... presently the moonlight fell on a black shape sprawled amidst the dabbled coverings of the couch on the floor; a grayish, shambling form moved silently across the chamber toward the window whose broken bars leaned out against the stars.

2

'Tuthmes!' The voice was urgent, urgent as the fist that hammered on the teak door of the chamber where slept Shumballa's most ambitious nobleman. 'Tuthmes! Let me in! The devil is loose in Shumballa!'

The door was opened, and the speaker burst into the room – a lean, wiry man in a white djebbeh, dark-skinned, the whites of his eyes gleaming. He was met by Tuthmes, tall, slender, dusky, with the straight features of his caste.

'What are you saying, Afari?'

Afari closed the door before he answered; he was panting as if from a long run. He was shorter than Tuthmes, and the negroid was more predominant in his features.

'Amboola! He is dead! In the Red Tower!'

'What?' exclaimed Tuthmes. 'Tananda dared execute him?'

'No! No, no! She would not be such a fool, surely. He was not executed, but murdered. Something broke through the bars of his cell and tore his throat out, and stamped in his ribs, and broke his skull – Set, I have seen many dead men, but never one less lovely in his death than Amboola! Tuthmes, it is the work of some demon!

His throat was bitten out, and the prints of the teeth were not like those of a lion or an ape. It was as if they had been made by chisels, sharp as razors!'

'When was this done?'

'Sometime about midnight. Guards in the lower part of the tower, watching the stair that leads up to the cell in which he was imprisoned, heard him cry out, and rushing up the stairs, burst into the cell and found him lying as I have said. I was sleeping in the lower part of the tower as you bade me, and having seen, I came straight here, bidding the guards say naught to anyone.'

Tuthmes smiled and his smile was not pleasant to see.

'Gods and demons work for a bold man,' he said. 'I do not think Tananda was fool enough to have Amboola murdered, however she desired it. The blacks have been sullen, ever since she cast him into prison. She could not have kept him imprisoned much longer.

'But this matter puts a weapon into our hands. If the Gallahs *think* she did it, so much the better. Each resentment against the dynasty is a weapon for us. Go, now, and strike before the king can learn of it. First, take a detachment of black spearmen to the Red Tower and execute the guards for sleeping at their duty. Be sure you take care to do it by my orders. That will show the Gallahs that I have avenged their commander, and remove a weapon from Tananda's hands. Kill them before she can have it done.

'Then go into Punt and find old Ageera, the witch-finder. Do not tell him flatly that Tananda had this deed done, but hint at it.'

Afari shuddered visibly.

'How can a common man lie to that black devil? His eyes are like coals of red fire that look into depths unnameable. I have seen him make corpses rise and walk, and skulls champ and grind their naked jaws.'

'Don't lie,' answered Tuthmes. 'Simply hint to him your own suspicions. After all, even if a demon *did* slay Amboola, some human summoned it out of the night. Perhaps Tananda is behind this, after all!'

When Afari had left, mulling intensely over what his patron had told him, Tuthmes drew a silken cloak about his otherwise naked limbs and mounting a short, wide staircase of polished mahogany, he came out upon the flat roof of his palace.

Looking over the parapet, he saw below him the silent streets of the inner city of Shumballa, the palaces and gardens, and the great square, into which, at an instant's notice, a thousand black horsemen could ride, from the courts of adjoining barracks.

Looking further, he saw the great bronze gates, and beyond them, the outer city that men called Punt, to distinguish it from El Shebbeh, the inner city. Shumballa stood in the midst of a great plain, of rolling grass lands that stretched to the horizons, broken only by occasional low hills. A narrow, deep river, meandering across the grass lands, touched the straggling edges of the city. El Shebbeh was separated from Punt by a tall and massive wall, which enclosed the palaces of the ruling caste, descendants of those Stygians who centuries ago had come southward to hack out a black empire, and to mix their proud blood with the blood of their dusky subjects. El Shebbeh was well laid out, with regular streets and squares, stone buildings and gardens; Punt was a sprawling wilderness of mud huts; the streets straggled into squares that were squares in name only. The black people of Kush, the Gallahs, the original inhabitants of the country, lived in Punt; none but the ruling caste, the Chagas, dwelt in El Shebbeh, except for their servants, and the black horsemen who served as their guardsmen.

Tuthmes glanced out over that vast expanse of huts. Fires glowed in the ragged squares, torches swayed to and fro in the wandering streets, and from time to time he caught a snatch of song, a barbaric chanting that thrummed with an undertone of wrath or bloodlust. Tuthmes drew his cloak closer about him and shivered.

Advancing across the roof, he halted by a figure which slept in the shadow of a palm growing in the artifical garden. When stirred by Tuthmes's toe, this man awoke and sprang up.

'There is no need for speech,' cautioned Tuthmes. 'The deed is done. Amboola is dead, and before dawn, all Punt will know he was murdered by Tananda.'

'And the – the devil?' whispered the man, shivering.

'Shh! Gone back into the darkness whence it was invoked. Harken, Shubba, it is time you were gone. Search among the Shemites until you find a woman suitable – a white woman. Bring her here speedily. If you return within the moon, I will give you her weight in silver. If you fail, I will hang your head from that palm tree.'

Shubba prostrated himself and touched his head to the dust. Then rising, he hurried from the roof. Tuthmes glanced again into Punt. The fires seemed to glow more fiercely, somehow, and a drum had begun an ominous monotone. A sudden clamor of bestial yells welled up to his ears.

'They have heard that Amboola is dead,' he muttered, and again he was shaken by a strong shudder.

3

Life flowed on its accustomed course in the filth-littered streets of Punt. Giant black men squatted in the doorways of their thatched huts, or lolled on the ground in their shade. Black women went up and down the streets with water-gourds or baskets of food on their heads. Children played or fought in the dust, laughing or squalling shrilly. In the squares the black folk chaffered and bargained over plantains, beer and hammered brass ornaments. Smiths crouched over tiny charcoal fires, laboriously beating out spear blades. The hot sun beat down on all, the sweat, mirth, anger, nakedness and squalor of the black people.

Suddenly there came a change in the pattern, a new note in the timbre. With a clatter of hoofs a group of horsemen rode by, half a dozen men, and a woman. It was the woman who dominated the group. Her skin was dusky, her hair, a thick black mass, caught back and confined by a gold fillet. Her only garment, besides the sandals on her feet, was a short silk skirt girdled at the waist. Gold plates, crusted with jewels, partially covered her dusky breasts. Her features were straight, her bold, scintillant eyes full of challenge and sureness. She rode and handled her steed with ease and certitude, the slim Kushite horse, with the jeweled bridle, the reins of scarlet leather, as broad as a man's palm and worked with gilt, and her sandalled feet in the wide silver stirrups.

As she rode by, work and chatter ceased suddenly. The black faces grew sullen, and the murky eyes burned redly. The blacks turned their heads to whisper in each other's ears, and the whispers grew to a sullen, audible murmur.

The youth who rode at the woman's stirrup grew nervous. He glanced ahead, along the winding street, measured the distance to the bronze gates, not yet in view along the flat-topped houses, and whispered: 'The people grow ugly, Tananda; it was foolish to ride in Punt.'

'All the black dogs in Kush shall not keep me from my hunting,' answered the woman. 'If any seem threatening, ride them down.'

'Easier said than done,' muttered the youth, scanning the silent throng. 'They are coming from their houses and massing thick along the street – look there!'

They were entering a broad, ragged square, where the black folk swarmed. On one side of this square stood a house of mud and rough-hewn beams, larger than its neighbors, with a cluster of skulls above the wide doorway. This was the temple of Jullah, which the black folk worshipped in opposition to Set, the Serpent-god worshipped by the Chagas in imitation of their Stygian ancestors. The black folk were thronged in this square, sullenly staring at the horsemen. There was a distinct menace in their attitude, and Tananda, for the first time feeling a slight nervousness, did not notice another rider approaching the square along another street. This rider would have attracted attention in ordinary times, for he was neither Chaga nor Gallah, but a white man, a powerful figure in chain-mail and helmet, with a scarlet cloak whipping its folds about him.

'These dogs mean mischief,' muttered the youth at Tananda's side, half drawing his curved sword. The others, guardsmen, black men like the folk about them, drew closer about her, but did not draw their blades. A low sullen muttering rose louder, though no movement was made.

'Push through them,' ordered Tananda, reining her horse forward. The blacks gave back sullenly before her advance, and suddenly, from the devil-devil house came a lean black figure. It was old Ageera, clad only in a loin-cloth. Pointing his finger at Tananda, he yelled: 'There she rides, she whose hands are dipped in blood! She who murdered Amboola!'

His yell was the spark that set off the explosion. A vast roar rose from the mob, and they surged forward, yelling: 'Death to Tananda!' In an instant a hundred black hands were clawing at the legs of the riders. The youth reined between Tananda and the mob, but a stone, cast from a black hand, shattered his skull. The guardsmen, slashing and hacking, were torn from their steeds and beaten, stamped and stabbed to death. Tananda, beset at last with terror, screamed as her horse reared. A score of wild black figures, men and women, were clawing at her.

A giant grasped her thigh and plucked her from her saddle, full into the eager and furious hands which awaited her. Her skirt was ripped from her body and waved in the air above her, while a bellow of primitive laughter went up from the surging mob. A woman spat in her face and tore off her breastplates, scratching her breasts with her fingernails. A stone hurled at her grazed her head. She screamed in frantic fear; a score of brutal hands were tearing at her, threatening to dismember her. She saw a stone clenched in a black hand, while the owner sought to reach her in the press and brain her. Daggers glinted. Only the hindering numbers of the jammed mass kept them from doing her to death instantly. 'To the devil-devil house!' went up a roar, followed by a responsive clamor, and Tananda felt herself half carried, half dragged along with the surging mob, grasped by her hair, arms, legs, wherever a black hand could grip. Blows aimed at her in the press were blocked or diverted by the mass; and then there came a shock under which the whole throng staggered as a horseman on a powerful steed crashed full into the press.

Men went down screaming, to be crushed under the flailing hoofs; Tananda got a dizzy glimpse of a figure towering above the press, of a dark scarred face under a steel helmet, of a scarlet cloak unfurled from mighty mailed shoulders, and a great sword lashing up and down, spattering crimson splashes. But from somewhere in the press a spear licked upward, disembowelling the steed. It screamed, plunged and went down, but the rider landed on his feet, smiting right and left. Wildly driven spears and knives glanced from his helmet or the shield on his left arm, while his broadsword cleft flesh and bone, split skulls, scattered brains and spilled entrails into the bloody dust.

Flesh and blood could not stand before it. Clearing a space he stooped, caught up the terrified girl and, covering her with his shield, fell back, cutting a ruthless way. He backed into the angle of a wall and, dropping her behind him, stood before her, beating back the frothing, screaming onslaught.

Then there was a clatter of hoofs and a regiment of the guardsmen swept into the square, driving the rioters before them. The captain approached, a giant negro resplendent in crimson silk and gold-worked harness.

'You were long in coming,' said Tananda, who had risen and regained much of her poise. The captain turned ashy, but before he could turn, Tananda had made a sign that was caught by his men behind him. One of them grasped his spear with both hands and drove it between his captain's shoulders with such force that the point started out from his breast. The captain sank to his knees, and thrusts from half a dozen more spears finished the task.

Tananda shook back her long black disheveled hair and faced her rescuer. She was bleeding from a score of scratches on her breasts and thighs, her locks fell in confusion down her back, and she was as naked as the day she was born; but she stared at him without perturbation or uncertainty, and he gave back her stare, frank admiration in his expression of her cool bearing, and the ripeness of her brown limbs.

'Who are you?' she demanded.

'Conan, a Cimmerian,' he answered.

'What are you doing in Shumballa?'

'I came here to seek my fortune. I was formerly a corsair.'

'Oh!' New interest shone in her dark eyes; she gathered her hair back in her hands. 'We have heard tales of you, whom men call Amra the Lion. But if you are no longer a corsair, what are you now?'

'A penniless wanderer.'

She shook her head. 'No, by Set! You are captain of the royal guard.'

He glanced casually at the sprawling figure in silk and steel, and the sight did not alter the zest of his sudden grin.

4

Shubba returned to Shumballa, and coming to Tuthmes in his chamber where leopard skins carpeted the marble floor, he said: 'I have found the woman you desired. A Nemedian girl, captured from a trading vessel of Argos. I paid the Shemitish slave-trader many broad gold pieces.'

'Let me see her,' commanded Tuthmes, and Shubba left the room, returning a moment later leading a girl by the wrist. She was supple, her white skin almost dazzling in contrast with the brown and black bodies to which Tuthmes was accustomed. Her hair fell in a curly rippling gold stream over her white shoulders. She was clad only in a tattered shift. This Shubba removed, leaving her shrinking in complete nudity.

Tuthmes nodded, impersonally.

'She is a fine bit of merchandise. If I were not gambling for a throne, I might be tempted to keep her for myself. Have you taught her Kushite, as I commanded?'

'Aye; in the city of the Shemites, and later daily on the caravan trail, I taught her, and impressed upon her the need of learning by means of a slipper, after the Shemite fashion. Her name is Diana.'

Tuthmes seated himself on a couch, and indicated that the girl should sit cross-legged on the floor at his feet, which she did.

'I am going to give you to the king of Kush as a present,' he said. 'You will nominally be his slave, but actually you will belong to me. You will receive your orders regularly, and you will not fail to carry them out. The king is degenerate, slothful, dissipated. It should not be hard for you to achieve complete dominance over him. But lest you might be tempted to disobey, when you fancy yourself out of my reach in the palace of the king, I will demonstrate my power to you.'

He took her hand and led her through a corridor, down a flight of stone stairs and into a long chamber, dimly lighted. The chamber was divided in equal halves by a wall of crystal, clear as water though some three feet in thickness and of such strength as to have resisted the lunge of a bull elephant. He led her to this wall and made her stand, facing it, while he stepped back. Abruptly the light went out. She stood there in darkness, her slender limbs trembling with an unreasoning panic, then light began to float in the darkness. She saw a hideous malformed head grow out of the blackness; she saw a bestial snout, chisel-like teeth, bristles – turned and ran, frantic with fear, and forgetful of the sheet of crystal that kept the brute from her. She ran full into the arms of Tuthmes in the darkness, and heard his hiss in her ear: 'You have seen my servant; do not fail me, for if you do he will search you out wherever you may be, and you cannot hide from him.' And when he hissed something else into the quivering ear of the Nemedian girl, she promptly fainted.

Tuthmes carried her up the stairs and gave her into the hands of a black wench with instructions to revive her, to see that she had food and wine, and to bathe, comb, perfume and dress her for her presentation to the king.

BLACK COLOSSUS

'The Night of Power, when Fate stalked through the corridors of the world like a colossus just risen from an age-old throne of granite—'

E. HOFFMAN PRICE: THE GIRL FROM SAMARKAND

1

Only the age-old silence brooded over the mysterious ruins of Kuthchemes, but Fear was there; Fear quivered in the mind of Shevatas, the thief, driving his breath quick and sharp against his clenched teeth.

He stood, the one atom of life amidst the colossal monuments of desolation and decay. Not even a vulture hung like a black dot in the vast blue vault of the sky that the sun glazed with its heat. On every hand rose the grim relics of another, forgotten age: huge broken pillars, thrusting up their jagged pinnacles into the sky; long wavering lines of crumbling walls; fallen cyclopean blocks of stone; shattered images, whose horrific features the corroding winds and dust-storms had half erased. From horizon to horizon no sign of life: only the sheer breathtaking sweep of the naked desert, bisected by the wandering line of a long-dry river course; in the midst of that vastness the glimmering fangs of the ruins, the columns standing up like broken masts of sunken ships – all dominated by the towering ivory dome before which Shevatas stood trembling.

The base of this dome was a gigantic pedestal of marble rising from what had once been a terraced eminence on the banks of the ancient river. Broad steps led up to a great bronze door in the dome, which rested on its base like the half of some titanic egg. The dome itself was of pure ivory, which shone as if unknown hands kept it polished. Likewise shone the spired gold cap of the pinnacle, and the inscription which sprawled about the curve of the dome in golden hieroglyphics yards long. No man on earth could read those characters, but Shevatas shuddered at the dim conjectures they raised. For he came of a very old race, whose myths ran back to shapes undreamed of by contemporary tribes.

Shevatas was wiry and lithe, as became a master-thief of Zamora. His small round head was shaven, his only garment a loin-cloth of scarlet silk. Like all his race, he was very dark, his narrow vulture-like face set off by his keen black eyes. His long, slender and tapering fingers were quick and nervous as the wings of a moth. From a gold-scaled girdle hung a short, narrow, jewel-hilted sword in a sheath of ornamented leather. Shevatas handled the weapon with apparently exaggerated care. He even seemed to flinch away from the contact of the sheath with his naked thigh. Nor was his care without reason.

This was Shevatas, a thief among thieves, whose name was spoken with awe in the dives of the Maul and the dim shadowy recesses beneath the temples of Bel, and who lived in songs and myths for a thousand years. Yet fear ate at the heart of Shevatas as he stood before the ivory dome of Kuthchemes. Any fool could see there was something unnatural about the structure; the winds and suns of three thousand years had lashed it, yet its gold and ivory rose bright and glistening as the day it was reared by nameless hands on the bank of the nameless river.

This unnaturalness was in keeping with the general aura of these devil-haunted ruins. This desert was the mysterious expanse lying southeast of the lands of Shem. A few days' ride on camel-back to the southwest, as Shevatas knew, would bring the traveller within sight of the great river Styx at the point where it turned at right angles with its former course, and flowed westward to empty at last into the distant sea. At the point of its bend began the land of Stygia, the dark-bosomed mistress of the south, whose domains, watered by the great river, rose sheer out of the surrounding desert.

Eastward, Shevatas knew, the desert shaded into steppes stretching to the Hyrkanian kingdom of Turan, rising in barbaric splendor on the shores of the great inland sea. A week's ride northward the desert ran into a tangle of barren hills, beyond which lay the fertile uplands of Koth, the southernmost realm of the Hyborian races. Westward the desert merged into the meadowlands of Shem, which stretched away to the ocean.

All this Shevatas knew without being particularly conscious of the knowledge, as a man knows the streets of his town. He was a far traveller and had looted the treasures of many kingdoms. But now he hesitated and shuddered before the highest adventure and the mightiest treasure of all.

In that ivory dome lay the bones of Thugra Khotan, the dark sorcerer who had reigned in Kuthchemes three thousand years ago, when the kingdoms of Stygia stretched far northward of the great river, over the meadows of Shem, and into the uplands. Then the great drift of the Hyborians swept southward from the cradle-land of their race near the northern pole. It was a titanic drift, extending over centuries and ages. But in the reign of Thugra Khotan, the last magician of Kuthchemes, gray-eyed, tawny-haired barbarians in wolfskins and scale-mail had ridden from the north into the rich uplands to carve out the kingdom of Koth with their iron swords. They had stormed over Kuthchemes like a tidal wave, washing the marble towers in blood, and the northern Stygian kingdom had gone down in fire and ruin.

But while they were shattering the streets of his city and cutting down his archers like ripe corn, Thugra Khotan had swallowed a strange terrible poison, and his masked priests had locked him into the tomb he himself had prepared. His devotees died about that tomb in a crimson holocaust, but the barbarians could not burst the door, nor ever mar the structure by maul or fire. So they rode away, leaving the great city in ruins, and in his ivory-domed sepulcher great Thugra Khotan slept unmolested, while the lizards of desolation gnawed at the crumbling pillars, and the very river that watered his land in old times sank into the sands and ran dry.

Many a thief sought to gain the treasure which fables said lay heaped about the moldering bones inside the dome. And many a thief died at the door of the tomb, and many another was harried by monstrous dreams to die at last with the froth of madness on his lips.

So Shevatas shuddered as he faced the tomb, nor was his shudder altogether occasioned by the legend of the serpent said to guard the sorcerer's bones. Over all myths of Thugra Khotan hung horror and death like a pall. From where the thief stood he could see the ruins of the great hall wherein chained captives had knelt by the hundreds during festivals to have their heads hacked off by the priest-king in honor of Set, the Serpent-god of Stygia. Somewhere near by had been the pit, dark and awful, wherein screaming victims were fed to a nameless amorphic monstrosity which came up out of a deeper, more hellish cavern. Legend made Thugra Khotan more than human; his worship yet lingered in a mongrel degraded cult, whose votaries stamped his likeness on coins to pay the way of their dead over the great river of darkness of which the Styx was but the material shadow. Shevatas had seen this likeness, on coins stolen from under the tongues of the dead, and its image was etched indelibly in his brain.

But he put aside his fears and mounted to the bronze door, whose smooth surface offered no bolt or catch. Not for naught had he gained access into darksome cults, had harkened to the grisly whispers of the votaries of Skelos under midnight trees, and read the forbidden iron-bound books of Vathelos the Blind.

Kneeling before the portal, he searched the sill with nimble fingers; their sensitive tips found projections too small for the eye to detect, or for less-skilled fingers to discover. These he pressed carefully and according to a peculiar system, muttering a long-forgotten incantation as he did so. As he pressed the last projection, he sprang up with frantic haste and struck the exact center of the door a quick sharp blow with his open hand.

There was no rasp of spring or hinge, but the door retreated inward, and the breath hissed explosively from Shevatas's clenched teeth. A short narrow corridor was disclosed. Down this the door had slid, and was now in place at the other end. The floor, ceiling and sides of the tunnel-like aperture were of ivory, and now from an opening on one side came a silent writhing horror that reared up and glared on the intruder with awful luminous eyes; a serpent twenty feet long, with shimmering, iridescent scales.

The thief did not waste time in conjecturing what night-black pits lying below the dome had given sustenance to the monster. Gingerly he drew the sword, and from it dripped a greenish liquid exactly like that which slavered from the scimitar-fangs of the reptile. The blade was steeped in the poison of the snake's own kind, and the obtaining of that venom from the fiend-haunted swamps of Zingara would have made a saga in itself.

Shevatas advanced warily on the balls of his feet, knees bent slightly, ready to spring either way like a flash of light. And he needed all his co-ordinate speed when the snake arched its neck and struck, shooting out its full length like a stroke of lightning. For all his quickness of nerve and eye, Shevatas had died then but for chance. His well-laid plans of leaping aside and striking down on the outstretched neck were put at naught by the blinding speed of the reptile's attack. The thief had but time to extend the sword in front of him, involuntarily closing his eyes and crying out. Then the sword was wrenched from his hand and the corridor was filled with a horrible thrashing and lashing.

Opening his eyes, amazed to find himself still alive, Shevatas saw the monster heaving and twisting its slimy form in fantastic contortions, the sword transfixing its giant jaws. Sheer chance had hurled it full against the point he had held out blindly. A few moments later the serpent sank into shining, scarcely quivering coils, as the poison on the blade struck home.

Gingerly stepping over it, the thief thrust against the door, which this time slid aside, revealing the interior of the dome. Shevatas cried out; instead of utter darkness he had come into a crimson light that throbbed and pulsed almost beyond the endurance of mortal eyes. It came from a gigantic red jewel high up in the vaulted arch of the dome. Shevatas gaped, inured though he was to the sight of riches. The treasure was there, heaped in staggering profusion – piles of diamonds, sapphires, rubies, turquoises, opals, emeralds; zikkurats of jade, jet and lapis lazuli; pyramids of gold wedges; teocallis of silver ingots; jewel-hilted swords in cloth-of-gold sheaths; golden helmets with colored horsehair crests, or black and scarlet plumes; silver-scaled corselets; gem-crusted harness worn by warrior-kings three thousand years in their tombs; goblets carven of single jewels; skulls plated with gold, with moonstones for eyes; necklaces of human teeth set with jewels. The ivory floor was covered inches deep with gold dust that sparkled and shimmered under the crimson glow with a million scintillant lights. The thief stood in a wonderland of magic and splendor, treading stars under his sandalled feet.

But his eyes were focussed on the dais of crystal which rose in the midst of the shimmering array, directly under the red jewel, and on which should be lying the moldering bones, turning to dust with the crawling of the centuries. And as Shevatas looked, the blood drained from his dark features; his marrow turned to ice, and the skin of his back crawled and wrinkled with horror, while his lips worked soundlessly. But suddenly he found his voice in one awful scream that rang hideously under the arching dome. Then again the silence of the ages lay among the ruins of mysterious Kuthchemes.

2

Rumors drifted up through the meadowlands, into the cities of the Hyborians. The word ran along the caravans, the long camel-trains plodding through the sands, herded by lean, hawk-eyed men in white kaftans. It was passed on by the hook-nosed herdsmen of the grasslands, from the dwellers in tents to the dwellers in the squat stone cities where kings with curled blue-black beards worshipped round-bellied gods with curious rites. The word passed up through the fringe of hills where gaunt tribesmen took toll of the caravans.

The rumors came into the fertile uplands where stately cities rose above blue lakes and rivers: the rumors marched along the broad white roads thronged with ox-wains, with lowing herds, with rich merchants, knights in steel, archers and priests.

They were rumors from the desert that lies east of Stygia, far south of the Kothian hills. A new prophet had risen among the nomads. Men spoke of tribal war, of a gathering of vultures in the southeast, and a terrible leader who led his swiftly increasing hordes to victory. The Stygians, ever a menace to the northern nations, were apparently not connected with this movement; for they were massing armies on their eastern borders and their priests were making magic to fight that of the desert sorcerer, whom men called Natohk, the Veiled One; for his features were always masked.

But the tide swept northwestward, and the blue-bearded kings died before the altars of their pot-bellied gods, and their squat-walled cities were drenched in blood. Men said that the uplands of the Hyborians were the goal of Natohk and his chanting votaries.

Raids from the desert were not uncommon, but this latest movement seemed to promise more than a raid. Rumor said Natohk had welded thirty nomadic tribes and fifteen cities into his following, and that a rebellious Stygian prince had joined him. This latter lent the affair an aspect of real war.

Characteristically, most of the Hyborian nations were prone to ignore the growing menace. But in Khoraja, carved out of Shemite lands by the swords of Kothic adventurers, heed was given. Lying southeast of Koth, it would bear the brunt of the invasion. And its young king was captive to the treacherous king of Ophir, who hesitated between restoring him for a huge ransom, or handing him over to his enemy, the penurious king of Koth, who offered no gold, but an advantageous treaty. Meanwhile, the rule of the struggling kingdom was in the white hands of young princess Yasmela, the king's sister.

Minstrels sang her beauty throughout the western world, and the pride of a kingly dynasty was hers. But on that night her pride was dropped from her like a cloak. In her chamber whose ceiling was a lapis lazuli dome, whose marble floor was littered with rare furs, and whose walls were lavish with golden frieze-work, ten girls, daughters of nobles, their slender limbs weighted with gem-crusted armlets and anklets, slumbered on velvet couches about the royal bed with its golden dais and silken canopy. But princess Yasmela lolled not on that silken bed. She lay naked on her supple belly upon the bare marble like the most abased suppliant, her dark hair streaming over her white shoulders, her slender fingers intertwined. She lay and writhed in pure horror that froze the blood in her lithe limbs and dilated her beautiful eyes, that pricked the roots of her dark hair and made goose-flesh rise along her supple spine.

Above her, in the darkest corner of the marble chamber, lurked a vast shapeless shadow. It was no living thing of form or flesh and blood. It was a clot of darkness, a blur in the sight, a monstrous night-born incubus that might have been deemed a figment of a sleep-drugged brain, but for the points of blazing yellow fire that glimmered like two eyes from the blackness.

Moreover, a voice issued from it – a low subtle inhuman sibilance that was more like the soft abominable hissing of a serpent than anything else, and that apparently could not emanate from anything with human lips. Its sound as well as its import filled Yasmela with a shuddering horror so intolerable that she writhed and twisted her slender body as if beneath a lash, as though to rid her mind of its insinuating vileness by physical contortion.

'You are marked for mine, princess,' came the gloating whisper. 'Before I wakened from the long sleep I had marked you, and yearned for you, but I was held fast by the ancient spell by which I escaped mine enemies. I am the soul of Natohk, the Veiled One! Look well upon me, princess! Soon you shall behold me in my bodily guise, and shall love me!'

The ghostly hissing dwindled off in lustful titterings, and Yasmela moaned and beat the marble tiles with her small fists in her ecstasy of terror.

'I sleep in the palace chamber of Akbatana,' the sibilances continued. 'There my body lies in its frame of bones and flesh. But it is but an empty shell from which the spirit has flown for a brief space. Could you gaze from that palace casement you would realize the futility of resistance. The desert is a rose-garden beneath the moon, where blossom the fires of a hundred thousand warriors. As an avalanche sweeps onward, gathering bulk and momentum, I will sweep into the lands of mine ancient enemies. Their kings shall furnish me skulls for goblets, their women and children shall be slaves of my slaves' slaves. I have grown strong in the long years of dreaming …

'But thou shalt be my queen, oh princess! I will teach thee the ancient forgotten ways of pleasure. We—' Before the stream of cosmic obscenity which poured from the shadowy colossus, Yasmela cringed and writhed as if from a whip that flayed her dainty bare flesh.

'Remember!' whispered the horror. 'The days will not be many before I come to claim mine own!'

Yasmela, pressing her face against the tiles and stopping her pink ears with her dainty fingers, yet seemed to hear a strange sweeping noise, like the beat of bat wings. Then, looking fearfully up, she saw only the moon that shone through the window with a beam that rested like a silver sword across the spot where the phantom had lurked. Trembling in every limb, she rose and staggered to a satin couch, where she threw herself down, weeping hysterically. The girls slept on, but one, who roused, yawned, stretched her slender figure and blinked about. Instantly she was on her knees beside the couch, her arms about Yasmela's supple waist.

'Was it – was it—?' Her dark eyes were wide with fright. Yasmela caught her in a convulsive grasp.

'Oh, Vateesa. *It* came again! I saw It – heard It speak! It spoke Its name – Natohk! It is Natohk! It is not a nightmare – it towered over me while the girls slept like drugged ones. What – oh, *what* shall I do?'

Vateesa twisted a golden bracelet about her rounded arm in meditation.

'Oh, princess,' she said, 'it is evident that no mortal power can deal with It, and the charm is useless that the priests of Ishtar gave you. Therefore seek you the forgotten oracle of Mitra.'

In spite of her recent fright, Yasmela shuddered. The gods of yesterday become the devils of tomorrow. The Kothians had long since abandoned the worship of Mitra, forgetting the attributes of the universal Hyborian god. Yasmela had a vague idea that, being very ancient, it followed that the deity was very terrible. Ishtar was much to be feared, and all the gods of Koth. Kothian culture and religion had suffered from a subtle admixture of Shemite and Stygian strains. The simple ways of the Hyborians had become modified to a large extent by the sensual, luxurious, yet despotic habits of the East.

'Will Mitra aid me?' Yasmela caught Vateesa's wrist in her eagerness. 'We have worshipped Ishtar so long—'

'To be sure he will!' Vateesa was the daughter of an Ophirean priest who had brought his customs with him when he fled from political enemies to Khoraja. 'Seek the shrine! I will go with you.'

'I will!' Yasmela rose, but objected when Vateesa prepared to dress her. 'It is not fitting that I come before the shrine clad in silk. I will go naked, on my knees, as befits a suppliant, lest Mitra deem I lack humility.'

'Nonsense!' Vateesa had scant respect for the ways of what she deemed a false cult. 'Mitra would have folks stand upright before him – not crawling on their bellies like worms, or spilling blood of animals all over his altars.'

Thus objurgated, Yasmela allowed the girl to garb her in the light sleeveless silk shirt, over which was slipped a silken tunic, bound at the waist by a wide velvet girdle. Satin slippers were put upon her slender feet, and a few deft touches of Vateesa's pink fingers arranged her dark wavy tresses. Then the princess followed the girl, who drew aside a heavy gilt-worked tapestry and threw the golden bolt of the door it concealed. This let into a narrow winding corridor, and down this the two girls went swiftly, through another door and into a broad hallway. Here stood a guardsman in crested gilt helmet, silvered cuirass and gold-chased greaves, with a long-shafted battle-ax in his hands.

A motion from Yasmela checked his exclamation and, saluting, he took his stand again beside the doorway, motionless as a brazen image. The girls traversed the hallway, which seemed immense and eery in the light of the cressets along the lofty walls, and went down a stairway where Yasmela shivered at the blots of shadows which hung in the angles of the walls. Three levels down they halted at last in a narrow corridor whose arched ceiling was crusted with jewels, whose floor was set with blocks of crystal, and whose walls were decorated with golden frieze-work. Down this shining way they stole, holding each other's hands, to a wide portal of gilt.

Vateesa thrust open the door, revealing a shrine long forgotten except by a faithful few, and royal visitors to Khoraja's court, mainly for whose benefit the fane was maintained. Yasmela had never entered it before, though she was born in the palace. Plain and unadorned in comparison to the lavish display of Ishtar's shrines, there was about it a simplicity of dignity and beauty characteristic of the Mitran religion.

The ceiling was lofty, but it was not domed, and was of plain white marble, as were the walls and floor, the former with a narrow gold frieze running about them. Behind an altar of clear green jade, unstained with sacrifice, stood the pedestal whereon sat the material manifestation of the deity. Yasmela looked in awe at the sweep of the magnificent shoulders, the clear-cut features – the wide straight eyes, the patriarchal beard, the thick curls of the hair, confined by a simple band about the temples. This, though she did not know it, was art in its highest form – the free, uncramped artistic expression of a highly esthetic race, unhampered by conventional symbolism.

She fell on her knees and thence prostrate, regardless of Vateesa's admonition, and Vateesa, to be on the safe side, followed her example; for after all, she was only a girl, and it was very awesome in Mitra's shrine. But even so she could not refrain from whispering in Yasmela's ear.

'This is but the emblem of the god. None pretends to know what Mitra looks like. This but represents him in idealized human form, as near perfection as the human mind can conceive. He does not inhabit this cold stone, as your priests tell you Ishtar does. He is everywhere – above us, and about us, and he dreams betimes in the high places among the stars. But here his being focusses. Therefore call upon him.'

'What shall I say?' whispered Yasmela in stammering terror.

'Before you can speak, Mitra knows the contents of your mind—' began Vateesa. Then both girls started violently as a voice began in the air above them. The deep, calm, bell-like tones emanated no more from the image than from anywhere else in the chamber. Again Yasmela trembled before a bodiless voice speaking to her, but this time it was not from horror or repulsion.

'Speak not, my daughter, for I know your need,' came the intonations like deep musical waves beating rhythmically along a golden beach. 'In one manner may you save your kingdom, and saving it, save all the world from the fangs of the serpent which has crawled up out of the darkness of the ages. Go forth upon the streets alone, and place your kingdom in the hands of the first man you meet there.'

The unechoing tones ceased, and the girls stared at each other. Then, rising, they stole forth, nor did they speak until they stood once more in Yasmela's chamber. The princess stared out of the gold-barred windows. The moon had set. It was long past midnight. Sounds of revelry had died away in the gardens and on the roofs of the city. Khoraja slumbered beneath the stars, which seemed to be reflected in the cressets that twinkled among the gardens and along the streets and on the flat roofs of houses where folk slept.

'What will you do?' whispered Vateesa, all a-tremble.

'Give me my cloak,' answered Yasmela, setting her teeth.

'But alone, in the streets, at this hour!' expostulated Vateesa.

'Mitra has spoken,' replied the princess. 'It might have been the voice of the god, or a trick of a priest. No matter. I will go!'

Wrapping a voluminous silken cloak about her lithe figure and donning a velvet cap from which depended a filmy veil, she passed hurriedly through the corridors and approached a bronze door where a dozen spearmen gaped at her as she passed through. This was in a wing of the palace which let directly onto the street; on all other sides it was surrounded by broad gardens, bordered by a high wall. She emerged into the street, lighted by cressets placed at regular intervals.

She hesitated; then, before her resolution could falter, she closed the door behind her. A slight shudder shook her as she glanced up and down the street, which lay silent and bare. This daughter of aristocrats had never before ventured unattended outside her ancestral palace. Then, steeling herself, she went swiftly up the street. Her satin-slippered feet fell lightly on the pave, but their soft sound brought her heart into her throat. She imagined their fall echoing thunderously through the cavernous city, rousing ragged rat-eyed figures in hidden lairs among the sewers. Every shadow seemed to hide a lurking assassin, every blank doorway to mask the slinking hounds of darkness.

Then she started violently. Ahead of her a figure appeared on the eery street. She drew quickly into a clump of shadows, which now seemed like a haven of refuge, her pulse pounding. The approaching figure went not furtively, like a thief, or timidly, like a fearful traveller. He strode down the nighted street as one who has no need or desire to walk softly. An unconscious swagger was in his stride, and his footfalls resounded on the pave. As he passed near a cresset she saw him plainly – a tall man, in the chain-mail hauberk of a mercenary. She braced herself, then darted from the shadow, holding her cloak close about her.

'Sa-ha!' his sword flashed half out of his sheath. It halted when he saw it was only a woman that stood before him, but his quick glance went over her head, seeking the shadows for possible confederates.

He stood facing her, his hand on the long hilt that jutted forward from beneath the scarlet cloak which flowed carelessly from his mailed shoulders. The torchlight glinted dully on the polished blue steel of his greaves and basinet. A more baleful fire glittered bluely in his eyes. At first glance she saw he was no Kothian; when he spoke she knew he was no Hyborian. He was clad like a captain of the mercenaries, and in that desperate command there were men of many lands, barbarians as well as civilized foreigners. There was a wolfishness about this warrior that marked the barbarian. The eyes of no civilized man, however wild or criminal, ever blazed with such a fire. Wine scented his breath, but he neither staggered nor stammered.

'Have they shut you into the street?' he asked in barbarous Kothic, reaching for her. His fingers closed lightly about her rounded wrist, but she felt that he could splinter its bones without effort. 'I've but come from the last wine-shop open – Ishtar's curse on these white-livered reformers who close the grog-houses! "Let men sleep rather than guzzle," they say – aye, so they can work and fight better for their masters! Soft-gutted eunuchs, I call them. When I served with the mercenaries of Corinthia we swilled and wenched all night and fought all day – aye, blood ran down the channels of our swords. But what of you, my girl? Take off that cursed mask—'

She avoided his clutch with a lithe twist of her body, trying not to appear to repulse him. She realized her danger, alone with a drunken barbarian. If she revealed her identity, he might laugh at her, or take himself off. She was not sure he would not cut her throat. Barbaric men did strange inexplicable things. She fought a rising fear.

'Not here,' she laughed. 'Come with me—'

'Where?' His wild blood was up, but he was wary as a wolf. 'Are you taking me to some den of robbers?'

'No, no, I swear it!' She was hard put to avoid the hand which was again fumbling at her veil.

'Devil bite you, hussy!' he growled disgustedly. 'You're as bad as a Hyrkanian woman, with your damnable veil. Here – let me look at your figure, anyway.'

Before she could prevent it, he wrenched the cloak from her, and she heard his breath hiss between his teeth. He stood holding the cloak, eyeing her as if the sight of her rich garments had somewhat sobered him. She saw suspicion flicker sullenly in his eyes.

'Who the devil are you?' he muttered. 'You're no street-waif – unless your leman robbed the king's seraglio for your clothes.'

'Never mind.' She dared to lay her white hand on his massive iron-clad arm. 'Come with me off the street.'

He hesitated, then shrugged his mighty shoulders. She saw that he half believed her to be some noble lady, who, weary of polite lovers, was taking this means of amusing herself. He allowed her to don the cloak again, and followed her. From the corner of her eye she watched him as they went down the street together. His mail could not conceal his hard lines of tigerish strength. Everything about him was tigerish, elemental, untamed. He was alien as the jungle to her in his difference from the debonair courtiers to whom she was accustomed. She feared him, told herself she loathed his raw brute strength and unashamed barbarism, yet something breathless and perilous inside her leaned toward him; the hidden primitive chord that lurks in every woman's soul was sounded and responded. She had felt his hardened hand on her arm, and something deep in her tingled to the memory of that contact. Many men had knelt before Yasmela. Here was one she felt had never knelt before any one. Her sensations were those of one leading an unchained tiger; she was frightened, and fascinated by her fright.

She halted at the palace door and thrust lightly against it. Furtively watching her companion, she saw no suspicion in his eyes.

'Palace, eh?' he rumbled. 'So you're a maid-in-waiting?'

She found herself wondering, with a strange jealousy, if any of her maids had ever led this war-eagle into her palace. The guards made no sign as she led him between them, but he eyed them as a fierce dog might eye a strange pack. She led him through a curtained doorway into an inner chamber, where he stood, naïvely scanning the tapestries, until he saw a crystal jar of wine on an ebony table. This he took up with a gratified sigh, tilting it toward his lips. Vateesa ran from an inner room, crying breathlessly, 'Oh my princess—'

'Princess!'

The wine-jar crashed to the floor. With a motion too quick for sight to follow, the mercenary snatched off Yasmela's veil, glaring. He recoiled with a curse, his sword leaping into his hand with a broad shimmer of blue steel. His eyes blazed like a trapped tiger's. The air was supercharged with tension that was like the pause before the bursting of a storm. Vateesa sank to the floor, speechless with terror, but Yasmela faced the infuriated barbarian without flinching. She realized her very life hung in the balance: maddened with suspicion and unreasoning panic, he was ready to deal death at the slightest provocation. But she experienced a certain breathless exhilaration in the crisis.

'Do not be afraid,' she said. 'I am Yasmela, but there is no reason to fear me.'

'Why did you lead me here?' he snarled, his blazing eyes darting all about the chamber. 'What manner of trap is this?'

'There is no trickery,' she answered. 'I brought you here because you can aid me. I called on the gods – on Mitra – and he bade me go into the streets and ask aid of the first man I met.'

This was something he could understand. The barbarians had their oracles. He lowered his sword, though he did not sheathe it.

'Well, if you're Yasmela, you need aid,' he grunted. 'Your kingdom's in a devil of a mess. But how can I aid you? If you want a throat cut, of course—'

'Sit down,' she requested. 'Vateesa, bring him wine.'

He complied, taking care, she noticed, to sit with his back against a solid wall, where he could watch the whole chamber. He laid his naked sword across his mail-sheathed knees. She glanced at it in fascination. Its dull blue glimmer seemed to reflect tales of bloodshed and rapine; she doubted her ability to lift it, yet she knew that the mercenary could wield it with one hand as lightly as she could wield a riding-whip. She noted the breadth and power of his hands; they were not the stubby undeveloped paws of a troglodyte. With a guilty start she found herself imagining those strong fingers locked in her dark hair.

He seemed reassured when she deposited herself on a satin divan opposite him. He lifted off his basinet and laid it on the table, and drew back his coif, letting the mail folds fall upon his massive shoulders. She saw more fully now his unlikeness to the Hyborian races. In his dark, scarred face there was a suggestion of moodiness; and without being marked by depravity, or definitely evil, there was more than a suggestion of the sinister about his features, set off by his smoldering blue eyes. A low broad forehead was topped by a square-cut tousled mane as black as a raven's wing.

'Who are you?' she asked abruptly.

'Conan, a captain of the mercenary spearmen,' he answered, emptying the wine-cup at a gulp and holding it out for more. 'I was born in Cimmeria.'

The name meant little to her. She only knew vaguely that it was a wild grim hill-country which lay far to the north, beyond the last outposts of the Hyborian nations, and was peopled by a fierce moody race. She had never before seen one of them.

Resting her chin on her hands, she gazed at him with the deep dark eyes that had enslaved many a heart.

'Conan of Cimmeria,' she said, 'you said I needed aid. Why?'

'Well,' he answered, 'any man can see that. Here is the king your brother in an Ophirean prison; here is Koth plotting to enslave you; here is this sorcerer screaming hell-fire and destruction down in Shem – and what's worse, here are your soldiers deserting every day.'

She did not at once reply; it was a new experience for a man to speak so forthrightly to her, his words not couched in courtier phrases.

'Why are my soldiers deserting, Conan?' she asked.

'Some are being hired away by Koth,' he replied, pulling at the wine-jar with relish. 'Many think Khoraja is doomed as an independent state. Many are frightened by tales of this dog Natohk.'

'Will the mercenaries stand?' she asked anxiously.

'As long as you pay us well,' he answered frankly. 'Your politics are nothing to us. You can trust Amalric, our general, but the rest of us are only common men who love loot. If you pay the ransom Ophir asks, men say you'll be unable to pay us. In that case we might go over to the king of Koth, though that cursed miser is no friend of mine. Or we might loot this city. In a civil war the plunder is always plentiful.'

'Why would you not go over to Natohk?' she inquired.

'What could he pay us?' he snorted. 'With fat-bellied brass

idols he looted from the Shemite cities? As long as you're fighting Natohk, you may trust us.'

'Would your comrades follow you?' she asked abruptly.

'What do you mean?'

'I mean,' she answered deliberately, 'that I am going to make you commander of the armies of Khoraja!'

He stopped short, the goblet at his lips, which curved in a broad grin. His eyes blazed with a new light.

'Commander? Crom! But what will your perfumed nobles say?'

'They will obey me!' She clasped her hands to summon a slave, who entered, bowing deeply. 'Have Count Thespides come to me at once, and the chancellor Taurus, lord Amalric, and the Agha Shupras.

'I place my trust in Mitra,' she said, bending her gaze on Conan, who was now devouring the food placed before him by the trembling Vateesa. 'You have seen much war?'

'I was born in the midst of a battle,' he answered, tearing a chunk of meat from a huge joint with his strong teeth. 'The first sound my ears heard was the clang of swords and the yells of the slaying. I have fought in blood-feuds, tribal wars, and imperial campaigns.'

'But can you lead men and arrange battle-lines?'

'Well, I can try,' he returned imperturbably. 'It's no more than sword-play on a larger scale. You draw his guard, then – stab, slash! And either his head is off, or yours.'

The slave entered again, announcing the arrival of the men sent for, and Yasmela went into the outer chamber, drawing the velvet curtains behind her. The nobles bent the knee, in evident surprise at her summons at such an hour.

'I have summoned you to tell you of my decision,' said Yasmela. 'The kingdom is in peril—'

'Right enough, my princess.' It was Count Thespides who spoke – a tall man, whose black locks were curled and scented. With one white hand he smoothed his pointed mustache, and with the other he held a velvet chaperon with a scarlet feather fastened by a golden clasp. His pointed shoes were satin, his cote-hardie of gold-broidered velvet. His manner was slightly affected, but the thews under his silks were steely. 'It were well to offer Ophir more gold for your royal brother's release.'

'I strongly disagree,' broke in Taurus the chancellor, an elderly man in an ermine-fringed robe, whose features were lined with the cares of his long service. 'We have already offered what will beggar the kingdom to pay. To offer more would further excite Ophir's cupidity. My princess, I say as I have said before: Ophir will not move until we have met this invading horde. If we lose, he will give king Khossus to Koth; if we win, he will doubtless restore his majesty to us on payment of the ransom.'

'And in the meantime,' broke in Amalric, 'the soldiers desert daily, and the mercenaries are restless to know why we dally.' He was a Nemedian, a large man with a lion-like yellow mane. 'We must move swiftly, if at all—'

'Tomorrow we march southward,' she answered. 'And there is the man who shall lead you!'

Jerking aside the velvet curtains she dramatically indicated the Cimmerian. It was perhaps not an entirely happy moment for the disclosure. Conan was sprawled in his chair, his feet propped on the ebony table, busily engaged in gnawing a beef-bone which he gripped firmly in both hands. He glanced casually at the astounded nobles, grinned faintly at Amalric, and went on munching with undisguised relish.

'Mitra protect us!' exploded Amalric. 'That's Conan the northron, the most turbulent of all my rogues! I'd have hanged him long ago, were he not the best swordsman that ever donned hauberk—'

'Your highness is pleased to jest!' cried Thespides, his aristocratic features darkening. 'This man is a savage – a fellow of no culture or breeding! It is an insult to ask gentlemen to serve under him! I—'

'Count Thespides,' said Yasmela, 'you have my glove under your baldric. Please give it to me, and then go.'

'Go?' he cried, starting. 'Go where?'

'To Koth or to Hades!' she answered. 'If you will not serve me as I wish, you shall not serve me at all.'

'You wrong me, princess,' he answered, bowing low, deeply hurt. 'I would not forsake you. For your sake I will even put my sword at the disposal of this savage.'

'And you, my lord Amalric?'

Amalric swore beneath his breath, then grinned. True soldier of fortune, no shift of fortune, however outrageous, surprised him much.

'I'll serve under him. A short life and a merry one, say I – and with Conan the Throat-slitter in command, life is likely to be both merry and short. Mitra! If the dog ever commanded more than a company of cut-throats before, I'll eat him, harness and all!'

'And you, my Agha?' she turned to Shupras.

He shrugged his shoulders resignedly. He was typical of the race evolved along Koth's southern borders – tall and gaunt, with features leaner and more hawk-like than his purer-blooded desert kin.

'Ishtar gives, princess.' The fatalism of his ancestors spoke for him.

'Wait here,' she commanded, and while Thespides fumed and gnawed his velvet cap, Taurus muttered wearily under his breath, and Amalric strode back and forth, tugging at his yellow beard and grinning like a hungry lion, Yasmela disappeared again through the curtains and clapped her hands for her slaves.

At her command they brought harness to replace Conan's chain-mail – gorget, sollerets, cuirass, pauldrons, jambes, cuisses and sallet. When Yasmela again drew the curtains, a Conan in burnished steel stood before his audience. Clad in the plate-armor, vizor lifted and dark face shadowed by the black plumes that nodded above his helmet, there was a grim impressiveness about him that even Thespides grudgingly noted. A jest died suddenly on Amalric's lips.

'By Mitra,' said he slowly, 'I never expected to see you cased in coat-armor, but you do not put it to shame. By my finger-bones, Conan, I have seen kings who wore their harness less regally than you!'

Conan was silent. A vague shadow crossed his mind like a prophecy. In years to come he was to remember Amalric's words, when the dream became the reality.

3

In the early haze of dawn the streets of Khoraja were thronged by crowds of people who watched the hosts riding from the southern gate. The army was on the move at last. There were the knights, gleaming in richly wrought plate-armor, colored plumes waving above their burnished sallets. Their steeds, caparisoned with silk, lacquered leather and gold buckles, caracoled and curvetted as their riders put them through their paces. The early light struck glints from lance-points that rose like a forest above the array, their pennons flowing in the breeze. Each knight wore a lady's token, a glove, scarf or rose, bound to his helmet or fastened to his sword-belt. They were the chivalry of Khoraja, five hundred strong, led by Count Thespides, who, men said, aspired to the hand of Yasmela herself.

They were followed by the light cavalry on rangy steeds. The riders were typical hillmen, lean and hawk-faced; peaked steel caps were on their heads and chain-mail glinted under their flowing kaftans. Their main weapon was the terrible Shemitish bow, which could send a shaft five hundred paces. There were five thousand of these, and Shupras rode at their head, his lean face moody beneath his spired helmet.

Close on their heels marched the Khoraja spearmen, always comparatively few in any Hyborian state, where men thought cavalry the only honorable branch of service. These, like the knights, were of ancient Kothic blood – sons of ruined families, broken men, penniless youths, who could not afford horses and plate-armor, five hundred of them.

The mercenaries brought up the rear, a thousand horsemen, two thousand spearmen. The tall horses of the cavalry seemed hard and savage as their riders; they made no curvets or gambades.

There was a grimly business-like aspect to these professional killers, veterans of bloody campaigns. Clad from head to foot in chain-mail, they wore their vizorless head-pieces over linked coifs. Their shields were unadorned, their long lances without guidons. At their saddle-bows hung battle-axes or steel maces, and each man wore at his hip a long broadsword. The spearmen were armed in much the same manner, though they bore pikes instead of cavalry lances.

They were men of many races and many crimes. There were tall Hyperboreans, gaunt, big-boned, of slow speech and violent natures; tawny-haired Gundermen from the hills of the north-west; swaggering Corinthian renegades; swarthy Zingarians, with bristling black mustaches and fiery tempers; Aquilonians from the distant west. But all, except the Zingarians, were Hyborians.

Behind all came a camel in rich housings, led by a knight on a great war-horse, and surrounded by a clump of picked fighters from the royal house-troops. Its rider, under the silken canopy of the seat, was a slim, silk-clad figure, at the sight of which the populace, always mindful of royalty, threw up its leather cap and cheered wildly.

Conan the Cimmerian, restless in his plate-armor, stared at the bedecked camel with no great approval, and spoke to Amalric, who rode beside him, resplendent in chain-mail threaded with gold, golden breastplate and helmet with flowing horsehair crest.

'The princess would go with us. She's supple, but too soft for this work. Anyway, she'll have to get out of these robes.'

Amalric twisted his yellow mustache to hide a grin. Evidently Conan supposed Yasmela intended to strap on a sword and take part in the actual fighting, as the barbarian women often fought.

'The women of the Hyborians do not fight like your Cimmerian women, Conan,' he said. 'Yasmela rides with us to watch the battle. Anyway,' he shifted in his saddle and lowered his voice, 'between you and me, I have an idea that the princess dares not remain behind. She fears something—'

'An uprising? Maybe we'd better hang a few citizens before we start—'

'No. One of her maids talked – babbled about *Something* that came into the palace by night and frightened Yasmela half out of her wits. It's some of Natohk's deviltry, I doubt not. Conan, it's more than flesh and blood we fight!'

'Well,' grunted the Cimmerian, 'it's better to go meet an enemy than to wait for him.'

He glanced at the long line of wagons and camp-followers, gathered the reins in his mailed hand, and spoke from habit the phrase of the marching mercenaries, 'Hell or plunder, comrades – march!'

Behind the long train the ponderous gates of Khoraja closed. Eager heads lined the battlements. The citizens well knew they were watching life or death go forth. If the host was overthrown, the future of Khoraja would be written in blood. In the hordes swarming up from the savage south, mercy was a quality unknown.

All day the columns marched, through grassy rolling meadowlands, cut by small rivers, the terrain gradually beginning to slope upward. Ahead of them lay a range of low hills, sweeping in an unbroken rampart from east to west. They camped that night on the northern slopes of those hills, and hook-nosed, fiery-eyed men of the hill tribes came in scores to squat about the fires and repeat news that had come up out of the mysterious desert. Through their tales ran the name of Natohk like a crawling serpent. At his bidding the demons of the air brought thunder and wind and fog, the fiends of the underworld shook the earth with awful roaring. He brought fire out of the air and consumed the gates of walled cities, and burnt armored men to bits of charred bone. His warriors covered the desert with their numbers, and he had five thousand Stygian troops in war-chariots under the rebel prince Kutamun.

Conan listened unperturbed. War was his trade. Life was a continual battle, or series of battles, since his birth. Death had been a constant companion. It stalked horrifically at his side; stood at his shoulder beside the gaming-tables; its bony fingers rattled the wine-cups. It loomed above him, a hooded and monstrous shadow, when he lay down to sleep. He minded its presence no more than a king minds the presence of his cup-bearer. Some day its bony grasp would close; that was all. It was enough that he lived through the present.

However, others were less careless of fear than he. Striding back from the sentry lines, Conan halted as a slender cloaked figure stayed him with an outstretched hand.

'Princess! You should be in your tent.'

'I could not sleep.' Her dark eyes were haunted in the shadow. 'Conan, I am afraid!'

'Are there men in the host you fear?' His hand locked on his hilt.

'No man,' she shuddered. 'Conan, is there anything you fear?'

He considered, tugging at his chin. 'Aye,' he admitted at last, 'the curse of the gods.'

Again she shuddered. 'I am cursed. A fiend from the abysses has set his mark upon me. Night after night he lurks in the shadows, whispering awful secrets to me. He will drag me down to be his queen in hell. I dare not sleep – he will come to me in my pavilion as he came in the palace. Conan, you are strong – keep me with you! I am afraid!'

She was no longer a princess, but only a terrified girl. Her pride had fallen from her, leaving her unashamed in her nakedness. In her frantic fear she had come to him who seemed strongest. The ruthless power that had repelled her, drew her now.

For answer he drew off his scarlet cloak and wrapped it about her, roughly, as if tenderness of any kind were impossible to him. His iron hand rested for an instant on her slender shoulder, and she shivered again, but not with fear. Like an electric shock a surge of animal vitality swept over her at his mere touch, as if some of his superabundant strength had been imparted to her.

'Lie here.' He indicated a clean-swept space close to a small flickering fire. He saw no incongruity in a princess lying down on the naked ground beside a campfire, wrapped in a warrior's cloak. But she obeyed without question.

He seated himself near her on a boulder, his broadsword across his knees. With the firelight glinting from his blue steel armor, he seemed like an image of steel – dynamic power for the moment quiescent; not resting, but motionless for the instant, awaiting the signal to plunge again into terrific action. The firelight played on his features, making them seem as if carved out of substance shadowy yet hard as steel. They were immobile, but his eyes smoldered with fierce life. He was not merely a wild man; he was part of the wild, one with the untameable elements of life; in his veins ran the blood of the wolf-pack; in his brain lurked the brooding depths of the northern night; his heart throbbed with the fire of blazing forests.

So, half meditating, half dreaming, Yasmela dropped off to sleep, wrapped in a sense of delicious security. Somehow she knew that no flame-eyed shadow would bend over her in the darkness, with this grim figure from the outlands standing guard above her. Yet once again she wakened, to shudder in cosmic fear, though not because of anything she saw.

It was a low mutter of voices that roused her. Opening her eyes, she saw that the fire was burning low. A feeling of dawn was in the air. She could dimly see that Conan still sat on the boulder; she glimpsed the long blue glimmer of his blade. Close beside him crouched another figure, on which the dying fire cast a faint glow. Yasmela drowsily made out a hooked beak of a nose, a glittering bead of an eye, under a white turban. The man was speaking rapidly in a Shemite dialect she found hard to understand.

'Let Bel wither my arm! I speak truth! By Derketo, Conan, I am a prince of liars, but I do not lie to an old comrade. I swear by the days when we were thieves together in the land of Zamora, before you donned hauberk!

'I saw Natohk; with the others I knelt before him when he made incantations to Set. But I did not thrust my nose in the sand as the rest did. I am a thief of Shumir, and my sight is keener than a weasel's. I squinted up and saw his veil blowing in the wind. It blew aside, and I saw – I saw – Bel aid me, Conan, I say I *saw*! My blood froze in my veins and my hair stood up. What I had seen burned my soul like a red-hot iron. I could not rest until I had made sure.

'I journeyed to the ruins of Kuthchemes. The door of the ivory dome stood open; in the doorway lay a great serpent, transfixed by a sword. Within the dome lay the body of a man, so shrivelled and distorted I could scarce make it out at first – it was Shevatas, the Zamorian, the only thief in the world I acknowledged as my superior. The treasure was untouched; it lay in shimmering heaps about the corpse. That was all.'

'There were no bones—' began Conan.

'There was nothing!' broke in the Shemite passionately. 'Nothing! Only the *one* corpse!'

Silence reigned an instant, and Yasmela shrank with a crawling nameless horror.

'Whence came Natohk?' rose the Shemite's vibrant whisper. 'Out of the desert on a night when the world was blind and wild with mad clouds driven in frenzied flight across the shuddering stars, and the howling of the wind was mingled with the shrieking of the spirits of the wastes. Vampires were abroad that night, witches rode naked on the wind, and werewolves howled across the wilderness. On a black camel he came, riding like the wind, and an unholy fire played about him; the cloven tracks of the camel glowed in the darkness. When Natohk dismounted before Set's shrine by the oasis of Aphaka, the beast swept into the night and vanished. And I have talked with tribesmen who swore that it suddenly spread gigantic wings and rushed upwards into the clouds, leaving a trail of fire behind it. No man has seen that camel since that night, but a black brutish man-like shape shambles to Natohk's tent and gibbers to him in the blackness before dawn. I will tell you, Conan, Natohk is – look, I will show you an image of what I saw that day by Shushan when the wind blew aside his veil!'

Yasmela saw the glint of gold in the Shemite's hand, as the men bent closely over something. She heard Conan grunt; and suddenly blackness rolled over her. For the first time in her life, princess Yasmela had fainted.

4

Dawn was still a hint of whiteness in the east when the army was again on the march. Tribesmen had raced into camp, their steeds reeling from the long ride, to report the desert horde encamped at the Well of Altaku. So through the hills the soldiers pushed hastily, leaving the wagon trains to follow. Yasmela rode with them; her eyes were haunted. The nameless horror had been taking even more awful shape, since she had recognized the coin in the Shemite's hand the night before – one of those secretly molded by the degraded Zugite cult, bearing the features of a man dead three thousand years.

The way wound between ragged cliffs and gaunt crags towering over narrow valleys. Here and there villages perched, huddles of stone huts, plastered with mud. The tribesmen swarmed out to join their kin, so that before they had traversed the hills, the host had been swelled by some three thousand wild archers.

Abruptly they came out of the hills and caught their breath at the vast expanse that swept away to the south. On the southern side the hills fell away sheerly, marking a distinct geographical division between the Kothian uplands and the southern desert. The hills were the rim of the uplands, stretching in an almost unbroken wall. Here they were bare and desolate, inhabited only by the Zaheemi clan, whose duty it was to guard the caravan road. Beyond the hills the desert stretched bare, dusty, lifeless. Yet beyond its horizon lay the Well of Altaku, and the horde of Natohk.

The army looked down on the Pass of Shamla, through which flowed the wealth of the north and the south, and through which had marched the armies of Koth, Khoraja, Shem, Turan and Stygia. Here the sheer wall of the rampart was broken. Promontories ran out into the desert, forming barren valleys, all but one of which were closed on the northern extremity by rugged cliffs. This one was the Pass. It was much like a great hand extended from the hills; two fingers, parted, formed a fan-shaped valley. The fingers were represented by a broad ridge on either hand, the outer sides sheer, the inner, steep slopes. The vale pitched upward as it narrowed, to come out on a plateau, flanked by gully-torn slopes. A well was there, and a cluster of stone towers, occupied by the Zaheemis.

There Conan halted, swinging off his horse. He had discarded the plate-armor for the more familiar chain-mail. Thespides reined in and demanded, 'Why do you halt?'

'We'll await them here,' answered Conan.

''T'were more knightly to ride out and meet them,' snapped the count.

'They'd smother us with numbers,' answered the Cimmerian. 'Besides, there's no water out there. We'll camp on the plateau—'

'My knights and I camp in the valley,' retorted Thespides angrily. 'We are the vanguard, and *we*, at least, do not fear a ragged desert swarm.'

Conan shrugged his shoulders and the angry nobleman rode away. Amalric halted in his bellowing order, to watch the glittering company riding down the slope into the valley.

'The fools! Their canteens will soon be empty, and they'll have to ride back up to the well to water their horses.'

'Let them be,' replied Conan. 'It goes hard for them to take orders from me. Tell the dog-brothers to ease their harness and rest. We've marched hard and fast. Water the horses and let the men munch.'

No need to send out scouts. The desert lay bare to the gaze, though just now this view was limited by low-lying clouds which rested in whitish masses on the southern horizon. The monotony was broken only by a jutting tangle of stone ruins, some miles out on the desert, reputedly the remnants of an ancient Stygian temple. Conan dismounted the archers and ranged them along the ridges, with the wild tribesmen. He stationed the mercenaries and the Khoraji spearmen on the plateau about the well. Farther back, in the angle where the hill road debouched on the plateau, was pitched Yasmela's pavilion.

With no enemy in sight, the warriors relaxed. Basinets were doffed, coifs thrown back on mailed shoulders, belts let out. Rude jests flew back and forth as the fighting-men gnawed beef and thrust their muzzles deep into ale-jugs. Along the slopes the hill-men made themselves at ease, nibbling dates and olives. Amalric strode up to where Conan sat bareheaded on a boulder.

'Conan, have you heard what the tribesmen say about Natohk? They say – Mitra, it's too mad even to repeat. What do you think?'

'Seeds rest in the ground for centuries without rotting, sometimes,' answered Conan. 'But surely Natohk is a man.'

'I am not sure,' grunted Amalric. 'At any rate, you've arranged your lines as well as a seasoned general could have done. It's certain Natohk's devils can't fall on us unawares. Mitra, what a fog!'

'I thought it was clouds at first,' answered Conan. 'See how it rolls!'

What had seemed clouds was a thick mist moving northward like a great unstable ocean, rapidly hiding the desert from view. Soon it engulfed the Stygian ruins, and still it rolled onward. The army watched in amazement. It was a thing unprecedented – unnatural and inexplicable.

'No use sending out scouts,' said Amalric disgustedly. 'They couldn't see anything. Its edges are near the outer flanges of the ridges. Soon the whole Pass and these hills will be masked—'

Conan, who had been watching the rolling mist with growing nervousness, bent suddenly and laid his ear to the earth. He sprang up with frantic haste, swearing.

'Horses and chariots, thousands of them! The ground vibrates to their tread! Ho, there!' His voice thundered out across the valley to electrify the lounging men. 'Burganets and pikes, you dogs! Stand to your ranks!'

At that, as the warriors scrambled into their lines, hastily donning head-pieces and thrusting arms through shield-straps, the mist rolled away, as something no longer useful. It did not slowly lift and fade like a natural fog; it simply vanished, like a blown-out flame. One moment the whole desert was hidden with the rolling fleecy billows, piled mountainously, stratum above stratum; the next, the sun shone from a cloudless sky on a naked desert

– no longer empty, but thronged with the living pageantry of war. A great shout shook the hills.

At first glance the amazed watchers seemed to be looking down upon a glittering sparkling sea of bronze and gold, where steel points twinkled like a myriad stars. With the lifting of the fog the invaders had halted as if frozen, in long serried lines, flaming in the sun.

First was a long line of chariots, drawn by the great fierce horses of Stygia, with plumes on their heads – snorting and rearing as each naked driver leaned back, bracing his powerful legs, his dusky arms knotted with muscles. The fighting-men in the chariots were tall figures, their hawk-like faces set off by bronze helmets crested with a crescent supporting a golden ball. Heavy bows were in their hands. No common archers these, but nobles of the South, bred to war and the hunt, who were accustomed to bringing down lions with their arrows.

Behind these came a motley array of wild men on half-wild horses – the warriors of Kush, the first of the great black kingdoms of the grasslands south of Stygia. They were shining ebony, supple and lithe, riding stark naked and without saddle or bridle.

After these rolled a horde that seemed to encompass all the desert. Thousands on thousands of the war-like Sons of Shem: ranks of horsemen in scale-mail corselets and cylindrical helmets – the *asshuri* of Nippr, Shumir and Eruk and their sister cities; wild white-robed hordes – the nomad clans.

Now the ranks began to mill and eddy. The chariots drew off to one side while the main host came uncertainly onward. Down in the valley the knights had mounted, and now Count Thespides galloped up the slope to where Conan stood. He did not deign to dismount but spoke abruptly from the saddle.

'The lifting of the mist has confused them! Now is the time to charge! The Kushites have no bows and they mask the whole advance. A charge of my knights will crush them back into the ranks of the Shemites, disrupting their formation. Follow me! We will win this battle with one stroke!'

Conan shook his head. 'Were we fighting a natural foe, I would agree. But this confusion is more feigned than real, as if to draw us into a charge. I fear a trap.'

'Then you refuse to move?' cried Thespides, his face dark with passion.

'Be reasonable,' expostulated Conan. 'We have the advantage of position—'

With a furious oath Thespides wheeled and galloped back down the valley where his knights waited impatiently.

Amalric shook his head. 'You should not have let him return, Conan. I – look there!'

Conan sprang up with a curse. Thespides had swept in beside his men. They could hear his impassioned voice faintly, but his gesture toward the approaching horde was significant enough. In another instant five hundred lances dipped and the steel-clad company was thundering down the valley.

A young page came running from Yasmela's pavilion, crying to Conan in a shrill, eager voice. 'My Lord, the princess asks why you do not follow and support Count Thespides?'

'Because I am not so great a fool as he,' grunted Conan, reseating himself on the boulder and beginning to gnaw a huge beef-bone.

'You grow sober with authority,' quoth Amalric. 'Such madness as that was always your particular joy.'

'Aye, when I had only my own life to consider,' answered Conan. 'Now – what in hell—'

The horde had halted. From the extreme wing rushed a chariot, the naked charioteer lashing the steeds like a madman; the other occupant was a tall figure whose robe floated spectrally on the wind. He held in his arms a great vessel of gold and from it poured a thin stream that sparkled in the sunlight. Across the whole front of the desert horde the chariot swept, and behind its thundering wheels was left, like the wake behind a ship, a long thin powdery line that glittered in the sands like the phosphorescent track of a serpent.

'That's Natohk!' swore Amalric. 'What hellish seed is he sowing?'

The charging knights had not checked their headlong pace.

Another fifty paces and they would crash into the uneven Kushite ranks, which stood motionless, spears lifted. Now the foremost knights had reached the thin line that glittered across the sands. They did not heed that crawling menace. But as the steel-shod hoofs of the horses struck it, it was as when steel strikes flint – but with more terrible result. A terrific explosion rocked the desert, which seemed to split apart along the strewn line with an awful burst of white flame.

In that instant the whole foremost line of the knights was seen enveloped in that flame, horses and steel-clad riders withering in the glare like insects in an open blaze. The next instant the rear ranks were piling up on their charred bodies. Unable to check their headlong velocity, rank after rank crashed into the ruins. With appalling suddenness the charge had turned into a shambles where armored figures died amid screaming, mangled horses.

Now the illusion of confusion vanished as the horde settled into orderly lines. The wild Kushites rushed into the shambles, spearing the wounded, bursting the helmets of the knights with stones and iron hammers. It was all over so quickly that the watchers on the slopes stood dazed; and again the horde moved forward, splitting to avoid the charred waste of corpses. From the hills went up a cry: 'We fight not men but devils!'

On either ridge the hillmen wavered. One rushed toward the plateau, froth dripping from his beard.

'Flee, flee!' he slobbered. 'Who can fight Natohk's magic?'

With a snarl Conan bounded from his boulder and smote him with the beef-bone; he dropped, blood starting from nose and mouth. Conan drew his sword, his eyes slits of blue bale-fire.

'Back to your posts!' he yelled. 'Let another take a backward step and I'll shear off his head! Fight, damn you!'

The rout halted as quickly as it had begun. Conan's fierce personality was like a dash of ice-water in their whirling blaze of terror.

'Take your places,' he directed quickly. 'And stand to it! Neither man nor devil comes up Shamla Pass this day!'

Where the plateau rim broke to the valley slope the mercenaries braced their belts and gripped their spears. Behind them the lancers sat their steeds, and to one side were stationed the Khoraja spearmen as reserves. To Yasmela, standing white and speechless at the door of her tent, the host seemed a pitiful handful in comparison to the thronging desert horde.

Conan stood among the spearmen. He knew the invaders would not try to drive a chariot charge up the Pass in the teeth of the archers, but he grunted with surprise to see the riders dismounting. These wild men had no supply trains. Canteens and pouches hung at their saddle-peaks. Now they drank the last of their water and threw the canteens away.

'This is the death-grip,' he muttered as the lines formed on foot. 'I'd rather have had a cavalry charge; wounded horses bolt and ruin formations.'

The horde had formed into a huge wedge, of which the tip was the Stygians and the body, the mailed *asshuri*, flanked by the nomads. In close formation, shields lifted, they rolled onward, while behind them a tall figure in a motionless chariot lifted wide-robed arms in grisly invocation.

As the horde entered the wide valley mouth the hillmen loosed their shafts. In spite of the protective formation, men dropped by dozens. The Stygians had discarded their bows; helmeted heads bent to the blast, dark eyes glaring over the rims of their shields, they came on in an inexorable surge, striding over their fallen comrades. But the Shemites gave back the fire, and the clouds of arrows darkened the skies. Conan gazed over the billowing waves of spears and wondered what new horror the sorcerer would invoke. Somehow he felt that Natohk, like all his kind, was more terrible in defense than in attack; to take the offensive against him invited disaster.

But surely it was magic that drove the horde on in the teeth of death. Conan caught his breath at the havoc wrought in the onsweeping ranks. The edges of the wedge seemed to be melting away, and already the valley was strewn with dead men. Yet the survivors came on like madmen unaware of death. By the very numbers of their bows, they began to swamp the archers on the cliffs. Clouds of shafts sped upward, driving the hillmen to cover. Panic struck at their hearts at that unwavering advance, and they plied their bows madly, eyes glaring like trapped wolves.

As the horde neared the narrower neck of the Pass, boulders thundered down, crushing men by the scores, but the charge did not waver. Conan's wolves braced themselves for the inevitable concussion. In their close formation and superior armor, they took little hurt from the arrows. It was the impact of the charge Conan feared, when the huge wedge should crash against his thin ranks. And he realized now there was no breaking of that onslaught. He gripped the shoulder of a Zaheemi who stood near.

'Is there any way by which mounted men can get down into the blind valley beyond that western ridge?'

'Aye, a steep, perilous path, secret and eternally guarded. But—'

Conan was dragging him along to where Amalric sat upon his great war-horse.

'Amalric!' he snapped. 'Follow this man! He'll lead you into yon outer valley. Ride down it, circle the end of the ridge, and strike the horde from the rear. Speak not, but go! I know it's madness, but we're doomed anyway; we'll do all the damage we can before we die! Haste!'

Amalric's mustache bristled in a fierce grin, and a few moments later his lancers were following the guide into a tangle of gorges leading off from the plateau. Conan ran back to the pikemen, sword in hand.

He was not too soon. On either ridge Shupras's hillmen, mad with anticipation of defeat, rained down their shafts desperately. Men died like flies in the valley and along the slopes – and with a roar and an irresistible upward surge the Stygians crashed against the mercenaries.

In a hurricane of thundering steel, the lines twisted and swayed. It was war-bred noble against professional soldier. Shields crashed against shields, and between them spears drove in and blood spurted.

Conan saw the mighty form of prince Kutamun across the sea

of swords, but the press held him hard, breast to breast with dark shapes that gasped and slashed. Behind the Stygians the *asshuri* were surging and yelling.

On either hand the nomads climbed the cliffs and came to handgrips with their mountain kin. All along the crests of the ridges the combat raged in blind, gasping ferocity. Tooth and nail, frothing mad with fanaticism and ancient feuds, the tribesmen rent and slew and died. Wild hair flying, the naked Kushites ran howling into the fray.

It seemed to Conan that his sweat-blinded eyes looked down into a rising ocean of steel that seethed and eddied, filling the valley from ridge to ridge. The fight was at a bloody deadlock. The hillmen held the ridges, and the mercenaries, gripping their dipping pikes, bracing their feet in the bloody earth, held the Pass. Superior position and armor for a space balanced the advantage of overwhelming numbers. But it could not endure. Wave after wave of glaring faces and flashing spears surged up the slope, the *asshuri* filling the gaps in the Stygian ranks.

Conan looked to see Amalric's lancers rounding the western ridge, but they did not come, and the pikemen began to reel back under the shocks. And Conan abandoned all hope of victory and of life. Yelling a command to his gasping captains, he broke away and raced across the plateau to the Khoraja reserves who stood trembling with eagerness. He did not glance toward Yasmela's pavilion. He had forgotten the princess; his one thought was the wild beast instinct to slay before he died.

'This day you become knights!' he laughed fiercely, pointing with his dripping sword toward the hillmen's horses, herded nearby. 'Mount and follow me to hell!'

The hill steed reared wildly under the unfamiliar clash of the Kothic armor, and Conan's gusty laugh rose above the din as he led them to where the eastern ridge branched away from the plateau. Five hundred footmen – pauper patricians, younger sons, black sheep – on half-wild Shemite horses, charging an army, down a slope where no cavalry had ever dared charge before!

Past the battle-choked mouth of the Pass they thundered, out onto the corpse-littered ridge. Down the steep slope they rushed, and a score lost their footing and rolled under the hoofs of their comrades. Below them men screamed and threw up their arms – and the thundering charge ripped through them as an avalanche cuts through a forest of saplings. On through the close-packed throngs the Khorajis hurtled, leaving a crushed-down carpet of dead.

And then, as the horde writhed and coiled upon itself, Amalric's lancers, having cut through a cordon of horsemen encountered in the outer valley, swept around the extremity of the western ridge and smote the host in a steel-tipped wedge, splitting it asunder. His attack carried all the dazing demoralization of a surprise on the rear. Thinking themselves flanked by a superior force and frenzied at the fear of being cut off from the desert, swarms of nomads broke and stampeded, working havoc in the ranks of their more steadfast comrades. These staggered and the horsemen rode through them. Up on the ridges the desert fighters wavered, and the hillmen fell on them with renewed fury, driving them down the slopes.

Stunned by surprise, the horde broke before they had time to see it was but a handful which assailed them. And once broken, not even a magician could weld such a horde again. Across the sea of heads and spears Conan's madmen saw Amalric's riders forging steadily through the rout, to the rise and fall of axes and maces, and a mad joy of victory exalted each man's heart and made his arm steel.

Bracing their feet in the wallowing sea of blood whose crimson waves lapped about their ankles, the pikemen in the Pass mouth drove forward, crushing strongly against the milling ranks before them. The Stygians held, but behind them the press of the *asshuri* melted; and over the bodies of the nobles of the South who died in their tracks to a man, the mercenaries rolled, to split and crumple the wavering mass behind.

Up on the cliffs old Shupras lay with an arrow through his heart; Amalric was down, swearing like a pirate, a spear through his mailed thigh. Of Conan's mounted infantry, scarce a hundred and fifty remained in the saddle. But the horde was shattered. Nomads and mailed spearmen broke away, fleeing to their camp where their horses were, and the hillmen swarmed down the slopes, stabbing the fugitives in the back, cutting the throats of the wounded.

In the swirling red chaos a terrible apparition suddenly appeared before Conan's rearing steed. It was prince Kutamun, naked but for a loin-cloth, his harness hacked away, his crested helmet dented, his limbs splashed with blood. With a terrible shout he hurled his broken hilt full into Conan's face, and leaping, seized the stallion's bridle. The Cimmerian reeled in his saddle, half stunned, and with awful strength the dark-skinned giant forced the screaming steed upward and backward, until it lost its footing and crashed into the muck of bloody sand and writhing bodies.

Conan sprang clear as the horse fell, and with a roar Kutamun was on him. In that mad nightmare of battle, the barbarian never exactly knew how he killed his man. He only knew that a stone in the Stygian's hand crashed again and again on his basinet, filling his sight with flashing sparks, as Conan drove his dagger again and again into his foe's body, without apparent effect on the prince's terrible vitality. The world was swimming to Conan's sight, when with a convulsive shudder the frame that strained against his stiffened and then went limp.

Reeling up, blood streaming down his face from under his dented helmet, Conan glared dizzily at the profusion of destruction which spread before him. From crest to crest the dead lay strewn, a red carpet that choked the valley. It was like a red sea, with each wave a straggling line of corpses. They choked the neck of the Pass, they littered the slopes. And down in the desert the slaughter continued, where the survivors of the horde had reached their horses and streamed out across the waste, pursued by the weary victors – and Conan stood appalled as he noted how few of these were left to pursue.

Then an awful scream rent the clamor. Up the valley a chariot came flying, making nothing of the heaped corpses. No horses drew it, but a great black creature that was like a camel. In the chariot stood Natohk, his robes flying; and gripping the reins and lashing like mad, crouched a black anthropomorphic being that might have been a monster ape.

With a rush of burning wind the chariot swept up the corpse-littered slope, straight toward the pavilion where Yasmela stood alone, deserted by her guards in the frenzy of pursuit. Conan, standing frozen, heard her frenzied scream as Natohk's long arm swept her up into the chariot. Then the grisly steed wheeled and came racing back down the valley, and no man dared speed arrow or spear lest he strike Yasmela, who writhed in Natohk's arms.

With an inhuman cry Conan caught up his fallen sword and leaped into the path of the hurtling horror. But even as his sword went up, the forefeet of the black beast smote him like a thunderbolt and sent him hurtling a score feet away, dazed and bruised. Yasmela's cry came hauntingly to his stunned ears as the chariot roared by.

A yell that had nothing of the human in its timbre rang from his lips as Conan rebounded from the bloody earth and seized the rein of a riderless horse that raced past him, throwing himself into the saddle without bringing the charger to a halt. With mad abandon he raced after the rapidly receding chariot. He struck the levels flying, and passed like a whirlwind through the Shemite camp. Into the desert he fled, passing clumps of his own riders, and hard-spurring desert horsemen.

On flew the chariot, and on raced Conan, though his horse began to reel beneath him. Now the open desert lay all about them, bathed in the lurid desolate splendor of sunset. Before him rose up the ancient ruins, and with a shriek that froze the blood in Conan's veins, the unhuman charioteer cast Natohk and the girl from him. They rolled on the sand, and to Conan's dazed gaze, the chariot and its steed altered awfully. Great wings spread from a black horror that in no way resembled a camel, and it rushed upward into the sky, bearing in its wake a shape of blinding flame, in which a black man-like shape gibbered in ghastly triumph. So quickly it passed, that it was like the rush of a nightmare through a horror-haunted dream.

Natohk sprang up, cast a swift look at his grim pursuer, who had not halted but came riding hard, with sword swinging low and spattering red drops; and the sorcerer caught up the fainting girl and ran with her into the ruins.

Conan leaped from his horse and plunged after them. He came into a room that glowed with unholy radiance, though outside the dusk was falling swiftly. On a black jade altar lay Yasmela, her naked body gleaming like ivory in the weird light. Her garments lay strewn on the floor, as if ripped from her in brutal haste. Natohk faced the Cimmerian – inhumanly tall and lean, clad in shimmering green silk. He tossed back his veil, and Conan looked into the features he had seen depicted on the Zugite coin.

'Aye, blench, dog!' The voice was like the hiss of a giant serpent. 'I am Thugra Khotan! Long I lay in my tomb, awaiting the day of awakening and release. The arts which saved me from the barbarians long ago likewise imprisoned me, but I knew one would come in time – and he came, to fulfill his destiny, and to die as no man has died in three thousand years!

'Fool, do you think you have conquered because my people are scattered? Because I have been betrayed and deserted by the demon I enslaved? I am Thugra Khotan, who shall rule the world despite your paltry gods! The desert is filled with my people; the demons of the earth shall do my bidding, as the reptiles of the earth obey me. Lust for a woman weakened my sorcery. Now the woman is mine, and feasting on her soul, I shall be unconquerable! Back, fool! You have not conquered Thugra Khotan!'

He cast his staff and it fell at the feet of Conan, who recoiled with an involuntary cry. For as it fell it altered horribly; its outline melted and writhed, and a hooded cobra reared up hissing before the horrified Cimmerian. With a furious oath Conan struck, and his sword sheared the horrid shape in half. And there at his feet lay only the two pieces of a severed ebon staff. Thugra Khotan laughed awfully, and wheeling, caught up something that crawled loathsomely in the dust of the floor.

In his extended hand something alive writhed and slavered. No tricks of shadows this time. In his naked hand Thugra Khotan gripped a black scorpion, more than a foot in length, the deadliest creature of the desert, the stroke of whose spiked tail was instant death. Thugra Khotan's skull-like countenance split in a mummy-like grin. Conan hesitated; then without warning he threw his sword.

Caught off guard, Thugra Khotan had no time to avoid the cast. The point struck beneath his heart and stood out a foot behind his shoulders. He went down, crushing the poisonous monster in his grasp as he fell.

Conan strode to the altar, lifting Yasmela in his blood-stained arms. She threw her white arms convulsively about his mailed neck, sobbing hysterically, and would not let him go.

'Crom's devils, girl!' he grunted. 'Loose me! Fifty thousand men have perished today, and there is work for me to do—'

'No!' she gasped, clinging with convulsive strength, as barbaric for the instant as he in her fear and passion. 'I will not let you go! I am yours, by fire and steel and blood! You are mine! Back there, I belong to others – here I am mine – and yours! You shall not go!'

He hesitated, his own brain reeling with the fierce upsurging of his violent passions. The lurid unearthly glow still hovered in the shadowy chamber, lighting ghostlily the dead face of Thugra Khotan, which seemed to grin mirthlessly and cavernously at them. Out on the desert, in the hills among the oceans of dead, men were dying, were howling with wounds and thirst and madness, and kingdoms were staggering. Then all was swept away by the crimson tide that rode madly in Conan's soul, as he crushed fiercely in his iron arms the slim white body that shimmered like a witch-fire of madness before him.

SHADOWS IN THE MOONLIGHT

1

A swift crashing of horses through the tall reeds; a heavy fall, a despairing cry. From the dying steed there staggered up its rider, a slender girl in sandals and girdled tunic. Her dark hair fell over her white shoulders, her eyes were those of a trapped animal. She did not look at the jungle of reeds that hemmed in the little clearing, nor at the blue waters that lapped the low shore behind her. Her wide-eyed gaze was fixed in agonized intensity on the horseman who pushed through the reedy screen and dismounted before her.

He was a tall man, slender, but hard as steel. From head to heel he was clad in light silvered mesh-mail that fitted his supple form like a glove. From under the dome-shaped, gold-chased helmet his brown eyes regarded her mockingly.

'Stand back!' her voice shrilled with terror. 'Touch me not, Shah Amurath, or I will throw myself into the water and drown!'

He laughed, and his laughter was like the purr of a sword sliding from a silken sheath.

'No, you will not drown, Olivia, daughter of confusion, for the marge is too shallow, and I can catch you before you can reach the deeps. You gave me a merry chase, by the gods, and all my men are far behind us. But there is no horse west of Vilayet that can distance Irem for long.' He nodded at the tall, slender-legged desert stallion behind him.

'Let me go!' begged the girl, tears of despair staining her face. 'Have I not suffered enough? Is there any humiliation, pain or degradation you have not heaped on me? How long must my torment last?'

'As long as I find pleasure in your whimperings, your pleas, tears and writhings,' he answered with a smile that would have seemed gentle to a stranger. 'You are strangely virile, Olivia. I wonder if I shall ever weary of you, as I have always wearied of women before. You are ever fresh and unsullied, in spite of me. Each new day with you brings a new delight.

'But come – let us return to Akif, where the people are still feting the conqueror of the miserable *kozaki*; while he, the conqueror, is engaged in recapturing a wretched fugitive, a foolish, lovely, idiotic runaway!'

'No!' She recoiled, turning toward the waters lapping bluely among the reeds.

'Yes!' His flash of open anger was like a spark struck from flint. With a quickness her tender limbs could not approximate, he caught her wrist, twisting it in pure wanton cruelty until she screamed and sank to her knees.

'Slut! I should drag you back to Akif at my horse's tail, but I will be merciful and carry you on my saddle-bow, for which favor you shall humbly thank me, while—'

He released her with a startled oath and sprang back, his saber flashing out, as a terrible apparition burst from the reedy jungle sounding an inarticulate cry of hate.

Olivia, staring up from the ground, saw what she took to be either a savage or a madman advancing on Shah Amurath in an attitude of deadly menace. He was powerfully built, naked but for a girdled loin-cloth, which was stained with blood and crusted with dried mire. His black mane was matted with mud and clotted blood; there were streaks of dried blood on his chest and limbs, dried blood on the long straight sword he gripped in his right hand. From under the tangle of his locks, bloodshot eyes glared like coals of blue fire.

'You Hyrkanian dog!' mouthed this apparition in a barbarous accent. 'The devils of vengeance have brought you here!'

'*Kozak!*' ejaculated Shah Amurath, recoiling. 'I did not know a dog of you escaped! I thought you all lay stiff on the steppe, by Ilbars River.'

'All but me, damn you!' cried the other. 'Oh, I've dreamed of such a meeting as this, while I crawled on my belly through the brambles, or lay under rocks while the ants gnawed my flesh, or crouched in the mire up to my mouth – I dreamed, but never hoped it would come to pass. Oh, gods of Hell, how I have yearned for this!'

The stranger's bloodthirsty joy was terrible to behold. His jaws champed spasmodically, froth appeared on his blackened lips.

'Keep back!' ordered Shah Amurath, watching him narrowly.

'Ha!' It was like the bark of a timber wolf. 'Shah Amurath, the great Lord of Akif! Oh, damn you, how I love the sight of you – you, who fed my comrades to the vultures, who tore them between wild horses, blinded and maimed and mutilated them – *ai*, you dog, you filthy dog!' His voice rose to a maddened scream, and he charged.

In spite of the terror of his wild appearance, Olivia looked to see him fall at the first crossing of the blades. Madman or savage, what could he do, naked, against the mailed chief of Akif?'

There was an instant when the blades flamed and licked, seeming barely to touch each other and leap apart; then the broadsword flashed past the saber and descended terrifically on Shah Amurath's shoulder. Olivia cried out at the fury of that stroke. Above the crunch of the rending mail, she distinctly heard the snap of the shoulder-bone. The Hyrkanian reeled back, suddenly ashen, blood spurting over the links of his hauberk; his saber slipped from his nerveless fingers.

'Quarter!' he gasped.

'Quarter?' There was a quiver of frenzy in the stranger's voice. 'Quarter such as you gave us, you swine!'

Olivia closed her eyes. This was no longer battle, but butchery, frantic, bloody, impelled by an hysteria of fury and hate, in which culminated the sufferings of battle, massacre, torture, and fear-ridden, thirst-maddened, hunger-haunted flight. Though Olivia knew that Shah Amurath deserved no mercy or pity from any living creature, yet she closed her eyes and pressed her hands over her ears, to shut out the sight of that dripping sword that rose and fell with the sound of a butcher's cleaver, and the gurgling cries that dwindled away and ceased.

She opened her eyes, to see the stranger turning away from a gory travesty that only vaguely resembled a human being. The man's breast heaved with exhaustion or passion; his brow was beaded with sweat; his right hand was splashed with blood.

He did not speak to her, or even glance toward her. She saw him stride through the reeds that grew at the water's edge, stoop, and tug at something. A boat wallowed out of its hiding-place among the stalks. Then she divined his intention, and was galvanized into action.

'Oh, wait!' she wailed, staggering up and running toward him. 'Do not leave me! Take me with you!'

He wheeled and stared at her. There was a difference in his bearing. His bloodshot eyes were sane. It was as if the blood he had just shed had quenched the fire of his frenzy.

'Who are you?' he demanded.

'I am called Olivia. I was *his* captive. I ran away. He followed me. That's why he came here. Oh, do not leave me here! His warriors are not far behind him. They will find his corpse – they will find me near it – oh!' She moaned in her terror and wrung her white hands.

He stared at her in perplexity.

'Would you be better off with me?' he demanded. 'I am a barbarian, and I know from your looks that you fear me.'

'Yes, I fear you,' she replied, too distracted to dissemble. 'My flesh crawls at the horror of your aspect. But I fear the Hyrkanians more. Oh, let me go with you! They will put me to the torture if they find me beside their dead lord.'

'Come, then.' He drew aside, and she stepped quickly into the boat, shrinking from contact with him. She seated herself in the bow, and he stepped into the boat, pushed off with an oar, and using it as a paddle, worked his way tortuously among the tall stalks until they glided out into open water. Then he set to work with both oars, rowing with great, smooth, even strokes, the heavy muscles of arms and shoulders and back rippling in rhythm to his exertions.

There was silence for some time, the girl crouching in the bows, the man tugging at the oars. She watched him with timorous fascination. It was evident that he was not an Hyrkanian, and he did not resemble the Hyborian races. There was a wolfish hardness about him that marked the barbarian. His features, allowing for the strains and stains of battle and his hiding in the marshes, reflected that same untamed wildness, but they were neither evil nor degenerate.

'Who are you?' she asked. 'Shah Amurath called you a *kozak*; were you of that band?'

'I am Conan, of Cimmeria,' he grunted. 'I was with the *kozaki*, as the Hyrkanian dogs called us.'

She knew vaguely that the land he named lay far to the northwest, beyond the farthest boundaries of the different kingdoms of her race.

'I am a daughter of the King of Ophir,' she said. 'My father sold me to a Shemite chief, because I would not marry a prince of Koth.'

The Cimmerian grunted in surprise.

Her lips twisted in a bitter smile. 'Aye, civilized men sell their children as slaves to savages, sometimes. They call your race barbaric, Conan of Cimmeria.'

'We do not sell our children,' he growled, his chin jutting truculently.

'Well – I was sold. But the desert man did not misuse me. He wished to buy the good will of Shah Amurath, and I was among the gifts he brought to Akif of the purple gardens. Then—' She shuddered and hid her face in her hands.

'I should be lost to all shame,' she said presently. 'Yet each memory stings me like a slaver's whip. I abode in Shah Amurath's palace, until some weeks agone he rode out with his hosts to do battle with a band of invaders who were ravaging the borders of Turan. Yesterday he returned in triumph, and a great fete was made to honor him. In the drunkenness and rejoicing, I found an opportunity to steal out of the city on a stolen horse. I had thought to escape – but he followed, and about midday came up with me. I outran his vassals, but him I could not escape. Then you came.'

'I was lying hid in the reeds,' grunted the barbarian. 'I was one of those dissolute rogues, the Free Companions, who burned and looted along the borders. There were five thousand of us, from a score of races and tribes. We had been serving as mercenaries for a rebel prince in eastern Koth, most of us, and when he made peace with his cursed sovereign, we were out of employment; so we took to plundering the outlying dominions of Koth, Zamora and Turan impartially. A week ago Shah Amurath trapped us near the banks of Ilbars with fifteen thousand men. Mitra! The skies were black with vultures. When the lines broke, after a whole day of fighting, some tried to break through to the north, some to the west. I doubt if any escaped. The steppes were covered with horsemen riding down the fugitives. I broke for the east, and finally reached the edge of the marshes that border this part of Vilayet.

'I've been hiding in the morasses ever since. Only the day before yesterday the riders ceased beating up the reed-brakes, searching for just such fugitives as I. I've squirmed and burrowed and hidden like a snake, feasting on musk-rats I caught and ate raw, for lack of fire to cook them. This dawn I found this boat hidden among the reeds. I hadn't intended going out on the sea until night, but after I killed Shah Amurath, I knew his mailed dogs would be close at hand.'

'And what now?'

'We shall doubtless be pursued. If they fail to see the marks left by the boat, which I covered as well as I could, they'll guess anyway that we took to sea, after they fail to find us among the marshes. But we have a start, and I'm going to haul at these oars until we reach a safe place.'

'Where shall we find that?' she asked hopelessly. 'Vilayet is an Hyrkanian pond.'

'Some folk don't think so,' grinned Conan grimly; 'notably the slaves that have escaped from galleys and become pirates.'

'But what are your plans?'

'The southwestern shore is held by the Hyrkanians for hundreds of miles. We still have a long way to go before we pass beyond their northern boundaries. I intend to go northward until I think we have passed them. Then we'll turn westward, and try to land on the shore bordered by the uninhabited steppes.'

'Suppose we meet pirates, or a storm?' she asked. 'And we shall starve on the steppes.'

'Well,' he reminded her, 'I didn't ask you to come with me.'

'I am sorry.' She bowed her shapely dark head. 'Pirates, storms, starvation – they are all kinder than the people of Turan.'

'Aye.' His dark face grew somber. 'I haven't done with them yet. Be at ease, girl. Storms are rare on Vilayet at this time of year. If we make the steppes, we shall not starve. I was reared in a naked land. It was those cursed marshes, with their stench and stinging flies, that nigh unmanned me. I am at home in the high lands. As for pirates—' He grinned enigmatically, and bent to the oars.

The sun sank like a dull-glowing copper ball into a lake of fire. The blue of the sea merged with the blue of the sky, and both turned to soft dark velvet, clustered with stars and the mirrors of stars. Olivia reclined in the bows of the gently rocking boat, in a state dreamy and unreal. She experienced an illusion that she was floating in midair, stars beneath her as well as above. Her silent companion was etched vaguely against the softer darkness. There was no break or falter in the rhythm of his oars; he might have been a fantasmal oarsman, rowing her across the dark lake of Death. But the edge of her fear was dulled, and, lulled by the monotony of motion, she passed into a quiet slumber.

Dawn was in her eyes when she awakened, aware of a ravenous hunger. It was a change in the motion of the boat that had roused her; Conan was resting on his oars, gazing beyond her. She realized that he had rowed all night without pause, and marvelled at his iron endurance. She twisted about to follow his stare, and saw a green wall of trees and shrubbery rising from the water's edge and sweeping away in a wide curve, enclosing a small bay whose waters lay still as blue glass.

'This is one of the many islands that dot this inland sea,' said Conan. 'They are supposed to be uninhabited. I've heard the

Hyrkanians seldom visit them. Besides, they generally hug the shores in their galleys, and we have come a long way. Before sunset we were out of sight of the mainland.'

With a few strokes he brought the boat in to shore and made the painter fast to the arching root of a tree which rose from the water's edge. Stepping ashore, he reached out a hand to help Olivia. She took it, wincing slightly at the bloodstains upon it, feeling a hint of the dynamic strength that lurked in the barbarian's thews.

A dreamy quiet lay over the woods that bordered the blue bay. Then somewhere, far back among the trees, a bird lifted its morning song. A breeze whispered through the leaves, and set them to murmuring. Olivia found herself listening intently for something, she knew not what. What might be lurking amid those nameless woodlands?

As she peered timidly into the shadows between the trees, something swept into the sunlight with a swift whirl of wings: a great parrot which dropped on to a leafy branch and swayed there, a gleaming image of jade and crimson. It turned its crested head sidewise and regarded the invaders with glittering eyes of jet.

'Crom!' muttered the Cimmerian. 'Here is the grandfather of all parrots. He must be a thousand years old! Look at the evil wisdom of his eyes. What mysteries do you guard, Wise Devil?'

Abruptly the bird spread its flaming wings and, soaring from its perch, cried out harshly: *'Yagkoolan yok tha, xuthalla!'* and with a wild screech of horribly human laughter, rushed away through the trees to vanish in the opalescent shadows.

Olivia stared after it, feeling the cold hand of nameless foreboding touch her supple spine.

'What did it say?' she whispered.

'Human words, I'll swear,' answered Conan; 'but in what tongue I can't say.'

'Nor I,' returned the girl. 'Yet it must have learned them from human lips. Human, or—' she gazed into the leafy fastness and shuddered slightly, without knowing why.

'Crom, I'm hungry!' grunted the Cimmerian. 'I could eat a whole buffalo. We'll look for fruit; but first I'm going to cleanse myself of this dried mud and blood. Hiding in marshes is foul business.'

So saying, he laid aside his sword, and wading out shoulder-deep into the blue water, went about his ablutions. When he emerged, his clean-cut bronze limbs shone, his streaming black mane was no longer matted. His blue eyes, though they smoldered with unquenchable fire, were no longer murky or bloodshot. But the tigerish suppleness of limb and the dangerous aspect of feature were not altered.

Strapping on his sword once more, he motioned the girl to follow him, and they left the shore, passing under the leafy arches of the great branches. Underfoot lay a short green sward which cushioned their tread. Between the trunks of the trees they caught glimpses of faery-like vistas.

Presently Conan grunted in pleasure at the sight of golden and russet globes hanging in clusters among the leaves. Indicating that the girl should seat herself on a fallen tree, he filled her lap with the exotic delicacies, and then himself fell to with unconcealed gusto.

'Ishtar!' said he, between mouthfuls. 'Since Ilbars I have lived on rats, and roots I dug out of the stinking mud. This is sweet to the palate, though not very filling. Still, it will serve if we eat enough.'

Olivia was too busy to reply. The sharp edge of the Cimmerian's hunger blunted, he began to gaze at his fair companion with more interest than previously, noting the lustrous clusters of her dark hair, the peach-bloom tints of her dainty skin, and the rounded contours of her lithe figure which the scanty silk tunic displayed to full advantage.

Finishing her meal, the object of his scrutiny looked up, and meeting his burning, slit-eyed gaze, she changed color and the remnants of the fruit slipped from her fingers.

Without comment, he indicated with a gesture that they should continue their explorations, and rising, she followed him out of the trees and into a glade, the farther end of which was bounded by a dense thicket. As they stepped into the open there was a ripping crash in this thicket, and Conan, bounding aside and carrying the girl with him, narrowly saved them from something that rushed through the air and struck a tree-trunk with a thunderous impact.

Whipping out his sword, Conan bounded across the glade and plunged into the thicket. Silence ensued, while Olivia crouched on the sward, terrified and bewildered. Presently Conan emerged, a puzzled scowl on his face.

'Nothing in that thicket,' he growled. 'But there was something—'

He studied the missile that had so narrowly missed them, and grunted incredulously, as if unable to credit his own senses. It was a huge block of greenish stone which lay on the sward at the foot of the tree, whose wood its impact had splintered.

'A strange stone to find on an uninhabited island,' growled Conan.

Olivia's lovely eyes dilated in wonder. The stone was a symmetrical block, indisputably cut and shaped by human hands. And it was astonishingly massive. The Cimmerian grasped it with both hands, and with legs braced and the muscles standing out on his arms and back in straining knots, he heaved it above his head and cast it from him, exerting every ounce of nerve and sinew. It fell a few feet in front of him. Conan swore.

'No man living could throw that rock across this glade. It's a task for siege engines. Yet here there are no mangonels or ballistas.'

'Perhaps it was thrown by some such engine from afar,' she suggested.

He shook his head. 'It didn't fall from above. It came from yonder thicket. See how the twigs are broken? It was thrown as a man might throw a pebble. But who? What? Come!'

She hesitantly followed him into the thicket. Inside the outer ring of leafy brush, the undergrowth was less dense. Utter silence brooded over all. The springy sward gave no sign of footprint. Yet from this mysterious thicket had hurtled that boulder, swift and deadly. Conan bent closer to the sward, where the grass was crushed down here and there. He shook his head angrily. Even to his keen eyes it gave no clue as to what had stood or trodden there.

His gaze roved to the green roof above their heads, a solid ceiling of thick leaves and interwoven arches. And he froze suddenly.

Then rising, sword in hand, he began to back away, thrusting Olivia behind him.

'Out of here, quick!' he urged in a whisper that congealed the girl's blood.

'What is it? What do you see?'

'Nothing,' he answered guardedly, not halting his wary retreat.

'But what is it, then? What lurks in this thicket?'

'Death!' he answered, his gaze still fixed on the brooding jade arches that shut out the sky.

Once out of the thicket, he took her hand and led her swiftly through the thinning trees, until they mounted a grassy slope, sparsely treed, and emerged upon a low plateau, where the grass grew taller and the trees were few and scattered. And in the midst of that plateau rose a long broad structure of crumbling greenish stone.

They gazed in wonder. No legends named such a building on any island of Vilayet. They approached it warily, seeing that moss and lichen crawled over the stones, and the broken roof gaped to the sky. On all sides lay bits and shards of masonry, half hidden in the waving grass, giving the impression that once many buildings rose there, perhaps a whole town. But now only the long hall-like structure rose against the sky, and its walls leaned drunkenly among the crawling vines.

Whatever doors had once guarded its portals had long rotted away. Conan and his companion stood in the broad entrance and stared inside. Sunlight streamed in through gaps in the walls and roof, making the interior a dim weave of light and shadow. Grasping his sword firmly, Conan entered, with the slouching gait of a hunting panther, sunken head and noiseless feet. Olivia tiptoed after him.

Once within, Conan grunted in surprise, and Olivia stifled a scream.

'Look! Oh, look!'

'I see,' he answered. 'Nothing to fear. They are statues.'

'But how life-like – and how evil!' she whispered, drawing close to him.

They stood in a great hall, whose floor was of polished stone, littered with dust and broken stones, which had fallen from the ceiling. Vines, growing between the stones, masked the apertures. The lofty roof, flat and undomed, was upheld by thick columns, marching in rows down the sides of the walls. And in each space between these columns stood a strange figure.

They were statues, apparently of iron, black and shining as if continually polished. They were life-sized, depicting tall, lithely powerful men, with cruel hawk-like faces. They were naked, and every swell, depression and contour of joint and sinew was represented with incredible realism. But the most life-like feature was their proud, intolerant faces. These features were not cast in the same mold. Each face possessed its own individual characteristics, though there was a tribal likeness between them all. There was none of the monotonous uniformity of decorative art, in the faces at least.

'They seem to be listening – and waiting!' whispered the girl uneasily.

Conan rang his hilt against one of the images.

'Iron,' he pronounced. 'But Crom! In what molds were they cast?'

He shook his head and shrugged his massive shoulders in puzzlement.

Olivia glanced timidly about the great silent hall. Only the ivy-grown stones, the tendril-clasped pillars, with the dark figures brooding between them, met her gaze. She shifted uneasily and wished to be gone, but the images held a strange fascination for her companion. He examined them in detail, and barbarian-like, tried to break off their limbs. But their material resisted his best efforts. He could neither disfigure nor dislodge from its niche a single image. At last he desisted, swearing in his wonder.

'What manner of men were these copied from?' he inquired of the world at large. 'These figures are black, yet they are not like negroes. I have never seen their like.'

'Let us go into the sunlight,' urged Olivia, and he nodded, with a baffled glance at the brooding shapes along the walls.

So they passed out of the dusky hall into the clear blaze of the summer sun. She was surprised to note its position in the sky; they had spent more time in the ruins than she had guessed.

'Let us take to the boat again,' she suggested. 'I am afraid here. It is a strange evil place. We do not know when we may be attacked by whatever cast the rock.'

'I think we're safe as long as we're not under the trees,' he answered. 'Come.'

The plateau, whose sides fell away toward the wooded shores on the east, west and south, sloped upward toward the north to abut on a tangle of rocky cliffs, the highest point of the island. Thither Conan took his way, suiting his long stride to his companion's gait. From time to time his glance rested inscrutably upon her, and she was aware of it.

They reached the northern extremity of the plateau, and stood gazing up the steep pitch of the cliffs. Trees grew thickly along the rim of the plateau east and west of the cliffs, and clung to the precipitous incline. Conan glanced at these trees suspiciously, but he began the ascent, helping his companion on the climb. The slope was not sheer, and was broken by ledges and boulders. The Cimmerian, born in a hill country, could have run up it like a cat, but Olivia found the going difficult. Again and again she felt herself lifted lightly off her feet and over some obstacle that would have taxed her strength to surmount, and her wonder grew at the sheer physical power of the man. She no longer found his touch repugnant. There was a promise of protection in his iron clasp.

At last they stood on the ultimate pinnacle, their hair stirring in the sea wind. From their feet the cliffs fell away sheerly three or four hundred feet to a narrow tangle of woodlands bordering the beach. Looking southward they saw the whole island lying like a great oval mirror, its bevelled edges sloping down swiftly into a rim of green, except where it broke in the pitch of the cliffs. As far as they could see, on all sides stretched the blue waters, still, placid, fading into dreamy hazes of distance.

'The sea is still,' sighed Olivia. 'Why should we not take up our journey again?'

Conan, poised like a bronze statue on the cliffs, pointed northward. Straining her eyes, Olivia saw a white fleck that seemed to hang suspended in the aching haze.

'What is it?'

'A sail.'

'Hyrkanians?'

'Who can tell, at this distance?'

'They will anchor here – search the island for us!' she cried in quick panic.

'I doubt it. They come from the north, so they can not be searching for us. They may stop for some other reason, in which case we'll have to hide as best we can. But I believe it's either pirate, or an Hyrkanian galley returning from some northern raid. In the latter case they are not likely to anchor here. But we can't put to sea until they've gone out of sight, for they're coming from the direction in which we must go. Doubtless they'll pass the island tonight, and at dawn we can go on our way.'

'Then we must spend the night here?' she shivered.

'It's safest.'

'Then let us sleep here, on the crags,' she urged.

He shook his head, glancing at the stunted trees, at the marching woods below, a green mass which seemed to send out tendrils straggling up the sides of the cliffs.

'Here are too many trees. We'll sleep in the ruins.'

She cried out in protest.

'Nothing will harm you there,' he soothed. 'Whatever threw the stone at us did not follow us out of the woods. There was nothing to show that any wild thing lairs in the ruins. Besides, you are soft-skinned, and used to shelter and dainties. I could sleep naked in the snow and feel no discomfort, but the dew would give you cramps, were we to sleep in the open.'

Olivia helplessly acquiesced, and they descended the cliffs, crossed the plateau and once more approached the gloomy, age-haunted ruins. By this time the sun was sinking below the plateau rim. They had found fruit in the trees near the cliffs, and these formed their supper, both food and drink.

The southern night swept down quickly, littering the dark blue sky with great white stars, and Conan entered the shadowy ruins, drawing the reluctant Olivia after him. She shivered at the sight of those tense black shadows in their niches along the walls. In the darkness that the starlight only faintly touched, she could not make out their outlines; she could only sense their attitude of waiting – waiting as they had waited for untold centuries.

Conan had brought a great armful of tender branches, well leafed. These he heaped to make a couch for her, and she lay upon it, with a curious sensation as of one lying down to sleep in a serpent's lair.

Whatever her forebodings, Conan did not share them. The Cimmerian sat down near her, his back against a pillar, his sword across his knees. His eyes gleamed like a panther's in the dusk.

'Sleep, girl,' said he. 'My slumber is light as a wolf's. Nothing can enter this hall without awaking me.'

Olivia did not reply. From her bed of leaves she watched the immobile figure, indistinct in the soft darkness. How strange, to move in fellowship with a barbarian, to be cared for and protected by one of a race, tales of which had frightened her as a child! He came of a people bloody, grim and ferocious. His kinship to the wild was apparent in his every action; it burned in his smoldering eyes. Yet he had not harmed her, and her worst oppressor had been a man the world called civilized. As a delicious languor stole over her relaxing limbs and she sank into foamy billows of slumber, her last waking thought was a drowsy recollection of the firm touch of Conan's fingers on her soft flesh.

2

Olivia dreamed, and through her dreams crawled a suggestion of lurking evil, like a black serpent writhing through flower gardens. Her dreams were fragmentary and colorful, exotic shards of a broken, unknown pattern, until they crystalized into a scene of horror and madness, etched against a background of cyclopean stones and pillars.

She saw a great hall, whose lofty ceiling was upheld by stone columns marching in even rows along the massive walls. Among these pillars fluttered great green and scarlet parrots, and the hall was thronged with black-skinned, hawk-faced warriors. They were not negroes. Neither they nor their garments nor weapons resembled anything of the world the dreamer knew.

They were pressing about one bound to a pillar: a slender white-skinned youth, with a cluster of golden curls about his alabaster brow. His beauty was not altogether human – like the dream of a god, chiseled out of living marble.

The black warriors laughed at him, jeered and taunted in a strange tongue. The lithe naked form writhed beneath their cruel hands. Blood trickled down the ivory thighs to spatter on the polished floor. The screams of the victim echoed through the hall; then lifting his head toward the ceiling and the skies beyond, he cried out a name in an awful voice. A dagger in an ebon hand cut short his cry, and the golden head rolled on the ivory breast.

As if in answer to that desperate cry, there was a rolling thunder as of celestial chariot-wheels, and a figure stood before the slayers, as if materialized out of empty air. The form was of a man, but no mortal man ever wore such an aspect of inhuman beauty. There was an unmistakable resemblance between him and the youth who dropped lifeless in his chains, but the alloy of humanity that softened the godliness of the youth was lacking in the features of the stranger, awful and immobile in their beauty.

The blacks shrank back before him, their eyes slits of fire. Lifting a hand, he spoke, and his tones echoed through the silent halls in deep rich waves of sound. Like men in a trance the black warriors fell back until they were ranged along the walls in regular lines. Then from the stranger's chiseled lips rang a terrible invocation and command: '*Yagkoolan yok tha, xuthalla!*'

At the blast of that awful cry, the black figures stiffened and froze. Over their limbs crept a curious rigidity, an unnatural petrification. The stranger touched the limp body of the youth, and the chains fell away from it. He lifted the corpse in his arms; then ere he turned away, his tranquil gaze swept again over the silent rows of ebony figures, and he pointed to the moon, which gleamed in through the casements. And they understood, those tense, waiting statues that had been men …

Olivia awoke, starting up on her couch of branches, a cold sweat beading her skin. Her heart pounded loud in the silence. She glanced wildly about. Conan slept against his pillar, his head fallen upon his massive breast. The silvery radiance of the late moon crept through the gaping roof, throwing long white lines along the dusty floor. She could see the images dimly, black, tense – waiting. Fighting down a rising hysteria, she saw the moonbeams rest lightly on the pillars and the shapes between.

What was that? A tremor among the shadows where the moonlight fell. A paralysis of horror gripped her, for where there should have been the immobility of death, there was movement: a slow twitching, a flexing and writhing of ebon limbs – an awful scream burst from her lips as she broke the bonds that held her mute and motionless. At her shriek Conan shot erect, teeth gleaming, sword lifted.

'The statues! The statues! – *Oh my God, the statues are coming to life!*'

And with the cry she sprang through a crevice in the wall, burst madly through the hindering vines, and ran, ran, ran – blind, screaming, witless – until a grasp on her arm brought her up short and she shrieked and fought against the arms that caught her, until a familiar voice penetrated the mists of her terror, and she saw Conan's face, a mask of bewilderment in the moonlight.

'What in Crom's name, girl? Did you have a nightmare?' His voice sounded strange and far away. With a sobbing gasp she threw her arms about his thick neck and clung to him convulsively, crying in panting catches.

'Where are they? Did they follow us?'

'Nobody followed us,' he answered.

She sat up, still clinging to him, and looked fearfully about. Her blind flight had carried her to the southern edge of the plateau. Just below them was the slope, its foot masked in the thick shadows of the woods. Behind them she saw the ruins looming in the high-swinging moon.

'Did you not see them? – The statues, moving, lifting their hands, their eyes glaring in the shadows?'

'I saw nothing,' answered the barbarian uneasily. 'I slept more soundly than usual, because it has been so long since I have slumbered the night through; yet I don't think anything could have entered the hall without waking me.'

'Nothing entered,' a laugh of hysteria escaped her. 'It was something there already. Ah, Mitra, we lay down to sleep among them, like sheep making their bed in the shambles!'

'What are you talking about?' he demanded. 'I woke at your cry, but before I had time to look about me, I saw you rush out through the crack in the wall. I pursued you, lest you come to harm. I thought you had a nightmare.'

'So I did!' she shivered. 'But the reality was more grisly than the dream. Listen!' And she narrated all that she had dreamed and thought to see.

Conan listened attentively. The natural skepticism of the sophisticated man was not his. His mythology contained ghouls, goblins, and necromancers. After she had finished, he sat silent, absently toying with his sword.

'The youth they tortured was like the tall man who came?' he asked at last.

'As like as son to father,' she answered, and hesitantly: 'If the mind could conceive of the offspring of a union of divinity with humanity, it would picture that youth. The gods of old times mated sometimes with mortal women, our legends tell us.'

'What gods?' he muttered.

'The nameless, forgotten ones. Who knows? They have gone back into the still waters of the lakes, the quiet hearts of the hills, the gulfs beyond the stars. Gods are no more stable than men.'

'But if these shapes were men, blasted into iron images by some god or devil, how can they come to life?'

'There is witchcraft in the moon,' she shuddered. '*He* pointed at the moon; while the moon shines on them, they live. So I believe.'

'But we were not pursued,' muttered Conan, glancing toward the brooding ruins. 'You might have dreamed they moved. I am of a mind to return and see.'

'No, no!' she cried, clutching him desperately. 'Perhaps the spell upon them holds them in the hall. Do not go back! They will rend you limb from limb! Oh, Conan, let us go into our boat and flee this awful island! Surely the Hyrkanian ship has passed us now! Let us go!'

So frantic was her pleading that Conan was impressed. His curiosity in regard to the images was balanced by his superstition. Foes of flesh and blood he did not fear, however great the odds, but any hint of the supernatural roused all the dim monstrous instincts of fear that are the heritage of the barbarian.

He took the girl's hand and they went down the slope and plunged into the dense woods, where the leaves whispered, and nameless night-birds murmured drowsily. Under the trees the shadows clustered thick, and Conan swerved to avoid the denser patches. His eyes roved continuously from side to side, and often flitted into the branches above them. He went quickly yet warily, his arm girdling the girl's waist so strongly that she felt as if she were being carried rather than guided. Neither spoke. The only sound was the girl's quick nervous panting, the rustle of her small feet in the grass. So they came through the trees to the edge of the water, shimmering like molten silver in the moonlight.

'We should have brought fruit for food,' muttered Conan; 'but doubtless we'll find other islands. As well leave now as later; it's but a few hours till dawn—'

His voice trailed away. The painter was still made fast to the looping root. But at the other end was only a smashed and shattered ruin, half submerged in the shallow water.

A stifled cry escaped Olivia. Conan wheeled and faced the dense shadows, a crouching image of menace. The noise of the night-birds was suddenly silent. A brooding stillness reigned over the woods. No breeze moved the branches, yet somewhere the leaves stirred faintly.

Quick as a great cat Conan caught up Olivia and ran. Through the shadows he raced like a phantom, while somewhere above and behind them sounded a curious rushing among the leaves, that implacably drew closer and closer. Then the moonlight burst full upon their faces, and they were speeding up the slope of the plateau.

At the crest Conan laid Olivia down, and turned to glare back at the gulf of shadows they had just quitted. The leaves shook in a sudden breeze; that was all. He shook his mane with an angry growl. Olivia crept to his feet like a frightened child. Her eyes looked up at him, dark wells of horror.

'What are we to do, Conan?' she whispered.

He looked at the ruins, stared again into the woods below.

'We'll go to the cliffs,' he declared, lifting her to her feet. 'Tomorrow I'll make a raft, and we'll trust our luck to the sea again.'

'It was not – not *they* that destroyed our boat?' It was half question, half assertion.

He shook his head, grimly taciturn.

Every step of the way across that moon-haunted plateau was a sweating terror for Olivia, but no black shapes stole subtly from the looming ruins, and at last they reached the foot of the crags, which rose stark and gloomily majestic above them. There Conan halted in some uncertainty, at last selecting a place sheltered by a broad ledge, nowhere near any trees.

'Lie down and sleep if you can, Olivia,' he said. 'I'll keep watch.'

But no sleep came to Olivia, and she lay watching the distant ruins and the wooded rim until the stars paled, the east whitened, and dawn in rose and gold struck fire from the dew on the grass-blades.

She rose stiffly, her mind reverting to all the happenings of the night. In the morning light some of its terrors seemed like figments of an overwrought imagination. Conan strode over to her, and his words electrified her.

'Just before dawn I heard the creak of timbers and the rasp and clack of cordage and oars. A ship has put in and anchored at the beach not far away – probably the ship whose sail we saw yesterday. We'll go up the cliffs and spy on her.'

Up they went, and lying on their bellies among the boulders, saw a painted mast jutting up beyond the trees to the west.

'An Hyrkanian craft, from the cut of her rigging,' muttered Conan. 'I wonder if the crew—'

A distant medley of voices reached their ears, and creeping to the southern edge of the cliffs, they saw a motley horde emerge from the fringe of trees along the western rim of the plateau, and stand there a space in debate. There was much flourishing of arms, brandishing of swords, and loud rough argument. Then the whole band started across the plateau toward the ruins, at a slant that would take them close by the foot of the cliffs.

'Pirates!' whispered Conan, a grim smile on his thin lips. 'It's an Hyrkanian galley they've captured. Here – crawl among these rocks.

'Don't show yourself unless I call to you,' he instructed, having secreted her to his satisfaction among a tangle of boulders along the crest of the cliffs. 'I'm going to meet these dogs. If I succeed in my plan, all will be well, and we'll sail away with them. If I don't succeed – well, hide yourself in the rocks until they're gone, for no devils on this island are as cruel as these sea-wolves.'

And tearing himself from her reluctant grasp, he swung quickly down the cliffs.

Looking fearfully from her eyrie, Olivia saw the band had neared the foot of the cliffs. Even as she looked, Conan stepped out from among the boulders and faced them, sword in hand. They gave back with yells of menace and surprise; then halted uncertainly to glare at this figure which had appeared so suddenly from the rocks. There were some seventy of them, a wild horde made up of men from many nations: Kothians, Zamorians, Brythunians, Corinthians, Shemites. Their features reflected the wildness of their natures. Many bore the scars of the lash or the branding-iron. There were cropped ears, slit noses, gaping eye-sockets, stumps of wrists – marks of the hangman as well as scars of battle. Most of them were half naked, but the garments they wore were fine; gold-braided jackets, satin girdles, silken breeches, tattered, stained with tar and blood, vied with pieces of silver-chased armor. Jewels glittered in nose-rings and ear-rings, and in the hilts of their daggers.

Over against this bizarre mob stood the tall Cimmerian in strong contrast with his hard bronzed limbs and clean-cut vital features.

'Who are you?' they roared.

'Conan the Cimmerian!' His voice was like the deep challenge of a lion. 'One of the Free Companions. I mean to try my luck with the Red Brotherhood. Who's your chief?'

'I, by Ishtar!' bellowed a bull-like voice, as a huge figure swaggered forward: a giant, naked to the waist, where his capacious belly was girdled by a wide sash that upheld voluminous silken pantaloons. His head was shaven except for a scalp-lock, his mustaches dropped over a rat-trap mouth. Green Shemitish slippers with upturned toes were on his feet, a long straight sword in his hand.

Conan stared and glared.

'Sergius of Khrosha, by Crom!'

'Aye, by Ishtar!' boomed the giant, his small black eyes glittering with hate. 'Did you think I had forgot? Ha! Sergius never forgets an enemy. Now I'll hang you up by the heels and skin you alive. At him, lads!'

'Aye, send your dogs at me, big-belly,' sneered Conan with bitter scorn. 'You were always a coward, you Kothic cur.'

'Coward! To me?' The broad face turned black with passion. 'On guard, you northern dog! I'll cut out your heart!'

In an instant the pirates had formed a circle about the rivals, their eyes blazing, their breath sucking between their teeth in bloodthirsty enjoyment. High up among the crags Olivia watched, sinking her nails into her palms in her painful excitement.

Without formality the combatants engaged, Sergius coming in with a rush, quick on his feet as a giant cat, for all his bulk. Curses hissed between his clenched teeth as he lustily swung and parried.

Conan fought in silence, his eyes slits of blue bale-fire.

The Kothian ceased his oaths to save his breath. The only sounds were the quick scuff of feet on the sward, the panting of the pirate, the ring and clash of steel. The swords flashed like white fire in the early sun, wheeling and circling. They seemed to recoil from each other's contact, then leap together again instantly. Sergius was giving back; only his superlative skill had saved him thus far from the blinding speed of the Cimmerian's onslaught. A louder clash of steel, a sliding rasp, a choking cry – from the pirate horde a fierce yell split the morning as Conan's sword plunged through their captain's massive body. The point quivered an instant from between Sergius's shoulders, a hand's breadth of white fire in the sunlight; then the Cimmerian wrenched back his steel and the pirate chief fell heavily, face down, and lay in a widening pool of blood, his broad hands twitching for an instant.

Conan wheeled toward the gaping corsairs.

'Well, you dogs!' he roared. 'I've sent your chief to hell. What says the law of the Red Brotherhood?'

Before any could answer, a rat-faced Brythunian, standing behind his fellows, whirled a sling swiftly and deadly. Straight as an arrow sped the stone to its mark, and Conan reeled and fell as a tall tree falls to the woodsman's ax. Up on the cliff Olivia caught at the boulders for support. The scene swam dizzily before her eyes; all she could see was the Cimmerian lying limply on the sward, blood oozing from his head.

The rat-faced one yelped in triumph and ran to stab the prostrate man, but a lean Corinthian thrust him back.

'What, Aratus, would you break the law of the Brotherhood, you dog?'

'No law is broken,' snarled the Brythunian.

'No law? Why, you dog, this man you have just struck down is by just rights our captain!'

'Nay!' shouted Aratus. 'He was not of our band, but an outsider. He had not been admitted to fellowship. Slaying Sergius does not make him captain, as would have been the case had one of us killed him.'

'But he wished to join us,' retorted the Corinthian. 'He said so.'

At that a great clamor arose, some siding with Aratus, some with the Corinthian, whom they called Ivanos. Oaths flew thick, challenges were passed, hands fumbled at sword-hilts.

At last a Shemite spoke up above the clamor: 'Why do you argue over a dead man?'

'He's not dead,' answered the Corinthian, rising from beside the prostrate Cimmerian. 'It was a glancing blow; he's only stunned.'

At that the clamor rose anew, Aratus trying to get at the senseless man and Ivanos finally bestriding him, sword in hand, and defying all and sundry. Olivia sensed that it was not so much in defense of Conan that the Corinthian took his stand, but in opposition to Aratus. Evidently these men had been Sergius's lieutenants, and there was no love lost between them. After more arguments, it was decided to bind Conan and take him along with them, his fate to be voted on later.

The Cimmerian, who was beginning to regain consciousness, was bound with leather girdles, and then four pirates lifted him, and with many complaints and curses, carried him along with the band, which took up its journey across the plateau once more. The body of Sergius was left where it had fallen; a sprawling, unlovely shape on the sun-washed sward.

Up among the rocks, Olivia lay stunned by the disaster. She was incapable of speech or action, and could only lie there and stare with horrified eyes as the brutal horde dragged her protector away.

How long she lay there, she did not know. Across the plateau she saw the pirates reach the ruins and enter, dragging their captive. She saw them swarming in and out of the doors and crevices, prodding into the heaps of debris, and clambering about the walls. After awhile a score of them came back across the plateau and vanished among the trees on the western rim, dragging the body of Sergius after them, presumably to cast into the sea. About the ruins the others were cutting down trees and securing material for a fire. Olivia heard their shouts, unintelligible in the distance, and she heard the voices of those who had gone into the woods, echoing among the trees. Presently they came back into sight, bearing casks of liquor and leathern sacks of food. They headed for the ruins, cursing lustily under their burdens.

Of all this Olivia was but mechanically cognizant. Her overwrought brain was almost ready to collapse. Left alone and unprotected, she realized how much the protection of the Cimmerian had meant to her. There intruded vaguely a wonderment at the mad pranks of Fate, that could make the daughter of a king the companion of a red-handed barbarian. With it came a revulsion toward her own kind. Her father, and Shah Amurath, they were civilized men. And from them she had had only suffering. She had never encountered any civilized man who treated her with kindness unless there was an ulterior motive behind his actions. Conan had shielded her, protected her, and – so far – demanded nothing in return. Laying her head in her rounded arms she wept, until distant shouts of ribald revelry roused her to her own danger.

She glanced from the dark ruins about which the fantastic figures, small in the distance, weaved and staggered, to the dusky depths of the green forest. Even if her terrors in the ruins the night before had been only dreams, the menace that lurked in those green leafy depths below was no figment of nightmare. Were Conan slain or carried away captive, her only choice would lie between giving herself up to the human wolves of the sea, or remaining alone on that devil-haunted island.

As the full horror of her situation swept over her, she fell forward in a swoon.

3

The sun was hanging low when Olivia regained her senses. A faint wind wafted to her ears distant shouts and snatches of ribald song. Rising cautiously, she looked out across the plateau. She saw the pirates clustered about a great fire outside the ruins, and her heart leaped as a group emerged from the interior dragging some object she knew was Conan. They propped him against the wall, still evidently bound fast, and there ensued a long discussion, with much brandishing of weapons. At last they dragged him back into the hall, and took up anew the business of ale-guzzling. Olivia sighed; at least she knew that the Cimmerian still lived. Fresh determination steeled her. As soon as night fell, she would steal to those grim ruins and free him or be taken herself in the attempt. And she knew it was not selfish interest alone which prompted her decision.

With this in mind she ventured to creep from her refuge to pluck and eat nuts which grew sparsely near at hand. She had not eaten since the day before. It was while so occupied that she was troubled by a sensation of being watched. She scanned the rocks nervously, then, with a shuddering suspicion, crept to the north edge of the cliff and gazed down into the waving green mass below, already dusky with the sunset. She saw nothing; it was impossible that she could be seen, when not on the cliff's edge, by anything lurking in those woods. Yet she distinctly felt the glare of hidden eyes, and felt that *something* animate and sentient was aware of her presence and her hiding-place.

Stealing back to her rocky eyrie, she lay watching the distant ruins until the dusk of night masked them, and she marked their position by the flickering flames about which black figures leaped and cavorted groggily.

Then she rose. It was time to make her attempt. But first she stole back to the northern edge of the cliffs, and looked down into the woods that bordered the beach. And as she strained her eyes in the dim starlight, she stiffened, and an icy hand touched her heart.

Far below her something moved. It was as if a black shadow detached itself from the gulf of shadows below her. It moved slowly up the sheer face of the cliff – a vague bulk, shapeless in the semi-darkness. Panic caught Olivia by the throat, and she struggled with the scream that tugged at her lips. Turning, she fled down the southern slope.

That flight down the shadowed cliffs was a nightmare in which she slid and scrambled, catching at jagged rocks with cold fingers. As she tore her tender skin and bruised her soft limbs on the rugged boulders over which Conan had so lightly lifted her, she realized again her dependence on the iron-thewed barbarian. But this thought was but one in a fluttering maelstrom of dizzy fright.

The descent seemed endless, but at last her feet struck the grassy levels, and in a very frenzy of eagerness she sped away toward the fire that burned like the red heart of night. Behind her, as she fled, she heard a shower of stones rattle down the steep slope, and the sound lent wings to her heels. What grisly climber dislodged those stones she dared not try to think.

Strenuous physical action dissipated her blind terror somewhat and before she had reached the ruin, her mind was clear, her reasoning faculties alert, though her limbs trembled from her efforts.

She dropped to the sward and wriggled along on her belly until, from behind a small tree that had escaped the axes of the pirates, she watched her enemies. They had completed their supper, but were still drinking, dipping pewter mugs or jewelled goblets into the broken heads of the wine-casks. Some were already snoring drunkenly on the grass, while others had staggered into the ruins. Of Conan she saw nothing. She lay there, while the dew formed on the grass about her and the leaves overhead, and the men about the fire cursed, gambled and argued. There were only a few about the fire; most of them had gone into the ruins to sleep.

She lay watching them, her nerves taut with the strain of waiting, the flesh crawling between her shoulders at the thought of what might be watching her in turn – of what might be stealing up behind her. Time dragged on leaden feet. One by one the revellers sank down in drunken slumber, until all were stretched senseless beside the dying fire.

Olivia hesitated – then was galvanized by a distant glow rising through the trees. The moon was rising!

With a gasp she rose and hurried toward the ruins. Her flesh crawled as she tiptoed among the drunken shapes that sprawled beside the gaping portal. Inside were many more; they shifted and mumbled in their besotted dreams, but none awakened as she glided among them. A sob of joy rose to her lips as she saw Conan. The Cimmerian was wide awake, bound upright to a pillar, his eyes gleaming in the faint reflection of the waning fire outside.

Picking her way among the sleepers, she approached him. Lightly as she had come, he had heard her; had seen her when first framed in the portal. A faint grin touched his hard lips.

She reached him and clung to him an instant. He felt the quick beating of her heart against his breast. Through a broad crevice in the wall stole a beam of moonlight, and the air was instantly super-charged with subtle tension. Conan felt it and stiffened. Olivia felt it and gasped. The sleepers snored on. Bending quickly, she drew a dagger from its senseless owner's belt, and set to work on Conan's bonds. They were sail cords, thick and heavy, and tied with the craft of a sailor. She toiled desperately, while the tide of moonlight crept slowly across the floor toward the feet of the crouching black figures between the pillars.

Her breath came in gasps; Conan's wrists were free, but his elbows and legs were still bound fast. She glanced fleetingly at the figures along the walls – waiting, waiting. They seemed to watch her with the awful patience of the undead. The drunkards beneath her feet began to stir and groan in their sleep. The moonlight crept down the hall, touching the black feet. The cords fell from Conan's arms, and taking the dagger from her, he ripped the bonds from his legs with a single quick slash. He stepped out from the pillar, flexing his limbs, stoically enduring the agony of returning circulation. Olivia crouched against him, shaking like a leaf. Was it some trick of the moonlight that touched the eyes of the black figures with fire, so that they glimmered redly in the shadows?

Conan moved with the abruptness of a jungle cat. Catching up his sword from where it lay in a stack of weapons near by, he lifted Olivia lightly from her feet and glided through an opening that gaped in the ivy-grown wall.

No word passed between them. Lifting her in his arms he set off swiftly across the moon-bathed sward. Her arms about his iron neck, the Ophirean closed her eyes, cradling her dark curly head against his massive shoulder. A delicious sense of security stole over her.

In spite of his burden, the Cimmerian crossed the plateau swiftly, and Olivia, opening her eyes, saw that they were passing under the shadow of the cliffs.

'Something climbed the cliffs,' she whispered. 'I heard it scrambling behind me as I came down.'

'We'll have to chance it,' he grunted.

'I am not afraid – now,' she sighed.

'You were not afraid when you came to free me, either,' he answered. 'Crom, what a day it has been! Such haggling and wrangling I never heard. I'm nearly deaf. Aratus wished to cut out my heart, and Ivanos refused, to spite Aratus, whom he hates. All day long they snarled and spat at one another, and the crew quickly grew too drunk to vote either way—'

He halted suddenly, an image of bronze in the moonlight. With a quick gesture he tossed the girl lightly to one side and behind him. Rising to her knees on the soft sward, she screamed at what she saw.

Out of the shadows of the cliffs moved a monstrous shambling bulk – an anthropomorphic horror, a grotesque travesty of creation.

In general outline it was not unlike a man. But its face, limned in the bright moonlight, was bestial, with close-set ears, flaring nostrils, and a great flabby-lipped mouth in which gleamed white tusk-like fangs. It was covered with shaggy grayish hair, shot with silver which shone in the moonlight, and its great misshapen paws hung nearly to the earth. Its bulk was tremendous; as it stood on its short bowed legs, its bullet-head rose above that of the man who faced it; the sweep of the hairy breast and giant shoulders was breathtaking; the huge arms were like knotted trees.

The moonlight scene swam, to Olivia's sight. This, then, was the end of the trail – for what human being could withstand the fury of that hairy mountain of thews and ferocity? Yet as she stared in wide-eyed horror at the bronzed figure facing the monster, she sensed a kinship in the antagonists that was almost appalling. This was less a struggle between man and beast than a conflict between two creatures of the wild, equally merciless and ferocious. With a flash of white tusks, the monster charged.

The mighty arms spread wide as the beast plunged, stupefyingly quick for all his vast bulk and stunted legs.

Conan's action was a blur of speed Olivia's eye could not follow. She only saw that he evaded that deadly grasp, and his sword, flashing like a jet of white lightning, sheared through one of those massive arms between shoulder and elbow. A great spout of blood deluged the sward as the severed member fell, twitching horribly, but even as the sword bit through, the other malformed hand locked in Conan's black mane.

Only the iron neck-muscles of the Cimmerian saved him from a broken neck that instant. His left hand darted out to clamp on the beast's squat throat, his left knee was jammed hard against the brute's hairy belly. Then began a terrific struggle, which lasted only seconds, but which seemed like ages to the paralyzed girl.

The ape maintained his grasp in Conan's hair, dragging him toward the tusks that glistened in the moonlight. The Cimmerian resisted this effort, with his left arm rigid as iron, while the sword in his right hand, wielded like a butcher-knife, sank again and again into the groin, breast and belly of his captor. The beast took its punishment in awful silence, apparently unweakened by the blood that gushed from its ghastly wounds. Swiftly the terrible strength of the anthropoid overcame the leverage of braced arm and knee. Inexorably Conan's arm bent under the strain; nearer and nearer he was drawn to the slavering jaws that gaped for his life. Now the blazing eyes of the barbarian glared into the bloodshot eyes of the ape. But as Conan tugged vainly at his sword, wedged deep in the hairy body, the frothing jaws snapped spasmodically shut, an inch from the Cimmerian's face, and he was hurled to the sward by the dying convulsions of the monster.

Olivia, half fainting, saw the ape heaving, thrashing and writhing, gripping, man-like, the hilt that jutted from its body. A sickening instant of this, then the great bulk quivered and lay still.

Conan rose and limped over to the corpse. The Cimmerian

breathed heavily, and walked like a man whose joints and muscles have been wrenched and twisted almost to their limit of endurance. He felt his bloody scalp and swore at the sight of the long black red-stained strands still grasped in the monster's shaggy hand.

'Crom!' he panted. 'I feel as if I'd been racked! I'd rather fight a dozen men. Another instant and he'd have bitten off my head. Blast him, he's torn a handful of my hair out by the roots.'

Gripping his hilt with both hands he tugged and worked it free. Olivia stole close to clasp his arm and stare down wide-eyed at the sprawling monster.

'What – what is it?' she whispered.

'A gray man-ape,' he grunted. 'Dumb, and man-eating. They dwell in the hills that border the eastern shore of this sea. How this one got to this island, I can't say. Maybe he floated here on driftwood, blown out from the mainland in a storm.'

'And it was he that threw the stone?'

'Yes; I suspected what it was when we stood in the thicket and I saw the boughs bending over our heads. These creatures always lurk in the deepest woods they can find, and seldom emerge. What brought him into the open, I can't say, but it was lucky for us; I'd have had no chance with him among the trees.'

'It followed me,' she shivered. 'I saw it climbing the cliffs.'

'And following his instinct, he lurked in the shadow of the cliff, instead of following you out across the plateau. His kind are creatures of darkness and the silent places, haters of sun and moon.'

'Do you suppose there are others?'

'No, else the pirates had been attacked when they went through the woods. The gray ape is wary, for all his strength, as shown by his hesitancy in falling upon us in the thicket. His lust for you must have been great, to have driven him to attack us finally in the open. What—'

He started and wheeled back toward the way they had come. The night had been split by an awful scream. It came from the ruins.

Instantly there followed a mad medley of yells, shrieks and cries of blasphemous agony. Though accompanied by a ringing of steel, the sounds were of massacre rather than battle.

Conan stood frozen, the girl clinging to him in a frenzy of terror. The clamor rose to a crescendo of madness, and then the Cimmerian turned and went swiftly toward the rim of the plateau, with its fringe of moon-limned trees. Olivia's legs were trembling so that she could not walk; so he carried her, and her heart calmed its frantic pounding as she nestled into his cradling arms.

They passed under the shadowy forest, but the clusters of blackness held no terrors, the rifts of silver discovered no grisly shape. Night-birds murmured slumberously. The yells of slaughter dwindled behind them, masked in the distance to a confused jumble of sound. Somewhere a parrot called, like an eery echo: '*Yagkoolan yok tha, xuthalla!*' So they came to the tree-fringed water's edge and saw the galley lying at anchor, her sail shining white in the moonlight. Already the stars were paling for dawn.

4

In the ghastly whiteness of dawn a handful of tattered, bloodstained figures staggered through the trees and out on to the narrow beach. There were forty-four of them, and they were a cowed and demoralized band. With panting haste they plunged into the water and began to wade toward the galley, when a stern challenge brought them up standing.

Etched against the whitening sky they saw Conan the Cimmerian standing in the bows, sword in hand, his black mane tossing in the dawn wind.

'Stand!' he ordered. 'Come no nearer. What would you have, dogs?'

'Let us come aboard!' croaked a hairy rogue fingering a bloody stump of ear. 'We'd be gone from this devil's island.'

'The first man who tries to climb over the side, I'll split his skull,' promised Conan.

They were forty-four to one, but he held the whip-hand. The fight had been hammered out of them.

'Let us come aboard, good Conan,' whined a red-sashed Zamorian, glancing fearfully over his shoulder at the silent woods. 'We have been so mauled, bitten, scratched and rended, and are so weary from fighting and running, that not one of us can lift a sword.'

'Where is that dog Aratus?' demanded Conan.

'Dead, with the others! It was devils fell upon us! They were rending us to pieces before we could awake – a dozen good rovers died in their sleep. The ruins were full of flame-eyed shadows, with tearing fangs and sharp talons.'

'Aye!' put in another corsair. 'They were the demons of the isle, which took the forms of molten images, to befool us. Ishtar! We lay down to sleep among them. We are no cowards. We fought them as long as mortal man may strive against the powers of darkness. Then we broke away and left them tearing at the corpses like jackals. But surely they'll pursue us.'

'Aye, let us come aboard!' clamored a lean Shemite. 'Let us come in peace, or we must come sword in hand, and though we be so weary you will doubtless slay many of us, yet you can not prevail against us many.'

'Then I'll knock a hole in the planks and sink her,' answered Conan grimly. A frantic chorus of expostulation rose, which Conan silenced with a lion-like roar.

'Dogs! Must I aid my enemies? Shall I let you come aboard and cut out my heart?'

'Nay, nay!' they cried eagerly. 'Friends – friends, Conan . We are thy comrades! We be all lusty rogues together. We hate the king of Turan, not each other.'

Their gaze hung on his brown, frowning face.

'Then if I am one of the Brotherhood,' he grunted, 'the laws of the Trade apply to me; and since I killed your chief in fair fight, then I am your captain!'

There was no dissent. The pirates were too cowed and battered to have any thought except a desire to get away from that island of fear. Conan's gaze sought out the blood-stained figure of the Corinthian.

'How, Ivanos!' he challenged. 'You took my part, once. Will you uphold my claims again?'

'Aye, by Mitra!' The pirate, sensing the trend of feeling, was eager to ingratiate himself with the Cimmerian. 'He is right, lads; he is our lawful captain!'

A medley of acquiescence rose, lacking enthusiasm perhaps, but with sincerity accentuated by the feel of the silent woods behind them which might mask creeping ebony devils with red eyes and dripping talons.

'Swear by the hilt,' Conan demanded.

Forty-four sword-hilts were lifted toward him, and forty-four voices blended in the corsair's oath of allegiance.

Conan grinned and sheathed his sword. 'Come aboard, my bold swashbucklers, and take the oars.'

He turned and lifted Olivia to her feet, from where she had crouched shielded by the gunwales.

'And what of me, sir?' she asked.

'What would you?' he countered, watching her narrowly.

'To go with you, wherever your path may lie!' she cried, throwing her white arms about his bronzed neck.

The pirates, clambering over the rail, gasped in amazement.

'To sail a road of blood and slaughter?' he questioned. 'This keel will stain the blue waves crimson wherever it plows.'

'Aye, to sail with you on blue seas or red,' she answered passionately. 'You are a barbarian, and I am an outcast, denied by my people. We are both pariahs, wanderers of earth. Oh, take me with you!'

With a gusty laugh he lifted her to his fierce lips.

'I'll make you Queen of the Blue Sea! Cast off there, dogs! We'll scorch King Yildiz's pantaloons yet, by Crom!'

A WITCH SHALL BE BORN

1

The Blood-Red Crescent

Taramis, Queen of Khauran, awakened from a dream-haunted slumber to a silence that seemed more like the stillness of nighted catacombs than the normal quiet of a sleeping place. She lay staring into the darkness, wondering why the candles in their golden candelabra had gone out. A flecking of stars marked a gold-barred casement that lent no illumination to the interior of the chamber. But as Taramis lay there, she became aware of a spot of radiance glowing in the darkness before her. She watched, puzzled. It grew and its intensity deepened as it expanded, a widening disk of lurid light hovering against the dark velvet hangings of the opposite wall. Taramis caught her breath, starting up to a sitting position. A dark object was visible in that circle of light – *a human head.*

In a sudden panic the queen opened her lips to cry out for her maids; then she checked herself. The glow was more lurid, the head more vividly limned. It was a woman's head, small, delicately molded, superbly poised, with a high-piled mass of lustrous black hair. The face grew distinct as she stared – and it was the sight of this face which froze the cry in Taramis's throat. The features were her own! She might have been looking into a mirror which subtly altered her reflection, lending it a tigerish gleam of eye, a vindictive curl of lip.

'Ishtar!' gasped Taramis. 'I am bewitched!'

Appallingly, the apparition spoke, and its voice was like honeyed venom.

'Bewitched? No, sweet sister! Here is no sorcery.'

'Sister?' stammered the bewildered girl. 'I have no sister.'

'You never had a sister?' came the sweet, poisonously mocking voice. 'Never a twin sister whose flesh was as soft as yours to caress or hurt?'

'Why, once I had a sister,' answered Taramis, still convinced that she was in the grip of some sort of nightmare. 'But she died.'

The beautiful face in the disk was convulsed with the aspect of a fury; so hellish became its expression that Taramis, cowering back, half expected to see snaky locks writhe hissing about the ivory brow.

'You lie!' The accusation was spat from between the snarling red lips. 'She did not die! Fool! Oh, enough of this mummery! Look – and let your sight be blasted!'

Light ran suddenly along the hangings like flaming serpents, and incredibly the candles in the golden sticks flared up again. Taramis crouched on her velvet couch, her lithe legs flexed beneath her, staring wide-eyed at the pantherish figure which posed mockingly before her. It was as if she gazed upon another Taramis, identical with herself in every contour of feature and limb, yet animated by an alien and evil personality. The face of this stranger waif reflected the opposite of every characteristic the countenance of the queen denoted. Lust and mystery sparkled in her scintillant eyes, cruelty lurked in the curl of her full red lips. Each movement of her supple body was subtly suggestive. Her coiffure imitated that of the queen's, on her feet were gilded sandals such as Taramis wore in her boudoir. The sleeveless, low-necked silk tunic, girdled at the waist with a cloth-of-gold cincture, was a duplicate of the queen's night-garment.

'Who are you?' gasped Taramis, an icy chill she could not explain creeping along her spine. 'Explain your presence before I call my ladies-in-waiting to summon the guard!'

'Scream until the roof beams crack,' callously answered the stranger. 'Your sluts will not wake till dawn, though the palace spring into flames about them. Your guardsmen will not hear your squeals; they have been sent out of this wing of the palace.'

'What!' exclaimed Taramis, stiffening with outraged majesty. 'Who dared give my guardsmen such a command?'

'I did, sweet sister,' sneered the other girl. 'A little while ago, before I entered. They thought it was their darling adored queen. Ha! How beautifully I acted the part! With what imperious dignity, softened by womanly sweetness, did I address the great louts who knelt in their armor and plumed helmets!'

Taramis felt as if a stifling net of bewilderment were being drawn about her.

'Who are you?' she cried desperately. 'What madness is this? Why do you come here?'

'Who am I?' There was the spite of a she-cobra's hiss in the soft response. The girl stepped to the edge of the couch, grasped the queen's white shoulders with fierce fingers, and bent to glare full into the startled eyes of Taramis. And under the spell of that hypnotic glare, the queen forgot to resent the unprecedented outrage of violent hands laid on regal flesh.

'Fool!' gritted the girl between her teeth. 'Can you ask? Can you wonder? I am Salome!'

'Salome!' Taramis breathed the word, and the hairs prickled on her scalp as she realized the incredible, numbing truth of the statement. 'I thought you died within the hour of your birth,' she said feebly.

'So thought many,' answered the woman who called herself Salome. 'They carried me into the desert to die, damn them! I, a mewing, puling babe whose life was so young it was scarcely the flicker of a candle. And do you know why they bore me forth to die?'

'I – I have heard the story—' faltered Taramis.

Salome laughed fiercely, and slapped her bosom. The low-necked tunic left the upper parts of her firm breasts bare, and between them there shone a curious mark – a crescent, red as blood.

'The mark of the witch!' cried Taramis, recoiling.

'Aye!' Salome's laughter was dagger-edged with hate. 'The curse of the kings of Khauran! Aye, they tell the tale in the market-places, with wagging beards and rolling eyes, the pious fools! They tell how the first queen of our line had traffic with a fiend of darkness and bore him a daughter who lives in foul legendry to this day. And thereafter in each century a girl baby was born into the Askhaurian dynasty, with a scarlet half-moon between her breasts, that signified her destiny.

'"Every century a witch shall be born." So ran the ancient curse. And so it has come to pass. Some were slain at birth, as they sought to slay me. Some walked the earth as witches, proud daughters of Khauran, with the moon of hell burning upon their ivory bosoms. Each was named Salome. I too am Salome. It was always Salome, the witch. It will always be Salome, the witch, even when the mountains of ice have roared down from the pole and ground the civilizations to ruin, and a new world has risen from the ashes and dust – even then there shall be Salomes to walk the earth, to trap men's hearts by their sorcery, to dance before the kings of the world, to see the heads of the wise men fall at their pleasure.'

'But – but you—' stammered Taramis.

'I?' The scintillant eyes burned like dark fires of mystery. 'They carried me into the desert far from the city, and laid me naked on the hot sand, under the flaming sun. And then they rode away and left me for the jackals and the vultures and the desert wolves.

'But the life in me was stronger than the life in common folk, for it partakes of the essence of the forces that seethe in the black gulfs beyond mortal ken. The hours passed, and the sun slashed down like the molten flames of hell, but I did not die – aye, something of that torment I remember, faintly and far away, as one remembers a dim, formless dream. Then there were camels, and yellow-skinned men who wore silk robes and spoke in a weird tongue. Strayed from the caravan road, they passed close by, and their leader saw me, and recognized the scarlet crescent on my bosom. He took me up and gave me life.

'He was a magician from far Khitai, returning to his native kingdom after a journey to Stygia. He took me with him to purple-towering Paikang, its minarets rising amid the vine-festooned jungles of bamboo, and there I grew to womanhood under his teaching.

Age had steeped him deep in black wisdom, not weakened his powers of evil. Many things he taught me—'

She paused, smiling enigmatically, with wicked mystery gleaming in her dark eyes. Then she tossed her head.

'He drove me from him at last, saying that I was but a common witch in spite of his teachings, and not fit to command the mighty sorcery he would have taught me. He would have made me queen of the world and ruled the nations through me, he said, but I was only a harlot of darkness. But what of it? I could never endure to seclude myself in a golden tower, and spend the long hours staring into a crystal globe, mumbling over incantations written on serpent's skin in the blood of virgins, poring over musty volumes in forgotten languages.

'He said I was but an earthly sprite, knowing naught of the deeper gulfs of cosmic sorcery. Well, this world contains all I desire – power, and pomp, and glittering pageantry, handsome men and soft women for my paramours and my slaves. He had told me who I was, of the curse and my heritage. I have returned to take that to which I have as much right as you. Now it is mine by right of possession.'

'What do you mean?' Taramis sprang up and faced her sister, stung out of her bewilderment and fright. 'Do you imagine that by drugging a few of my maids and tricking a few of my guardsmen you have established a claim to the throne of Khauran? Do not forget that I am Queen of Khauran! I shall give you a place of honor, as my sister, but—'

Salome laughed hatefully.

'How generous of you, dear, sweet sister! But before you begin putting me in my place – perhaps you will tell me whose soldiers camp in the plain outside the city walls?'

'They are the Shemitish mercenaries of Constantius, the Kothic *voivode* of the Free Companies.'

'And what do they in Khauran?' cooed Salome.

Taramis felt that she was being subtly mocked, but she answered with an assumption of dignity which she scarcely felt.

'Constantius asked permission to pass along the borders of

Khauran on his way to Turan. He himself is hostage for their good behavior as long as they are within my domains.'

'And Constantius,' pursued Salome. 'Did he not ask your hand today?'

Taramis shot her a clouded glance of suspicion.

'How did you know that?'

An insolent shrug of the slim naked shoulders was the only reply.

'You refused, dear sister?'

'Certainly I refused!' exclaimed Taramis angrily. 'Do you, an Askhaurian princess yourself, suppose that the Queen of Khauran could treat such a proposal with anything but disdain? Wed a bloody-handed adventurer, a man exiled from his own kingdom because of his crimes, and the leader of organized plunderers and hired murderers?

'I should never have allowed him to bring his black-bearded slayers into Khauran. But he is virtually a prisoner in the south tower, guarded by my soldiers. Tomorrow I shall bid him order his troops to leave the kingdom. He himself shall be kept captive until they are over the border. Meantime, my soldiers man the walls of the city, and I have warned him that he will answer for any outrages perpetrated on the villagers or shepherds by his mercenaries.'

'He is confined in the south tower?' asked Salome.

'That is what I said. Why do you ask?'

For answer Salome clapped her hands, and lifting her voice, with a gurgle of cruel mirth in it, called: 'The queen grants you an audience, Falcon!'

A gold-arabesqued door opened and a tall figure entered the chamber, at the sight of which Taramis cried out in amazement and anger.

'Constantius! You dare enter my chamber!'

'As you see, Your Majesty!' He bent his dark, hawk-like head in mock humility.

Constantius, whom men called Falcon, was tall, broad-shouldered, slim-waisted, lithe and strong as pliant steel. He was handsome in an aquiline, ruthless way. His face was burnt dark by the sun, and his hair, which grew far back from his high, narrow forehead, was black as a raven. His dark eyes were penetrating and alert, the hardness of his thin lips not softened by his thin black mustache. His boots were of Kordavan leather, his hose and doublet of plain, dark silk, tarnished with the wear of the camps and the stains of armor rust.

Twisting his mustache, he let his gaze travel up and down the shrinking queen with an effrontery that made her wince.

'By Ishtar, Taramis,' he said silkily, 'I find you more alluring in your night-tunic than in your queenly robes. Truly, this is an auspicious night!'

Fear grew in the queen's dark eyes. She was no fool; she knew that Constantius would never dare this outrage unless he was sure of himself.

'You are mad!' she said. 'If I am in your power in this chamber, you are no less in the power of my subjects, who will rend you to pieces if you touch me. Go at once, if you would live.'

Both laughed mockingly, and Salome made an impatient gesture.

'Enough of this farce; let us on to the next act in the comedy. Listen, dear sister: it was I who sent Constantius here. When I decided to take the throne of Khauran, I cast about for a man to aid me, and chose the Falcon, because of his utter lack of all characteristics men call good.'

'I am overwhelmed, princess,' murmured Constantius sardonically, with a profound bow.

'I sent him to Khauran, and, once his men were camped in the plain outside, and he was in the palace, I entered the city by that small gate in the west wall – the fools guarding it thought it was you returning from some nocturnal adventure—'

'You hell-cat!' Taramis's cheeks flamed and her resentment got the better of her regal reserve.

Salome smiled hardly.

'They were properly surprised and shocked, but admitted me without question. I entered the palace the same way, and gave the order to the surprised guards that sent them marching away, as well as the men who guarded Constantius in the south tower. Then I came here, attending to the ladies-in-waiting on the way.'

Taramis's fingers clenched and she paled.

'Well, what next?' she asked in a shaky voice.

'Listen!' Salome inclined her head. Faintly through the casement there came the clank of marching men in armor; gruff voices shouted in an alien tongue, and cries of alarm mingled with the shouts.

'The people awaken and grow fearful,' said Constantius sardonically. 'You had better go and reassure them, Salome!'

'Call me Taramis,' answered Salome. 'We must become accustomed to it.'

'What have you done?' cried Taramis. 'What have you done?'

'I have gone to the gates and ordered the soldiers to open them,' answered Salome. 'They were astounded, but they obeyed. That is the Falcon's army you hear, marching into the city.'

'You devil!' cried Taramis. 'You have betrayed my people, in my guise! You have made me seem a traitor! Oh, I shall go to them—'

With a cruel laugh Salome caught her wrist and jerked her back. The magnificent suppleness of the queen was helpless against the vindictive strength that steeled Salome's slender limbs.

'You know how to reach the dungeons from the palace, Constantius?' said the witch-girl. 'Good. Take this spitfire and lock her into the strongest cell. The jailers are all sound in drugged sleep. I saw to that. Send a man to cut their throats before they can awaken. None must ever know what has occurred tonight. Thenceforward I am Taramis, and Taramis is a nameless prisoner in an unknown dungeon.'

Constantius smiled with a glint of strong white teeth under his thin mustache.

'Very good; but you would not deny me a little – ah – amusement first?'

'Not I! Tame the scornful hussy as you will.' With a wicked laugh Salome flung her sister into the Kothian's arms, and turned away through the door that opened into the outer corridor.

Fright widened Taramis's lovely eyes, her supple figure rigid and straining against Constantius's embrace. She forgot the men marching in the streets, forgot the outrage to her queenship, in the face of the menace to her womanhood. She forgot all sensations but terror and shame as she faced the complete cynicism of Constantius's burning, mocking eyes, felt his hard arms crushing her writhing body.

Salome, hurrying along the corridor outside, smiled spitefully as a scream of despair and agony rang shuddering through the palace.

2

The Tree of Death

The young soldier's hose and shirt were smeared with dried blood, wet with sweat and gray with dust. Blood oozed from the deep gash in his thigh, from the cuts on his breast and shoulder. Perspiration glistened on his livid face and his fingers were knotted in the cover of the divan on which he lay. Yet his words reflected mental suffering that outweighed physical pain.

'She must be mad!' he repeated again and again, like one still stunned by some monstrous and incredible happening. 'It's like a nightmare! Taramis, whom all Khauran loves, betraying her people to that devil from Koth! Oh, Ishtar, why was I not slain? Better die than live to see our queen turn traitor and harlot!'

'Lie still, Valerius,' begged the girl who was washing and bandaging his wounds with trembling hands. 'Oh, please lie still, darling! You will make your wounds worse. I dared not summon a leech—'

'No,' muttered the wounded youth. 'Constantius's blue-bearded devils will be searching the quarters for wounded Khaurani; they'll hang every man who has wounds to show he fought against them. Oh, Taramis, how could you betray the people who worshipped you?' In his fierce agony he writhed, weeping in rage and shame, and the terrified girl caught him in her arms, straining his tossing head against her bosom, imploring him to be quiet.

'Better death than the black shame that has come upon Khauran this day,' he groaned. 'Did you see it, Ivga?'

'No, Valerius.' Her soft, nimble fingers were again at work, gently cleansing and closing the gaping edges of his raw wounds. 'I was awakened by the noise of fighting in the streets – I looked out a casement and saw the Shemites cutting down people; then presently I heard you calling me faintly from the alley door.'

'I had reached the limits of my strength,' he muttered. 'I fell in the alley and could not rise. I knew they'd find me soon if I lay there – I killed three of the blue-bearded beasts, by Ishtar! They'll never swagger through Khauran's streets, by the gods! The fiends are tearing their hearts in hell!'

The trembling girl crooned soothingly to him, as to a wounded child, and closed his panting lips with her own cool sweet mouth. But the fire that raged in his soul would not allow him to lie silent.

'I was not on the wall when the Shemites entered,' he burst out. 'I was asleep in the barracks, with the others not on duty. It was just before dawn when our captain entered, and his face was pale under his helmet. "The Shemites are in the city," he said. "The queen came to the southern gate and gave orders that they should be admitted. She made the men come down from the walls, where they've been on guard since Constantius entered the kingdom. I don't understand it, and neither does anyone else, but I heard her give the order, and we obeyed as we always do. We are ordered to assemble in the square before the palace. Form ranks outside the barracks and march – leave your arms and armor here. Ishtar knows what this means, but it is the queen's order."

'Well, when we came to the square the Shemites were drawn up on foot opposite the palace, ten thousand of the blue-bearded devils, fully armed, and people's heads were thrust out of every window and door on the square. The streets leading into the square were thronged by bewildered folk. Taramis was standing on the steps of the palace, alone except for Constantius, who stood stroking his mustache like a great lean cat who has just devoured a sparrow. But fifty Shemites with bows in their hands were ranged below them.

'That's where the queen's guard should have been, but they were drawn up at the foot of the palace stair, as puzzled as we, though they had come fully armed, in spite of the queen's order.

'Taramis spoke to us then, and told us that she had reconsidered the proposal made her by Constantius – why, only yesterday she threw it in his teeth in open court – and that she had decided to make him her royal consort. She did not explain why she had brought the Shemites into the city so treacherously. But she said that, as Constantius had control of a body of professional fighting-men, the army of Khauran would no longer be needed, and therefore she disbanded it, and ordered us to go quietly to our homes.

'Why, obedience to our queen is second nature to us, but we were struck dumb and found no word to answer. We broke ranks almost before we knew what we were doing, like men in a daze.

'But when the palace guard was ordered to disarm likewise and disband, the captain of the guard, Conan, interrupted. Men said he was off duty the night before, and drunk. But he was wide awake now. He shouted to the guardsmen to stand as they were until they received an order from him – and such is his dominance of his men, that they obeyed in spite of the queen. He strode up to the palace steps and glared at Taramis – and then he roared: '"This is not the queen! This isn't Taramis! It's some devil in masquerade!"

'Then hell was to pay! I don't know just what happened. I think a Shemite struck Conan, and Conan killed him. The next instant the square was a battleground. The Shemites fell on the guardsmen, and their spears and arrows struck down many soldiers who had already disbanded.

'Some of us grabbed up such weapons as we could and fought back. We hardly knew what we were fighting for, but it was against Constantius and his devils – not against Taramis, I swear it! Constantius shouted to cut the traitors down. We were not traitors!' Despair and bewilderment shook his voice. The girl murmured pityingly, not understanding it all, but aching in sympathy with her lover's suffering.

'The people did not know which side to take. It was a madhouse of confusion and bewilderment. We who fought didn't have a chance, in no formation, without armor and only half armed. The guards were fully armed and drawn up in a square, but there were only five hundred of them. They took a heavy toll before they were cut down, but there could be only one conclusion to such a battle. And while her people were being slaughtered before her, Taramis stood on the palace steps, with Constantius's arm about her waist, and laughed like a heartless, beautiful fiend! Gods, it's all mad – mad!

'I never saw a man fight as Conan fought. He put his back to the courtyard wall, and before they overpowered him the dead men were strewn in heaps thigh-deep about him. But at last they dragged him down, a hundred against one. When I saw him fall I dragged myself away feeling as if the world had burst under my very fingers. I heard Constantius call to his dogs to take the captain alive – stroking his mustache, with that hateful smile on his lips!'

That smile was on the lips of Constantius at that very moment. He sat his horse among a cluster of his men – thick-bodied Shemites with curled blue-black beards and hooked noses; the low-swinging sun struck glints from their peaked helmets and the silvered scales of their corselets. Nearly a mile behind, the walls and towers of Khauran rose sheer out of the meadowlands.

By the side of the caravan road a heavy cross had been planted, and on this grim tree a man hung, nailed there by iron spikes through his hands and feet. Naked but for a loin-cloth, the man was almost a giant in stature, and his muscles stood out in thick corded ridges on limbs and body, which the sun had long ago burned brown. The perspiration of agony beaded his face and his mighty breast, but from under the tangled black mane that fell over his low, broad forehead, his blue eyes blazed with an unquenched fire. Blood oozed sluggishly from the lacerations in his hands and feet.

Constantius saluted him mockingly.

'I am sorry, captain,' he said, 'that I cannot remain to ease your last hours, but I have duties to perform in yonder city – I must not keep your delicious queen waiting!' He laughed softly. 'So

I leave you to your own devices – and those beauties!' He pointed meaningly at the black shadows which swept incessantly back and forth, high above.

'Were it not for them, I imagine that a powerful brute like yourself should live on the cross for days. Do not cherish any illusions of rescue because I am leaving you unguarded. I have had it proclaimed that anyone seeking to take your body, living or dead, from the cross, will be flayed alive together with all the members of his family, in the public square. I am so firmly established in Khauran that my order is as good as a regiment of guardsmen. I am leaving no guard, because the vultures will not approach as long as anyone is near, and I do not wish them to feel any constraint. That is also why I brought you so far from the city. These desert vultures approach the walls no closer than this spot.

'And so, brave captain, farewell! I will remember you when, in an hour, Taramis lies in my arms.'

Blood started afresh from the pierced palms as the victim's mallet-like fists clenched convulsively on the spike-heads. Knots and bunches of muscle started out of the massive arms, and Conan beat his head forward and spat savagely at Constantius's face. The *voivode* laughed coolly, wiped the saliva from his gorget and reined his horse about.

'Remember me when the vultures are tearing at your living flesh,' he called mockingly. 'The desert scavengers are a particularly voracious breed. I have seen men hang for hours on a cross, eyeless, earless, and scalpless, before the sharp beaks had eaten their way into their vitals.'

Without a backward glance he rode toward the city, a supple, erect figure, gleaming in his burnished armor, his stolid, bearded henchmen jogging beside him. A faint rising of dust from the worn trail marked their passing.

The man hanging on the cross was the one touch of sentient life in a landscape that seemed desolate and deserted in the late evening. Khauran, less than a mile away, might have been on the other side of the world, and existing in another age.

Shaking the sweat out of his eyes, Conan stared blankly at the familiar terrain. On either side of the city, and beyond it, stretched the fertile meadowlands, with cattle browsing in the distance where fields and vineyards checkered the plain. The western and northern horizons were dotted with villages, miniature in the distance. A lesser distance to the southeast a silvery gleam marked the course of a river, and beyond that river sandy desert began abruptly to stretch away and away beyond the horizon. Conan stared at that expanse of empty waste shimmering tawnily in the late sunlight as a trapped hawk stares at the open sky. A revulsion shook him when he glanced at the gleaming towers of Khauran. The city had betrayed him – trapped him into circumstances that left him hanging to a wooden cross like a hare nailed to a tree.

A red lust for vengeance swept away the thought. Curses ebbed fitfully from the man's lips. All his universe contracted, focused, became incorporated in the four iron spikes that held him from life and freedom. His great muscles quivered, knotting like iron cables. With the sweat starting out on his graying skin, he sought to gain leverage, to tear the nails from the wood. It was useless. They had been driven deep. Then he tried to tear his hands off the spikes, and it was not the knifing, abysmal agony that finally caused him to cease his efforts, but the futility of it. The spike-heads were broad and heavy; he could not drag them through the wounds. A surge of helplessness shook the giant, for the first time in his life. He hung motionless, his head resting on his breast, shutting his eyes against the aching glare of the sun.

A beat of wings caused him to look, just as a feathered shadow shot down out of the sky. A keen beak, stabbing at his eyes, cut his cheek, and he jerked his head aside, shutting his eyes involuntarily. He shouted, a croaking, desperate shout of menace, and the vultures swerved away and retreated, frightened by the sound. They resumed their wary circling above his head. Blood trickled over Conan's mouth, and he licked his lips involuntarily, spat at the salty taste.

Thirst assailed him savagely. He had drunk deeply of wine the night before, and no water had touched his lips since before the battle in the square, that dawn. And killing was thirsty, salt-sweaty work. He glared at the distant river as a man in hell glares through the opened grille. He thought of gushing freshets of white water he had breasted, laved to the shoulders in liquid jade. He remembered great horns of foaming ale, jacks of sparkling wine gulped carelessly or spilled on the tavern floor. He bit his lip to keep from bellowing in intolerable anguish as a tortured animal bellows.

The sun sank, a lurid ball in a fiery sea of blood. Against a crimson rampart that banded the horizon the towers of the city floated unreal as a dream. The very sky was tinged with blood to his misted glare. He licked his blackened lips and stared with bloodshot eyes at the distant river. It too seemed crimson with blood, and the shadows crawling up from the east seemed black as ebony.

In his dulled ears sounded the louder beat of wings. Lifting his head he watched with the burning glare of a wolf the shadows wheeling above him. He knew that his shouts would frighten them away no longer. One dipped – dipped – lower and lower. Conan drew his head back as far as he could, waiting with terrible patience. The vulture swept in with a swift roar of wings. Its beak flashed down, ripping the skin on Conan's chin as he jerked his head aside; then before the bird could flash away, Conan's head lunged forward on his mighty neck muscles, and his teeth, snapping like those of a wolf, locked on the bare, wattled neck.

Instantly the vulture exploded into squawking, flapping hysteria. Its thrashing wings blinded the man, and its talons ripped his chest. But grimly he hung on, the muscles starting out in lumps on his jaws. And the scavenger's neck-bones crunched between those powerful teeth. With a spasmodic flutter the bird hung limp. Conan let go, spat blood from his mouth. The other vultures, terrified by the fate of their companion, were in full flight to a distant tree, where they perched like black demons in conclave.

Ferocious triumph surged through Conan's numbed brain. Life beat strongly and savagely through his veins. He could still deal death; he still lived. Every twinge of sensation, even of agony, was a negation of death.

'By Mitra!' Either a voice spoke, or he suffered from hallucination. 'In all my life I have never seen such a thing!'

Shaking the sweat and blood from his eyes, Conan saw four

horsemen sitting their steeds in the twilight and staring up at him. Three were lean, white-robed hawks, Zuagir tribesmen without a doubt, nomads from beyond the river. The other was dressed like them in a white, girdled *khalat* and a flowing head-dress which, banded about the temples with a triple circlet of braided camel-hair, fell to his shoulders. But he was not a Shemite. The dust was not so thick, nor Conan's hawk-like sight so clouded, that he could not perceive the man's facial characteristics.

He was as tall as Conan, though not so heavy-limbed. His shoulders were broad and his supple figure was hard as steel and whalebone. A short black beard did not altogether mask the aggressive jut of his lean jaw, and gray eyes cold and piercing as a sword gleamed from the shadow of the *kafieh*. Quieting his restless steed with a quick, sure hand, this man spoke: 'By Mitra, I should know this man!'

'Aye!' It was the guttural accents of a Zuagir. 'It is the Cimmerian who was captain of the queen's guard!'

'She must be casting off all her old favorites,' muttered the rider. 'Who'd have ever thought it of Queen Taramis? I'd rather have had a long, bloody war. It would have given us desert folk a chance to plunder. As it is we've come this close to the walls and found only this nag' – he glanced at a fine gelding led by one of the nomads – 'and this dying dog.'

Conan lifted his bloody head.

'If I could come down from this beam I'd make a dying dog out of you, you Zaporoskan thief!' he rasped through blackened lips.

'Mitra, the knave knows me!' exclaimed the other. 'How, knave, do you know me?'

'There's only one of your breed in these parts,' muttered Conan. 'You are Olgerd Vladislav, the outlaw chief.'

'Aye! and once a hetman of the *kozaki* of the Zaporoskan River, as you have guessed. Would you like to live?'

'Only a fool would ask that question,' panted Conan.

'I am a hard man,' said Olgerd, 'and toughness is the only quality I respect in a man. I shall judge if you are a man, or only a dog after all, fit only to lie here and die.'

'If we cut him down we may be seen from the walls,' objected one of the nomads.

Olgerd shook his head.

'The dusk is deep. Here, take this ax, Djebal, and cut down the cross at the base.'

'If it falls forward it will crush him,' objected Djebal. 'I can cut it so it will fall backward, but then the shock of the fall may crack his skull and tear loose all his entrails.'

'If he's worthy to ride with me he'll survive it,' answered Olgerd imperturbably. 'If not, then he doesn't deserve to live. Cut!'

The first impact of the battle-ax against the wood and its accompanying vibrations sent lances of agony through Conan's swollen feet and hands. Again and again the blade fell, and each stroke reverberated on his bruised brain, setting his tortured nerves aquiver. But he set his teeth and made no sound. The ax cut through, the cross reeled on its splintered base and toppled backward. Conan made his whole body a solid knot of iron-hard muscle, jammed his head back hard against the wood and held it rigid there. The beam struck the ground heavily and rebounded slightly. The impact tore his wounds and dazed him for an instant. He fought the rushing tide of blackness, sick and dizzy, but realized that the iron muscles that sheathed his vitals had saved him from permanent injury.

And he had made no sound, though blood oozed from his nostrils and his belly-muscles quivered with nausea. With a grunt of approval Djebal bent over him with a pair of pincers used to draw horse-shoe nails, and gripped the head of the spike in Conan's right hand, tearing the skin to get a grip on the deeply embedded head. The pincers were small for that work. Djebal sweated and tugged, swearing and wrestling with the stubborn iron, working it back and forth – in swollen flesh as well as in wood. Blood started, oozing over the Cimmerian's fingers. He lay so still he might have been dead, except for the spasmodic rise and fall of his great chest. The spike gave way, and Djebal held up the blood-stained thing with a grunt of satisfaction, then flung it away and bent over the other.

The process was repeated, and then Djebal turned his attention to Conan's skewered feet. But the Cimmerian, struggling up to a sitting posture, wrenched the pincers from his fingers and sent him staggering backward with a violent shove. Conan's hands were swollen to almost twice their normal size. His fingers felt like misshapen thumbs, and closing his hands was an agony that brought blood streaming from under his grinding teeth. But somehow, clutching the pincers clumsily with both hands, he managed to wrench out first one spike and then the other. They were not driven so deeply into the wood as the others had been.

He rose stiffly and stood upright on his swollen, lacerated feet, swaying drunkenly, the icy sweat dripping from his face and body. Cramps assailed him and he clamped his jaws against the desire to retch.

Olgerd, watching him impersonally, motioned him toward the stolen horse. Conan stumbled toward it, and every step was a stabbing, throbbing hell that flecked his lips with bloody foam. One misshapen, groping hand fell clumsily on the saddle-bow, a bloody foot somehow found the stirrup. Setting his teeth, he swung up, and he almost fainted in midair; but he came down in the saddle – and as he did so, Olgerd struck the horse sharply with his whip. The startled beast reared, and the man in the saddle swayed and slumped like a sack of sand, almost unseated. Conan had wrapped a rein about each hand, holding it in place with a clamping thumb. Drunkenly he exerted the strength of his knotted biceps, wrenching the horse down; it screamed, its jaw almost dislocated.

One of the Shemites lifted a water-flask questioningly.

Olgerd shook his head.

'Let him wait until we get to camp. It's only ten miles. If he's fit to live in the desert he'll live that long without a drink.'

The group rode like swift ghosts toward the river; among them Conan swayed like a drunken man in the saddle, bloodshot eyes glazed, foam drying on his blackened lips.

3

A Letter to Nemedia

The savant Astreas, traveling in the East in his never-tiring search for knowledge, wrote a letter to his friend and fellow-philosopher Alcemides, in his native Nemedia, which constitutes the entire knowledge of the Western nations concerning the events of that period in the East, always a hazy, half-mythical region in the minds of the Western folk.

Astreas wrote, in part: 'You can scarcely conceive, my dear old friend, of the conditions now existing in this tiny kingdom since Queen Taramis admitted Constantius and his mercenaries, an event which I briefly described in my last, hurried letter. Seven months have passed since then, during which time it seems as though the devil himself had been loosed in this unfortunate realm. Taramis seems to have gone quite mad; whereas formerly she was famed for her virtue, justice and tranquillity, she is now notorious for qualities precisely opposite to those just enumerated. Her private life is a scandal – or perhaps "private" is not the correct term, since the queen makes no attempt to conceal the debauchery of her court. She constantly indulges in the most infamous revelries, in which the unfortunate ladies of the court are forced to join, young married women as well as virgins.

'She herself has not bothered to marry her paramour, Constantius, who sits on the throne beside her and reigns as her royal consort, and his officers follow his example, and do not hesitate to debauch any woman they desire, regardless of her rank or station. The wretched kingdom groans under exorbitant taxation, the farms are stripped to the bone, and the merchants go in rags which are all that is left them by the tax-gatherers. Nay, they are lucky if they escape with a whole skin.

'I sense your incredulity, good Alcemides; you will fear that I exaggerate conditions in Khauran. Such conditions would be unthinkable in any of the Western countries, admittedly. But you must realize the vast difference that exists between West and East, especially this part of the East. In the first place, Khauran is a kingdom of no great size, one of the many principalities which at one time formed the eastern part of the empire of Koth, and which later regained the independence which was theirs at a still earlier age. This part of the world is made up of these tiny realms, diminutive in comparison with the great kingdoms of the West, or the great sultanates of the farther East, but important in their control of the caravan routes, and in the wealth concentrated in them.

'Khauran is the most southeasterly of these principalities, bordering on the very deserts of eastern Shem. The city of Khauran is the only city of any magnitude in the realm, and stands within sight of the river which separates the grasslands from the sandy desert, like a watch-tower to guard the fertile meadows behind it. The land is so rich that it yields three and four crops a year, and the plains north and west of the city are dotted with villages. To one accustomed to the great plantations and stock-farms of the West, it is strange to see these tiny fields and vineyards; yet wealth in grain and fruit pours from them as from a horn of plenty. The villagers are agriculturists, nothing else. Of a mixed, aboriginal race, they are unwarlike, unable to protect themselves, and forbidden the possession of arms. Dependent wholly upon the soldiers of the city for protection, they are helpless under the present conditions. So the savage revolt of the rural sections, which would be a certainty in any Western nation, is here impossible.

'They toil supinely under the iron hand of Constantius, and his black-bearded Shemites ride incessantly through the fields, with whips in their hands, like the slave-drivers of the black serfs who toil in the plantations of southern Zingara.

'Nor do the people of the city fare any better. Their wealth is stripped from them, their fairest daughters taken to glut the insatiable lust of Constantius and his mercenaries. These men are utterly without mercy or compassion, possessed of all the characteristics our armies learned to abhor in our wars against the Shemitish allies of Argos – inhuman cruelty, lust, and wild-beast ferocity. The people of the city are Khauran's ruling caste, predominantly Hyborian, and valorous and war-like. But the treachery of their queen delivered them into the hands of their oppressors. The Shemites are the only armed force in Khauran, and the most hellish punishment is inflicted on any Khaurani found possessing weapons. A systematic persecution to destroy the young Khaurani men able to bear arms has been savagely pursued. Many have ruthlessly been slaughtered, others sold as slaves to the Turanians. Thousands have fled the kingdom and either entered the service of other rulers, or become outlaws, lurking in numerous bands along the borders.

'At present there is some possibility of invasion from the desert, which is inhabited by tribes of Shemitish nomads. The mercenaries of Constantius are men from the Shemitish cities of the west, Pelishtim, Anakim, Akkharim, and are ardently hated by the Zuagirs and other wandering tribes. As you know, good Alcemides, the countries of these barbarians are divided into the western meadowlands which stretch to the distant ocean, and in which rise the cities of the town-dwellers, and the eastern deserts, where the lean nomads hold sway; there is incessant warfare between the dwellers of the cities and the dwellers of the desert.

'The Zuagirs have fought with and raided Khauran for centuries, without success, but they resent its conquest by their western kin. It is rumored that their natural antagonism is being fomented by the man who was formerly the captain of the queen's guard, and who, somehow escaping the hate of Constantius, who actually had him upon the cross, fled to the nomads. He is called Conan, and is himself a barbarian, one of those gloomy Cimmerians whose ferocity our soldiers have more than once learned to their bitter cost. It is rumored that he has become the right-hand man of Olgerd Vladislav, the *kozak* adventurer who wandered down from the northern steppes and made himself chief of a band of Zuagirs. There are also rumors that this band has increased vastly in the last few months, and that Olgerd, incited no doubt by this Cimmerian, is even considering a raid on Khauran.

'It can not be anything more than a raid, as the Zuagirs are without siege-machines, or the knowledge of investing a city, and it has been proven repeatedly in the past that the nomads in their loose formation, or rather lack of formation, are no match in hand-to-hand fighting for the well-disciplined, fully-armed warriors of the Shemitish cities. The natives of Khauran would perhaps welcome this conquest, since the nomads could deal with them no more harshly than their present masters, and even total extermination would be preferable to the suffering they have to endure. But they are so cowed and helpless that they could give no aid to the invaders.

'Their plight is most wretched. Taramis, apparently possessed of a demon, stops at nothing. She has abolished the worship of Ishtar, and turned the temple into a shrine of idolatry. She has destroyed the ivory image of the goddess which these eastern Hyborians worship (and which, inferior as it is to the true religion of Mitra which we Western nations recognize, is still superior to the devil-worship of the Shemites) and filled the temple of Ishtar with obscene images of every imaginable sort – gods and goddesses of the night, portrayed in all the salacious and perverse poses and with all the revolting characteristics that a degenerate brain could conceive. Many of these images are to be identified as foul deities of the Shemites, the Turanians, the Vendhyans, and the Khitans, but others are reminiscent of a hideous and half-remembered antiquity, vile shapes forgotten except in the most obscure legends. Where the queen gained the knowledge of them I dare not even hazard a guess.

'She has instituted human sacrifice, and since her mating with Constantius, no less then five hundred men, women and children have been immolated. Some of these have died on the altar she has set up in the temple, herself wielding the sacrificial dagger, but most have met a more horrible doom.

'Taramis has placed some sort of monster in a crypt in the temple. What it is, and whence it came, none knows. But shortly after she had crushed the desperate revolt of her soldiers against Constantius, she spent a night alone in the desecrated temple, alone except for a dozen bound captives, and the shuddering people saw thick, foul-smelling smoke curling up from the dome, heard all night the frenetic chanting of the queen, and the agonized cries of her tortured captives; and toward dawn another voice mingled with these sounds – a strident, inhuman croaking that froze the blood of all who heard.

'In the full dawn Taramis reeled drunkenly from the temple, her eyes blazing with demoniac triumph. The captives were never seen again, nor the croaking voice heard. But there is a room in the temple into which none ever goes but the queen, driving a human sacrifice before her. And this victim is never seen again. All know that in that grim chamber lurks some monster from the black night of ages, which devours the shrieking humans Taramis delivers up to it.

'I can no longer think of her as a mortal woman, but as a rabid she-fiend, crouching in her blood-fouled lair amongst the bones and fragments of her victims, with taloned, crimsoned fingers. That the gods allow her to pursue her awful course unchecked almost shakes my faith in divine justice.

'When I compare her present conduct with her deportment when first I came to Khauran, seven months ago, I am confused with bewilderment, and almost inclined to the belief held by many of the people – that a demon has possessed the body of Taramis. A young soldier, Valerius, had another belief. He believed that a witch had assumed a form identical with that of Khauran's adored ruler. He believed that Taramis had been spirited away in the night, and confined in some dungeon, and that this being ruling in her place was but a female sorcerer. He swore that he would find the real queen, if she still lived, but I greatly fear that he himself has fallen victim to the cruelty of Constantius. He was implicated in the revolt of the palace guards, escaped and remained in hiding for some time, stubbornly refusing to seek safety abroad, and it was during this time that I encountered him and he told me his beliefs.

'But he has disappeared, as so many have, whose fate one dares not conjecture, and I fear he has been apprehended by the spies of Constantius.

'But I must conclude this letter and slip it out of the city by means of a swift carrier-pigeon, which will carry it to the post whence I purchased it, on the borders of Koth. By rider and camel-train it will eventually come to you. I must haste, before dawn. It is late, and the stars gleam whitely on the gardened roofs of Khauran. A shuddering silence envelops the city, in which I hear the throb of a sullen drum from the distant temple. I doubt not that Taramis is there, concocting more devilry.'

But the savant was incorrect in his conjecture concerning the whereabouts of the woman he called Taramis. The girl whom the world knew as queen of Khauran stood in a dungeon, lighted only by a flickering torch which played on her features, etching the diabolical cruelty of her beautiful countenance.

On the bare stone floor before her crouched a figure whose nakedness was scarcely covered with tattered rags.

This figure Salome touched contemptuously with the upturned toe of her gilded sandal, and smiled vindictively as her victim shrank away.

'You do not love my caresses, sweet sister?'

Taramis was still beautiful, in spite of her rags and the imprisonment and abuse of seven weary months. She did not reply to her sister's taunts, but bent her head as one grown accustomed to mockery.

This resignation did not please Salome. She bit her red lip, and stood tapping the toe of her shoe against the floor as she frowned down at the passive figure. Salome was clad in the barbaric splendor of a woman of Shushan. Jewels glittered in the torchlight on her gilded sandals, on her gold breast-plates and the slender chains that held them in place. Gold anklets clashed as she moved, jeweled bracelets weighted her bare arms. Her tall coiffure was that of a Shemitish woman, and jade pendants hung from gold hoops in her ears, flashing and sparkling with each impatient movement of her haughty head. A gem-crusted girdle supported a silk shirt so transparent that it was in the nature of a cynical mockery of convention.

Suspended from her shoulders and trailing down her back hung a darkly scarlet cloak, and this was thrown carelessly over the crook of one arm and the bundle that arm supported.

Salome stooped suddenly and with her free hand grasped her sister's dishevelled hair and forced back the girl's head to stare into her eyes. Taramis met that tigerish glare without flinching.

'You are not so ready with your tears as formerly, sweet sister,' muttered the witch-girl.

'You shall wring no more tears from me,' answered Taramis. 'Too often you have reveled in the spectacle of the queen of Khauran sobbing for mercy on her knees. I know that you have spared me only to torment me; that is why you have limited your tortures to such torments as neither slay nor permanently disfigure. But I fear you no longer; you have strained out the last vestige of hope, fright and shame from me. Slay me and be done with it, for I have shed my last tear for your enjoyment, you she-devil from hell!'

'You flatter yourself, my dear sister,' purred Salome. 'So far it is only your handsome body that I have caused to suffer, only your pride and self-esteem that I have crushed. You forget that, unlike myself, you are capable of mental torment. I have observed this when I have regaled you with narratives concerning the comedies I have enacted with some of your stupid subjects. But this time I have brought more vivid proof of these farces. Did you know that Krallides, your faithful councillor, had come skulking back from Turan and been captured?'

Taramis turned pale.

'What – what have you done to him?'

For answer Salome drew the mysterious bundle from under her cloak. She shook off the silken swathings and held it up – the head of a young man, the features frozen in a convulsion as if death had come in the midst of inhuman agony.

Taramis cried out as if a blade had pierced her heart.

'Oh, Ishtar! Krallides!'

'Aye! He was seeking to stir up the people against me, poor fool, telling them that Conan spoke the truth when he said I was not Taramis. How would the people rise against the Falcon's Shemites?

With sticks and pebbles? Bah! Dogs are eating his headless body in the market-place, and this foul carrion shall be cast into the sewer to rot.

'How, sister!' She paused, smiling down at her victim. 'Have you discovered that you still have unshed tears? Good! I reserved the mental torment for the last. Hereafter I shall show you many such sights as – this!'

Standing there in the torchlight with the severed head in her hand she did not look like anything ever borne by a human woman, in spite of her awful beauty. Taramis did not look up. She lay face down on the slimy floor, her slim body shaken in sobs of agony, beating her clenched hands against the stones. Salome sauntered toward the door, her anklets clashing at each step, her ear pendants winking in the torch-glare.

A few moments later she emerged from a door under a sullen arch that led into a court which in turn opened upon a winding alley. A man standing there turned toward her – a giant Shemite, with sombre eyes and shoulders like a bull, his great black beard falling over his mighty, silver-mailed breast.

'She wept?' His rumble was like that of a bull, deep, low-pitched and stormy. He was the general of the mercenaries, one of the few even of Constantius's associates who knew the secret of the queens of Khauran.

'Aye, Khumbanigash. There are whole sections of her sensibilities that I have not touched. When one sense is dulled by continual laceration, I will discover a newer, more poignant pang. Here, dog!' A trembling, shambling figure in rags, filth and matted hair approached, one of the beggars that slept in the alleys and open courts. Salome tossed the head to him. 'Here, deaf one; cast that in the nearest sewer. Make the sign with your hands, Khumbanigash. He can not hear.'

The general complied, and the tousled head bobbed, as the man turned painfully away.

'Why do you keep up this farce?' rumbled Khumbanigash. 'You are so firmly established on the throne that nothing can unseat you. What if Khaurani fools learn the truth? They can do nothing.

Proclaim yourself in your true identity! Show them their beloved ex-queen – and cut off her head in the public square!'

'Not yet, good Khumbanigash—'

The arched door slammed on the hard accents of Salome, the stormy reverberations of Khumbanigash. The mute beggar crouched in the courtyard, and there was none to see that the hands which held the severed head were quivering strongly – brown, sinewy hands, strangely incongruous with the bent body and filthy tatters.

'I knew it!' It was a fierce, vibrant whisper, scarcely audible. 'She lives! Oh, Krallides, your martyrdom was not in vain! They have her locked in that dungeon! Oh, Ishtar, if you love true men, aid me now!'

4

Wolves of the Desert

Olgerd Vladislav filled his jeweled goblet with crimson wine from a golden jug and thrust the vessel across the ebony table to Conan the Cimmerian. Olgerd's apparel would have satisfied the vanity of any Zaporoskan hetman.

His *khalat* was of white silk, with pearls sewn on the bosom. Girdled at the waist with a Bakhauriot belt, its skirts were drawn back to reveal his wide silken breeches, tucked into short boots of soft green leather, adorned with gold thread. On his head was a green silk turban, wound about a spired helmet chased with gold. His only weapon was a broad curved Cherkees knife in an ivory sheath girdled high on his left hip, *kozak* fashion. Throwing himself back in his gilded chair with its carven eagles, Olgerd spread his booted legs before him, and gulped down the sparkling wine noisily.

To his splendor the huge Cimmerian opposite him offered a strong contrast, with his square-cut black mane, brown scarred countenance and burning blue eyes. He was clad in black mesh-mail, and the only glitter about him was the broad gold buckle of the belt which supported his sword in its worn leather scabbard.

They were alone in the silk-walled tent, which was hung with gilt-worked tapestries and littered with rich carpets and velvet cushions, the loot of the caravans. From outside came a low, incessant murmur, the sound that always accompanies a great throng of men, in camp or otherwise. An occasional gust of desert wind rattled the palm-leaves.

'Today in the shadow, tomorrow in the sun,' quoth Olgerd, loosening his crimson girdle a trifle and reaching again for the wine-jug. 'That's the way of life. Once I was a hetman on the Zaporoska; now I'm a desert chief. Seven months ago you were hanging on a cross outside Khauran. Now you're lieutenant to the most powerful raider between Turan and the western meadows. You should be thankful to me!'

'For recognizing my usefulness?' Conan laughed and lifted the jug. 'When you allow the elevation of a man, one can be sure that you'll profit by his advancement. I've earned everything I've won, with my blood and sweat.' He glanced at the scars on the insides of his palms. There were scars, too, on his body, scars that had not been there seven months ago.

'You fight like a regiment of devils,' conceded Olgerd. 'But don't get to thinking that you've had anything to do with the recruits who've swarmed in to join us. It was our success at raiding, guided by my wit, that brought them in. These nomads are always looking for a successful leader to follow, and they have more faith in a foreigner than in one of their own race.

'There's no limit to what we may accomplish! We have eleven thousand men now. In another year we may have three times that number. We've contented ourselves, so far, with raids on the Turanian outposts and the city-states to the west. With thirty or forty thousand men we'll raid no longer. We'll invade and conquer and establish ourselves as rulers. I'll be emperor of all Shem yet, and you'll be my vizier, so long as you carry out my orders unquestioningly. In the meantime, I think we'll ride eastward and storm that Turanian outpost at Vezek, where the caravans pay toll.'

Conan shook his head. 'I think not.'

Olgerd glared, his quick temper irritated.

'What do you mean, *you* think not? I do the thinking for this army!'

'There are enough men in this band now for my purpose,' answered the Cimmerian. 'I'm sick of waiting. I have a score to settle.'

'Oh!' Olgerd scowled, and gulped wine, then grinned. 'Still thinking of that cross, eh? Well, I like a good hater. But that can wait.'

'You told me once you'd aid me in taking Khauran,' said Conan.

'Yes, but that was before I began to see the full possibilities of our power,' answered Olgerd. 'I was only thinking of the loot in the city. I don't want to waste our strength unprofitably. Khauran is too strong a nut for us to crack now. Maybe in a year—'

'Within the week,' answered Conan, and the *kozak* stared at the certainty in his voice.

'Listen,' said Olgerd, 'even if I were willing to throw away men on such a hare-brained attempt – what could you expect? Do you think these wolves could besiege and take a city like Khauran?'

'There'll be no siege,' answered the Cimmerian. 'I know how to draw Constantius out into the plain.'

'And what then?' cried Olgerd with an oath. 'In the arrow-play our horsemen would have the worst of it, for the armor of the *asshuri* is the better, and when it came to sword-strokes their close-marshaled ranks of trained swordsmen would cleave through our loose lines and scatter our men like chaff before the wind.'

'Not if there were three thousand desperate Hyborian horsemen fighting in a solid wedge such as I could teach them,' answered Conan.

'And where would you secure three thousand Hyborians?' asked Olgerd with vast sarcasm. 'Will you conjure them out of the air?'

'I *have* them,' answered the Cimmerian imperturbably. 'Three thousand men of Khauran camp at the oasis of Akrel awaiting my orders.'

'*What?*' Olgerd glared like a startled wolf.

'Aye. Men who had fled from the tyranny of Constantius. Most of them have been living the lives of outlaws in the deserts east of Khauran, and are gaunt and hard and desperate as man-eating tigers. One of them will be a match for any three squat mercenaries. It takes oppression and hardship to stiffen men's guts and put the fire of hell into their thews. They were broken up into small bands; all they needed was a leader. They believed the word I sent them by my riders, and assembled at the oasis and put themselves at my disposal.'

'All this without my knowledge?' A feral light began to gleam in Olgerd's eye. He hitched at his weapon-girdle.

'It was *I* they wished to follow, not *you*.'

'And what did you tell these outcasts to gain their allegiance?' There was a dangerous ring in Olgerd's voice.

'I told them that I'd use this horde of desert wolves to help them destroy Constantius and give Khauran back into the hands of its citizens.'

'You fool!' whispered Olgerd. 'Do you deem yourself chief already?'

The men were on their feet, facing each other across the ebony board, devil-lights dancing in Olgerd's cold gray eyes, a grim smile on the Cimmerian's hard lips.

'I'll have you torn between four palm-trees,' said the *kozak* calmly.

'Call the men and bid them do it!' challenged Conan. 'See if they obey you!'

Baring his teeth in a snarl, Olgerd lifted his hand – then paused. There was something about the confidence in the Cimmerian's dark face that shook him. His eyes began to burn like those of a wolf.

'You scum of the western hills,' he muttered, 'have you dared seek to undermine my power?'

'I didn't have to,' answered Conan. 'You lied when you said I had nothing to do with bringing in the new recruits. I had everything to do with it. They took your orders, but they fought for me. There is not room for two chiefs of the Zuagirs. They know I am the stronger man. I understand them better than you, and they, me; because I am a barbarian too.'

'And what will they say when you ask them to fight for Khauran?' asked Olgerd sardonically.

'They'll follow me. I'll promise them a camel-train of gold from the palace. Khauran will be willing to pay that as a guerdon for getting rid of Constantius. After that, I'll lead them against the Turanians as you have planned. They want loot, and they'd as soon fight Constantius for it as anybody.'

In Olgerd's eyes grew a recognition of defeat. In his red dreams of empire he had missed what was going on about him. Happenings and events that had seemed meaningless before now flashed into his mind, with their true significance, bringing a realization that Conan spoke no idle boast. The giant black-mailed figure before him was the real chief of the Zuagirs.

'Not if you die!' muttered Olgerd, and his hand flickered toward his hilt. But quick as the stroke of a great cat, Conan's arm shot across the table and his fingers locked on Olgerd's forearm. There was a snap of breaking bones, and for a tense instant the scene held: the men facing each other as motionless as images, perspiration starting out on Olgerd's forehead. Conan laughed, never easing his grip on the broken arm.

'Are you fit to live, Olgerd?'

His smile did not alter as the corded muscles rippled in knotting ridges along his forearm and his fingers ground into the *kozak*'s quivering flesh. There was the sound of broken bones grating together and Olgerd's face turned the color of ashes; blood oozed from his lip where his teeth sank, but he uttered no sound.

With a laugh Conan released him and drew back, and the *kozak* swayed, caught the table edge with his good hand to steady himself.

'I give you life, Olgerd, as you gave it to me,' said Conan tranquilly, 'though it was for your own ends that you took me down from the cross. It was a bitter test you gave me then; you couldn't have endured it; neither could anyone, but a western barbarian.

'Take your horse and go. It's tied behind the tent, and food and water are in the saddle-bags. None will see your going, but go quickly. There's no room for a fallen chief on the desert. If the warriors see you, maimed and deposed, they'll never let you leave the camp alive.'

Olgerd did not reply. Slowly, without a word, he turned and stalked across the tent, through the flapped opening. Unspeaking he climbed into the saddle of the great white stallion that stood tethered there in the shade of a spreading palm-tree; and unspeaking, with his broken arm thrust in the bosom of his *khalat*, he reined the steed about and rode eastward into the open desert, out of the life of the people of the Zuagir.

Inside the tent Conan emptied the wine-jug and smacked his lips with relish. Tossing the empty vessel into a corner, he braced his belt and strode out through the front opening, halting for a moment to let his gaze sweep over the lines of camel-hair tents that stretched before him, and the white-robed figures that moved among them, arguing, singing, mending bridles or whetting tulwars.

He lifted his voice in a thunder that carried to the farthest confines of the encampment: '*Aie*, you dogs, sharpen your ears and listen! Gather around here. I have a tale to tell you.'

5

The Voice from the Crystal

In a chamber in a tower near the city wall a group of men listened attentively to the words of one of their number. They were young men, but hard and sinewy, with a bearing that comes only to men rendered desperate by adversity. They were clad in mail shirts and worn leather; swords hung at their girdles.

'I knew that Conan spoke the truth when he said it was not Taramis!' the speaker exclaimed. 'For months I have haunted the outskirts of the palace, playing the part of a deaf beggar. At last I learned what I had believed – that our queen was a prisoner in the dungeons that adjoin the palace. I watched my opportunity and captured a Shemitish jailer – knocked him senseless as he left the courtyard late one night – dragged him into a cellar near by and questioned him. Before he died he told me what I have just told you, and what we have suspected all along – that the woman ruling Khauran is a witch: Salome. Taramis, he said, is imprisoned in the lowest dungeon.

'This invasion of the Zuagirs gives us the opportunity we sought. What Conan means to do, I can not say. Perhaps he merely wishes vengeance on Constantius. Perhaps he intends sacking the city and destroying it. He is a barbarian and no one can understand their minds.

'But this is what we must do: rescue Taramis while the battle rages! Constantius will march out into the plain to give battle. Even now his men are mounting. He will do this because there is not sufficient food in the city to stand a siege. Conan burst out of the desert so suddenly that there was no time to bring in supplies. And the Cimmerian is equipped for a siege. Scouts have reported that the Zuagirs have siege engines, built, undoubtedly, according to the instructions of Conan, who learned all the arts of war among the Western nations.

'Constantius does not desire a long siege; so he will march with his warriors into the plain, where he expects to scatter Conan's forces at one stroke. He will leave only a few hundred men in the city, and they will be on the walls and in the towers commanding the gates.

'The prison will be left all but unguarded. When we have freed Taramis our next actions will depend upon circumstances. If Conan wins, we must show Taramis to the people and bid them rise – they will! Oh, they will! With their bare hands they are enough to overpower the Shemites left in the city and close the gates against both the mercenaries and the nomads. Neither must get within the walls! Then we will parley with Conan. He was always loyal to Taramis. If he knows the truth, and she appeals to him, I believe he will spare the city. If, which is more probable, Constantius prevails, and Conan is routed, we must steal out of the city with the queen and seek safety in flight.

'Is all clear?'

They replied with one voice.

'Then let us loosen our blades in our scabbards, commend our souls to Ishtar, and start for the prison, for the mercenaries are already marching through the southern gate.'

This was true. The dawnlight glinted on peaked helmets pouring in a steady stream through the broad arch, on the bright housings of the chargers. This would be a battle of horsemen, such as is possible only in the lands of the East. The riders flowed through the gates like a river of steel – sombre figures in black and silver mail, with their curled beards and hooked noses, and their inexorable eyes in which glimmered the fatality of their race – the utter lack of doubt or of mercy.

The streets and the walls were lined with throngs of people who watched silently these warriors of an alien race riding forth to defend their native city. There was no sound; dully, expressionless they watched, those gaunt people in shabby garments, their caps in their hands.

In a tower that overlooked the broad street that led to the southern gate, Salome lolled on a velvet couch cynically watching Constantius as he settled his broad sword-belt about his lean hips and drew on his gauntlets. They were alone in the chamber. Outside, the rhythmical clank of harness and shuffle of horses' hoofs welled up through the gold-barred casements.

'Before nightfall,' quoth Constantius, giving a twirl to his thin mustache, 'you'll have some captives to feed to your temple-devil. Does it not grow weary of soft, city-bred flesh? Perhaps it would relish the harder thews of a desert man.'

'Take care you do not fall prey to a fiercer beast than Thaug,' warned the girl. 'Do not forget who it is that leads these desert animals.'

'I am not likely to forget,' he answered. 'That is one reason why I am advancing to meet him. The dog has fought in the West and knows the art of siege. My scouts had some trouble in approaching his columns, for his outriders have eyes like hawks; but they did get close enough to see the engines he is dragging on ox-cart wheels drawn by camels – catapults, rams, ballistas, mangonels – by Ishtar! he must have had ten thousand men working day and night for a month. Where he got the material for their construction is more than I can understand. Perhaps he has a treaty with the Turanians, and gets supplies from them.

'Anyway, they won't do him any good. I've fought these desert wolves before – an exchange of arrows for awhile, in which the armor of my warriors protects them – then a charge and my squadrons sweep through the loose swarms of the nomads, wheel and sweep back through, scattering them to the four winds. I'll ride back through the south gate before sunset, with hundreds of naked captives staggering at my horse's tail. We'll hold a fête tonight, in the great square. My soldiers delight in flaying their enemies alive – we will have a wholesale skinning, and make these weak-kneed townsfolk watch. As for Conan, it will afford me intense pleasure, if we take him alive, to impale him on the palace steps.'

'Skin as many as you like,' answered Salome indifferently. 'I would like a dress made of human hide. But at least a hundred captives you must give to me – for the altar, and for Thaug.'

'It shall be done,' answered Constantius, with his gauntleted hand brushing back the thin hair from his high bald forehead, burned dark by the sun. 'For victory and the fair honor of Taramis!' he said sardonically, and, taking his vizored helmet under his arm, he lifted a hand in salute, and strode clanking from the chamber. His voice drifted back, harshly lifted in orders to his officers.

Salome leaned back on the couch, yawned, stretched herself like a great supple cat, and called: 'Zang!'

A cat-footed priest, with features like yellowed parchment stretched over a skull, entered noiselessly.

Salome turned to an ivory pedestal on which stood two crystal globes, and taking from it the smaller, she handed the glistening sphere to the priest.

'Ride with Constantius,' she said. 'Give me the news of the battle. Go!'

The skull-faced man bowed low, and hiding the globe under his dark mantle, hurried from the chamber.

Outside in the city there was no sound, except the clank of hoofs and after a while the clang of a closing gate. Salome mounted a wide marble stair that led to the flat, canopied, marble-battlemented roof. She was above all other buildings in the city. The streets were deserted, the great square in front of the palace was empty. In normal times folk shunned the grim temple which rose on the opposite side of that square, but now the town looked like a dead city. Only on the southern wall and the roofs that overlooked it was there any sign of life. There the people massed thickly. They made no demonstration, did not know whether to hope for the victory or defeat of Constantius. Victory meant further misery under his intolerable rule; defeat probably meant the sack of the city and red massacre. No word had come from Conan. They did not know what to expect at his hands. They remembered that he was a barbarian.

The squadrons of the mercenaries were moving out into the plain. In the distance, just this side of the river, other dark masses were moving, barely recognizable as men on horses. Objects dotted the farther bank; Conan had not brought his siege engines across the river, apparently fearing an attack in the midst of the crossing. But he had crossed with his full force of horsemen. The sun rose and struck glints of fire from the dark multitudes. The squadrons from the city broke into a gallop; a deep roar reached the ears of the people on the wall.

The rolling masses merged, intermingled; at that distance it was a tangled confusion in which no details stood out. Charge and countercharge were not to be identified. Clouds of dust rose from the plains, under the stamping hoofs, veiling the action. Through these swirling clouds masses of riders loomed, appearing and disappearing, and spears flashed.

Salome shrugged her shoulders and descended the stair. The palace lay silent. All the slaves were on the wall, gazing vainly southward with the citizens.

She entered the chamber where she had talked with Constantius, and approached the pedestal, noting that the crystal globe was clouded, shot with bloody streaks of crimson. She bent over the ball, swearing under her breath.

'Zang!' she called. 'Zang!'

Mists swirled in the sphere, resolving themselves into billowing dust-clouds through which black figures rushed unrecognizably; steel glinted like lightning in the murk. Then the face of Zang leaped into startling distinctness; it was as if the wide eyes gazed up at Salome. Blood trickled from a gash in the skull-like head, the skin was gray with sweat-runneled dust. The lips parted, writhing; to other ears than Salome's it would have seemed that the face in the crystal contorted silently. But sound to her came as plainly from those ashen lips as if the priest had been in the same room with her, instead of miles away, shouting into the smaller crystal. Only the gods of darkness knew what unseen, magic filaments linked together those shimmering spheres.

'Salome! shrieked the bloody head. '*Salome!*'

'I hear!' she cried. 'Speak! How goes the battle?'

'Doom is upon us!' screamed the skull-like apparition. 'Khauran is lost! *Aie*, my horse is down and I can not win clear! Men are falling around me! They are dying like flies, in their silvered mail!'

'Stop yammering and tell me what happened!' she cried harshly.

'We rode at the desert-dogs and they came on to meet us!' yowled the priest. 'Arrows flew in clouds between the hosts, and the nomads wavered. Constantius ordered the charge. In even ranks we thundered upon them.

'Then the masses of their horde opened to right and left, and through the cleft rushed three thousand Hyborian horsemen whose presence we had not even suspected. Men of Khauran, mad with hate! Big men in full armor on massive horses! In a solid wedge of steel they smote us like a thunderbolt. They split our ranks asunder before we knew what was upon us, and then the desert-men swarmed on us from either flank.

'They have ripped our ranks apart, broken and scattered us! It is a trick of that devil Conan! The siege engines are false – mere frames of palm trunks and painted silk, that fooled our scouts who saw them from afar. A trick to draw us out to our doom! Our warriors flee! Khumbanigash is down – Conan slew him. I do not see Constantius. The Khaurani rage through our milling masses like blood-mad lions, and the desert-men feather us with arrows. I – ahh!'

There was a flicker as of lightning, or trenchant steel, a burst of bright blood – then abruptly the image vanished, like a bursting bubble, and Salome was staring into an empty crystal ball that mirrored only her own furious features.

She stood perfectly still for a few moments, erect and staring into space. Then she clapped her hands and another skull-like priest entered, as silent and immobile as the first.

'Constantius is beaten,' she said swiftly. 'We are doomed. Conan will be crashing at our gates within the hour. If he catches me, I have no illusions as to what I can expect. But first I am going to make sure that my cursed sister never ascends the throne again. Follow me! Come what may, we shall give Thaug a feast.'

As she descended the stairs and galleries of the palace, she heard a faint rising echo from the distant walls. The people there had begun to realize that the battle was going against Constantius. Through the dust clouds masses of horsemen were visible, racing toward the city.

Palace and prison were connected by a long closed gallery, whose vaulted roof rose on gloomy arches. Hurrying along this, the false queen and her slave passed through a heavy door at the other end that let them into the dim-lit recesses of the prison. They had emerged into a wide, arched corridor at a point near where a stone stair descended into the darkness. Salome recoiled suddenly, swearing. In the gloom of the hall lay a motionless form – a Shemitish jailer, his short beard tilted toward the roof as his head hung on a half-severed neck. As panting voices from below reached the girl's ears, she shrank back into the black shadow of an arch, pushing the priest behind her, her hand groping in her girdle.

6

The Vulture's Wings

It was the smoky light of a torch which roused Taramis, Queen of Khauran, from the slumber in which she sought forgetfulness. Lifting herself on her hand she raked back her tangled hair and blinked up, expecting to meet the mocking countenance of Salome, malign with new torments. Instead a cry of pity and horror reached her ears.

'Taramis! Oh, my Queen!'

The sound was so strange to her ears that she thought she was still dreaming. Behind the torch she could make out figures now, the glint of steel, then five countenances bent toward her, not swarthy and hook-nosed, but lean, aquiline faces, browned by the sun. She crouched in her tatters, staring wildly.

One of the figures sprang forward and fell on one knee before her, arms stretched appealingly toward her.

'Oh, Taramis! Thank Ishtar we have found you! Do you not remember me, Valerius? Once with your own lips you praised me, after the battle of Korveka!'

'Valerius!' she stammered. Suddenly tears welled into her eyes. 'Oh, I dream! It is some magic of Salome's to torment me!'

'No!' The cry rang with exultation. 'It is your own true vassals come to rescue you! Yet we must hasten. Constantius fights in the plain against Conan, who has brought the Zuagirs across the river, but three hundred Shemites yet hold the city. We slew the jailer and took his keys, and have seen no other guards. But we must be gone. Come!'

The queen's legs gave way, not from weakness but from the reaction. Valerius lifted her like a child, and with the torch-bearer hurrying before them, they left the dungeon and went up a slimy stone stair. It seemed to mount endlessly, but presently they emerged into a corridor.

They were passing a dark arch when the torch was suddenly

struck out, and the bearer cried out in fierce, brief agony. A burst of blue fire glared in the dark corridor, in which the furious face of Salome was limned momentarily, with a beast-like figure crouching beside her – then the eyes of the watchers were blinded by that blaze.

Valerius tried to stagger along the corridor with the queen; dazedly he heard the sound of murderous blows driven deep in flesh, accompanied by gasps of death and a bestial grunting. Then the queen was torn brutally from his arms, and a savage blow on his helmet dashed him to the floor.

Grimly he crawled to his feet, shaking his head in an effort to rid himself of the blue flame which seemed still to dance devilishly before him. When his blinded sight cleared, he found himself alone in the corridor – alone except for the dead. His four companions lay in their blood, heads and bosoms cleft and gashed. Blinded and dazed in that hell-born glare, they had died without an opportunity of defending themselves. The queen was gone.

With a bitter curse Valerius caught up his sword, tearing his cleft helmet from his head to clatter on the flags; blood ran down his cheek from a cut in his scalp.

Reeling, frantic with indecision, he heard a voice calling his name in desperate urgency: 'Valerius! *Valerius!*'

He staggered in the direction of the voice, and rounded a corner just in time to have his arms filled with a soft, supple figure which flung itself frantically at him.

'Ivga! Are you mad!'

'I had to come!' she sobbed. 'I followed you – hid in an arch of the outer court. A moment ago I saw *her* emerge with a brute who carried a woman in his arms. I knew it was Taramis, and that you had failed! Oh, you are hurt!'

'A scratch!' He put aside her clinging hands. 'Quick, Ivga, tell me which way they went!'

'They fled across the square toward the temple.'

He paled. 'Ishtar! Oh, the fiend! She means to give Taramis to the devil she worships! Quick, Ivga! Run to the south wall where the people watch the battle! Tell them that their real queen has been found – that the impostor has dragged her to the temple! Go!'

Sobbing, the girl sped away, her light sandals pattering on the cobblestones, and Valerius raced across the court, plunged into the street, dashed into the square upon which it debouched, and raced for the great structure that rose on the opposite side.

His flying feet spurned the marble as he darted up the broad stair and through the pillared portico. Evidently their prisoner had given them some trouble. Taramis, sensing the doom intended for her, was fighting against it with all the strength of her splendid young body. Once she had broken away from the brutish priest, only to be dragged down again.

The group was halfway down the broad nave, at the other end of which stood the grim altar and beyond that the great metal door, obscenely carven, through which many had gone, but from which only Salome had ever emerged. Taramis's breath came in panting gasps; her tattered garment had been torn from her in the struggle. She writhed in the grasp of her apish captor like a white, naked nymph in the arms of a satyr. Salome watched cynically, though impatiently, moving toward the carven door, and from the dusk that lurked along the lofty walls the obscene gods and gargoyles leered down, as if imbued with salacious life.

Choking with fury, Valerius rushed down the great hall, sword in hand. At a sharp cry from Salome, the skull-faced priest looked up, then released Taramis, drew a heavy knife, already smeared with blood, and ran at the oncoming Khaurani.

But cutting down men blinded by the devil's-flame loosed by Salome was different from fighting a wiry young Hyborian afire with hate and rage.

Up went the dripping knife, but before it could fall Valerius's keen narrow blade slashed through the air, and the fist that held the knife jumped from its wrist in a shower of blood. Valerius, berserk, slashed again and yet again before the crumpling figure could fall. The blade licked through flesh and bone. The skull-like head fell one way, the half-sundered torso the other.

Valerius whirled on his toes, quick and fierce as a jungle-cat, glaring about for Salome. She must have exhausted her fire-dust in the prison. She was bending over Taramis, grasping her sister's black locks in one hand, in the other lifting a dagger. Then with a fierce cry Valerius's sword was sheathed in her breast with such fury that the point sprang out between her shoulders. With an awful shriek the witch sank down, writhing in convulsions, grasping at the naked blade as it was withdrawn, smoking and dripping. Her eyes were inhuman; with a more than human vitality she clung to the life that ebbed through the wound that split the crimson crescent on her ivory bosom. She groveled on the floor, clawing and biting at the naked stones in her agony.

Sickened at the sight, Valerius stooped and lifted the half-fainting queen. Turning his back on the twisting figure on the floor, he ran toward the door, stumbling in his haste. He staggered out upon the portico, halted at the head of the steps. The square thronged with people. Some had come at Ivga's incoherent cries; others had deserted the walls in fear of the onsweeping hordes out of the desert, fleeing unreasoningly toward the centre of the city. Dumb resignation had vanished. The throng seethed and milled, yelling and screaming. About the road there sounded somewhere the splintering of stone and timbers.

A band of grim Shemites cleft the crowd – the guards of the northern gates, hurrying toward the south gate to reinforce their comrades there. They reined up short at the sight of the youth on the steps, holding the limp, naked figure in his arms. The heads of the throng turned toward the temple; the crowd gaped, a new bewilderment added to their swirling confusion.

'Here is your queen!' yelled Valerius, straining to make himself understood above the clamor. The people gave back a bewildered roar. They did not understand, and Valerius sought in vain to lift his voice above their bedlam. The Shemites rode toward the temple steps, beating a way through the crowd with their spears.

Then a new, grisly element introduced itself into the frenzy. Out of the gloom of the temple behind Valerius wavered a slim white figure, laced with crimson. The people screamed; there in the arms of Valerius hung the woman they thought their queen; yet there in the temple door staggered another figure, like a reflection of the other. Their brains reeled. Valerius felt his blood congeal as he stared at the swaying witch-girl. His sword had transfixed her, sundered her heart. She should be dead; by all laws of nature she should be dead. Yet there she swayed, on her feet, clinging horribly to life.

'Thaug!' she screamed, reeling in the doorway. '*Thaug!*' As in answer to that frightful invocation there boomed a thunderous croaking from within the temple, the snapping of wood and metal.

'That is the queen!' roared the captain of the Shemites, lifting his bow. 'Shoot down the man and other woman!'

But the roar of a roused hunting-pack rose from the people; they had guessed the truth at last, understood Valerius's frenzied appeals, knew that the girl who hung limply in his arms was their true queen. With a soul-shaking yell they surged on the Shemites, tearing and smiting with tooth and nail and naked hands, with the desperation of hard-pent fury loosed at last. Above them Salome swayed and tumbled down the marble stairs, dead at last.

Arrows flickered about him as Valerius ran back between the pillars of the portico, shielding the body of the queen with his own. Shooting and slashing ruthlessly, the mounted Shemites were holding their own with the maddened crowd. Valerius darted to the temple door – with one foot on the threshold he recoiled, crying out in horror and despair.

Out of the gloom at the other end of the great hall a vast dark form heaved up – came rushing toward him in gigantic frog-like hops. He saw the gleam of great unearthly eyes, the shimmer of fangs or talons. He fell back from the door, and then the whir of a shaft past his ear warned him that death was also behind him. He wheeled desperately. Four or five Shemites had cut their way through the throng and were spurring their horses up the steps, their bows lifted to shoot him down. He sprang behind a pillar, on which the arrows splintered. Taramis had fainted. She hung like a dead woman in his arms.

Before the Shemites could loose again, the doorway was blocked by a gigantic shape. With affrighted yells the mercenaries wheeled and began beating a frantic way through the throng, which crushed back in sudden, galvanized horror, trampling one another in their stampede.

But the monster seemed to be watching Valerius and the girl. Squeezing its vast, unstable bulk through the door, it bounded toward him, as he ran down the steps. He felt it looming behind him, a giant shadowy thing, like a travesty of nature cut out of the heart of night, a black shapelessness in which only the staring eyes and gleaming fangs were distinct.

There came a sudden thunder of hoofs; a rout of Shemites, bloody and battered, streamed across the square from the south, plowing blindly through the packed throng. Behind them swept a horde of horsemen yelling in a familiar tongue, waving red swords – the exiles, returned! With them rode fifty black-bearded desert-riders, and at their head a giant figure in black mail.

'Conan!' shrieked Valerius. *'Conan!'*

The giant yelled a command. Without checking their headlong pace, the desert men lifted their bows, drew and loosed. A cloud of arrows sang across the square, over the seething heads of the multitudes, and sank feather-deep in the black monster. It halted, wavered, reared, a black blot against the marble pillars. Again the sharp cloud sang, and yet again, and the horror collapsed and rolled down the steps, as dead as the witch who had summoned it out of the night of ages.

Conan drew rein beside the portico, leaped off. Valerius had laid the queen on the marble, sinking beside her in utter exhaustion. The people surged about, crowding in. The Cimmerian cursed them back, lifted her dark head, pillowed it against his mailed shoulder.

'By Crom, what is this? The real Taramis! But who is that yonder?'

'The demon who wore her shape,' panted Valerius.

Conan swore heartily. Ripping a cloak from the shoulders of a soldier, he wrapped it about the naked queen. Her long dark lashes quivered on her cheeks; her eyes opened, stared up unbelievingly into the Cimmerian's scarred face.

'Conan!' Her soft fingers caught at him. 'Do I dream? *She* told me you were dead—'

'Scarcely!' He grinned hardly. 'You do not dream. You are Queen of Khauran again. I broke Constantius, out there by the river. Most of his dogs never lived to reach the walls, for I gave orders that no prisoners be taken – except Constantius. The city guard closed the gate in our faces, but we burst in with rams swung from our saddles. I left all my wolves outside, except this fifty. I didn't trust them in here, and these Khaurani lads were enough for the gate guards.'

'It has been a nightmare!' she whimpered. 'Oh, my poor people! You must help me try to repay them for all they have suffered, Conan, henceforth councilor as well as captain!'

Conan laughed, but shook his head. Rising, he set the queen upon her feet, and beckoned to a number of his Khaurani horsemen who had not continued the pursuit of the fleeing Shemites. They sprang from their horses, eager to do the bidding of their new-found queen.

'No, lass, that's over with. I'm chief of the Zuagirs now, and must lead them to plunder the Turanians, as I promised. This lad, Valerius, will make you a better captain than I. I wasn't made to dwell among marble walls, anyway. But I must leave you now, and complete what I've begun. Shemites still live in Khauran.'

As Valerius started to follow Taramis across the square towards the palace, through a lane opened by the wildly cheering multitude, he felt a soft hand slipped timidly into his sinewy fingers and turned to receive the slender body of Ivga in his arms. He crushed her to him and drank her kisses with the gratitude of a weary fighter who has attained rest at last through tribulation and storm.

But not all men seek rest and peace; some are born with the spirit of the storm in their blood, restless harbingers of violence and bloodshed, knowing no other path ...

The sun was rising. The ancient caravan road was thronged with white-robed horsemen, in a wavering line that stretched from the walls of Khauran to a spot far out in the plain. Conan the Cimmerian sat at the head of that column, near the jagged end of a wooden beam that stuck up out of the ground. Near that stump rose a heavy cross, and on that cross a man hung by spikes through his hands and feet.

'Seven months ago, Constantius,' said Conan, 'it was I who hung there, and you who sat here.'

Constantius did not reply; he licked his gray lips and his eyes were glassy with pain and fear. Muscles writhed like cords along his lean body.

'You are more fit to inflict torture than to endure it,' said Conan tranquilly. 'I hung there on a cross as you are hanging, and I lived, thanks to circumstances and a stamina peculiar to barbarians. But you civilized men are soft; your lives are not nailed to your spines as are ours. Your fortitude consists mainly in inflicting torment, not in enduring it. You will be dead before sundown. And so, Falcon of the desert, I leave you to the companionship of another bird of the desert.'

He gestured toward the vultures whose shadows swept across the sands as they wheeled overhead. From the lips of Constantius came an inhuman cry of despair and horror.

Conan lifted his reins and rode toward the river that shone like silver in the morning sun. Behind him the white-clad riders struck into a trot; the gaze of each, as he passed a certain spot, turned impersonally and with the desert man's lack of compassion, toward the cross and the gaunt figure that hung there, black against the sunrise. Their horses' hoofs beat out a knell in the dust. Lower and lower swept the wings of the hungry vultures.

SHADOWS IN ZAMBOULA

1
A Drum Begins

'Peril hides in the house of Aram Baksh!'

The speaker's voice quivered with earnestness and his lean, black-nailed fingers clawed at Conan's mightily muscled arm as he croaked his warning. He was a wiry, sun-burnt man with a straggling black beard, and his ragged garments proclaimed him a nomad. He looked smaller and meaner than ever in contrast to the giant Cimmerian with his black brows, broad chest, and powerful limbs. They stood in a corner of the Sword-Makers' Bazar, and on either side of them flowed past the many-tongued, many-colored stream of the Zamboula streets, which is exotic, hybrid, flamboyant and clamorous.

Conan pulled his eyes back from following a bold-eyed, red-lipped Ghanara whose short skirt bared her brown thigh at each insolent step, and frowned down at his importunate companion.

'What do you mean by peril?' he demanded.

The desert man glanced furtively over his shoulder before replying, and lowered his voice.

'Who can say? But desert men and travelers *have* slept in the house of Aram Baksh, and never been seen or heard of again. What became of them? *He* swore they rose and went their way – and it is true that no citizen of the city has ever disappeared from his house. But no one saw the travelers again, and men say that goods and equipment recognized as theirs have been seen in the bazars. If Aram did not sell them, after doing away with their owners, how came they here?'

'I have no goods,' growled the Cimmerian, touching the

shagreen-bound hilt of the broadsword that hung at his hip. 'I have even sold my horse.'

'But it is not always rich strangers who vanish by night from the house of Aram Baksh!' chattered the Zuagir. 'Nay, poor desert men have slept there – because his score is less than that of the other taverns – and have been seen no more. Once a chief of the Zuagirs whose son had thus vanished complained to the satrap, Jungir Khan, who ordered the house searched by soldiers.'

'And they found a cellar full of corpses?' asked Conan in good-humored derision.

'Nay! They found naught! And drove the chief from the city with threats and curses! But – ' he drew closer to Conan and shivered – 'something else was found! At the edge of the desert, beyond the houses, there is a clump of palm trees, and within that grove there is a pit. And within that pit have been found human bones, charred and blackened! Not once, but many times!'

'Which proves what?' grunted the Cimmerian.

'Aram Baksh is a demon! Nay, in this accursed city which Stygians built and which Hyrkanians rule – where white, brown and black folk mingle together to produce hybrids of all unholy hues and breeds – who can tell who is a man, and who a demon in disguise? Aram Baksh is a demon in the form of a man! At night he assumes his true guise and carries his guests off into the desert where his fellow demons from the waste meet in conclave.'

'Why does he always carry off strangers?' asked Conan skeptically.

'The people of the city would not suffer him to slay their people, but they care naught for the strangers who fall into his hands. Conan, you are of the West, and know not the secrets of this ancient land. But, since the beginning of happenings, the demons of the desert have worshipped Yog, the Lord of the Empty Abodes, with fire – fire that devours human victims.

'Be warned! You have dwelt for many moons in the tents of the Zuagirs, and you are our brother! Go not to the house of Aram Baksh!'

'Get out of sight!' Conan said suddenly. 'Yonder comes a squad of the city-watch. If they see you they may remember a horse that was stolen from the satrap's stable—'

The Zuagir gasped, and moved convulsively. He ducked between a booth and a stone horse-trough, pausing only long enough to chatter: 'Be warned, my brother! There are demons in the house of Aram Baksh!' Then he darted down a narrow alley and was gone.

Conan shifted his broad sword-belt to his liking, and calmly returned the searching stares directed at him by the squad of watchmen as they swung past. They eyed him curiously and suspiciously, for he was a man who stood out even in such a motley throng as crowded the winding streets of Zamboula. His blue eyes and alien features distinguished him from the Eastern swarms, and the straight sword at his hip added point to the racial difference.

The watchmen did not accost him, but swung on down the street, while the crowd opened a lane for them. They were Pelishtim, squat, hook-nosed, with blue-black beards sweeping their mailed breasts – mercenaries hired for work the ruling Turanians considered beneath themselves, and no less hated by the mongrel population for that reason.

Conan glanced at the sun, just beginning to dip behind the flat-topped houses on the western side of the bazar, and hitching once more at his belt, moved off in the direction of Aram Baksh's tavern.

With a hillman's stride he moved through the ever-shifting colors of the streets, where the ragged tunics of whining beggars brushed against the ermine-trimmed khalats of lordly merchants, and the pearl-sewn satin of rich courtezans. Giant black slaves slouched along, jostling blue-bearded wanderers from the Shemitish cities, ragged nomads from the surrounding deserts, traders and adventurers from all the lands of the East.

The native population was no less heterogenous. Here, centuries ago, the armies of Stygia had come, carving an empire out of the eastern desert. Zamboula was but a small trading-town then, lying amidst a ring of oases, and inhabited by descendants of nomads. The Stygians built it into a city and settled it with their own people, and with Shemite and Kushite slaves. The ceaseless caravans, threading the desert from east to west and back again, brought riches and more mingling of races. Then came the conquering Turanians, riding out of the East to thrust back the boundaries of Stygia, and now for a generation Zamboula had been Turan's westernmost outpost, ruled by a Turanian satrap.

The babel of a myriad tongues smote on the Cimmerian's ears as the restless pattern of the Zamboula streets weaved about him – cleft now and then by a squad of clattering horsemen, the tall, supple warriors of Turan, with dark hawk-faces, clinking metal and curved swords. The throng scampered from under their horses' hoofs, for they were the lords of Zamboula. But tall, somber Stygians, standing back in the shadows, glowered darkly, remembering their ancient glories. The hybrid population cared little whether the king who controlled their destinies dwelt in dark Khemi or gleaming Aghrapur. Jungir Khan ruled Zamboula, and men whispered that Nafertari, the satrap's mistress, ruled Jungir Khan; but the people went their way, flaunting their myriad colors in the streets, bargaining, disputing, gambling, swilling, loving, as the people of Zamboula have done for all the centuries its towers and minarets have lifted over the sands of the Kharamun.

Bronze lanterns, carved with leering dragons, had been lighted in the streets before Conan reached the house of Aram Baksh. The tavern was the last occupied house on the street, which ran west. A wide garden, enclosed by a wall, where date-palms grew thick, separated it from the houses farther east. To the west of the inn stood another grove of palms, through which the street, now become a road, wound out into the desert. Across the road from the tavern stood a row of deserted huts, shaded by straggling palm trees, and occupied only by bats and jackals. As Conan came down the road he wondered why the beggars, so plentiful in Zamboula, had not appropriated these empty houses for sleeping quarters. The lights ceased some distance behind him. Here were no lanterns, except the one hanging before the tavern gate: only the stars, the soft dust of the road underfoot, and the rustle of the palm leaves in the desert breeze.

Aram's gate did not open upon the road, but upon the alley which ran between the tavern and the garden of the date-palms. Conan jerked lustily at the rope which depended from the bell beside the lantern, augmenting its clamor by hammering on the iron-bound teakwork gate with the hilt of his sword. A wicket opened in the gate and a black face peered through.

'Open, blast you,' requested Conan. 'I'm a guest. I've paid Aram for a room, and a room I'll have, by Crom!'

The black craned his neck to stare into the starlit road behind Conan; but he opened the gate without comment, and closed it again behind the Cimmerian, locking and bolting it. The wall was unusually high; but there were many thieves in Zamboula, and a house on the edge of the desert might have to be defended against a nocturnal nomad raid. Conan strode through a garden where great pale blossoms nodded in the starlight, and entered the tap-room, where a Stygian with the shaven head of a student sat at a table brooding over nameless mysteries, and some nondescripts wrangled over a game of dice in a corner.

Aram Baksh came forward, walking softly, a portly man, with a black beard that swept his breast, a jutting hook-nose, and small black eyes which were never still.

'You wish food?' he asked. 'Drink?'

'I ate a joint of beef and a loaf of bread in the *suk*,' grunted Conan. 'Bring me a tankard of Ghazan wine – I've got just enough left to pay for it.' He tossed a copper coin on the wine-splashed board.

'You did not win at the gaming-tables?'

'How could I, with only a handful of silver to begin with? I paid you for the room this morning, because I knew I'd probably lose. I wanted to be sure I had a roof over my head tonight. I notice nobody sleeps in the streets in Zamboula. The very beggars hunt a niche they can barricade before dark. The city must be full of a particularly bloodthirsty brand of thieves.'

He gulped the cheap wine with relish, and then followed Aram out of the tap-room. Behind him the players halted their game to stare after him with a cryptic speculation in their eyes. They said nothing, but the Stygian laughed, a ghastly laugh of inhuman cynicism and mockery. The others lowered their eyes uneasily, avoiding one another's glance. The arts studied by a Stygian scholar are not calculated to make him share the feelings of a normal human being.

Conan followed Aram down a corridor lighted by copper lamps, and it did not please him to note his host's noiseless tread. Aram's feet were clad in soft slippers and the hallway was carpeted with thick Turanian rugs; but there was an unpleasant suggestion of stealthiness about the Zamboulan.

At the end of the winding corridor Aram halted at a door, across which a heavy iron bar rested in powerful metal brackets. This Aram lifted and showed the Cimmerian into a well-appointed chamber, the windows of which, Conan instantly noted, were small and strongly set with twisted bars of iron, tastefully gilded. There were rugs on the floor, a couch, after the Eastern fashion, and ornately carved stools. It was a much more elaborate chamber than Conan could have procured for the price nearer the center of the city – a fact that had first attracted him, when, that morning, he discovered how slim a purse his roisterings for the past few days had left him. He had ridden into Zamboula from the desert a week before.

Aram had lighted a bronze lamp, and he now called Conan's attention to the two doors. Both were provided with heavy bolts.

'You may sleep safely tonight, Cimmerian,' said Aram, blinking over his bushy beard from the inner doorway.

Conan grunted and tossed his naked broadsword on the couch.

'Your bolts and bars are strong; but I always sleep with steel by my side.'

Aram made no reply; he stood fingering his thick beard for a moment as he stared at the grim weapon. Then silently he withdrew, closing the door behind him. Conan shot the bolt into place, crossed the room, opened the opposite door and looked out. The room was on the side of the house that faced the road running west from the city. The door opened into a small court that was enclosed by a wall of its own. The end-walls, which shut it off from the rest of the tavern compound, were high and without entrances; but the wall that flanked the road was low, and there was no lock on the gate.

Conan stood for a moment in the door, the glow of the bronze lamp behind him, looking down the road to where it vanished among the dense palms. Their leaves rustled together in the faint breeze; beyond them lay the naked desert. Far up the street, in the other direction, lights gleamed and the noises of the city came faintly to him. Here was only starlight, the whispering of the palm leaves, and beyond that low wall, the dust of the road and the deserted huts thrusting their flat roofs against the low stars. Somewhere beyond the palm groves a drum began.

The garbled warnings of the Zuagir returned to him, seeming somehow less fantastic than they had seemed in the crowded, sunlit streets. He wondered again at the riddle of those empty huts. Why did the beggars shun them? He turned back into the chamber, shut the door and bolted it.

The light began to flicker, and he investigated, swearing when he found the palm oil in the lamp was almost exhausted. He started to shout for Aram, then shrugged his shoulders and blew out the light. In the soft darkness he stretched himself fully clad on the couch, his sinewy hand by instinct searching for and closing on the hilt of his broadsword. Glancing idly at the stars framed in the barred windows, with the murmur of the breeze through the palms in his ears, he sank into slumber with a vague consciousness of the muttering drum, out on the desert – the low rumble and mutter of a leather-covered drum, beaten with soft, rhythmic strokes of an open black hand . . .

2

The Night Skulkers

It was the stealthy opening of a door which awakened the Cimmerian. He did not awake as civilized men do, drowsy and drugged and stupid. He awoke instantly, with a clear mind, recognizing the sound that had interrupted his sleep. Lying there tensely in the dark he saw the outer door slowly open. In a widening crack of starlit sky he saw framed a great black bulk, broad, stooping shoulders and a misshapen head blocked out against the stars.

Conan felt the skin crawl between his shoulders. He had bolted that door securely. How could it be opening now, save by supernatural agency? And how could a human being possess a head like that outlined against the stars? All the tales he had heard in the Zuagir tents of devils and goblins came back to bead his flesh with clammy sweat. Now the monster slid noiselessly into the room, with a crouching posture and a shambling gait; and a familiar scent assailed the Cimmerian's nostrils, but did not reassure him, since Zuagir legendry represented demons as smelling like that.

Noiselessly Conan coiled his long legs under him; his naked sword was in his right hand, and when he struck it was as suddenly and murderously as a tiger lunging out of the dark. Not even a demon could have avoided that catapulting charge. His sword met and clove through flesh and bone, and something went heavily to the floor with a strangling cry. Conan crouched in the dark above it, sword dripping in his hand. Devil or beast or man, the thing was dead there on the floor. He sensed death as any wild thing senses it. He glared through the half-open door into the starlit court beyond. The gate stood open, but the court was empty.

Conan shut the door but did not bolt it. Groping in the darkness he found the lamp and lighted it. There was enough oil in it to burn for a minute or so. An instant later he was bending over the figure that sprawled on the floor in a pool of blood.

It was a gigantic black man, naked but for a loin-cloth. One hand still grasped a knotty-headed bludgeon. The fellow's kinky wool was built up into horn-like spindles with twigs and dried mud. This barbaric coiffure had given the head its misshapen appearance in the starlight. Provided with a clue to the riddle, Conan pushed back the thick red lips, and grunted as he stared down at teeth filed to points.

He understood now the mystery of the strangers who had

disappeared from the house of Aram Baksh; the riddle of the black drum thrumming out there beyond the palm groves, and of that pit of charred bones – that pit where strange meat might be roasted under the stars, while black beasts squatted about to glut a hideous hunger. The man on the floor was a cannibal slave from Darfar.

There were many of his kind in the city. Cannibalism was not tolerated openly in Zamboula. But Conan knew now why people locked themselves in so securely at night, and why even beggars shunned the open alleys and doorless ruins. He grunted in disgust as he visualized brutish black shadows skulking up and down the nighted streets, seeking human prey – and such men as Aram Baksh to open the doors to them. The innkeeper was not a demon; he was worse. The slaves from Darfar were notorious thieves; there was no doubt that some of their pilfered loot found its way into the hands of Aram Baksh. And in return he sold them human flesh.

Conan blew out the light, stepped to the door and opened it, and ran his hand over the ornaments on the outer side. One of them was movable and worked the bolt inside. The room was a trap to catch human prey like rabbits. But this time instead of a rabbit it had caught a saber-toothed tiger.

Conan returned to the other door, lifted the bolt and pressed against it. It was immovable and he remembered the bolt on the other side. Aram was taking no chances either with his victims or the men with whom he dealt. Buckling on his sword-belt, the Cimmerian strode out into the court, closing the door behind him. He had no intention of delaying the settlement of his reckoning with Aram Baksh. He wondered how many poor devils had been bludgeoned in their sleep and dragged out of that room and down the road that ran through the shadowed palm groves to the roasting-pit.

He halted in the court. The drum was still muttering, and he caught the reflection of a leaping red glare through the groves. Cannibalism was more than a perverted appetite with the black men of Darfar; it was an integral element of their ghastly cult.

The black vultures were already in conclave. But whatever flesh filled their bellies that night, it would not be his.

To reach Aram Baksh he must climb one of the walls which separated the small enclosure from the main compound. They were high, meant to keep out the man-eaters; but Conan was no swamp-bred black man; his thews had been steeled in boyhood on the sheer cliffs of his native hills. He was standing at the foot of the nearer wall when a cry echoed under the trees.

In an instant Conan was crouching at the gate, glaring down the road. The sound had come from the shadows of the huts across the road. He heard a frantic choking and gurgling such as might result from a desperate attempt to shriek, with a black hand fastened over the victim's mouth. A close-knit clump of figures emerged from the shadows beyond the huts, and started down the road – three huge black men carrying a slender, struggling figure between them. Conan caught the glimmer of pale limbs writhing in the starlight, even as, with a convulsive wrench, the captive slipped from the grasp of the brutal fingers and came flying up the road, a supple young woman, naked as the day she was born. Conan saw her plainly before she ran out of the road and into the shadows between the huts. The blacks were at her heels, and back in the shadows the figures merged and an intolerable scream of anguish and horror rang out.

Stirred to red rage by the ghoulishness of the episode, Conan raced across the road.

Neither victim nor abductors were aware of his presence until the soft swish of the dust about his feet brought them about, and then he was almost upon them, coming with the gusty fury of a hill wind. Two of the blacks turned to meet him, lifting their bludgeons. But they failed to estimate properly the speed at which he was coming. One of them was down, disemboweled, before he could strike, and wheeling cat-like, Conan evaded the stroke of the other's cudgel and lashed in a whistling counter-cut. The black's head flew into the air; the headless body took three staggering steps, spurting blood and clawing horribly at the air with groping hands, and then slumped to the dust.

The remaining cannibal gave back with a strangled yell, hurling his captive from him. She tripped and rolled in the dust, and the black fled in blind panic toward the city. Conan was at his heels. Fear winged the black feet, but before they reached the easternmost hut, he sensed death at his back, and bellowed like an ox in the slaughter-yards.

'Black dog of hell!' Conan drove his sword between the dusky shoulders with such vengeful fury that the broad blade stood out half its length from the black breast. With a choking cry the black stumbled headlong, and Conan braced his feet and dragged out his sword as his victim fell.

Only the breeze disturbed the leaves. Conan shook his head as a lion shakes its mane and growled his unsatiated blood-lust. But no more shapes slunk from the shadows, and before the huts the starlit road stretched empty. He whirled at the quick patter of feet behind him, but it was only the girl, rushing to throw herself on him and clasp his neck in a desperate grasp, frantic from terror of the abominable fate she had just escaped.

'Easy, girl,' he grunted. 'You're all right. How did they catch you?'

She sobbed something unintelligible. He forgot all about Aram Baksh as he scrutinized her by the light of the stars. She was white, though a very definite brunette, obviously one of Zamboula's many mixed breeds. She was tall, with a slender, supple form, as he was in a good position to observe. Admiration burned in his fierce eyes as he looked down on her splendid bosom and her lithe limbs, which still quivered from fright and exertion. He passed an arm around her flexible waist and said, reassuringly: 'Stop shaking, wench; you're safe enough.'

His touch seemed to restore her shaken sanity. She tossed back her thick, glossy locks and cast a fearful glance over her shoulder, while she pressed closer to the Cimmerian as if seeking security in the contact.

'They caught me in the streets,' she muttered, shuddering. 'Lying in wait, beneath a dark arch – black men, like great, hulking apes! Set have mercy on me! I shall dream of it!'

'What were you doing out on the streets this time of night?' he inquired, fascinated by the satiny feel of her sleek skin under his questing fingers.

She raked back her hair and stared blankly up into his face. She did not seem aware of his caresses.

'My lover,' she said. 'My lover drove me into the streets. He went mad and tried to kill me. As I fled from him I was seized by those beasts.'

'Beauty like yours might drive a man mad,' quoth Conan, running his fingers experimentally through her glossy tresses.

She shook her head, like one emerging from a daze. She no longer trembled, and her voice was steady.

'It was the spite of a priest – of Totrasmek, the high priest of Hanuman, who desires me for himself – the dog!'

'No need to curse him for that,' grinned Conan. 'The old hyena has better taste than I thought.'

She ignored the bluff compliment. She was regaining her poise swiftly.

'My lover is a – a young Turanian soldier. To spite me, Totrasmek gave him a drug that drove him mad. Tonight he snatched up a sword and came at me to slay me in his madness, but I fled from him into the streets. The negroes seized me and brought me to this – *what was that?*'

Conan had already moved. Soundlessly as a shadow he drew her behind the nearest hut, beneath the straggling palms. They stood in tense stillness, while the low mutterings both had heard grew louder until voices were distinguishable. A group of negroes, some nine or ten, were coming along the road from the direction of the city. The girl clutched Conan's arm and he felt the terrified quivering of her supple body against his.

Now they could understand the gutturals of the black men.

'Our brothers have already assembled at the pit,' said one. 'We have had no luck. I hope they have enough for us.'

'Aram promised us a man,' muttered another, and Conan mentally promised Aram something.

'Aram keeps his word,' grunted yet another. 'Many a man we

have taken from his tavern. But we pay him well. I myself have given him ten bales of silk I stole from my master. It was good silk, by Set!'

The blacks shuffled past, bare splay feet scuffing up the dust, and their voices dwindled down the road.

'Well for us those corpses are lying behind these huts,' muttered Conan. 'If they look in Aram's death-room they'll find another. Let's begone.'

'Yes, let us hasten!' begged the girl, almost hysterical again. 'My lover is wandering somewhere in the streets alone. The negroes may take him.'

'A devil of a custom this is!' growled Conan, as he led the way toward the city, paralleling the road but keeping behind the huts and straggling trees. 'Why don't the citizens clean out these black dogs?'

'They are valuable slaves,' murmured the girl. 'There are so many of them they might revolt if they were denied the flesh for which they lust. The people of Zamboula know they skulk the streets at night, and all are careful to remain within locked doors, except when something unforeseen happens, as it did to me. The blacks prey on anything they catch, but they seldom catch anybody but strangers. The people of Zamboula are not concerned with the strangers that pass through the city.

'Such men as Aram Baksh sell these strangers to the blacks. He would not dare attempt such a thing with a citizen.'

Conan spat in disgust, and a moment later led his companion out into the road which was becoming a street, with still, unlighted houses on each side. Slinking in the shadows was not congenial to his nature.

'Where do you want to go?' he asked. The girl did not seem to object to his arm about her waist.

'To my house, to rouse my servants,' she answered. 'To bid them search for my lover. I do not wish the city – the priests – anyone – to know of his madness. He – he is a young officer with a promising future. Perhaps we can drive this madness from him if we can find him.'

'If *we* find him?' rumbled Conan. 'What makes you think I want to spend the night scouring the streets for a lunatic?'

She cast a quick glance into his face, and properly interpreted the gleam in his blue eyes. Any woman could have known that he would follow her wherever she led – for a while, at least. But being a woman, she concealed her knowledge of that fact.

'Please,' she began with a hint of tears in her voice, 'I have no one else to ask for help – you have been kind—'

'All right!' he grunted. 'All right! What's the young reprobate's name?'

'Why – Alafdhal. I am Zabibi, a dancing-girl. I have danced often before the satrap, Jungir Khan, and his mistress Nafertari, and before all the lords and royal ladies of Zamboula. Totrasmek desired me, and because I repulsed him, he made me the innocent tool of his vengeance against Alafdhal. I asked a love potion of Totrasmek, not suspecting the depth of his guile and hate. He gave me a drug to mix with my lover's wine, and he swore that when Alafdhal drank it, he would love me even more madly than ever, and grant my every wish. I mixed the drug secretly with my lover's wine. But having drunk, my lover went raving mad and things came about as I have told you. Curse Totrasmek, the hybrid snake – ahhh!'

She caught his arm convulsively and both stopped short. They had come into a district of shops and stalls, all deserted and unlighted, for the hour was late. They were passing an alley, and in its mouth a man was standing, motionless and silent. His head was lowered, but Conan caught the weird gleam of eery eyes regarding them unblinkingly. His skin crawled, not with fear of the sword in the man's hand, but because of the uncanny suggestion of his posture and silence. They suggested madness. Conan pushed the girl aside and drew his sword.

'Don't kill him!' she begged. 'In the name of Set, do not slay him! You are strong – overpower him!'

'We'll see,' he muttered, grasping his sword in his right hand and clenching his left into a mallet-like fist.

He took a wary step toward the alley – and with a horrible moaning laugh the Turanian charged. As he came he swung his sword, rising on his toes as he put all the power of his body behind the blows. Sparks flashed blue as Conan parried the blade, and the next instant the madman was stretched senseless in the dust from a thundering buffet of Conan's left fist.

The girl ran forward.

'Oh, he is not – he is not—'

Conan bent swiftly, turned the man on his side and ran quick fingers over him.

'He's not hurt much,' he grunted. 'Bleeding at the nose, but anybody's likely to do that, after a clout on the jaw. He'll come to after a bit, and maybe his mind will be right. In the meantime I'll tie his wrists with his sword-belt – so. Now where do you want me to take him?'

'Wait!' She knelt beside the senseless figure, seized the bound hands and scanned them avidly. Then, shaking her head as if in baffled disappointment, she rose. She came close to the giant Cimmerian, and laid her slender hands on his arching breast. Her dark eyes, like wet black jewels in the starlight, gazed up into his.

'You are a man! Help me! Totrasmek must die! Slay him for me!'

'And put my neck into a Turanian noose?' he grunted.

'Nay!' The slender arms, strong as pliant steel, were around his corded neck. Her supple body throbbed against his. 'The Hyrkanians have no love for Totrasmek. The priests of Set fear him. He is a mongrel, who rules men by fear and superstition. I worship Set, and the Turanians bow to Erlik, but Totrasmek sacrifices to Hanuman the accursed! The Turanian lords fear his black arts and his power over the hybrid population, and they hate him. If he were slain in his temple at night, they would not seek his slayer very closely.'

'And what of his magic?' rumbled the Cimmerian.

'You are a fighting-man,' she answered. 'To risk your life is part of your profession.'

'For a price,' he admitted.

'There will be a price!' she breathed, rising on tiptoe, to gaze into his eyes.

The nearness of her vibrant body drove a flame through his veins. The perfume of her breath mounted to his brain. But as his arms closed about her supple figure she avoided them with a lithe movement, saying: 'Wait! First serve me in this matter.'

'Name your price.' He spoke with some difficulty.

'Pick up my lover,' she directed, and the Cimmerian stooped and swung the tall form easily to his broad shoulder. At the moment he felt as if he could have toppled over Jungir Khan's palace with equal ease. The girl murmured an endearment to the unconscious man, and there was no hypocrisy in her attitude. She obviously loved Alafdhal sincerely. Whatever business arrangement she made with Conan would have no bearing on her relationship with Alafdhal. Women are more practical about these things than men.

'Follow me!' She hurried along the street, while the Cimmerian strode easily after her, in no way discomforted by his limp burden. He kept a wary eye out for black shadows skulking under arches, but saw nothing suspicious. Doubtless the men of Darfar were all gathered at the roasting-pit. The girl turned down a narrow side street, and presently knocked cautiously at an arched door.

Almost instantly a wicket opened in the upper panel, and a black face glanced out. She bent close to the opening, whispering swiftly. Bolts creaked in their sockets, and the door opened. A giant black man stood framed against the soft glow of a copper lamp. A quick glance showed Conan the man was not from Darfar. His teeth were unfiled and his kinky hair was cropped close to his skull. He was from the Wadai.

At a word from Zabibi, Conan gave the limp body into the black's arms, and saw the young officer laid on a velvet divan. He showed no signs of returning consciousness. The blow that had rendered him senseless might have felled an ox. Zabibi bent over him for an instant, her fingers nervously twining and twisting. Then she straightened and beckoned the Cimmerian.

The door closed softly, the locks clicked behind them, and the closing wicket shut off the glow of the lamps. In the starlight of the street Zabibi took Conan's hand. Her own hand trembled a little.

'You will not fail me?'

He shook his maned head, massive against the stars.

'Then follow me to Hanuman's shrine, and the gods have mercy on our souls!'

Along the silent streets they moved like phantoms of antiquity. They went in silence. Perhaps the girl was thinking of her lover lying senseless on the divan under the copper lamps; or was shrinking with fear of what lay ahead of them in the demon-haunted shrine of Hanuman. The barbarian was thinking only of the woman moving so supplely beside him. The perfume of her scented hair was in his nostrils, the sensuous aura of her presence filled his brain and left room for no other thoughts.

Once they heard the clank of brass-shod feet, and drew into the shadows of a gloomy arch while a squad of Pelishtim watchmen swung past. There were fifteen of them; they marched in close formation, pikes at the ready, and the rearmost men had their broad brass shields slung on their backs, to protect them from a knife-stroke from behind. The skulking menace of the black man-eaters was a threat even to armed men.

As soon as the clang of their sandals had receded up the street, Conan and the girl emerged from their hiding-place and hurried on. A few moments later they saw the squat, flat-topped edifice they sought looming ahead of them.

The temple of Hanuman stood alone in the midst of a broad square, which lay silent and deserted beneath the stars. A marble wall surrounded the shrine, with a broad opening directly before the portico. This opening had no gate or any sort of barrier.

'Why don't the blacks seek their prey here?' muttered Conan. 'There's nothing to keep them out of the temple.'

He could feel the trembling of Zabibi's body as she pressed close to him.

'They fear Totrasmek, as all in Zamboula fear him, even Jungir Khan and Nafertari. Come! Come quickly, before my courage flows from me like water!'

The girl's fear was evident, but she did not falter. Conan drew his sword and strode ahead of her as they advanced through the open gateway. He knew the hideous habits of the priests of the East, and was aware that an invader of Hanuman's shrine might expect to encounter almost any sort of nightmare horror. He knew there was a good chance that neither he nor the girl would ever leave the shrine alive, but he had risked his life too many times before to devote much thought to that consideration.

They entered a court paved with marble which gleamed whitely in the starlight. A short flight of broad marble steps led up to the pillared portico. The great bronze doors stood wide open as they had stood for centuries. But no worshippers burnt incense within. In the day men and women might come timidly into the shrine and place offerings to the ape-god on the black altar. At night the people shunned the temple of Hanuman as hares shun the lair of the serpent.

Burning censers bathed the interior in a soft weird glow that created an illusion of unreality. Near the rear wall, behind the black stone altar, sat the god with his gaze fixed for ever on the open door, through which for centuries his victims had come, dragged by chains of roses. A faint groove ran from the sill to the altar, and when Conan's foot felt it, he stepped away as quickly as if he had trodden upon a snake. That groove had been worn by the faltering feet of the multitude of those who had died screaming on that grim altar.

Bestial in the uncertain light Hanuman leered with his carven mask. He sat, not as an ape would crouch, but cross-legged as a man would sit, but his aspect was no less simian for that reason. He was carved from black marble, but his eyes were rubies, which glowed red and lustful as the coals of hell's deepest pits. His great hands lay upon his lap, palms upward, taloned fingers spread and grasping. In the gross emphasis of his attributes, in the leer of his satyr-countenance, was reflected the abominable cynicism of the degenerate cult which deified him.

The girl moved around the image, making toward the back wall, and when her sleek flank brushed against a carven knee, she shrank aside and shuddered as if a reptile had touched her. There was a space of several feet between the broad back of the idol and the marble wall with its frieze of gold leaves. On either hand, flanking the idol, an ivory door under a gold arch was set in the wall.

'Those doors open into each end of a hair-pin shaped corridor,' she said hurriedly. 'Once I was in the interior of the shrine – once!' She shivered and twitched her slim shoulders at a memory both terrifying and obscene. 'The corridor is bent like a horseshoe, with each horn opening into this room. Totrasmek's chambers are enclosed within the curve of the corridor and open into it. But there is a secret door in this wall which opens directly into an inner chamber—'

She began to run her hands over the smooth surface, where no crack or crevice showed. Conan stood beside her, sword in hand, glancing warily about him. The silence, the emptiness of the shrine, with imagination picturing what might lie behind that wall, made him feel like a wild beast nosing a trap.

'Ah!' The girl had found a hidden spring at last; a square opening gaped blackly in the wall. 'Set!' she screamed, and even as Conan leaped toward her, he saw that a great misshapen hand had fastened itself in her hair. She was snatched off her feet and jerked headfirst through the opening. Conan, grabbing ineffectually at her, felt his fingers slip from a naked limb, and in an instant she had vanished and the wall showed blank as before. Only from beyond it came briefly the muffled sounds of a struggle, a scream, faintly heard, and a low laugh that made Conan's blood congeal in his veins.

3

Black Hands Gripping

With an oath the Cimmerian smote the wall a terrific blow with the pommel of his sword, and the marble cracked and chipped. But the hidden door did not give way, and reason told him that doubtless it had been bolted on the other side of the wall. Turning, he sprang across the chamber to one of the ivory doors.

He lifted his sword to shatter the panels, but on a venture tried the door first with his left hand. It swung open easily, and he glared into a long corridor that curved away into dimness under the weird light of censers similar to those in the shrine. A heavy gold bolt showed on the jamb of the door, and he touched it lightly with his finger tips. The faint warmness of the metal could have been detected only by a man whose faculties were akin to those of a wolf. That bolt had been touched – and therefore drawn – within the last few seconds. The affair was taking on more and more of the aspect of a baited trap. He might have known Totrasmek would know when anyone entered the temple.

To enter the corridor would undoubtedly be to walk into whatever trap the priest had set for him. But Conan did not hesitate. Somewhere in that dim-lit interior Zabibi was a captive, and, from what he knew of the characteristics of Hanuman's priests, he was sure that she needed help badly. Conan stalked into the corridor with a pantherish tread, poised to strike right or left.

On his left, ivory, arched doors opened into the corridor, and he tried each in turn. All were locked. He had gone perhaps seventy-five feet when the corridor bent sharply to the left, describing the curve the girl had mentioned. A door opened into this curve, and it gave under his hand.

He was looking into a broad, square chamber, somewhat more clearly lighted than the corridor. Its walls were of white marble, the floor of ivory, the ceiling of fretted silver. He saw divans of rich satin, gold-worked footstools of ivory, a disk-shaped table of some massive, metal-like substance. On one of the divans a man was reclining, looking toward the door. He laughed as he met the Cimmerian's startled glare.

This man was naked except for a loin-cloth and high-strapped sandals. He was brown-skinned, with close-cropped black hair and restless black eyes that set off a broad, arrogant face. In girth and breadth he was enormous, with huge limbs on which the great muscles swelled and rippled at each slightest movement. His hands were the largest Conan had ever seen. The assurance of gigantic physical strength colored his every action and inflection.

'Why not enter, barbarian?' he called mockingly, with an exaggerated gesture of invitation.

Conan's eyes began to smolder ominously, but he trod warily into the chamber, his sword ready.

'Who the devil are you?' he growled.

'I am Baal-pteor,' the man answered. 'Once, long ago and in another land, I had another name. But this is a good name, and why Totrasmek gave it to me, any temple wench can tell you.'

'So you're his dog!' grunted Conan. 'Well, curse your brown hide, Baal-pteor, where's the wench you jerked through the wall?'

'My master entertains her!' laughed Baal-pteor. 'Listen!'

From beyond a door opposite the one by which Conan had entered there sounded a woman's scream, faint and muffled in the distance.

'Blast your soul!' Conan took a stride toward the door, then wheeled with his skin tingling. Baal-pteor was laughing at him, and that laugh was edged with menace that made the hackles rise on Conan's neck and sent a red wave of murder-lust driving across his vision.

He started toward Baal-pteor, the knuckles on his sword-hand showing white. With a swift motion the brown man threw something at him – a shining crystal sphere that glistened in the weird light.

Conan dodged instinctively, but, miraculously, the globe stopped short in midair, a few feet from his face. It did not fall to the floor. It hung suspended, as if by invisible filaments, some five feet above the floor. And as he glared in amazement, it began to rotate with growing speed. And as it revolved it grew, expanded, became nebulous. It filled the chamber. It enveloped him. It blotted out furniture, walls, the smiling countenance of Baal-pteor. He was lost in the midst of a blinding bluish blur of whirling speed. Terrific winds screamed past Conan, tugging, tearing at him, striving to wrench him from his feet, to drag him into the vortex that spun madly before him.

With a choking cry Conan lurched backward, reeled, felt the solid wall against his back. At the contact the illusion ceased to be. The whirling, titanic sphere vanished like a bursting bubble. Conan reeled upright in the silver-ceilinged room, with a gray mist coiling about his feet, and saw Baal-pteor lolling on the divan, shaking with silent laughter.

'Son of a slut!' Conan lunged at him. But the mist swirled up from the floor, blotting out that giant brown form. Groping in a rolling cloud that blinded him, Conan felt a rending sensation of dislocation – and then room and mist and brown man were gone together. He was standing alone among the high reeds of a marshy fen, and a buffalo was lunging at him, head down. He leaped aside from the ripping scimitar-curved horns, and drove his sword in behind the foreleg, through ribs and heart. And then it was not a buffalo dying there in the mud, but the brown-skinned Baal-pteor. With a curse Conan struck off his head; and the head soared from the ground and snapped beast-like tusks into his throat. For all his mighty strength he could not tear it loose – he was choking – strangling; then there was a rush and roar through space, the dislocating shock of an immeasurable impact, and he was back in the chamber with Baal-pteor, whose head was once more set firmly on his shoulders, and who laughed silently at him from the divan.

'Mesmerism!' muttered Conan, crouching and digging his toes hard against the marble.

His eyes blazed. This brown dog was playing with him, making sport of him! But this mummery, this child's play of mists and shadows of thought, it could not harm him. He had but to leap and strike and the brown acolyte would be a mangled corpse under his heel. This time he would not be fooled by shadows of illusion – but he was.

A blood-curdling snarl sounded behind him, and he wheeled and struck in a flash at the panther crouching to spring on him from the metal-colored table. Even as he struck, the apparition vanished and his blade clashed deafeningly on the adamantine surface. Instantly he sensed something abnormal. The blade stuck to the table! He wrenched at it savagely. It did not give. This was no mesmeristic trick. The table was a giant magnet. He gripped the hilt with both hands, when a voice at his shoulder brought him about, to face the brown man, who had at last risen from the divan.

Slightly taller than Conan, and much heavier, Baal-pteor loomed before him, a daunting image of muscular development. His mighty arms were unnaturally long, and his great hands opened and closed, twitching convulsively. Conan released the hilt of his imprisoned sword and fell silent, watching his enemy through slitted lids.

'Your head, Cimmerian!' taunted Baal-pteor. 'I shall take it with my bare hands, twisting it from your shoulders as the head of a fowl is twisted! Thus the sons of Kosala offer sacrifice to Yajur. Barbarian, you look upon a strangler of Yota-pong. I was chosen by the priests of Yajur in my infancy, and throughout childhood, boyhood and youth I trained in the art of slaying with the naked hands – for only thus are the sacrifices enacted. Yajur loves blood, and we waste not a drop from the victim's veins. When I was a child they gave me infants to throttle; when I was a boy I strangled young girls; as a youth, women, old men and young boys. Not until I reached my full manhood was I given a strong man to slay on the altar of Yota-pong.

'For years I offered the sacrifices to Yajur. Hundreds of necks have snapped between these fingers—' he worked them before the Cimmerian's angry eyes. 'Why I fled from Yota-pong to become Totrasmek's servant is no concern of yours. In a moment you will be beyond curiosity. The priests of Kosala, the stranglers of Yajur, are strong beyond the belief of men. And I was stronger than any. With my hands, barbarian, I shall break your neck!'

And like the stroke of twin cobras, the great hands closed on Conan's throat. The Cimmerian made no attempt to dodge or fend them away, but his own hands darted to the Kosalan's bull-neck. Baal-pteor's black eyes widened as he felt the thick cords of muscles that protected the barbarian's throat. With a snarl he exerted his inhuman strength, and knots and lumps and ropes of thews rose along his massive arms. And then a choking gasp burst from him as Conan's fingers locked on his throat. For an instant they stood there like statues, their faces masks of effort, veins beginning to stand out purply on their temples. Conan's thin lips drew back from his teeth in a grinning snarl. Baal-pteor's eyes were distended; in them grew an awful surprize and the glimmer of fear. Both men stood motionless as images, except for the expanding of their muscles on rigid arms and braced legs, but strength beyond common conception was warring there – strength that might have uprooted trees and crushed the skulls of bullocks.

The wind whistled suddenly from between Baal-pteor's parted teeth. His face was growing purple. Fear flooded his eyes. His thews seemed ready to burst from his arms and shoulders, yet the muscles of the Cimmerian's thick neck did not give; t3hey felt like masses of woven iron cords under his desperate fingers. But his own flesh was giving way under the iron fingers of the Cimmerian which ground deeper and deeper into the yielding throat-muscles, crushing them in upon jugular and windpipe.

The statuesque immobility of the group gave way to sudden, frenzied motion, as the Kosalan began to wrench and heave, seeking to throw himself backward. He let go of Conan's throat and grasped his wrists, trying to tear away those inexorable fingers.

With a sudden lunge Conan bore him backward until the small of his back crashed against the table. And still farther over its edge Conan bent him, back and back, until his spine was ready to snap.

Conan's low laugh was merciless as the ring of steel.

'You fool!' he all but whispered. 'I think you never saw a man from the West before. Did you deem yourself strong, because you were able to twist the heads off civilized folk, poor weaklings with muscles like rotten string? Hell! Break the neck of a wild Cimmerian bull before you call yourself strong. I did that, before I was a full-grown man – like this!'

And with a savage wrench he twisted Baal-pteor's head around until the ghastly face leered over the left shoulder, and the vertebrae snapped like a rotten branch.

Conan hurled the flopping corpse to the floor, turned to the sword again and gripped the hilt with both hands, bracing his feet against the floor. Blood trickled down his broad breast from the wounds Baal-pteor's finger nails had torn in the skin of his neck.

His black hair was damp, sweat ran down his face, and his chest heaved. For all his vocal scorn of Baal-pteor's strength, he had almost met his match in the inhuman Kosalan. But without pausing to catch his breath, he exerted all his strength in a mighty wrench that tore the sword from the magnet where it clung.

Another instant and he had pushed open the door from behind which the scream had sounded, and was looking down a long straight corridor, lined with ivory doors. The other end was masked by a rich velvet curtain, and from beyond that curtain came the devilish strains of such music as Conan had never heard, not even in nightmares. It made the short hairs bristle on the back of his neck. Mingled with it was the panting, hysterical sobbing of a woman. Grasping his sword firmly, he glided down the corridor.

4

Dance, Girl, Dance!

When Zabibi was jerked head-first through the aperture which opened in the wall behind the idol, her first, dizzy, disconnected thought was that her time had come. She instinctively shut her eyes and waited for the blow to fall. But instead she felt herself dumped unceremoniously onto the smooth marble floor, which bruised her knees and hip. Opening her eyes she stared fearfully around her, just as a muffled impact sounded from beyond the wall. She saw a brown-skinned giant in a loin-cloth standing over her, and, across the chamber into which she had come, a man sat on a divan, with his back to a rich velvet curtain, a broad, fleshy man, with fat white hands and snaky eyes. And her flesh crawled, for this man was Totrasmek, the priest of Hanuman, who for years had spun his slimy webs of power throughout the city of Zamboula.

'The barbarian seeks to batter his way through the wall,' said Totrasmek sardonically, 'but the bolt will hold.'

The girl saw that a heavy golden bolt had been shot across the hidden door, which was plainly discernible from this side of the wall. The bolt and its sockets would have resisted the charge of an elephant.

'Go open one of the doors for him, Baal-pteor,' ordered Totrasmek. 'Slay him in the square chamber at the other end of the corridor.'

The Kosalan salaamed and departed by the way of a door in the side wall of the chamber. Zabibi rose, staring fearfully at the priest, whose eyes ran avidly over her splendid figure. To this she was indifferent. A dancer of Zamboula was accustomed to nakedness. But the cruelty in his eyes started her limbs to quivering.

'Again you come to me in my retreat, beautiful one,' he purred with cynical hypocrisy. 'It is an unexpected honor. You seemed to enjoy your former visit so little, that I dared not hope for you to repeat it. Yet I did all in my power to provide you with an interesting experience.'

For a Zamboulan dancer to blush would be an impossibility, but a smolder of anger mingled with the fear in Zabibi's dilated eyes.

'Fat pig! You know I did not come here for love of you.'

'No,' laughed Totrasmek, 'you came like a fool, creeping through the night with a stupid barbarian to cut my throat. Why should you seek my life?'

'You know why!' she cried, knowing the futility of trying to dissemble.

'You are thinking of your lover,' he laughed. 'The fact that you are here seeking my life shows that he quaffed the drug I gave you. Well, did you not ask for it? And did I not send what you asked for, out of the love I bear you?'

'I asked you for a drug that would make him slumber harmlessly for a few hours,' she said bitterly. 'And you – you sent your servant with a drug that drove him mad! I was a fool ever to trust you. I might have known your protestations of friendship were lies, to disguise your hate and spite.'

'Why did you wish your lover to sleep?' he retorted. 'So you could steal from him the only thing he would never give you – the ring with the jewel men call the Star of Khorala – the star stolen from the Queen of Ophir, who would pay a roomful of gold for its return. He would not give it to you willingly, because he knew that it holds a magic which, when properly controlled, will enslave the hearts of any of the opposite sex. You wished to steal it from him, fearing that his magicians would discover the key to that magic and he would forget you in his conquests of the queens of the world. You would sell it back to the queen of Ophir, who understands its power and would use it to enslave men, as she did before it was stolen.'

'And why did *you* want it?' she demanded sulkily.

'I understand its powers. It would increase the power of my arts.'

'Well,' she snapped, 'you have it now!'

'*I* have the Star of Khorala? Nay, you err.'

'Why bother to lie?' she retorted bitterly. 'He had it on his finger when he drove me into the streets. He did not have it when I found him again. Your servant must have been watching the house, and have taken it from him, after I escaped him. To the devil with it! I want my lover back sane and whole. You have the ring; you have punished us both. Why do you not restore his mind to him? Can you?'

'I could,' he assured her, in evident enjoyment of her distress. He drew a phial from among his robes. 'This contains the juice of the golden lotus. If your lover drank it he would be sane again. Yes, I will be merciful. You have both thwarted and flouted me, not once but many times; he has constantly opposed my wishes. But I will be merciful. Come and take the phial from my hand.'

She stared at Totrasmek, trembling with eagerness to seize it, but fearing it was but some cruel jest. She advanced timidly, with a hand extended, and he laughed heartlessly and drew back out of her reach. Even as her lips parted to curse him, some instinct snatched her eyes upward. From the gilded ceiling four jade-hued vessels were falling. She dodged, but they did not strike her. They crashed to the floor about her, forming the four corners of a square. And she screamed, and screamed again. For out of each ruin reared the hooded head of a cobra, and one struck at her bare leg. Her convulsive movement to evade it brought her within reach of the one on the other side and again she had to shift like lightning to avoid the flash of its hideous head.

She was caught in a frightful trap. All four serpents were swaying and striking at foot, ankle, calf, knee, thigh, hip, whatever portion of her voluptuous body chanced to be nearest to them, and she could not spring over them or pass between them to safety. She could only whirl and spring aside and twist her body to avoid the strokes, and each time she moved to dodge one snake, the motion brought her within range of another, so that she had to keep shifting with the speed of light. She could move only a short space in any direction, and the fearful hooded crests were menacing her every second. Only a dancer of Zamboula could have lived in that grisly square.

She became, herself, a blur of bewildering motion. The heads missed her by hair's breadths, but they missed, as she pitted her twinkling feet, flickering limbs and perfect eye against the blinding speed of the scaly demons her enemy had conjured out of thin air.

Somewhere a thin whining music struck up, mingling with the hissing of the serpents, like an evil night-wind blowing through the empty sockets of a skull. Even in the flying speed of her urgent haste she realized that the darting of the serpents was no longer at random. They obeyed the grisly piping of the eery music. They struck with a horrible rhythm, and perforce her swaying, writhing, spinning body attuned itself to their rhythm. Her frantic motions melted into the measures of a dance compared to which the most obscene tarantella of Zamora would have seemed sane and restrained. Sick with shame and terror Zabibi heard the hateful mirth of her merciless tormentor.

'The Dance of the Cobras, my lovely one!' laughed Totrasmek. 'So maidens danced in the sacrifice to Hanuman centuries ago – but never with such beauty and suppleness. Dance, girl, dance! How long can you avoid the fangs of the Poison People? Minutes? Hours? You will weary at last. Your swift, sure feet will stumble, your legs falter, your hips slow in their rotations. Then the fangs will begin to sink deep into your ivory flesh—'

Behind him the curtain shook as if struck by a gust of wind, and Totrasmek screamed. His eyes dilated and his hands caught convulsively at the length of bright steel which jutted suddenly from his breast.

The music broke off short. The girl swayed dizzily in her dance, crying out in dreadful anticipation of the flickering fangs – and then only four wisps of harmless blue smoke curled up from the floor about her, as Totrasmek sprawled headlong from the divan.

Conan came from behind the curtain, wiping his broad blade. Looking through the hangings he had seen the girl dancing desperately between four swaying spirals of smoke, but he had guessed that their appearance was very different to her. He knew he had killed Totrasmek.

Zabibi sank down on the floor, panting, but even as Conan started toward her, she staggered up again, though her legs trembled with exhaustion.

'The phial!' she gasped. 'The phial!'

Totrasmek still grasped it in his stiffening hand. Ruthlessly she tore it from his locked fingers, and then began frantically to ransack his garments.

'What the devil are you looking for?' Conan demanded.

'A ring – he stole it from Alafdhal. He must have, while my lover walked in madness through the streets. Set's devils!'

She had convinced herself that it was not on the person of Totrasmek. She began to cast about the chamber, tearing up divan-covers and hangings, and upsetting vessels.

She paused and raked a damp lock of hair out of her eyes.

'I forgot Baal-pteor!'

'He's in hell with his neck broken,' Conan assured her.

She expressed vindictive gratification at the news, but an instant later swore expressively.

'We can't stay here. It's not many hours until dawn. Lesser priests are likely to visit the temple at any hour of the night, and if we're discovered here with his corpse, the people will tear us to pieces. The Turanians could not save us.'

She lifted the bolt on the secret door, and a few moments later they were in the streets and hurrying away from the silent square where brooded the age-old shrine of Hanuman.

In a winding street a short distance away Conan halted and checked his companion with a heavy hand on her naked shoulder.

'Don't forget there was a price—'

'I have not forgotten!' She twisted free. 'But we must go to – to Alafdhal first!'

A few minutes later the black slave let them through the wicket door. The young Turanian lay upon the divan, his arms and legs bound with heavy velvet ropes. His eyes were open, but they were like those of a mad dog, and foam was thick on his lips. Zabibi shuddered.

'Force his jaws open!' she commanded, and Conan's iron fingers accomplished the task.

Zabibi emptied the phial down the maniac's gullet. The effect was like magic. Instantly he became quiet. The glare faded from his eyes; he stared up at the girl in a puzzled way, but with recognition and intelligence. Then he fell into a normal slumber.

'When he awakes he will be quite sane,' she whispered, motioning to the silent slave.

With a deep bow he gave into her hands a small leathern bag, and drew about her shoulders a silken cloak. Her manner had subtly changed when she beckoned Conan to follow her out of the chamber.

In an arch that opened on the street, she turned to him, drawing herself up with a new regality.

'I must now tell you the truth,' she said. 'I am not Zabibi. I am Nafertari. And *he* is not Alafdhal, a poor captain of the guardsmen. He is Jungir Khan, satrap of Zamboula.'

Conan made no comment; his scarred dark countenance was immobile.

'I lied to you because I dared not divulge the truth to anyone,' she said. 'We were alone when Jungir Khan went mad. None knew of it but myself. Had it been known that the satrap of Zamboula was a madman, there would have been instant revolt and rioting, even as Totrasmek planned, who plotted our destruction.

'You see now how impossible is the reward for which you hoped. The satrap's mistress is not – cannot be for you. But you shall not go unrewarded. Here is a sack of gold.'

She gave him the bag she had received from the slave.

'Go, now, and when the sun is come up to the palace, I will have Jungir Khan make you captain of his guard. But you will take your orders from me, secretly. Your first duty will be to march a squad to the shrine of Hanuman, ostensibly to search for clues of the priest's slayer; in reality to search for the Star of Khorala. It must be hidden there somewhere. When you find it, bring it to me. You have my leave to go now.'

He nodded, still silent, and strode away. The girl, watching the swing of his broad shoulders, was piqued to note that there was nothing in his bearing to show that he was in any way chagrined or abashed.

When he had rounded a corner, he glanced back, and then changed his direction and quickened his pace. A few moments later he was in the quarter of the city containing the Horse Market. There he smote on a door until from the window above a bearded head was thrust to demand the reason for the disturbance.

'A horse,' demanded Conan. 'The swiftest steed you have.'

'I open no gates at this time of night,' grumbled the horse-trader.

Conan rattled his coins.

'Dog's son knave! Don't you see I'm white, and alone? Come down, before I smash your door!'

Presently, on a bay stallion, Conan was riding toward the house of Aram Baksh.

He turned off the road into the alley that lay between the tavern compound and the date-palm garden, but he did not pause at the gate. He rode on to the northeast corner of the wall, then turned and rode along the north wall, to halt within a few paces of the northwest angle. No trees grew near the wall, but there were some low bushes. To one of these he tied his horse, and was about to climb into the saddle again, when he heard a low muttering of voices beyond the corner of the wall.

Drawing his foot from the stirrup he stole to the angle and peered around it. Three men were moving down the road toward the palm groves, and from their slouching gait he knew they were negroes. They halted at his low call, bunching themselves as he strode toward them, his sword in his hand. Their eyes gleamed whitely in the starlight. Their brutish lust shone in their ebony faces, but they knew their three cudgels could not prevail against his sword, just as he knew it.

'Where are you going?' he challenged.

'To bid our brothers put out the fire in the pit beyond the groves,' was the sullen, guttural reply. 'Aram Baksh promised us a man, but he lied. We found one of our brothers dead in the trap-chamber. We go hungry this night.'

'I think not,' smiled Conan. 'Aram Baksh will give you a man. Do you see that door?'

He pointed to a small, iron-bound portal set in the midst of the western wall.

'Wait there. Aram Baksh will give you a man.'

Backing warily away until he was out of reach of a sudden bludgeon blow, he turned and melted around the northwest angle of the wall. Reaching his horse he paused to ascertain that the blacks were not sneaking after him, and then he climbed into the saddle and stood upright on it, quieting the uneasy steed with a low word. He reached up, grasped the coping of the wall and drew himself up and over. There he studied the grounds for an instant. The tavern was built in the southwest corner of the enclosure, the remaining space of which was occupied by groves and gardens. He saw no one in the grounds. The tavern was dark and silent, and he knew all the doors and windows were barred and bolted.

Conan knew that Aram Baksh slept in a chamber that opened into a cypress-bordered path that led to the door in the western wall. Like a shadow he glided among the trees and a few moments later he rapped lightly on the chamber door.

'What is it?' asked a rumbling voice within.

'Aram Baksh!' hissed Conan. 'The blacks are stealing over the wall!'

Almost instantly the door opened, framing the tavern-keeper, naked but for his shirt, with a dagger in his hand.

He craned his neck to stare into the Cimmerian's face.

'What tale is this – *you*!'

Conan's vengeful fingers strangled the yell in his throat. They went to the floor together and Conan wrenched the dagger from his enemy's hand. The blade glinted in the starlight, and blood spurted. Aram Baksh made hideous noises, gasping and gagging on a mouthful of blood. Conan dragged him to his feet and again the dagger slashed, and most of the curly beard fell to the floor.

Still gripping his captive's throat – for a man can scream incoherently even with his tongue slit – Conan dragged him out of the dark chamber and down the cypress-shadowed path, to the iron-bound door in the outer wall. With one hand he lifted the bolt and threw the door open, disclosing the three shadowy figures which waited like black vultures outside. Into their eager arms Conan thrust the innkeeper.

A horrible, blood-choked scream rose from the Zamboulan's throat, but there was no response from the silent tavern. The people there were used to screams outside the wall. Aram Baksh fought like a wild man, his distended eyes turned frantically on the Cimmerian's face. He found no mercy there. Conan was thinking of the scores of wretches who owed their bloody doom to this man's greed.

In glee the negroes dragged him down the road, mocking his frenzied gibberings. How could they recognize Aram Baksh in this half-naked, bloodstained figure, with the grotesquely shorn beard and unintelligible babblings? The sounds of the struggle came back to Conan, standing beside the gate, even after the clump of figures had vanished among the palms.

Closing the door behind him, Conan returned to his horse, mounted and turned westward, toward the open desert, swinging wide to skirt the sinister belt of palm groves. As he rode, he drew from his belt a ring in which gleamed a jewel that snared the starlight in a shimmering iridescence. He held it up to admire it, turning it this way and that. The compact bag of gold pieces clinked gently at his saddle-bow, like a promise of the greater riches to come.

'I wonder what she'd say if she knew I recognized her as Nafertari and him as Jungir Khan the instant I saw them,' he mused. 'I knew the Star of Khorala, too. There'll be a fine scene if she ever guesses that I slipped it off his finger while I was tying him with his sword-belt. But they'll never catch me, with the start I'm getting.'

He glanced back at the shadowy palm groves, among which a red glare was mounting. A chanting rose to the night, vibrating with savage exultation. And another sound mingled with it, a mad, incoherent screaming, a frenzied gibbering in which no words could be distinguished. The noise followed Conan as he rode westward beneath the paling stars.

THE DEVIL IN IRON

1

The fisherman loosened his knife in its scabbard. The gesture was instinctive, for what he feared was nothing a knife could slay, not even the saw-edged crescent blade of the Yuetshi that could disembowel a man with an upward stroke. Neither man nor beast threatened him in the solitude which brooded over the castellated isle of Xapur.

He had climbed the cliffs, passed through the jungle that bordered them, and now stood surrounded by evidences of a vanished state. Broken columns glimmered among the trees, the straggling lines of crumbling walls meandered off into the shadows, and under his feet were broad paves, cracked and bowed by roots growing beneath.

The fisherman was typical of his race, that strange people whose origin is lost in the gray dawn of the past, and who have dwelt in their rude fishing huts along the southern shore of the Sea of Vilayet since time immemorial. He was broadly built, with long apish arms and a mighty chest, but with lean loins and thin bandy legs. His face was broad, his forehead low and retreating, his hair thick and tangled. A belt for a knife and a rag for a loin-cloth were all he wore in the way of clothing.

That he was where he was proved that he was less dully incurious than most of his people. Men seldom visited Xapur. It was uninhabited, all but forgotten, merely one among the myriad isles which dotted the great inland sea. Men called it Xapur, the Fortified, because of its ruins, remnants of some prehistoric kingdom, lost and forgotten before the conquering Hyborians had ridden southward. None knew who reared those stones, though dim legends lingered among the Yuetshi which half intelligibly suggested a connection of immeasurable antiquity between the fishers and the unknown island kingdom.

But it had been a thousand years since any Yuetshi had understood the import of these tales; they repeated them now as a meaningless formula, a gibberish framed by their lips by custom. No Yuetshi had come to Xapur for a century. The adjacent coast of the mainland was uninhabited, a reedy marsh given over to the grim beasts that haunted it. The fisher's village lay some distance to the south, on the mainland. A storm had blown his frail fishing craft far from his accustomed haunts, and wrecked it in a night of flaring lightning and roaring waters on the towering cliffs of the isle. Now in the dawn the sky shone blue and clear, the rising sun made jewels of the dripping leaves. He had climbed the cliffs to which he had clung through the night because, in the midst of the storm, he had seen an appalling lance of lightning fork out of the black heavens, and the concussion of its stroke, which had shaken the whole island, had been accompanied by a cataclysmic crash that he doubted could have resulted from a riven tree.

A dull curiosity had caused him to investigate; and now he had found what he sought and an animal-like uneasiness possessed him, a sense of lurking peril.

Among the trees reared a broken dome-like structure, built of gigantic blocks of the peculiar iron-like green stone found only on the islands of Vilayet. It seemed incredible that human hands could have shaped and placed them, and certainly it was beyond human power to have overthrown the structure they formed. But the thunderbolt had splintered the ton-heavy blocks like so much glass, reduced others to green dust, and ripped away the whole arch of the dome.

The fisherman climbed over the debris and peered in, and what he saw brought a grunt from him. Within the ruined dome, surrounded by stone-dust and bits of broken masonry, lay a man on the golden block. He was clad in a sort of skirt and a shagreen girdle. His black hair, which fell in a square mane to his massive shoulders, was confined about his temples by a narrow gold band. On his bare, muscular breast lay a curious dagger with a jeweled pommel, shagreen-bound hilt, and a broad crescent blade. It was much like the knife the fisherman wore at his hip, but it lacked the serrated edge, and was made with infinitely greater skill.

The fisherman lusted for the weapon. The man, of course, was dead; had been dead for many centuries. This dome was his tomb. The fisherman did not wonder by what art the ancients had preserved the body in such a vivid likeness of life, which kept the muscular limbs full and unshrunken, the dark flesh vital. The dull brain of the Yuetshi had room only for his desire for the knife with its delicate waving lines along the dully gleaming blade.

Scrambling down into the dome, he lifted the weapon from the man's breast. And as he did so, a strange and terrible thing came to pass. The muscular dark hands knotted convulsively, the lids flared open, revealing great dark magnetic eyes whose stare struck the startled fisherman like a physical blow. He recoiled, dropping the jeweled dagger in his perturbation. The man on the dais heaved up to a sitting position, and the fisherman gaped at the full extent of his size, thus revealed. His narrowed eyes held the Yuetshi and in those slitted orbs he read neither friendliness nor gratitude; he saw only a fire as alien and hostile as that which burns in the eyes of a tiger.

Suddenly the man rose and towered above him, menace in his every aspect. There was no room in the fisherman's dull brain for fear, at least for such fear as might grip a man who has just seen the fundamental laws of nature defied. As the great hands fell to his shoulders, he drew his saw-edged knife and struck upward with the same motion. The blade splintered against the stranger's corded belly as against a steel column, and then the fisherman's thick neck broke like a rotten twig in the giant hands.

2

Jehungir Agha, lord of Khawarizm and keeper of the coastal border, scanned once more the ornate parchment scroll with its peacock seal, and laughed shortly and sardonically.

'Well?' bluntly demanded his counsellor Ghaznavi.

Jehungir shrugged his shoulders. He was a handsome man, with the merciless pride of birth and accomplishment.

'The king grows short of patience,' said he. 'In his own hand he complains bitterly of what he calls my failure to guard the frontier. By Tarim, if I can not deal a blow to these robbers of the steppes, Khawarizm may own a new lord.'

Ghaznavi tugged his gray-shot beard in meditation. Yezdigerd, king of Turan, was the mightiest monarch in the world. In his palace in the great port city of Aghrapur was heaped the plunder of empires. His fleets of purple-sailed war galleys had made Vilayet an Hyrkanian lake. The dark-skinned people of Zamora paid him tribute, as did the eastern provinces of Koth. The Shemites bowed to his rule as far west as Shushan. His armies ravaged the borders of Stygia in the south and the snowy lands of the Hyperboreans in the north. His riders bore torch and sword westward into Brythunia and Ophir and Corinthia, even to the borders of Nemedia. His gilt-helmeted swordsmen had trampled hosts under their horses' hoofs, and walled cities went up in flames at his command. In the glutted slave markets of Aghrapur, Sultanapur, Khawarizm, Shahpur and Khorusun, women were sold for three small silver coins – blond Brythunians, tawny Stygians, dark-haired Zamorians, ebon Kushites, olive-skinned Shemites.

Yet, while his swift horsemen overthrew armies far from his frontiers, at his very borders an audacious foe plucked his beard with a red-dripping and smoke-stained hand.

On the broad steppes between the Sea of Vilayet and the borders of the easternmost Hyborian kingdoms, a new race had sprung up in the past half-century, formed originally of fleeing criminals, broken men, escaped slaves, and deserting soldiers. They were men of many crimes and countries, some born on the steppes, some fleeing from the kingdoms in the west. They were called *kozak*, which means wastrel.

Dwelling on the wild, open steppes, owning no law but their own peculiar code, they had become a people capable of defying the Grand Monarch. Ceaselessly they raided the Turanian frontier, retiring in the steppes when defeated; with the pirates of Vilayet, men of much the same breed, they harried the coast, preying off the merchant ships which plied between the Hyrkanian ports.

'How am I to crush these wolves?' demanded Jehungir. 'If I follow them into the steppes, I run the risk either of being cut off and destroyed, or having them elude me entirely and burn the city in my absence. Of late they have been more daring than ever.'

'That is because of the new chief who has risen among them,' answered Ghaznavi. 'You know whom I mean.'

'Aye!' replied Jehungir feelingly. 'It is that devil Conan; he is even wilder than the *kozaks*, yet he is crafty as a mountain lion.'

'It is more through wild animal instinct than through intelligence,' answered Ghaznavi. 'The other *kozaks* are at least descendants of civilized men. He is a barbarian. But to dispose of him would be to deal them a crippling blow.'

'But how?' demanded Jehungir. 'He has repeatedly cut his way out of spots that seemed certain death for him. And, by instinct or cunning, he has avoided or escaped every trap set for him.'

'For every beast and for every man there is a trap he will not escape,' quoth Ghaznavi. 'When we have parleyed with the *kozaks* for the ransom of captives, I have observed this man Conan. He has a keen relish for women and strong drink. Have your captive Octavia fetched here.'

Jehungir clapped his hands, and an impassive Kushite eunuch, an image of shining ebony in silken pantaloons, bowed before him and went to do his bidding. Presently he returned, leading by the wrist a tall handsome girl, whose yellow hair, clear eyes and fair skin identified her as a pure-blooded member of her race. Her scanty silk tunic, girded at the waist, displayed the marvelous contours of her magnificent figure. Her fine eyes flashed with resentment and her red lips were sulky, but submission had been taught her during her captivity. She stood with hanging head before her master until he motioned her to a seat on the divan beside him. Then he looked inquiringly at Ghaznavi.

'We must lure Conan away from the *kozaks*,' said the counsellor abruptly. 'Their war camp is at present pitched somewhere on the lower reaches of the Zaporoska River – which, as you well know, is a wilderness of reeds, a swampy jungle in which our last expedition was cut to pieces by those masterless devils.'

'I am not likely to forget that,' said Jehungir wryly.

'There is an uninhabited island near the mainland,' said Ghaznavi, 'known as Xapur, the Fortified, because of some ancient ruins upon it. There is a peculiarity about it which makes it perfect for our purpose. It has no shore-line, but rises sheer out of the sea in cliffs a hundred and fifty feet tall. Not even an ape could negotiate them. The only place where a man can go up or down is a narrow path on the western side that has the appearance of a worn stair, carved into the solid rock of the cliffs.

'If we could trap Conan on that island, alone, we could hunt him down at our leisure, with bows, as men hunt a lion.'

'As well wish for the moon,' said Jehungir impatiently. 'Shall we send him a messenger, bidding him climb the cliffs and await our coming?'

'In effect, yes!' Seeing Jehungir's look of amazement, Ghaznavi continued: 'We will ask for a parley with the *kozaks* in regard to prisoners, at the edge of the steppes by Fort Ghori. As usual, we will go with a force and encamp outside the castle. They will come, with an equal force, and the parley will go forward with the usual distrust and suspicion. But this time we will take with us, as if by casual chance, your beautiful captive.' Octavia changed color and listened with intensified interest as the counsellor nodded toward her. 'She will use all her wiles to attract Conan's attention. That should not be difficult. To that wild reaver she should appear a dazzling vision of loveliness. Her vitality and substantial figure should appeal to him more vividly than would one of the doll-like beauties of your seraglio.'

Octavia sprang up, her white fists clenched, her eyes blazing and her figure quivering with outraged anger.

'You would force me to play the trollop with this barbarian?' she exclaimed. 'I will not! I am no market-block slut to smirk and ogle at a steppes-robber. I am the daughter of a Nemedian lord—'

'You were of the Nemedian nobility before my riders carried you off,' returned Jehungir cynically. 'Now you are merely a slave who will do as she is bid.'

'I will not!' she raged.

'On the contrary,' rejoined Jehungir with studied cruelty, 'you will. I like Ghaznavi's plan. Continue, prince among counsellors.'

'Conan will probably wish to buy her. You will refuse to sell her, of course, or to exchange her for Hyrkanian prisoners. He may then try to steal her, or take her by force – though I do not think even he would break the parley-truce. Anyway, we must be prepared for whatever he might attempt.

'Then, shortly after the parley, before he has time to forget all about her, we will send a messenger to him, under a flag of truce, accusing him of stealing the girl, and demanding her return. He may kill the messenger, but at least he will think that she has escaped.

'Then we will send a spy – a Yuetshi fisherman will do – to the *kozak* camp, who will tell Conan that Octavia is hiding on Xapur. If I know my man, he will go straight to that place.'

'But we do not know that he will go alone,' Jehungir argued.

'Does a man take a band of warriors with him, when going to a rendezvous with a woman he desires?' retorted Ghaznavi. 'The chances are all that he *will* go alone. But we will take care of the other alternative. We will not await him on the island, where we might be trapped ourselves, but among the reeds of a marshy point which juts out to within a thousand yards of Xapur. If he brings a large force, we'll beat a retreat and think up another plot. If he comes alone or with a small party, we will have him. Depend upon it, he will come, remembering your charming slave's smiles and meaning glances.'

'I will never descend to such shame!' Octavia was wild with fury and humiliation. 'I will die first!'

'You will not die, my rebellious beauty,' said Jehungir, 'but you will be subjected to a very painful and humiliating experience.'

He clapped his hands, and Octavia paled. This time it was not the Kushite who entered, but a Shemite, a heavily muscled man of medium height with a short, curled, blue-black beard.

'Here is work for you, Gilzan,' said Jehungir. 'Take this fool, and play with her awhile. Yet be careful not to spoil her beauty.'

With an inarticulate grunt the Shemite seized Octavia's wrist, and at the grasp of his iron fingers, all the defiance went out of her. With a piteous cry she tore away and threw herself on her knees before her implacable master, sobbing incoherently for mercy.

Jehungir dismissed the disappointed torturer with a gesture, and said to Ghaznavi: 'If your plan succeeds, I will fill your lap with gold.'

3

In the darkness before dawn an unaccustomed sound disturbed the solitude that slumbered over the reedy marshes and the misty waters of the coast. It was not a drowsy water-fowl nor a waking beast. It was a human who struggled through the thick reeds, which were taller than a man's head.

It was a woman, had there been anyone to see, tall and yellow-haired, her splendid limbs molded by her draggled tunic. Octavia had escaped in good earnest, every outraged fiber of her still tingling from her experience in a captivity that had become unendurable.

Jehungir's mastery of her had been bad enough; but with deliberate fiendishness Jehungir had given her to a nobleman whose name was a byword for degeneracy even in Khawarizm.

Octavia's resilient flesh crawled and quivered at her memories. Desperation had nerved her climb from Jelal Khan's castle on a rope made of strips from torn tapestries, and chance had led her to a picketed horse. She had ridden all night, and dawn found her with a foundered steed on the swampy shores of the sea. Quivering with the abhorrence of being dragged back to the revolting destiny planned for her by Jelal Khan, she plunged into the morass, seeking a hiding-place from the pursuit she expected. When the reeds grew thinner around her and the water rose about her thighs, she saw the dim loom of an island ahead of her. A broad span of water lay between, but she did not hesitate. She waded out until the low waves were lapping about her waist; then she struck out strongly, swimming with a vigor that promised unusual endurance.

As she neared the island, she saw that it rose sheer from the water in castle-like cliffs. She reached them at last, but found neither ledge to stand on below the water, not to cling to above. She swam on, following the curve of the cliffs, the strain of her long flight beginning to weight her limbs. Her hands fluttered along the sheer stone, and suddenly they found a depression. With a sobbing gasp of relief, she pulled herself out of the water and clung there, a dripping white goddess in the dim starlight.

She had come upon what seemed to be steps carved in the cliff. Up them she went, flattening herself against the stone as she caught the faint clack of muffled oars. She strained her eyes and thought she made out a vague bulk moving toward the reedy point she had just quitted. But it was too far away for her to be sure, in the darkness, and presently the faint sound ceased, and she continued her climb. If it were her pursuers, she knew of no better course than to hide on the island. She knew that most of the islands off that marshy coast were uninhabited. This might be a pirate's lair, but even pirates would be preferable to the beast she had escaped.

A vagrant thought crossed her mind as she climbed, in which she mentally compared her former master with the *kozak* chief with whom – by compulsion – she had shamelessly flirted in the pavilions of the camp by Fort Ghori, where the Hyrkanian lords had parleyed with the warriors of the steppes. His burning gaze had frightened and humiliated her, but his cleanly elemental fierceness set him above Jelal Khan, a monster such as only an overly opulent civilization can produce.

She scrambled up over the cliff edge and looked timidly at the dense shadows which confronted her. The trees grew close to the cliffs, presenting a solid mass of blackness. Something whirred above her head and she cowered, even though realizing it was only a bat.

She did not like the look of those ebony shadows, but she set her teeth and went toward them, trying not to think of snakes. Her bare feet made no sound in the spongy loam under the trees. Once among them, the darkness closed frighteningly about her. She had not taken a dozen steps when she was no longer able to look back and see the cliffs and the sea beyond. A few steps more and she became hopelessly confused and lost her sense of direction. Through the tangled branches not even a star peered. She groped and floundered on, blindly, and then came to a sudden halt.

Somewhere ahead there began the rhythmical booming of a drum. It was not such a sound as she would have expected to hear in that time and place. Then she forgot it as she was aware of a presence near her. She could not see, but she knew that something was standing beside her in the darkness.

With a stifled cry she shrank back, and as she did so, something that even in her panic she recognized as a human arm curved about her waist. She screamed and threw all her supple young strength into a wild lunge for freedom, but her captor caught her up like a child, crushing her frantic resistance with ease. The silence with which her frenzied pleas and protests were received added to her terror as she felt herself being carried through the darkness toward the distant drum which still pulsed and muttered.

4

As the first tinge of dawn reddened the sea, a small boat with a solitary occupant approached the cliffs. The man in the boat was a picturesque figure. A crimson scarf was knotted about his head; his wide silk breeches, of flaming hue, were upheld by a broad sash which likewise supported a scimitar in a shagreen scabbard.

His gilt-worked leather boots suggested the horseman rather than the seaman, but he handled his boat with skill. Through his widely open white silk shirt showed his broad muscular breast, burned brown by the sun.

The muscles of his heavy bronzed arms rippled as he pulled the oars with an almost feline ease of motion. A fierce vitality that was evident in each feature and motion set him apart from common men; yet his expression was neither savage nor somber, though the smoldering blue eyes hinted at ferocity easily wakened. This was Conan, who had wandered into the armed camps of the *kozak*s with no other possession than his wits and his sword, and who had carved his way to leadership among them.

He paddled to the carven stair as one familiar with his environs, and moored the boat to a projection of the rock. Then he went up the worn steps without hesitation. He was keenly alert, not because he consciously suspected hidden danger, but because alertness was a part of him, whetted by the wild existence he followed.

What Ghaznavi had considered animal intuition or some sixth sense was merely the razor-edge faculties and savage wit of the barbarian. Conan had no instinct to tell him that men were watching him from a covert among the reeds of the mainland.

As he climbed the cliff, one of these men breathed deeply and stealthily lifted a bow. Jehungir caught his wrist and hissed an oath into his ear. 'Fool! Will you betray us? Don't you realize he is out of range? Let him get upon the island. He will go looking for the girl. We will stay here awhile. He *may* have sensed our presence or guessed our plot. He may have warriors hidden somewhere. We will wait. In an hour, if nothing suspicious occurs, we'll row up to the foot of the stair and await him there. If he does not return in a reasonable time, some of us will go upon the island and hunt him down. But I do not wish to do that if it can be helped. Some of us are sure to die if we have to go into the bush after him. I had rather catch him descending the stair, where we can feather him with arrows from a safe distance.'

Meanwhile the unsuspecting *kozak* had plunged into the forest. He went silently in his soft leather boots, his gaze sifting every shadow in eagerness to catch sight of the splendid tawny-haired beauty of whom he had dreamed ever since he had seen her in the pavilion of Jehungir Agha by Fort Ghori. He would have desired her even if she had displayed repugnance toward him. But her cryptic smiles and glances had fired his blood, and with all the lawless violence which was his heritage he desired that white-skinned golden-haired woman of civilization.

He had been on Xapur before. Less than a month ago he had held a secret conclave here with a pirate crew. He knew that he was approaching a point where he could see the mysterious ruins which gave the island its name, and he wondered if he would find the girl hiding among them. Even with the thought he stopped as though struck dead.

Ahead of him, among the trees, rose something that his reason told him was not possible. *It was a great dark green wall, with towers rearing beyond the battlements.*

Conan stood paralyzed in the disruption of the faculties which demoralizes anyone who is confronted by an impossible negation of sanity. He doubted neither his sight nor his reason, but something was monstrously out of joint. Less than a month ago only broken ruins had showed among the trees. What human hands could rear such a mammoth pile as now met his eyes, in the few weeks which had elapsed? Besides, the buccaneers who roamed Vilayet ceaselessly would have learned of any work going on on such a stupendous scale, and would have informed the *kozaks*.

There was no explaining this thing, but it was so. He was on Xapur and that fantastic heap of towering masonry was on Xapur, and all was madness and paradox; yet it was all true.

He wheeled back through the jungle, down the carven stair and across the blue waters to the distant camp at the mouth of the Zaporoska. In that moment of unreasoning panic even the thought of halting so near the inland sea was repugnant. He would leave it behind him, would quit the armed camps and the steppes, and put a thousand miles between him and the blue mysterious East where the most basic laws of nature could be set at naught, by what diabolism he could not guess.

For an instant the future fate of kingdoms that hinged on this gay-clad barbarian hung in the balance. It was a small thing that tipped the scales – merely a shred of silk hanging on a bush that caught his uneasy glance. He leaned to it, his nostrils expanding, his nerves quivering to a subtle stimulant. On that bit of torn cloth, so faint that it was less with his physical faculties than by some obscure instinctive sense that he recognized it, lingered the tantalizing perfume that he connected with the sweet firm flesh of the woman he had seen in Jehungir's pavilion. The fisherman had not lied, then; she *was* here! Then in the soil he saw a single track of a bare foot, long and slender, but a man's not a woman's, and sunk deeper than was natural. The conclusion was obvious; the man who made that track was carrying a burden, and what should it be but the girl the *kozak* was seeking?

He stood silently facing the dark towers that loomed through the trees, his eyes slits of blue bale-fire. Desire for the yellow-haired woman vied with a sullen primordial rage at whoever had taken her. His human passion fought down his ultra-human fears, and dropping into the stalking crouch of a hunting panther, he glided toward the walls, taking advantage of the dense foliage to escape detection from the battlements.

As he approached he saw that the walls were composed of the same green stone that had formed the ruins, and he was haunted by a vague sense of familiarity. It was as if he looked upon something he had never seen before, but had dreamed of, or pictured mentally. At last he recognized the sensation. The walls and towers followed the plan of the ruins. It was as if the crumbling lines had grown back into the structures they originally were.

No sound disturbed the morning quiet as Conan stole to the foot of the wall which rose sheer from the luxuriant growth. On the southern reaches of the inland sea the vegetation was almost tropical. He saw no one on the battlements, heard no sounds within. He saw a massive gate a short distance to his left, and had had no reason to suppose that it was not locked and guarded. But he believed that the woman he sought was somewhere beyond that wall, and the course he took was characteristically reckless.

Above him vine-festooned branches reached out toward the battlements. He went up a great tree like a cat, and reaching a point above the parapet, he gripped a thick limb with both hands, swung back and forth at arm's length until he had gained momentum, and then let go and catapulted through the air, landing cat-like on the battlements. Crouching there he stared down into the streets of a city.

The circumference of the wall was not great, but the number of green stone buildings it contained was surprising. They were three or four stories in height, mainly flat-roofed, reflecting a fine architectural style. The streets converged like the spokes of a wheel into an octagon-shaped court in the center of the town which gave upon a lofty edifice, which, with its domes and towers, dominated the whole city. He saw no one moving in the streets or looking out of the windows, though the sun was already coming up. The silence that reigned there might have been that of a dead and deserted city. A narrow stone stair ascended the wall near him; down this he went.

Houses shouldered so closely to the wall that halfway down the stair he found himself within arm's length of a window, and halted to peer in. There were no bars, and the silk curtains were caught back with satin cords. He looked into a chamber whose walls were hidden by dark velvet tapestries. The floor was covered with thick rugs, and there were benches of polished ebony, and an ivory dais heaped with furs.

He was about to continue his descent, when he heard the sound of someone approaching in the street below. Before the unknown person could come round a corner and see him on the stair, he stepped quickly across the intervening space and dropped lightly into the room, drawing his scimitar. He stood for an instant statue-like; then as nothing happened he was moving across the rugs toward an arched doorway when a hanging was drawn aside, revealing a cushioned alcove from which a slender, dark-haired girl regarded him with languid eyes.

Conan glared at her tensely, expecting her momentarily to start screaming. But she merely smothered a yawn with a dainty hand, rose from the alcove and leaned negligently against the hanging which she held with one hand.

She was undoubtedly a member of a white race, though her skin was very dark. Her square-cut hair was black as midnight, her only garment a wisp of silk about her supple hips.

Presently she spoke, but the tongue was unfamiliar to him, and he shook his head. She yawned again, stretched lithely, and without any show of fear or surprise, shifted to a language he did understand, a dialect of Yuetshi which sounded strangely archaic.

'Are you looking for someone?' she asked, as indifferently as if the invasion of her chamber by an armed stranger were the most common thing imaginable.

'Who are you?' he demanded.

'I am Yateli,' she answered languidly. 'I must have feasted late last night, I am so sleepy now. Who are you?'

'I am Conan, a *hetman* among the *kozaks*,' he answered, watching her narrowly. He believed her attitude to be a pose, and expected her to try to escape from the chamber or rouse the house. But, though a velvet rope that might be a signal cord hung near her, she did not reach for it.

'Conan,' she repeated drowsily. 'You are not a Dagonian. I suppose you are a mercenary. Have you cut the heads off many Yuetshi?'

'I do not war on water rats!' he snorted.

'But they are very terrible,' she murmured. 'I remember when they were our slaves. But they revolted and burned and slew. Only the magic of Khosatral Khel has kept them from the walls—' She paused, a puzzled look struggling with the sleepiness of her expression. 'I forgot,' she muttered. 'They *did* climb the walls, last night. There was shouting and fire, and people calling in vain on Khosatral.' She shook her head as if to clear it. 'But that can not be,' she murmured, 'because I am alive, and I thought I was dead. Oh, to the devil with it!'

She came across the chamber, and taking Conan's hand, drew him to the dais. He yielded in bewilderment and uncertainty. The girl smiled at him like a sleepy child; her long silky lashes drooped over dusky, clouded eyes. She ran her fingers through his thick black locks as if to assure herself of his reality.

'It was a dream,' she yawned. 'Perhaps it's all a dream. I feel like a dream now. I don't care. I can't remember something – I have forgotten – there is something I can not understand, but I grow so sleepy when I try to think. Anyway, it doesn't matter.'

'What do you mean?' he asked uneasily. 'You said they climbed the walls last night? Who?'

'The Yuetshi. I thought so, anyway. A cloud of smoke hid everything, but a naked, blood-stained devil caught me by the throat and drove his knife into my breast. Oh, it hurt! But it was a dream, because see, there is no scar.' She idly inspected her smooth bosom, and then sank upon Conan's lap and passed her supple arms around his massive neck. 'I can not remember,' she murmured, nestling her dark head against his mighty breast. 'Everything is dim and misty. It does not matter. You are no dream. You are strong. Let us live while we can. Love me!'

He cradled the girl's glossy head in the bend of his heavy arm, and kissed her full red lips with unfeigned relish.

'You are strong,' she repeated, her voice waning. 'Love me – love—' The sleepy murmur faded away; the dusky eyes closed, the long lashes drooping over the sensuous cheeks; the supple body relaxed in Conan's arms.

He scowled down at her. She seemed to partake of the illusion that haunted this whole city, but the firm resilience of her limbs under his questing fingers convinced him that he had a living human girl in his arms, and not the shadow of a dream. No less disturbed, he hastily laid her on the furs upon the dais. Her sleep was too deep to be natural. He decided that she must be an addict of some drug, perhaps like the black lotus of Xuthal.

Then he found something else to make him wonder. Among the furs on the dais was a gorgeous spotted skin, whose predominant hue was golden. It was not a clever copy, but the skin of an actual beast. And that beast, Conan knew, had been extinct for at least a thousand years; it was the great golden leopard which figures so predominantly in Hyborian legendry, and which the ancient artists delighted to portray in pigments and marble.

Shaking his head in bewilderment, Conan passed through the archway into a winding corridor. Silence hung over the house, but outside he heard a sound which his keen ears recognized as something ascending the stair on the wall from which he had entered the building. An instant later he was startled to hear something land with a soft but weighty thud on the floor of the chamber he had just quitted. Turning quickly away, he hurried along the twisting hallway until something on the floor before him brought him to a halt.

It was a human figure, which lay half in the hall and half in an opening that obviously was normally concealed by a door which was a duplicate of the panels of the wall. It was a man, dark and lean, clad only in a silk loin-cloth, with a shaven head and cruel features, and he lay as if death had struck him just as he was emerging from the panel. Conan bent above him, seeking the cause of his death, and discovered him to be merely sunk in the same deep sleep as the girl in the chamber.

But why should he select such a place for his slumbers? While meditating on the matter, Conan was galvanized by a sound behind him. Something was moving up the corridor in his direction. A quick glance down it showed that it ended in a great door which might be locked. Conan jerked the supine body out of the panel-entrance and stepped through, pulling the panel shut after him. A click told him it was locked in place. Standing in utter darkness, he heard a shuffling tread halt just outside the door, and a faint chill trickled along his spine. That was no human step, nor that of any beast he had ever encountered.

There was an instant of silence, then a faint creak of wood and metal. Putting out his hand he felt the door straining and bending inward, as if a great weight were being steadily borne against it from the outside. As he reached for his sword, this ceased and he heard a strange slobbering mouthing that prickled the short hairs on his scalp. Scimitar in hand he began backing away, and his heels felt steps, down which he nearly tumbled. He was in a narrow staircase leading downward.

He groped his way down in the blackness, feeling for, but not finding, some other opening in the walls. Just as he decided that he was no longer in the house, but deep in the earth under it, the steps ceased in a level tunnel.

5

Along the black silent tunnel Conan groped, momentarily dreading a fall into some unseen pit; but at last his feet struck steps again, and he went up them until he came to a door on which his fumbling fingers found a metal catch. He came out into a dim and lofty room of enormous proportions. Fantastic columns marched around the mottled walls, upholding a ceiling, which, at once translucent and dusky, seemed like a cloudy midnight sky, giving an illusion of impossible height. If any light filtered in from the outside it was curiously altered.

In a brooding twilight Conan moved across the bare green floor. The great room was circular, pierced on one side by the great bronze valves of a giant door. Opposite this, on a dais against the wall, up to which led broad curving steps, there stood a throne of copper, and when Conan saw what was coiled on this throne, he retreated hastily, lifting his scimitar.

Then, as the thing did not move, he scanned it more closely, and presently mounted the glass steps and stared down at it. It was a gigantic snake, apparently carved in some jade-like substance. Each scale stood out as distinctly as in real life, and the iridescent colors were vividly reproduced. The great wedge-shaped head was half submerged in the folds of its trunk; so neither the eyes nor jaws were visible. Recognition stirred in his mind. This snake was evidently meant to represent one of those grim monsters of the marsh which in past ages had haunted the reedy edges of Vilayet's southern shores. But, like the golden leopard, they had been extinct for hundreds of years. Conan had seen rude images of them, in miniature, among the idol-huts of the Yuetshi, and there was a description of them in the *Book of Skelos*, which drew on prehistoric sources.

Conan admired the scaly torso, thick as his thigh and obviously of great length, and he reached out and laid a curious hand on the thing. And as he did so, his heart nearly stopped. An icy chill congealed the blood in his veins and lifted the short hair on his scalp. Under his hand there was not the smooth, brittle surface of glass or metal or stone, but the yielding, fibrous mass of a *living* thing. He felt cold, sluggish life flowing under his fingers.

His hand jerked back in instinctive repulsion. Sword shaking in his grasp, horror and revulsion and fear almost choking him, he backed away and down the glass steps with painful care, glaring in awful fascination at the grisly thing that slumbered on the copper throne. It did not move.

He reached the bronze door and tried it, with his heart in his teeth, sweating with fear that he should find himself locked in with that slimy horror. But the valves yielded to his touch, and he glided through and closed them behind him.

He found himself in a wide hallway with lofty tapestried walls, where the light was the same twilight gloom. It made distant objects indistinct and that made him uneasy, rousing thoughts of serpents gliding unseen through the dimness. A door at the other end seemed miles away in the illusive light. Nearer at hand the tapestry hung in such a way as to suggest an opening behind it, and lifting it cautiously he discovered a narrow stair leading up.

While he hesitated he heard in the great room he had just left, the same shuffling tread he had heard outside the locked panel. Had he been followed through the tunnel? He went up the stair hastily, dropping the tapestry in place behind him.

Emerging presently into a twisting corridor, he took the first doorway he came to. He had a twofold purpose in his apparently aimless prowling: to escape from the building and its mysteries, and to find the Nemedian girl who, he felt, was imprisoned somewhere in this palace, temple, or whatever it was. He believed it was the great domed edifice in the center of the city, and it was likely that here dwelt the ruler of the town, to whom a captive woman would doubtless be brought.

He found himself in a chamber, not another corridor, and was about to retrace his steps, when he heard a voice which came from behind one of the walls. There was no door in that wall, but he leaned close and heard distinctly. And an icy chill crawled slowly along his spine. The tongue was Nemedian, but the voice was not human. There was a terrifying resonance about it, like a bell tolling at midnight.

'There was no life in the Abyss, save that which was incorporated in me,' it tolled. 'Nor was there light, nor motion, nor any sound. Only the urge behind and beyond life guided and impelled me on my upward journey, blind, insensate, inexorable. Through ages upon ages, and the changeless strata of darkness I climbed—'

Ensorcelled by that belling resonance, Conan crouched forgetful of all else, until its hypnotic power caused a strange replacement of faculties and perception, and sound created the illusion of sight. Conan was no longer aware of the voice, save as far-off rhythmical waves of sound. Transported beyond his age and his own individuality, he was seeing the transmutation of the being men called Khosatral Khel which crawled up from Night and the Abyss ages ago to clothe itself in the substance of the material universe.

But human flesh was too frail, too paltry to hold the terrific essence that was Khosatral Khel. So he stood up in the shape and aspect of a man, but his flesh was not flesh, nor the bone, bone, nor blood, blood. He became a blasphemy against all nature, for he caused to live and think and act a basic substance that before had never known the pulse and stir of animate being.

He stalked through the world like a god, for no earthly weapon could harm him, and to him a century was like an hour. In his wanderings he came upon a primitive people inhabiting the island of Dagonia, and it pleased him to give this race culture and civilization, and by his aid they built the city of Dagon and they abode there and worshipped him. Strange and grisly were his servants, called from the dark corners of the planet where grim survivals of forgotten ages yet lurked. His house in Dagon was connected with every other house by tunnels through which his shaven-headed priests bore victims for the sacrifice.

But after many ages a fierce and brutish people appeared on the shores of the sea. They called themselves Yuetshi, and after a fierce battle they were defeated and enslaved, and for nearly a generation they died on the altars of Khosatral.

His sorcery kept them in bonds. Then their priest, a strange gaunt man of unknown race, plunged into the wilderness, and when he returned he bore a knife that was of no earthly substance. It was forged of a meteor which flashed through the sky like a flaming arrow and fell in a far valley. The slaves rose. Their saw-edged crescents cut down the men of Dagon like sheep, and against that unearthly knife the magic of Khosatral was impotent. While carnage and slaughter bellowed through the red smoke that choked the streets, the grimmest act of that grim drama was played in the cryptic dome behind the great daised chamber with its copper throne and its walls mottled like the skin of serpents.

From that dome the Yuetshi priest emerged alone. He had not slain his foe, because he wished to hold the threat of his loosing over the heads of his own rebellious subjects. He had left Khosatral lying upon the golden dais with the mystic knife across his breast for a spell to hold him senseless and inanimate until doomsday.

But the ages passed and the priest died, the towers of deserted Dagon crumbled, the tales became dim, and the Yuetshi were reduced by plagues and famines and war to scattered remnants, dwelling in squalor along the seashore.

Only the cryptic dome resisted the rot of time, until a chance thunderbolt and the curiosity of a fisherman lifted from the breast of the god the magic knife and broke the spell. Khosatral Khel rose and lived and waxed mighty once more. It pleased him to restore the city as it was in the days before its fall. By his necromancy he lifted the towers from the dust of forgotten millenniums, and the folk which had been dust for ages moved in life again.

But folk who have tasted death are only partly alive. In the dark corners of their souls and minds death still lurks unconquered. By night the people of Dagon moved and loved, hated and feasted, and remembered the fall of Dagon and their own slaughter only as a dim dream; they moved in an enchanted mist of illusion, feeling the strangeness of their existence but not inquiring the reasons therefor. With the coming of day they sank into deep sleep, to be roused again only by the coming of night, which is akin to death.

All this rolled in a terrible panorama before Conan's consciousness as he crouched beside the tapestried wall. His reason staggered. All certainty and sanity were swept away, leaving a shadowy universe through which stole hooded figures of grisly potentialities. Through the belling of the voice which was like a tolling of triumph over the ordered laws of a sane planet, a human sound anchored Conan's mind from its flight through spheres of madness. It was the hysterical sobbing of a woman.

Involuntarily he sprang up.

6

Jehungir Agha waited with growing impatience in his boat among the reeds. More than an hour passed, and Conan had not reappeared. Doubtless he was still searching the island for the girl he thought to be hidden there. But another surmise occurred to the Agha. Suppose the *hetman* had left his warriors near by, and that they should grow suspicious and come to investigate his long absence? Jehungir spoke to the oarsmen, and the long boat slid from among the reeds and glided toward the carven stairs.

Leaving half a dozen men in the boat, he took the rest, ten mighty archers of Khawarizm, in spired helmets and tiger-skin cloaks. Like hunters invading the retreat of the lion, they stole forward under the trees, arrows on string. Silence reigned over the forest except when a great green thing that might have been a parrot swirled over their heads with a low thunder of broad wings, and then sped off through the trees. With a sudden gesture Jehungir halted his party, and they stared incredulously at the towers that showed through the verdure in the distance.

'Tarim!' muttered Jehungir. 'The pirates have rebuilt the ruins! Doubtless Conan is there. We must investigate this. A fortified town this close to the mainland! – Come!'

With renewed caution they glided through the trees. The game had altered; from pursuers and hunters they had become spies.

And as they crept through the tangled growth, the man they sought was in peril more deadly than their filigreed arrows.

Conan realized with a crawling of his skin that beyond the wall the belling voice had ceased. He stood motionless as a statue, his gaze fixed on a curtained door through which he knew that a culminating horror would presently appear.

It was dim and misty in the chamber, and Conan's hair began to lift on his scalp as he looked. He saw a head and a pair of gigantic shoulders grow out of the twilight gloom. There was no sound of footsteps, but the great dusky form grew more distinct until Conan recognized the figure of a man. He was clad in sandals, a skirt and a broad shagreen girdle. His square-cut mane was confined by a circlet of gold. Conan stared at the sweep of the monstrous shoulders, the breadth of the swelling breast, the bands and ridges and clusters of muscles on torso and limbs. The face was without weakness and without mercy. The eyes were balls of dark fire. And Conan knew that this was Khosatral Khel, the ancient from the Abyss, the god of Dagonia.

No word was spoken. No word was necessary. Khosatral spread his great arms, and Conan, crouching beneath them, slashed at the giant's belly. Then he bounded back, eyes blazing with surprise. The keen edge had rung on the mighty body as on an anvil, rebounding without cutting. Then Khosatral came upon him in an irresistible surge.

There was a fleeting concussion, a fierce writhing and intertwining of limbs and bodies, and then Conan sprang clear, every thew quivering from the violence of his efforts; blood started where the grazing fingers had torn the skin. In that instant of contact he had experienced the ultimate madness of blasphemed nature; no human flesh had bruised his, but *metal* animated and sentient; it was a body of living iron which opposed his.

Khosatral loomed above the warrior in the gloom. Once let those great fingers lock and they would not loosen until the human body hung limp in their grasp. In that twilit chamber it was as if a man fought with a dream-monster in a nightmare.

Flinging down his useless sword, Conan caught up a heavy bench and hurled it with all his power. It was such a missile as few men could even lift. On Khosatral's mighty breast it smashed into shreds and splinters. It did not even shake the giant on his braced legs. His face lost something of its human aspect, a nimbus of fire played about his awesome head, and like a moving tower he came on.

With a desperate wrench Conan ripped a whole section of tapestry from the wall and whirling it, with a muscular effort greater than that required for throwing the bench, he flung it over the giant's head. For an instant Khosatral floundered, smothered and blinded by the clinging stuff that resisted his strength as wood or steel could not have done, and in that instant Conan caught up his scimitar and shot out into the corridor. Without checking his speed he hurled himself through the door of the adjoining chamber, slammed the door and shot the bolt.

Then as he wheeled he stopped short, all the blood in him seeming to surge to his head. Crouching on a heap of silk cushions, golden hair streaming over her naked shoulders, eyes blank with terror, was the woman for whom he had dared so much. He almost forgot the horror at his heels until a splintering crash behind him brought him to his senses. He caught up the girl and sprang for the opposite door. She was too helpless with fright either to resist or to aid him. A faint whimper was the only sound of which she seemed capable.

Conan wasted no time trying the door. A shattering stroke of his scimitar hewed the lock asunder, and as he sprang through to the stair that loomed beyond it, he saw the head and shoulders of Khosatral crash through the other door. The colossus was splintering the massive panels as if they were of cardboard.

Conan raced up the stair, carrying the big girl over one shoulder as easily as if she had been a child. Where he was going he had no idea, but the stair ended at the door of a round, domed chamber. Khosatral was coming up the stair behind them, silently as a wind of death, and as swiftly.

The chamber's walls were of solid steel, and so was the door. Conan shut it and dropped in place the great bars with which it was furnished. The thought struck him that this was Khosatral's chamber, where he locked himself in to sleep securely from the monsters he had loosed from the Pits to do his bidding.

Hardly were the bolts in place when the great door shook and trembled to the giant's assault. Conan shrugged his shoulders. This was the end of the trail. There was no other door in the chamber, nor any window. Air, and the strange misty light, evidently came from interstices in the dome. He tested the nickel edge of his scimitar, quite cool now that he was at bay. He had done his volcanic best to escape; when the giant came crashing through that door he would explode in another savage onslaught with his useless sword, not because he expected it to do any good, but because it was his nature to die fighting. For the moment there was no course of action to take, and his calmness was not forced or feigned.

The gaze he turned on his fair companion was as admiring and intense as if he had a hundred years to live. He had dumped her unceremoniously on the floor when he turned to close the door, and she had risen to her knees, mechanically arranging her streaming locks and her scanty garment. Conan's fierce eyes glowed with approval as they devoured her thick golden hair, her clear wide eyes, her milky skin, sleek with exuberant health, the firm swell of her breasts, the contours of her splendid hips.

A low cry escaped her as the door shook and a bolt gave way with a groan.

Conan did not look around. He knew the door would hold a little while longer.

'They told me you had escaped,' he said. 'A Yuetshi fisher told me you were hiding here. What is your name?'

'Octavia,' she gasped mechanically. Then words came in a rush. She caught at him with desperate fingers. 'Oh Mitra! what nightmare is this? The people – the dark-skinned people – one of them caught me in the forest and brought me here. They carried me to – to that – that *thing*. He told me – he said – am I mad? Is this a dream?'

He glanced at the door which bulged inward as if from the impact of a battering-ram.

'No,' he said, 'it's no dream. That hinge is giving way. Strange that a devil has to break down a door like a common man; but after all, his strength itself is a diabolism.'

'Can you not kill him?' she panted. 'You are strong.'

Conan was too honest to lie. 'If a mortal man could kill him, he'd be dead now,' he answered. 'I nicked my blade on his belly.'

Her eyes dulled. 'Then you must die, and I must – oh Mitra!' she screamed in sudden frenzy, and Conan caught her hands, fearing that she would harm herself. 'He told me what he was going to do to me!' she panted. 'Kill me! Kill me with your sword before he bursts the door!'

Conan looked at her, and shook his head.

'I'll do what I can,' he said. 'That won't be much, but it'll give you a chance to get past him down the stair. Then run for the cliffs. I have a boat tied at the foot of the steps. If you can get out of the palace you may escape him yet. The people of this city are all asleep.'

She dropped her head in her hands. Conan took up his scimitar and moved over to stand before the echoing door. One watching him would have realized that he was waiting for a death he regarded as inevitable. His eyes smoldered more vividly; his muscular hand knotted harder on his hilt; that was all.

The hinges had given under the giant's terrible assault and the door rocked crazily, held only by the bolts. And these solid steel bars were buckling, bending, bulging out of their sockets. Conan watched in an almost impersonal fascination, envying the monster his inhuman strength.

Then without warning the bombardment ceased. In the stillness Conan heard other noises on the landing outside – the beat of wings, and a muttering voice that was like the whining of wind through midnight branches. Then presently there was silence, but there was a new *feel* in the air. Only the whetted instincts of barbarism could have sensed it, but Conan knew, without seeing or hearing him leave, that the master of Dagon no longer stood outside the door.

He glared through a crack that had been started in the steel of the portal. The landing was empty. He drew the warped bolts and cautiously pulled aside the sagging door. Khosatral was not on the stair, but far below he heard the clang of a metal door. He did not know whether the giant was plotting new devilries or had been summoned away by that muttering voice, but he wasted no time in conjectures.

He called to Octavia, and the new note in his voice brought her up to her feet and to his side almost without her conscious volition.

'What is it?' she gasped.

'Don't stop to talk!' He caught her wrist. 'Come on!' The chance for action had transformed him; his eyes blazed, his voice crackled. 'The knife!' he muttered, while almost dragging the girl down the stair in his fierce haste. 'The magic Yuetshi blade! He left it in the dome! I—' his voice died suddenly as a clear mental picture sprang up before him. The dome adjoined the great room where stood the copper throne – sweat started out on his body. The only way to that dome was through that room with its copper throne and the foul thing that slumbered in it.

But he did not hesitate. Swiftly they descended the stair, crossed the chamber, descended the next stair, and came into the great dim hall with its mysterious hangings. They had seen no sign of the colossus. Halting before the great bronze-valved door, Conan caught Octavia by her shoulders and shook her in his intensity.

'Listen!' he snapped. 'I'm going into that room and fasten the door. Stand here and listen; if Khosatral comes, call to me. If you hear me cry for you to go, run as though the devil were on your heels – which he probably will be. Make for that door at the other end of the hall, because I'll be past helping you. I'm going for the Yuetshi knife!'

Before she could voice the protest her lips were framing, he had slid through the valves and shut them behind him. He lowered the bolt cautiously, not noticing that it could be worked from the outside. In the dim twilight his gaze sought that grim copper throne; yes, the scaly brute was still there, filling the throne with its loathsome coils. He saw a door behind the throne and knew that it led into the dome. But to reach it he must mount the dais, a few feet from the throne itself.

A wind blowing across the green floor would have made more noise than Conan's slinking feet. Eyes glued on the sleeping reptile he reached the dais and mounted the glass steps. The snake had not moved. He was reaching for the door . . .

The bolt on the bronze portal clanged and Conan stifled an awful oath as he saw Octavia come into the room. She stared about, uncertain in the deeper gloom, and he stood frozen, not daring to shout a warning. Then she saw his shadowy figure and ran toward the dais, crying: 'I want to go with you! I'm afraid to stay alone – *oh*!' She threw up her hands with a terrible scream as for the first time she saw the occupant of the throne. The wedge-shaped head had lifted from its coils and thrust out toward her on a yard of shining neck.

Conan cleared the space between him and the throne with a desperate bound, his scimitar swinging with all his power. And with such blinding speed did the serpent move that it whipped about and met him in full midair, lapping his limbs and body with half a dozen coils. His half-checked stroke fell futilely as he crashed down on the dais, gashing the scaly trunk but not severing it.

Then he was writhing on the glass steps with fold after slimy fold knotting about him, twisting, crushing, killing him. His right arm was still free, but he could get no purchase to strike a killing blow, and he knew one blow must suffice. With a groaning convulsion of muscular expansion that bulged his veins almost to bursting on his temples and tied his muscles in quivering, tortured knots, he heaved up on his feet, lifting almost the full weight of that forty-foot devil.

An instant he reeled on wide-braced legs, feeling his ribs caving in on his vitals and his sight growing dark, while his scimitar gleamed above his head. Then it fell, shearing through the scales and flesh and vertebrae. And where there had been one huge writhing cable, now there were horribly two, lashing and flopping in the death throes. Conan staggered away from their blind strokes. He was sick and dizzy, and blood oozed from his nose. Groping in a dark mist he clutched Octavia and shook her until she gasped for breath.

'Next time I tell you to stay somewhere,' he gasped, 'you stay!'

He was too dizzy even to know whether she replied. Taking her wrist like a truant schoolgirl, he led her around the hideous stumps that still looped and knotted on the floor. Somewhere, in the distance, he thought he heard men yelling, but his ears were still roaring so that he could not be sure.

The door gave to his efforts. If Khosatral had placed the snake there to guard the thing he feared, evidently he considered it ample precaution. Conan half expected some other monstrosity to leap at him with the opening of the door, but in the dimmer light he saw only the vague sweep of the arch above, a dully gleaming block of gold, and a half-moon glimmer on the stone.

With a gasp of gratification he scooped it up, and did not linger for further exploration. He turned and fled across the room and down the great hall toward the distant door that he felt led to the outer air. He was correct. A few minutes later he emerged into the silent streets, half carrying, half guiding his companion. There was no one to be seen, but beyond the western wall there sounded cries and moaning wails that made Octavia tremble. He led her to the southwestern wall, and without difficulty found a stone stair that mounted the rampart. He had appropriated a thick tapestry rope in the great hall, and now, having reached the parapet, he looped the soft strong cord about the girl's hips and lowered her to the earth. Then, making one end fast to a merlon, he slid down after her. There was but one way of escape from the island – the stair on the western cliffs. In that direction he hurried, swinging wide around the spot from which had come the cries and the sound of terrible blows.

Octavia sensed that grim peril lurked in those leafy fastnesses. Her breath came pantingly and she pressed close to her protector. But the forest was silent now, and they saw no shape of menace until they emerged from the trees and glimpsed a figure standing on the edge of the cliffs.

Jehungir Agha had escaped the doom that had overtaken his warriors when an iron giant sallied suddenly from the gate and battered and crushed them into bits of shredded flesh and splintered bone. When he saw the swords of his archers break on that man-like juggernaut, he had known it was no human foe they faced, and he had fled, hiding in the deep woods until the sounds of slaughter ceased. Then he crept back to the stair, but his boatmen were not waiting for him.

They had heard the screams, and presently, waiting nervously, had seen, on the cliff above them, a blood-smeared monster waving gigantic arms in awful triumph. They had waited for no more. When Jehungir came upon the cliffs they were just vanishing among the reeds beyond ear-shot. Khosatral was gone – had either returned to the city or was prowling the forest in search of the man who had escaped him outside the walls.

Jehungir was just preparing to descend the stairs and depart in Conan's boat, when he saw the *hetman* and the girl emerge from the trees. The experience which had congealed his blood and almost blasted his reason had not altered Jehungir's intentions toward the *kozak* chief. The sight of the man he had come to kill filled him with gratification. He was astonished to see the girl he had given to Jelal Khan, but he wasted no time on her. Lifting his bow he drew the shaft to its head and loosed. Conan crouched and the arrow splintered on a tree, and Conan laughed.

'Dog!' he taunted. 'You can't hit me! I was not born to die on Hyrkanian steel! Try again, pig of Turan!'

Jehungir did not try again. That was his last arrow. He drew his scimitar and advanced, confident in his spired helmet and close-meshed mail. Conan met him half-way in a blinding whirl of swords. The curved blades ground together, sprang apart, circled in glittering arcs that blurred the sight which tried to follow them. Octavia, watching, did not see the stroke, but she heard its chopping impact, and saw Jehungir fall, blood spurting from his side where the Cimmerian's steel had sundered his mail and bitten to his spine.

But Octavia's scream was not caused by the death of her former master. With a crash of bending boughs Khosatral Khel was upon them. The girl could not flee; a moaning cry escaped her as her knees gave way and pitched her grovelling to the sward.

Conan, stooping above the body of the Agha, made no move to escape. Shifting his reddened scimitar to his left hand, he drew the great half-blade of the Yuetshi. Khosatral Khel was towering above him, his arms lifted like mauls, but as the blade caught the sheen of the sun, the giant gave back suddenly.

But Conan's blood was up. He rushed in, slashing with the crescent blade. And it did not splinter. Under its edge the dusky metal of Khosatral's body gave way like common flesh beneath a cleaver. From the deep gash flowed a strange ichor, and Khosatral cried out like the dirging of a great bell. His terrible arms flailed down, but Conan, quicker than the archers who had died beneath those awful flails, avoided their strokes and struck again and yet again. Khosatral reeled and tottered; his cries were awful to hear, as if metal were given a tongue of pain, as if iron shrieked and bellowed under torment.

Then wheeling away he staggered into the forest; he reeled in his gait, crashed through bushes and caromed off trees. Yet though Conan followed him with the speed of hot passion, the walls and towers of Dagon loomed through the trees before the man came within dagger-reach of the giant.

Then Khosatral turned again, flailing the air with desperate blows, but Conan, fired to berserk fury, was not to be denied. As a panther strikes down a bull moose at bay, so he plunged under the bludgeoning arms and drove the crescent blade to the hilt under the spot where a human's heart would be.

Khosatral reeled and fell. In the shape of a man he reeled, but it was not the shape of a man that struck the loam. Where there had been the likeness of a human face, there was no face at all, and the metal limbs melted and changed ... Conan, who had not shrunk from Khosatral living, recoiled blenching from Khosatral dead, for he had witnessed an awful transmutation; in his dying throes Khosatral Khel had become again the *thing* that had crawled up from the Abyss millenniums gone. Gagging with intolerable repugnance, Conan turned to flee the sight; and he was suddenly aware that the pinnacles of Dagon no longer glimmered through the trees. They had faded like smoke – the battlements, the crenellated towers, the great bronze gates, the velvets, the gold, the ivory, and the dark-haired women, and the men with their shaven skulls. With the passing of the inhuman intellect which had given them rebirth, they had faded back into the dust which they had been for ages uncounted. Only the stumps of broken columns rose above crumbling walls and broken paves and shattered dome. Conan again looked upon the ruins of Xapur as he remembered them.

The wild *hetman* stood like a statue for a space, dimly grasping something of the cosmic tragedy of the fitful ephemera called mankind and the hooded shapes of darkness which prey upon it. Then as he heard his name called in accents of fear, he started, as one awaking from a dream, glanced again at the thing on the ground, shuddered and turned away toward the cliffs and the girl that waited there.

She was peering fearfully under the trees, and she greeted him with a half-stifled cry of relief. He had shaken off the dim monstrous visions which had momentarily haunted him, and was his exuberant self again.

'Where is *he*?' she shuddered.

'Gone back to hell whence he crawled,' he replied cheerfully. 'Why didn't you climb the stair and make your escape in my boat?'

'I wouldn't desert—' she began, then changed her mind, and amended rather sulkily, 'I have nowhere to go. The Hyrkanians would enslave me again, and the pirates would—'

'What of the *kozaks*?' he suggested.

'Are they better than the pirates?' she asked scornfully. Conan's admiration increased to see how well she had recovered her poise after having endured such frantic terror. Her arrogance amused him.

'You seemed to think so in the camp by Ghori,' he answered. 'You were free enough with your smiles then.'

Her red lip curled in disdain. 'Do you think I was enamored of you? Do you dream that I would have shamed myself before an ale-guzzling, meat-gorging barbarian unless I had to? My master – whose body lies there – forced me to do as I did.'

'Oh!' Conan seemed rather crestfallen. Then he laughed with undiminished zest. 'No matter. You belong to me now. Give me a kiss.'

'You dare ask—' she began angrily, when she felt herself snatched off her feet and crushed to the *hetman*'s muscular breast. She fought him fiercely, with all the supple strength of her magnificent youth, but he only laughed exuberantly, drunk with his possession of this splendid creature writhing in his arms.

He crushed her struggles easily, drinking the nectar of her lips with all the unrestrained passion that was his, until the arms that strained against him melted and twined convulsively about his massive neck. Then he laughed down into the clear eyes, and said: 'Why should not a chief of the Free People be preferable to a city-bred dog of Turan?'

She shook back her tawny locks, still tingling in every nerve from the fire of his kisses. She did not loosen her arms from his neck. 'Do you deem yourself an Agha's equal?' she challenged.

He laughed and strode with her in his arms toward the stair. 'You shall judge,' he boasted. 'I'll burn Khawarizm for a torch to light your way to my tent.'

THE PEOPLE OF THE BLACK CIRCLE

1

Death Strikes a King

The King of Vendhya was dying. Through the hot, stifling night the temple gongs boomed and the conchs roared. Their clamor was a faint echo in the gold-domed chamber where Bunda Chand struggled on the velvet-cushioned dais. Beads of sweat glistened on his dark skin; his fingers twisted the gold-worked fabric beneath him. He was young; no spear had touched him, no poison lurked in his wine. But his veins stood out like blue cords on his temples, and his eyes dilated with the nearness of death. Trembling slave-girls knelt at the foot of the dais, and leaning down to him, watching him with passionate intensity, was his sister, the Devi Yasmina. With her was the *wazam*, a noble grown old in the royal court.

She threw up her head in a gusty gesture of wrath and despair as the thunder of the distant drums reached her ears.

'The priests and their clamor!' she exclaimed. 'They are no wiser than the leeches who are helpless! Nay, he dies and none can say why. He is dying now – and I stand here helpless, who would burn the whole city and spill the blood of thousands to save him.'

'Not a man of Ayodhya but would die in his place, if it might be, Devi,' answered the *wazam*. 'This poison—'

'I tell you it is not poison!' she cried. 'Since his birth he has been guarded so closely that the cleverest poisoners of the East could not reach him. Five skulls bleaching on the Tower of the Kites can testify to attempts which were made – and which failed. As you well know, there are ten men and ten women whose sole duty is to taste his food and wine, and fifty armed warriors guard his chamber as they guard it now. No, it is not poison; it is sorcery – black, ghastly magic—'

She ceased as the king spoke; his livid lips did not move, and there was no recognition in his glassy eyes. But his voice rose in an eery call, indistinct and far away, as if called to her from beyond vast, wind-blown gulfs.

'Yasmina! Yasmina! My sister, where are you? I can not find you. All is darkness, and the roaring of great winds!'

'Brother!' cried Yasmina, catching his limp hand in a convulsive grasp. 'I am here! Do you not know me—'

Her voice died at the utter vacancy of his face. A low confused moan waned from his mouth. The slave-girls at the foot of the dais whimpered with fear, and Yasmina beat her breast in anguish.

In another part of the city a man stood in a latticed balcony overlooking a long street in which torches tossed luridly, smokily revealing upturned dark faces and the whites of gleaming eyes. A long-drawn wailing rose from the multitude.

The man shrugged his broad shoulders and turned back into the arabesque chamber. He was a tall man, compactly built, and richly clad.

'The king is not yet dead, but the dirge is sounded,' he said to another man who sat cross-legged on a mat in a corner. This man was clad in a brown camel-hair robe and sandals, and a green turban was on his head. His expression was tranquil, his gaze impersonal.

'The people know he will never see another dawn,' this man answered.

The first speaker favored him with a long, searching stare.

'What I can not understand,' he said, 'is why I have had to wait so long for your masters to strike. If they have slain the king now, why could they not have slain him months ago?'

'Even the arts you call sorcery are governed by cosmic laws,' answered the man in the green turban. 'The stars direct these actions, as in other affairs. Not even my masters can alter the stars. Not until the heavens were in the proper order could they perform this necromancy.' With a long, stained fingernail he mapped the constellations on the marble-tiled floor. 'The slant of the moon presaged evil for the king of Vendhya; the stars are in turmoil, the Serpent in the House of the Elephant. During such juxtaposition, the invisible guardians are removed from the spirit of Bhunda Chand. A path is opened in the unseen realms, and once a point of contact was established, mighty powers were put in play along that path.'

'Point of contact?' inquired the other. 'Do you mean that lock of Bhunda Chand's hair?'

'Yes. All discarded portions of the human body still remain part of it, attached to it by intangible connections. The priests of Asura have a dim inkling of this truth, and so all nail trimmings, hair and other waste products of the persons of the royal family are carefully reduced to ashes and the ashes hidden. But at the urgent entreaty of the princess of Khosala, who loved Bhunda Chand vainly, he gave her a lock of his long black hair as a token of remembrance. When my masters decided upon his doom, the lock, in its golden, jewel-encrusted case, was stolen from under her pillow while she slept, and another substituted, so like the first that she never knew the difference. Then the genuine lock travelled by camel-caravan up the long, long road to Peshkhauri, thence up the Zhaibar Pass, until it reached the hands of those for whom it was intended.'

'Only a lock of hair,' murmured the nobleman.

'By which a soul is drawn from its body and across gulfs of echoing space,' returned the man on the mat.

The nobleman studied him curiusly.

'I do not know if you are a man or a demon, Khemsa,' he said at last. 'Few of us are what we seem. I, whom the Kshatriyas know as Kerim Shah, a prince from Iranistan, am no greater a masquerader than most men. They are all traitors in one way or another, and half of them know not whom they serve. There at least I have no doubts; for I serve King Yezdigerd of Turan.'

'And I the Black Seers of Yimsha,' said Khemsa; 'and my masters are greater than yours, for they have accomplished by their arts what Yezdigerd could not with a hundred thousand swords.'

*

Outside, the moan of the tortured thousands shuddered up to the stars which crusted the sweating Vendhyan night, and the conchs bellowed like oxen in pain.

In the gardens of the palace the torches glinted on polished helmets and curved swords and gold-chased corselets. All the noble-born fighting-men of Ayodhya were gathered in the great palace or about it, and at each broad-arched gate and door fifty archers stood on guard, with bows in their hands. But Death stalked through the royal palace and none could stay his ghostly tread.

On the dais under the golden dome the king cried out again, racked by awful paroxysms. Again his voice came faintly and far away, and again the Devi bent to him, trembling with a fear that was darker than the terror of death.

'Yasmina!' Again that far, weirdly dreeing cry, from realms immeasurable. 'Aid me! I am far from my mortal house! Wizards have drawn my soul through the wind-blown darkness. They seek to snap the silver cord that binds me to my dying body. They cluster around me; their hands are taloned, their eyes are red like flame burning in darkness. *Aie*, save me, my sister! Their fingers sear me like fire! They would slay my body and damn my soul! What is this they bring before me?—*Aie!*'

At the terror in his hopeless cry Yasmina screamed uncontrollably and threw herself bodily upon him in the abandon of her anguish. He was torn by a terrible convulsion; foam flew from his contorted lips and his writhing fingers left their marks on the girl's shoulders. But the glassy blankness passed from his eyes like smoke blown from a fire, and he looked up at his sister with recognition.

'Brother!' she sobbed. 'Brother—'

'Swift!' he gasped, and his weakening voice was rational. 'I know now what brings me to the pyre. I have been on a far journey and I understand. I have been ensorcelled by the wizards of the Himelians. They drew my soul out of my body and far away, into a stone room. There they strove to break the silver cord of life, and thrust my soul into the body of a foul night-weird their sorcery summoned up from hell. Ah! I feel their pull upon me now! Your cry and the grip of your fingers brought me back, but I am going fast. My soul clings to my body, but its hold weakens. Quick – kill me, before they can trap my soul for ever!'

'I cannot!' she wailed, smiting her naked breasts.

'Swiftly, I command you!' There was the old imperious note in his failing whisper. 'You have never disobeyed me – obey my last command! Send my soul clean to Asura! Haste, lest you damn me to spend eternity as a filthy gaunt of darkness. Strike, I command you! *Strike!*'

Sobbing wildly, Yasmina plucked a jeweled dagger from her girdle and plunged it to the hilt in his breast. He stiffened and then went limp, a grim smile curving his dead lips. Yasmina hurled herself face-down on the rush-covered floor, beating the reeds with her clenched hands. Outside, the gongs and conchs brayed and thundered and the priests gashed themselves with copper knives.

2

A Barbarian from the Hills

Chunder Shan, governor of Peshkhauri, laid down his golden pen and carefully scanned that which he had written on parchment that bore his official seal. He had ruled Peshkhauri so long only because he weighed his every word, spoken or written. Danger breeds caution, and only a wary man lives long in that wild country where the hot Vendhyan plains meet the crags of the Himelians. An hour's ride westward or northward and one crossed the border and was among the Hills where men lived by the law of the knife.

The governor was alone in his chamber, seated at his ornately carven table of inlaid ebony. Through the wide window, open for the coolness, he could see a square of the blue Himelian night, dotted with great white stars. An adjacent parapet was a shadowy line, and further crenelles and embrasures were barely hinted at in the dim starlight. The governor's fortress was strong, and situated outside the walls of the city it guarded. The breeze that stirred the tapestries on the wall brought faint noises from the streets of Peshkhauri – occasional snatches of wailing song, or the thrum of a cithern.

The governor read what he had written, slowly, with his open hand shading his eyes from the bronze butterlamp, his lips moving. Absently, as he read, he heard the drum of horses' hoofs outside the barbican, the sharp staccato of the guards' challenge. He did not heed, intent upon his letter. It was addressed to the *wazam* of Vendhya, at the royal court of Ayodhya, and it stated, after the customary salutations:

> 'Let it be known to your excellency that I have faithfully carried out your excellency's instructions. The seven tribesmen are well guarded in their prison, and I have repeatedly sent word into the hills that their chief come in person to bargain for their release. But he has made no move, except to send word that unless they are freed he will burn Peshkhauri and cover his saddle with my hide, begging your excellency's indulgence. This he is quite capable of attempting, and I have tripled the numbers of the lance guards. The man is not a native of Ghulistan. I cannot with certainty predict his next move. But since it is the wish of the Devi—'

He was out of his ivory chair and on his feet facing the arched door, all in one instant. He snatched at the curved sword lying in its ornate scabbard on the table, and then checked the movement.

It was a woman who had entered unannounced, a woman whose gossamer robes did not conceal the rich garments beneath them any more than they concealed the suppleness and beauty of her tall, slender figure. A filmy veil fell below her breasts, supported by a flowing head-dress bound about with a triple gold braid and adorned with a golden crescent. Her dark eyes regarded the astonished governor over the veil, and then with an imperious gesture of her white hand, she uncovered her face.

'Devi!' The governor dropped to his knees before her, surprise and confusion somewhat spoiling the stateliness of his obeisance.

With a gesture she motioned him to rise, and he hastened to lead her to the ivory chair, all the while bowing level with his girdle. But his first words were of reproof.

'Your Majesty! This was most unwise! The border is unsettled. Raids from the hills are incessant. You came with a large attendance?'

'An ample retinue followed me to Peshkhauri,' she answered. 'I lodged my people there and came on to the fort with my maid, Gitara.'

Chunder Shan groaned in horror.

'Devi! You do not understand the peril. An hour's ride from this spot the hills swarm with barbarians who make a profession of murder and rapine. Women have been stolen and men stabbed between the fort and the city. Peshkhauri is not like your southern provinces—'

'But I am here, and unharmed,' she interrupted with a trace of impatience. 'I showed my signet ring to the guard at the gate, and to the one outside your door, and they admitted me unannounced, not knowing me, but supposing me to be a secret courier from Ayodhya. Let us not now waste time.

'You have received no word from the chief of the barbarians?'

'None save threats and curses, Devi. He is wary and suspicious. He deems it a trap, and perhaps he is not to be blamed. The Kshatriyas have not always kept their promises to the hill people.'

'He must be brought to terms!' broke in Yasmina, the knuckles of her clenched hands showing white.

'I do not understand.' The governor shook his head. 'When I chanced to capture these seven hillmen, I reported their capture to the *wazam*, as is the custom, and then, before I could hang them, there came an order to hold them and communicate with their chief. This I did, but the man holds aloof, as I have said. These men are of the tribe of Afghulis, but he is a foreigner from the west, and he is called Conan. I have threatened to hang them tomorrow at dawn, if he does not come.'

'Good!' exclaimed the Devi. 'You have done well. And I will tell you why I have given these orders. My brother—' she faltered, choking, and the governor bowed his head, with the customary gesture of respect for a departed sovereign.

'The king of Vendhya was destroyed by magic,' she said at last. 'I have devoted my life to the destruction of his murderers. As he died he gave me a clue, and I have followed it. I have read the *Book of Skelos*, and talked with nameless hermits in the caves below Jhelai. I learned how, and by whom, he was destroyed. His enemies were the Black Seers of Mount Yimsha.'

'Asura!' whispered Chunder Shan, paling.

Her eyes knifed him through. 'Do you fear them?'

'Who does not, Your Majesty?' he replied. 'They are black devils, haunting the uninhabited hills beyond the Zhaibar. But the sages say that they seldom interfere in the lives of mortal men.'

'Why they slew my brother I do not know,' she answered. 'But I have sworn on the altar of Asura to destroy them! And I need the aid of a man beyond the border. A Kshatriya army, unaided, would never reach Yimsha.'

'Aye,' muttered Chunder Shan. 'You speak the truth there. It would be fight every step of the way, with hairy hillmen hurling down boulders from every height, and rushing us with their long knives in every valley. The Turanians fought their way through the Himelians once, but how many returned to Khurusun? Few of those who escaped the swords of the Kshatriyas, after the king, your brother, defeated their host on the Jhumda River, ever saw Secunderam again.'

'And so I must control men across the border,' she said, 'men who know the way to Mount Yimsha—'

'But the tribes fear the Black Seers and shun the unholy mountain,' broke in the governor.

'Does the chief, Conan, fear them?' she asked.

'Well, as to that,' muttered the governor, 'I doubt if there is anything that devil fears.'

'So I have been told. Therefore he is the man I must deal with. He wishes the release of his seven men. Very well; their ransom shall be the heads of the Black Seers!' Her voice thrummed with hate as she uttered the last words, and her hands clenched at her sides. She looked an image of incarnate passion as she stood there with her head thrown high and her bosom heaving.

Again the governor knelt, for part of his wisdom was the knowledge that a woman in such an emotional tempest is as perilous as a blind cobra to any about her.

'It shall be as you wish, Your Majesty.' Then as she presented a calmer aspect, he rose and ventured to drop a word of warning. 'I can not predict what the chief Conan's action will be. The tribesmen are always turbulent, and I have reason to believe that emissaries from the Turanians are stirring them up to raid our borders. As your majesty knows, the Turanians have established themselves in Secunderam and other northern cities, though the hill tribes remain unconquered. King Yezdigerd has long looked southward with greedy lust and perhaps is seeking to gain by treachery what he could not win by force of arms. I have thought that Conan might well be one of his spies.'

'We shall see,' she answered. 'If he loves his followers, he will be at the gates at dawn, to parley. I shall spend the night in the fortress. I came in disguise to Peshkhauri, and lodged my retinue at an inn instead of the palace. Besides my people, only yourself knows of my presence here.'

'I shall escort you to your quarters, Your Majesty,' said the governor, and as they emerged from the doorway, he beckoned the warrior on guard there, and the man fell in behind them, spear held at salute.

The maid waited, veiled like her mistress, outside the door, and the group traversed a wide, winding corridor, lighted by smoky torches, and reached the quarters reserved for visiting notables – generals and viceroys, mostly; none of the royal family had ever honored the fortress before. Chunder Shan had a perturbed feeling that the suite was not suitable to such an exalted personage as the Devi, and though she sought to make him feel at ease in her presence, he was glad when she dismissed him and he bowed himself out. All the menials of the fort had been summoned to serve his royal guest – though he did not divulge her identity – and he stationed a squad of spearmen before her doors, among them the warrior who had guarded his own chamber. In his preoccupation he forgot to replace the man.

The governor had not been long gone from her when Yasmina suddenly remembered something else which she had wished to discuss with him, but had forgotten until that moment. It concerned the past actions of one Kerim Shah, a nobleman from Iranistan, who had dwelt for a while in Peshkhauri before coming on to the court at Ayodhya. A vague suspicion concerning the man had been stirred by a glimpse of him in Peshkhauri that night. She wondered if he had followed her from Ayodhya. Being a truly remarkable Devi, she did not summon the governor to her again, but hurried out into the corridor alone, and hastened toward his chamber.

Chunder Shan, entering his chamber, closed the door and went to his table. There he took the letter he had been writing and tore it to bits. Scarcely had he finished when he heard something drop softly onto the parapet adjacent to the window. He looked up to see a figure loom briefly against the stars, and then a man dropped lightly into the room. The light glinted on a long sheen of steel in his hand.

'Shhhh!' he warned. 'Don't make a noise, or I'll send the devil a henchman!'

The governor checked his motion toward the sword on the table. He was within reach of the yard-long Zhaibar knife that glittered in the intruder's fist, and he knew the desperate quickness of a hillman.

The invader was a tall man, at once strong and supple. He was dressed like a hillman, but his dark features and blazing blue eyes did not match his garb. Chunder Shan had never seen a man like him; he was not an Easterner, but some barbarian from the West. But his aspect was as untamed and formidable as any of the hairy tribesmen who haunt the hills of Ghulistan.

'You come like a thief in the night,' commented the governor, recovering some of his composure, although he remembered that there was no guard within call. Still, the hillman could not know that.

'I climbed a bastion,' snarled the intruder. 'A guard thrust his head over the battlement in time for me to rap it with my knife-hilt.'

'You are Conan?'

'Who else? You sent word into the hills that you wished for me to come and parley with you. Well, by Crom, I've come! Keep away from that table or I'll gut you.'

'I merely wish to seat myself,' answered the governor, carefully sinking into the ivory chair, which he wheeled away from the table. Conan moved restlessly before him, glancing suspiciously at the door, thumbing the razor edge of his three-foot knife. He did not walk like an Afghuli, and was bluntly direct where the East is subtle.

'You have seven of my men,' he said abruptly. 'You refused the ransom I offered. What the devil do you want?'

'Let us discuss terms,' answered Chunder Shan cautiously.

'Terms?' There was a timbre of dangerous anger in his voice. 'What do you mean? Haven't I offered you gold?'

Chunder Shan laughed.

'Gold? There is more gold in Peshkhauri than you ever saw.'

'You're a liar,' retorted Conan. 'I've seen the *suk* of the goldsmiths in Khurusun.'

'Well, more than an Afghuli ever saw,' amended Chunder Shan. 'And it is but a drop of all the treasure of Vendhya. Why should we desire gold? It would be more to our advantage to hang these seven thieves.'

Conan ripped out a sulfurous oath and the long blade quivered in his grip as the muscles rose in ridges on his brown arm.

'I'll split your head like a ripe melon!'

A wild blue flame flickered in the hillman's eyes, but Chunder Shan shrugged his shoulders, though keeping an eye on the keen steel.

'You can kill me easily, and probably escape over the wall afterward. But that would not save the seven tribesmen. My men would surely hang them. And these men are headmen among the Afghulis.'

'I know it,' snarled Conan. 'The tribe is baying like wolves at my heels because I have not procured their release. Tell me in plain words what you want, because, by Crom! if there's no other way, I'll raise a horde and lead it to the very gates of Peshkhauri!'

Looking at the man as he stood squarely, knife in fist and eyes glaring, Chunder Shan did not doubt that he was capable of it. The governor did not believe any hill-horde could take Peshkhauri, but he did not wish a devastated countryside.

'There is a mission you must perform,' he said, choosing his words with as much care as if they had been razors. 'There—'

Conan had sprung back, wheeling to face the door at the same instant, lips asnarl. His barbarian ears had caught the quick tread of soft slippers outside the door. The next instant the door was thrown open and a slim, silk-robed form entered hastily, pulling the door shut – then stopping short at sight of the hillman.

Chunder Shan sprang up, his heart jumping into his mouth.

'Devi!' he cried involuntarily, losing his head momentarily in his fright.

'Devi!' It was like an explosive echo from the hillman's lips. Chunder Shan saw recognition and intent flame up in the fierce blue eyes.

The governor shouted desperately and caught at his sword, but the hillman moved with the devastating speed of a hurricane. He sprang, knocked the governor sprawling with a savage blow of his knife-hilt, swept up the astounded Devi in one brawny arm and leaped for the window. Chunder Shan, struggling frantically to his feet, saw the man poise an instant on the sill in a flutter of silken skirts and white limbs that was his royal captive, and heard his fierce, exultant snarl: '*Now* dare to hang my men!' and then Conan leaped to the parapet and was gone. A wild scream floated back to the governor's ears.

'Guard! *Guard!*' screamed the governor, struggling up and running drunkenly to the door. He tore it open and reeled into the hall. His shouts re-echoed along the corridors, and warriors came running, gaping to see the governor holding his broken head, from which the blood streamed.

'Turn out the lancers!' he roared. 'There has been an abduction!' Even in his frenzy he had enough sense left to withhold the full truth. He stopped short as he heard a sudden drum of hoofs outside, a frantic scream and a wild yell of barbaric exultation.

Followed by the bewildered guardsmen, the governor raced for the stair. In the courtyard of the fort a force of lancers stood by saddled steeds, ready to ride at an instant's notice. Chunder Shan led his squadron flying after the fugitive, though his head swam so he had to hold with both hands to the saddle. He did not divulge the identity of the victim, but said merely that the noblewoman who had borne the royal signet-ring had been carried away by the chief of the Afghulis. The abductor was out of sight and hearing, but they knew the path he would strike – the road that runs straight to the mouth of the Zhaibar. There was no moon; peasant huts rose dimly in the starlight. Behind them fell away the grim bastion of the fort, and the towers of Peshkhauri. Ahead of them loomed the black walls of the Himelians.

3

Khemsa Uses Magic

In the confusion that reigned in the fortress while the guard was being turned out, no one noticed that the girl who had accompanied the Devi slipped out the great arched gate and vanished in the darkness. She ran straight for the city, her garments tucked high. She did not follow the open road, but cut straight through fields and over slopes, avoiding fences and leaping irrigation ditches as surely as if it were broad daylight, and as easily as if she were a trained masculine runner. The hoof-drum of the guardsmen had faded away up the hill before she reached the city wall. She did not go to the great gate, beneath whose arch men leaned on spears and craned their necks into the darkness, discussing the unwonted activity about the fortress. She skirted the wall until she reached a certain point where the spire of the tower was visible above the battlements. Then she placed her hands to her mouth and voiced a low weird call that carried strangely.

Almost instantly a head appeared at an embrasure and a rope came wriggling down the wall. She seized it, placed a foot in the loop at the end, and waved her arm. Then quickly and smoothly she was drawn up the sheer stone curtain. An instant later she scrambled over the merlons and stood up on a flat roof which covered a house that was built against the wall. There was an open trap there, and a man in a camel-hair robe who silently coiled the rope, not showing in any way the strain of hauling a full-grown woman up a forty-foot wall.

'Where is Kerim Shah?' she gasped, panting after her long run.

'Asleep in the house below. You have news?'

'Conan has stolen the Devi out of the fortress and carried her away into the hills!' She blurted out her news in a rush, the words stumbling over one another.

Khemsa showed no emotion, but merely nodded his turbaned head. 'Kerim Shah will be glad to hear that,' he said.

'Wait!' The girl threw her supple arms about his neck. She was panting hard, but not only from exertion. Her eyes blazed like black jewels in the starlight. Her upturned face was close to Khemsa's, but though he submitted to her embrace, he did not return it.

'Do not tell the Hyrkanian!' she panted. 'Let us use this knowledge ourselves! The governor has gone into the hills with his riders, but he might as well chase a ghost. He has not told anyone that it was the Devi who was kidnapped. None in Peshkhauri or the fort knows it except us.'

'But what good does it do us?' the man expostulated. 'My masters sent me with Kerim Shah to aid him in every way—'

'Aid yourself!' she cried fiercely. 'Shake off your yoke!'

'You mean – disobey my masters?' he gasped, and she felt his whole body turn cold under her arms.

'Aye!' she shook him in the fury of her emotion. 'You too are a magician! Why will you be a slave, using your powers only to elevate others? Use your arts for yourself!'

'That is forbidden!' He was shaking as if with an ague. 'I am not one of the Black Circle. Only by the command of the masters do I dare to use the knowledge they have taught me.'

'But you *can* use it!' she argued passionately. 'Do as I beg you! Of course Conan has taken the Devi to hold as hostage against the seven tribesmen in the governor's prison. Destroy them, so Chunder Shan can not use them to buy back the Devi. Then let us go into the mountains and take her from the Afghulis. They can not stand against your sorcery with their knives. The treasure of the Vendhyan kings will be ours as ransom – and then when we have it in our hands, we can trick them, and sell her to the king of Turan. We shall have wealth beyond our maddest dreams. With it we can buy warriors. We will take Khorbhul, oust the Turanians from the hills, and send our hosts southward; become king and queen of an empire!'

Khemsa too was panting, shaking like a leaf in her grasp; his face showed gray in the starlight, beaded with great drops of perspiration.

'I love you!' she cried fiercely, writhing her body against his, almost strangling him in her wild embrace, shaking him in her abandon. 'I will make a king of you! For love of you I betrayed my mistress; for love of me betray your masters! Why fear the Black Seers? By your love for me you have broken one of their laws already! Break the rest! You are as strong as they!'

A man of ice could not have withstood the searing heat of her passion and fury. With an inarticulate cry he crushed her to him, bending her backward and showering gasping kisses on her eyes, face and lips.

'I'll do it!' His voice was thick with laboring emotions. He staggered like a drunken man. 'The arts they have taught me shall work for me, not for my masters. We shall be rulers of the world – of the world—'

'Come then!' Twisting lithely out of his embrace, she seized his hand and led him toward the trap-door. 'First we must make sure that the governor does not exchange those seven Afghulis for the Devi.'

He moved like a man in a daze, until they had descended a ladder and she paused in the chamber below. Kerim Shah lay on a couch motionless, an arm across his face as though to shield his sleeping eyes from the soft light of a brass lamp. She plucked Khemsa's arm and made a quick gesture across her own throat. Khemsa lifted his hand; then his expression changed and he drew away.

'I have eaten his salt,' he muttered. 'Besides, he can not interfere with us.'

He led the girl through a door that opened on a winding stair. After their soft tread had faded into silence, the man on the couch sat up. Kerim Shah wiped the sweat from his face. A knife-thrust he did not dread, but he feared Khemsa as a man fears a poisonous reptile.

'People who plot on roofs should remember to lower their voices,' he muttered. 'But as Khemsa has turned against his masters, and as he was my only contact between them, I can count on their aid no longer. From now on I play the game in my own way.'

Rising to his feet he went quickly to a table, drew pen and parchment from his girdle and scribbled a few succinct lines.

> 'To Khosru Khan, governor of Secunderam: the Cimmerian Conan has carried the Devi Yasmina to the villages of the Afghulis. It is an opportunity to get the Devi into our hands, as the king has so long desired. Send three thousand horsemen at once. I will meet them in the valley of Gurashah with native guides.'

And he signed it with a name that was not in the least like Kerim Shah.

Then from a golden cage he drew forth a carrier pigeon, to whose leg he made fast the parchment, rolled into a tiny cylinder and secured with gold wire. Then he went quickly to a casement and tossed the bird into the night. It wavered on fluttering wings, balanced, and was gone like a flitting shadow. Catching up helmet, sword and cloak, Kerim Shah hurried out of the chamber and down the winding stair.

The prison quarters of Peshkhauri were separated from the rest of the city by a massive wall, in which was set a single iron-bound door under an arch. Over the arch burned a lurid red cresset, and beside the door squatted a warrior with spear and shield.

This warrior, leaning on his spear, and yawning from time to time, started suddenly to his feet. He had not thought he had dozed, but a man was standing before him, a man he had not heard approach. The man wore a camel-hair robe and a green turban. In the flickering light of the cresset his features were shadowy, but a pair of lambent eyes shone surprisingly in the lurid glow.

'Who comes?' demanded the warrior, presenting his spear. 'Who are you?'

The stranger did not seem perturbed, though the spear-point touched his bosom. His eyes held the warrior's with strange intensity.

'What are you obliged to do?' he asked, strangely.

'To guard the gate!' The warrior spoke thickly and mechanically; he stood rigid as a statue, his eyes slowly glazing.

'You lie! You are obliged to obey me! You have looked into my eyes, and your soul is no longer your own. Open that door!'

Stiffly, with the wooden features of an image, the guard wheeled about, drew a great key from his girdle, turned it in the massive lock and swung open the door. Then he stood at attention, his unseeing stare straight ahead of him.

A woman glided from the shadows and laid an eager hand on the mesmerist's arm.

'Bid him fetch us horses, Khemsa,' she whispered.

'No need of that,' answered the Rakhsha. Lifting his voice slightly he spoke to the guardsman. 'I have no more use for you. Kill yourself!'

Like a man in a trance the warrior thrust the butt of his spear against the base of the wall, and placed the keen head against his body, just below the ribs. Then slowly, stolidly, he leaned against it with all his weight, so that it transfixed his body and came out between his shoulders. Sliding down the shaft he lay still, the spear jutting above him its full length, like a horrible stalk growing out of his back.

The girl stared down at him in morbid fascination, until Khemsa took her arm and led her through the gate. Torches lighted a narrow space between the outer wall and a lower inner one, in which were arched doors at regular intervals. A warrior paced this enclosure, and when the gate opened he came sauntering up, so secure in his knowledge of the prison's strength that he was not suspicious until Khemsa and the girl emerged from the archway. Then it was too late. The Rakhsha did not waste time in hypnotism, though his action savored of magic to the girl. The guard lowered his spear threateningly, opening his mouth to shout an alarm that would bring spearmen swarming out of the guardrooms at either end of the alleyway. Khemsa flicked the spear aside with his left hand, as a man might flick a straw, and his right flashed out and back, seeming gently to caress the warrior's neck in passing. And the guard pitched on his face without a sound, his head lolling on a broken neck.

Khemsa did not glance at him, but went straight to one of the arched doors and placed his open hand against the heavy bronze lock. With a rending shudder the portal buckled inward. As the girl followed him through, she saw that the thick teakwood hung in splinters, the bronze bolts were bent and twisted from their sockets, and the great hinges broken and disjointed. A thousand-pound battering-ram with forty men to swing it could have shattered the barrier no more completely. Khemsa was drunk with freedom and the exercise of his power, glorying in his might and flinging his strength about as a young giant exercises his thews with unnecessary vigor in the exultant pride of his prowess.

The broken door let them into a small courtyard, lit by a cresset. Opposite the door was a wide grille of iron bars. A hairy hand was visible, gripping one of these bars, and in the darkness behind them glimmered the whites of eyes.

Khemsa stood silent for a space, gazing into the shadows from which those glimmering eyes gave back his stare with burning intensity. Then his hand went into his robe and came out again, and from his opening fingers a shimmering feather of sparkling dust sifted to the flags. Instantly a flare of green fire lighted the enclosure. In the brief glare the forms of seven men, standing motionless behind the bars, were limned in vivid detail; tall, hairy men in ragged hillmen's garments. They did not speak, but in their eyes blazed the fear of death, and their hairy fingers gripped the bars.

The fire died out but the glow remained, a quivering ball of lambent green that pulsed and shimmered on the flags before Khemsa's feet. The wide gaze of the tribesmen was fixed upon it. It wavered, elongated; it turned into a luminous greensmoke spiraling upward. It twisted and writhed like a great shadowy serpent, then broadened and billowed out in shining folds and whirls. It grew to a cloud moving silently over the flags – straight toward the grille. The men watched its coming with dilated eyes; the bars quivered with the grip of their desperate fingers. Bearded lips parted but no sound came forth. The green cloud rolled on the bars and blotted them from sight; like a fog it oozed through the grille and hid the men within. From the enveloping folds came a strangled gasp, as of a man plunged suddenly under the surface of water. That was all.

Khemsa touched the girl's arm, as she stood with parted lips and dilated eyes. Mechanically she turned away with him, looking back over her shoulder. Already the mist was thinning; close to the bars she saw a pair of sandalled feet, the toes turned upward – she glimpsed the indistinct outlines of seven still, prostrate shapes.

'And now for a steed swifter than the fastest horse ever bred in a mortal stable,' Khemsa was saying. 'We will be in Afghulistan before dawn.'

4

An Encounter in the Pass

Yasmina Devi could never clearly remember the details of her abduction. The unexpectedness and violence stunned her; she had only a confused impression of a whirl of happenings – the terrifying grip of a mighty arm, the blazing eyes of her abductor, and his hot breath burning on her flesh. The leap through the window to the parapet, the mad race across battlements and roofs when the fear of falling froze her, the reckless descent of a rope bound to a merlon – he went down almost at a run, his captive folded limply over his brawny shoulder – all this was a befuddled tangle in the Devi's mind. She retained a more vivid memory of him running fleetly into the shadows of the trees, carrying her like a child, and vaulting into the saddle of a fierce Bhalkhana stallion which reared and snorted. Then there was a sensation of flying, and the racing hoofs were striking sparks of fire from the flinty road as the stallion swept up the slopes.

As the girl's mind cleared, her first sensations were furious rage and shame. She was appalled. The rulers of the golden kingdoms south of the Himelians were considered little short of divine; and she was the Devi of Vendhya! Fright was submerged in regal wrath. She cried out furiously and began struggling. She, Yasmina, to be carried on the saddle-bow of a hill chief, like a common wench of the market-place! He merely hardened his massive thews slightly against her writhings, and for the first time in her life she experienced the coercion of superior physical strength. His arms felt like iron about her slender limbs. He glanced down at her and grinned hugely. His teeth glimmered whitely in the starlight. The reins lay loose on the stallion's flowing mane, and every thew and fiber of the great beast strained as he hurtled along the boulder-strewn trail. But Conan sat easily, almost carelessly, in the saddle, riding like a centaur.

'You hill-bred dog!' she panted, quivering with the impact of shame, anger, and the realization of helplessness. 'You dare – you *dare*! Your life shall pay for this! Where are you taking me?'

'To the villages of Afghulistan,' he answered, casting a glance over his shoulder.

Behind them, beyond the slopes they had traversed, torches were tossing on the walls of the fortress, and he glimpsed a flare of light that meant the great gate had been opened. And he laughed, a deep-throated boom gusty as the hill wind.

'The governor has sent his riders after us,' he laughed. 'By Crom, we will lead him a merry chase! What do you think, Devi

– will they pay seven lives for a Kshatriya princess?'

'They will send an army to hang you and your spawn of devils,' she promised him with conviction.

He laughed gustily and shifted her to a more comfortable position in his arms. But she took this as a fresh outrage, and renewed her vain struggle, until she saw that her efforts were only amusing him. Besides, her light silken garments, floating on the wind, were being outrageously disarranged by her struggles. She concluded that a scornful submission was the better part of dignity, and lapsed into a smoldering quiescence.

She felt even her anger being submerged by awe as they entered the mouth of the Pass, lowering like a black well mouth in the blacker walls that rose like colossal ramparts to bar their way. It was as if a gigantic knife had cut the Zhaibar out of walls of solid rock. On either hand sheer slopes pitched up for thousands of feet, and the mouth of the Pass was dark as hate. Even Conan could not see with any accuracy, but he knew the road, even by night. And knowing that armed men were racing through the starlight after him, he did not check the stallion's speed. The great brute was not yet showing fatigue. He thundered along the road that followed the valley bed, labored up a slope, swept along a low ridge where treacherous shale on either hand lurked for the unwary, and came upon a trail that followed the lap of the left-hand wall.

Not even Conan could spy, in that darkness, an ambush set by Zhaibar tribesmen. As they swept past the black mouth of a gorge that opened into the Pass, a javelin swished through the air and thudded home behind the stallion's straining shoulder. The great beast let out his life in a shuddering sob and stumbled, going headlong in mid-stride. But Conan had recognized the flight and stroke of the javelin, and he acted with spring-steel quickness.

As the horse fell he leaped clear, holding the girl aloft to guard her from striking boulders. He lit on his feet like a cat, thrust her into a cleft of rock, and wheeled toward the outer darkness, drawing his knife.

Yasmina, confused by the rapidity of events, not quite sure just what had happened, saw a vague shape rush out of the darkness, bare feet slapping softly on the rock, ragged garments whipping on the wind of his haste. She glimpsed the flicker of steel, heard the lightning crack of stroke, parry and counter-stroke, and the crunch of bone as Conan's long knife split the other's skull.

Conan sprang back, crouching in the shelter of the rocks. Out in the night men were moving and a stentorian voice roared: 'What, you dogs! Do you flinch? In, curse you, and take them!'

Conan started, peered into the darkness and lifted his voice.

'Yar Afzal! Is it you?'

There sounded a startled imprecation, and the voice called warily.

'Conan? Is it you, Conan?'

'Aye!' the Cimmerian laughed. 'Come forth, you old war-dog. I've slain one of your men.'

There was movement among the rocks, a light flared dimly, and then a flame appeared and came bobbing toward him, and as it approached, a fierce bearded countenance grew out of the darkness. The man who carried it held it high, thrust forward, and craned his neck to peer among the boulders it lighted; the other hand gripped a great curved tulwar. Conan stepped forward, sheathing his knife, and the other roared a greeting.

'Aye, it is Conan! Come out of your rocks, dogs! It is Conan!'

Others pressed into the wavering circle of light – wild, ragged, bearded men, with eyes like wolves, and long blades in their fists. They did not see Yasmina, for she was hidden by Conan's massive body. But peeping from her covert, she knew icy fear for the first time that night. These men were more like wolves than human beings.

'What are you hunting in the Zhaibar by night, Yar Afzal?' Conan demanded of the burly chief, who grinned like a bearded ghoul.

'Who knows what might come up the Pass after dark? We Wazulis are night-hawks. But what of you, Conan?'

'I have a prisoner,' answered the Cimmerian. And moving aside he disclosed the cowering girl. Reaching a long arm into the crevice he drew her trembling forth.

Her imperious bearing was gone. She stared timidly at the ring of bearded faces that hemmed her in, and was grateful for the strong arm that clasped her possessively. The torch was thrust close to her, and there was a sucking intake of breath about the ring.

'She is my captive,' Conan warned, glancing pointedly at the feet of the man he had slain, just visible within the ring of light. 'I was taking her to Afghulistan, but now you have slain my horse, and the Kshatriyas are close behind me.'

'Come with us to my village,' suggested Yar Afzal. 'We have horses hidden in the gorge. They can never follow us in the darkness. They are close behind you, you say?'

'So close that I hear now the clink of their hoofs on the flint,' answered Conan grimly.

Instantly there was movement; the torch was dashed out and the ragged shapes melted like phantoms into the darkness. Conan swept up the Devi in his arms, and she did not resist. The rocky ground hurt her slim feet in their soft slippers and she felt very small and helpless in that brutish, primordial blackness among those colossal, nighted crags.

Feeling her shiver in the wind that moaned down the defiles, Conan jerked a ragged cloak from its owner's shoulders and wrapped it about her. He also hissed a warning in her ear, ordering her to make no sound. She did not hear the distant clink of shod hoofs on rock that warned the keen-eared hillmen; but she was far too frightened to disobey, in any event.

She could see nothing but a few faint stars far above, but she knew by the deepening darkness when they entered the gorge mouth. There was a stir about them, the uneasy movement of horses. A few muttered words, and Conan mounted the horse of the man he had killed, lifting the girl up in front of him. Like phantoms except for the click of their hoofs, the band swept away up the shadowy gorge. Behind them on the trail they left the dead horse and the dead man, which were found less than half an hour later by the riders from the fortress, who recognized the man as a Wazuli and drew their own conclusions accordingly.

Yasmina, snuggled warmly in her captor's arms, grew drowsy in spite of herself. The motion of the horse, though it was uneven, uphill and down, yet possessed a certain rhythm which combined with weariness and emotional exhaustion to force sleep upon her. She had lost all sense of time or direction. They moved in soft thick darkness, in which she sometimes glimpsed vaguely gigantic walls sweeping up like black ramparts, or great crags shouldering the stars; at times she sensed echoing depths beneath them, or felt the wind of dizzy heights blowing cold about her. Gradually these things faded into a dreamy unwakefulness in which the clink of hoofs and the creak of saddles were like the irrelevant sounds in a dream.

She was vaguely aware when the motion ceased and she was lifted down and carried a few steps. Then she was laid down on something soft and rustling, and something – a folded coat perhaps – was thrust under her head, and the cloak in which she was wrapped was carefully tucked about her. She heard Yar Afzal laugh.

'A rare prize, Conan; fit mate for a chief of the Afghulis.'

'Not for me,' came Conan's answering rumble. 'This wench will buy the lives of my seven headmen, blast their souls.'

That was the last she heard as she sank into dreamless slumber.

She slept while armed men rode through the dark hills, and the fate of kingdoms hung in the balance. Through the shadowy gorges and defiles that night there rang the hoofs of galloping horses, and the starlight glimmered on helmets and curved blades, until the ghoulish shapes that haunt the crags stared into the darkness from ravine and boulder and wondered what things were afoot.

A band of these sat gaunt horses in the black pitmouth of a gorge as the hurrying hoofs swept past. Their leader, a well-built man in a helmet and gilt-braided cloak, held up his hand warningly, until the riders had sped on. Then he laughed softly.

'They must have lost the trail! Or else they have found that Conan has already reached the Afghuli villages. It will take many riders to smoke out that hive. There will be squadrons riding up the Zhaibar by dawn.'

'If there is fighting in the hills there will be looting,' muttered a voice behind him, in the dialect of the Irakzai.

'There will be looting,' answered the man with the helmet. 'But first it is our business to reach the valley of Gurashah and await the riders that will be galloping southward from Secunderam before daylight.'

He lifted his reins and rode out of the defile, his men falling in behind him – thirty ragged phantoms in the starlight.

5

The Black Stallion

The sun was well up when Yasmina awoke. She did not start and stare blankly, wondering where she was. She awoke with full knowledge of all that had occurred. Her supple limbs were stiff from her long ride, and her firm flesh seemed to feel the contact of the muscular arm that had borne her so far.

She was lying on a sheepskin covering a pallet of leaves on a hard-beaten dirt floor. A folded sheepskin coat was under her head, and she was wrapped in a ragged cloak. She was in a large room, the walls of which were crudely but strongly built of uncut rocks, plastered with sun-baked mud. Heavy beams supported a roof of the same kind, in which showed a trap-door up to which led a ladder. There were no windows in the thick walls, only loop-holes. There was one door, a sturdy bronze affair that must have been looted from some Vendhyan border tower. Opposite it was a wide opening in the wall, with no door, but several strong wooden bars in place. Beyond them Yasmina saw a magnificent black stallion munching a pile of dried grass. The building was fort, dwelling-place and stable in one.

At the other end of the room a girl in the vest and baggy trousers of a hill-woman squatted beside a small fire, cooking strips of meat on an iron grid laid over blocks of stone. There was a sooty cleft in the wall a few feet from the floor, and some of the smoke found its way out there. The rest floated in blue wisps about the room.

The hill-girl glanced at Yasmina over her shoulder, displaying a bold, handsome face, and then continued her cooking. Voices boomed outside; then the door was kicked open, and Conan strode in. He looked more enormous than ever with the morning sunlight behind him, and Yasmina noted some details that had escaped her the night before. His garments were clean and not ragged. The broad Bakhariot girdle that supported his knife in its ornamented scabbard would have matched the robes of a prince, and there was a glint of fine Turanian mail under his shirt.

'Your captive is awake, Conan,' said the Wazuli girl, and he grunted, strode up to the fire and swept the strips of mutton off into a stone dish.

The squatting girl laughed up at him, with some spicy jest, and he grinned wolfishly, and hooking a toe under her haunches, tumbled her sprawling onto the floor. She seemed to derive considerable amusement from this bit of rough horse-play, but Conan paid no more heed to her. Producing a great hunk of bread from somewhere, with a copper jug of wine, he carried the lot to Yasmina, who had risen from her pallet and was regarding him doubtfully.

'Rough fare for a Devi, girl, but our best,' he grunted. 'It will fill your belly, at least.'

He set the platter on the floor, and she was suddenly aware of a ravenous hunger. Making no comment, she seated herself cross-legged on the floor, and taking the dish in her lap, she began to eat, using her fingers, which were all she had in the way of table utensils. After all, adaptability is one of the tests of true aristocracy. Conan stood looking down at her, his thumbs hooked in his girdle. He never sat cross-legged, after the Eastern fashion.

'Where am I?' she asked abruptly.

'In the hut of Yar Afzal, the chief of the Khurum Wazulis,' he answered. 'Afghulistan lies a good many miles farther on to the west. We'll hide here awhile. The Kshatriyas are beating up the hills for you – several of their squads have been cut up by the tribes already.'

'What are you going to do?' she asked.

'Keep you until Chunder Shan is willing to trade back my seven cow-thieves,' he grunted. 'Women of the Wazulis are crushing ink out of *shoki* leaves, and after a while you can write a letter to the governor.'

A touch of her old imperious wrath shook her, as she thought how maddeningly her plans had gone awry, leaving her captive of the very man she had plotted to get into her power. She flung down the dish, with the remnants of her meal, and sprang to her feet, tense with anger.

'I will not write a letter! If you do not take me back, they will hang your seven men, and a thousand more besides!'

The Wazuli girl laughed mockingly, Conan scowled, and then the door opened and Yar Afzal came swaggering in. The Wazuli chief was as tall as Conan, and of greater girth, but he looked fat and slow beside the hard compactness of the Cimmerian. He plucked his red-stained beard and stared meaningly at the Wazuli girl, and that wench rose and scurried out without delay. Then Yar Afzal turned to his guest.

'The damnable people murmur, Conan,' quoth he. 'They wish me to murder you and take the girl to hold for ransom. They say that anyone can tell by her garments that she is a noble lady. They say why should the Afghuli dogs profit by her, when it is the people who take the risk of guarding her?'

'Lend me your horse,' said Conan. 'I'll take her and go.'

'Pish!' boomed Yar Afzal. 'Do you think I can't handle my own people? I'll have them dancing in their shirts if they cross me! They don't love you – or any other outlander – but you saved my life once, and I will not forget. Come out, though, Conan; a scout has returned.'

Conan hitched at his girdle and followed the chief outside. They closed the door after them, and Yasmina peeped through a loophole. She looked out on a level space before the hut. At the farther end of that space there was a cluster of mud and stone huts, and she saw naked children playing among the boulders, and the slim erect women of the hills going about their tasks.

Directly before the chief's hut a circle of hairy, ragged men squatted, facing the door. Conan and Yar Afzal stood a few paces before the door, and between them and the ring of warriors another man sat cross-legged. This one was addressing his chief in the harsh accents of the Wazuli which Yasmina could scarcely understand, though as part of her royal education she had been taught the languages of Iranistan and the kindred tongues of Ghulistan.

'I talked with a Dagozai who saw the riders last night,' said the scout. 'He was lurking near when they came to the spot where we ambushed the lord Conan. He overheard their speech. Chunder Shan was with them. They found the dead horse, and one of the men recognized it as Conan's. Then they found the man Conan slew, and knew him for a Wazuli. It seemed to them that Conan had been slain and the girl taken by the Wazuli; so they turned aside from their purpose of following to Afghulistan. But they did not know from which village the dead man was come, and we had left no trail a Kshatriya could follow.

'So they rode to the nearest Wazuli village, which was the village of Jugra, and burnt it and slew many of the people. But the men of Khojur came upon them in darkness and slew some of them, and wounded the governor. So the survivors retired down the Zhaibar in the darkness before dawn, but they returned with reinforcements before sunrise, and there has been skirmishing and fighting in the hills all morning. It is said that a great army is being raised to sweep the hills about the Zhaibar. The tribes are whetting their knives and laying ambushes in every pass from here to Gurashah valley. Moreover, Kerim Shah has returned to the hills.'

A grunt went around the circle, and Yasmina leaned closer to the loop-hole at the name she had begun to mistrust.

'Where went he?' demanded Yar Afzal.

'The Dagozai did not know; with him were thirty Irakzai of the lower villages. They rode into the hills and disappeared.'

'These Irakzai are jackals that follow a lion for crumbs,' growled Yar Afzal. 'They have been lapping up the coins Kerim Shah scatters among the border tribes to buy men like horses. I like him not, for all he is our kinsman from Iranistan.'

'He's not even that,' said Conan. 'I know him of old. He's an Hyrkanian, a spy of Yezdigerd's. If I catch him I'll hang his hide to a tamarisk.'

'But the Kshatriyas!' clamored the men in the semicircle. 'Are we to squat on our haunches until they smoke us out? They will learn at last in which Wazuli village the wench is held. We are not loved by the Zhaibari; they will help the Kshatriyas hunt us out.'

'Let them come,' grunted Yar Afzal. 'We can hold the defiles against a host.'

One of the men leaped up and shook his fist at Conan.

'Are we to take all the risks while he reaps the rewards?' he howled. 'Are we to fight his battles for him?'

With a stride Conan reached him and bent slightly to stare full into his hairy face. The Cimmerian had not drawn his long knife, but his left hand grasped the scabbard, jutting the hilt suggestively forward.

'I ask no man to fight my battles,' he said softly. 'Draw your blade if you dare, you yapping dog!'

The Wazuli started back, snarling like a cat.

'Dare to touch me and here are fifty men to rend you apart!' he screeched.

'What!' roared Yar Afzal, his face purpling with wrath. His whiskers bristled, his belly swelled with his rage. 'Are you chief of Khurum? Do the Wazulis take orders from Yar Afzal, or from a low-bred cur?'

The man cringed before his invincible chief, and Yar Afzal, striding up to him, seized him by the throat and choked him until his face was turning black. Then he hurled the man savagely against the ground and stood over him with his tulwar in his hand.

'Is there any who questions my authority?' he roared, and his warriors looked down sullenly as his bellicose glare swept their semicircle. Yar Afzal grunted scornfully and sheathed his weapon with a gesture that was the apex of insult. Then he kicked the fallen agitator with a concentrated vindictiveness that brought howls from his victim.

'Get down the valley to the watchers on the heights and bring word if they have seen anything,' commanded Yar Afzal, and the man went, shaking with fear and grinding his teeth with fury.

Yar Afzal then seated himself ponderously on a stone, growling in his beard. Conan stood near him, legs braced apart, thumbs hooked in his girdle, narrowly watching the assembled warriors. They stared at him sullenly, not daring to brave Yar Afzal's fury, but hating the foreigner as only a hillman can hate.

'Now listen to me, you sons of nameless dogs, while I tell you what the lord Conan and I have planned to fool the Kshatriyas.' The boom of Yar Afzal's bull-like voice followed the discomfited warrior as he slunk away from the assembly.

The man passed by the cluster of huts, where women who had seen his defeat laughed at him and called stinging comments, and hastened on along the trail that wound among spurs and rocks toward the valley head.

Just as he rounded the first turn that took him out of sight of the village, he stopped short, gaping stupidly. He had not believed it possible for a stranger to enter the valley of Khurum without being detected by the hawk-eyed watchers along the heights; yet a man sat cross-legged on a low ledge beside the path – a man in a camel-hair robe and a green turban.

The Wazuli's mouth gaped for a yell, and his hand leaped to his knife-hilt. But at that instant his eyes met those of the stranger and the cry died in his throat, his fingers went limp. He stood like a statue, his own eyes glazed and vacant.

For minutes the scene held motionless; then the man on the ledge drew a cryptic symbol in the dust on the rock with his forefinger. The Wazuli did not see him place anything within the compass of that emblem, but presently something gleamed there – a round, shiny black ball that looked like polished jade. The man in the green turban took this up and tossed it to the Wazuli, who mechanically caught it.

'Carry this to Yar Afzal,' he said, and the Wazuli turned like an automaton and went back along the path, holding the black jade ball in his outstretched hand. He did not even turn his head to the renewed jeers of the women as he passed the huts. He did not seem to hear.

The man on the ledge gazed after him with a cryptic smile. A girl's head rose above the rim of the ledge and she looked at him with admiration and a touch of fear that had not been present the night before.

'Why did you do that?' she asked.

He ran his fingers through her dark locks caressingly.

'Are you still dizzy from your flight on the horse-of-air, that you doubt my wisdom?' he laughed. 'As long as Yar Afzal lives, Conan will bide safe among the Wazuli fighting-men. Their knives are sharp, and there are many of them. What I plot will be safer, even for me, than to seek to slay him and take her from among them. It takes no wizard to predict what the Wazulis will do, and what Conan will do, when my victim hands the globe of Yezud to the chief of Khurum.'

Back before the hut, Yar Afzal halted in the midst of some tirade, surprised and displeased to see the man he had sent up the valley, pushing his way through the throng.

'I bade you go to the watchers!' the chief bellowed. 'You have not had time to come from them.'

The other did not reply; he stood woodenly, staring vacantly into the chief's face, his palm outstretched holding the jade ball. Conan, looking over Yar Afzal's shoulder, murmured something and reached to touch the chief's arm, but as he did so, Yar Afzal, in a paroxysm of anger, struck the man with his clenched fist and felled him like an ox. As he fell, the jade sphere rolled to Yar Afzal's foot, and the chief, seeming to see it for the first time, bent and picked it up. The men, staring perplexedly at their senseless comrade, saw their chief bend, but they did not see what he picked up from the ground.

Yar Afzal straightened, glanced at the jade, and made a motion to thrust it into his girdle.

'Carry that fool to his hut,' he growled. 'He has the look of a lotus-eater. He returned me a blank stare. I – *aie*!'

In his right hand, moving toward his girdle, he had suddenly felt movement where movement should not be. His voice died away as he stood and glared at nothing; and inside his clenched right hand he felt the quivering of *change*, of *motion*, of *life*. He no longer held a smooth shining sphere in his fingers. And he dared not look; his tongue clove to the roof of his mouth, and he could not open his hand. His astonished warriors saw Yar Afzal's eyes distend, the color ebb from his face. Then suddenly a bellow of agony burst from his bearded lips; he swayed and fell as if struck by lightning, his right arm tossed out in front of him. Face down he lay, and from between his opening fingers crawled a spider – a hideous, black, hairy-legged monster whose body shone like black jade. The men yelled and gave back suddenly, and the creature scuttled into a crevice of the rocks and disappeared.

The warriors started up, glaring wildly, and a voice rose above their clamor, a far-carrying voice of command which came from none knew where. Afterward each man there – who still lived – denied that he had shouted, but all there heard it.

'Yar Afzal is dead! Kill the outlander!'

That shout focused their whirling minds as one. Doubt, bewilderment and fear vanished in the uproaring surge of the blood-lust. A furious yell rent the skies as the tribesmen responded instantly to the suggestion. They came headlong across the open space, cloaks flapping, eyes blazing, knives lifted.

Conan's action was as quick as theirs. As the voice shouted he sprang for the hut door. But they were closer to him than he was to the door, and with one foot on the sill he had to wheel and parry the swipe of a yard-long blade. He split the man's skull – ducked another swinging knife and gutted the wielder – felled a man with his left fist and stabbed another in the belly – and heaved back mightily against the closed door with his shoulders. Hacking blades were nicking chips out of the jambs about his ears, but the door flew open under the impact of his shoulders, and he went stumbling backward into the room. A bearded tribesman, thrusting with all his fury as Conan sprang back, overreached and pitched head-first through the doorway. Conan stopped, grasped the slack of his garments and hauled him clear, and slammed the door in the faces of the men who came surging into it. Bones snapped under the impact, and the next instant Conan slammed the bolts into place and whirled with desperate haste to meet the man who sprang from the floor and tore into action like a madman.

Yasmina cowered in a corner, staring in horror as the two men fought back and forth across the room, almost trampling her at times; the flash and clangor of their blades filled the room, and outside the mob clamored like a wolf-pack, hacking deafeningly at the bronze door with their long knives, and dashing huge rocks against it. Somebody fetched a tree trunk, and the door began to stagger under the thunderous assault. Yasmina clasped her ears, staring wildly. Violence and fury within, cataclysmic madness without. The stallion in his stall neighed and reared, thundering with his heels against the walls. He wheeled and launched his hoofs through the bars just as the tribesman, backing away from Conan's murderous swipes, stumbled against them. His spine cracked in three places like a rotten branch and he was hurled headlong against the Cimmerian, bearing him backward so that they both crashed to the beaten floor.

Yasmina cried out and ran forward; to her dazed sight it seemed that both were slain. She reached them just as Conan threw aside the corpse and rose. She caught his arm, trembling from head to foot.

'Oh, you live! I thought – I thought you were dead!'

He glanced down at her quickly, into the pale, upturned face and the wide staring dark eyes.

'Why are you trembling?' he demanded. 'Why should you care if I live or die?'

A vestige of her poise returned to her, and she drew away, making a rather pitiful attempt at playing the Devi.

'You are preferable to those wolves howling without,' she answered, gesturing toward the door, the stone sill of which was beginning to splinter away.

'That won't hold long,' he muttered, then turned and went swiftly to the stall of the stallion.

Yasmina clenched her hands and caught her breath as she saw him tear aside the splintered bars and go into the stall with the maddened beast. The stallion reared above him, neighing terribly, hoofs lifted, eyes and teeth flashing and ears laid back, but Conan leaped and caught his mane with a display of sheer strength that seemed impossible, and dragged the beast down on his forelegs. The steed snorted and quivered, but stood still while the man bridled him and clapped on the gold-worked saddle, with the wide silver stirrups.

Wheeling the beast around in the stall, Conan called quickly to Yasmina, and the girl came, sidling nervously past the stallion's heels. Conan was working at the stone wall, talking swiftly as he worked.

'A secret door in the wall here, that not even the Wazuli know about. Yar Afzal showed it to me once when he was drunk. It opens out into the mouth of the ravine behind the hut. Ha!'

As he tugged at a projection that seemed casual, a whole section of the wall slid back on oiled iron runners. Looking through, the girl saw a narrow defile opening in a sheer stone cliff within a few feet of the hut's back wall. Then Conan sprang into the saddle and hauled her up before him. Behind them the great door groaned like a living thing and crashed in, and a yell rang to the roof as the entrance was instantly flooded with hairy faces and knives in hairy fists. And then the great stallion went through the wall like a javelin from a catapult, and thundered into the defile, running low, foam flying from the bit-rings.

That move came as an absolute surprise to the Wazulis. It was a surprise, too, to those stealing down the ravine. It happened so quickly – the hurricane-like charge of the great horse – that a man in a green turban was unable to get out of the way. He went down under the frantic hoofs, and a girl screamed. Conan got one glimpse of her as they thundered by – a slim, dark girl in silk trousers and a jeweled breast-band, flattening herself against the ravine wall. Then the black horse and his riders were gone up the gorge like the spume blown before a storm, and the men who came tumbling through the wall into the defile after them met that which changed their yells of blood-lust to shrill screams of fear and death.

6

The Mountain of the Black Seers

'Where now?' Yasmina was trying to sit erect on the rocking saddle-bow, clutching her captor. She was conscious of a recognition of shame that she should not find unpleasant the feel of his muscular flesh under her fingers.

'To Afghulistan,' he answered. 'It's a perilous road, but the stallion will carry us easily, unless we fall in with some of your friends, or my tribal enemies. Now that Yar Afzal is dead, those damned Wazulis will be on our heels. I'm surprised we haven't sighted them behind us already.'

'Who was that man you rode down?' she asked.

'I don't know. I never saw him before. He's no Ghuli, that's certain. What the devil he was doing there is more than I can say. There was a girl with him, too.'

'Yes.' Her gaze was shadowed. 'I can not understand that. That girl was my maid, Gitara. Do you suppose she was coming to aid me? That the man was a friend? If so, the Wazulis have captured them both.'

'Well,' he answered, 'there's nothing we can do. If we go back, they'll skin us both. I can't understand how a girl like that could get this far into the mountains with only one man – and he a robed scholar, for that's what he looked like. There's something infernally queer in all this. That fellow Yar Afzal beat and sent away – he moved like a man walking in his sleep. I've seen the priests of Zamora perform their abominable rituals in their forbidden temples, and their victims had a stare like that man. The priests looked into their eyes and muttered incantations, and then the people became the walking dead men, with glassy eyes, doing as they were ordered.

'And then I saw what the fellow had in his hand, which Yar Afzal picked up. It was like a big black jade bead, such as the temple girls of Yezud wear when they dance before the black stone spider which is their god. Yar Afzal held it in his hand, and he didn't pick up anything else. Yet when he fell dead, a spider, like the god at Yezud, only smaller, ran out of his fingers. And then, when the Wazulis stood uncertain there, a voice cried out for them to kill me, and I know that voice didn't come from any of the warriors, nor from the women who watched by the huts. It seemed to come from *above*.'

Yasmina did not reply. She glanced at the stark outlines of the mountains all about them and shuddered. Her soul shrank from their gaunt brutality. This was a grim, naked land where anything might happen. Age-old traditions invested it with shuddery horror for anyone born in the hot, luxuriant southern plains.

The sun was high, beating down with fierce heat, yet the wind that blew in fitful gusts seemed to sweep off slopes of ice. Once she heard a strange rushing above them that was not the sweep of the wind, and from the way Conan looked up, she knew it was not a common sound to him, either. She thought that a strip of the cold blue sky was momentarily blurred, as if some all but invisible object had swept between it and herself, but she could not be sure. Neither made any comment, but Conan loosened his knife in his scabbard.

They were following a faintly marked path dipping down into ravines so deep the sun never struck bottom, laboring up steep slopes where loose shale threatened to slide from beneath their feet, and following knife-edge ridges with blue-hazed echoing depths on either hand.

The sun had passed its zenith when they crossed a narrow trail winding among the crags. Conan reined the horse aside and followed it southward, going almost at right angles to their former course.

'A Galzai village is at one end of this trail,' he explained. 'Their women follow it to a well, for water. You need new garments.'

Glancing down at her filmy attire, Yasmina agreed with him. Her cloth-of-gold slippers were in tatters, her robes and silken under-garments torn to shreds that scarcely held together decently. Garments meant for the streets of Peshkhauri were scarcely appropriate for the crags of the Himelians.

Coming to a crook in the trail, Conan dismounted, helped Yasmina down and waited. Presently he nodded, though she heard nothing.

'A woman coming along the trail,' he remarked. In sudden panic she clutched his arm.

'You will not – not kill her?'

'I don't kill women ordinarily,' he grunted; 'though some of the hill-women are she-wolves. No,' he grinned as at a huge jest. 'By Crom, I'll *pay* for her clothes! How is that?' He displayed a large handful of gold coins, and replaced all but the largest. She nodded, much relieved. It was perhaps natural for men to slay and die; her flesh crawled at the thought of watching the butchery of a woman.

Presently a woman appeared around the crook of the trail – a tall, slim Galzai girl, straight as a young sapling, bearing a great empty gourd. She stopped short and the gourd fell from her hands when she saw them; she wavered as though to run, then realized that Conan was too close to her to allow her to escape, and so stood still, staring at them with a mixed expression of fear and curiosity.

Conan displayed the gold coin.

'If you will give this woman your garments,' he said, 'I will give you this money.'

The response was instant. The girl smiled broadly with surprise and delight, and, with the disdain of a hill-woman for prudish conventions, promptly yanked off her sleeveless embroidered vest, slipped down her wide trousers and stepped out of them, twitched off her wide-sleeved shirt, and kicked off her sandals. Bundling them all in a bunch, she proffered them to Conan, who handed them to the astonished Devi.

'Get behind that rock and put these on,' he directed, further proving himself no native hill-man. 'Fold your robes up into a bundle and bring them to me when you come out.'

'The money!' clamored the hill-girl, stretching out her hands eagerly. 'The gold you promised me!'

Conan flipped the coin to her, she caught it, bit, then thrust it into her hair, bent and caught up the gourd and went on down the path, as devoid of self-consciousness as of garments. Conan waited with some impatience while the Devi, for the first time in her pampered life, dressed herself. When she stepped from behind the rock he swore in surprise, and she felt a curious rush of emotions at the unrestrained admiration burning in his fierce blue eyes. She felt shame, embarrassment, yet a stimulation of vanity she had never before experienced, and a tingling when meeting the impact of his eyes. He laid a heavy hand on her shoulder and turned her about, staring avidly at her from all angles.

'By Crom!' said he. 'In those smoky, mystic robes you were aloof and cold and far off as a star! Now you are a woman of warm flesh and blood! You went behind that rock as the Devi of Vendhya; you come out as a hill-girl – though a thousand times more beautiful than any wench of the Zhaibar! You were a goddess – now you are real!'

He spanked her resoundingly, and she, recognizing this as merely another expression of admiration, did not feel outraged. It was indeed as if the changing of her garments had wrought a change in her personality. The feelings and sensations she had suppressed rose to domination in her now, as if the queenly robes she had cast off had been material shackles and inhibitions.

But Conan, in his renewed admiration, did not forget that peril lurked all about them. The farther they drew away from the region of the Zhaibar, the less likely he was to encounter any Kshatriya troops. On the other hand he had been listening all throughout their flight for sounds that would tell him the vengeful Wazulis of Khurum were on their heels.

Swinging the Devi up, he followed her into the saddle and again reined the stallion westward. The bundle of garments she had given him, he hurled over a cliff, to fall into the depths of a thousand-foot gorge.

'Why did you do that?' she asked. 'Why did you not give them to the girl?'

'The riders from Peshkhauri are combing these hills,' he said. 'They'll be ambushed and harried at every turn, and by way of reprisal they'll destroy every village they can take. They may turn westward any time. If they found a girl wearing your garments, they'd torture her into talking, and she might put them on my trail.'

'What will she do?' asked Yasmina.

'Go back to her village and tell her people that a stranger attacked her,' he answered. 'She'll have them on our track, all right. But she had to go on and get the water first; if she dared go back without it, they'd whip the skin off her. That gives us a long start. They'll never catch us. By nightfall we'll cross the Afghuli border.'

'There are no paths or signs of human habitation in these parts,' she commented. 'Even for the Himelians this region seems singularly deserted. We have not seen a trail since we left the one where we met the Galzai woman.'

For answer he pointed to the northwest, where she glimpsed a peak in a notch of the crags.

'Yimsha,' grunted Conan. 'The tribes build their villages as far from the mountain as they can.'

She was instantly rigid with attention.

'Yimsha!' she whispered. 'The mountain of the Black Seers!'

'So they say,' he answered. 'This is as near as I ever approached it. I have swung north to avoid any Kshatriya troops that might be prowling through the hills. The regular trail from Khurum to Afghulistan lies farther south. This is an ancient one, and seldom used.'

She was staring intently at the distant peak. Her nails bit into her pink palms.

'How long would it take to reach Yimsha from this point?'

'All the rest of the day, and all night,' he answered, and grinned. 'Do you want to go there? By Crom, it's no place for an ordinary human, from what the hill-people say.'

'Why do they not gather and destroy the devils that inhabit it?' she demanded.

'Wipe out wizards with swords? Anyway, they never interfere with people, unless the people interfere with them. I never saw one of them, though I've talked with men who swore they had. They say they've glimpsed people from the tower among the crags at sunset or sunrise – tall, silent men in black robes.'

'Would you be afraid to attack them?'

'I?' The idea seemed a new one to him. 'Why, if they imposed upon me, it would be my life or theirs. But I have nothing to do with them. I came to these mountains to raise a following of human beings, not to war with wizards.'

Yasmina did not at once reply. She stared at the peak as at a human enemy, feeling all her anger and hatred stir in her bosom anew. And another feeling began to take dim shape. She had plotted to hurl against the masters of Yimsha the man in whose arms she was now carried. Perhaps there was another way, besides the method she had planned, to accomplish her purpose. She could not mistake the look that was beginning to dawn in this wild man's eyes as they rested on her. Kingdoms have fallen when a woman's slim white hands pulled the strings of destiny. Suddenly she stiffened, pointing.

'Look!'

Just visible on the distant peak there hung a cloud of peculiar aspect. It was a frosty crimson in color, veined with sparkling gold. This cloud was in motion; it rotated, and as it whirled it contracted. It dwindled to a spinning taper that flashed in the sun. And suddenly it detached itself from the snow-tipped peak, floated out over the void like a gay-hued feather, and became invisible against the cerulean sky.

'What could that have been?' asked the girl uneasily, as a shoulder of rock shut the distant mountain from view; the phenomenon had been disturbing, even in its beauty.

'The hill-men call it Yimsha's Carpet, whatever that means,' answered Conan. 'I've seen five hundred of them running as if the devil were at their heels, to hide themselves in caves and crags, because they saw that crimson cloud float up from the peak. What in—'

They had advanced through a narrow, knife-cut gash between turreted walls and emerged upon a broad ledge, flanked by a series of rugged slopes on one hand, and a gigantic precipice on the other. The dim trail followed this ledge, bent around a shoulder and reappeared at intervals far below, working a tedious way downward. And emerging from the cut that opened upon the ledge, the black stallion halted short, snorting. Conan urged him on impatiently, and the horse snorted and threw his head up and down, quivering and straining as if against an invisible barrier.

Conan swore and swung off, lifting Yasmina down with him. He went forward, with a hand thrown out before him as if expecting to encounter unseen resistance, but there was nothing to hinder him, though when he tried to lead the horse, it neighed shrilly and jerked back. Then Yasmina cried out, and Conan wheeled, hand starting to knife-hilt.

Neither of them had seen him come, but he stood there, with his arms folded, a man in a camel-hair robe and a green turban. Conan grunted with surprise to recognize the man the stallion had spurned in the ravine outside the Wazuli village.

'Who the devil are you?' he demanded.

The man did not answer. Conan noticed that his eyes were wide, fixed, and of a peculiar luminous quality. And those eyes held his like a magnet.

Khemsa's sorcery was based on hypnotism, as is the case with most Eastern magic. The way has been prepared for the hypnotist for untold centuries of generations who have lived and died in the firm conviction of the reality and power of hypnotism, building up, by mass thought and practise, a colossal though intangible atmosphere against which the individual, steeped in the traditions of the land, finds himself helpless.

But Conan was not a son of the East. Its traditions were meaningless to him; he was the product of an utterly alien atmosphere. Hypnotism was not even a myth in Cimmeria. The heritage that prepared a native of the East for submission to the mesmerist was not his.

He was aware of what Khemsa was trying to do to him; but

he felt the impact of the man's uncanny power only as a vague impulsion, a tugging and pulling that he could shake off as a man shakes spider-webs from his garments.

Aware of hostility and black magic, he ripped out his long knife and lunged, as quick on his feet as a mountain lion.

But hypnotism was not all of Khemsa's magic. Yasmina, watching, did not see by what roguery of movement or illusion the man in the green turban avoided the terrible disembowelling thrust. But the keen blade whickered between side and lifted arm, and to Yasmina it seemed that Khemsa merely brushed his open palm lightly against Conan's bull-neck. But the Cimmerian went down like a slain ox.

Yet Conan was not dead; breaking his fall with his left hand, he slashed at Khemsa's legs even as he went down, and the Rakhsha avoided the scythe-like swipe only by a most unwizardly bound backward. Then Yasmina cried out sharply as she saw a woman she recognized as Gitara glide out from among the rocks and come up to the man. The greeting died in the Devi's throat as she saw the malevolence in the girl's beautiful face.

Conan was rising slowly, shaken and dazed by the cruel craft of that blow which, delivered with an art forgotten of men before Atlantis sank, would have broken like a rotten twig the neck of a lesser man. Khemsa gazed at him cautiously and a trifle uncertainly. The Rakhsha had learned the full flood of his own power when he faced at bay the knives of the maddened Wazulis in the ravine behind Khurum village; but the Cimmerian's resistance had perhaps shaken his new-found confidence a trifle. Sorcery thrives on success, not on failure.

He stepped forward, lifting his hand – then halted as if frozen, head tilted back, eyes wide open, hand raised. In spite of himself Conan followed his gaze, and so did the women – the girl cowering by the trembling stallion, and the girl beside Khemsa.

Down the mountain slopes, like a whirl of shining dust blown before the wind, a crimson, conoid cloud came dancing. Khemsa's dark face turned ashen; his hand began to tremble, then sank to his side. The girl beside him, sensing the change in him, stared at him inquiringly.

The crimson shape left the mountain slope and came down in a long arching sweep. It struck the ledge between Conan and Khemsa, and the Rakhsha gave back with a stifled cry. He backed away, pushing the girl Gitara back with groping, fending hands.

The crimson cloud balanced like a spinning top for an instant, whirling in a dazzling sheen on its point. Then without warning it was gone, vanished as a bubble vanishes when burst. There on the ledge stood four men. It was miraculous, incredible, impossible, yet it was true. They were not ghosts or phantoms. They were four tall men, with shaven, vulture-like heads, and black robes that hid their feet. Their hands were concealed by their wide sleeves. They stood in silence, their naked heads nodding slightly in unison. They were facing Khemsa, but behind them Conan felt his own blood turning to ice in his veins. Rising, he backed stealthily away, until he could feel the stallion's shoulder trembling against his back, and the Devi crept into the shelter of his arm. There was no word spoken. Silence hung like a stifling pall.

All four of the men in black robes stared at Khemsa. Their vulture-like faces were immobile, their eyes introspective and contemplative. But Khemsa shook like a man in an ague. His feet were braced on the rock, his calves straining as if in physical combat. Sweat ran in streams down his dark face. His right hand locked on something under his brown robe so desperately that the blood ebbed from that hand and left it white. His left hand fell on the shoulder of Gitara and clutched in agony like the grasp of a drowning man. She did not flinch or whimper, though his fingers dug like talons into her firm flesh.

Conan had witnessed hundreds of battles in his wild life, but never one like this, wherein four diabolical wills sought to beat down one lesser but equally devilish will that opposed them. But he only faintly sensed the monstrous quality of that hideous struggle. With his back to the wall, driven to bay by his former masters, Khemsa was fighting for his life with all the dark power, all the frightful knowledge they had taught him through long, grim years of neophytism and vassalage.

He was stronger than even he had guessed, and the free exercise of his powers in his own behalf had tapped unsuspected reservoirs of forces. And he was nerved to super-energy by frantic fear and desperation. He reeled before the merciless impact of those hypnotic eyes, but he held his ground. His features were distorted into a bestial grin of agony, and his limbs were twisted as on a rack. It was a war of souls, of frightful brains steeped in lore forbidden to men for a million years, of mentalities which had plumbed the abysses and explored the dark stars where spawn the shadows.

Yasmina understood this better than did Conan. And she dimly understood why Khemsa could withstand the concentrated impact of those four hellish wills which might have blasted into atoms the very rock on which he stood. The reason was the girl that he clutched with the strength of his despair. She was like an anchor to his staggering soul, battered by the waves of those psychic emanations. His weakness was now his strength. His love for the girl, violent and evil though it might be, was yet a tie that bound him to the rest of humanity, providing an earthly leverage for his will, a chain that his inhuman enemies could not break; at least not break through Khemsa.

They realized that before he did. And one of them turned his gaze from the Rakhsha full upon Gitara. There was no battle there. The girl shrank and wilted like a leaf in the drought. Irresistibly impelled, she tore herself from her lover's arms before he realized what was happening. Then a hideous thing came to pass. She began to back toward the precipice, facing her tormentors, her eyes wide and blank as dark gleaming glass from behind which a lamp has been blown out. Khemsa groaned and staggered toward her, falling into the trap set for him. A divided mind could not maintain the unequal battle. He was beaten, a straw in their hands. The girl went backward, walking like an automaton, and Khemsa reeled drunkenly after her, hands vainly outstretched, groaning, slobbering in his pain, his feet moving heavily like dead things.

On the very brink she paused, standing stiffly, her heels on the edge, and he fell on his knees and crawled whimpering toward her, groping for her, to drag her back from destruction. And just before his clumsy fingers touched her, one of the wizards laughed, like the sudden, bronze note of a bell in hell. The girl reeled suddenly and, consummate climax of exquisite cruelty, reason and understanding flooded back into her eyes, which flared with awful fear. She screamed, clutched wildly at her lover's straining hand, and then, unable to save herself, fell headlong with a moaning cry.

Khemsa hauled himself to the edge and stared over, haggardly, his lips working as he mumbled to himself. Then he turned and stared for a long minute at his torturers, with wide eyes that held no human light. And then with a cry that almost burst the rocks, he reeled up and came rushing toward them, a knife lifted in his hand.

One of the Rakhshas stepped forward and stamped his foot, and as he stamped, there came a rumbling that grew swiftly to a grinding roar. Where his foot struck, a crevice opened in the solid rock that widened instantly. Then, with a deafening crash, a whole section of the ledge gave way. There was a last glimpse of Khemsa, with arms wildly upflung, and then he vanished amidst the roar of the avalanche that thundered down into the abyss.

The four looked contemplatively at the ragged edge of rock that formed the new rim of the precipice, and then turned suddenly. Conan, thrown off his feet by the shudder of the mountain, was rising, lifting Yasmina. He seemed to move as slowly as his brain was working. He was befogged and stupid. He realized that there was a desperate need for him to lift the Devi on the black stallion and ride like the wind, but an unaccountable sluggishness weighted his every thought and action.

And now the wizards had turned toward him; they raised their arms, and to his horrified sight, he saw their outlines fading, dimming, becoming hazy and nebulous, as a crimson smoke billowed around their feet and rose about them. They were blotted out by a sudden whirling cloud – and then he realized that he too was enveloped in a blinding crimson mist – he heard Yasmina scream, and the stallion cried out like a woman in pain. The Devi was torn from his arm, and as he lashed out with his knife blindly, a terrific blow like a gust of storm wind knocked him sprawling against a rock. Dazedly he saw a crimson conoid cloud spinning up and over the mountain slopes. Yasmina was gone, and so were the four men in black. Only the terrified stallion shared the ledge with him.

7

On to Yimsha

As mists vanish before a strong wind, the cobwebs vanished from Conan's brain. With a searing curse he leaped into the saddle and the stallion reared neighing beneath him. He glared up the slopes, hesitated, and then turned down the trail in the direction he had been going when halted by Khemsa's trickery. But now he did not ride at a measured gait. He shook loose the reins and the stallion went like a thunderbolt, as if frantic to lose hysteria in violent physical exertion. Across the ledge and around the crag and down the narrow trail threading the great steep they plunged at breakneck speed. The path followed a fold of rock, winding interminably down from tier to tier of striated escarpment, and once, far below, Conan got a glimpse of the ruin that had fallen – a mighty pile of broken stone and boulders at the foot of a gigantic cliff.

The valley floor was still far below him when he reached a long and lofty ridge that led out from the slope like a natural causeway. Out upon this he rode, with an almost sheer drop on either hand. He could trace ahead of him the trail and made a great horseshoe back into the riverbed at his left hand. He cursed the necessity of traversing those miles, but it was the only way. To try to descend to the lower lap of the trail here would be to attempt the impossible. Only a bird could get to the river-bed with a whole neck.

So he urged on the wearying stallion, until a clink of hoofs reached his ears, welling up from below. Pulling up short and reining to the lip of the cliff, he stared down into the dry river-bed that wound along the foot of the ridge. Along that gorge rode a motley throng – bearded men on half-wild horses, five hundred strong, bristling with weapons. And Conan shouted suddenly, leaning over the edge of the cliff, three hundred feet above them.

At his shout they reined back, and five hundred bearded faces were tilted up towards him; a deep, clamorous roar filled the canyon. Conan did not waste words.

'I was riding for Ghor!' he roared. 'I had not hoped to meet you dogs on the trail. Follow me as fast as your nags can push! I'm going to Yimsha, and—'

'Traitor!' The howl was like a dash of ice-water in his face.

'What?' He glared down at them, jolted speechless. He saw wild eyes blazing up at him, faces contorted with fury, fists brandishing blades.

'Traitor!' they roared back, wholeheartedly. 'Where are the seven chiefs held captive in Peshkhauri?'

'Why, in the governor's prison, I suppose,' he answered.

A bloodthirsty yell from a hundred throats answered him, with such a waving of weapons and a clamor that he could not understand what they were saying. He beat down the din with a bull-like roar, and bellowed: 'What devil's play is this? Let one of you speak, so I can understand what you mean!'

A gaunt old chief elected himself to this position, shook his tulwar at Conan as a preamble, and shouted accusingly: 'You would not let us go raiding Peshkhauri to rescue our brothers!'

'No, you fools!' roared the exasperated Cimmerian. 'Even if you'd breached the wall, which is unlikely, they'd have hanged the prisoners before you could reach them.'

'And you went alone to traffic with the governor!' yelled the Afghuli, working himself into a frothing frenzy.

'Well?'

'Where are the seven chiefs?' howled the old chief, making his tulwar into a glimmering wheel of steel about his head. 'Where are they? Dead!'

'What!' Conan nearly fell off his horse in his surprise.

'Aye, dead!' five hundred bloodthirsty voices assured him.

The old chief brandished his arms and got the floor again. 'They were not hanged!' he screeched. 'A Wazuli in another cell saw them die! The governor sent a wizard to slay them by craft!'

'That must be a lie,' said Conan. 'The governor would not dare. Last night I talked with him—'

The admission was unfortunate. A yell of hate and accusation split the skies.

'Aye! You went to him alone! To betray us! It is no lie. The Wazuli escaped through the doors the wizard burst in his entry, and told the tale to our scouts whom he met in Zhaibar. They had been sent forth to search for you, when you did not return. When they heard the Wazuli's tale, they returned with all haste to Ghor, and we saddled our steeds and girt our swords!'

'And what do you fools mean to do?' demanded the Cimmerian.

'To avenge our brothers!' they howled. 'Death to the Kshatriyas! Slay him, brothers, he is a traitor!'

Arrows began to rattle around him. Conan rose in his stirrups, striving to make himself heard above the tumult, and then, with a roar of mingled rage, defiance and disgust, he wheeled and galloped back up the trail. Behind him and below him the Afghulis came pelting, mouthing their rage, too furious even to remember that the only way they could reach the height whereon he rode was to traverse the riverbed in the other direction, make the broad bend and follow the twisting trail up over the ridge. When they did remember this, and turned back, their repudiated chief had almost reached the point where the ridge joined the escarpment.

At the cliff he did not take the trail by which he had descended, but turned off on another, a mere trace along a rock-fault, where the stallion scrambled for footing. He had not ridden far when the stallion snorted and shied back from something lying in the trail. Conan stared down on the travesty of a man, a broken, shredded, bloody heap that gibbered and gnashed splintered teeth.

Impelled by some obscure reason, Conan dismounted and stood looking down at the ghastly shape, knowing that he was witness of a thing miraculous and opposed to nature. The Rakhsha lifted his gory head, and his strange eyes, glazed with agony and approaching death, rested on Conan with recognition.

'Where are they?' It was a racking croak not even remotely resembling a human voice.

'Gone back to their damnable castle on Yimsha,' grunted Conan. 'They took the Devi with them.'

'I will go!' muttered the man. 'I will follow them! They killed Gitara; I will kill them – the acolytes, the Four of the Black Circle, the Master himself! Kill – kill them all!' He strove to drag his mutilated frame along the rock, but not even his indomitable will could animate that gory mass longer, where the splintered bones hung together only by torn tissue and ruptured fibre.

'Follow them!' raved Khemsa, drooling a bloody slaver. 'Follow!'

'I'm going to,' growled Conan. 'I went to fetch my Afghulis, but they've turned on me. I'm going on to Yimsha alone. I'll have the Devi back if I have to tear down that damned mountain with my bare hands. I didn't think the governor would dare kill my headmen, when I had the Devi, but it seems he did. I'll have his head for that. She's no use to me now as a hostage, but—'

'The curse of Yizil on them!' gasped Khemsa. 'Go! I am dying. Wait – take my girdle.'

He tried to fumble with a mangled hand at his tatters, and Conan, understanding what he sought to convey, bent and drew from about his gory waist a girdle of curious aspect.

'Follow the golden vein through the abyss,' muttered Khemsa. 'Wear the girdle. I had it from a Stygian priest. It will aid you, though it failed me at last. Break the crystal globe with the four golden pomegranates. Beware of the Master's transmutations – I am going to Gitara – she is waiting for me in hell – *aie, ya Skelos yar!*' And so he died.

Conan stared down at the girdle. The hair of which it was woven was not horsehair. He was convinced that it was woven of the thick black tresses of a woman. Set in the thick mesh were tiny jewels such as he had never seen before. The buckle was strangely made, in the form of a golden serpent-head, flat, wedge-shaped and scaled with curious art. A strong shudder shook Conan as he handled it, and he turned as though to cast it over the precipice;

then he hesitated, and finally buckled it about his waist, under the Bakhariot girdle. Then he mounted and pushed on.

The sun had sunk behind the crags. He climbed the trail in the vast shadow of the cliffs that was thrown out like a dark blue mantle over valleys and ridges far below. He was not far from the crest when, edging around the shoulder of a jutting crag, he heard the clink of shod hoofs ahead of him. He did not turn back. Indeed, so narrow was the path that the stallion could not have wheeled his great body upon it. He rounded the jut of the rock and came upon a portion of the path that broadened somewhat. A chorus of threatening yells broke on his ear, but his stallion pinned a terrified horse hard against the rock, and Conan caught the arm of the rider in an iron grip, checking the lifted sword in midair.

'Kerim Shah!' muttered Conan, red glints smoldering luridly in his eyes. The Turanian did not struggle; they sat their horses almost breast to breast, Conan's fingers locking the other's sword-arm. Behind Kerim Shah filed a group of lean Irakzai on gaunt horses. They glared like wolves, fingering bows and knives, but rendered uncertain because of the narrowness of the path and the perilous proximity of the abyss that yawned beneath them.

'Where is the Devi?' demanded Kerim Shah.

'What's it to you, you Hyrkanian spy?' snarled Conan.

'I know you have her,' answered Kerim Shah. 'I was on my way northward with some tribesmen when we were ambushed by enemies in Shalizah Pass. Many of my men were slain, and the rest of us harried through the hills like jackals. When we had beaten off our pursuers, we turned westward, toward Amir Jehun Pass, and this morning we came upon a Wazuli wandering through the hills. He was quite mad, but I learned much from his incoherent gibberings before he died. I learned that he was the sole survivor of a band which followed a chief of the Afghulis and a captive Kshatriya woman into a gorge behind Khurum village. He babbled much of a man in a green turban whom the Afghuli rode down, but who, when attacked by the Wazulis who pursued, smote them with a nameless doom that wiped them out as a gust of wind-driven fire wipes out a cluster of locusts.

'How that one man escaped, I do not know, nor did he; but I knew from his maunderings that Conan of Ghor had been in Khurum with his royal captive. And as we made our way through the hills, we overtook a naked Galzai girl bearing a gourd of water, who told us a tale of having been stripped and ravished by a giant foreigner in the garb of an Afghuli chief, who, she said, gave her garments to a Vendhyan woman who accompanied him. She said you rode westward.'

Kerim Shah did not consider it necessary to explain that he had been on his way to keep his rendezvous with the expected troops from Secunderam when he found his way barred by hostile tribesmen. The road to Gurashah valley through Shalizah Pass was longer than the road that wound through Amir Jehun Pass, but the latter traversed part of the Afghuli country, which Kerim Shah had been anxious to avoid until he came with an army. Barred from the Shalizah road, however, he had turned to the forbidden route, until news that Conan had not yet reached Afghulistan with his captive had caused him to turn southward and push on recklessly in the hope of overtaking the Cimmerian in the hills.

'So you had better tell me where the Devi is,' suggested Kerim Shah. 'We outnumber you—'

'Let one of your dogs nock a shaft and I'll throw you over the cliff,' Conan promised. 'It wouldn't do you any good to kill me, anyhow. Five hundred Afghulis are on my trail, and if they find you've cheated them, they'll flay you alive. Anyway, I haven't got the Devi. She's in the hands of the Black Seers of Yimsha.'

'*Tarim!*' swore Kerim Shah softly, shaken out of his poise for the first time. 'Khemsa—'

'Khemsa's dead,' grunted Conan. 'His masters sent him to hell on a landslide. And now get out of my way. I'd be glad to kill you if I had the time, but I'm on my way to Yimsha.'

'I'll go with you,' said the Turanian abruptly.

Conan laughed at him. 'Do you think I'd trust you, you Hyrkanian dog?'

'I don't ask you to,' returned Kerim Shah. 'We both want the Devi. You know my reason; King Yezdigerd desires to add her kingdom to his empire, and herself in his seraglio. And I knew you, in the days when you were a hetman of the *kozak* steppes; so I know your ambition is wholesale plunder. You want to loot Vendhya, and to twist out a huge ransom for Yasmina. Well, let us for the time being, without any illusion about each other, unite our forces, and try to rescue the Devi from the Seers. If we succeed, and live, we can fight it out to see who keeps her.'

Conan narrowly scrutinized the other for a moment, and then nodded, releasing the Turanian's arm. 'Agreed; what about your men?'

Kerim Shah turned to the silent Irakzai and spoke briefly: 'This chief and I are going to Yimsha to fight the wizards. Will you go with us, or stay here to be flayed by the Afghulis who are following this man?'

They looked at him with eyes grimly fatalistic. They were doomed and they knew it – had known it ever since the singing arrows of the ambushed Dagozai had driven them back from the pass of Shalizah. The men of the lower Zhaibar had too many reeking bloodfeuds among the crag-dwellers. They were too small a band to fight their way back through the hills to the villages of the border, without the guidance of the crafty Turanian. They counted themselves as dead already, so they made the reply that only dead men would make: 'We will go with thee and die on Yimsha.'

'Then in Crom's name let us be gone,' grunted Conan, fidgeting with impatience as he started into the blue gulfs of the deepening twilight. 'My wolves were hours behind me, but we've lost a devilish lot of time.'

Kerim Shah backed his steed from between the black stallion and the cliff, sheathed his sword and cautiously turned the horse. Presently the band was filing up the path as swiftly as they dared. They came out upon the crest nearly a mile east of the spot where Khemsa had halted the Cimmerian and the Devi. The path they had traversed was a perilous one, even for hill-men, and for that reason Conan had avoided it that day when carrying Yasmina, though Kerim Shah, following him, had taken it supposing the

Cimmerian had done likewise. Even Conan sighed with relief when the horses scrambled up over the last rim. They moved like phantom riders through an enchanted realm of shadows. The soft creak of leather, the clink of steel marked their passing, then again the dark mountain slopes lay naked and silent in the starlight.

8

Yasmina Knows Stark Terror

Yasmina had time but for one scream when she felt herself enveloped in that crimson whirl and torn from her protector with appalling force. She screamed once, and then she had no breath to scream. She was blinded, deafened, rendered mute and eventually senseless by the terrific rushing of the air about her. There was a dazed consciousness of dizzy height and numbing speed, a confused impression of natural sensations gone mad, and then vertigo and oblivion.

A vestige of these sensations clung to her as she recovered consciousness; so she cried out and clutched wildly as though to stay a headlong and involuntary flight. Her fingers closed on soft fabric, and a relieving sense of stability pervaded her. She took cognizance of her surroundings.

She was lying on a dais covered with black velvet. This dais stood in a great, dim room whose walls were hung with dusky tapestries across which crawled dragons reproduced with repellent realism. Floating shadows merely hinted at the lofty ceiling, and gloom that lent itself to illusion lurked in the corners. There seemed to be neither windows nor doors in the walls, or else they were concealed by the nighted tapestries. Where the dim light came from, Yasmina could not determine. The great room was a realm of mysteries, or shadows, and shadowy shapes in which she could not have sworn to observe movement, yet which invaded her mind with a dim and formless terror.

But her gaze fixed itself on a tangible object. On another, smaller dais of jet, a few feet away, a man sat cross-legged, gazing contemplatively at her. His long black velvet robe, embroidered with gold thread, fell loosely about him, masking his figure. His hands were folded in his sleeves. There was a velvet cap upon his head. His face was calm, placid, not unhandsome, his eyes lambent and slightly oblique. He did not move a muscle as he sat regarding her, nor did his expression alter when he saw she was conscious.

Yasmina felt fear crawl like a trickle of ice-water down her supple spine. She lifted herself on her elbows and stared apprehensively at the stranger.

'Who are you?' she demanded. Her voice sounded brittle and inadequate.

'I am the Master of Yimsha.' The tone was rich and resonant, like the mellow tones of a temple bell.

'Why did you bring me here?' she demanded.

'Were you not seeking me?'

'If you are one of the Black Seers – yes!' she answered recklessly, believing that he could read her thoughts anyway.

He laughed softly, and chills crawled up and down her spine again.

'You would turn the wild children of the hills against the Seers of Yimsha!' He smiled. 'I have read it in your mind, princess. Your weak, human mind, filled with petty dreams of hate and revenge.'

'You slew my brother!' A rising tide of anger was vying with her fear; her hands were clenched, her lithe body rigid. 'Why did you persecute him? He never harmed you. The priests say the Seers are above meddling in human affairs. Why did you destroy the king of Vendhya?'

'How can an ordinary human understand the motives of a Seer?' returned the Master calmly. 'My acolytes in the temples of Turan, who are the priests behind the priests of Tarim, urged me to bestir myself in behalf of Yezdigerd. For reasons of my own, I complied. How can I explain my mystic reasons to your puny intellect? You could not understand.'

'I understand this: that my brother died!' Tears of grief and rage shook in her voice. She rose upon her knees and stared at him with wide blazing eyes, as supple and dangerous in that moment as a she-panther.

'As Yezdigerd desired,' agreed the Master calmly. 'For a while it was my whim to further his ambitions.'

'Is Yezdigerd your vassal?' Yasmina tried to keep the timbre of her voice unaltered. She had felt her knee pressing something hard and symmetrical under a fold of velvet. Subtly she shifted her position, moving her hand under the fold.

'Is the dog that licks up the offal in the temple yard the vassal of the god?' returned the Master.

He did not seem to notice the actions she sought to dissemble. Concealed by the velvet, her fingers closed on what she knew was the golden hilt of a dagger. She bent her head to hide the light of triumph in her eyes.

'I am weary of Yezdigerd,' said the Master. 'I have turned to other amusements – ha!'

With a fierce cry Yasmina sprang like a jungle cat, stabbing murderously. Then she stumbled and slid to the floor, where she cowered, staring up at the man on the dais. He had not moved; his cryptic smile was unchanged. Tremblingly she lifted her hand and stared at it with dilated eyes. There was no dagger in her fingers; they grasped a stalk of golden lotus, the crushed blossoms drooping on the bruised stem.

She dropped it as if it had been a viper, and scrambled away from the proximity of her tormenter. She returned to her own dais, because that was at least more dignified for a queen than groveling on the floor at the feet of a sorcerer, and eyed him apprehensively, expecting reprisals.

But the Master made no move.

'All substance is one to him who holds the key of the cosmos,' he said cryptically. 'To an adept nothing is immutable. At will, steel blossoms bloom in unnamed gardens, or flower-swords flash in the moonlight.'

'You are a devil,' she sobbed.

'Not I!' he laughed. 'I was born on this planet, long ago. Once I was a common man, nor have I lost all human attributes in the numberless eons of my adeptship. A human steeped in the dark arts is greater than a devil. I am of human origin, but I rule demons. You have seen the Lords of the Black Circle – it would blast your soul to hear from what far realm I summoned them and from what doom I guard them with ensorcelled crystal and golden serpents.

'But only I can rule them. My foolish Khemsa thought to make himself great – poor fool, bursting material doors and hurtling himself and his mistress through the air from hill to hill! Yet if he had not been destroyed his power might have grown to rival mine.'

He laughed again. 'And you, poor, silly thing! Plotting to send a hairy hill chief to storm Yimsha! It was such a jest that I myself could have designed, had it occurred to me, that you should fall in his hands. And I read in your childish mind an intention to seduce by your feminine wiles to attempt your purpose, anyway.

'But for all your stupidity, you are a woman fair to look upon. It is my whim to keep you for my slave.'

The daughter of a thousand proud emperors gasped with shame and fury at the word.

'You dare not!'

His mocking laughter cut her like a whip across her naked shoulders.

'The king dares not trample a worm in the road? Little fool, do you not realize that your royal pride is no more than a straw blown on the wind? I, who have known the kisses of the queens of Hell! You have seen how I deal with a rebel!'

Cowed and awed, the girl crouched on the velvet-covered dais. The light grew dimmer and more phantom-like. The features of the Master became shadowy. His voice took on a newer tone of command.

'I will never yield to you!' Her voice trembled with fear but it carried a ring of resolution.

'You will yield,' he answered with horrible conviction. 'Fear and pain shall teach you. I will lash you with horror and agony to the last quivering ounce of your endurance, until you become as melted wax to be bent and molded in my hands as I desire. You shall know such discipline as no mortal woman ever knew, until my slightest command is to you as the unalterable will of the gods. And first, to humble your pride, you shall travel back through the lost ages, and view all the shapes that have been you. *Aie, yil la khosa!'*

At these words the shadowy room swam before Yasmina's affrighted gaze. The roots of her hair prickled her scalp, and her tongue clove to her palate. Somewhere a gong sounded a deep, ominous note. The dragons on the tapestries glowed like blue fire, and then faded out. The Master on his dais was but a shapeless shadow. The dim light gave way to soft, thick darkness, almost tangible, that pulsed with strange radiations. She could no longer see the Master. She could see nothing. She had a strange sensation that the walls and ceiling had withdrawn immensely from her.

Then somewhere in the darkness a glow began, like a firefly that rhythmically dimmed and quickened. It grew to a golden ball, and as it expanded its light grew more intense, flaming whitely. It burst suddenly, showering the darkness with white sparks that did not illumine the shadows. But like an impression left in the gloom, a faint luminance remained, and revealed a slender dusky shaft shooting up from the shadowy floor. Under the girl's dilated gaze it spread, took shape; stems and broad leaves appeared, and great black poisonous blossoms that towered above her as she cringed against the velvet. A subtle perfume pervaded the atmosphere. It was the dread figure of the black lotus that had grown up as she watched, as it grows in the haunted, forbidden jungles of Khitai.

The broad leaves were murmurous with evil life. The blossoms bent toward her like sentient things, nodding serpent-like on pliant stems. Etched against soft, impenetrable darkness it loomed over her, gigantic, blackly visible in some mad way. Her brain reeled with the drugging scent and she sought to crawl from the dais. Then she clung to it as it seemed to be pitching at an impossible slant. She cried out with terror and clung to the velvet, but she felt her fingers ruthlessly torn away. There was a sensation as of all sanity and stability crumbling and vanishing. She was a quivering atom of sentiency driven through a black, roaring, icy void by a thundering wind that threatened to extinguish her feeble flicker of animate life like a candle blown out in a storm.

Then there came a period of blind impulse and movement, when the atom that was she mingled and merged with myriad other atoms of spawning life in the yeasty morass of existence, molded by formative forces until she emerged again a conscious individual, whirling down an endless spiral of lives.

In a mist of terror she relived all her former existences, recognized and *was* again all the bodies that had carried her ego throughout the changing ages. She bruised her feet again over the long, weary road of life that stretched out behind her into the immemorial past. Back beyond the dimmest dawns of Time she crouched shuddering in primordial jungles, hunted by slavering beasts of prey. Skin-clad, she waded thigh-deep in rice swamps, battling with squawking water-fowl for the precious grains. She labored with the oxen to drag the pointed stick through the stubborn soil, and she crouched endlessly over looms in peasant huts.

She saw walled cities burst into flame, and fled screaming before the slayers. She reeled naked and bleeding over burning sands, dragged at the slaver's stirrup, and she knew the grip of hot, fierce hands on her writhing flesh, the shame and agony of brutal lust. She screamed under the bite of the lash, and moaned on the rack; mad with terror she fought against the hands that forced her head inexorably down on the bloody block.

She knew the agonies of childbirth, and the bitterness of love betrayed. She suffered all the woes and wrongs and brutalities that man has inflicted on woman throughout the eons; and she endured all the spite and malice of women for woman. And like the flick of a fiery whip throughout was the consciousness she retained of her Devi-ship. She was all the women she had ever been, yet in her knowing she was Yasmina. This consciousness was not lost in the throes of reincarnation. At one and the same time she was a naked slave-wench groveling under the whip, and the proud Devi of Vendhya. And she suffered not only as the slave-girl suffered, but as Yasmina, to whose pride the whip was like a white-hot brand.

Life merged into life in flying chaos, each with its burden of woe and shame and agony, until she dimly heard her own voice screaming unbearably, like one long-drawn cry of suffering echoing down the ages.

Then she awakened on the velvet-covered dais in the mystic room.

In a ghostly gray light she saw again the dais and the cryptic robed figure seated upon it. The hooded head was bent, the high shoulders faintly etched against the uncertain dimness. She could make out no details clearly, but the hood, where the velvet cap had been, stirred a formless uneasiness in her. As she stared, there stole over her a nameless fear that froze her tongue to her palate – a feeling that it was not the Master who sat so silently on that black dais.

Then the figure moved and rose upright, towering above her. It stooped over her and the long arms in their wide black sleeves bent about her. She fought against them in speechless fright, surprized by their lean hardness. The hooded head bent down toward her averted face. And she screamed, and screamed again in poignant fear and loathing. Bony arms gripped her lithe body, and from that hood looked forth a countenance of death and decay – features like rotting parchment on a moldering skull.

She screamed again, and then, as those champing, grinning jaws bent toward her lips, she lost consciousness . . .

9

The Castle of the Wizards

The sun had risen over the white Himelian peaks. At the foot of a long slope a group of horsemen halted and stared upward. High above them a stone tower poised on the pitch of the mountainside. Beyond and above that gleamed the walls of a greater keep, near the line where the snow began that capped Yimsha's pinnacle. There was a touch of unreality about the whole – purple slopes pitching up to that fantastic castle, toy-like with distance, and above it the white glistening peak shouldering the cold blue.

'We'll leave the horses here,' grunted Conan. 'That treacherous slope is safer for a man on foot. Besides, they're done.'

He swung down from the black stallion which stood with wide-braced legs and drooping head. They had pushed hard throughout the night, gnawing at scraps from saddle-bags, and pausing only to give the horses the rests they had to have.

'That first tower is held by the acolytes of the Black Seers,' said Conan. 'Or so men say; watch-dogs for their masters – lesser sorcerers. They won't sit sucking their thumbs as we climb this slope.'

Kerim Shah glanced up the mountain, then back the way they had come; they were already far up Yimsha's side, and a vast expanse of lesser peaks and crags spread out beneath them. Among these labyrinths the Turanian sought in vain for a movement of color that would betray men. Evidently the pursuing Afghulis had lost their chief's trail in the night.

'Let us go, then.' They tied the weary horses in a clump of tamarisk and without further comment turned up the slope. There was no cover. It was a naked incline, strewn with boulders not big enough to conceal a man. But they did conceal something else.

The party had not gone fifty steps when a snarling shape burst from behind a rock. It was one of the gaunt savage dogs that infested the hill villages, and its eyes glared redly, its jaws dripped foam. Conan was leading, but it did not attack him. It dashed past him and leaped at Kerim Shah. The Turanian leaped aside, and the great dog flung itself upon the Irakzai behind him. The man yelled and threw up his arm, which was torn by the brute's fangs as it bore him backward, and the next instant half a dozen tulwars were hacking at the beast. Yet not until it was literally dismembered did the hideous creature cease its efforts to seize and rend its attackers.

Kerim Shah bound up the wounded warrior's gashed arm, looked at him narrowly, and then turned away without a word. He rejoined Conan, and they renewed the climb in silence.

Presently Kerim Shah said: 'Strange to find a village dog in this place.'

'There's no offal here,' grunted Conan.

Both turned their heads to glance back at the wounded warrior toiling after them among his companions. Sweat glistened on his dark face and his lips were drawn back from his teeth in a grimace of pain. Then both looked again at the stone tower squatting above them.

A slumberous quiet lay over the uplands. The tower showed no sign of life, nor did the strange pyramidal structure beyond it. But the men who toiled upward went with the tenseness of men walking on the edge of a crater. Kerim Shah had unslung the powerful Turanian bow that killed at five hundred paces, and the Irakzai looked to their own lighter and less lethal bows.

But they were not within bow-shot of the tower when something shot down out of the sky without warning. It passed so close to Conan that he felt the wind of rushing wings, but it was an Irakzai who staggered and fell, blood jetting from a severed jugular. A hawk with wings like burnished steel shot up again, blood dripping from the scimitar-beak, to reel against the sky as Kerim Shah's bowstring twanged. It dropped like a plummet, but no man saw where it struck the earth.

Conan bent over the victim of the attack, but the man was already dead. No one spoke; useless to comment on the fact that never before had a hawk been known to swoop on a man. Red rage began to vie with fatalistic lethargy in the wild souls of the Irakzai. Hairy fingers nocked arrows and men glared vengefully at the tower whose very silence mocked them.

But the next attack came swiftly. They all saw it – a white puffball of smoke that tumbled over the tower-rim and came drifting and rolling down the slope toward them. Others followed it. They seemed harmless, mere woolly globes of cloudy foam, but Conan stepped aside to avoid contact with the first. Behind him one of the Irakzai reached out and thrust his sword into the unstable mass. Instantly a sharp report shook the mountainside. There was a burst of blinding flame, and then the puffball had vanished, and the too-curious warrior remained only a heap of charred and blackened bones. The crisped hand still gripped the ivory sword-hilt, but the blade was gone – melted and destroyed by that awful heat. Yet men standing almost within reach of the victim had not suffered except to be dazzled and half blinded by the sudden flare.

'Steel touches it off,' grunted Conan. 'Look out – here they come!'

The slope above them was almost covered by the billowing spheres. Kerim Shah bent his bow and sent a shaft into the mass, and those touched by the arrow burst like bubbles in spurting flame. His men followed his example and for the next few minutes it was as if a thunderstorm raged on the mountain slope, with bolts of lightning striking and bursting in showers of flame. When the barrage ceased, only a few arrows were left in the quivers of the archers.

They pushed on grimly, over soil charred and blackened, where the naked rock had in places been turned to lava by the explosion of those diabolical bombs.

Now they were almost within arrow-flight of the silent tower, and they spread their line, nerves taut, ready for any horror that might descend upon them.

On the tower appeared a single figure, lifting a ten-foot bronze horn. Its strident bellow roared out across the echoing slopes, like the blare of trumpets on Judgment Day. And it began to be fearfully answered. The ground trembled under the feet of the invaders, and rumblings and grindings welled up from the subterranean depths.

The Irakzai screamed, reeling like drunken men on the shuddering slope, and Conan, eyes glaring, charged recklessly up the incline, knife in hand, straight at the door that showed in the tower-wall. Above him the great horn roared and bellowed in brutish mockery. And then Kerim Shah drew a shaft to his ear and loosed.

Only a Turanian could have made that shot. The bellowing of the horn ceased suddenly, and a high, thin scream shrilled in its place. The green-robed figure on the tower staggered, clutching at the long shaft which quivered in its bosom, and then pitched across the parapet. The great horn tumbled upon the battlement and hung precariously, and another robed figure rushed to seize it, shrieking in horror. Again the Turanian bow twanged, and again it was answered by a death-howl. The second acolyte, in falling, struck the horn with his elbow and knocked it clattering over the parapet to shatter on the rocks far below.

At such headlong speed had Conan covered the ground that before the clattering echoes of that fall had died away, he was hacking at the door. Warned by his savage instinct, he gave back suddenly as a tide of molten lead splashed down from above. But the next instant he was back again, attacking the panels with redoubled fury. He was galvanized by the fact that his enemies had resorted to earthly weapons. The sorcery of the acolytes was limited. Their necromantic resources might well be exhausted.

Kerim Shah was hurrying up the slope, his hill-men behind him in a straggling crescent. They loosed as they ran, their arrows splintering against the walls or arching over the parapet.

The heavy teak portal gave way beneath the Cimmerian's assault, and he peered inside warily, expecting anything. He was looking into a circular chamber from which a stair wound upward. On the opposite side of the chamber a door gaped open, revealing the outer slope – and the backs of half a dozen green-robed figures in full retreat.

Conan yelled, took a step into the tower, and then native caution jerked him back, just as a great block of stone fell crashing to the floor where his foot had been an instant before. Shouting to his followers, he raced around the tower.

The acolytes had evacuated their first line of defence. As Conan rounded the tower he saw their green robes twinkling up the mountain ahead of him. He gave chase, panting with earnest blood-lust, and behind him Kerim Shah and the Irakzai came pelting, the latter yelling like wolves at the flight of their enemies, their fatalism momentarily submerged by temporary triumph.

The tower stood on the lower edge of a narrow plateau whose upward slant was barely perceptible. A few hundred yards away this plateau ended abruptly in a chasm which had been invisible farther down the mountain. Into this chasm the acolytes apparently leaped without checking their speed. Their pursuers saw the green robes flutter and disappear over the edge.

A few moments later they themselves were standing on the brink of the mighty moat that cut them off from the castle of the Black Seers. It was a sheer-walled ravine that extended in either direction as far as they could see, apparently girdling the mountain, some four hundred yards in width and five hundred feet deep. And in it, from rim to rim, a strange, translucent mist sparkled and shimmered.

Looking down, Conan grunted. Far below him, moving across the glimmering floor, which shone like burnished silver, he saw the forms of the green-robed acolytes. Their outline was wavering and indistinct, like figures seen under deep water. They walked in single file, moving toward the opposite wall.

Kerim Shah nocked an arrow and sent it singing downward. But when it struck the mist that filled the chasm it seemed to lose momentum and direction, wandering widely from its course.

'If they went down, so can we!' grunted Conan, while Kerim Shah stared after his shaft in amazement. 'I saw them last at this spot—'

Squinting down he saw something shining like a golden thread across the canyon floor far below. The acolytes seemed to be following this thread, and there suddenly came to him Khemsa's cryptic words – 'Follow the golden vein!' On the brink, under his very hand as he crouched, he found it, a thin vein of sparkling gold running from an outcropping of ore to the edge and down across the silvery floor. And he found something else, which had before been invisible to him because of the peculiar refraction of the light. The gold vein followed a narrow ramp which slanted down into the ravine, fitted with niches for hand and foot hold.

'Here's where they went down,' he grunted to Kerim Shah. 'They're no adepts, to waft themselves through the air! We'll follow them—'

It was at that instant that the man who had been bitten by the mad dog cried out horribly and leaped at Kerim Shah, foaming and gnashing his teeth. The Turanian, quick as a cat on his feet, sprang aside and the madman pitched head-first over the brink. The others rushed to the edge and glared after him in amazement. The maniac did not fall plummet-like. He floated slowly down through the rosy haze like a man sinking in deep water. His limbs moved like a man trying to swim, and his features were purple and convulsed beyond the contortions of his madness. Far down at last on the shining floor his body settled and lay still.

'There's death in that chasm,' muttered Kerim Shah, drawing back from the rosy mist that shimmered almost at his feet. 'What now, Conan?'

'On!' answered the Cimmerian grimly. 'Those acolytes are human; if the mist doesn't kill them, it won't kill me.'

He hitched his belt, and his hands touched the girdle Khemsa had given him; he scowled, then smiled bleakly. He had forgotten that girdle; yet thrice had death passed him by to strike another victim.

The acolytes had reached the farther wall and were moving up it like great green flies. Letting himself upon the ramp, he descended warily. The rosy cloud lapped about his ankles, ascending as he lowered himself. It reached his knees, his thighs, his waist, his armpits. He felt as one feels a thick heavy fog on a damp night. With it lapping about his chin he hesitated, and then ducked under. Instantly his breath ceased; all air was shut off from him and he felt his ribs caving in on his vitals. With a frantic effort he heaved himself up, fighting for life. His head rose above the surface and he drank air in great gulps.

Kerim Shah leaned down toward him, spoke to him, but Conan neither heard nor heeded. Stubbornly, his mind fixed on what the dying Khemsa had told him, the Cimmerian groped for the gold vein, and found that he had moved off it in his descent. Several series of hand-holds were niched in the ramp. Placing himself directly over the thread, he began climbing down once more. The rosy mist rose about him, engulfed him. Now his head was under, but he was still drinking pure air. Above him he saw his companions staring down at him, their features blurred by the haze that shimmered over his head. He gestured for them to follow, and went down swiftly, without waiting to see whether they complied or not.

Kerim Shah sheathed his sword without comment and followed, and the Irakzai, more fearful of being left alone than of the terrors that might lurk below, scrambled after him. Each man clung to the golden thread as they saw the Cimmerian do.

Down the slanting ramp they went to the ravine floor and moved out across the shining level, treading the gold vein like rope-walkers. It was as if they walked along an invisible tunnel through which air circulated freely. They felt death pressing in on them above and on either hand, but it did not touch them.

The vein crawled up a similar ramp on the other wall up which the acolytes had disappeared, and up it they went with taut nerves, not knowing what might be waiting for them among the jutting spurs of rock that fanged the lip of the precipice.

It was the green-robed acolytes who awaited them, with knives in their hands. Perhaps they had reached the limits to which they could retreat. Perhaps the Stygian girdle about Conan's waist could have told why their necromantic spells had proven so weak and so quickly exhausted. Perhaps it was knowledge of death decreed for failure that sent them leaping from among the rocks, eyes glaring and knives glittering, resorting in their desperation to material weapons.

There among the rocky fangs on the precipice lip was no war of wizard craft. It was a whirl of blades, where real steel bit and real blood spurted, where sinewy arms dealt forthright blows that severed quivering flesh, and men went down to be trodden under foot as the fight raged over them.

One of the Irakzai bled to death among the rocks, but the acolytes were down – slashed and hacked asunder or hurled over the edge to float sluggishly down to the silver floor that shone so far below.

Then the conquerors shook blood and sweat from their eyes, and looked at one another. Conan and Kerim Shah still stood upright, and four of the Irakzai.

They stood among the rocky teeth that serrated the precipice brink, and from that spot a path wound up a gentle slope to a broad stair, consisting of half a dozen steps, a hundred feet across, cut out of a green jade-like substance. They led up to a broad stage or roofless gallery of the same polished stone, and above it rose, tier upon tier, the castle of the Black Seers. It seemed to have been carved out of the sheer stone of the mountain. The architecture was faultless, but unadorned. The many casements were barred and masked with curtains within. There was no sign of life, friendly or hostile.

They went up the path in silence, and warily as men treading the lair of a serpent. The Irakzai were dumb, like men marching to a certain doom. Even Kerim Shah was silent. Only Conan seemed unaware what a monstrous dislocating and uprooting of accepted thought and action their invasion constituted, what an unprecedented violation of tradition. He was not of the East; and he came of a breed who fought devils and wizards as promptly and matter-of-factly as they battled human foes.

He strode up the shining stairs and across the wide green gallery straight toward the great golden-bound teak door that opened upon it. He cast but a single glance upward at the higher tiers of the great pyramidal structure towering above him. He reached a hand for the bronze prong that jutted like a handle from the door – then checked himself, grinning hardly. The handle was made in the shape of a serpent, head lifted on arched neck; and Conan had a suspicion that that metal head would come to grisly life under his hand.

He struck it from the door with one blow, and its bronze clink on the glassy floor did not lessen his caution. He flipped it aside with his knife-point, and again turned to the door. Utter silence reigned over the towers. Far below them the mountain slopes fell away into a purple haze of distance. The sun glittered on snow-clad peaks on either hand. High above, a vulture hung like a black dot in the cold blue of the sky. But for it, the men before the gold-bound door were the only evidence of life, tiny figures on a green jade gallery poised on the dizzy height, with that fantastic pile of stone towering above them.

A sharp wind off the snow slashed them, whipping their tatters about. Conan's long knife splintering through the teak panels roused the startled echoes. Again and again he struck, hewing through polished wood and metal bands alike. Through the sundered ruins he glared into the interior, alert and suspicious as a wolf. He saw a broad chamber, the polished stone walls untapestried, the mosaic floor uncarpeted. Square, polished ebon stools and a stone dais formed the only furnishings. The room was empty of human life. Another door showed in the opposite wall.

'Leave a man on guard outside,' grunted Conan. 'I'm going in.'

Kerim Shah designated a warrior for that duty, and the man fell back toward the middle of the gallery, bow in hand. Conan strode into the castle, followed by the Turanian and the three remaining Irakzai. The one outside spat, grumbled in his beard, and started suddenly as a low mocking laugh reached his ears.

He lifted his head and saw, on the tier above him, a tall, black-robed figure, naked head nodding slightly as he stared down. His whole attitude suggested mockery and malignity. Quick as a flash the Irakzai bent his bow and loosed, and the arrow streaked upward to strike full in the black-robed breast. The mocking smile did not alter. The Seer plucked out the missile and threw it back at the bowman, not as a weapon is hurled, but with a contemptuous gesture. The Irakzai dodged, instinctively throwing up his arm. His fingers closed on the revolving shaft.

Then he shrieked. In his hand the wooden shaft suddenly *writhed*. Its rigid outline became pliant, melting in his grasp. He tried to throw it from him, but it was too late. He held a living serpent in his naked hand, and already it had coiled about his wrist and its wicked wedge-shaped head darted at his muscular arm. He screamed again and his eyes became distended, his features purple. He went to his knees shaken by an awful convulsion, and then lay still.

The men inside had wheeled at his first cry. Conan took a swift stride toward the open doorway, and then halted short, baffled. To the men behind him it seemed that he strained against empty air. But though he could see nothing, there was a slick, smooth, hard surface under his hands, and he knew that a sheet of crystal had been let down in the doorway. Through it he saw the Irakzai lying motionless on the glassy gallery, an ordinary arrow sticking in his arm.

Conan lifted his knife and smote, and the watchers were dumbfounded to see his blow checked apparently in midair, with the loud clang of steel that meets an unyielding substance. He wasted no more effort. He knew that not even the legendary tulwar of Amir Khurum could shatter that invisible curtain.

In a few words he explained the matter to Kerim Shah, and the Turanian shrugged his shoulders. 'Well, if our exit is barred, we must find another. In the meanwhile our way lies forward, does it not?'

With a grunt the Cimmerian turned and strode across the chamber to the opposite door, with a feeling of treading on the threshold of doom. As he lifted his knife to shatter the door, it swung silently open as if of its own accord. He strode into the great hall, flanked with tall glassy columns. A hundred feet from the door began the broad jade-green steps of a stair that tapered toward the top like the side of a pyramid. What lay beyond that stair he could not tell. But between him and its shimmering foot stood a curious altar of gleaming black jade. Four great golden serpents twined their tails about this altar and reared their wedge-shaped heads in the air, facing the four quarters of the compass like the enchanted guardians of a fabled treasure. But on the altar, between the arching necks, stood only a crystal globe filled with a cloudy smoke-like substance, in which floated four golden pomegranates.

The sight stirred some dim recollection in his mind; then Conan heeded the altar no longer, for on the lower steps of the stair stood four black-robed figures. He had not seen them come. They were simply there, tall, gaunt, their vulture-heads nodding in unison, their feet and hands hidden by their flowing garments.

One lifted his arm and the sleeve fell away revealing his hand – and it was not a hand at all. Conan halted in mid-stride, compelled against his will. He had encountered a force differing subtly from

Khemsa's mesmerism, and he could not advance, though he felt it in his power to retreat if he wished. His companions had likewise halted, and they seemed even more helpless than he, unable to move in either direction.

The seer whose arm was lifted beckoned to one of the Irakzai, and the man moved toward him like one in a trance, eyes staring and fixed, blade hanging in limp fingers. As he pushed past Conan, the Cimmerian threw an arm across his breast to arrest him. Conan was so much stronger than the Irakzai that in ordinary circumstances he could have broken his spine between his hands. But now the muscular arm was brushed aside like straw and the Irakzai moved toward the stair, treading jerkily and mechanically. He reached the steps and knelt stiffly, proffering his blade and bending his head. The Seer took the sword. It flashed as he swung it up and down. The Irakzai's head tumbled from his shoulders and thudded heavily on the black marble floor. An arch of blood jetted from the severed arteries and the body slumped over and lay with arms spread wide.

Again a malformed hand lifted and beckoned, and another Irakzai stumbled stiffly to his doom. The ghastly drama was reenacted and another headless form lay beside the first.

As the third tribesman clumped his way past Conan to his death, the Cimmerian, his veins bulging in his temples with his efforts to break past the unseen barrier that held him, was suddenly aware of allied forces, unseen, but waking into life about him. This realization came without warning, but so powerfully that he could not doubt his instinct. His left hand slid involuntarily under his Bakhariot belt and closed on the Stygian girdle. And as he gripped it he felt new strength flood his numbed limbs; the will to live was a pulsing white-hot fire, matched by the intensity of his burning rage.

The third Irakzai was a decapitated corpse, and the hideous finger was lifting again when Conan felt the bursting of the invisible barrier. A fierce, involuntary cry burst from his lips as he leaped with the explosive suddenness of pent-up ferocity. His left hand gripped the sorcerer's girdle as a drowning man grips a floating log, and the long knife was a sheen of light in his right. The men on the steps did not move. They watched calmly, cynically; if they felt surprise they did not show it. Conan did not allow himself to think what might chance when he came within knife-reach of them. His blood was pounding in his temples, a mist of crimson swam before his sight. He was afire with the urge to kill – to drive his knife deep into flesh and bone, and twist the blade in blood and entrails.

Another dozen strides would carry him to the steps where the sneering demons stood. He drew his breath deep, his fury rising redly as his charge gathered momentum. He was hurtling past the altar with its golden serpents when like a levin-flash there shot across his mind again as vividly as if spoken in his external ear, the cryptic words of Khemsa: *'Break the crystal ball!'*

His reaction was almost without his own volition. Execution followed impulse so spontaneously that the greatest sorcerer of the age would not have had time to read his mind and prevent his action. Wheeling like a cat from his headlong charge, he brought his knife crashing down upon the crystal. Instantly the air vibrated with a peal of terror, whether from the stairs, the altar, or the crystal itself he could not tell. Hisses filled his ears as the golden serpents, suddenly vibrant with hideous life, writhed and smote at him. But he was fired to the speed of a maddened tiger. A whirl of steel sheared through the hideous trunks that waved toward him, and he smote the crystal sphere again and yet again. And the globe burst with a noise like a thunderclap, raining fiery shards on the black marble, and the gold pomegranates, as if released from captivity, shot upward toward the lofty roof and were gone.

A mad screaming, bestial and ghastly, was echoing through the great hall. On the steps writhed four black-robed figures, twisting in convulsions, froth dripping from their livid mouths. Then with one frenzied crescendo of inhuman ululation they stiffened and lay still, and Conan knew that they were dead. He stared down at the altar and the crystal shards. Four headless golden serpents still coiled about the altar, but no alien life now animated the dully gleaming metal.

Kerim Shah was rising slowly from his knees, whither he had been dashed by some unseen force. He shook his head to clear the ringing from his ears.

'Did you hear that crash when you struck? It was as if a thousand crystal panels shattered all over the castle as that globe burst. Were the souls of the wizards imprisoned in those golden balls? – Ha!'

Conan wheeled as Kerim Shah drew his sword and pointed.

Another figure stood at the head of the stair. His robe, too, was black, but of richly embroidered velvet, and there was a velvet cap on his head. His face was calm, and not unhandsome.

'Who the devil are you?' demanded Conan, staring up at him, knife in hand.

'I am the Master of Yimsha!' His voice was like the chime of a temple bell, but a note of cruel mirth ran through it.

'Where is Yasmina?' demanded Kerim Shah.

The Master laughed down at him.

'What is that to you, dead man? Have you so quickly forgotten my strength, once lent to you, that you come armed against me, you poor fool? I think I will take your heart, Kerim Shah!'

He held out his hand as if to receive something, and the Turanian cried out sharply like a man in mortal agony. He reeled drunkenly, and then, with a splintering of bones, a rending of flesh and muscle and a snapping of mail-links, his breast burst outward with a shower of blood, and through the ghastly aperture something red and dripping shot through the air into the Master's outstretched hand, as a bit of steel leaps to the magnet. The Turanian slumped to the floor and lay motionless, and the Master laughed and hurled the object to fall before Conan's feet – a still-quivering human heart.

With a roar and a curse Conan charged the stair. From Khemsa's girdle he felt strength and deathless hate flow into him to combat the terrible emanation of power that met him on the steps. The air filled with a shimmering steely haze through which he plunged like a swimmer, head lowered, left arm bent about his face, knife gripped low in his right hand. His half-blinded eyes, glaring over the crook of his elbow, made out the hated shape of the Seer before and above him, the outline wavering as a reflection wavers in disturbed water.

He was racked and torn by forces beyond his comprehension, but he felt a driving power outside and beyond his own lifting him inexorably upward and onward, despite the wizard's strength and his own agony.

Now he had reached the head of the stairs, and the Master's face floated in the steely haze before him, and a strange fear shadowed the inscrutable eyes. Conan waded through the mist as through a surf, and his knife lunged upward like a live thing. The keen point ripped the Master's robe as he sprang back with a low cry. Then before Conan's gaze, the wizard vanished – simply disappeared like a burst bubble, and something long and undulating darted up one of the smaller stairs that led up to left and right from the landing.

Conan charged after it, up the left-hand stair, uncertain as to just what he had seen whip up those steps, but in a berserk mood that drowned the nausea and horror whispering at the back of his consciousness.

He plunged out into a broad corridor whose uncarpeted floor and untapestried walls were of polished jade, and something long and swift whisked down the corridor ahead of him, and into a curtained door. From within the chamber rose a scream of urgent terror. The sound lent wings to Conan's flying feet and he hurtled through the curtains and headlong into the chamber within.

A frightful scene met his glare. Yasmina cowered on the farther edge of a velvet-covered dais, screaming her loathing and horror, an arm lifted as if to ward off attack, while before her swayed the hideous head of a giant serpent, shining neck arching up from dark-gleaming coils. With a choked cry Conan threw his knife.

Instantly the monster whirled and was upon him like the rush of wind through tall grass. The long knife quivered in its neck, point and a foot of blade showing on one side, and the hilt and a hand's-breadth of steel on the other, but it only seemed to madden the giant reptile. The great head towered above the man who faced it, and then darted down, the venom-dripping jaws gaping wide. But Conan had plucked a dagger from his girdle and he stabbed upward as the head dipped down. The point tore through the lower jaw and transfixed the upper, pinning them together. The next instant the great trunk had looped itself about the Cimmerian as the snake, unable to use its fangs, employed its remaining form of attack.

Conan's left arm was pinioned among the bone-crushing folds, but his right was free. Bracing his feet to keep upright, he stretched forth his hand, gripped the hilt of the long knife jutting from the serpent's neck, and tore it free in a shower of blood. As if divining his purpose with more than bestial intelligence, the snake writhed and knotted, seeking to cast its loops about his right arm. But with the speed of light the long knife rose and fell, shearing halfway through the reptile's giant trunk.

Before he could strike again, the great pliant loops fell from him and the monster dragged itself across the floor, gushing blood from its ghastly wounds. Conan sprang after it, knife lifted, but his vicious swipe cut empty air as the serpent writhed away from him and struck its blunt nose against a paneled screen of sandalwood. One of the panels gave inward and the long, bleeding barrel whipped through it and was gone.

Conan instantly attacked the screen. A few blows rent it apart and he glared into the dim alcove beyond. No horrific shape coiled there; there was blood on the marble floor, and bloody tracks led to a cryptic arched door. Those tracks were of a man's bare feet . . .

'Conan!' He wheeled back into the chamber just in time to catch the Devi of Vendhya in his arms as she rushed across the room and threw herself upon him, catching him about the neck with a frantic clasp, half hysterical with terror and gratitude and relief.

His wild blood had been stirred to its uttermost by all that had passed. He caught her to him in a grasp that would have made her wince at another time, and crushed her lips with his. She made no resistance; the Devi was drowned in the elemental woman. She closed her eyes and drank in his fierce, hot, lawless kisses with all the abandon of passionate thirst. She was panting with his violence when he ceased for breath, and glared down at her lying limp in his mighty arms.

'I knew you'd come for me,' she murmured. 'You would not leave me in this den of devils.'

At her words recollection of their environment came to him suddenly. He lifted his head and listened intently. Silence reigned over the castle of Yimsha, but it was a silence impregnated with menace. Peril crouched in every corner, leered invisibly from every hanging.

'We'd better go while we can,' he muttered. 'Those cuts were enough to kill any common beast – or *man* – but a wizard has a dozen lives. Wound one, and he writhes away like a crippled snake to soak up fresh venom from some source of sorcery.'

He picked up the girl and carrying her in his arms like a child, he strode out into the gleaming jade corridor and down the stairs, nerves tautly alert for any sign or sound.

'I met the Master,' she whispered, clinging to him and shuddering. 'He worked his spells on me to break my will. The most awful thing was a moldering corpse which seized me in its arms – I fainted then and lay as one dead, I do not know how long. Shortly after I regained consciousness I heard sounds of strife below, and cries, and then that snake came slithering through the curtains – ah!' She shook at the memory of that horror. 'I knew somehow that it was not an illusion, but a real serpent that sought my life.'

'It was not a shadow, at least,' answered Conan cryptically. 'He knew he was beaten, and chose to slay you rather than let you be rescued.'

'What do you mean, *he*?' she asked uneasily, and then shrank against him, crying out, and forgetting her question. She had seen the corpses at the foot of the stairs. Those of the Seers were not good to look at; as they lay twisted and contorted, their hands and feet were exposed to view, and at the sight Yasmina went livid and hid her face against Conan's powerful shoulder.

10

Yasmina and Conan

Conan passed through the hall quickly enough, traversed the outer chamber and approached the door that led upon the gallery. Then he saw the floor sprinkled with tiny, glittering shards. The crystal sheet that had covered the doorway had been shivered to bits, and he remembered the crash that had accompanied the shattering of the crystal globe. He believed that every piece of crystal in the castle had broken at that instant, and some dim instinct or memory of esoteric lore vaguely suggested the truth of the monstrous connection between the Lords of the Black Circle and the golden pomegranates. He felt the short hair bristle chilly at the back of his neck and put the matter hastily out of his mind.

He breathed a deep sigh of relief as he stepped out upon the green jade gallery. There was still the gorge to cross, but at least he could see the white peaks glistening in the sun, and the long slopes falling away into the distant blue hazes.

The Irakzai lay where he had fallen, an ugly blotch on the glassy smoothness. As Conan strode down the winding path, he was surprised to note the position of the sun. It had not yet passed its zenith; and yet it seemed to him that hours had passed since he plunged into the castle of the Black Seers.

He felt an urge to hasten, not a mere blind panic, but an instinct of peril growing behind his back. He said nothing to Yasmina, and she seemed content to nestle her dark head against his arching breast and find security in the clasp of his iron arms. He paused an instant on the brink of the chasm, frowning down. The haze which danced in the gorge was no longer rose-hued and sparkling. It was smoky, dim, ghostly, like the life-tide that flickered thinly in a wounded man. The thought came vaguely to Conan that the spells of magicians were more closely bound to their personal beings than were the actions of common men to the actors.

But far below, the floor shone like tarnished silver, and the gold thread sparkled undimmed. Conan shifted Yasmina across his shoulder, where she lay docilely, and began the descent. Hurriedly he descended the ramp, and hurriedly he fled across the echoing floor. He had a conviction that they were racing with time, that their chances of survival depended upon crossing that gorge of horrors before the wounded Master of the castle should regain enough power to loose some other doom upon them.

When he toiled up the farther ramp and came out upon the crest, he breathed a gusty sigh of relief and stood Yasmina upon her feet.

'You walk from here,' he told her; 'it's downhill all the way.'

She stole a glance at the gleaming pyramid across the chasm; it reared up against the snowy slope like the citadel of silence and immemorial evil.

'Are you a magician, that you have conquered the Black Seers of Yimsha, Conan of Ghor?' she asked, as they went down the path, with his heavy arm about her supple waist.

'It was a girdle Khemsa gave me before he died,' Conan answered. 'Yes, I found him on the trail. It is a curious one, which I'll show you when I have time. Against some spells it was weak, but against others it was strong, and a good knife is always a hearty incantation.'

'But if the girdle aided you in conquering the Master,' she argued, 'why did it not aid Khemsa?'

He shook his head. 'Who knows? But Khemsa had been the Master's slave; perhaps that weakened its magic. He had no hold on me as he had on Khemsa. Yet I can't say that I conquered him. He retreated, but I have a feeling that we haven't seen the last of him. I want to put as many miles between us and his lair as we can.'

He was further relieved to find horses tethered among the tamarisks as he had left them. He loosed them swiftly and mounted the black stallion, swinging the girl up before him. The others followed, freshened by their rest.

'And what now?' she asked. 'To Afghulistan?'

'Not just now!' He grinned hardly. 'Somebody – maybe the

governor – killed my seven headmen. My idiotic followers think I had something to do with it, and unless I am able to convince them otherwise, they'll hunt me like a wounded jackal.'

'Then what of me? If the headmen are dead, I am useless to you as a hostage. Will you slay me, to avenge them?'

He looked down at her, with eyes fiercely aglow, and laughed at the suggestion.

'Then let us ride to the border,' she said. 'You'll be safe from the Afghulis there—'

'Yes, on a Vendhyan gibbet.'

'I am Queen of Vendhya,' she reminded him with a touch of her old imperiousness. 'You have saved my life. You shall be rewarded.'

She did not intend it as it sounded, but he growled in his throat, ill pleased.

'Keep your bounty for your city-bred dogs, princess! If you're a queen of the plains, I'm a chief of the hills, and not one foot toward the border will I take you!'

'But you would be safe—' she began bewilderedly.

'And you'd be the Devi again,' he broke in. 'No, girl; I prefer you as you are now – a woman of flesh and blood, riding on my saddle-bow.'

'But you can't *keep* me!' she cried. 'You can't—'

'Watch and see!' he advised grimly.

'But I will pay you a vast ransom—'

'Devil take your ransom!' he answered roughly, his arms hardening about her supple figure. 'The kingdom of Vendhya could give me nothing I desire half so much as I desire you. I took you at the risk of my neck; if your courtiers want you back, let them come up the Zhaibar and fight for you.'

'But you have no followers now!' she protested. 'You are hunted! How can you preserve your own life, much less mine?'

'I still have friends in the hills,' he answered. 'There is a chief of the Khurakzai who will keep you safely while I bicker with the Afghulis. If they will have none of me, by Crom! I will ride northward with you to the steppes of the *kozaki*. I was a hetman among the Free Companions before I rode southward. I'll make you a queen on the Zaporoska River!'

'But I can not!' she objected. 'You must not hold me—'

'If the idea's so repulsive,' he demanded, 'why did you yield your lips to me so willingly?'

'Even a queen is human,' she answered, coloring. 'But because I am a queen, I must consider my kingdom. Do not carry me away into some foreign country. Come back to Vendhya with me!'

'Would you make me your king?' he asked sardonically.

'Well, there are customs—' she stammered, and he interrupted her with a hard laugh.

'Yes, civilized customs that won't let you do as you wish. You'll marry some withered old king of the plains, and I can go my way with only the memory of a few kisses snatched from your lips. Ha!'

'But I must return to my kingdom!' she repeated helplessly.

'Why?' he demanded angrily. 'To chafe your rump on gold thrones, and listen to the plaudits of smirking, velvet-skirted fools? Where is the gain? Listen: I was born in the Cimmerian hills where the people are all barbarians. I have been a mercenary soldier, a corsair, a *kozak*, and a hundred other things. What king has roamed the countries, fought the battles, loved the women, and won the plunder that I have?

'I came into Ghulistan to raise a horde and plunder the kingdoms to the south – your own among them. Being chief of the Afghulis was only a start. If I can conciliate them, I'll have a dozen tribes following me within a year. But if I can't I'll ride back to the steppes and loot the Turanian borders with the *kozaki*. And you'll go with me. To the devil with your kingdom; they fended for themselves before you were born.'

She lay in his arms looking up at him, and she felt a tug at her spirit, a lawless, reckless urge that matched his own and was by it called into being. But a thousand generations of sovereignship rode heavy upon her.

'I can't! I can't!' she repeated helplessly.

'You haven't any choice,' he assured her. 'You – what the devil!'

They had left Yimsha some miles behind them, and were riding along a high ridge that separated two deep valleys. They had just topped a steep crest where they could gaze down into the valley on their right hand. And there was a running fight in progress. A strong wind was blowing away from them, carrying the sound from their ears, but even so the clashing of steel and thunder of hoofs welled up from far below.

They saw the glint of the sun on lance-tip and spired helmet. Three thousand mailed horsemen were driving before them a ragged band of turbaned riders, who fled snarling and striking like fleeing wolves.

'Turanians,' muttered Conan. 'Squadrons from Secunderam. What the devil are they doing here?'

'Who are the men they pursue?' asked Yasmina. 'And why do they fall back so stubbornly? They can not stand against such odds.'

'Five hundred of my mad Afghulis,' he growled, scowling down into the vale. 'They're in a trap, and they know it.'

The valley was indeed a cul-de-sac at that end. It narrowed to a high-walled gorge, opening out further into a round bowl, completely rimmed with lofty, unscalable walls.

The turbaned riders were being forced into this gorge, because there was nowhere else for them to go, and they went reluctantly, in a shower of arrows and a whirl of swords. The helmeted riders harried them, but did not press in too rashly. They knew the desperate fury of the hill tribes, and they knew too that they had their prey in a trap from which there was no escape. They had recognized the hill-men as Afghulis, and they wished to hem them in and force a surrender. They needed hostages for the purpose they had in mind.

Their emir was a man of decision and initiative. When he reached the Gurashah valley, and found neither guides nor emissary waiting for him, he pushed on, trusting to his own knowledge of the country. All the way from Secunderam there had been fighting, and tribesmen were licking their wounds in many a crag-perched village. He knew there was a good chance that neither he nor any of his helmeted spearmen would ever ride through the gates of

Secunderam again, for the tribes would all be up behind him now, but he was determined to carry out his orders – which were to take Yasmina Devi from the Afghulis at all costs, and to bring her captive to Secunderam, or if confronted by impossibility, to strike off her head before he himself died.

Of all this, of course, the watchers on the ridge were not aware. But Conan fidgeted with nervousness.

'Why the devil did they get themselves trapped?' he demanded of the universe at large. 'I know what they're doing in these parts – they were hunting me, the dogs! Poking into every valley – and found themselves penned in before they knew it. The poor fools! They're making a stand in the gorge, but they can't hold out for long. When the Turanians have pushed them back into the bowl, they'll slaughter them at their leisure.'

The din welling up from below increased in volume and intensity. In the strait of the narrow gut, the Afghulis, fighting desperately, were for the time holding their own against the mailed riders, who could not throw their whole weight against them.

Conan scowled darkly, moved restlessly, fingering his hilt, and finally spoke bluntly: 'Devi, I must go down to them. I'll find a place for you to hide until I come back to you. You spoke of your kingdom – well, I don't pretend to look on those hairy devils as my children, but after all, such as they are, they're my henchmen. A chief should never desert his followers, even if they desert him first. They think they were right in kicking me out – hell, I won't be cast off! I'm still chief of the Afghulis, and I'll prove it! I can climb down on foot into the gorge.'

'But what of me?' she queried. 'You carried me away forcibly from *my* people; now will you leave me to die in the hills alone while you go down and sacrifice yourself uselessly?'

His veins swelled with the conflict of his emotions.

'That's right,' he muttered helplessly. 'Crom knows what I *can* do.'

She turned her head slightly, a curious expression dawning on her beautiful face. Then:

'Listen!' she cried. 'Listen!'

A distant fanfare of trumpets was borne faintly to their ears. They stared into the deep valley on the left, and caught a glint of steel on the farther side. A long line of lances and polished helmets moved along the vale, gleaming in the sunlight.

'The riders of Vendhya!' she cried exultingly.

'There are thousands of them!' muttered Conan. 'It has been long since a Kshatriya host has ridden this far into the hills.'

'They are searching for me!' she exclaimed. 'Give me your horse! I will ride to my warriors! The ridge is not so precipitous on the left, and I can reach the valley floor. I will lead my horsemen into the valley at the upper end and fall upon the Turanians! We will crush them in the vise! Quick, Conan! Will you sacrifice your men to your own desire?'

The burning hunger of the steppes and the wintry forests glared out of his eyes, but he shook his head and swung off the stallion, placing the reins in her hands.

'You win!' he grunted. 'Ride like the devil!'

She wheeled away down the left-hand slope and he ran swiftly along the ridge until he reached the long ragged cleft that was the defile in which the fight raged. Down the rugged wall he scrambled like an ape, clinging to projections and crevices, to fall at last, feet first, into the mêlée that raged in the mouth of the gorge. Blades were whickering and clanging about him, horses rearing and stamping, helmet plumes nodding among turbans that were stained crimson.

As he hit, he yelled like a wolf, caught a gold-worked rein, and dodging the sweep of a scimitar, drove his long knife upward through the rider's vitals. In another instant he was in the saddle, yelling ferocious orders to the Afghulis. They stared at him stupidly for an instant; then as they saw the havoc his steel was wreaking among their enemies, they fell to their work again, accepting him without comment. In that inferno of licking blades and spurting blood there was no time to ask or answer questions.

The riders in their spired helmets and gold-worked hauberks swarmed about the gorge mouth, thrusting and slashing, and the narrow defile was packed and jammed with horses and men, the warriors crushed breast to breast, stabbing with shortened blades, slashing murderously when there was an instant's room to swing a sword. When a man went down he did not get up from beneath the stamping, swirling hoofs. Weight and sheer strength counted heavily there, and the chief of the Afghulis did the work of ten. At such times accustomed habits sway men strongly, and the warriors, who were used to seeing Conan in their vanguard, were heartened mightily, despite their distrust of him.

But superior numbers counted too. The pressure of the men behind forced the horsemen of Turan deeper and deeper into the gorge, in the teeth of the flickering tulwars. Foot by foot the Afghulis were shoved back, leaving the defile-floor carpeted with dead, on which the riders trampled. As he hacked and smote like a man possessed, Conan had time for some chilling doubts – would Yasmina keep her word? She had but to join her warriors, turn southward and leave him and his band to perish.

But at last, after what seemed centuries of desperate battling, in the valley outside there rose another sound above the clash of steel and yells of slaughter. And then with a burst of trumpets that shook the walls, and rushing thunder of hoofs, five thousand riders of Vendhya smote the hosts of Secunderam.

That stroke split the Turanian squadrons asunder, shattered, tore and rent them and scattered their fragments all over the valley. In an instant the surge had ebbed back out of the gorge; there was a chaotic, confused swirl of fighting, horsemen wheeling and smiting singly and in clusters, and then the emir went down with a Kshatriya lance through his breast, and the riders in their spired helmets turned their horses down the valley, spurring like mad and seeking to slash a way through the swarms which had come upon them from the rear. As they scattered in flight, the conquerors scattered in pursuit, and all across the valley floor, and up on the slopes near the mouth and over the crests streamed the fugitives and the pursuers. The Afghulis, those left to ride, rushed out of the gorge and joined in the harrying of their foes, accepting the unexpected alliance as unquestioningly as they had accepted the return of their repudiated chief.

The sun was sinking toward the distant crags when Conan, his garments hacked to tatters and the mail under them reeking and clotted with blood, his knife dripping and crusted to the hilt, strode over the corpses to where Yasmina Devi sat her horse among her nobles on the crest of the ridge, near a lofty precipice.

'You kept your word, Devi!' he roared. 'By Crom, though, I had some bad seconds down in that gorge – *look out!*'

Down from the sky swooped a vulture of tremendous size with a thunder of wings that knocked men sprawling from their horses.

The scimitar-like beak was slashing for the Devi's soft neck, but Conan was quicker – a short run, a tigerish leap, the savage thrust of a dripping knife, and the vulture voiced a horribly human cry, pitched sideways and went tumbling down the cliffs to the rocks and river a thousand feet below. As it dropped, its black wings thrashing the air, it took on the semblance, not of a bird, but of a black-robed human body that fell, arms in wide black sleeves thrown abroad.

Conan turned to Yasmina, his red knife still in his hand, his blue eyes smoldering, blood oozing from wounds on his thickly muscled arms and thighs.

'You are the Devi again,' he said, grinning fiercely at the gold-clasped gossamer robe she had donned over her hill-girl attire, and awed not at all by the imposing array of chivalry about him. 'I have you to thank for the lives of some three hundred and fifty of my rogues, who are at least convinced that I didn't betray them. You have put my hands on the reins of conquest again.'

'I still owe you my ransom,' she said, her dark eyes glowing as they swept over him. 'Ten thousand pieces of gold I will pay you—'

He made a savage, impatient gesture, shook the blood from his knife and thrust it back in its scabbard, wiping his hands on his mail.

'I will collect your ransom in my own way, at my own time,' he said. 'I will collect it in your palace at Ayodhya, and I will come with fifty thousand men to see that the scales are fair.'

She laughed, gathering her reins into her hands. 'And I will meet you on the shores of the Jhumda with a hundred thousand!'

His eyes shone with fierce appreciation and admiration, and stepping back, he lifted his hand with a gesture that was like the assumption of kingship, indicating that her road was clear before her.

THE SLITHERING SHADOW

1

The desert shimmered in the heat waves. Conan the Cimmerian stared out over the aching desolation and involuntarily drew the back of his powerful hand over his blackened lips. He stood like a bronze image in the sand, apparently impervious to the murderous sun, though his only garment was a silk loin-cloth, girdled by a wide gold-buckled belt from which hung a saber and a broad-bladed poniard. On his clean-cut limbs were evidences of scarcely healed wounds.

At his feet rested a girl, one white arm clasping his knee, against which her blond head drooped. Her white skin contrasted with his hard bronzed limbs; her short silken tunic, low-necked and sleeveless, girdled at the waist, emphasized rather than concealed her lithe figure.

Conan shook his head, blinking. The sun's glare half blinded him. He lifted a small canteen from his belt and shook it, scowling at the faint splashing within.

The girl moved wearily, whimpering.

'Oh, Conan, we shall die here! I am so thirsty!'

The Cimmerian growled wordlessly, glaring truculently at the surrounding waste, with outthrust jaw, and blue eyes smoldering savagely from under his black tousled mane, as if the desert were a tangible enemy.

He stooped and put the canteen to the girl's lips.

'Drink till I tell you to stop, Natala,' he commanded.

She drank with little panting gasps, and he did not check her. Only when the canteen was empty did she realize that he had deliberately allowed her to drink all their water supply, little enough that it was.

Tears sprang to her eyes. 'Oh, Conan,' she wailed, wringing her hands, 'why did you let me drink it all? I did not know – now there is none for you!'

'Hush,' he growled. 'Don't waste your strength in weeping.'

Straightening, he threw the canteen from him.

'Why did you do that?' she whispered.

He did not reply, standing motionless and immobile, his fingers closing slowly about the hilt of his saber. He was not looking at the girl; his fierce eyes seemed to plumb the mysterious purple hazes of the distance.

Endowed with all the barbarian's ferocious love of life and instinct to live, Conan the Cimmerian yet knew that he had reached the end of his trail. He had not come to the limits of his endurance, but he knew another day under the merciless sun in those waterless wastes would bring him down. As for the girl, she had suffered enough. Better a quick painless sword-stroke than the lingering agony that faced him. Her thirst was temporarily quenched; it was a false mercy to let her suffer until delirium and death brought relief. Slowly he slid the saber from its sheath.

He halted suddenly, stiffening. Far out on the desert to the south, something glimmered through the heat waves.

At first he thought it was a phantom, one of the mirages which had mocked and maddened him in that accursed desert. Shading his sun-dazzled eyes, he made out spires and minarets, and gleaming walls. He watched it grimly, waiting for it to fade and vanish. Natala had ceased to sob; she struggled to her knees and followed his gaze.

'Is it a city, Conan?' she whispered, too fearful to hope. 'Or is it but a shadow?'

The Cimmerian did not reply for a space. He closed and opened his eyes several times; he looked away, then back. The city remained where he had first seen it.

'The devil knows,' he grunted. 'It's worth a try, though.'

He thrust the saber back in its sheath. Stooping, he lifted Natala in his mighty arms as though she had been an infant. She resisted weakly.

'Don't waste your strength carrying me, Conan,' she pleaded. 'I can walk.'

'The ground gets rockier here,' he answered. 'You would soon wear your sandals to shreds,' glancing at her soft green foot-wear. 'Besides, if we are to reach that city at all, we must do it quickly, and I can make better time this way.'

The chance for life had lent fresh vigor and resilience to the Cimmerian's steely thews. He strode out across the sandy waste as if he had just begun the journey. A barbarian of barbarians, the vitality and endurance of the wild were his, granting him survival where civilized men would have perished.

He and the girl were, so far as he knew, the sole survivors of Prince Almuric's army, that mad motley horde which, following the defeated rebel prince of Koth, swept through the Lands of Shem like a devastating sandstorm and drenched the outlands of Stygia with blood. With a Stygian host on its heels, it had cut its way through the black kingdom of Kush, only to be annihilated on the edge of the southern desert. Conan likened it in his mind to a great torrent, dwindling gradually as it rushed southward, to run dry at last in the sands of the naked desert. The bones of its members – mercenaries, outcasts, broken men, outlaws – lay strewn from the Kothic uplands to the dunes of the wilderness.

From that final slaughter, when the Stygians and the Kushites closed in on the trapped remnants, Conan had cut his way clear and fled on a camel with the girl. Behind them the land swarmed with enemies; the only way open to them was the desert to the south. Into those menacing depths they had plunged.

The girl was Brythunian, whom Conan had found in the slave-market of a stormed Shemite city, and appropriated. She had had nothing to say in the matter, but her new position was so far superior to the lot of any Hyborian woman in a Shemitish seraglio, that she accepted it thankfully. So she had shared in the adventures of Almuric's damned horde.

For days they had fled into the desert, pursued so far by Stygian horsemen that when they shook off the pursuit, they dared not turn back. They pushed on, seeking water, until the camel died. Then they went on foot. For the past few days their suffering had been intense. Conan had shielded Natala all he could, and the rough life of the camp had given her more stamina and strength than the average woman possesses; but even so, she was not far from collapse.

The sun beat fiercely on Conan's tangled black mane. Waves of dizziness and nausea rose in his brain, but he set his teeth and strode on unwaveringly. He was convinced that the city was a reality and not a mirage. What they would find there he had no idea. The inhabitants might be hostile. Nevertheless it was a fighting chance, and that was as much as he had ever asked.

The sun was nigh to setting when they halted in front of the massive gate, grateful for the shade. Conan stood Natala on her feet, and stretched his aching arms. Above them the walls towered some thirty feet in height, composed of a smooth greenish substance that shone almost like glass. Conan scanned the parapets, expecting to be challenged, but saw no one. Impatiently he shouted, and banged on the gate with his saber-hilt, but only the hollow echoes mocked him. Natala cringed close to him, frightened by the silence. Conan tried the portal, and stepped back, drawing his saber, as it swung silently inward. Natala stifled a cry.

'Oh, look, Conan!'

Just inside the gate lay a human body. Conan glared at it narrowly, then looked beyond it. He saw a wide open expanse, like a court, bordered by the arched doorways of houses composed of the same greenish material as the outer walls. These edifices were lofty and imposing, pinnacled with shining domes and minarets. There was no sign of life among them. In the center of the court rose the square curb of a well, and the sight stung Conan, whose mouth felt caked with dry dust. Taking Natala's wrist he drew her through the gate, and closed it behind them.

'Is he dead?' she whispered, shrinkingly indicating the man who lay limply before the gate. The body was that of a tall powerful individual, apparently in his prime; the skin was yellow, the eyes slightly slanted; otherwise the man differed little from the Hyborian type. He was clad in high-strapped sandals and a tunic of purple silk, and a short sword in a cloth-of-gold scabbard hung from his girdle. Conan felt his flesh. It was cold. There was no sign of life in the body.

'Not a wound on him,' grunted the Cimmerian, 'but he's dead as Almuric with forty Stygian arrows in him. In Crom's name, let's see to the well! If there's water in it, we'll drink, dead men or no.'

There was water in the well, but they did not drink of it. Its level was a good fifty feet below the curb, and there was nothing to draw it up with. Conan cursed blackly, maddened by the sight of the stuff just out of his reach, and turned to look for some means of obtaining it. Then a scream from Natala brought him about.

The supposedly dead man was rushing upon him, eyes blazing with indisputable life, his short sword gleaming in his hand. Conan cursed amazedly, but wasted no time in conjecture. He met the hurtling attacker with a slashing cut of his saber that sheared through flesh and bone. The fellow's head thudded on the flags; the body staggered drunkenly, an arch of blood jetting from the severed jugular; then it fell heavily.

Conan glared down, swearing softly.

'This fellow is no deader now than he was a few minutes agone. Into what madhouse have we strayed?'

Natala, who had covered her eyes with her hands at the sight, peeked between her fingers and shook with fear.

'Oh, Conan, will the people of the city not kill us, because of this?'

'Well,' he growled, 'this creature would have killed us if I hadn't lopped off his head.'

He glanced at the archways that gaped blankly from the green walls above them. He saw no hint of movement, heard no sound.

'I don't think any one saw us,' he muttered. 'I'll hide the evidence—'

He lifted the limp carcass by its swordbelt with one hand, and grasping the head by its long hair in the other, he half carried, half dragged the ghastly remains over to the well.

'Since we can't drink this water,' he gritted vindictively, 'I'll see that nobody else enjoys drinking it. Curse such a well, anyway!' He heaved the body over the curb and let it drop, tossing the head after it. A dull splash sounded far beneath.

'There's blood on the stones,' whispered Natala.

'There'll be more unless I find water soon,' growled the Cimmerian, his short store of patience about exhausted. The girl had almost forgotten her thirst and hunger in her fear, but not Conan.

'We'll go into one of these doors,' he said. 'Surely we'll find people after awhile.'

'Oh, Conan!' she wailed, snuggling up as close to him as she could. 'I'm afraid! This is a city of ghosts and dead men! Let us go back into the desert! Better to die there, than to face these terrors!'

'We'll go into the desert when they throw us off the walls,' he snarled. 'There's water somewhere in this city, and I'll find it, if I have to kill every man in it.'

'But what if they come to life again?' she whispered.

'Then I'll keep killing them until they stay dead!' he snapped. 'Come on! That doorway is as good as another! Stay behind me, but don't run unless I tell you to.'

She murmured a faint assent and followed him so closely that she stepped on his heels, to his irritation. Dusk had fallen, filling the strange city with purple shadows. They entered the open doorway, and found themselves in a wide chamber, the walls of which were hung with velvet tapestries, worked in curious designs. Floor, walls and ceiling were of the green glassy stone, the walls decorated with gold frieze-work. Furs and satin cushions littered the floor. Several doorways let into other rooms. They passed through, and traversed several chambers, counterparts of the first. They saw no one, but the Cimmerian grunted suspiciously.

'Some one was here not long ago. This couch is still warm from contact with a human body. That silk cushion bears the imprint of some one's hips. Then there's a faint scent of perfume lingering in the air.'

A weird unreal atmosphere hung over all. Traversing this dim silent palace was like an opium dream. Some of the chambers were unlighted, and these they avoided. Others were bathed in a soft weird light that seemed to emanate from jewels set in the walls in fantastic designs. Suddenly, as they passed into one of these illumined chambers, Natala cried out and clutched her companion's arm. With a curse he wheeled, glaring for an enemy, bewildered because he saw none.

'What's the matter?' he snarled. 'If you ever grab my sword-arm again, I'll skin you. Do you want me to get my throat cut? What were you yelling about?'

'Look there,' she quavered, pointing.

Conan grunted. On a table of polished ebony stood golden vessels, apparently containing food and drink. The room was unoccupied.

'Well, whoever this feast is prepared for,' he growled, 'he'll have to look elsewhere tonight.'

'Dare we eat it, Conan?' ventured the girl nervously. 'The people might come upon us, and—'

'Lir an mannanan mac lir!' he swore, grabbing her by the nape of her neck and thrusting her into a gilded chair at the end of the table with no great ceremony. 'We starve and you make objections! Eat!'

He took the chair at the other end, and seizing a jade goblet, emptied it at a gulp. It contained a crimson wine-like liquor of a peculiar tang, unfamiliar to him, but it was like nectar to his parched gullet. His thirst allayed, he attacked the food before him with rare gusto. It too was strange to him: exotic fruits and unknown meats. The vessels were of exquisite workmanship, and there were golden knives and forks as well. These Conan ignored, grasping the meat-joints in his fingers and tearing them with his strong teeth. The Cimmerian's table manners were rather wolfish at any time. His civilized companion ate more daintily, but just as ravenously. It occurred to Conan that the food might be poisoned, but the thought did not lessen his appetite; he preferred to die of poisoning rather than starvation.

His hunger satisfied, he leaned back with a deep sigh of relief. That there were humans in that silent city was evidenced by the fresh food, and perhaps every dark corner concealed a lurking enemy. But he felt no apprehension on that score, having a large confidence in his own fighting ability. He began to feel sleepy, and considered the idea of stretching himself on a near-by couch for a nap.

Not so Natala. She was no longer hungry and thirsty, but she felt no desire to sleep. Her lovely eyes were very wide indeed as she timidly glanced at the doorways, boundaries of the unknown. The silence and mystery of the strange place preyed on her. The chamber seemed larger, the table longer than she had first noticed, and she realized that she was farther from her grim protector than she wished to be. Rising quickly, she went around the table and seated herself on his knee, glancing nervously at the arched doorways. Some were lighted and some were not, and it was at the unlighted ones she gazed longest.

'We have eaten, drunk and rested,' she urged. 'Let us leave this place, Conan. It's evil. I can feel it.'

'Well, we haven't been harmed so far,' he began, when a soft but sinister rustling brought him about. Thrusting the girl off his knee he rose with the quick ease of a panther, drawing his saber, facing the doorway from which the sound had seemed to come. It was not repeated, and he stole forward noiselessly, Natala following with her heart in her mouth. She knew he suspected peril. His outthrust head was sunk between his giant shoulders, he glided forward in a half crouch, like a stalking tiger. He made no more noise than a tiger would have made.

At the doorway he halted, Natala peering fearfully from behind him. There was no light in the room, but it was partially illuminated by the radiance behind them, which streamed across it into yet another chamber. And in this chamber a man lay on a raised dais. The soft light bathed him, and they saw he was a counterpart of the man Conan had killed before the outer gate, except that his garments were richer, and ornamented with jewels which twinkled in the uncanny light. Was he dead, or merely sleeping? Again came that faint sinister sound, as if some one had thrust aside a hanging. Conan drew back, drawing the clinging Natala with him. He clapped his hand over her mouth just in time to check her shriek.

From where they now stood, they could no longer see the dais, but they could see the shadow it cast on the wall behind it. And now another shadow moved across the wall: a huge shapeless black blot. Conan felt his hair prickle curiously as he watched. Distorted though it might be, he felt that he had never seen a man or beast which cast such a shadow. He was consumed with curiosity, but some instinct held him frozen in his tracks. He heard Natala's quick panting gasps as she stared with dilated eyes. No other sound disturbed the tense stillness. The great shadow engulfed that of the dais. For a long instant only its black bulk was thrown on the smooth wall. Then slowly it receded, and once more the dais was etched darkly against the wall. But the sleeper was no longer upon it.

An hysterical gurgle rose in Natala's throat, and Conan gave her an admonitory shake. He was aware of an iciness in his own veins. Human foes he did not fear; anything understandable, however grisly, caused no tremors in his broad breast. But this was beyond his ken.

After a while, however, his curiosity conquered his uneasiness, and he moved out into the unlighted chamber again, ready for anything. Looking into the other room, he saw it was empty. The dais stood as he had first seen it, except that no bejeweled human lay thereon. Only on its silken covering shone a single drop of blood, like a great crimson gem. Natala saw it and gave a low choking cry, for which Conan did not punish her. Again he felt the icy hand of fear. On that dais a man had lain; *something* had crept into the chamber and carried him away. What that something was, Conan had no idea, but an aura of unnatural horror hung over those dim-lit chambers.

He was ready to depart. Taking Natala's hand, he turned back, then hesitated. Somewhere back among the chambers they had traversed, he heard the sound of a footfall. A human foot, bare or softly shod, had made that sound, and Conan, with the wariness of a wolf, turned quickly aside. He believed he could come again into the outer court, and yet avoid the room from which the sound had appeared to come.

But they had not crossed the first chamber on their new route, when the rustle of a silken hanging brought them about suddenly. Before a curtained alcove stood a man eyeing them intently.

He was exactly like the others they had encountered: tall, well made, clad in purple garments, with a jeweled girdle. There was neither surprise nor hostility in his amber eyes. They were dreamy as a lotus-eater's. He did not draw the short sword at his side. After a tense moment he spoke, in a far-away detached tone, and a language his hearers did not understand.

On a venture Conan replied in Stygian, and the stranger answered in the same tongue: 'Who are you?'

'I am Conan, a Cimmerian,' answered the barbarian. 'This is Natala, of Brythunia. What city is this?'

The man did not at once reply. His dreamy sensuous gaze rested on Natala, and he drawled, 'Of all my rich visions, this is the strangest! Oh, girl of the golden locks, from what far dreamland do you come? From Andarra, or Tothra, or Kuth of the star-girdle?'

'What madness is this?' growled the Cimmerian harshly, not relishing the man's words or manner.

The other did not heed him.

'I have dreamed more gorgeous beauties,' he murmured; 'lithe women with hair dusky as night, and dark eyes of unfathomed mystery. But your skin is white as milk, your eyes as clear as dawn, and there is about you a freshness and daintiness alluring as honey. Come to my couch, little dream-girl!'

He advanced and reached for her, and Conan struck aside his hand with a force that might have broken his arm. The man reeled back, clutching the numbed member, his eyes clouding.

'What rebellion of ghosts is this?' he muttered. 'Barbarian,

I command ye – begone! Fade! Dissipate! Fade! Vanish!'

'I'll vanish your head from your shoulders!' snarled the infuriated Cimmerian, his saber gleaming in his hand. 'Is this the welcome you give strangers? By Crom, I'll drench these hangings in blood!'

The dreaminess had faded from the other's eyes, to be replaced by a look of bewilderment.

'Thog!' he ejaculated. 'You are real! Whence come you? Who are you? What do you in Xuthal?'

'We came from the desert,' Conan growled. 'We wandered into the city at dusk, famishing. We found a feast set for some one, and we ate it. I have no money to pay for it. In my country, no starving man is denied food, but you civilized people must have your recompense – if you are like all I ever met. We have done no harm and we were just leaving. By Crom, I do not like this place, where dead men rise, and sleeping men vanish into the bellies of shadows!'

The man started violently at the last comment, his yellow face turning ashy.

'What do you say? Shadows? Into the bellies of shadows?'

'Well,' answered the Cimmerian cautiously, 'whatever it is that takes a man from a sleeping-dais and leaves only a spot of blood.'

'You have seen? You have *seen*?' The man was shaking like a leaf; his voice cracked on the high-pitched note.

'Only a man sleeping on a dais, and a shadow that engulfed him,' answered Conan.

The effect of his words on the other was horrifying. With an awful scream the man turned and rushed from the chamber. In his blind haste he caromed from the side of the door, righted himself, and fled through the adjoining chambers, still screaming at the top of his voice. Amazed, Conan stared after him, the girl trembling as she clutched the giant's arm. They could no longer see the flying figure, but they still heard his frightful screams, dwindling in the distance, and echoing as from vaulted roofs. Suddenly one cry, louder than the others, rose and broke short, followed by blank silence.

'Crom!'

Conan wiped the perspiration from his forehead with a hand that was not entirely steady.

'Surely this is a city of the mad! Let's get out of here, before we meet other madmen!'

'It is all a nightmare!' whimpered Natala. 'We are dead and damned! We died out on the desert and are in hell! We are disembodied spirits – *ow*!' Her yelp was induced by a resounding spank from Conan's open hand.

'You're no spirit when a pat makes you yell like that,' he commented, with the grim humor which frequently manifested itself at inopportune times. 'We are alive, though we may not be if we loiter in this devil-haunted pile. Come!'

They had traversed but a single chamber when again they stopped short. Some one or something was approaching. They faced the doorway whence the sounds came, waiting for they knew not what. Conan's nostrils widened, and his eyes narrowed. He caught the faint scent of the perfume he had noticed earlier in the night. A figure framed itself in the doorway. Conan swore under his breath; Natala's red lips opened wide.

It was a woman who stood there staring at them in wonder. She was tall, lithe, shaped like a goddess; clad in a narrow girdle crusted with jewels. A burnished mass of night-black hair set off the whiteness of her ivory body. Her dark eyes, shaded by long dusky lashes, were deep with sensuous mystery. Conan caught his breath at her beauty, and Natala stared with dilated eyes. The Cimmerian had never seen such a woman; her facial outline was Stygian, but she was not dusky-skinned like the Stygian women he had known; her limbs were like alabaster.

But when she spoke, in a deep rich musical voice, it was in the Stygian tongue.

'Who are you? What do you in Xuthal? Who is that girl?'

'Who are you?' bluntly countered Conan, who quickly wearied of answering questions.

'I am Thalis the Stygian,' she replied. 'Are you mad, to come here?'

'I've been thinking I must be,' he growled. 'By Crom, if I am sane, I'm out of place here, because these people are all maniacs. We stagger in from the desert, dying of thirst and hunger, and we come upon a dead man who tries to stab me in the back. We enter a palace rich and luxuriant, yet apparently empty. We find a meal set, but with no feasters. Then we see a shadow devour a sleeping man—' He watched her narrowly and saw her change color slightly. 'Well?'

'Well what?' she demanded, apparently regaining control of herself.

'I was just waiting for you to run through the rooms howling like a wild woman,' he answered. 'The man I told about the shadow did.'

She shrugged her slim ivory shoulders. 'That was the screams I heard, then. Well, to every man his fate, and it's foolish to squeal like a rat in a trap. When Thog wants me, he will come for me.'

'Who is Thog?' demanded Conan suspiciously.

She gave him a long appraising stare that brought color to Natala's face and made her bite her small red lip.

'Sit down on that divan and I will tell you,' she said. 'But first tell me your names.'

'I am Conan, a Cimmerian, and this is Natala, a daughter of Brythunia,' he answered. 'We are refugees of an army destroyed on the borders of Kush. But I am not desirous of sitting down, where black shadows might steal up on my back.'

With a light musical laugh, she seated herself, stretching out her supple limbs with studied abandon.

'Be at ease,' she advised. 'If Thog wishes you, he will take you, wherever you are. That man you mentioned, who screamed and ran – did you not hear him give one great cry, and then fall silent? In his frenzy, he must have run full into that which he sought to escape. No man can avoid his fate.'

Conan grunted non-committally, but he sat down on the edge of a couch, his saber across his knees, his eyes wandering suspiciously about the chamber. Natala nestled against him, clutching him jealously, her legs tucked up under her. She eyed the stranger woman with suspicion and resentment. She felt small and dust-stained and insignificant before this glamorous beauty, and she could not mistake the look in the dark eyes which feasted on every detail of the bronzed giant's physique.

'What is this place, and who are these people?' demanded Conan.

'This city is called Xuthal; it is very ancient. It is built over an oasis, which the founders of Xuthal found in their wanderings. They came from the east, so long ago that not even their descendants remember the age.'

'Surely there are not many of them; these palaces seem empty.'

'No; and yet more than you might think. The city is really one great palace, with every building inside the walls closely connected with the others. You might walk among these chambers for hours and see no one. At other times, you would meet hundreds of the inhabitants.'

'How is that?' Conan inquired uneasily; this savored too strongly of sorcery for comfort.

'Much of the time these people lie in sleep. Their dream-life is as important – and to them as real – as their waking life. You have heard of the black lotus? In certain pits of the city it grows. Through the ages they have cultivated it, until, instead of death, its juice induces dreams, gorgeous and fantastic. In these dreams they spend most of their time. Their lives are vague, erratic, and without plan. They dream, they wake, drink, love, eat and dream again. They seldom finish anything they begin, but leave it half completed and sink back again into the slumber of the black lotus. That meal you found – doubtless one awoke, felt the urge of hunger, prepared the meal for himself, then forgot about it and wandered away to dream again.'

'Where do they get their food?' interrupted Conan. 'I saw no fields or vineyards outside the city. Have they orchards and cattle-pens within the walls?'

She shook her head. 'They manufacture their own food out of the primal elements. They are wonderful scientists, when they are not drugged with their dream-flower. Their ancestors were mental giants, who built this marvelous city in the desert, and though the race became slaves to their curious passions, some of their wonderful knowledge still remains. Have you wondered about these lights? They are jewels, fused with radium. You rub them with your thumb to make them glow, and rub them again, the opposite way, to extinguish them. That is but a single example of their science. But much they have forgotten. They take little interest in waking life, choosing to lie most of the time in death-like sleep.'

'Then the dead man at the gate—' began Conan.

'Was doubtless slumbering. Sleepers of the lotus are like the dead. Animation is apparently suspended. It is impossible to detect the slightest sign of life. The spirit has left the body and is roaming at will through other, exotic worlds. The man at the gate was a good example of the irresponsibility of these people's lives. He was guarding the gate, where custom decrees a watch be kept, though no enemy has ever advanced across the desert. In other parts of the city you would find other guards, generally sleeping as soundly as the man at the gate.'

Conan mulled over this for a space.

'Where are the people now?'

'Scattered in different parts of the city; lying on couches, on silken divans, in cushion-littered alcoves, on fur-covered daises; all wrapt in the shining veil of dreams.'

Conan felt the skin twitch between his massive shoulders. It was not soothing to think of hundreds of people lying cold and still throughout the tapestried palaces, their glassy eyes turned unseeingly upward. He remembered something else.

'What of the thing that stole through the chambers and carried away the man on the dais?'

A shudder twitched her ivory limbs.

'That was Thog, the Ancient, the god of Xuthal, who dwells in the sunken dome in the center of the city. He has always dwelt in Xuthal. Whether he came here with the ancient founders, or was here when they built the city, none knows. But the people of Xuthal worship him. Mostly he sleeps below the city, but sometimes at irregular intervals he grows hungry, and then he steals through the secret corridors and the dim-lit chambers, seeking prey. Then none is safe.'

Natala moaned with terror and clasped Conan's mighty neck as if to resist an effort to drag her from her protector's side.

'Crom!' he ejaculated aghast. 'You mean to tell me these people lie down calmly and sleep, with this demon crawling among them?'

'It is only occasionally that he is hungry,' she repeated. 'A god must have his sacrifices. When I was a child in Stygia the people lived under the shadow of the priests. None ever knew when he or she would be seized and dragged to the altar. What difference whether the priests give a victim to the gods, or the god comes for his own victim?'

'Such is not the custom of my people,' Conan growled, 'nor of Natala's either. The Hyborians do not sacrifice humans to their god, Mitra, and as for my people – by Crom, I'd like to see a priest try to drag a Cimmerian to the altar! There'd be blood spilt, but not as the priest intended.'

'You are a barbarian,' laughed Thalis, but with a glow in her luminous eyes. 'Thog is very ancient and very terrible.'

'These folk must be either fools or heroes,' grunted Conan, 'to lie down and dream their idiotic dreams, knowing they might awaken in his belly.'

She laughed. 'They know nothing else. For untold generations Thog has preyed on them. He has been one of the factors which have reduced their numbers from thousands to hundreds. A few more generations and they will be extinct, and Thog must either fare forth into the world for new prey, or retire to the underworld whence he came so long ago.

'They realize their ultimate doom, but they are fatalists, incapable of resistance or escape. Not one of the present generation has been out of sight of these walls. There is an oasis a day's march to the south – I have seen it on the old maps their ancestors drew on parchment – but no man of Xuthal has visited it for three generations, much less made any attempt to explore the fertile grasslands which the maps show lying another day's march beyond it. They are a fast-fading race, drowned in lotus-dreams, stimulating their waking hours by means of the golden wine which heals wounds, prolongs life, and invigorates the most sated debauchee.

'Yet they cling to life, and fear the deity they worship. You saw how one went mad at the knowledge that Thog was roving the palaces. I have seen the whole city screaming and tearing its hair, and running frenziedly out of the gates, to cower outside the walls and draw lots to see which would be bound and flung back through the arched doorways to satisfy Thog's lust and hunger. Were they not all slumbering now, the word of his coming would send them raving and shrieking again through the outer gates.'

'Oh, Conan!' begged Natala hysterically. 'Let us flee!'

'In good time,' muttered Conan, his eyes burning on Thalis' ivory limbs. 'What are you, a Stygian woman, doing here?'

'I came here when a young girl,' she answered, leaning lithely back against the velvet divan, and intertwining her slender fingers behind her dusky head. 'I am the daughter of a king, no common woman, as you can see by my skin, which is as white as that of your little blond there. I was abducted by a rebel prince, who, with an army of Kushite bowmen, pushed southward into the wilderness, searching for a land he could make his own. He and all his warriors perished in the desert, but one, before he died, placed me on a camel and walked beside it until he dropped and died in his tracks. The beast wandered on, and I finally passed into delirium from thirst and hunger, and awakened in this city. They told me I had been seen from the walls, early in the dawn, lying senseless beside a dead camel. They went forth and brought me in and revived me with their wonderful golden wine. And only the sight of a woman would have led them to have ventured that far from their walls.

'They were naturally much interested in me, especially the men. As I could not speak their language, they learned to speak mine. They are very quick and able of intellect; they learned my language long before I learned theirs. But they were more interested in me than in my language. I have been, and am, the only thing for which a man of them will forgo his lotus-dreams for a space.'

She laughed wickedly, flashing her audacious eyes meaningly at Conan.

'Of course the women are jealous of me,' she continued tranquilly. 'They are handsome enough in their yellow-skinned way, but they are dreamy and uncertain as the men, and these latter like me not only for my beauty, but for my reality. I am no dream! Though I have dreamed the dreams of the lotus, I am a normal woman, with earthly emotions and desires. With such these moon-eyed yellow women can not compare.

'That is why it would be better for you to cut that girl's throat with your saber, before the men of Xuthal waken and catch her. They will put her through paces she never dreamed of! She is too soft to endure what I have thrived on. I am a daughter of Luxur, and before I had known fifteen summers I had been led through the temples of Derketo, the dusky goddess, and had been initiated into the mysteries. Not that my first years in Xuthal were years of unmodified pleasure! The people of Xuthal have forgotten more than the priestesses of Derketo ever dreamed. They live only for sensual joys. Dreaming or waking, their lives are filled with exotic ecstasies, beyond the ken of ordinary men.'

'Damned degenerates!' growled Conan.

'It is all in the point of view,' smiled Thalis lazily.

'Well,' he decided, 'we're merely wasting time. I can see this is no place for ordinary mortals. We'll be gone before your morons awake, or Thog comes to devour us. I think the desert would be kinder.'

Natala, whose blood had curdled in her veins at Thalis's words, fervently agreed. She could speak Stygian only brokenly, but she understood it well enough. Conan stood up, drawing her up beside him.

'If you'll show us the nearest way out of this city,' he grunted, 'we'll take ourselves off.' But his gaze lingered on the Stygian's sleek limbs and ivory breasts.

She did not miss his look, and she smiled enigmatically as she rose with the lithe ease of a great lazy cat.

'Follow me,' she directed and led the way, conscious of Conan's eyes fixed on her supple figure and perfectly poised carriage. She did not go the way they had come, but before Conan's suspicions could be roused, she halted in a wide ivory-cased chamber, and pointed to a tiny fountain which gurgled in the center of the ivory floor.

'Don't you want to wash your face, child?' she asked Natala. 'It is stained with dust, and there is dust in your hair.'

Natala colored resentfully at the suggestion of malice in the Stygian's faintly mocking tone, but she complied, wondering miserably just how much havoc the desert sun and wind had wrought on her complexion – a feature for which women of her race were justly noted. She knelt beside the fountain, shook back her hair, slipped her tunic down to her waist, and began to lave not only her face, but her white arms and shoulders as well.

'By Crom!' grumbled Conan. 'A woman will stop to consider her beauty, if the devil himself were on her heels. Haste, girl; you'll be dusty again before we've got out of sight of this city. And Thalis, I'd take it kindly if you'd furnish us with a bit of food and drink.'

For answer Thalis leaned herself against him, slipping one white arm about his bronzed shoulders. Her sleek naked flank pressed against his thigh and the perfume of her foamy hair was in his nostrils.

'Why dare the desert?' she whispered urgently. 'Stay here! I will teach you the ways of Xuthal. I will protect you. I will love you! You are a real man: I am sick of these moon-calves who sigh and dream and wake, and dream again. I am hungry for the hard, clean passion of a man from the earth. The blaze of your dynamic eyes makes my heart pound in my bosom, and the touch of your iron-thewed arm maddens me.

'Stay here! I will make you king of Xuthal! I will show you all the ancient mysteries, and the exotic ways of pleasure! I—' She had thrown both arms about his neck and was standing on tiptoe, her vibrant body shivering against his. Over her ivory shoulder he saw Natala, throwing back her damp tousled hair, stop short, her lovely eyes dilating, her red lips parting in a shocked O. With an embarrassed grunt, Conan disengaged Thalis's clinging arms and put her aside with one massive arm. She threw a swift glance at the Brythunian girl and smiled enigmatically, seeming to nod her splendid head in mysterious cogitation.

Natala rose and jerked up her tunic, her eyes blazing, her lips pouting sulkily. Conan swore under his breath. He was no more monogamous in his nature than the average soldier of fortune, but there was an innate decency about him that was Natala's best protection.

Thalis did not press her suit. Beckoning them with her slender hand to follow, she turned and walked across the chamber. There, close to the tapestried wall, she halted suddenly. Conan, watching her, wondered if she had heard the sounds that might be made by a nameless monster stealing through the midnight chambers, and his skin crawled at the thought.

'What do you hear?' he demanded.

'Watch that doorway,' she replied, pointing.

He wheeled, sword ready. Only the empty arch of the entrance met his gaze. Then behind him sounded a quick faint scuffling noise, a half-choked gasp. He whirled. Thalis and Natala had vanished. The tapestry was settling back in place, as if it had been lifted away from the wall. As he gaped bewilderedly, from behind that tapestried wall rang a muffled scream in the voice of the Brythunian girl.

2

When Conan turned, in compliance with Thalis's request, to glare at the doorway opposite, Natala had been standing just behind him, close to the side of the Stygian. The instant the Cimmerian's back was turned, Thalis, with a pantherish quickness almost incredible, clapped her hand over Natala's mouth, stifling the cry she tried to give. Simultaneously the Stygian's other arm was passed about the blond girl's supple waist, and she was jerked back against the wall, which seemed to give way as Thalis' shoulder pressed against it. A section of the wall swung inward, and through a slit that opened in the tapestry Thalis slid with her captive, just as Conan wheeled back.

Inside was utter blackness as the secret door swung to again. Thalis paused to fumble at it for an instant, apparently sliding home a bolt, and as she took her hand from Natala's mouth to perform this act, the Brythunian girl began to scream at the top of her voice. Thalis's laugh was like poisoned honey in the darkness.

'Scream if you will, little fool. It will only shorten your life.'

At that Natala ceased suddenly, and cowered shaking in every limb.

'Why did you do this?' she begged. 'What are you going to do?'

'I am going to take you down this corridor for a short distance,' answered Thalis, 'and leave you for one who will sooner or later come for you.'

'Ohhhhhh!' Natala's voice broke in a sob of terror. 'Why should you harm me? I have never injured you!'

'I want your warrior. You stand in my way. He desires me – I could read the look in his eyes. But for you, he would be willing to stay here and be my king. When you are out of the way, he will follow me.'

'He will cut your throat,' answered Natala with conviction, knowing Conan better than Thalis did.

'We shall see,' answered the Stygian coolly from the confidence of her power over men. 'At any rate, you will not know whether he stabs or kisses me, because you will be the bride of him who dwells in darkness. Come!'

Half mad with terror, Natala fought like a wild thing, but it availed her nothing. With a lithe strength she would not have believed possible in a woman, Thalis picked her up and carried her down the black corridor as if she had been a child. Natala did not scream again, remembering the Stygian's sinister words; the only sounds were her desperate quick panting and Thalis' soft taunting lascivious laughter. Then the Brythunian's fluttering hand closed on something in the dark – a jeweled dagger-hilt jutting from Thalis's gem-crusted girdle. Natala jerked it forth and struck blindly and with all her girlish power.

A scream burst from Thalis's lips, feline in its pain and fury. She reeled, and Natala slipped from her relaxing grasp, to bruise her tender limbs on the smooth stone floor. Rising, she scurried to the nearest wall and stood there panting and trembling, flattening herself against the stones. She could not see Thalis, but she could hear her. The Stygian was quite certainly not dead. She was cursing in a steady stream, and her fury was so concentrated and deadly that Natala felt her bones turn to wax, her blood to ice.

'Where are you, you little she-devil?' gasped Thalis. 'Let me get my fingers on you again, and I'll—' Natala grew physically sick as Thalis described the bodily injuries she intended to inflict on her rival. The Stygian's choice of language would have shamed the toughest courtesan in Aquilonia.

Natala heard her groping in the dark, and then a light sprang up. Evidently whatever fear Thalis felt of the black corridor was submerged in her anger. The light came from one of the radium gems which adorned the walls of Xuthal. This Thalis had rubbed, and now she stood bathed in its reddish glow: a light different from that which the others had emitted. One hand was pressed to her side and blood trickled between the fingers. But she did not seem weakened or badly hurt, and her eyes blazed fiendishly. What little courage remained to Natala ebbed away at sight of the Stygian standing limned in that weird glow, her beautiful face contorted with a passion that was no less than hellish. She now advanced with a pantherish tread, drawing her hand away from her wounded side, and shaking the blood drops impatiently from her fingers. Natala saw that she had not badly harmed her rival. The blade had glanced from the jewels of Thalis's girdle and inflicted only a very superficial flesh-wound, only enough to rouse the Stygian's unbridled fury.

'Give me that dagger, you fool!' she gritted, striding up to the cowering girl.

Natala knew she ought to fight while she had the chance, but she simply could not summon up the courage. Never much of a fighter, the darkness, violence and horror of her adventure had left her limp, mentally and physically. Thalis snatched the dagger from her lax fingers and threw it contemptuously aside.

'You little slut!' she ground between her teeth, slapping the girl viciously with either hand. 'Before I drag you down the corridor and throw you into Thog's jaws I'll have a little of your blood myself! You would dare to knife me – well, for that audacity you shall pay!'

Seizing her by the hair, Thalis dragged her down the corridor a short distance, to the edge of the circle of light. A metal ring showed in the wall, above the level of a man's head. From it depended a silken cord. As in a nightmare Natala felt her tunic being stripped from her, and the next instant Thalis had jerked up her wrists and bound them to the ring, where she hung, naked as the day she was born, her feet barely touching the floor. Twisting her head, Natala saw Thalis unhook a jewel-handled whip from where it hung on the wall, near the ring. The lashes consisted of seven round silk cords, harder yet more pliant than leather thongs.

With a hiss of vindictive gratification, Thalis drew back her arm, and Natala shrieked as the cords curled across her loins. The tortured girl writhed, twisted and tore agonizedly at the thongs which imprisoned her wrists. She had forgotten the lurking menace her cries might summon, and so apparently had Thalis. Every stroke evoked screams of anguish. The whippings Natala had received in the Shemite slave-markets paled to insignificance before this. She had never guessed the punishing power of hard-woven silk cords. Their caress was more exquisitely painful than any birch twigs or leather thongs. They whistled venomously as they cut the air.

Then, as Natala twisted her tear-stained face over her shoulder to shriek for mercy, something froze her cries. Agony gave place to paralyzing horror in her beautiful eyes.

Struck by her expression, Thalis checked her lifted hand and whirled quick as a cat. Too late! An awful cry rang from her lips as she swayed back, her arms upflung. Natala saw her for an instant, a white figure of fear etched against a great black shapeless mass that towered over her; then the white figure was whipped off its feet, the shadow receded with it, and in the circle of dim light Natala hung alone, half fainting with terror.

From the black shadows came sounds, incomprehensible and blood-freezing. She heard Thalis's voice pleading frenziedly, but no voice answered. There was no sound except the Stygian's panting voice, which suddenly rose to screams of agony, and then broke in hysterical laughter, mingled with sobs. This dwindled to a convulsive panting, and presently this too ceased, and a silence more terrible hovered over the secret corridor.

Nauseated with horror, Natala twisted about and dared to look fearfully in the direction the black shape had carried Thalis. She saw nothing, but she sensed an unseen peril, more grisly than she could understand. She fought against a rising tide of hysteria. Her bruised wrists, her smarting body were forgotten in the teeth of this menace which she dimly felt threatened not only her body, but her soul as well.

She strained her eyes into the blackness beyond the rim of the dim light, tense with fear of what she might see. A whimpering gasp escaped her lips. The darkness was taking form. Something huge and bulky grew up out of the void. She saw a great misshapen head emerging into the light. At least she took it for a head, though it was not the member of any sane or normal creature. She saw a great toad-like face, the features of which were as dim and unstable as those of a specter seen in a mirror of nightmare. Great pools of light that might have been eyes blinked at her, and she shook at the cosmic lust reflected there. She could tell nothing about the creature's body. Its outline seemed to waver and alter subtly even as she looked at it; yet its substance was apparently solid enough. There was nothing misty or ghostly about it.

As it came toward her, she could not tell whether it walked, wriggled, flew or crept. Its method of locomotion was absolutely beyond her comprehension. When it had emerged from the shadows she was still uncertain as to its nature. The light from the radium gem did not illumine it as it would have illumined an ordinary creature. Impossible as it seemed, the being seemed almost impervious to the light. Its details were still obscure and indistinct, even when it halted so near that it almost touched her shrinking flesh. Only the blinking toad-like face stood out with any distinctness. The thing was a blur in the sight, a black blot of shadow that normal radiance would neither dissipate nor illuminate.

She decided she was mad, because she could not tell whether the being looked up at her or towered above her. She was unable to say whether the dim repulsive face blinked up at her from the shadows at her feet, or looked down at her from an immense height. But if her sight convinced her that whatever its mutable qualities, it was yet composed of solid substance, her sense of feel further assured her of that fact. A dark tentacle-like member slid about her body, and she screamed at the touch of it on her naked flesh. It was neither warm nor cold, rough nor smooth; it was like nothing that had ever touched her before, and at its caress she knew such fear and shame as she had never dreamed of. All the obscenity and salacious infamy spawned in the muck of the abysmal pits of Life seemed to drown her in seas of cosmic filth. And in that instant she knew that whatever form of life this thing represented it was not a beast.

She began to scream uncontrollably, the monster tugged at her as if to tear her from the ring by sheer brutality; then something crashed above their heads, and a form hurtled down through the air to strike the stone floor.

3

When Conan wheeled to see the tapestry settling back in place and to hear Natala's muffled cry, he hurled himself against the wall with a maddened roar. Rebounding from the impact that would have splintered the bones of a lesser man, he ripped away the tapestry revealing what appeared to be a blank wall. Beside himself with fury he lifted his saber as though to hew through the marble, when a sudden sound brought him about, eyes blazing.

A score of figures faced him, yellow men in purple tunics, with shortswords in their hands. As he turned they surged in on him with hostile cries. He made no attempt to conciliate them. Maddened at the disappearance of his sweetheart, the barbarian reverted to type.

A snarl of bloodthirsty gratification hummed in his bull-throat as he leaped, and the first attacker, his short sword overreached by the whistling saber, went down with his brains gushing from his split skull. Wheeling like a cat, Conan caught a descending wrist on his edge, and the hand gripping the short sword flew into the air scattering a shower of red drops. But Conan had not paused or hesitated. A pantherish twist and shift of his body avoided the blundering rush of two yellow swordsmen, and the blade of one missing its objective, was sheathed in the breast of the other.

A yell of dismay went up at this mischance, and Conan allowed himself a short bark of laughter as he bounded aside from a whistling cut and slashed under the guard of yet another man of Xuthal. A long spurt of crimson followed his singing edge and the man crumpled screaming, his belly-muscles cut through.

The warriors of Xuthal howled like mad wolves. Unaccustomed to battle, they were ridiculously slow and clumsy compared to the tigerish barbarian whose motions were blurs of quickness possible only to steel thews knit to a perfect fighting-brain. They floundered and stumbled, hindered by their own numbers; they struck too quick or too soon, and cut only empty air. He was never motionless or in the same place an instant; springing, side-stepping, whirling, twisting, he offered a constantly shifting target for their swords, while his own curved blade sang death about their ears.

But whatever their faults, the men of Xuthal did not lack courage. They swarmed about him yelling and hacking, and through the arched doorways rushed others, awakened from their slumbers by the unwonted clamor.

Conan, bleeding from a cut on the temple, cleared a space for an instant with a devastating sweep of his dripping saber, and cast a quick glance about for an avenue of escape. At that instant he saw the tapestry on one of the walls drawn aside, disclosing a narrow stairway. On this stood a man in rich robes, vague-eyed and blinking, as if he had just awakened and had not yet shaken the dusts of slumber from his brain. Conan's sight and action were simultaneous.

A tigerish leap carried him untouched through the hemming ring of swords, and he bounded toward the stair with the pack giving tongue behind him. Three men confronted him at the foot of the marble steps, and he struck them with a deafening crash of steel. There was a frenzied instant when the blades flamed like summer lightning; then the group fell apart and Conan sprang up the stair. The oncoming horde tripped over three writhing forms at its foot: one lay face-down in a sickening welter of blood and brains; another propped himself on his hands, blood spurting blackly from his severed throat veins; the other howled like a dying dog as he clawed at the crimson stump that had been an arm.

As Conan rushed up the marble stair, the man above shook himself from his stupor and drew a sword that sparkled frostily in the radium light. He thrust downward as the barbarian surged upon him. But as the point sang toward his throat, Conan ducked deeply. The blade slit the skin of his back, and Conan straightened, driving his saber upward as a man might wield a butcher-knife, with all the power of his mighty shoulders.

So terrific was his headlong drive that the sinking of the saber to the hilt into the belly of his enemy did not check him. He caromed against the wretch's body, knocking it sideways. The impact sent Conan crashing against the wall; the other, the saber torn through his body, fell headlong down the stair, ripped open to the spine from groin to broken breastbone. In a ghastly mess of streaming entrails the body tumbled against the men rushing up the stairs, bearing them back with it.

Half stunned, Conan leaned against the wall an instant, glaring down upon them; then with a defiant shake of his dripping saber, he bounded up the steps.

Coming into an upper chamber, he halted only long enough

to see that it was empty. Behind him the horde was yelling with such intensified horror and rage, that he knew he had killed some notable man there on the stair, probably the king of that fantastic city.

He ran at random, without plan. He desperately wished to find and succor Natala, who he was sure needed aid badly; but harried as he was by all the warriors in Xuthal, he could only run on, trusting to luck to elude them and find her. Among those dark or dimly lighted upper chambers he quickly lost all sense of direction, and it was not strange that he eventually blundered into a chamber into which his foes were just pouring.

They yelled vengefully and rushed for him, and with a snarl of disgust he turned and fled back the way he had come. At least he thought it was the way he had come. But presently, racing into a particularly ornate chamber, he was aware of his mistake. All the chambers he had traversed since mounting the stair had been empty. This chamber had an occupant, who rose up with a cry as he charged in.

Conan saw a yellow-skinned woman, loaded with jeweled ornaments but otherwise nude, staring at him with wide eyes. So much he glimpsed as she raised her hand and jerked a silken rope hanging from the wall. Then the floor dropped from under him, and all his steel-trap coordination could not save him from the plunge into the black depths that opened beneath him.

He did not fall any great distance, though it was far enough to have snapped the leg bones of a man not built of steel springs and whalebone.

He hit cat-like on his feet and one hand, instinctively retaining his grasp on his saber hilt. A familiar cry rang in his ears as he rebounded on his feet as a lynx rebounds with snarling bared fangs. So Conan, glaring from under his tousled mane, saw the white naked figure of Natala writhing in the lustful grasp of a black nightmare shape that could have only been bred in the lost pits of hell.

The sight of that awful shape alone might have frozen the Cimmerian with fear. In juxtaposition to his girl, the sight sent a red wave of murderous fury through Conan's brain. In a crimson mist he smote the monster.

It dropped the girl, wheeling toward its attacker, and the maddened Cimmerian's saber, shrilling through the air, sheared clear through the black viscous bulk and rang on the stone floor, showering blue sparks. Conan went to his knees from the fury of the blow; the edge had not encountered the resistance he had expected. As he bounded up, the thing was upon him.

It towered above him like a clinging black cloud. It seemed to flow about him in almost liquid waves, to envelop and engulf him. His madly slashing saber sheared through it again and again, his ripping poniard tore and rent it; he was deluged with a slimy liquid that must have been its sluggish blood. Yet its fury was nowise abated.

He could not tell whether he was slashing off its members or whether he was cleaving its bulk, which knit behind the slicing blade. He was tossed to and fro in the violence of that awful battle, and had a dazed feeling that he was fighting not one, but an aggregation of lethal creatures. The thing seemed to be biting, clawing, crushing and clubbing him all at the same time. He felt fangs and talons rend his flesh; flabby cables that were yet hard as iron encircled his limbs and body, and worse than all, something like a whip of scorpions fell again and again across his shoulders, back and breast, tearing the skin and filling his veins with a poison that was like liquid fire.

They had rolled beyond the circle of light, and it was in utter blackness that the Cimmerian battled. Once he sank his teeth, beast-like, into the flabby substance of his foe, revolting as the stuff writhed and squirmed like living rubber from between his iron jaws.

In that hurricane of battle they were rolling over and over, farther and farther down the tunnel. Conan's brain reeled with the punishment he was taking. His breath came in whistling gasps between his teeth. High above him he saw a great toad-like face, dimly limned in an eery glow that seemed to emanate from it.

And with a panting cry that was half curse, half gasp of straining agony, he lunged toward it, thrusting with all his waning power. Hilt-deep the saber sank, somewhere below the grisly face, and a convulsive shudder heaved the vast bulk that half enveloped the Cimmerian. With a volcanic burst of contraction and expansion, it tumbled backward, rolling now with frantic haste down the corridor. Conan went with it, bruised, battered, invincible, hanging on like a bulldog to the hilt of his saber which he could not withdraw, tearing and ripping at the shuddering bulk with the poniard in his left hand, goring it to ribbons.

The thing glowed all over now with a weird phosphorous radiance, and this glow was in Conan's eyes, blinding him, as suddenly the heaving billowing mass fell away from beneath him, the saber tearing loose and remaining in his locked hand. This hand and arm hung down into space, and far below him the glowing body of the monster was rushing downward like a meteor. Conan dazedly realized that he lay on the brink of a great round well, the edge of which was slimy stone. He lay there watching the hurtling glow dwindling and dwindling until it vanished into a dark shining surface that seemed to surge upward to meet it. For an instant a dimming witchfire glimmered in those dusky depths; then it disappeared and Conan lay staring down into the blackness of the ultimate abyss from which no sound came.

4

Straining vainly at the silk cords which cut into her wrists, Natala sought to pierce the darkness beyond the radiant circle. Her tongue seemed frozen to the roof of her mouth. Into that blackness she had seen Conan vanish, locked in mortal combat with the unknown demon, and the only sounds that had come to her straining ears had been the panting gasps of the barbarian, the impact of struggling bodies, and the thud and rip of savage blows. These ceased, and Natala swayed dizzily on her cords, half fainting.

A footstep roused her out of her apathy of horror, to see Conan emerging from the darkness. At the sight she found her voice in a shriek which echoed down the vaulted tunnel. The manhandling the Cimmerian had received was appalling to behold. At every step he dripped blood. His face was skinned and bruised as if he had been beaten with a bludgeon. His lips were pulped, and blood oozed down his face from a wound in his scalp. There were deep gashes in his thighs, calves and forearms, and great bruises showed on his limbs and body from impacts against the stone floor. But his shoulders, back and upper-breast muscles had suffered most. The flesh was bruised, swollen and lacerated, the skin hanging in loose strips, as if he had been lashed with wire whips.

'Oh, Conan!' she sobbed. 'What has happened to you?'

He had no breath for conversation, but his smashed lips writhed in what might have been grim humor as he approached her. His hairy breast, glistening with sweat and blood, heaved with his panting. Slowly and laboriously he reached up and cut her cords, then fell back against the wall and leaned there, his trembling legs braced wide. She scrambled up from where she had fallen and caught him in a frenzied embrace, sobbing hysterically.

'Oh, Conan, you are wounded unto death! Oh, what shall we do?'

'Well,' he panted, 'you can't fight a devil out of hell and come off with a whole skin!'

'Where is it?' she whispered. 'Did you kill it?'

'I don't know. It fell into a pit. It was hanging in bloody shreds, but whether it can be killed by steel I know not.'

'Oh, your poor back!' she wailed, wringing her hands.

'It lashed me with a tentacle,' he grimaced, swearing as he moved. 'It cut like wire and burned like poison. But it was its damnable squeezing that got my wind. It was worse than a python. If half my guts are not mashed out of place, I'm much mistaken.'

'What shall we do?' she whimpered.

He glanced up. The trap was closed. No sound came from above.

'We can't go back through the secret door,' he muttered. 'That room is full of dead men, and doubtless warriors keep watch there. They must have thought my doom sealed when I plunged through the floor above, or else they dare not follow me into this tunnel. – Twist that radium gem off the wall. – As I groped my way back up the corridor I felt arches opening into other tunnels. We'll follow the first we come to. It may lead to another pit, or to the open air. We must chance it. We can't stay here and rot.'

Natala obeyed, and holding the tiny point of light in his left hand and his bloody saber in his right, Conan started down the corridor. He went slowly, stiffly, only his animal vitality keeping him on his feet. There was a blank glare in his bloodshot eyes, and Natala saw him involuntarily lick his battered lips from time to time. She knew his suffering was ghastly, but with the stoicism of the wilds he made no complaint.

Presently the dim light shone on a black arch, and into this Conan turned. Natala cringed at what she might see, but the light revealed only a tunnel similar to that they had just left.

How far they went she had no idea, before they mounted a long stair and came upon a stone door, fastened with a golden bolt.

She hesitated, glancing at Conan. The barbarian was swaying on his feet, the light in his unsteady hand flinging fantastic shadows back and forth along the wall.

'Open the door, girl,' he muttered thickly. 'The men of Xuthal will be waiting for us, and I would not disappoint them. By Crom, the city has not seen such a sacrifice as I will make!'

She knew he was half delirious. No sound came from beyond the door. Taking the radium gem from his blood-stained hand, she threw the bolt and drew the panel inward. The inner side of a cloth-of-gold tapestry met her gaze and she drew it aside and peeked through, her heart in her mouth. She was looking into an empty chamber in the center of which a silvery fountain tinkled.

Conan's hand fell heavily on her naked shoulder.

'Stand aside, girl,' he mumbled. 'Now is the feasting of swords.'

'There is no one in the chamber,' she answered. 'But there is water—'

'I hear it,' he licked his blackened lips. 'We will drink before we die.'

He seemed blinded. She took his darkly stained hand and led him through the stone door. She went on tiptoe, expecting a rush of yellow figures through the arches at any instant.

'Drink while I keep watch,' he muttered.

'No, I am not thirsty. Lie down beside the fountain and I will bathe your wounds.'

'What of the swords of Xuthal?' He continually raked his arm across his eyes as if to clear his blurred sight.

'I hear no one. All is silent.'

He sank down gropingly and plunged his face into the crystal jet, drinking as if he could not get enough. When he raised his head there was sanity in his bloodshot eyes and he stretched his massive limbs out on the marble floor as she requested, though he kept his saber in his hand, and his eyes continually roved toward the archways. She bathed his torn flesh and bandaged the deeper wounds with strips torn from a silk hanging. She shuddered at the appearance of his back; the flesh was discolored, mottled and spotted black and blue and a sickly yellow, where it was not raw. As she worked she sought frantically for a solution to their problem. If they stayed where they were, they would eventually be discovered. Whether the men of Xuthal were searching the palaces for them, or had returned to their dreams, she could not know.

As she finished her task, she froze. Under the hanging that partly concealed an alcove, she saw a hand's breadth of yellow flesh.

Saying nothing to Conan, she rose and crossed the chamber softly, grasping his poniard. Her heart pounded suffocatingly as she cautiously drew aside the hanging. On the dais lay a young yellow woman, naked and apparently lifeless. At her hand stood a jade jar nearly full of peculiar golden-colored liquid. Natala believed it to be the elixir described by Thalis, which lent vigor and vitality to the degenerate Xuthal. She leaned across the supine form and grasped the vessel, her poniard poised over the girl's bosom. The latter did not wake.

With the jar in her possession, Natala hesitated, realizing it would be the safer course to put the sleeping girl beyond the power of waking and raising an alarm. But she could not bring herself to plunge the Cimmerian poniard into that still bosom, and at last she drew back the hanging and returned to Conan, who lay where she had left him, seemingly only partly conscious.

She bent and placed the jar to his lips. He drank, mechanically at first, then with a suddenly roused interest. To her amazement he sat up and took the vessel from her hands. When he lifted his face, his eyes were clear and normal. Much of the drawn haggard look had gone from his features, and his voice was not the mumble of delirium.

'Crom! Where did you get this?'

She pointed. 'From that alcove, where a yellow hussy is sleeping.'

He thrust his muzzle again into the golden liquid.

'By Crom,' he said with a deep sigh, 'I feel new life and power rush like wildfire through my veins. Surely this is the very elixir of Life!'

'We had best go back into the corridor,' Natala ventured nervously. 'We shall be discovered if we stay here long. We can hide there until your wounds heal—'

'Not I,' he grunted. 'We are not rats, to hide in dark burrows. We leave this devil-city now, and let none seek to stop us.'

'But your wounds!' she wailed.

'I do not feel them,' he answered. 'It may be a false strength this liquor has given me, but I swear I am aware of neither pain nor weakness.'

With sudden purpose he crossed the chamber to a window she had not noticed. Over his shoulder she looked out. A cool breeze tossed her tousled locks. Above was the dark velvet sky, clustered with stars. Below them stretched a vague expanse of sand.

'Thalis said the city was one great palace,' said Conan. 'Evidently some of the chambers are built like towers on the wall. This one is. Chance has led us well.'

'What do you mean?' she asked, glancing apprehensively over her shoulder.

'There is a crystal jar on that ivory table,' he answered. 'Fill it with water and tie a strip of that torn hanging about its neck for a handle while I rip up this tapestry.'

She obeyed without question, and when she turned from her task she saw Conan rapidly tying together the long tough strips of silk to make a rope, one end of which he fastened to the leg of the massive ivory table.

'We'll take our chance with the desert,' said he. 'Thalis spoke of an oasis a day's march to the south, and grasslands beyond that. If we reach the oasis we can rest until my wounds heal. This wine is like sorcery. A little while ago I was little more than a dead man; now I am ready for anything. Here is enough silk left for you to make a garment of.'

Natala had forgotten her nudity. The mere fact caused her no qualms, but her delicate skin would need protection from the desert sun. As she knotted the silk length about her supple body, Conan turned to the window and with a contemptuous wrench tore away the soft gold bars that guarded it. Then, looping the loose end of his silk rope about Natala's hips, and cautioning her to hold on with both hands, he lifted her through the window and lowered her the thirty-odd feet to the earth. She stepped out of the loop, and drawing it back up, he made fast the vessels of water and wine, and lowered them to her. He followed them, sliding down swiftly, hand over hand.

As he reached her side, Natala gave a sigh of relief. They stood alone at the foot of the great wall, the paling stars overhead and the naked desert about them. What perils yet confronted them she could not know, but her heart sang with joy because they were out of that ghostly, unreal city.

'They may find the rope,' grunted Conan, slinging the precious jars across his shoulders, wincing at the contact with his mangled flesh. 'They may even pursue us, but from what Thalis said, I doubt it. That way is south,' a bronze muscular arm indicated their course; 'so somewhere in that direction lies the oasis. Come!'

Taking her hand with a thoughtfulness unusual for him, Conan strode out across the sands, suiting his stride to the shorter legs of his companion. He did not glance back at the silent city, brooding dreamily and ghostlily behind them.

'Conan,' Natala ventured finally, 'when you fought the monster, and later, as you came up the corridor, did you see anything of – of Thalis?'

He shook his head. 'It was dark in the corridor; but it was empty.'

She shuddered. 'She tortured me – yet I pity her.'

'It was a hot welcome we got in that accursed city,' he snarled. Then his grim humor returned. 'Well, they'll remember our visit long enough, I'll wager. There are brains and guts and blood to be cleaned off the marble tiles, and if their god still lives, he carries more wounds than I. We got off light, after all: we have wine and water and a good chance of reaching a habitable country, though I look as if I've gone through a meat-grinder, and you have a sore—'

'It's all your fault,' she interrupted. 'If you had not looked so long and admiringly at that Stygian cat—'

'Crom and his devils!' he swore. 'When the oceans drown the world, women will take time for jealousy. Devil take their conceit! Did I tell the Stygian to fall in love with me? After all, she was only human!'

DRUMS OF TOMBALKU

(Draft)

I

Three men squatted beside the water hole, beneath the sunset sky that painted the desert umber and red. Two were Ghanatas, desert warriors, their tatters scarcely concealing their wiry dark frames. Men called them Gobir and Saidu; they looked like vultures as they crouched beside the water hole. The third was yellow-haired and gray-eyed; he was called Amalric.

Nearby a camel ground its cud noisily, and a pair of weary horses vainly nuzzled the bare sand. The men munched dried dates cheerlessly, the desert men intent only on the working of their jaws, Amalric occasionally glancing at the dull red sky, or out across the level monotony where the shadows were gathering and deepening. He was first to see the horseman who rode up and drew rein with a jerk that set the steed rearing.

The rider was a dark-skinned giant. His wide silk pantaloons were gathered in about his bare ankles. They were supported by a broad girdle wrapped repeatedly about his huge belly; that girdle also supported a flaring-tipped scimitar few men could wield with one hand. With that scimitar the man was famed wherever the sons of the desert rode. He was Tilutan, the pride of the Ghanata.

Across his saddle bow a limp shape lay, or rather hung. Breath hissed through the teeth of the Ghanatas as they caught the gleam of smooth, white limbs. A girl hung across Tilutan's saddle bow, face down, her loose hair flowing over his stirrup in a rippling black wave. The giant grinned with a glint of white teeth, and cast her casually onto the sand, where she lay laxly, unconscious. Instinctively Gobir and Saidu turned toward Amalric, and Tilutan watched him from his saddle. Three Ghanatas and an outlander. The entrance of a woman into the scene wrought a subtle change in the atmosphere.

Almaric was the only one who was apparently oblivious to the tenseness. He raked back his rebellious yellow locks absently, and glanced indifferently at the girl's limp figure. If there was a momentary gleam in his grey eyes, the others did not catch it.

Tilutan swung down from his saddle, contemptuously tossing the rein to Amalric.

'Tend my horse,' he said. 'By Jhil, I did not find a desert antelope, but I found this little filly. She was reeling through the sands, and she fell just as I approached. I think she fainted from weariness and thirst. Get away from there, you jackals, and let me give her a drink.'

The big man stretched her out beside the water hole and began laving her face and wrists, trickling a few drops between her parched lips. She moaned presently and stirred vaguely. Gobir and Saidu crouched with their hands on their knees, staring at her over Tilutan's burly shoulder. Amalric stood a little apart from them, his interest seeming only casual.

'She is coming to,' announced Gobir.

Saidu said nothing, but he licked his lips involuntarily, animal-like.

Amalric's gaze travelled impersonally over the prostrate form, from the torn sandals to the loose crown of glossy black hair. Her only garment was a silk kirtle, girdled at the waist. It left her arms, neck and part of her bosom bare, and the skirt ended several inches above her knees. On the parts revealed rested the gaze of the Ghanatas with devouring intensity, taking in the soft contours, childish in their white tenderness, yet rounded with budding womanhood.

Amalric shrugged his shoulders.

'After Tilutan, who?' he asked carelessly.

A pair of lean heads turned toward him, bloodshot eyes rolled at the question, then the Ghanatas turned and mutually stared at one another. Sudden rivalry crackled electrically between them.

'Cast the dice,' urged Amalric. 'No need to fight.' His hand came from under his worn tunic, and he threw down a pair of dice before them. A claw-like hand seized them.

'Aye!' agreed Gobir. 'We cast – after Tilutan, the winner!'

Amalric cast a glance toward the giant who still bent above his captive, bringing life back into her exhausted body. As he looked, her long-lashed lids parted. Deep violet eyes stared up into the leering face bewilderedly. An explosive exclamation of gratification escaped the thick lips of Tilutan. Wrenching a flask from his girdle, he put it to her mouth. She drank the wine mechanically. Amalric avoided her wandering gaze. He was one man and the three Ghanatas were all his match.

Gobir and Saidu bent above the dice; Saidu cupped them in his palm, breathed on them for luck, shook and threw. Two vulture-like heads bent over the spinning cubes in the dim light. And Amalric drew and struck with the same motion. The edge sliced through a thick neck, severing the windpipe, and Gobir fell across the dice, spurting blood, his head hanging by a shred.

Simultaneously, Saidu, with the desperate quickness of a desert man, shot to his feet and hacked ferociously at the slayer's head. Amalric barely had time to catch the stroke on his lifted sword. The whistling scimitar beat the straight blade down on Amalric's head, staggering him. He released his sword and threw both arms about Saidu, dragging him into close quarters where his scimitar was useless. Under the desert man's rags, the wiry frame was like steel cords.

Tilutan, comprehending the matter instantly, had cast the girl down and risen with a roar. He rushed toward the struggling pair like a charging bull, his great scimitar flaming in his hand. Amalric saw him coming, and his flesh turned cold. Saidu was jerking and wrenching, handicapped by the scimitar he was still seeking futilely to turn against his antagonist. Their feet twisted and stamped in the sand, their bodies ground against one another. Amalric smashed his sandal heel down on the Ghanata's bare instep, feeling bones give way. Saidu howled and plunged convulsively, and Amalric gave a desperate heave. The pair lurched drunkenly about, just as Tilutan struck with a rolling drive of his broad shoulders. Amalric felt the steel rasp the under part of his arm, and chug deep into Saidu's body. The Ghanata gave an agonized scream, and his convulsive start tore himself free of Amalric's grasp. Tilutan roared a ferocious oath and, wrenching his steel free, hurled the dying man aside. Before he could srike again, Amalric, his skin crawling with the fear of that great curved blade, had grappled with him.

Despair swept over him as he felt the strength of the warrior. Tilutan was wiser than Saidu. He dropped the scimitar and with a bellow, caught Amalric's throat with both hands. The great fingers locked like iron, and Amalric, striving vainly to break their grip, was borne down, with the Ghanata's great weight pinning him to the earth. The smaller man was shaken like a rat in the jaws of a dog. His head was smashed savagely against the sandy earth. As in a red mist he saw the furious face of his opponent, lips writhed back in a bestial grin of hate, teeth glistening. An inhuman snarling slavered from his thick throat.

'You want her, you dog!' the Ghanata mouthed, insane with rage and lust. 'Arrrrghhh! I break your back! I tear out your throat! I – my scimitar! I cut off your head and make her kiss it!'

A final ferocious smash of Amalric's head against the hardpacked sand, and Tilutan half-lifted him and hurled him down in an excess of bestial passion. Rising, the man ran, stooping like an ape, and caught up his scimitar where it lay like a broad crescent of steel in the sand. Yelling in ferocious exultation, he turned and charged back, brandishing the blade on high. Amalric rose slowly to meet him, dazed, shaken, sick from the manhandling he had received.

Tilutan's girdle had become unwound in the fight, and now the end dangled about his feet. He tripped, stumbled, fell headlong, throwing out his arms to save himself. The scimitar flew from his hand.

Amalric, galvanized, caught up the scimitar and took a reeling step forward. The desert swam darkly to his gaze. In the dusk before him he saw Tilutan's face suddenly ashy. The wide mouth gaped, the whites of the eyeballs rolled up. The giant froze on one knee and a hand, as if incapable of further motion. Then the scimitar fell, cleaving the round, shaven head to the chin, where its downward course was checked with a sickening jerk. Amalric had a dim impression of a face divided by a widening red line, fading in the thickening shadows. Then darkness caught him with a rush.

Something soft and cool was touching Amalric's face with gentle persistence. He groped blindly and his hand closed on something warm, firm and resilient. Then his sight cleared and he looked into a soft oval face, framed in lustrous black hair. As in a trance he gazed unspeaking, hungrily dwelling on each detail of the full red lips, dark violet eyes, and alabaster throat. With a start he realized the vision was speaking in a soft musical voice. The words were strange, yet possessed an illusive familiarity. A small white hand holding a dripping bunch of silk was passed gently over his throbbing head and face. He sat up dizzily.

It was night, under the star-splashed skies. The camel still munched its cud; a horse whinnied restlessly. Not far away lay a hulking dark figure with its cleft head in a horrible puddle of blood and brains. Amalric looked up at the girl who knelt beside him, talking in her gentle, unknown tongue. As the mists cleared from his brain, he began to understand her. Harking back into half-forgotten tongues he had learned and spoken in the past, he remembered a language used by a scholarly class in a southern province of Koth.

'Who are you, girl?' he demanded, prisoning a small hand in his own hardened fingers.

'I am Lissa.' The name was spoken with almost the suggestion of a lisp. It was like the rippling of a slender stream.

'I am glad you are conscious. I feared you were not alive.'

'A little more and I wouldn't have been,' he muttered, glancing at the grisly sprawl that had been Tilutan. She paled, refusing to follow his gaze. Her hand trembled, and in their nearness, Amalric thought he could feel the quick throb of her heart.

'It was horrible,' she faltered. 'Like an awful dream. Anger – and blows – and blood—'

'It might have been worse,' he growled.

She seemed sensitive to every changing inflection of his voice or mood. Her free hand stole timidly to his arm.

'I did not mean to offend you. It was very brave for you to risk your life for a stranger. You are noble as the knights about which I have read.'

He cast a quick glance at her. Her wide clear eyes met his, reflecting only the thought she had spoken. He started to speak, then changed his mind and said another thing.

'What are you doing in the desert?'

'I came from Gazal,' she answered. 'I – I was running away. I could not stand it any longer. But it was hot and lonely and weary, and I saw only sand, sand – and the blazing blue sky. The sands burned my feet, and my sandals were worn out quickly. I was so thirsty, my canteen was soon empty. And then I wished to return to Gazal, but one direction looked like another. I did not know which way to go. I was terribly afraid, and started running in the direction in which I thought Gazal to be. I do not remember much after that. I ran until I could run no further, and I must have lain in the burning sand for a while. I remember rising and staggering on, and toward the last I thought I heard someone shouting, and saw a huge man on a black horse riding toward me, and then I knew no more until I awoke and found myself lying with my head in that man's lap, while he gave me wine to drink. Then there was shouting and fighting—' She shuddered. 'When it was all over, I crept to where you lay like a dead man, and I tried to bring you to—'

'Why?' he demanded.

She seemed at a loss. 'Why,' she floundered, 'why, you were hurt – and – why, it is what anyone would do. Besides, I realized that you were fighting to protect me from these men. The people of Gazal have always said that the desert people were wicked and would harm the helpless.'

'That's no exclusive characteristic,' muttered Amalric. 'Where is this Gazal?'

'It can not be far,' she answered. 'I walked a whole day – and then I do not know how far the warrior carried me after he found me.

But he must have discovered me about sunset, so he could not have come far.'

'In what direction?' he demanded.

'I do not know. I travelled eastward when I left the city.'

'City?' he muttered. 'A day's travel from this spot? I had thought there was only desert for a thousand miles.'

'Gazal is in the desert,' she answered. 'It is built amidst the palms of an oasis.'

Putting her aside, he got to his feet, swearing softly as he fingered his throat, the skin of which was bruised and lacerated. He examined the three Ghanatas in turn, finding no sign of life in them. Then, one by one, he dragged them a short distance out into the desert. Somewhere the jackals were yelping. Returning to the water hole where the girl squatted patiently, he cursed to find only the black stallion of Tilutan with the camel. The other horses had broken their tethers and bolted during the fight.

Amalric went to the girl and proffered her a handful of dried dates. She nibbled at them eagerly, while the other sat and watched her, his chin on his fists, an increasing impatience throbbing in his veins.

'Why did you run away?' he asked abruptly. 'Are you a slave?'

'We have no slaves in Gazal,' she answered. 'Oh, I was weary – so weary of the eternal monotony. I wished to see something of the outer world. Tell me, from what land do you come?'

'I was born in the western hills of Aquilonia,' he answered.

She clapped her hands like a delighted child.

'I know where it is! I have seen it on the maps. It is the westernmost country of the Hyborians, and its king is Epeus the Swordwielder!'

Amalric experienced a distinct shock. His head jerked up and he stared at his fair companion.

'Epeus? Why, Epeus has been dead for nine hundred years. The king's name is Vilerus.'

'Oh, of course,' she said, rather embarrassedly. 'I am foolish. Of course, Epeus was king nine centuries ago, as you say. But tell me – tell me all about the world!'

'Why, that is a big order,' he answered nonplussed. 'You have not travelled?'

'This is the very first time that I have ever been out of sight of the walls of Gazal,' she admitted to him.

His gaze was fixed on the curve of her white bosom. He was not interested in her adventures at the moment, and Gazal might have been Hell for all he cared.

He started to speak, then changing his mind caught her roughly in his arms, his muscles tensing for the struggle he expected. But he encountered no resistance. Her soft, yielding body lay across his knees, and she looked up at him somewhat in surprize, but without fear or embarrassment. She might have been a child submitting to a new kind of play. Something about her direct gaze confused him. If she had screamed, wept, fought, or smiled knowingly, he would have known how to deal with her.

'Who in Mitra's name are you, girl?' he asked roughly. 'You are neither touched with the sun, nor playing a game with me. Your speech shows you to be no ignorant country lass, innocent in ignorance. Yet you seem to know nothing of the world and its ways.'

'I am a daughter of Gazal,' she answered helplessly. 'If you saw Gazal, perhaps you would understand.'

He lifted her and placed her on the sand. Rising, he brought a saddle blanket and set it out for her.

'Sleep, Lissa,' he said, his voice harsh with conflicting emotions. 'Tomorrow I mean to see Gazal.'

At dawn they started westward. Amalric had lifted Lissa onto the camel, showing her how to maintain her balance. She clung to the seat with both hands, showing no knowledge whatever of camels, which again surprized the young Aquilonian. A girl raised in the desert, she had never before been on a camel, nor, until the preceding night, had she ever ridden or been carried on a horse. Amalric had manufactured a sort of cloak for her, and she wore it without question, not asking whence it came, accepting it as she accepted all things he did for her, gratefully but blindly, without asking the reason. Amalric did not tell her that the silk that shielded her from the sun had once covered the skin of her abductor.

As they rode she again begged him to tell her something of the world, like a child asking for a story.

'I know Aquilonia is far from this desert,' she said. 'Stygia lies between, and the Lands of Shem, and other countries. How is it that you are here, so far from your homeland?'

He rode for a space in silence, his hand on the camel's guide-rope.

'Argos and Stygia were at war,' he said abruptly. 'Koth became embroiled. The Kothians urged a simultaneous invasion of Stygia. Argos raised an army of mercenaries, which went into ships and sailed southward along the coast. At the same time, a Kothic army was to invade Stygia by land. I was one of that mercenary army. We met the Stygian fleet and defeated it, driving it back into Khemi. We should have landed, looted the city, and advanced along the course of the Styx – but our admiral was cautious. Our leader was Prince Zapayo da Kova, a Zingaran. We cruised southward until we reached the jungle-clad coasts of Kush. There we landed, and the ships anchored, while the army pushed eastward along the Stygian frontier, burning and pillaging as we went. It was our intention to turn northward at a certain point and strike into the heart of Stygia to form a juncture with the Kothic host which was supposed to be pushing down from the north. Then word came that we were betrayed. Koth had concluded a separate peace with the Stygians. A Stygian army was pushing southward to intercept us, while another already had cut us off from the coast.

'Prince Zapayo, in desperation, conceived the mad idea of marching eastward, hoping to skirt the Stygian border and eventually reach the eastern lands of Shem. But the army from the north overtook us. We turned and fought. All day we fought, and finally they gave before us, their retreat turning into rout. But the next day the pursuing army came up from the west, and crushed between the hosts, our army ceased to be. We were broken, annihilated, destroyed. There were few left to flee. But when night fell, I broke away with my companion, a Cimmerian named Conan, a brute of a man with the strength of a bull.

'We rode southward into the desert, because there was no other direction in which we might go. Conan had been in this part of the world before, and he believed we had a chance to survive. Far to the south we found an oasis, but Stygian riders harried us, and we fled again, from oasis to oasis, fleeing, starving, thirsting, until we found ourselves in a barren, unknown land of blazing and empty sand. We rode until our horses were reeling, and we were half delirious. Then one night we saw fires and rode up to them, taking a desperate chance that we might make friends. As soon as we came within range, a shower of arrows greeted us. Conan's horse was hit and it reared, throwing its rider. His neck must have broken like a twig, for he never moved. I got away in the darkness, somehow, though my horse died under me. I had only a glance at the attackers. They were tall, lean brown men, wearing strange, barbaric garments. I wandered on foot through the desert, and fell in with those three vultures you saw yesterday. They were jackals – Ghanatas – members of a robber tribe of mixed blood. The only reason they didn't murder me was because I had nothing they wished. For a month I have been wandering and thieving with them because there was nothing else I could do.'

'I did not know it was like that,' Lissa murmured faintly. 'They said there were wars and cruelty out in the world, but it seemed like a dream and far away. Listening to you speak of treachery and battle seems almost like seeing it.'

'Do no enemies ever come against Gazal?' he demanded.

She shook her head. 'Men ride wide of Gazal. Sometimes I have seen black dots moving in lines along the horizon, and the old men said they were armies moving to war. But they never come near to Gazal.'

Amalric felt a dim stirring of uneasiness. This desert, seemingly empty of life, nevertheless contained some of the fiercest tribes on earth – the Ghanatas, who ranged far to the east; the masked Tibu, whom he believed dwelt further to the south; and somewhere off to the southwest lay the semi-mythical empire of Tombalku, ruled by a wild and barbaric race. It was strange that a city in the midst of this savage land should be left so completely alone that one of its inhabitants did not even know the meaning of war.

When he turned his gaze elsewhere, strange thoughts assailed him. Was the girl touched by the sun? Was she a demon in womanly form come out of the desert to lure him to some cryptic doom? A glance at her clinging childishly to the high peak of the camel saddle was sufficient to dispel these broodings. Then again doubt assailed him. Was he bewitched? Had she cast a spell on him?

Westward they forged steadily, halting only to nibble dates and drink water at midday. Amalric fashioned a frail shelter out of his sword and sheath and the saddle blankets to shield her from the burning sun. Weary and stiff from the tossing, bucking gait of the camel, she had to be lifted down in his arms. As he felt again the voluptuous sweetness of her soft body, he felt a hot throb of passion sear through him, and he stood momentarily motionless, intoxicated with the nearness of her, before he laid her down in the shade of the makeshift tent.

He felt a touch of almost anger at the clear gaze with which she met his, at the docility with which she yielded her young body to his hands. It was as if she were unaware of things which might harm her; her innocent trust shamed him and pent a helpless wrath within him.

As they ate, he did not taste the dates he munched; his eyes burned on her, avidly drinking in every detail of her lithe young figure. She seemed as unaware of his intentness as a child. When he lifted her to place her again on the camel, and her arms went instinctively about his neck, he shuddered. But he lifted her up on her mount, and they took up the journey once more.

It was just before sundown when Lissa pointed and cried out: 'Look! The towers of Gazal!'

On the desert rim he saw them – spires and minarets, rising in a jade-green cluster against the blue sky. But for the girl, he would have thought it the phantom city of a mirage. He glanced at Lissa curiously. She showed no signs of eager joy at her homecoming. Instead, she sighed, and her slim shoulders seemed to droop.

As they approached, the details swam more plainly into view. Sheer from the desert sands rose the wall which enclosed the towers. And Amalric saw that the wall was crumbling in many places. The towers, too, he saw, were much in disrepair. Roofs sagged, broken battlements gaped, spires leaned drunkenly. Panic assailed him; was it a city of the dead to which he rode, guided by a vampire? A quick glance at the girl reassured him. No demon could lurk in that divinely molded exterior. She glanced at him with a strange and wistful questioning in her deep eyes, turned resolutely toward the desert, then, with a deep sigh, set her face toward the city, as if gripped by a subtle and fatalistic despair.

Now through the gaps of the jade-green wall, Amalric saw figures moving within the city. No one hailed them as they rode through a broad breach in the wall, and came out into a broad street. Close at hand, limned in the sinking sun, the decay was more apparent. Grass grew rank in the streets, pushing through shattered paving; grass grew rank in the small plazas. Streets and courts likewise were littered with rubbish of masonry and fallen stones.

Domes rose, cracked and discolored. Portals gaped, vacant of doors. Everywhere ruin had laid his hand. Then Amalric saw one spire untouched; a shining red cylindrical tower which rose in the extreme southeastern corner of the city.

It shone among the ruins, and Amalric pointed to it.

'Why is that tower less in ruins than the others?' he asked. Lissa turned pale; she trembled and caught his hand convulsively.

'Do not speak of it!' she whispered. 'Do not look toward it – do not even think of it!'

Amalric scowled; the nameless implication of her words somehow changed the aspect of the mysterious tower. Now it seemed like a serpent's head rearing among ruin and desolation.

The young Aquilonian looked warily about him. After all, he had no assurance that the people of Gazal would receive him in a friendly manner. He saw people moving leisurely about the streets. They halted and stared at him, and for some reason his flesh crawled. They were men and women with kindly features, and their looks were mild. But their interest seemed so slight – so vague and impersonal. They made no movement to approach him or to speak to him. It might have been the most common thing in the world for an armed horseman to ride into their city from the desert; yet Amalric knew that was not the case, and the casual manner in which the people of Gazal received him caused a faint uneasiness in his bosom.

Lissa spoke to them, indicating Amalric, whose hand she lifted like an affectionate child. 'This is Amalric of Aquilonia, who rescued me from the desert people and has brought me home.'

A polite murmur of welcome rose from the people, and several of them approached to extend their hands. Amalric thought he had never seen such vague, kindly faces. Their eyes were soft and mild, without fear and without wonder. Yet they were not the eyes of stupid oxen; rather, they were the eyes of people wrapped in dreams.

Their stare gave him a feeling of unreality; he hardly knew what was said to him. His mind was occupied by the strangeness of it all; these quiet, dreamy people in their silken tunics and soft sandals, moving with aimless vagueness among the discolored ruins. A lotus paradise of illusion? Somehow, the thought of that sinister red tower struck a discordant note.

One of the men, his face smooth and unlined, but his hair silver, was saying: 'Aquilonia? There was an invasion – we heard – King Bragorus of Nemedia – how went the war?'

'He was driven back,' answered Amalric briefly, resisting a shudder. Nine hundred years had passed since Bragorus led his spearmen across the marches of Aquilonia.

His questioner did not press him further; the people drifted away, and Lissa tugged at his hand. He turned, feasted his eyes upon her; in a realm of illusion and dream, her soft firm body anchored his wandering conjectures. She was no dream; she was real; her body was sweet and tangible as cream and honey.

'Come, let us go to rest and eat.'

'What of the people?' he demurred. 'Will you not tell them of your experiences?'

'They would not heed, except for a few minutes,' she answered. 'They would listen a little, and then drift away. They hardly know I have been gone. Come!'

Amalric led the horse and camel into an enclosed court where the grass grew high, and water seeped from a broken fountain into a marble trough. There he tethered them, and then turned to Lissa. Taking his hand, she led him across the court into an arched doorway. Night had fallen. In the open space above the court, the stars were clustering, etching the jagged pinnacles. Through a series of dark chambers Lissa went, moving with the sureness of long practice. Amalric groped after her, guided by her little hand in his. He found it no pleasant adventure. The scent of dust and decay hung in the thick darkness. At times, what felt like broken tiles underfoot caused him to move carefully. At other times there was the softness of worn carpets. His free hand touched the fretted arches of doorways. Then the stars gleamed through a broken roof, showing him a dim, winding hallway hung with rotting tapestries. They rustled in a faint wind, and their noise was like the whispering of witches, causing the hair to stir next his scalp.

Then they came into a chamber dimly lighted by the starshine streaming through open windows. Lissa released his hand, fumbled an instant, and produced a faint light of some sort. It was a glassy knob which glowed with a golden radiance. She set it on a marble table and indicated that Amalric should recline on a couch thickly littered with silks. Groping into some mysterious recess, she produced a gold vessel of wine and others containing food unfamiliar to Amalric. There were dates, but the other food, which he did not recognize, was pallid and insipid to his taste. The wine was pleasant to the palate, but no more heady than dish water.

Seated on a marble seat opposite him, Lissa nibbled daintily.

'What sort of place is this?' he demanded. 'You are like these people – yet strangely unlike.'

'They say I am like our ancestors,' answered Lissa. 'Long ago they came into the desert and built this city over a great oasis which was in reality only a series of springs. The stone they took from the ruins of a much older city – only the red tower—' her voice dropped and she glanced nervously at the star-framed windows – 'only the red tower stood there. It was empty – then.

'Our ancestors, who were called Gazali, once dwelt in the southern part of Koth. They were noted for their scholarly wisdom. But they sought to revive the worship of Mitra which the Kothians had long ago abandoned, and the king drove them from his kingdom. They came southward, many of them, priests, scholars, teachers, scientists, along with their Shemitish slaves.

'They reared Gazal in the desert; but the slaves revolted almost as soon as the city was built and, fleeing, mixed with the wild tribes of the desert. They were not treated badly, but word came to them in the night – a word which sent them fleeing madly from the city into the desert.

'My people dwelt here, learning to manufacture their food and drink from such material as was at hand. Their learning was a marvel. When the slaves fled, they took with them every camel, horse and donkey in the city. There was no communication with the outer world. There are whole chambers in Gazal that are filled with maps and books and chronicles. But they are all nine hundred years old, at the least, for it was nine hundred years ago that my people fled from Koth. Since then, no man of the outside world has set forth in Gazal. And the people are slowly vanishing. They have become so dreamy and introspective that they have neither human passions nor ambitions. The city falls into ruins and none moves hand to repair it. Horror—' she choked, and shuddered, 'when horror came upon them, they could neither flee nor fight.'

'What do you mean?' he whispered, a cold wind blowing on his spine. The rustling of rotten hangings down nameless black corridors stirred dim fear in his soul.

She shook her head, rose, and came around the marble table. She laid hands on his shoulders. Her eyes were wet and shone with horror and a desperate yearning that caught at his throat. Instinctively, his arm went around her lithe form, and he felt her tremble.

'Hold me!' she begged. 'I am afraid! Oh, I have dreamed of such a man as you. I am not like my people; they are dead men walking forgotten streets; but I am alive. I am warm and sentient. I hunger and thirst and yearn for life. I cannot abide the silent streets and ruined halls and dim people of Gazal, though I have never known anything else. That is why I ran away – I yearned for life—'

She was sobbing uncontrollably in his arms. Her hair streamed over his face; her fragrance made him dizzy. Her firm body strained against him. She was lying across his knees, her arms locked about his neck. Straining her to his breast, he crushed her lips with his. Eyes, lips, cheeks, hair, throat, breasts, he showered with hot kisses, until her sobs changed to panting gasps. The passion that slumbered in her woke in one overpowering wave. The glowing gold ball, struck by his groping fingers, tumbled to the floor and was extinguished. Only the starshine gleamed through the windows.

Lying in Amalric's arms on the silk-heaped couch, Lissa opened her heart and whispered her dreams and hopes and aspirations, childish, pathetic, terrible.

'I'll take you away,' he muttered. 'Tomorrow. You are right. Gazal is a city of the dead; we will seek life and the outer world. It is violent, rough, and cruel, but it is better than this living death—'

The night was broken by a shuddering cry of agony, horror and despair. Its timbre brought out cold sweat on Amalric's skin. He started upright from the couch, but Lissa clung to him desperately.

'No, no!' she begged in a frantic whisper. 'Do not go! Stay!'

'But murder is being done!' he exclaimed, fumbling for his sword. The cries seemed to come from across an outer court. Mingled with them there was an indescribable tearing, rending sound. They rose higher and thinner, unbearable in their hopeless agony, then sank away in a long, shuddering sob.

'I have heard men dying on the rack cry out like that!' muttered Amalric, shaking with horror. 'What devil's work is this?'

Lissa was trembling violently in a frenzy of terror. He felt the wild pounding of her heart.

'It is the Horror of which I spoke!' she whispered. 'The Horror which dwells in the red tower. Long ago it came – and some say it dwelt there in the lost years and returned after the building of Gazal. It devours human beings. What it is, no one knows, since none have seen it and lived to tell. It is a god or a devil. That is why the slaves fled; why the desert people shun Gazal. Many of us have gone into its awful belly. Eventually, all will have gone, and it will rule over an empty city, as men say it ruled over the ruins from which Gazal was reared.'

'Why have the people stayed to be devoured?' he demanded.

'I do not know,' she whimpered; 'they dream—'

'Hypnosis,' muttered Amalric; 'hypnosis coupled with decay. I saw it in their eyes. This devil has them mesmerized. Mitra, what a foul secret!'

Lissa pressed her face against his bosom and clung to him.

'But what are we to do?' he asked uneasily.

'There is nothing to do,' she whispered. 'Your sword would be helpless. Perhaps it will not harm us. It has taken a victim tonight. We must wait like sheep for the butcher.'

'I'll be damned if I will!' Amalric exclaimed, galvanized. 'We will not wait for morning. We'll go tonight. Make a bundle of food and drink. I'll get the horse and camel and bring them to the court outside. Meet me there!'

Since the unknown monster had already struck, Amalric felt that he was safe in leaving the girl alone for a few minutes. But his flesh crawled as he groped his way down the winding corridor and through the black chambers where the swinging tapestries whispered. He found the beasts huddled nervously together in the court where he had left them. The stallion whinnied anxiously and nuzzled him, as if sensing peril in the breathless night.

He saddled and bridled and hurriedly led them through the narrow opening onto the street. A few minutes later he was standing in the starlit court. And even as he reached it; he was electrified by an awful scream which rang shudderingly upon the air. It came from the chamber where he had left Lissa.

He answered that piteous cry with a wild yell; drawing his sword, he rushed across the court and hurled himself through the window. The golden ball was glowing again, carving out black shadows in the shrinking corners. Silks lay scattered on the floor. The marble seat was upset. But the chamber was empty.

A sick weakness overcame Amalric and he staggered against the marble table, the dim light waving dizzily to his sight. Then he was swept by a mad rage. The red tower! There the fiend would bear his victim!

He darted across the court, found the streets and raced toward the tower which glowed with an unholy light under the stars. The streets did not run straight. He cut through silent black buildings and crossed courts whose rank grass waved in the night wind.

Ahead of him, clustered about the crimson tower, rose a heap of ruins where decay had eaten more savagely than at the rest of the city. Apparently none dwelt among them. They reeled and tumbled, a crumbling mass of quaking masonry, with the red tower rearing up among them like a poisonous red flower from charnel-house ruin.

To reach the tower he would be forced to traverse the ruins. Recklessly, he plunged into the black mass, groping for a door. He found one and entered, thrusting his sword ahead of him. Then he saw such a vista as men sometimes see in fantastic dreams. Far ahead of him stretched a long corridor, visible in a faint, unhallowed glow, its black walls hung with strange shuddersome tapestries. Far down it he saw a receding figure – a white, naked, stooped figure, lurching along, dragging something the sight of which filled him with sweating horror. Then the apparition vanished from his sight, and with it vanished the eery glow. Amalric stood in the soundless dark, seeing nothing, hearing nothing; thinking only of that stooped white figure that dragged a limp human being down a long, black corridor.

As he groped onward, a vague memory stirred in his brain – the memory of a grisly tale mumbled to him over a dying fire in the skull-heaped, devil-devil hut of a black witchman – a tale of a god which dwelt in a crimson house in a ruined city and which was worshipped by darksome cults in dank jungles and along sullen dusky rivers. And there stirred, too, in his mind an incantation whispered in his ear in awed and shuddering tones, while the night had held its breath, the lions had ceased to roar along the river, and the very fronds had ceased their scraping one against the other.

Ollam-onga, whispered a dark wind down the sightless corridor. Ollam-onga whispered the dust that ground beneath his stealthy feet. Sweat stood on his skin and the sword shook in his hand. He stole through the house of a god, and fear held him by its bony hand. The house of the god – the full horror of the phrase filled his mind. All the ancestral fears and the fears that reached beyond ancestry and primordial race-memory crowded upon him; horror cosmic and unhuman sickened him. His weak humanity crushed him in its realization as he went through the house of darkness that was the house of a god.

About him shimmered a glow so faint that it was scarcely discernible; he knew that he was approaching the tower itself. Another instant and he groped his way through an arched door and stumbled upon strangely spaced steps. Up them he went and, as he climbed, that blind fury which is mankind's last defence against diabolism and all the hostile forces of the universe, surged in him, and he forgot his fear. Burning with terrible eagerness, he climbed up and up through the thick, evil darkness until he came into a chamber lit by a weird glow.

And before him stood a white, naked figure. Amalric halted, his tongue cleaving to his palate. It was a naked white man, to all appearance, who stood there, gazing at him with mighty arms folded on an alabaster breast. The features were classic, cleanly carven, with more than human beauty. But the eyes were balls of luminous fire, such as never looked from any human head. In those eyes, Amalric glimpsed the frozen fires of the ultimate hells, touched by awful shadows.

Then before him the form began to grow dim in outline – to waver. With a terrible effort, the Aquilonian burst the bonds of silence and spoke a cryptic and awful incantation. And as the frightful words cut the silence, the white giant halted – froze – again his outlines stood out clear and bold against the golden background.

'Now fall on, damn you!' cried Amalric hysterically. 'I have bound you into your human shape! The black wizard spoke truly! It was the master word he gave me! Fall on, Ollam-onga – till you break the spell by feasting on my heart, you are no more than a man like me!'

With a roar that was like the gust of a whirlwind, the creature charged. Amalric sprang aside from the clutch of those hands whose strength was more than that of a giant. A single taloned finger, spread wide and catching in his tunic, ripped the garment from him like a rotten rag as the monster plunged by. But Amalric, nerved to more than human quickness by the horror of the fight, wheeled and drove his sword through the thing's back, so that the point stood out a foot from the broad breast.

A fiendish howl of agony shook the tower; the monster whirled and rushed at Amalric, but the youth sprang aside and raced up the stairs to the dais. There he wheeled and, catching up a marble seat, hurled it down upon the horror that was lumbering up the stairs. Full in the face the massive missile struck, carrying the fiend back down the steps. He rose, an awful sight, streaming blood and again essayed the stairs. In desperation, Amalric lifted a jade bench whose weight wrenched a groan of effort from him, and hurled it.

Beneath the impact of the hurtling bulk, Ollam-onga pitched back down the stair and lay among the marble shards, which were flooded with his blood. With a last, desperate effort, he heaved himself up on his hands, eyes glazing, and throwing back his bloody head, voiced an awful cry. Amalric shuddered and recoiled from the abysmal horror of that scream. And it was answered. From somewhere in the air above the tower a faint medley of fiendish cries came back like an echo. Then the mangled white figure went limp among the blood-stained shards. And Amalric knew that one of the gods of Kush was no more. With the thought came blind, unreasoning horror.

In a fog of terror he rushed down the stair, shrinking from the thing that lay staring on the floor. The night seemed to cry out against him, aghast at the sacrilege. Reason, exultant over his triumph, was submerged in a flood of cosmic fear.

As he put foot on the head of the steps, he halted short. Up from the darkness Lissa came to him, her white arms outstretched, her eyes pools of horror and revulsion.

'Amalric!' It was a haunting cry. He crushed her in his arms.

'I saw It,' she whimpered – 'dragging a dead man through the corridor. I screamed and fled; then when I returned, I heard you cry out and knew you had gone to search for me in the red tower—'

'And you came to share my fate,' his voice was almost inarticulate. Then, as she tried to peer in trembling fascination past him, he covered her eyes with his hands and turned her about. Better that she should not see what lay on the crimson floor. As he half led, half carried her down the shadowed stairs, a glance over his shoulder showed him that a naked white figure lay no longer among the broken marble. The incantation had bound Ollam-onga into his human form in life, but not in death. Blindness momentarily assailed Amalric; then, galvanized into frantic haste, he hurried Lissa down the stairs and through the dark ruins.

He did not slacken pace until they reached the street where the camel and stallion huddled against one another. Quickly he placed the girl on the camel and swung up on the stallion. Taking the lead-line, he headed straight for the broken wall. A few minutes later he breathed gustily. The open air of the desert cooled his blood; it was free of the scent of decay and hideous antiquity.

There was a small water-pouch hanging from his saddle bow. They had no food, and his sword was in the chamber of the red tower. He had not dared touch it. Without food and unarmed, they faced the desert, but its peril seemed less grim than the horror of the city behind them.

Without speaking they rode. Amalric headed south; somewhere in that direction there was a water hole. Just at dawn, as they mounted a crest of sand, he looked back toward Gazal, unreal in the pink light. And he stiffened as Lissa, sharing his vision, cried out. From a breach in the wall rode seven horsemen; their steeds were black, and the riders were cloaked in black from head to foot. Horror swept over Amalric as he realized there had been no horses in Gazal. Turning, he urged their mounts on.

The sun rose, red, and then gold, and then a ball of white-beaten flame. On and on the fugitives pressed, reeling with heat and fatigue, blinded by the glare. They moistened their lips with water from time to time, and behind them, at an even pace, rode seven black dots. Evening began to fall, and the sun reddened and lurched toward the desert rim. And a cold hand clutched at Amalric's heart. The riders were closing in. As darkness came on, so came the black riders. Amalric glanced at Lissa, and a groan burst from him. His stallion stumbled and fell. The sun had gone down, the moon was blotted out suddenly by a bat-shaped shadow. In the utter darkness the stars glowed red, and behind him Amalric heard a rising rush as of an approaching wind. A black, speeding clump bulked against the night, in which glinted sparks of awful light.

'Ride girl!' he cried despairingly. 'Go on – save yourself; it is me they want!'

For answer she slid down from the camel and threw her arms about him.

'I will die with you!'

Seven black shapes loomed against the stars, racing like the wind. Under the hoods shone balls of evil fire. Jaw bones seemed to clack together. Suddenly, a horse swept past Amalric, a vague bulk in the unnatural darkness. There was the sound of an impact as the unknown steed caromed among the oncoming shapes. A horse screamed in frenzy, and a bull-like voice bellowed in a strange tongue. From somewhere in the night a clamor of yells answered.

Some sort of violent action was taking place. Horse's hoofs stamped and clattered. There was the impact of savage blows, and the same stentorian voice was cursing lustily. Then the moon abruptly came out and lit a fantastic scene.

A man on a giant horse whirled, slashed and smote apparently at thin air, and from another direction swept a wild horde of riders, their curved swords flashing in the moonlight. Away over the crest of a rise, seven black figures were vanishing, their cloaks floating out like the wings of bats.

Amalric was swamped by wild men who leaped from their horses and swarmed around him. Sinewy, naked arms pinioned him; fierce brown, hawk-like faces snarled at him. Lissa screamed.

Then the attackers were thrust right and left as the man on the great horse reined through the crowd. He bent from his saddle and glared closely at Amalric.

'The devil!' he roared. 'Amalric the Aquilonian!'

'Conan!' Amalric exclaimed bewilderedly. 'Conan! Alive!'

'More alive than you seem to be,' answered the other. 'By Crom, man, you look as if all the devils in this desert had been hunting you through the night. What things were those pursuing you? I was riding around the camp my men had pitched to make sure no enemies were in hiding, when the moon went out like a candle, and then I heard sounds of flight. I rode towards the sounds and, by Crom, I was among those devils before I knew what was happening. I had my sword in my hand and I laid about me – by Crom, their eyes blazed like fire in the dark! I know my edge bit them, but when the moon came out, they were gone like a puff of wind. Were they men or fiends?'

'Ghouls sent up from Hell,' shuddered Amalric. 'Ask me no more; there are some things that cannot be discussed.'

Conan did not press the matter, nor did he look incredulous. His beliefs included night fiends, ghosts, hobgoblins and dwarfs.

'Trust you to find a woman, even in a desert,' he said, glancing at Lissa, who had crept to Amalric and was clinging close to him, glancing fearfully at the wild figures which hemmed them in.

'Wine!' roared Conan. 'Bring flasks! Here!' He seized a leather flask from those who thrust it out to him, and placed it in Amalric's hand. 'Give the girl a swig and drink some yourself,' he advised. 'Then we'll put you on horses and take you to the camp. You need food, rest and sleep. I can see that.'

A richly caparisoned horse was brought, rearing and prancing, and willing hands helped Amalric into the saddle. Then the girl was handed up to him, and they moved off southward, surrounded by the wiry brown riders in their picturesque semi-nakedness. Conan rode ahead, humming a riding song of the mercenaries.

'Who is he?' whispered Lissa, her arms about her lover's neck; he was holding her on the saddle in front of him.

'Conan, the Cimmerian,' muttered Amalric. 'The man I

wandered with in the desert after the defeat of the mercenaries. These are the men who struck him down. I left him lying under their spears, apparently dead. Now we meet him obviously in command of, and respected by them.'

'He is a terrible man,' she whispered.

He smiled. 'You never saw a white-skinned barbarian before. He is a wanderer and a plunderer and a slayer, but he has his own code of morals. I don't think we have anything to fear from him.'

In his heart he was not sure. In a way, it might be said that he had forfeited Conan's comradeship when he had ridden away into the desert, leaving the Cimmerian senseless on the ground. But he had not known that Conan was alive. Doubt haunted Amalric. Savagely loyal to his companions, the Cimmerian's wild nature saw no reason why the rest of the world should not be plundered. He lived by the sword. And Amalric suppressed a shudder as he thought of what might chance did Conan desire Lissa.

Later on, having eaten and drunk in the camp of the riders, Amalric sat by a small fire in front of Conan's tent; Lissa, covered with a silken cloak, slumbered with her curly head on his knees. And across from him the firelight played on Conan's face, interchanging lights and shadows.

'Who are these men?' asked the young Aquilonian.

'The riders of Tombalku,' answered the Cimmerian.

'Tombalku!' exclaimed Amalric. 'Then it is no myth.'

'Far from it!' agreed Conan. 'When my accursed steed fell with me, I was knocked senseless, and when I recovered consciousness the devils had me bound hand and foot. This angered me, so I snapped several of the cords they had tied me with, but they re-bound them as fast as I could break them – never did I get a hand entirely free. But to them my strength seemed remarkable—'

Amalric gazed at Conan unspeaking. The man was tall and broad as Tilutan had been, without the dead man's surplus flesh. He could have broken the Ghanata's neck with his naked hands.

'They decided to carry me to their city instead of killing me out of hand,' Conan went on. 'They thought a man like me should be a long time in dying by torture, and so give them sport. Well, they bound me on a horse without a saddle, and we went to Tombalku.

'There were two kings of Tombalku. They took me before them – one a lean, brown-skinned devil named Zehbeh, the other a big, hulking black who dozed on his ivory-tusk throne. They spoke a dialect I could understand a little, it being much like that of the western Mandingo who dwell on the coast. Zehbeh asked one of his priests what should be done with me, and the priest cast dice made of sheep bone, and said I should be flayed alive before the altar of Jhil. Everyone cheered and that woke the other king.

'I spat at the priest and cursed him roundly, and the kings as well, telling them that if I were to be skinned, by Crom, I wanted a good belly-full of wine before they began. Then I damned them for thieves and cowards and sons of harlots.

'At this the black king roused and sat up to stare at me. Then he rose and shouted: "Amra!" and I knew him – Sakumbe, a Suba from the Black Coast, a fat adventurer I had known well in the days when I was a corsair along the coast. He trafficked in ivory, gold dust and slaves, and would cheat the devil out of his eye-teeth. Well, he knew me and descended from his throne and embraced me for joy – the fat, smelly devil – and took my cords off with his own hands. Then he announced that I was Amra, the Lion, his friend, and that no harm should come to me. Then followed much discussion because Zehbeh and his priest, Daura, wanted my life. But Sakumbe yelled for his witch-finder, Askia, and he came, all feathers and bells and snake-skins – a wizard of the Black Coast, and a son of the devil if there ever was one.

'Askia pranced and made incantations, and announced that Sakumbe was the chosen of Ajujo, the Dark One, and all the black people of Tombalku shouted, and Zehbeh backed down.

'The blacks in Tombalku are the real power. Several centuries ago, the Aphaki, a Shemitish race, pushed into the southern desert and established the kingdom of Tombalku. They mixed with the desert blacks and the result was a brown, straight-haired race. They are the dominant caste in Tombalku, but they are in the minority, and Sakumbe is the real ruler of Tombalku. The Aphaki worship

Jhil, but the blacks worship Ajujo the Dark One, and his kin. Askia came to Tombalku with Sakumbe and revived the worship of Ajujo, which was crumbling because of the Aphaki priests. Askia made black magic which defeated the wizardry of the Aphaki, and the blacks hailed him as a prophet sent by the dark gods. Sakumbe and Askia wax as Zehbeh and Daura wane.

'Well, as I am Sakumbe's friend, and Askia spoke for me, the blacks received me with great applause. Sakumbe had Kordofo, the general of the horsemen, poisoned, and gave me his place, which delighted the blacks and exasperated the Aphaki.

'You will like Tombalku! It was made for men like us to loot! There are half a dozen powerful factions plotting and intriguing against each other – there are continual brawls in the taverns and streets, secret murders, mutilations and executions. And there are women, gold, wine – all that a mercenary wants! By Crom, Amalric, you could not have come at a better time! I am high in favor and power! Why, what's the matter? You do not seem as enthusiastic as I remember you having once been in such matters.'

'I crave your pardon, Conan,' apologized Amalric. 'I do not lack interest, but weariness and want of sleep overcomes me.'

But it was not of gold, women and intrigue that the Aquilonian was thinking, but of the girl who slumbered on his lap. There was no joy in the thought of taking her into such a welter of intrigue and blood as Conan had described. A subtle change had come over Amalric, almost without his knowledge.

THE POOL OF THE BLACK ONE

Into the west, unknown of man,
Ships have sailed since the world began.
Read, if you dare, what Skelos wrote,
With dead hands fumbling his silken coat;
And follow the ships through the wind-blown wrack—
Follow the ships that come not back.

1

Sancha, once of Kordava, yawned daintily, stretched her supple limbs luxuriously, and composed herself more comfortably on the ermine-fringed silk spread on the carack's poop-deck. That the crew watched her with burning interest from waist and forecastle she was lazily aware, just as she was also aware that her short silk kirtle veiled little of her voluptuous contours from their eager eyes. Wherefore she smiled insolently and prepared to snatch a few more winks before the sun, which was just thrusting his golden disk above the ocean, should dazzle her eyes.

But at that instant a sound reached her ears unlike the creaking of timbers, thrum of cordage and lap of waves. She sat up, her gaze fixed on the rail, over which, to her amazement, a dripping figure clambered. Her dark eyes opened wide, her red lips parted in an O of surprise. The intruder was a stranger to her. Water ran in rivulets from his great shoulders and down his heavy arms. His single garment – a pair of bright crimson silk breeks – was soaking wet, as was his broad gold-buckled girdle and the sheathed sword it supported. As he stood at the rail, the rising sun etched him like a great bronze statue. He ran his fingers through his streaming black mane, and his blue eyes lit as they rested on the girl.

'Who are you?' she demanded. 'Whence did you come?'

He made a gesture toward the sea that took in a whole quarter of the compass, while his eyes did not leave her supple figure.

'Are you a merman, that you rise up out of the sea?' she asked, confused by the candor of his gaze, though she was accustomed to admiration.

Before he could reply, a quick step sounded on the boards, and the master of the carack was glaring at the stranger, fingers twitching at sword-hilt.

'Who the devil are you, sirrah?' this one demanded in no friendly tone.

'I am Conan,' the other answered imperturbably. Sancha pricked up her ears anew; she had never heard Zingaran spoken with such an accent as the stranger spoke it.

'And how did you get aboard my ship?' The voice grated with suspicion.

'I swam.'

'Swam!' exclaimed the master angrily. 'Dog, would you jest with me? We are far beyond sight of land. Whence do you come?'

Conan pointed with a muscular brown arm toward the east, banded in dazzling gold by the lifting sun.

'I came from the Islands.'

'Oh!' The other regarded him with increased interest. Black brows drew down over scowling eyes, and the thin lip lifted unpleasantly.

'So you are one of those dogs of the Barachans.'

A faint smile touched Conan's lips.

'And do you know who I am?' his questioner demanded.

'This ship is the *Wastrel*; so you must be Zaporavo.'

'Aye!' It touched the captain's grim vanity that the man should know him. He was a tall man, tall as Conan, though of leaner build. Framed in his steel morion his face was dark, saturnine and hawk-like, wherefore men called him the Hawk. His armor and garments were rich and ornate, after the fashion of a Zingaran grandee. His hand was never far from his sword-hilt.

There was little favor in the gaze he bent on Conan. Little love was lost between Zingaran renegades and the outlaws who infested the Baracha Islands off the southern coast of Zingara. These men were mostly sailors from Argos, with a sprinkling of other nationalities. They raided the shipping, and harried the Zingaran coast towns, just as the Zingaran buccaneers did, but these dignified their profession by calling themselves Freebooters, while they dubbed the Barachans pirates. They were neither the first nor the last to gild the name of thief.

Some of these thoughts passed through Zaporavo's mind as he toyed with his sword-hilt and scowled at his uninvited guest. Conan gave no hint of what his own thoughts might be. He stood with folded arms as placidly as if upon his own deck; his lips smiled and his eyes were untroubled.

'What are you doing here?' the Freebooter demanded abruptly.

'I found it necessary to leave the rendezvous at Tortage before moonrise last night,' answered Conan. 'I departed in a leaky boat, and rowed and bailed all night. Just at dawn I saw your topsails, and left the miserable tub to sink, while I made better speed in the water.'

'There are sharks in these waters,' growled Zaporavo, and was vaguely irritated by the answering shrug of the mighty shoulders. A glance toward the waist showed a screen of eager faces staring upward. A word would send them leaping up on the poop in a storm of swords that would overwhelm even such a fighting-man as the stranger looked to be.

'Why should I burden myself with every nameless vagabond that the sea casts up?' snarled Zaporavo, his look and manner more insulting than his words.

'A ship can always use another good sailor,' answered the other without resentment. Zaporavo scowled, knowing the truth of that assertion. He hesitated, and doing so, lost his ship, his command, his girl, and his life. But of course he could not see into the future, and to him Conan was only another wastrel, cast up, as he put it, by the sea. He did not like the man; yet the fellow had given him no provocation. His manner was not insolent, though rather more confident than Zaporavo liked to see.

'You'll work for your keep,' snarled the Hawk. 'Get off the poop. And remember, the only law here is my will.'

The smile seemed to broaden on Conan's thin lips. Without hesitation but without haste he turned and descended into the waist. He did not look again at Sancha, who, during the brief conversation, had watched eagerly, all eyes and ears.

As he came into the waist the crew thronged about him – Zingarans, all of them, half naked, their gaudy silk garments splashed with tar, jewels glinting in ear-rings and dagger-hilts. They were eager for the time-honored sport of baiting the stranger. Here he would be tested, and his future status in the crew decided. Up on the poop Zaporavo had apparently already forgotten the stranger's existence, but Sancha watched, tense with interest. She had become familiar with such scenes, and knew the baiting would be brutal and probably bloody.

But her familiarity with such matters was scanty compared to that of Conan. He smiled faintly as he came into the waist and saw the menacing figures pressing truculently about him. He paused and eyed the ring inscrutably, his composure unshaken. There was a certain code about these things. If he had attacked the captain, the whole crew would have been at his throat, but they would give him a fair chance against the one selected to push the brawl.

The man chosen for this duty thrust himself forward – a wiry brute, with a crimson sash knotted about his head like a turban. His lean chin jutted out, his scarred face was evil beyond belief. Every glance, each swaggering movement was an affront. His way of beginning the baiting was as primitive, raw and crude as himself.

'Baracha, eh?' he sneered. 'That's where they raise dogs for men. We of the Fellowship spit on 'em – like this!'

He spat in Conan's face and snatched at his own sword.

The Barachan's movement was too quick for the eye to follow. His sledge-like fist crunched with a terrible impact against his tormentor's jaw, and the Zingaran catapulted through the air and fell in a crumpled heap by the rail.

Conan turned towards the others. But for a slumbering glitter in his eyes, his bearing was unchanged. But the baiting was over as suddenly as it had begun. The seamen lifted their companion; his broken jaw hung slack, his head lolled unnaturally.

'By Mitra, his neck's broken!' swore a black-bearded sea-rogue.

'You Freebooters are a weak-boned race,' laughed the pirate. 'On the Barachas we take no account of such taps as that. Will you play at sword-strokes, now, any of you? No? Then all's well, and we're friends, eh?'

There were plenty of tongues to assure him that he spoke truth. Brawny arms swung the dead man over the rail, and a dozen fins cut the water as he sank. Conan laughed and spread his mighty arms as a great cat might stretch itself, and his gaze sought the deck above. Sancha leaned over the rail, red lips parted, dark eyes aglow with interest. The sun behind her outlined her lithe figure through the light kirtle which its glow made transparent. Then across her fell Zaporavo's scowling shadow and a heavy hand fell possessively on her slim shoulder. There were menace and meaning in the glare he bent on the man in the waist; Conan grinned back, as if at a jest none knew but himself.

Zaporavo made the mistake so many autocrats make; alone in somber grandeur on the poop, he underestimated the man below him. He had his opportunity to kill Conan, and he let it pass, engrossed in his own gloomy ruminations. He did not find it easy to think any of the dogs beneath his feet constituted a menace to him. He had stood in the high places so long, and had ground so many foes underfoot, that he unconsciously assumed himself to be above the machinations of inferior rivals.

Conan, indeed, gave him no provocation. He mixed with the crew, lived and made merry as they did. He proved himself a skilled sailor, and by far the strongest man any of them had seen. He did the work of three men, and was always first to spring to any heavy or dangerous task. His mates began to rely upon him. He did not quarrel with them, and they were careful not to quarrel with him. He gambled with them, putting up his girdle and sheath for a stake, won their money and weapons, and gave them back with a laugh. The crew instinctively looked toward him as the leader of the forecastle. He vouchsafed no information as to what had caused him to flee the Barachas, but the knowledge that he was capable of a deed bloody enough to have exiled him from that wild band increased the respect felt toward him by the fierce Freebooters. Toward Zaporavo and the mates he was imperturbably courteous, never insolent or servile.

The dullest was struck by the contrast between the harsh, taciturn, gloomy commander, and the pirate whose laugh was gusty and ready, who roared ribald songs in a dozen languages, guzzled ale like a toper, and – apparently – had no thought for the morrow.

Had Zaporavo known he was being compared, even though unconsciously, with a man before the mast, he would have been speechless with amazed anger. But he was engrossed with his broodings, which had become blacker and grimmer as the years crawled by, and with his vague grandiose dreams; and with the girl whose possession was a bitter pleasure, just as all his pleasures were.

And she looked more and more at the black-maned giant who towered among his mates at work or play. He never spoke to her, but there was no mistaking the candor of his gaze. She did not mistake it, and she wondered if she dared the perilous game of leading him on.

No great length of time lay between her and the palaces of Kordava, but it was as if a world of change separated her from the life she had lived before Zaporavo tore her screaming from the flaming caravel his wolves had plundered. She, who had been the spoiled and petted daughter of the Duke of Kordava, learned what it was to be a buccaneer's plaything, and because she was supple enough to bend without breaking, she lived where other women had died, and because she was young and vibrant with life, she came to find pleasure in the existence.

The life was uncertain, dream-like, with sharp contrasts of battle, pillage, murder, and flight. Zaporavo's red visions made it even more uncertain than that of the average Freebooter. No one knew what he planned next. Now they had left all charted coasts behind and were plunging further and further into that unknown billowy waste ordinarily shunned by seafarers, and into which, since the beginnings of Time, ships had ventured, only to vanish from the sight of man for ever. All known lands lay behind them, and day upon day the blue surging immensity lay empty to their sight. Here there was no loot – no towns to sack nor ships to burn. The men murmured, though they did not let their murmurings reach the ears of their implacable master, who tramped the poop day and night in gloomy majesty, or pored over ancient charts and time-yellowed maps, reading in tomes that were crumbling masses of worm-eaten parchment. At times he talked to Sancha, wildly it seemed to her, of lost continents, and fabulous isles dreaming unguessed amidst the blue foam of nameless gulfs, where horned dragons guarded treasures gathered by pre-human kings, long, long ago.

Sancha listened, uncomprehending, hugging her slim knees, her thoughts constantly roving away from the words of her grim companion back to a clean-limbed bronze giant whose laughter was gusty and elemental as the sea wind.

So, after many weary weeks, they raised land to westward, and at dawn dropped anchor in a shallow bay, and saw a beach which was like a white band bordering an expanse of gently grassy slopes, masked by green trees. The wind brought scents of fresh vegetation and spices, and Sancha clapped her hands with glee at the prospect of adventuring ashore. But her eagerness turned to sulkiness when Zaporavo ordered her to remain aboard until he sent for her. He never gave any explanation for his commands; so she never knew his reason, unless it was the lurking devil in him that frequently made him hurt her without cause.

So she lounged sulkily on the poop and watched the men row ashore through the calm water that sparkled like liquid jade in the morning sunlight. She saw them bunch together on the sands, suspicious, weapons ready, while several scattered out through the trees that fringed the beach. Among these, she noted, was Conan. There was no mistaking that tall brown figure with its springy step.

Men said he was no civilized man at all, but a Cimmerian, one of those barbaric tribesmen who dwelt in the gray hills of the far North, and whose raids struck terror in their southern neighbors. At least, she knew that there was something about him, some super-vitality or barbarism that set him apart from his wild mates.

Voices echoed along the shore, as the silence reassured the buccaneers. The clusters broke up, as men scattered along the beach in search of fruit. She saw them climbing and plucking among the trees, and her pretty mouth watered. She stamped a little foot and swore with a proficiency acquired by association with her blasphemous companions.

The men on shore had indeed found fruit, and were gorging on it, finding one unknown golden-skinned variety especially luscious. But Zaporavo did not seek or eat fruit. His scouts having found nothing indicating men or beasts in the neighborhood, he stood staring inland, at the long reaches of grassy slopes melting into one another. Then, with a brief word, he shifted his sword-belt and strode in under the trees. His mate expostulated with him against going alone, and was rewarded by a savage blow in the mouth. Zaporavo had his reasons for wishing to go alone. He desired to learn if this island were indeed that mentioned in the mysterious *Book of Skelos*, whereon, nameless sages aver, strange monsters guard crypts filled with hieroglyph-carven gold. Nor, for murky reasons of his own, did he wish to share his knowledge, if it were true, with any one, much less his own crew.

Sancha, watching eagerly from the poop, saw him vanish into the leafy fastness. Presently she saw Conan, the Barachan, turn, glance briefly at the men scattered up and down the beach; then the pirate went quickly in the direction taken by Zaporavo, and likewise vanished among the trees.

Sancha's curiosity was piqued. She waited for them to reappear, but they did not. The seamen still moved aimlessly up and down the beach, and some had wandered inland. Many had lain down in the shade to sleep. Time passed and she fidgeted about restlessly. The sun began to beat down hotly, in spite of the canopy above the poop-deck. Here it was warm, silent, draggingly monotonous; a few yards away across a band of blue shallow water, the cool shady mystery of tree-fringed beach and woodland-dotted meadow beckoned her. Moreover, the mystery concerning Zaporavo and Conan tempted her.

She well knew the penalty for disobeying her merciless master, and she sat for some time, squirming with indecision. At last she decided that it was worth even one of Zaporavo's whippings to play truant, and with no more ado she kicked off her soft leather sandals, slipped out of her kirtle and stood up on the deck naked as Eve. Clambering over the rail and down the chains, she slid into the water and swam ashore. She stood on the beach a few moments, squirming as the sands tickled her small toes, while she looked for the crew. She saw only a few, at some distance up or down the beach. Many were fast asleep under the trees, bits of golden fruit still clutched in their fingers. She wondered why they should sleep so soundly, so early in the day.

None hailed her as she crossed the white girdle of sand and entered the shade of the woodland. The trees, she found, grew in irregular clusters, and between these groves stretched rolling expanses of meadow-like slopes. As she progressed inland, in the direction taken by Zaporavo, she was entranced by the green vistas that unfolded gently before her, soft slope beyond slope, carpeted with green sward and dotted with groves. Between the slopes lay gentle declivities, likewise swarded. The scenery seemed to melt into itself, or each scene into the other; the view was singular, at once broad and restricted. Over all a dreamy silence lay like an enchantment.

Then she came suddenly onto the level summit of a slope, circled with tall trees, and the dreamily faery-like sensation vanished abruptly at the sight of what lay on the reddened and trampled grass. Sancha involuntarily cried out and recoiled, then stole forward, wide-eyed, trembling in every limb.

It was Zaporavo who lay there on the sward, staring sightlessly upward, a gaping wound in his breast. His sword lay near his nerveless hand. The Hawk had made his last swoop.

It is not to be said that Sancha gazed on the corpse of her lord without emotion. She had no cause to love him, yet she felt at least the sensation any girl might feel when looking on the body of the man who was first to possess her. She did not weep or feel any need of weeping, but she was seized by a strong trembling, her blood seemed to congeal briefly, and she resisted a wave of hysteria.

She looked about her for the man she expected to see. Nothing met her eyes but the ring of tall, thickly leafed forest giants, and the blue slopes beyond them. Had the Freebooter's slayer dragged himself away, mortally wounded? No bloody tracks led away from the body.

Puzzled, she swept the surrounding trees, stiffening as she caught a rustle in the emerald leaves that seemed not to be of the wind. She went toward the trees, staring into the leafy depths.

'Conan?' Her call was inquiring; her voice sounded strange and small in the vastness of silence that had grown suddenly tense.

Her knees began to tremble as a nameless panic swept over her.

'Conan!' she cried desperately. 'It is I – Sancha! Where are you? Please, Conan—' Her voice faltered away. Unbelieving horror dilated her brown eyes. Her red lips parted to an inarticulate scream. Paralysis gripped her limbs; where she had such desperate need of swift flight, she could not move. She could only shriek wordlessly.

2

When Conan saw Zaporavo stalk alone into the woodland, he felt that the chance he had watched for had come. He had eaten no fruit, nor joined in the horse-play of his mates; all his faculties were occupied with watching the buccaneer chief. Accustomed to Zaporavo's moods, his men were not particularly surprised that their captain should choose to explore an unknown and probably hostile isle alone. They turned to their own amusement, and did not notice Conan when he glided like a stalking panther after the chieftain.

Conan did not underrate his dominance of the crew. But he had not gained the right, through battle and foray, to challenge the captain to a duel to the death. In these empty seas there had been no opportunity for him to prove himself according to Freebooter law. The crew would stand solidly against him if he attacked the chieftain openly. But he knew that if he killed Zaporavo without their knowledge, the leaderless crew would not be likely to be swayed by loyalty to a dead man. In such wolf-packs only the living counted.

So he followed Zaporavo with sword in hand and eagerness in his heart, until he came out onto a level summit, circled with tall trees, between whose trunks he saw the green vistas of the slopes melting into the blue distance. In the midst of the glade Zaporavo, sensing pursuit, turned, hand on hilt.

The buccaneer swore.

'Dog, why do you follow me?'

'Are you mad, to ask?' laughed Conan, coming swiftly toward his erstwhile chief. His lips smiled, and in his blue eyes danced a wild gleam.

Zaporavo ripped out his sword with a black curse, and steel clashed against steel as the Barachan came in recklessly and wide open, his blade singing a wheel of blue flame about his head.

Zaporavo was the veteran of a thousand fights by sea and by land. There was no man in the world more deeply and thoroughly versed than he in the lore of swordcraft. But he had never been pitted against a blade wielded by thews bred in the wild lands beyond the borders of civilization. Against his fighting-craft was matched blinding speed and strength impossible to a civilized man. Conan's manner of fighting was unorthodox, but instinctive and natural as that of a timber wolf. The intricacies of the sword were as useless against his primitive fury as a human boxer's skill against the onslaughts of a panther.

Fighting as he had never fought before, straining every last ounce of effort to parry the blade that flickered like lightning about his head, Zaporavo in desperation caught a full stroke near his hilt, and felt his whole arm go numb beneath the terrific impact. That stroke was instantly followed by a thrust with such terrible drive behind it that the sharp point ripped through chain-mail and ribs like paper, to transfix the heart beneath. Zaporavo's lips writhed in brief agony, but, grim to the last, he made no sound. He was dead before his body relaxed on the trampled grass, where blood drops glittered like spilt rubies in the sun.

Conan shook the red drops from his sword, grinned with unaffected pleasure, stretched like a huge cat – and abruptly stiffened, the expression of satisfaction on his face being replaced by a stare of bewilderment. He stood like a statue, his sword trailing in his hand.

As he lifted his eyes from his vanquished foe, they had absently rested on the surrounding trees, and the vistas beyond. And he had seen a fantastic thing – a thing incredible and inexplicable. Over the soft rounded green shoulder of a distant slope had loped a tall black naked figure, bearing on its shoulder an equally naked white form. The apparition vanished as suddenly as it had appeared, leaving the watcher gasping in surprise.

The pirate stared about him, glanced uncertainly back the way he had come, and swore. He was nonplussed – a bit upset, if the term might be applied to one of such steely nerves as his. In the midst of realistic, if exotic surroundings, a vagrant image of fantasy and nightmare had been introduced. Conan doubted neither his eyesight nor his sanity. He had seen something alien and uncanny, he knew; the mere fact of a black figure racing across the landscape carrying a white captive was bizarre enough, but this black figure had been unnaturally tall.

Shaking his head doubtfully, Conan started off in the direction in which he had seen the thing. He did not argue the wisdom of his move; with his curiosity so piqued, he had no choice but to follow its promptings.

Slope after slope he traversed, each with its even sward and clustered groves. The general trend was always upward, though he ascended and descended the gentle inclines with monotonous regularity. The array of rounded shoulders and shallow declivities was bewildering and apparently endless. But at last he advanced up what he believed was the highest summit on the island, and halted at the sight of green shining walls and towers, which, until he had reached the spot on which he then stood, had merged so perfectly with the green landscape as to be invisible, even to his keen sight.

He hesitated, fingered his sword, then went forward, bitten by the worm of curiosity. He saw no one as he approached a tall archway in the curving wall. There was no door. Peering warily through, he saw what seemed to be a broad open court, grass-carpeted, surrounded by a circular wall of the green semi-translucent substance. Various arches opened from it. Advancing on the balls of his bare feet, sword ready, he chose one of these arches at random, and passed into another similar court. Over an inner wall he saw the pinnacles of strangely shaped tower-like structures. One of these towers was built in, or projected into the court in which he found himself, and a broad stair led up to it, along the side of the wall. Up this he went, wondering if it were all real, or if he were not in the midst of a black lotus dream.

At the head of the stair he found himself on a walled ledge, or balcony, he was not sure which. He could now make out more details of the towers, but they were meaningless to him. He realized uneasily that no ordinary human beings could have built them. There was symmetry about their architecture, and system, but it was a mad symmetry, a system alien to human sanity. As for the plan of the whole town, castle, or whatever it was intended for, he could see just enough to get the impression of a great number of courts, mostly circular, each surrounded by its own wall, and connected with the others by open arches, and all, apparently, grouped about the cluster of fantastic towers in the center.

Turning in the other direction from these towers, he got a fearful shock, and crouched down suddenly behind the parapet of the balcony, glaring amazedly.

The balcony or ledge was higher than the opposite wall, and he was looking over that wall into another swarded court. The inner curve of the further wall of that court differed from the others he had seen, in that, instead of being smooth, it seemed to be banded with long lines or ledges, crowded with small objects the nature of which he could not determine.

However, he gave little heed to the wall at the time. His attention was centered on the band of beings that squatted about a dark green pool in the midst of the court. These creatures were black and naked, made like men, but the least of them, standing upright, would have towered head and shoulders above the tall pirate. They were rangy rather than massive, but were finely formed, with no suggestion of deformity or abnormality, save as their great height was abnormal. But even at that distance Conan sensed the basic diabolism of their features.

In their midst, cringing and naked, stood a youth that Conan recognized as the youngest sailor aboard the *Wastrel*. He, then, had been the captive the pirate had seen borne across the grass-covered slope. Conan had heard no sound of fighting – saw no blood-stains or wounds on the sleek ebon limbs of the giants. Evidently the lad had wandered inland away from his companions and been snatched up by a black man lurking in ambush. Conan mentally termed the creatures black men, for lack of a better term; instinctively he knew that these tall ebony beings were not men, as he understood the term.

No sound came to him. The blacks nodded and gestured to one another, but they did not seem to speak – vocally, at least. One, squatting on his haunches before the cringing boy, held a pipe-like thing in his hand. This he set to his lips, and apparently blew, though Conan heard no sound. But the Zingaran youth heard or felt, and cringed. He quivered and writhed as if in agony; a regularity became evident in the twitching of his limbs, which quickly became rhythmic. The twitching became a violent jerking, the jerking regular movements. The youth began to dance, as cobras dance by compulsion to the tune of the faquir's fife. There was naught of zest or joyful abandon in that dance. There was, indeed, abandon that was awful to see, but it was not joyful. It was as if the mute tune of the pipes grasped the boy's inmost soul with salacious fingers and with brutal torture wrung from it every involuntary expression of secret passion. It was a convulsion of obscenity, a spasm of lasciviousness – an exudation of secret hungers framed by compulsion: desire without pleasure, pain mated awfully to lust. It was like watching a soul stripped naked, and all its dark and unmentionable secrets laid bare.

Conan glared frozen with repulsion and shaken with nausea. Himself as cleanly elemental as a timber wolf, he was yet not ignorant of the perverse secrets of rotting civilizations. He had roamed the cities of Zamora, and known the women of Shadizar the Wicked. But he sensed here a cosmic vileness transcending mere human degeneracy – a perverse branch on the tree of Life, developed along lines outside human comprehension. It was not at the agonized contortions and posturing of the wretched boy that he was shocked, but at the cosmic obscenity of these beings which could drag to light the abysmal secrets that sleep in the unfathomed darkness of the human soul, and find pleasure in the brazen flaunting of such things as should not be hinted at, even in restless nightmares.

Suddenly the black torturer laid down the pipes and rose, towering over the writhing white figure. Brutally grasping the boy by neck and haunch, the giant up-ended him and thrust him head-first into the green pool. Conan saw the white glimmer of his naked body amid the green water, as the black giant held his captive deep under the surface. Then there was a restless movement among the other blacks, and Conan ducked quickly below the balcony wall, not daring to raise his head lest he be seen.

After a while his curiosity got the better of him, and he cautiously peered out again. The blacks were filing out of an archway into another court. One of them was just placing something on a ledge of the further wall, and Conan saw it was the one who had tortured the boy. He was taller than the others, and wore a jeweled head-band. Of the Zingaran boy there was no trace. The giant followed his fellows, and presently Conan saw them emerge from the archway by which he had gained access to that castle of horror, and file away across the green slopes, in the direction from which he had come. They bore no arms, yet he felt that they planned further aggression against the Freebooters.

But before he went to warn the unsuspecting buccaneers, he wished to investigate the fate of the boy. No sound disturbed the quiet. The pirate believed that the towers and courts were deserted save for himself.

He went swiftly down the stair, crossed the court and passed through an arch into the court the blacks had just quitted. Now he saw the nature of the striated wall. It was banded by narrow ledges, apparently cut out of the solid stone, and ranged along these ledges or shelves were thousands of tiny figures, mostly grayish in color. These figures, not much longer than a man's hand, represented men, and so cleverly were they made that Conan recognized various racial characteristics in the different idols, features typical of Zingarans, Argoseans, Ophireans and Kushite corsairs. These last were black in color, just as their models were black in reality. Conan was aware of a vague uneasiness as he stared at the dumb sightless figures. There was a mimicry of reality about them that was somehow disturbing. He felt of them gingerly and could not decide of what material they were made. It felt like petrified bone; but he could not imagine petrified substance being found in the locality in such abundance as to be used so lavishly.

He noticed that the images representing types with which he was familiar were all on the higher ledges. The lower ledges were occupied by figures the features of which were strange to him. They either embodied merely the artists' imagination, or typified racial types long vanished and forgotten.

Shaking his head impatiently, Conan turned toward the pool. The circular court offered no place of concealment; as the body of the boy was nowhere in sight, it must be lying at the bottom of the pool.

Approaching the placid green disk, he stared into the glimmering surface. It was like looking through a thick green glass, unclouded, yet strangely illusory. Of no great dimensions, the pool was round as a well, bordered by a rim of green jade. Looking down he could see the rounded bottom – how far below the surface he could not decide. But the pool seemed incredibly deep – he was aware of a dizziness as he looked down, much as if he were looking into an abyss. He was puzzled by his ability to see the bottom; but it lay beneath his gaze, impossibly remote, illusive, shadowy, yet visible. At times he thought a faint luminosity was apparent deep in the jade-colored depth, but he could not be sure. Yet he was sure that the pool was empty except for the shimmering water.

Then where in the name of Crom was the boy whom he had seen brutally drowned in that pool? Rising, Conan fingered his sword, and gazed around the court again. His gaze focussed on a spot on one of the higher ledges. There he had seen the tall black place something – cold sweat broke suddenly out on Conan's brown hide.

Hesitantly, yet as if drawn by a magnet, the pirate approached the shimmering wall. Dazed by a suspicion too monstrous to voice, he glared up at the last figure on that ledge. A horrible familiarity made itself evident. Stony, immobile, dwarfish, yet unmistakable, the features of the Zingaran boy stared unseeingly at him. Conan recoiled, shaken to his soul's foundations. His sword trailed in his paralyzed hand as he glared, open-mouthed, stunned by the realization which was too abysmal and awful for the mind to grasp.

Yet the fact was indisputable; the secret of the dwarfish figures was revealed, though behind that secret lay the darker and more cryptic secret of their being.

3

How long Conan stood drowned in dizzy cogitation, he never knew. A voice shook him out of his gaze, a feminine voice that shrieked more and more loudly, as if the owner of the voice were being borne nearer. Conan recognized that voice, and his paralysis vanished instantly.

A quick bound carried him high up on the narrow ledges, where he clung, kicking aside the clustering images to obtain room for his feet. Another spring and a scramble, and he was clinging to the rim of the wall, glaring over it. It was an outer wall; he was looking into the green meadow that surrounded the castle.

Across the grassy level a giant black was striding, carrying a squirming captive under one arm as a man might carry a rebellious child. It was Sancha, her black hair falling in disheveled rippling waves, her olive skin contrasting abruptly with the glossy ebony of her captor. He gave no heed to her wrigglings and cries as he made for the outer archway.

As he vanished within, Conan sprang recklessly down the wall and glided into the arch that opened into the further court. Crouching there, he saw the giant enter the court of the pool, carrying his writhing captive. Now he was able to make out the creature's details.

The superb symmetry of body and limbs was more impressive at close range. Under the ebon skin long, rounded muscles rippled, and Conan did not doubt that the monster could rend an ordinary man limb from limb. The nails of the fingers provided further weapons, for they were grown like the talons of a wild beast. The face was a carven ebony mask. The eyes were tawny, a vibrant gold that glowed and glittered. But the face was inhuman; each line, each feature was stamped with evil – evil transcending the mere evil of humanity. The thing was not a human – it could not be; it was a growth of Life from the pits of blasphemous creation – a perversion of evolutionary development.

The giant cast Sancha down on the sward, where she grovelled, crying with pain and terror. He cast a glance about as if uncertain, and his tawny eyes narrowed as they rested on the images overturned and knocked from the wall. Then he stooped, grasped his captive by her neck and crotch, and strode purposefully toward the green pool. And Conan glided from his archway, and raced like a wind of death across the sward.

The giant wheeled, and his eyes flared as he saw the bronzed avenger rushing toward him. In the instant of surprise his cruel grip relaxed and Sancha wriggled from his hands and fell to the grass. The taloned hands spread and clutched, but Conan ducked beneath their swoop and drove his sword through the giant's groin. The black went down like a felled tree, gushing blood, and the next instant Conan was seized in a frantic grasp as Sancha sprang up and threw her arms around him in a frenzy of terror and hysterical relief.

He cursed as he disengaged himself, but his foe was already dead; the tawny eyes were glazed, the long ebony limbs had ceased to twitch.

'Oh, Conan,' Sancha was sobbing, clinging tenaciously to him, 'what will become of us? What are these monsters? Oh, surely this is hell and that was the devil—'

'Then hell needs a new devil.' The Barachan grinned fiercely. 'But how did he get hold of you? Have they taken the ship?'

'I don't know.' She tried to wipe away her tears, fumbled for her skirt, and then remembered that she wore none. 'I came ashore. I saw you follow Zaporavo, and I followed you both. I found Zaporavo – was – was it you who—'

'Who else?' he grunted. 'What then?'

'I saw a movement in the trees,' she shuddered. 'I thought it was you. I called – then I saw that – that black *thing* squatting like an ape among the branches, leering down at me. It was like a nightmare; I couldn't run. All I could do was squeal. Then it dropped from the tree and seized me – oh, oh, oh!' She hid her face in her hands, and was shaken anew at the memory of the horror.

'Well, we've got to get out of here,' he growled, catching her wrist. 'Come on; we've got to get to the crew—'

'Most of them were asleep on the beach as I entered the woods,' she said.

'Asleep?' he exclaimed profanely. 'What in the seven devils of hell's fire and damnation—'

'Listen!' She froze, a white quivering image of fright.

'I heard it!' he snapped. 'A moaning cry! Wait!'

He bounded up the ledges again and, glaring over the wall, swore with a concentrated fury that made even Sancha gasp. The black men were returning, but they came not alone or empty-handed. Each bore a limp human form; some bore two. Their captives were the Freebooters; they hung slackly in their captors' arms, and but for an occasional vague movement or twitching, Conan would have believed them dead. They had been disarmed but not stripped; one of the blacks bore their sheathed swords, a great armload of bristling steel. From time to time one of the seamen voiced a vague cry, like a drunkard calling out in sottish sleep.

Like a trapped wolf Conan glared about him. Three arches led out of the court of the pool. Through the eastern arch the blacks had left the court, and through it they would presumably return. He had entered by the southern arch. In the western arch he had hidden, and had not had time to notice what lay beyond it. Regardless of his ignorance of the plan of the castle, he was forced to make his decision promptly.

Springing down the wall, he replaced the images with frantic haste, dragged the corpse of his victim to the pool and cast it in. It sank instantly and, as he looked, he distinctly saw an appalling contraction – a shrinking, a hardening. He hastily turned away, shuddering. Then he seized his companion's arm and led her hastily toward the southern archway, while she begged to be told what was happening.

'They've bagged the crew,' he answered hastily. 'I haven't any plan, but we'll hide somewhere and watch. If they don't look in the pool, they may not suspect our presence.'

'But they'll see the blood on the grass!'

'Maybe they'll think one of their own devils spilled it,' he answered. 'Anyway, we'll have to take the chance.'

They were in the court from which he had watched the torture of the boy, and he led her hastily up the stair that mounted the southern wall, and forced her into a crouching position behind the balustrade of the balcony; it was poor concealment, but the best they could do.

Scarcely had they settled themselves, when the blacks filed into the court. There was a resounding clash at the foot of the stairs, and Conan stiffened, grasping his sword. But the blacks passed through an archway on the southwestern side, and they heard a series of thuds and groans. The giants were casting their victims down on the sward. An hysterical giggle rose to Sancha's lips, and Conan quickly clapped his hand over her mouth, stifling the sound before it could betray them.

After a while they heard the padding of many feet on the sward below, and then silence reigned. Conan peered over the wall. The court was empty. The blacks were once more gathered about the pool in the adjoining court, squatting on their haunches. They seemed to pay no heed to the great smears of blood on the sward and the jade rim of the pool. Evidently blood stains were nothing unusual. Nor were they looking into the pool. They were engrossed in some inexplicable conclave of their own; the tall black was playing again on his golden pipes, and his companions listened like ebony statues.

Taking Sancha's hand, Conan glided down the stair, stooping so that his head would not be visible above the wall. The cringing girl followed perforce, staring fearfully at the arch that let into the court of the pool, but through which, at that angle, neither the pool nor its grim throng were visible. At the foot of the stair lay the swords of the Zingarans. The clash they had heard had been the casting down of the captured weapons.

Conan drew Sancha toward the southwestern arch, and they silently crossed the sward and entered the court beyond. There the Freebooters lay in careless heaps, mustaches bristling, ear-rings glinting. Here and there one stirred or groaned restlessly. Conan bent down to them, and Sancha knelt beside him, leaning forward with her hands on her thighs.

'What is that sweet cloying smell?' she asked nervously. 'It's on all their breaths.'

'It's that damned fruit they were eating,' he answered softly. 'I remember the smell of it. It must have been like the black lotus, that makes men sleep. By Crom, they are beginning to awake – but they're unarmed, and I have an idea that those black devils won't wait long before they begin their magic on them. What chance will the lads have, unarmed and stupid with slumber?'

He brooded for an instant, scowling with the intentness of his thoughts; then seized Sancha's olive shoulder in a grip that made her wince.

'Listen! I'll draw those black swine into another part of the castle and keep them busy for a while. Meanwhile you shake these fools awake, and bring their swords to them – it's a fighting chance. Can you do it?'

'I – I – don't know!' she stammered, shaking with terror, and hardly knowing what she was saying.

With a curse, Conan caught her thick tresses near her head and shook her until the walls danced to her dizzy sight.

'You *must* do it!' he hissed at her. 'It's our only chance!'

'I'll do my best!' she gasped, and with a grunt of commendation and an encouraging slap on the back that nearly knocked her down, he glided away.

A few moments later he was crouching at the arch that opened into the court of the pool, glaring upon his enemies. They still sat about the pool, but were beginning to show evidences of an evil impatience. From the court where lay the rousing buccaneers he heard their groans growing louder, beginning to be mingled with incoherent curses. He tensed his muscles and sank into a pantherish crouch, breathing easily between his teeth.

The jeweled giant rose, taking his pipes from his lips – and at that instant Conan was among the startled blacks with a tigerish bound. And as a tiger leaps and strikes among his prey, Conan leaped and struck: thrice his blade flickered before any could lift a hand in defense; then he bounded from among them and raced across the sward. Behind him sprawled three black figures, their skulls split.

But though the unexpected fury of his surprise had caught the giants off guard, the survivors recovered quickly enough. They were at his heels as he ran through the western arch, their long legs sweeping them over the ground at headlong speed. However, he felt confident of his ability to outfoot them at will; but that was not his purpose. He intended leading them on a long chase, in order to give Sancha time to rouse and arm the Zingarans.

And as he raced into the court beyond the western arch, he swore. This court differed from the others he had seen. Instead of being round, it was octagonal, and the arch by which he had entered was the only entrance or exit.

Wheeling, he saw that the entire band had followed him in; a group clustered in the arch, and the rest spread out in a wide line as they approached. He faced them, backing slowly toward the northern wall. The line bent into a semicircle, spreading out to hem him in. He continued to move backward, but more and more slowly, noting the spaces widening between the pursuers. They feared lest he should try to dart around a horn of the crescent, and lengthened their line to prevent it.

He watched with the calm alertness of a wolf, and when he struck it was with the devastating suddenness of a thunderbolt – full at the center of the crescent. The giant who barred his way went down cloven to the middle of the breast-bone, and the pirate was outside their closing ring before the blacks to right and left could come to their stricken comrade's aid. The group at the gate prepared to receive his onslaught, but Conan did not charge them. He had turned and was watching his hunters without apparent emotion, and certainly without fear.

This time they did not spread out in a thin line. They had learned that it was fatal to divide their forces against such an incarnation of clawing, rending fury. They bunched up in a compact mass, and advanced on him without undue haste, maintaining their formation.

Conan knew that if he fell foul of that mass of taloned muscle and bone, there could be but one culmination. Once let them drag him down among them where they could reach him with their talons and use their greater body-weight to advantage, even his primitive ferocity would not prevail. He glanced around the wall and saw a ledge-like projection above a corner on the western side. What it was he did not know, but it would serve his purpose. He began backing toward that corner, and the giants advanced more rapidly. They evidently thought that they were herding him into the corner themselves, and Conan found time to reflect that they probably looked on him as a member of a lower order, mentally inferior to themselves. So much the better. Nothing is more disastrous than underestimating one's antagonist.

Now he was only a few yards from the wall, and the blacks were closing in rapidly, evidently thinking to pin him in the corner before he realized his situation. The group at the gate had deserted their post and were hastening to join their fellows. The giants half-crouched, eyes blazing like golden hell-fire, teeth glistening whitely, taloned hands lifted as if to fend off attack. They expected an abrupt and violent move on the part of their prey, but when it came, it took them by surprise.

Conan lifted his sword, took a step toward them, then wheeled and raced to the wall. With a fleeting coil and release of steel muscles, he shot high in the air, and his straining arm hooked its fingers over the projection. Instantly there was a rending crash and the jutting ledge gave way, precipitating the pirate back into the court.

He hit on his back, which for all its springy sinews would have broken but for the cushioning of the sward, and rebounding like a great cat, he faced his foes. The dancing recklessness was gone from his eyes. They blazed like blue bale-fire; his mane bristled, his thin lips snarled. In an instant the affair had changed from a daring game to a battle of life and death, and Conan's savage nature responded with all the fury of the wild.

The blacks, halted an instant by the swiftness of the episode, now made to sweep on him and drag him down. But in that instant a shout broke the stillness. Wheeling, the giants saw a disreputable throng crowding the arch. The buccaneers weaved drunkenly, they swore incoherently; they were addled and bewildered, but they grasped their swords and advanced with a ferocity not dimmed in the slightest by the fact that they did not understand what it was all about.

As the blacks glared in amazement, Conan yelled stridently and struck them like a razor-edged thunderbolt. They fell like ripe grains beneath his blade, and the Zingarans, shouting with muddled fury, ran groggily across the court and fell on their gigantic foes with bloodthirsty zeal. They were still dazed; emerging hazily from drugged slumber, they had felt Sancha frantically shaking them and shoving swords into their fists, and had vaguely heard her urging them to some sort of action. They had not understood all she said, but the sight of strangers, and blood streaming, was enough for them.

In an instant the court was turned into a battle-ground which soon resembled a slaughter-house. The Zingarans weaved and rocked on their feet, but they wielded their swords with power and effect, swearing prodigiously, and quite oblivious to all wounds except those instantly fatal. They far outnumbered the blacks, but these proved themselves no mean antagonists. Towering above their assailants, the giants wrought havoc with talons and teeth, tearing out men's throats, and dealing blows with clenched fists that crushed in skulls. Mixed and mingled in that mêlée, the buccaneers could not use their superior agility to the best advantage, and many were too stupid from their drugged sleep to avoid blows aimed at them. They fought with a blind wild-beast ferocity, too intent on dealing death to evade it. The sound of the hacking swords was like that of butchers' cleavers, and the shrieks, yells and curses were appalling.

Sancha, shrinking in the archway, was stunned by the noise and fury; she got a dazed impression of a whirling chaos in which steel flashed and hacked, arms tossed, snarling faces appeared and vanished, and straining bodies collided, rebounded, locked and mingled in a devil's dance of madness.

Details stood out briefly, like black etchings on a background of blood. She saw a Zingaran sailor, blinded by a great flap of scalp torn loose and hanging over his eyes, brace his straddling legs and drive his sword to the hilt in a black belly. She distinctly heard the buccaneer grunt as he struck, and saw the victim's tawny eyes roll up in sudden agony; blood and entrails gushed out over the driven blade. The dying black caught the blade with his naked hands, and the sailor tugged blindly and stupidly; then a black arm hooked about the Zingaran's head, a black knee was planted with cruel force in the middle of his back. His head was jerked back at a terrible angle, and something cracked above the noise of the fray, like the breaking of a thick branch. The conqueror dashed his victim's body to the earth – and as he did, something like a beam of blue light flashed across his shoulders from behind, from right to left. He staggered, his head toppled forward on his breast, and thence, hideously, to the earth.

Sancha turned sick. She gagged and wished to vomit. She made abortive efforts to turn and flee from the spectacle, but her legs would not work. Nor could she close her eyes. In fact, she opened them wider. Revolted, repelled, nauseated, yet she felt the awful fascination she had always experienced at sight of blood. Yet this battle transcended anything she had ever seen fought out between human beings in port raids or sea battles. Then she saw Conan.

Separated from his mates by the whole mass of the enemy, Conan had been enveloped in a black wave of arms and bodies, and dragged down. Then they would quickly have stamped the life out of him, but he had pulled down one of them with him, and the black's body protected that of the pirate beneath him. They kicked and tore at the Barachan and dragged at their writhing comrade, but Conan's teeth were set desperately in his throat, and the pirate clung tenaciously to his dying shield.

An onslaught of Zingarans caused a slackening of the press, and Conan threw aside the corpse and rose, blood-smeared and terrible. The giants towered above him like great black shadows, clutching, buffeting the air with terrible blows. But he was as hard to hit or grapple as a blood-mad panther, and at every turn or flash of his blade, blood jetted. He had already taken punishment enough to kill three ordinary men, but his bull-like vitality was undiminished.

His war cry rose above the medley of the carnage, and the bewildered but furious Zingarans took fresh heart and redoubled their strokes, until the rending of flesh and the crunching of bone beneath the swords almost drowned the howls of pain and wrath.

The blacks wavered, and broke for the gate, and Sancha squealed at their coming and scurried out of the way. They jammed in the narrow archway, and the Zingarans stabbed and hacked at their straining backs with strident yelps of glee. The gate was a shambles before the survivors broke through and scattered, each for himself.

The battle became a chase. Across grassy courts, up shimmering stairs, over the slanting roofs of fantastic towers, even along the broad coping of the walls, the giants fled, dripping blood at each step, harried by their merciless pursuers as by wolves. Cornered, some of them turned at bay and men died. But the ultimate result was always the same – a mangled black body twitching on the sward, or hurled writhing and twisting from parapet or tower roof.

Sancha had taken refuge in the court of the pool, where she crouched, shaking with terror. Outside rose a fierce yelling, feet pounded the sward, and through the arch burst a black, red-stained figure. It was the giant who wore the gemmed headband. A squat pursuer was close behind, and the black turned, at the very brink of the pool. In his extremity he had picked up a sword dropped by a dying sailor, and as the Zingaran rushed recklessly at him, he struck with the unfamiliar weapon. The buccaneer dropped with his skull crushed, but so awkwardly the blow was dealt, the blade shivered in the giant's hand.

He hurled the hilt at the figures which thronged the arch, and bounded toward the pool, his face a convulsed mask of hate. Conan burst through the men at the gate, and his feet spurned the sward in his headlong charge.

But the giant threw his great arms wide and from his lips rang an inhuman cry – the only sound made by a black during the entire fight. It screamed to the sky its awful hate; it was like a voice howling from the pits. At the sound the Zingarans faltered and hesitated. But Conan did not pause. Silently and murderously he drove at the ebon figure poised on the brink of the pool.

But even as his dripping sword gleamed in the air, the black wheeled and bounded high. For a flash of an instant they saw him poised in midair above the pool; then with an earth-shaking roar, the green waters rose and rushed up to meet him, enveloping him in a green volcano.

Conan checked his headlong rush just in time to keep from toppling into the pool, and he sprang back, thrusting his men behind him with mighty swings of his arms. The green pool was like a geyser now, the noise rising to deafening volume as the great column of water reared and reared, blossoming at the crest with a great crown of foam.

Conan was driving his men to the gate, herding them ahead of him, beating them with the flat of his sword; the roar of the water-spout seemed to have robbed them of their faculties. Seeing Sancha standing paralyzed, staring with wide-eyed terror at the seething pillar, he accosted her with a bellow that cut through the thunder of the water and made her jump out of her daze. She ran to him, arms outstretched, and he caught her up under one arm and raced out of the court.

In the court which opened on the outer world, the survivors had gathered, weary, tattered, wounded and blood-stained, and stood gaping dumbly at the great unstable pillar that towered momentarily nearer the blue vault of the sky. Its green trunk was laced with white; its foaming crown was thrice the circumference of its base. Momentarily it threatened to burst and fall in an engulfing torrent, yet it continued to jet skyward.

Conan's eyes swept the bloody, naked group, and he cursed to see only a score. In the stress of the moment he grasped a corsair by the neck and shook him so violently that blood from the man's wounds spattered all near them.

'Where are the rest?' he bellowed in his victim's ear.

'That's all!' the other yelled back, above the roar of the geyser. 'The others were all killed by those black—'

'Well, get out of here!' roared Conan, giving him a thrust that sent him staggering headlong toward the outer archway. 'That fountain is going to burst in a moment—'

'We'll all be drowned!' squawked a Freebooter, limping toward the arch.

'Drowned, hell!' yelled Conan. 'We'll be turned to pieces of petrified bone! Get out, blast you!'

He ran to the outer archway, one eye on the green roaring tower that loomed so awfully above him, the other on stragglers. Dazed with blood-lust, fighting, and the thunderous noise, some of the Zingarans moved like men in a trance. Conan hurried them up; his method was simple. He grasped loiterers by the scruff of the neck, impelled them violently through the gate, added impetus with a lusty kick in the rear, spicing his urgings for haste with pungent comments on the victim's ancestry. Sancha showed an inclination to remain with him, but he jerked away her twining arms, blaspheming luridly, and accelerated her movements with a tremendous slap on the posterior that sent her scurrying across the plateau.

Conan did not leave the gate until he was sure all his men who yet lived were out of the castle and started across the level meadow. Then he glanced again at the roaring pillar looming against the sky, dwarfing the towers, and he too fled that castle of nameless horrors.

The Zingarans had already crossed the rim of the plateau and were fleeing down the slopes. Sancha waited for him at the crest of the first slope beyond the rim, and there he paused for an instant to look back at the castle. It was as if a gigantic green-stemmed and white-blossomed flower swayed above the towers; the roar filled the sky. Then the jade-green and snowy pillar broke with a noise like the rending of the skies, and walls and towers were blotted out in a thunderous torrent.

Conan caught the girl's hand, and fled. Slope after slope rose and fell before them, and behind sounded the rushing of a river. A glance over his straining shoulder showed a broad green ribbon rising and falling as it swept over the slopes. The torrent had not spread out and dissipated; like a giant serpent it flowed over the depressions and the rounded crests. It held a consistent course – *it was following them.*

The realization roused Conan to a greater pitch of endurance. Sancha stumbled and went to her knees with a moaning cry of despair and exhaustion. Catching her up, Conan tossed her over his giant shoulder and ran on. His breast heaved, his knees trembled; his breath tore in great gasps through his teeth. He reeled in his gait. Ahead of him he saw the sailors toiling, spurred on by the terror that gripped them.

The ocean burst suddenly on his view, and in his swimming gaze floated the *Wastrel*, unharmed. Men tumbled into the boats helter-skelter. Sancha fell into the bottom and lay there in a crumpled heap. Conan, though the blood thundered in his ears and the world swam red to his gaze, took an oar with the panting sailors.

With hearts ready to burst from exhaustion, they pulled for the ship. The green river burst through the fringe of trees. Those trees fell as if their stems had been cut away, and as they sank into the jade-colored flood, they vanished. The tide flowed out over the beach, lapped at the ocean, and the waves turned a deeper, more sinister green.

Unreasoning, instinctive fear held the buccaneers, making them urge their agonized bodies and reeling brains to greater effort; what they feared they knew not, but they did know that in that abominable smooth green ribbon was a menace to body and to soul. Conan knew, and as he saw the broad line slip into the waves and stream through the water toward them, without altering its shape or course, he called up his last ounce of reserve strength so fiercely that the oar snapped in his hands.

But their prows bumped against the timbers of the *Wastrel*, and the sailors staggered up the chains, leaving the boats to drift as they would. Sancha went up on Conan's broad shoulder, hanging limp as a corpse, to be dumped unceremoniously on to the deck as the Barachan took the wheel, gasping orders to his skeleton of a crew. Throughout the affair, he had taken the lead without question, and they had instinctively followed him. They reeled about like drunken men, fumbling mechanically at ropes and braces. The anchor chain, unshackled, splashed into the water, the sails unfurled and bellied in a rising wind. The *Wastrel* quivered and shook herself, and swung majestically seaward. Conan glared shoreward; like a tongue of emerald flame, a ribbon licked out on the water futilely, an oar's length from the *Wastrel*'s keel. It advanced no further. From that end of the tongue, his gaze followed an unbroken stream of lambent green, across the white beach, and over the slopes, until it faded in the blue distance.

The Barachan, regaining his wind, grinned at the panting crew. Sancha was standing near him, hysterical tears coursing down her cheeks. Conan's breeks hung in blood-stained tatters; his girdle and sheath were gone, his sword, driven upright into the deck beside him, was notched and crusted with red. Blood thickly clotted his black mane, and one ear had been half torn from his head. His arms, legs, breast and shoulders were bitten and clawed as if by panthers. But he grinned as he braced his powerful legs, and swung on the wheel in sheer exuberance of muscular might.

'What now?' faltered the girl.

'The plunder of the seas!' he laughed. 'A paltry crew, and that chewed and clawed to pieces, but they can work the ship, and crews can always be found. Come here, girl, and give me a kiss.'

'A kiss?' she cried hysterically. 'You think of kisses at a time like this?'

His laughter boomed above the snap and thunder of the sails, as he caught her up off her feet in the crook of one mighty arm, and smacked her red lips with resounding relish.

'I think of Life!' he roared. 'The dead are dead, and what has passed is done! I have a ship and a fighting crew and a girl with lips like wine, and that's all I ever asked. Lick your wounds, bullies, and break out a cask of ale. You're going to work ship as she never was worked before. Dance and sing while you buckle to it, damn you! To the devil with empty seas! We're bound for waters where the seaports are fat, and the merchant ships are crammed with plunder!'

ALSO BY ROBERT E. HOWARD

NOVELS

Conan the Conqueror (1950)
Almuric (1964)
The Hour of the Dragon (1977)
Post Oaks and Sand Roughs (1990)

SHORT STORY COLLECTIONS

A Gent from Bear Creek (1937)
The Hyborian Age (1938)
Skull-Face and Others (1946)
The Sword of Conan (1952)
King Conan (1953)
The Coming of Conan (1953)
The Challenge from Beyond (1954) with C.L. Moore, A. Merritt, H.P. Lovecraft and Frank Belknap Long, Jr
Conan the Barbarian (1954)
Tales of Conan (1955) with L. Sprague de Camp
The Dark Man and Others (1963)
The Pride of Bear Creek (1966)
Conan the Adventurer (1966) with L. Sprague de Camp
Conan the Warrior (1967) with L. Sprague de Camp
Conan the Usurper (1967) with L. Sprague de Camp
King Kull (1967) with Lin Carter
Conan (1967) with L. Sprague de Camp and Lin Carter
Wolfshead (1968)
Red Shadows (1968)
Conan the Freebooter (1968) with L. Sprague de Camp
Conan the Wanderer (1968) with L. Sprague de Camp and Lin Carter
Conan of Cimmeria (1969) with L. Sprague de Camp and Lin Carter
Bran Mak Morn (1969)
The Moon of Skulls (1969)
The Hand of Kane (1970)
Solomon Kane (1971)
Red Blades of Black Cathay (1971) with Tevis Clyde Smith
Marchers of Valhalla (1972)
The Sowers of the Thunder (1973)
The Vultures (1973)
The Lost Valley of Iskander (1974)
The People of the Black Circle (1974)
Tigers of the Sea (1974)
The Incredible Adventures of Dennis Dorgan (1974)
The Swords of Shahrazar (1975)
A Witch Shall Be Born (1975)
Red Nails (1975)
The Tower of the Elephant (1975)
The Devil in Iron (1976)
Rogues in the House (1976)
The Book of Robert E. Howard (1976)
Black Vulmea's Vengeance (and Other Tales of Pirates) (1976)
The Second Book of Robert E. Howard (1976)
The Grim Land and Others (1976)
The Iron Man and Other Tales of the Ring (1976)
The Return of Skull-Face (1977) with Richard A. Lupoff
Son of the White Wolf (1977)
The Pride of Bear Creek (1977)
Three-Bladed Doom (1977)
The Sword Woman (1977)
The People of the Black Circle (1977)
Red Nails (1977)
The Robert E. Howard Omnibus (1977)

Skull-Face (1978)
Kull (1978)
Queen of the Black Coast (1978)
Black Canaan (1978)
The Last Ride (1978)
Solomon Kane: Skulls in the Stars (1978) with J. Ramsey Campbell
Solomon Kane: The Hills of the Dead (1979) with J. Ramsey Campbell
Black Colossus (1979)
The Jewels of Gwahlur (1979)
Hawks of Outremer (1979) with Richard L. Tierney
The Road of Azrael (1979)
The Gods of Bal-Sagoth (1979)
Pigeons from Hell (1979)
Mayhem on Bear Creek (1979)
Lord of the Dead (1981)
The Pool of the Black One (1986)
Cthulhu: The Mythos and Kindred Horrors (1987)
Robert E. Howard's World of Heroes (1989)
The Conan Chronicles (1989) with L. Sprague de Camp and Lin Carter
The Conan Chronicles 2 (1989) with L. Sprague de Camp and Lin Carter
Eons of the Night (1996)
Trails in Darkness (1996)
Beyond the Borders (1996)
Ghor Kin-Slayer: The Saga of Genseric's Fifth-Born Son (1997) with Divers Hands
The Essential Conan (1998)
The Savage Tales of Solomon Kane (1998)
The Ultimate Triumph (2000)
The Conan Chronicles Volume 1: The People of the Black Circle (2000)
The Conan Chronicles Volume 2: The Hour of the Dragon (2001)
Bran Mak Morn: The Last King (2001)
Nameless Cults: The Cthulhu Mythos Fiction of Robert E. Howard (2001)
Robert E. Howard: The Power of the Writing Mind (2003)
Robert E. Howard's Complete Conan of Cimmeria, Volume One (2003)
Waterfront Fists and Others: The Collected Fight Stories of Robert E. Howard (2003)
Graveyard Rats and Others (2003)
Complete Action Stories (2003)
The Coming of Conan the Cimmerian (2003)
Gates of Empire and Other Tales of the Crusades (2004)
Robert E. Howard's Complete Conan of Cimmeria, Volume Two (2004)
Treasures of Tartary and Other Heroic Tales (2004)
The Bloody Crown of Conan (2004)
Shadow Kingdoms: The Weird Works of Robert E. Howard, Volume 1 (2004)
Moon of Skulls: The Weird Works of Robert E. Howard, Volume 2 (2005)
The Black Stranger and Other American Tales (2005)
Lord of Samarcand and Other Adventure Tales of the Old Orient (2005)
The End of the Trail: Western Stories (2005)
Boxing Stories (2005)
The Riot at Bucksnort and Other Western Tales (2005)
Blood of the Gods and Other Stories (2005)
The Conquering Sword of Conan (2005)
People of the Dark: The Weird Works of Robert E. Howard, Volume 3 (2005)

Wings in the Night: The Weird Works of Robert E. Howard, Volume 4 (2005)
The Complete Chronicles of Conan: Centenary Edition (2006)
Valley of the Worm: The Weird Works of Robert E. Howard, Volume 5 (2006)
Kull: Exile of Atlantis (2006)
Gardens of Fear: The Weird Works of Robert E. Howard, Volume 6 (2006)
Treasure of Tartary and Other Heroic Tales (2006)
The Best of Robert E. Howard, Volume 1: Crimson Shadows (2007)
The Best of Robert E. Howard, Volume 2: Grim Lands (2007)
Beyond the Black River: The Weird Works of Robert E. Howard, Volume 7 (2007)

POETRY

Always Comes Evening (1957)
Etchings in Ivory (Poems in Prose) (1968)
Singers in the Shadows (1970)
Echoes from an Iron Harp (1972)
Rhymes of Death (1975)
Verses in Ebony (1975)
The Grim Land and Others (1976)
Night Images (1977)
The Ghost Ocean: Poems of Horror and Supernatural (1982)
Shadows of Dreams (1989)

ROBERT E. HOWARD was born and raised in rural Texas, where he lived all his life. The son of a pioneer physician, he began writing professionally at fifteen, and three years later sold his first story to *Weird Tales*. A prolific and proficient author, he published westerns, sports stories, horror tales, true confessions, historical adventures and detective thrillers, all the while developing a series of heroic characters with whom he would forever be identified with: Solomon Kane, King Kull, Bran Mak Morn and, of course, Conan the Cimmerian. Between 1932 and 1935, Howard wrote twenty-one sword and sorcery adventures of Conan, ranging in length from 3,500-word short stories to novel-length tales of 75,000 words. He committed suicide at the age of thirty, in June 1936. For more information about Robert E. Howard and Conan visit the REHupa website at http://www.rehupa.com

Vanaheim
Western Sea
(Atlantic)
Cimmeria
Pictish Wilderness
Marches
Gunderland
Galparan
Tanasul
Black River
Thunder River
Bossanian
Touran
Shirki River
Aquilonia
Tarantia
Khorotas R.
Ophir
Poitan
Zingara
Argos
Baracha Isles
Messantia
Meadows Cities
Khemi
Isle of the Black Ones
Kush
The Hyborian Age
From a map prepared by Robert E. Howard

HYPERBOREA
HYRKANIA
TO KHITAI
ZAMORA
Shadizar
Khauran
Khoraja
TURAN
later extended to Zamoran border
VILAYET SEA (CASPIAN)
Isle of Iron Statues
Agrapur
Khawarism
Kuthchemes
Xapur
ZAPOROSKA R.
Yuetshi
Ft. Ghori
Styx
Zamboula
to Vendhya
Keshan
Punt
ZEMBABWEI
D·S